the unbeatable Squirrel Girl

Big Squirrels Don't Cry

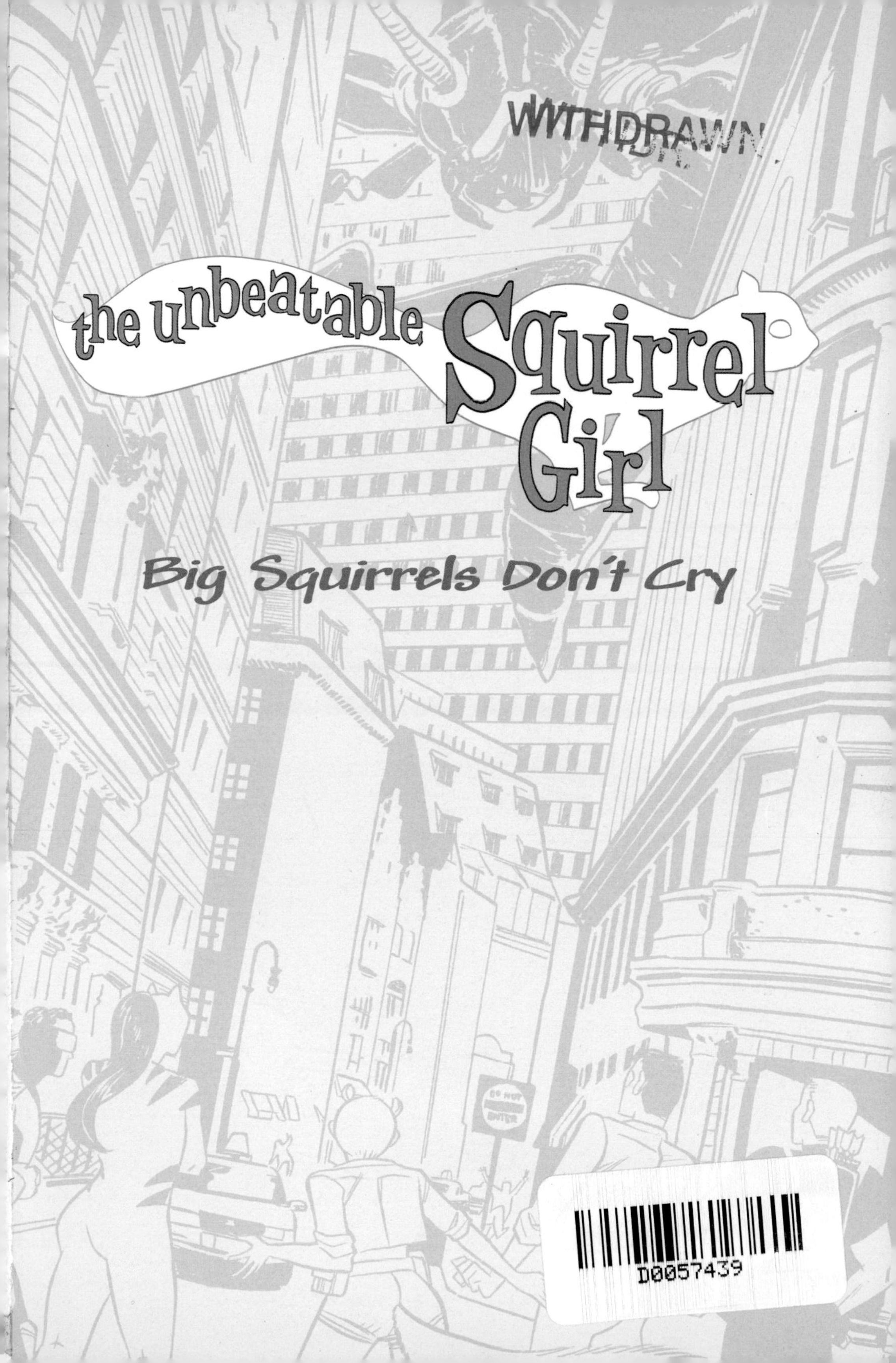

Contents

SQUIRREL GIRL
CREATED BY WILL MURRAY
& STEVE DITKO

collection editor JENNIFER GRÜNWALD
assistant managing editor MAIA LOY
assistant managing editor LISA MONTALBANO
editor, special projects MARK D. BEAZLEY
vp production & special projects JEFF YOUNGQUIST
director, licensed publishing SVEN LARSEN
svp print, sales & marketing DAVID GABRIEL
editor in chief C.B. CEBULSKI

THE UNBEATABLE SQUIRREL GIRL: BIG SQUIRRELS DON'T CRY. Contains material originally published in magazine form as THE UNBEATABLE SQUIRREL GIRL (2015B) #1-11and HOWARD THE DUCK (2015B) #6. First printing 2020. ISBN 978-1-302-92116-3. Published by MARVEL WORLDWIDE, INC., a subsidiary of MARVEL ENTERTAINMENT, LLC. OFFICE OF PUBLICATION: 1290 Avenue of the Americas, New York, NY 10104. © 2020 MARVEL No similarity between any of the names, characters, persons, and/or institutions in this magazine with those of any living or dead person or institution is intended, and any such similarity which may exist is purely coincidental. Printed in Canada. KEVIN FEIGE, Chief Creative Officer; DAN BUCKLEY, President, Marvel Entertainment; JOHN NEE, Publisher; JOE QUESADA, EVP & Creative Director; TOM BREVOORT, SVP of Publishing; DAVID BOGART, Associate Publisher & SVP of Talent Affairs; Publishing & Partnership; DAVID GABRIEL, VP of Print & Digital Publishing; JEFF YOUNGQUIST, VP of Production & Special Projects; DAN CARR, Executive Director of Publishing Technology; ALEX MORALES, Director of Publishing Operations; DAN EDINGTON, Managing Editor; SUSAN CRESPI, Production Manager; STAN LEE, Chairman Emeritus. For information regarding advertising in Marvel Comics or on Marvel.com, please contact Vit DeBellis, Custom Solutions & Integrated Advertising Manager, at vdebellis@marvel.com. For Marvel subscription inquiries, please call 888-511-5480. Manufactured between 2/21/2020 and 3/24/2020 by SOLISCO PRINTERS, SCOTT, QC, CANADA.

10 9 8 7 6 5 4 3 2 1

the unbeatable Squirrel Girl

Big Girl Don't Cry

WRITERS
RYAN NORTH
WITH CHIP ZDARSKY (#6)

PENCILERS
ERICA HENDERSON (#1-10) & **JACOB CHABOT** (#11)

INKERS
ERICA HENDERSON (#1-10), **TOM FOWLER** (#9-10)
& JACOB CHABOT (#11)

#8 1918 SEQUENCE ART	#9 "MOLE MAN'S DEAL…" ART	#10 FLASHBACK ART	#11 FINAL PANEL ART
ANDY HIRSH	DAVID MALKI	KYLE STARKS	ERICA HENDERSON

COLOR ARTISTS
RICO RENZI
WITH ERICA HENDERSON (#7)

LETTERERS
VC'S CLAYTON COWLES (#1-2, #4)
& TRAVIS LANHAM (#3, #5-6)

COVER ART
ERICA HENDERSON
WITH JOE QUINONES (#6)

HOWARD THE DUCK #6
WRITER: Chip Zdarsky with Ryan North
PENCILER: Joe Quinones
INKERS: Joe Rivera, Marc Deering & Joe Quinones
COLORISTS: Joe Quinones & Jordan Gibson
LETTERER: VC's Travis Lanham
COVER ART: Joe Quinones with Erica Henderson

ASSISTANT EDITORS
CHRIS ROBINSON & CHARLES BEACHAM

EDITOR
WIL MOSS

EXECUTIVE EDITOR
TOM BREVOORT

SPECIAL THANKS TO CK RUSSELL, DYLAN TODD, MICHAEL WIGGAM & CASSIE KELLY

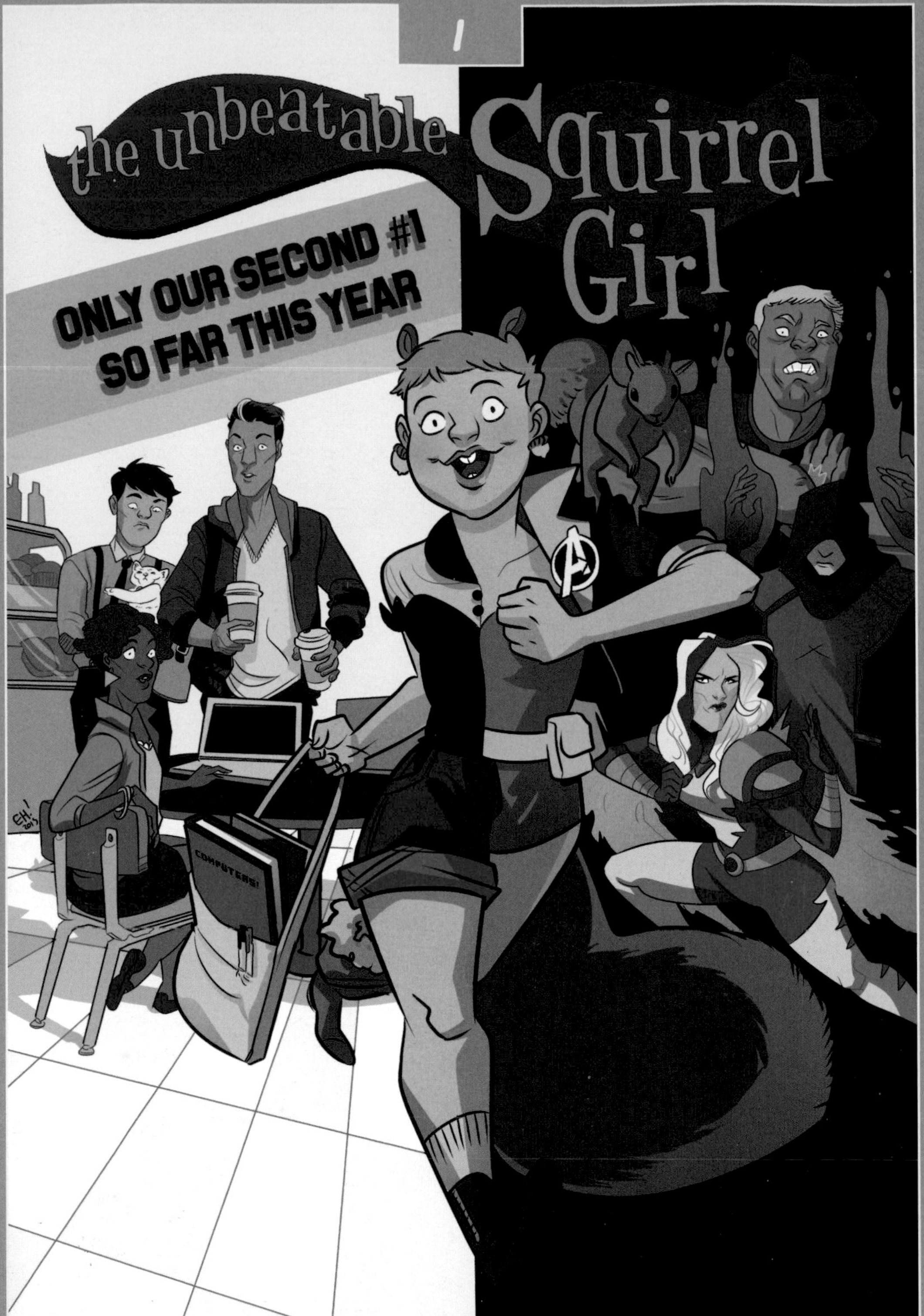
1
the unbeatable Squirrel Girl
ONLY OUR SECOND #1
SO FAR THIS YEAR
COMPUTERS!

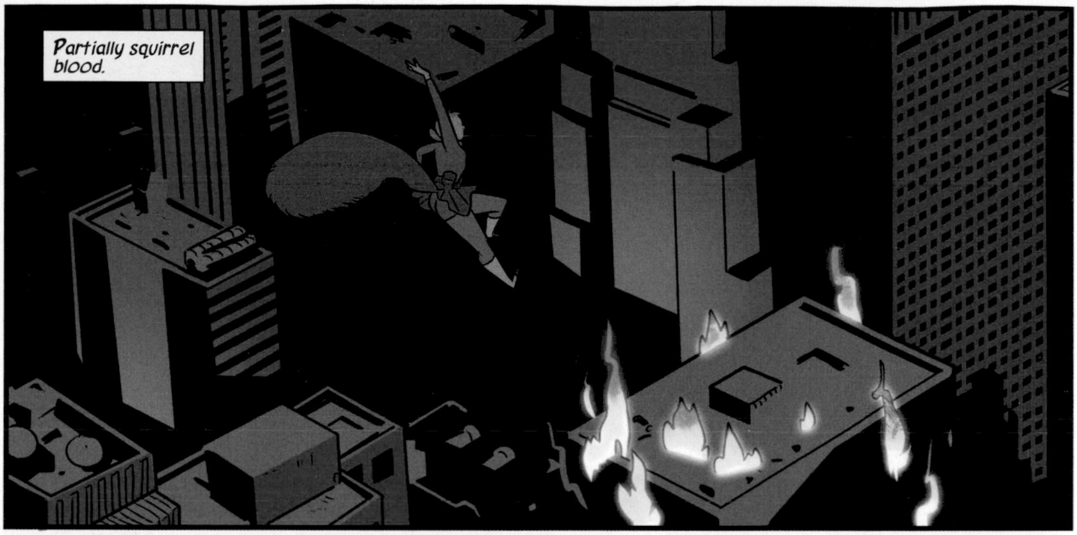
Partially squirrel blood.

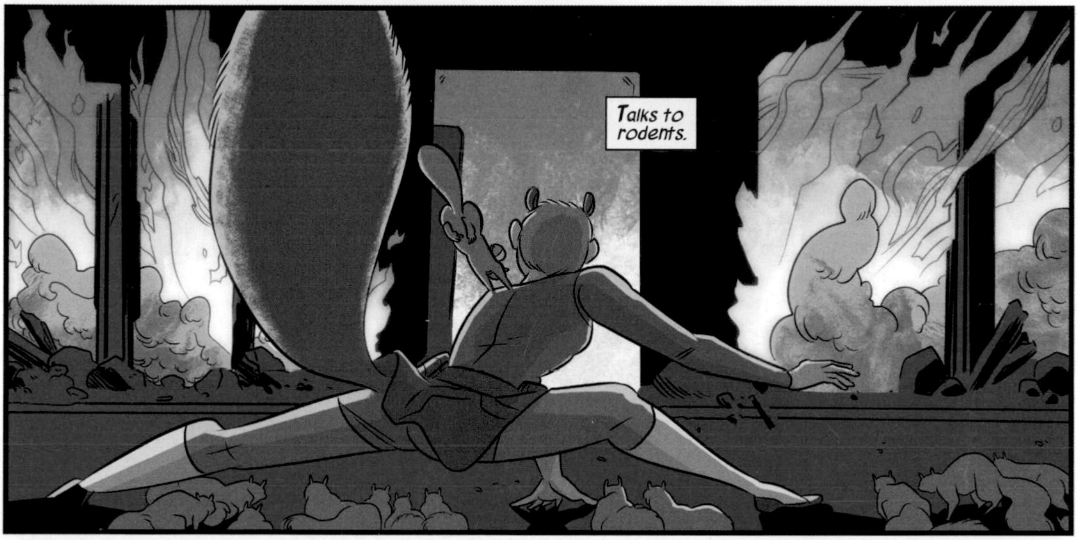
Talks to rodents.

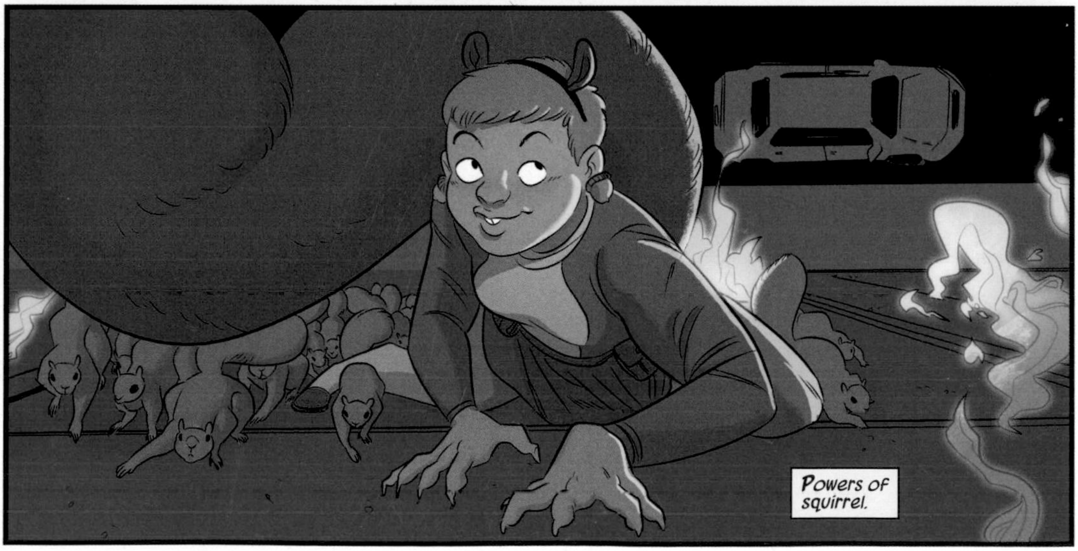
Powers of squirrel.

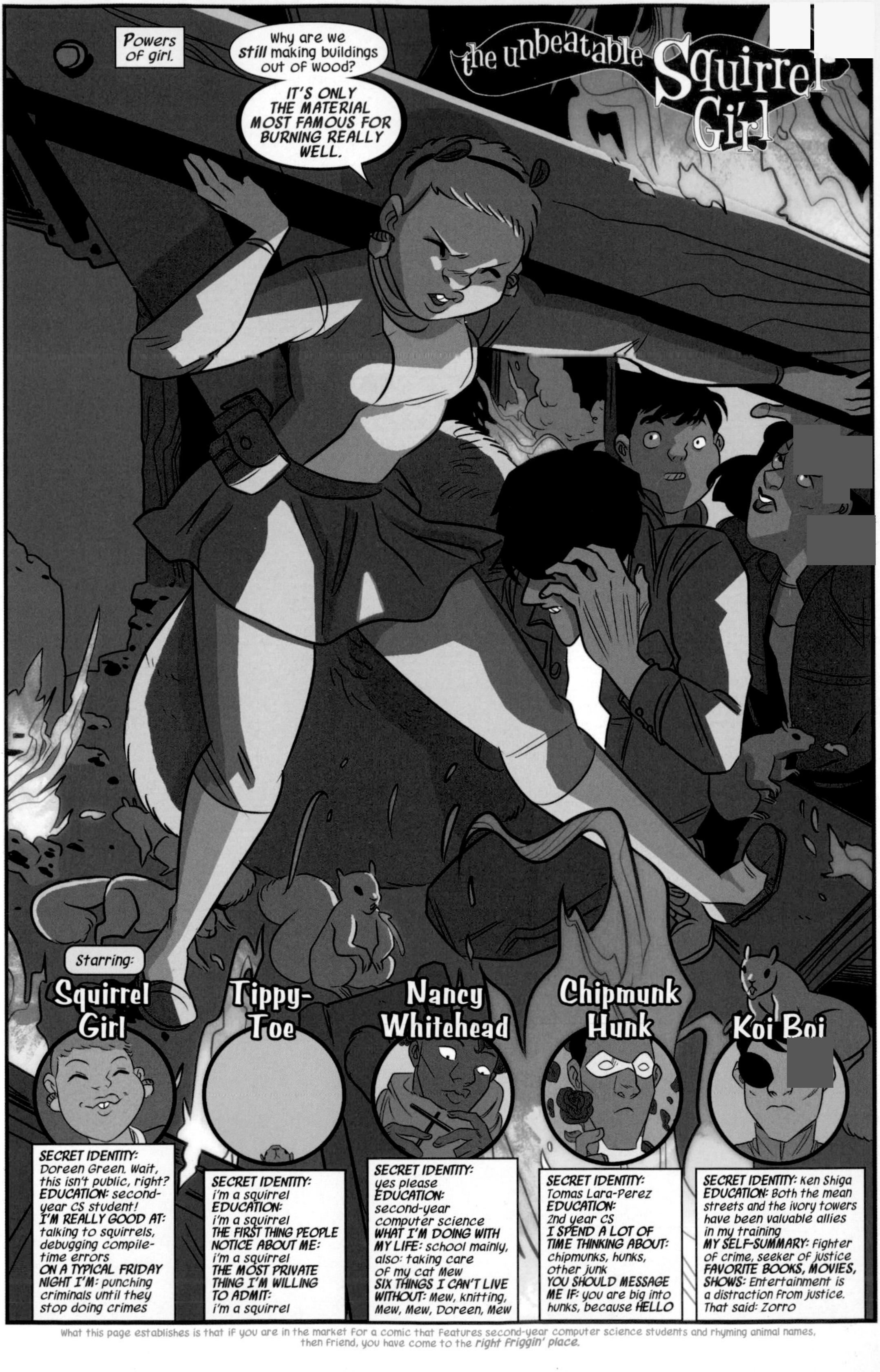
Powers of girl.
Why are we still making buildings out of wood?
IT'S ONLY THE MATERIAL MOST FAMOUS FOR BURNING REALLY WELL.
the unbeatable Squirrel Girl
Starring:
Squirrel Girl
Tippy-Toe
Nancy Whitehead
Chipmunk Hunk
Koi Boi
SECRET IDENTITY: Doreen Green. Wait, this isn't public, right? EDUCATION: second-year CS student! I'M REALLY GOOD AT: talking to squirrels, debugging compile-time errors ON A TYPICAL FRIDAY NIGHT I'M: punching criminals until they stop doing crimes
SECRET IDENTITY: i'm a squirrel EDUCATION: i'm a squirrel THE FIRST THING PEOPLE NOTICE ABOUT ME: i'm a squirrel THE MOST PRIVATE THING I'M WILLING TO ADMIT: i'm a squirrel
SECRET IDENTITY: yes please EDUCATION: second-year computer science WHAT I'M DOING WITH MY LIFE: school mainly, also: taking care of my cat Mew SIX THINGS I CAN'T LIVE WITHOUT: Mew, knitting, Mew, Mew, Doreen, Mew
SECRET IDENTITY: Tomas Lara-Perez EDUCATION: 2nd year CS I SPEND A LOT OF TIME THINKING ABOUT: chipmunks, hunks, other junk YOU SHOULD MESSAGE ME IF: you are big into hunks, because HELLO
SECRET IDENTITY: Ken Shiga EDUCATION: Both the mean streets and the ivory towers have been valuable allies in my training MY SELF-SUMMARY: Fighter of crime, seeker of justice FAVORITE BOOKS, MOVIES, SHOWS: Entertainment is a distraction from justice. That said: Zorro

What this page establishes is that if you are in the market for a comic that features second-year computer science students and rhyming animal names, then friend, you have come to the *right friggin' place.*

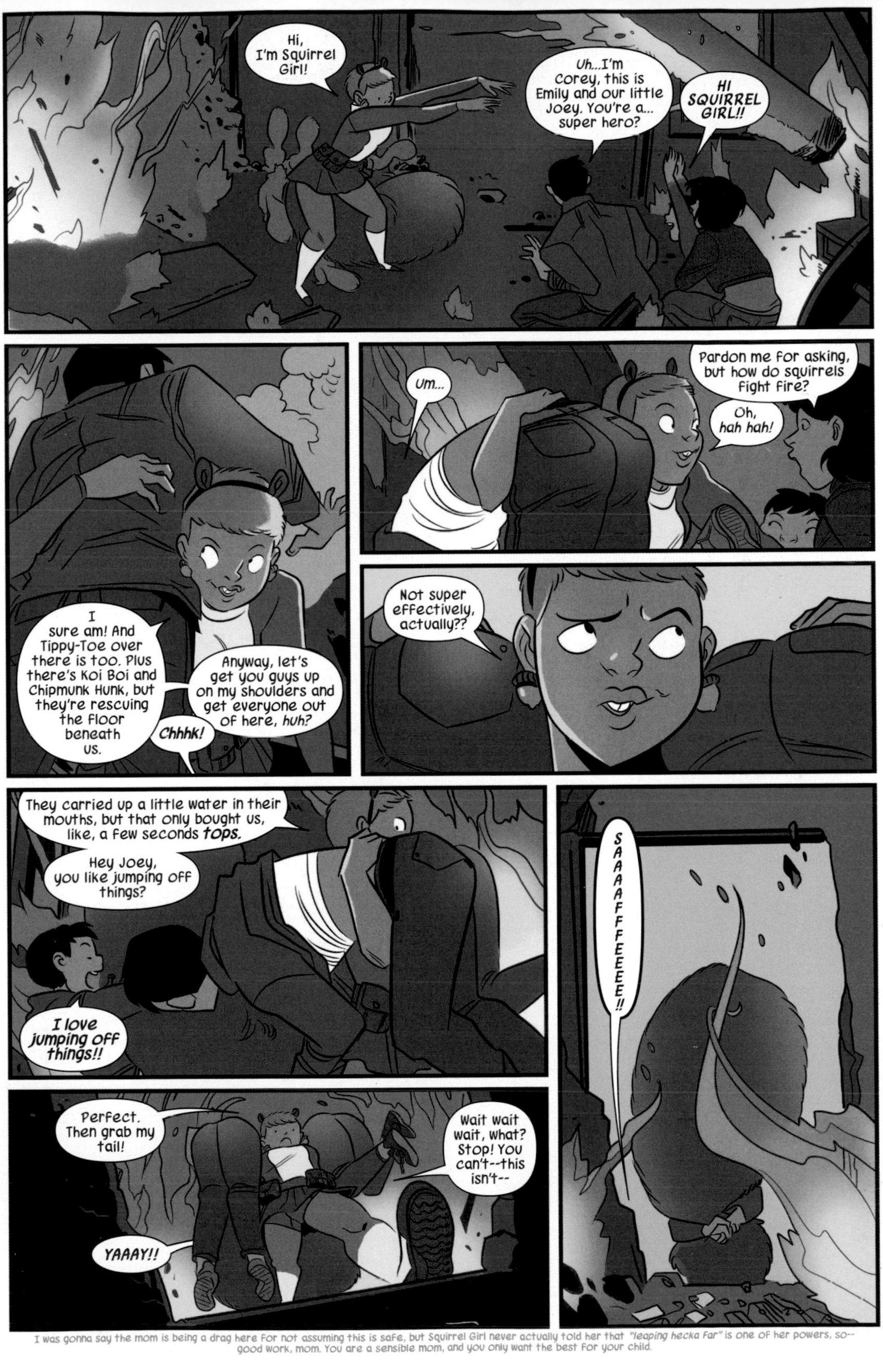
Hi, I'm Squirrel Girl!
Uh...I'm Corey, this is Emily and our little Joey. You're a... super hero?
HI SQUIRREL GIRL!!
I sure am! And Tippy-Toe over there is too. Plus there's Koi Boi and Chipmunk Hunk, but they're rescuing the floor beneath us.
Chhhk!
Anyway, let's get you guys up on my shoulders and get everyone out of here, huh?
Um...
Pardon me for asking, but how do squirrels fight fire?
Oh, hah hah!
Not super effectively, actually??
They carried up a little water in their mouths, but that only bought us, like, a few seconds tops.
Hey Joey, you like jumping off things?
I love jumping off things!!
Perfect. Then grab my tail!
Wait wait wait, what? Stop! You can't--this isn't--
YAAAY!!
SAAAAFFFEEEEE!!

I was gonna say the mom is being a drag here for not assuming this is safe, but Squirrel Girl never actually told her that *"leaping hecka far"* is one of her powers, so--good work, mom. You are a sensible mom, and you only want the best for your child.

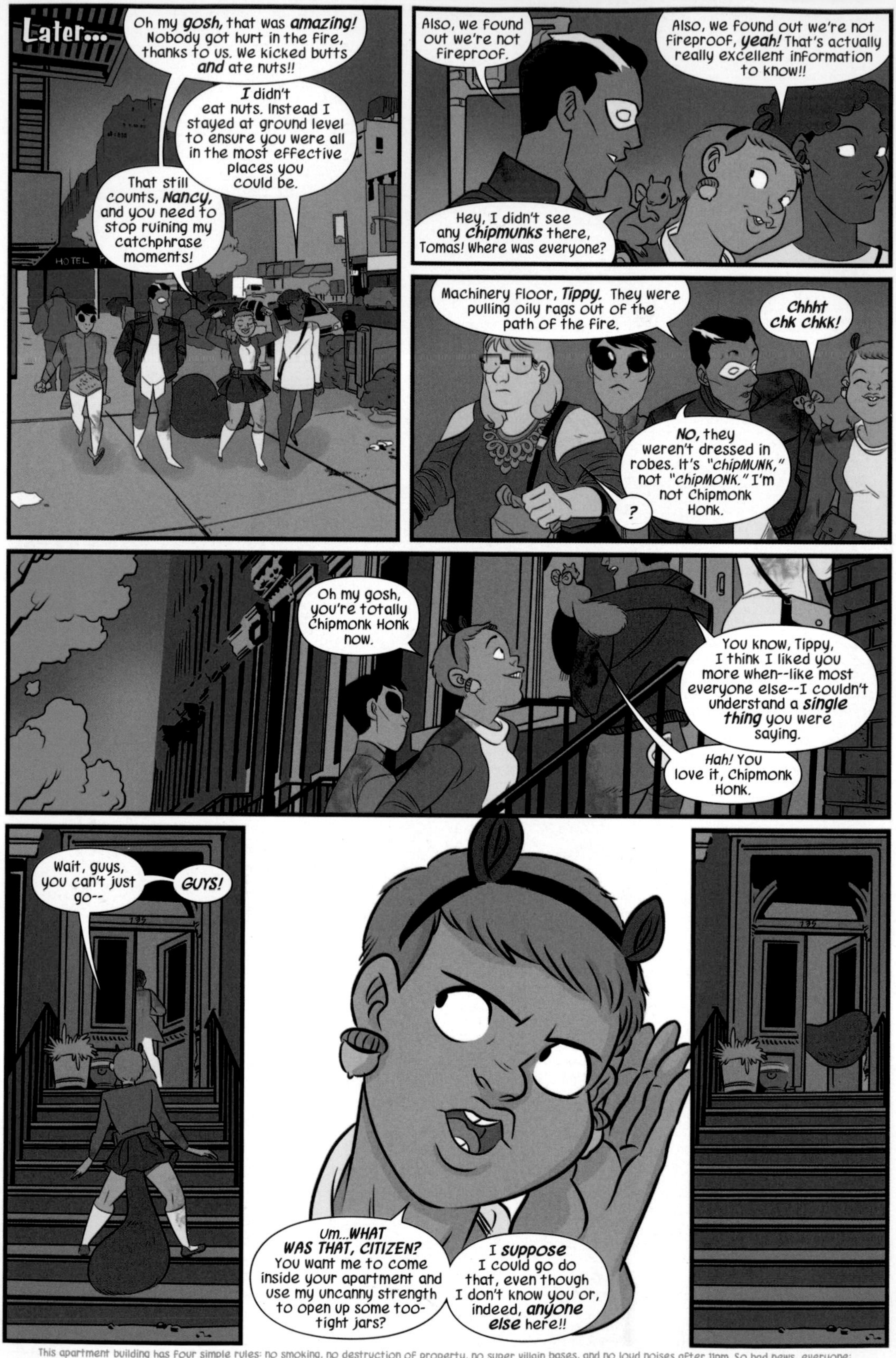

Later...
Oh my gosh, that was amazing! Nobody got hurt in the fire, thanks to us. We kicked butts and ate nuts!!
I didn't eat nuts. Instead I stayed at ground level to ensure you were all in the most effective places you could be.
That still counts, Nancy, and you need to stop ruining my catchphrase moments!
HOTEL
Also, we found out we're not fireproof.
Also, we found out we're not fireproof, yeah! That's actually really excellent information to know!!
Hey, I didn't see any chipmunks there, Tomas! Where was everyone?
Machinery floor, Tippy. They were pulling oily rags out of the path of the fire.
Chhht chk chkk!
NO, they weren't dressed in robes. It's "chipMUNK," not "chipMONK." I'm not Chipmonk Honk.
?
Oh my gosh, you're totally Chipmonk Honk now.
You know, Tippy, I think I liked you more when--like most everyone else--I couldn't understand a single thing you were saying.
Hah! You love it, Chipmonk Honk.
Wait, guys, you can't just go--
GUYS!
Um...WHAT WAS THAT, CITIZEN? You want me to come inside your apartment and use my uncanny strength to open up some too-tight jars?
I suppose I could go do that, even though I don't know you or, indeed, anyone else here!!

This apartment building has four simple rules: no smoking, no destruction of property, no super villain bases, and no loud noises after 11pm. So bad news, everyone: you'll have to find someplace else to have your *"loudly destroy super villain bases at 11:05pm while also smoking"* parties.

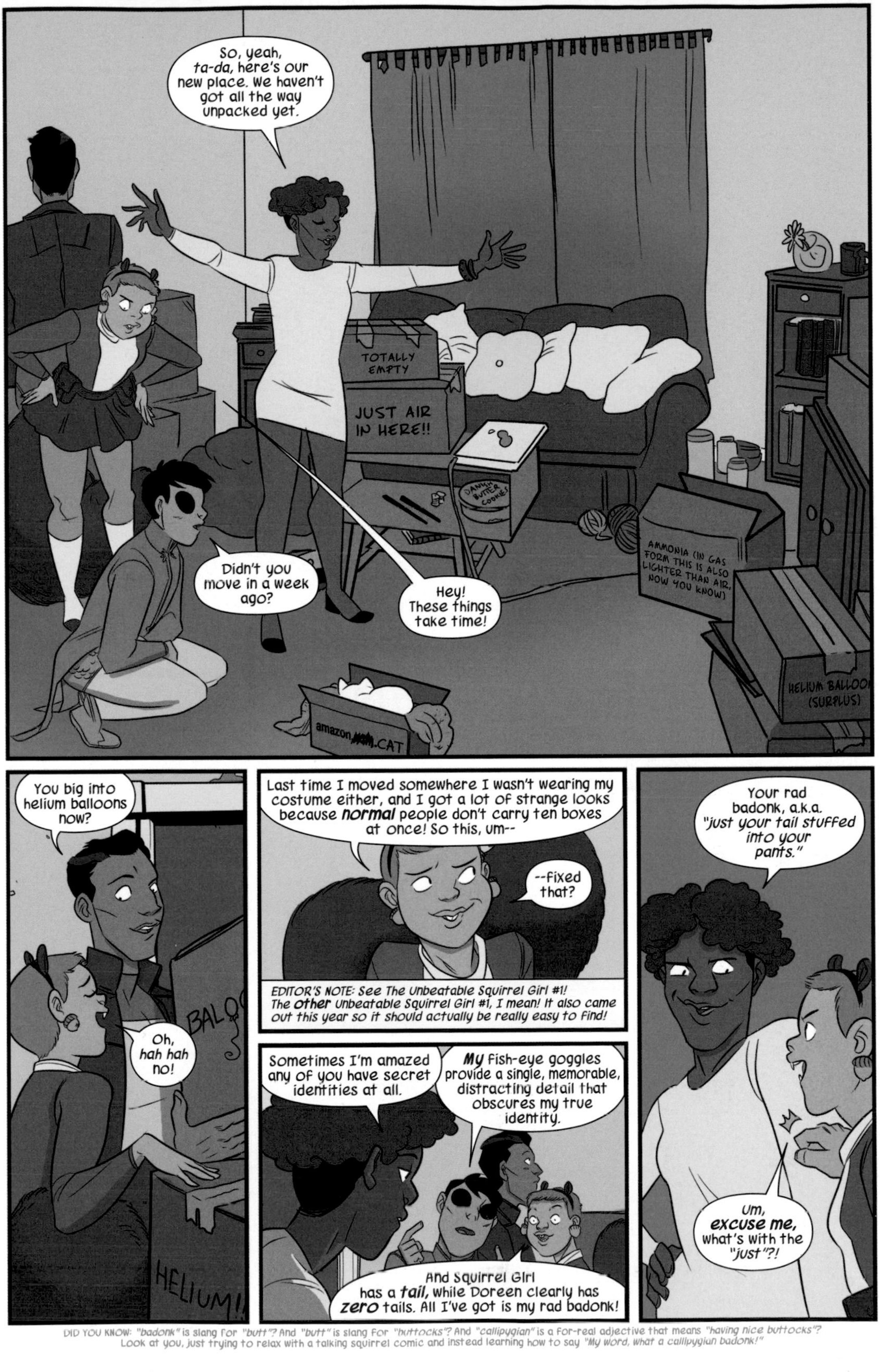

So, yeah, *ta-da*, here's our new place. We haven't got all the way unpacked yet.
TOTALLY EMPTY
JUST AIR IN HERE!!
AMMONIA (IN GAS FORM THIS IS ALSO LIGHTER THAN AIR, NOW YOU KNOW)
HELIUM BALLOO
(SURPLUS)
Didn't you move in a week ago?
Hey! These things take time!
amazon.CAT
You big into helium balloons now?
BALLO
Oh, *hah hah* no!
HELIUM!!
Last time I moved somewhere I wasn't wearing my costume either, and I got a lot of strange looks because **normal** people don't carry ten boxes at once! So this, um--
--fixed that?
EDITOR'S NOTE: See The Unbeatable Squirrel Girl #1! The **other** Unbeatable Squirrel Girl #1, I mean! It also came out this year so it should actually be really easy to find!
Sometimes I'm amazed any of you have secret identities at all.
My fish-eye goggles provide a single, memorable, distracting detail that obscures my true identity.
And Squirrel Girl has a ***tail,*** while Doreen clearly has ***zero*** tails. All I've got is my rad badonk!
Your rad badonk, a.k.a. *"just your tail stuffed into your pants."*
Um, ***excuse me,*** what's with the *"just"*?!

DID YOU KNOW: *"badonk"* is slang for *"butt"*? And *"butt"* is slang for *"buttocks"*? And *"callipygian"* is a for-real adjective that means *"having nice buttocks"*? Look at you, just trying to relax with a talking squirrel comic and instead learning how to say *"My word, what a callipygian badonk!"*

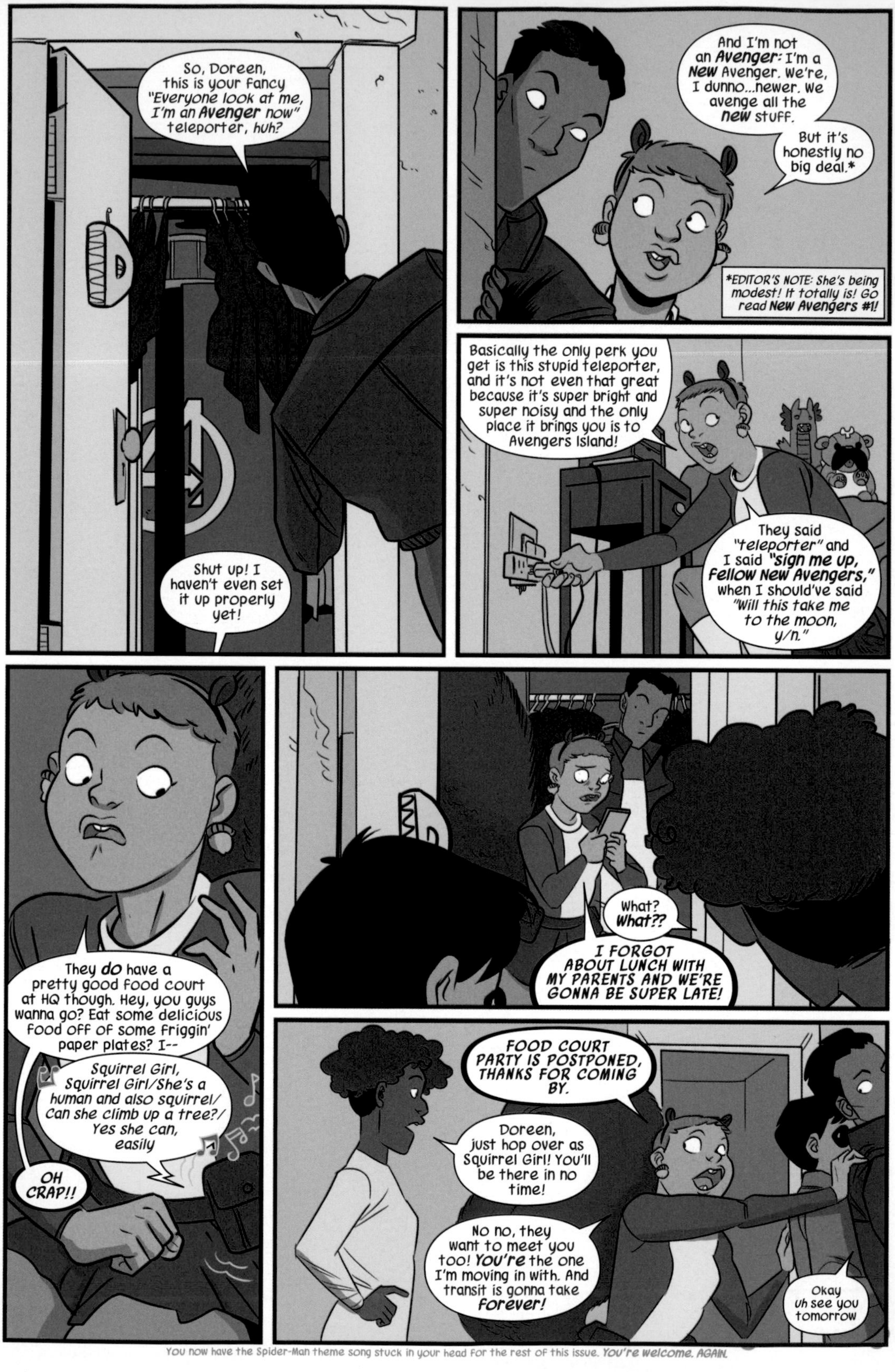
So, Doreen, this is your fancy "Everyone look at me, I'm an Avenger now" teleporter, huh?
Shut up! I haven't even set it up properly yet!
And I'm not an Avenger: I'm a New Avenger. We're, I dunno...newer. We avenge all the new stuff.
But it's honestly no big deal.*
*EDITOR'S NOTE: She's being modest! It totally is! Go read New Avengers #1!
Basically the only perk you get is this stupid teleporter, and it's not even that great because it's super bright and super noisy and the only place it brings you is to Avengers Island!
They said "teleporter" and I said "sign me up, fellow New Avengers," when I should've said "Will this take me to the moon, y/n."
They do have a pretty good food court at HQ though. Hey, you guys wanna go? Eat some delicious food off of some friggin' paper plates? I--
Squirrel Girl, Squirrel Girl/She's a human and also squirrel/ Can she climb up a tree?/ Yes she can, easily
OH CRAP!!
What? What??
I FORGOT ABOUT LUNCH WITH MY PARENTS AND WE'RE GONNA BE SUPER LATE!
FOOD COURT PARTY IS POSTPONED, THANKS FOR COMING BY.
Doreen, just hop over as Squirrel Girl! You'll be there in no time!
No no, they want to meet you too! You're the one I'm moving in with. And transit is gonna take forever!
Okay uh see you tomorrow

You now have the Spider-Man theme song stuck in your head for the rest of this issue. *You're welcome. AGAIN.*

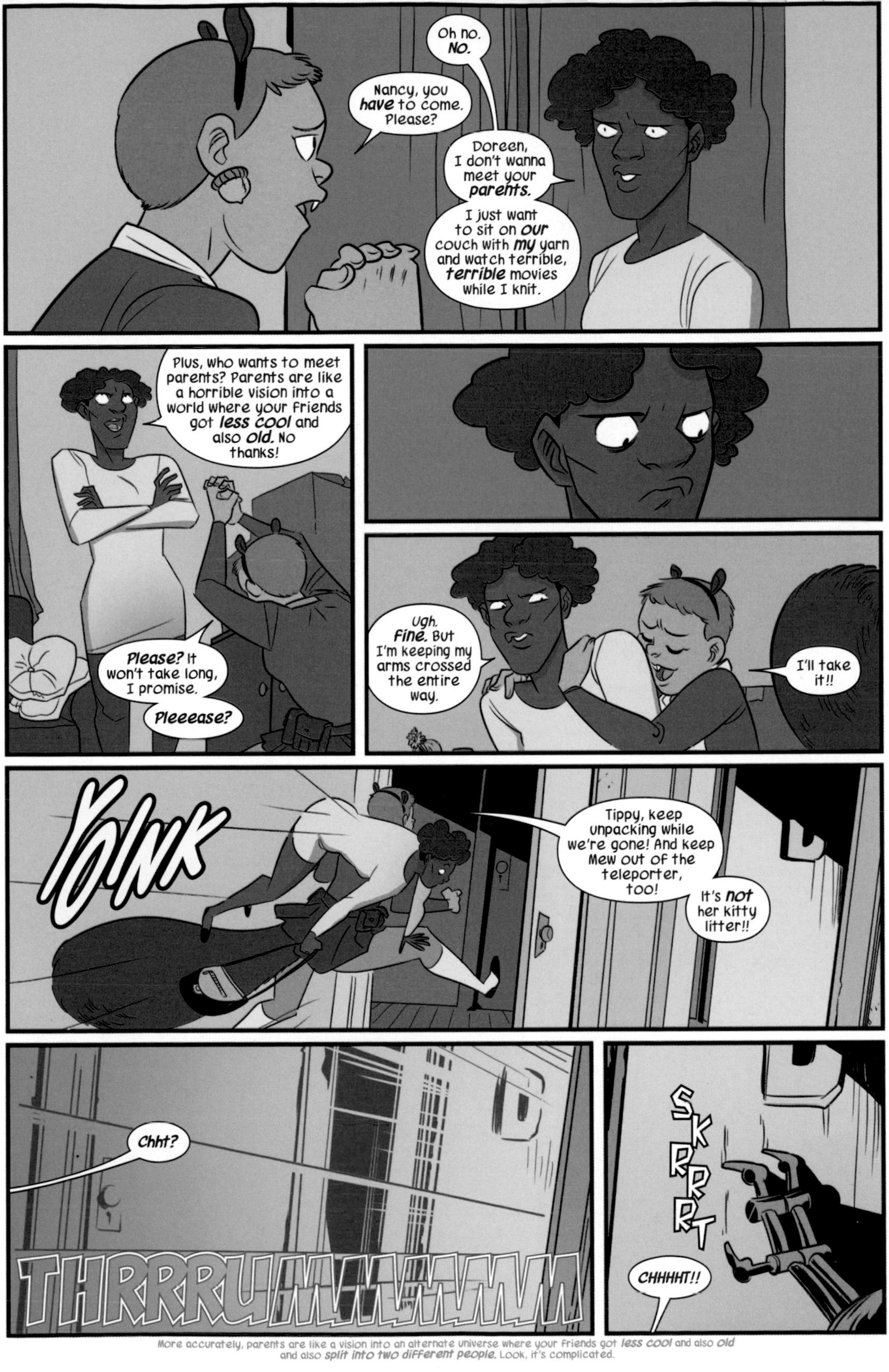
Nancy, you have to come. Please?
Oh no. NO.
Doreen, I don't wanna meet your parents.
I just want to sit on our couch with my yarn and watch terrible, terrible movies while I knit.
Plus, who wants to meet parents? Parents are like a horrible vision into a world where your friends got less cool and also old. No thanks!
Please? It won't take long, I promise.
Pleeease?
Ugh. Fine. But I'm keeping my arms crossed the entire way.
I'll take it!!
YOINK
Tippy, keep unpacking while we're gone! And keep Mew out of the teleporter, too!
It's not her kitty litter!!
Chht?
THRRRUMMMMMMMM
SKRRRT
CHHHHT!!

More accurately, parents are like a vision into an alternate universe where your friends got *less cool* and also *old* and also *split into two different people.* Look, it's complicated.

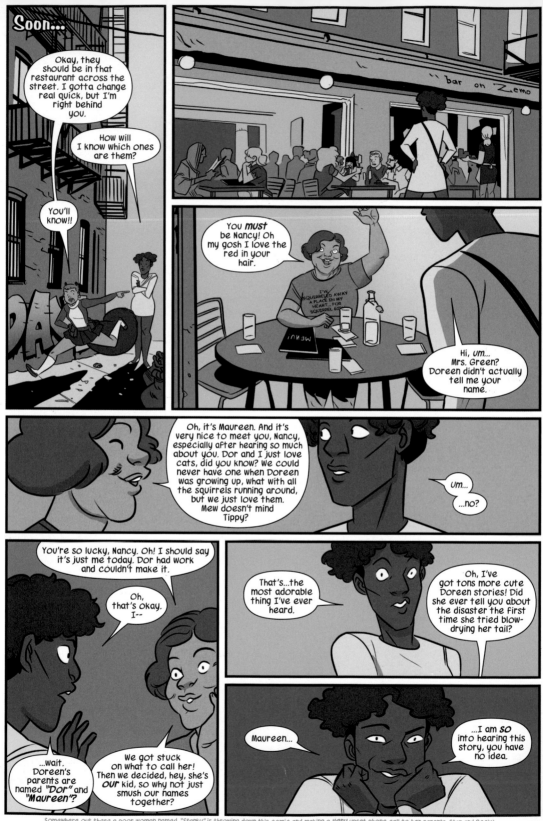

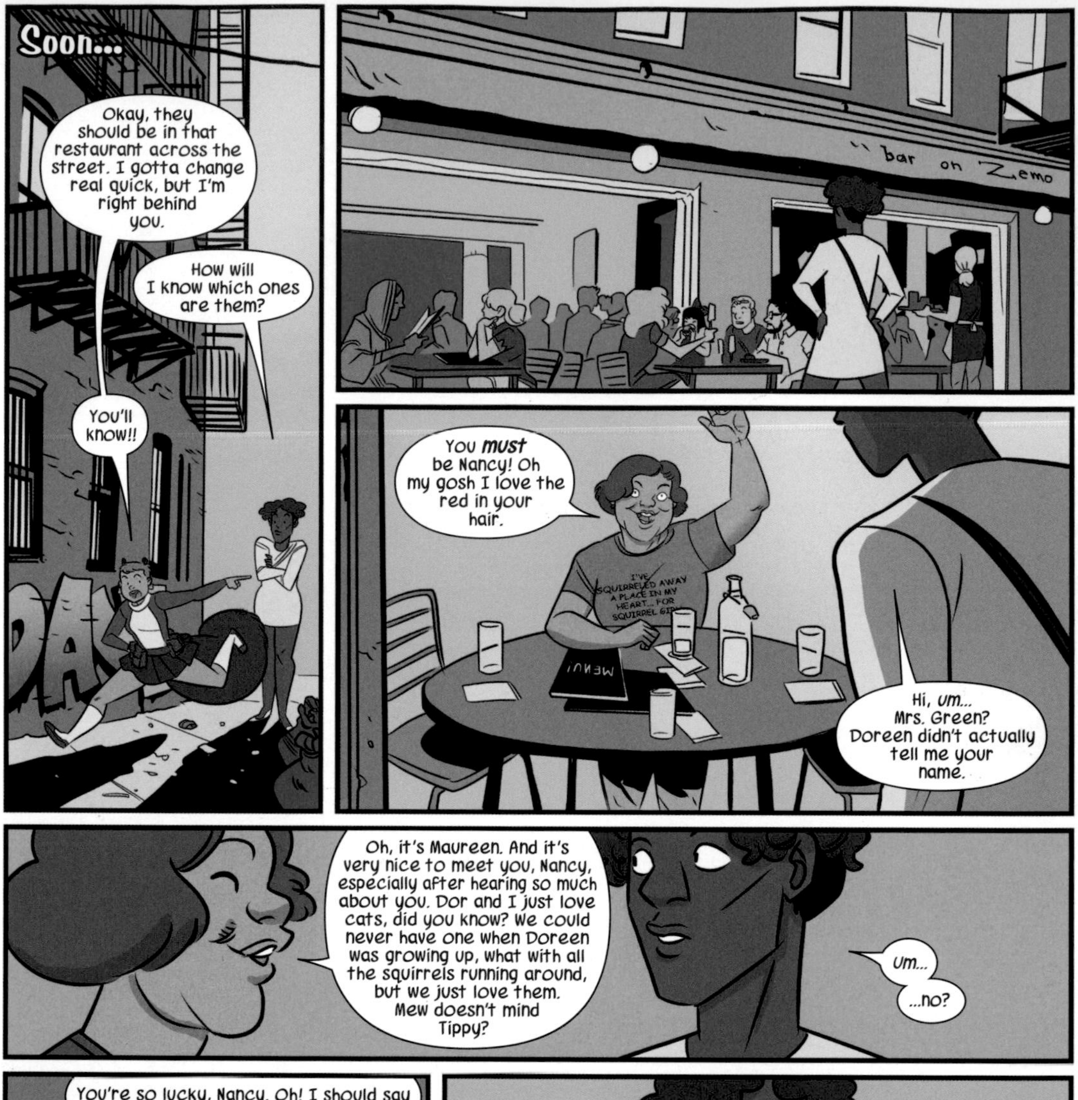
Soon...
Okay, they should be in that restaurant across the street. I gotta change real quick, but I'm right behind you.
How will I know which ones are them?
You'll know!!
bar on Zemo
You *must* be Nancy! Oh my gosh I love the red in your hair.
Hi, *um*... Mrs. Green? Doreen didn't actually tell me your name.
Oh, it's Maureen. And it's very nice to meet you, Nancy, especially after hearing so much about you. Dor and I just love cats, did you know? We could never have one when Doreen was growing up, what with all the squirrels running around, but we just love them. Mew doesn't mind Tippy?
Um...
...no?
You're so lucky, Nancy. Oh! I should say it's just me today. Dor had work and couldn't make it.
Oh, that's okay. I--
...wait. Doreen's parents are named *"Dor"* and *"Maureen"*?
We got stuck on what to call her! Then we decided, hey, she's *our* kid, so why not just smush our names together?
That's...the most adorable thing I've ever heard.
Oh, I've got tons more cute Doreen stories! Did she ever tell you about the disaster the first time she tried blow-drying her tail?
Maureen...
...I am *so* into hearing this story, you have no idea.

Somewhere out there a poor woman named *"Stanky"* is throwing down this comic and making a *very* upset phone call to her parents, Stan and Becky.

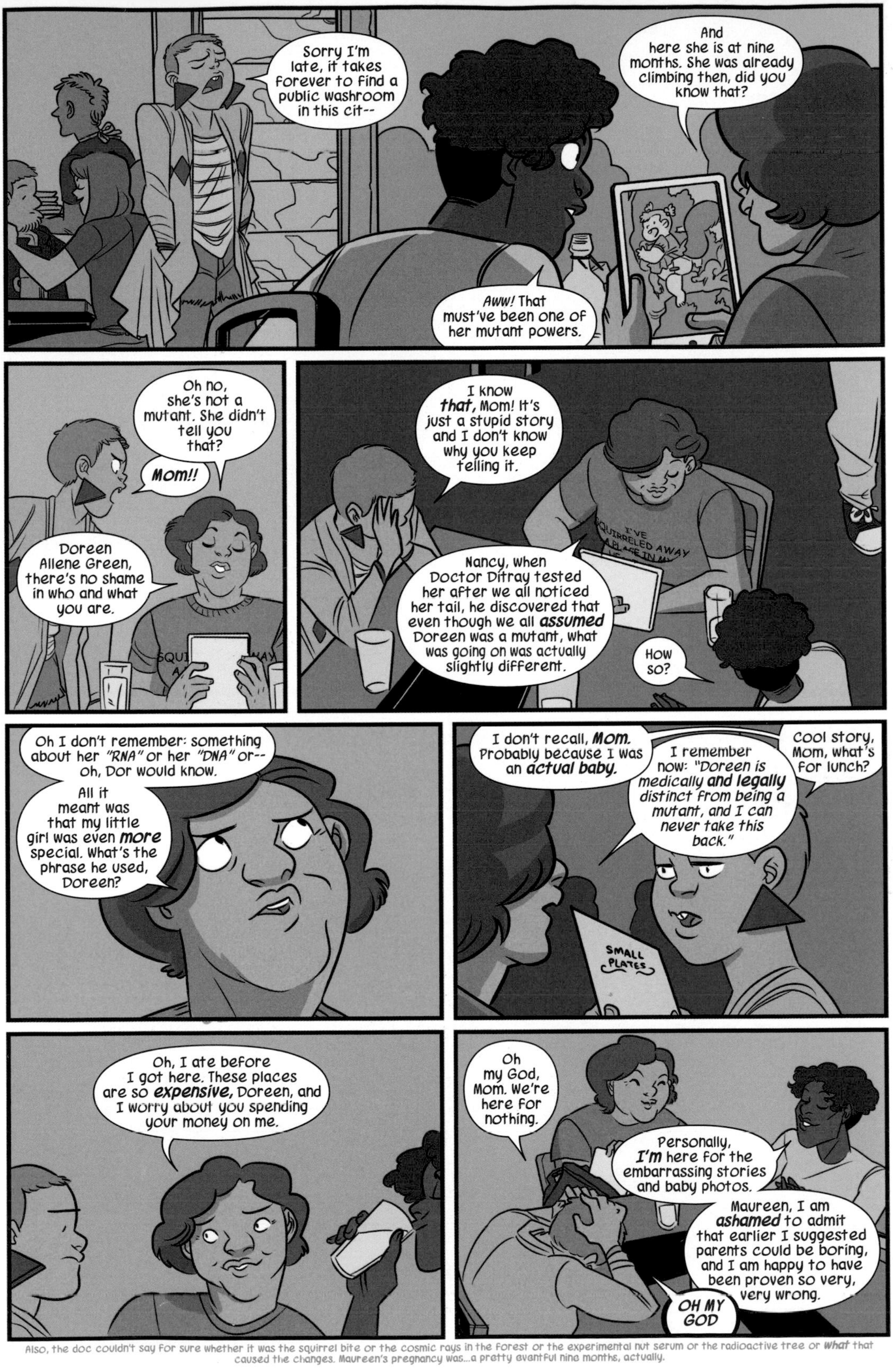
Sorry I'm late, it takes forever to find a public washroom in this cit--
And here she is at nine months. She was already climbing then, did you know that?
Aww! That must've been one of her mutant powers.
Oh no, she's not a mutant. She didn't tell you that?
Mom!!
Doreen Allene Green, there's no shame in who and what you are.
I know **that,** Mom! It's just a stupid story and I don't know why you keep telling it.
I'VE SQUIRRELED AWAY A PLACE IN MY
Nancy, when Doctor Ditray tested her after we all noticed her tail, he discovered that even though we all **assumed** Doreen was a mutant, what was going on was actually slightly different.
How so?
Oh I don't remember: something about her *"RNA"* or her *"DNA"* or-- oh, Dor would know.
All it meant was that my little girl was even **more** special. What's the phrase he used, Doreen?
I don't recall, **Mom.** Probably because I was an **actual baby.**
I remember now: *"Doreen is medically **and legally** distinct from being a mutant, and I can never take this back."*
Cool story, Mom, what's for lunch?
SMALL PLATES
Oh, I ate before I got here. These places are so **expensive,** Doreen, and I worry about you spending your money on me.
Oh my God, Mom. We're here for nothing.
Personally, ***I'm*** here for the embarrassing stories and baby photos.
Maureen, I am **ashamed** to admit that earlier I suggested parents could be boring, and I am happy to have been proven so very, very wrong.
OH MY GOD

Also, the doc couldn't say for sure whether it was the squirrel bite or the cosmic rays in the forest or the experimental nut serum or the radioactive tree or ***what*** that caused the changes. Maureen's pregnancy was...a pretty evantful nine months, actually.

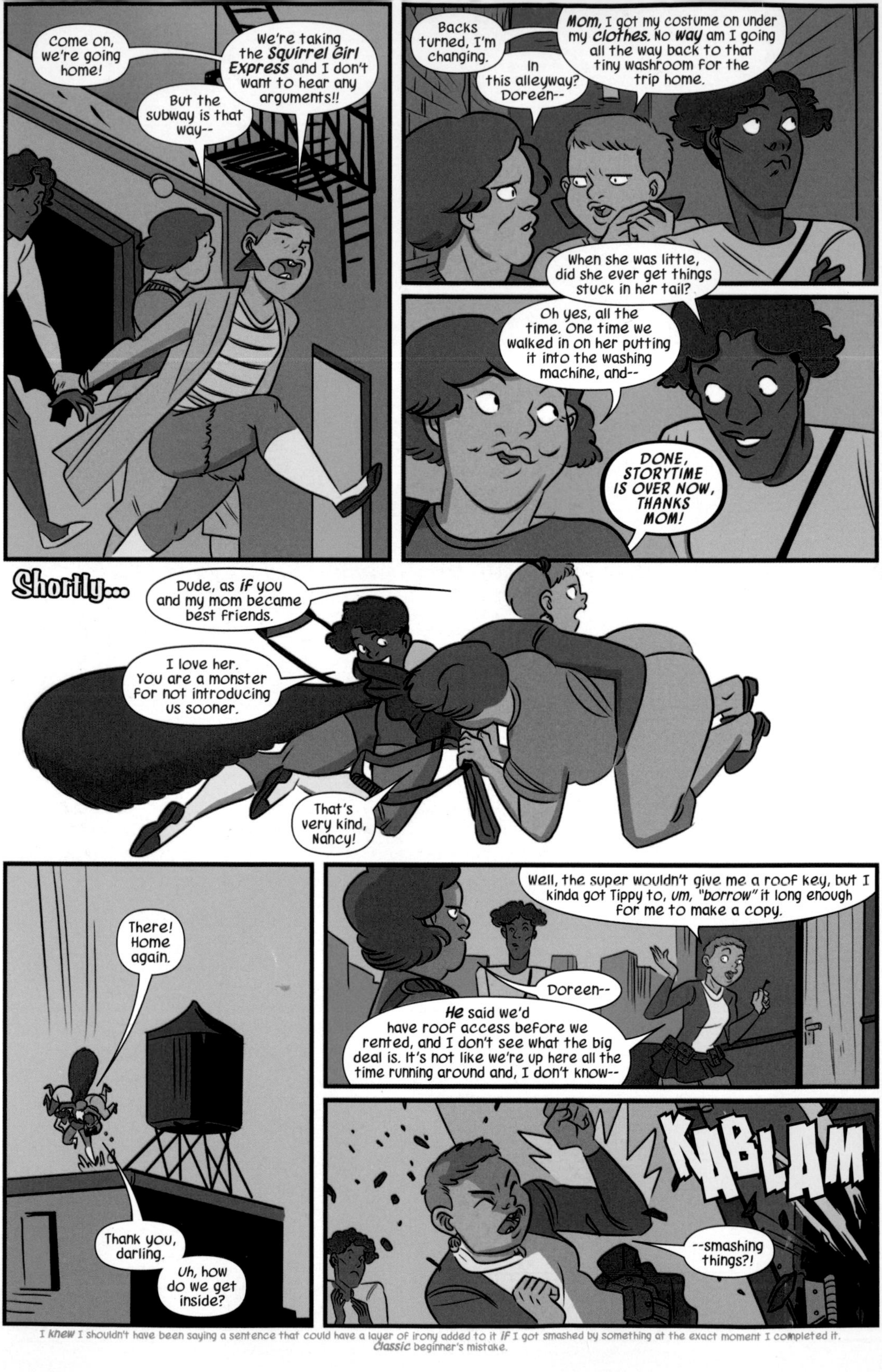

Come on, we're going home!
We're taking the Squirrel Girl Express and I don't want to hear any arguments!!
But the subway is that way--
Backs turned, I'm changing.
In this alleyway? Doreen--
Mom, I got my costume on under my clothes. No way am I going all the way back to that tiny washroom for the trip home.
When she was little, did she ever get things stuck in her tail?
Oh yes, all the time. One time we walked in on her putting it into the washing machine, and--
DONE, STORYTIME IS OVER NOW, THANKS MOM!
Shortly...
Dude, as if you and my mom became best friends.
I love her. You are a monster for not introducing us sooner.
That's very kind, Nancy!
There! Home again.
Thank you, darling.
Uh, how do we get inside?
Well, the super wouldn't give me a roof key, but I kinda got Tippy to, um, "borrow" it long enough for me to make a copy.
Doreen--
He said we'd have roof access before we rented, and I don't see what the big deal is. It's not like we're up here all the time running around and, I don't know--
KABLAM
--smashing things?!

I *knew* I shouldn't have been saying a sentence that could have a layer of irony added to it *if* I got smashed by something at the exact moment I completed it. *Classic* beginner's mistake.

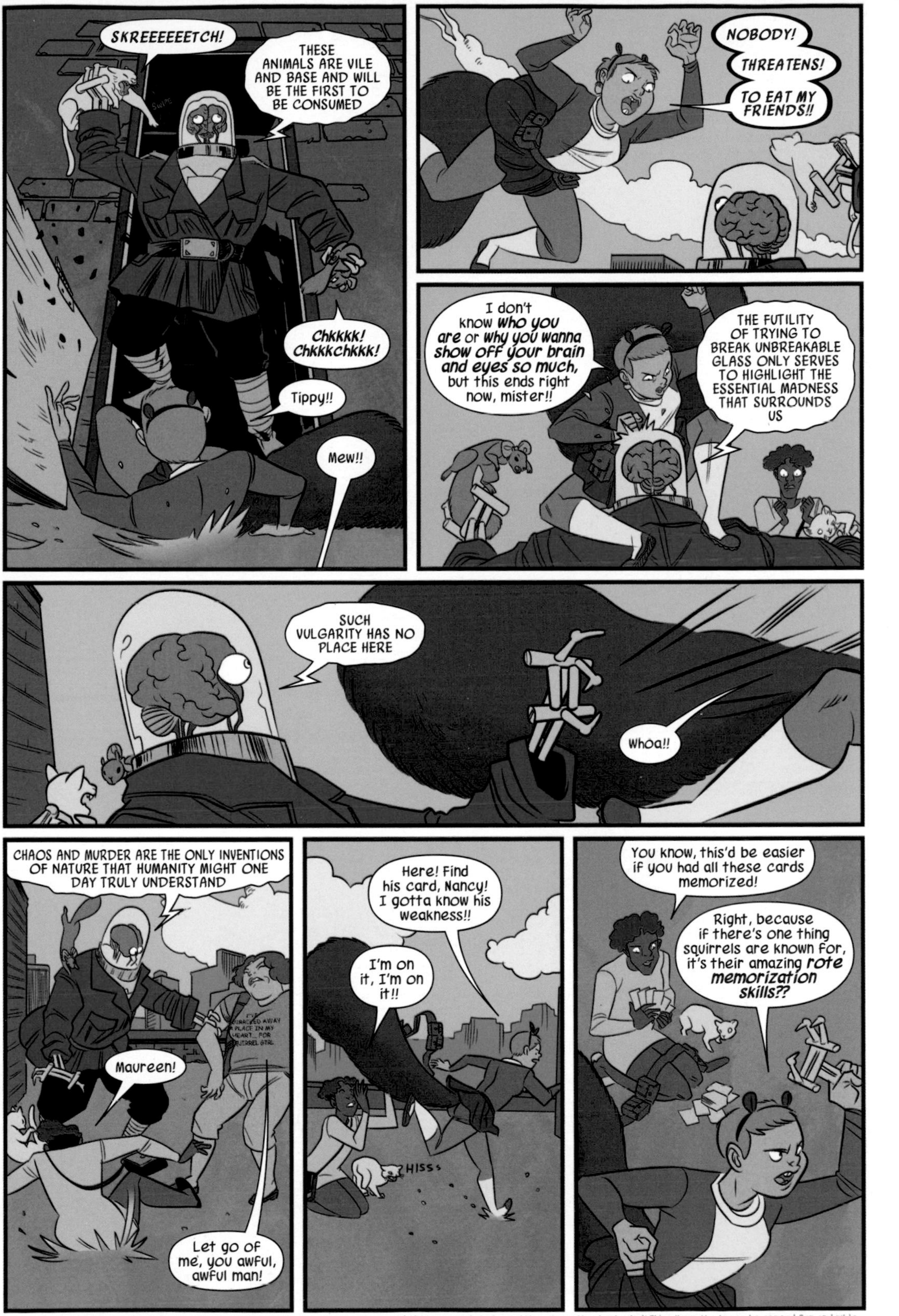
SKREEEEEETCH!
THESE ANIMALS ARE VILE AND BASE AND WILL BE THE FIRST TO BE CONSUMED
Chkkkk! Chkkkchkkk!
Tippy!!
Mew!!
NOBODY!
THREATENS!
TO EAT MY FRIENDS!!
I don't know who you are or why you wanna show off your brain and eyes so much, but this ends right now, mister!!
THE FUTILITY OF TRYING TO BREAK UNBREAKABLE GLASS ONLY SERVES TO HIGHLIGHT THE ESSENTIAL MADNESS THAT SURROUNDS US
SUCH VULGARITY HAS NO PLACE HERE
Whoa!!
CHAOS AND MURDER ARE THE ONLY INVENTIONS OF NATURE THAT HUMANITY MIGHT ONE DAY TRULY UNDERSTAND
Maureen!
Let go of me, you awful, awful man!
Here! Find his card, Nancy! I gotta know his weakness!!
I'm on it, I'm on it!!
HISSS
You know, this'd be easier if you had all these cards memorized!
Right, because if there's one thing squirrels are known for, it's their amazing rote memorization skills??

Actually, some tree species rely on squirrels stealing their nuts, burying them, and then completely forgetting where they're buried! This allows the trees to spread far and wide. THERE: now you know some squirrel facts *and* some *"fancy words for butts"* facts! I'd ***sincerely*** like to see each issue of *The Amazing Spider-Man* do ***that.***

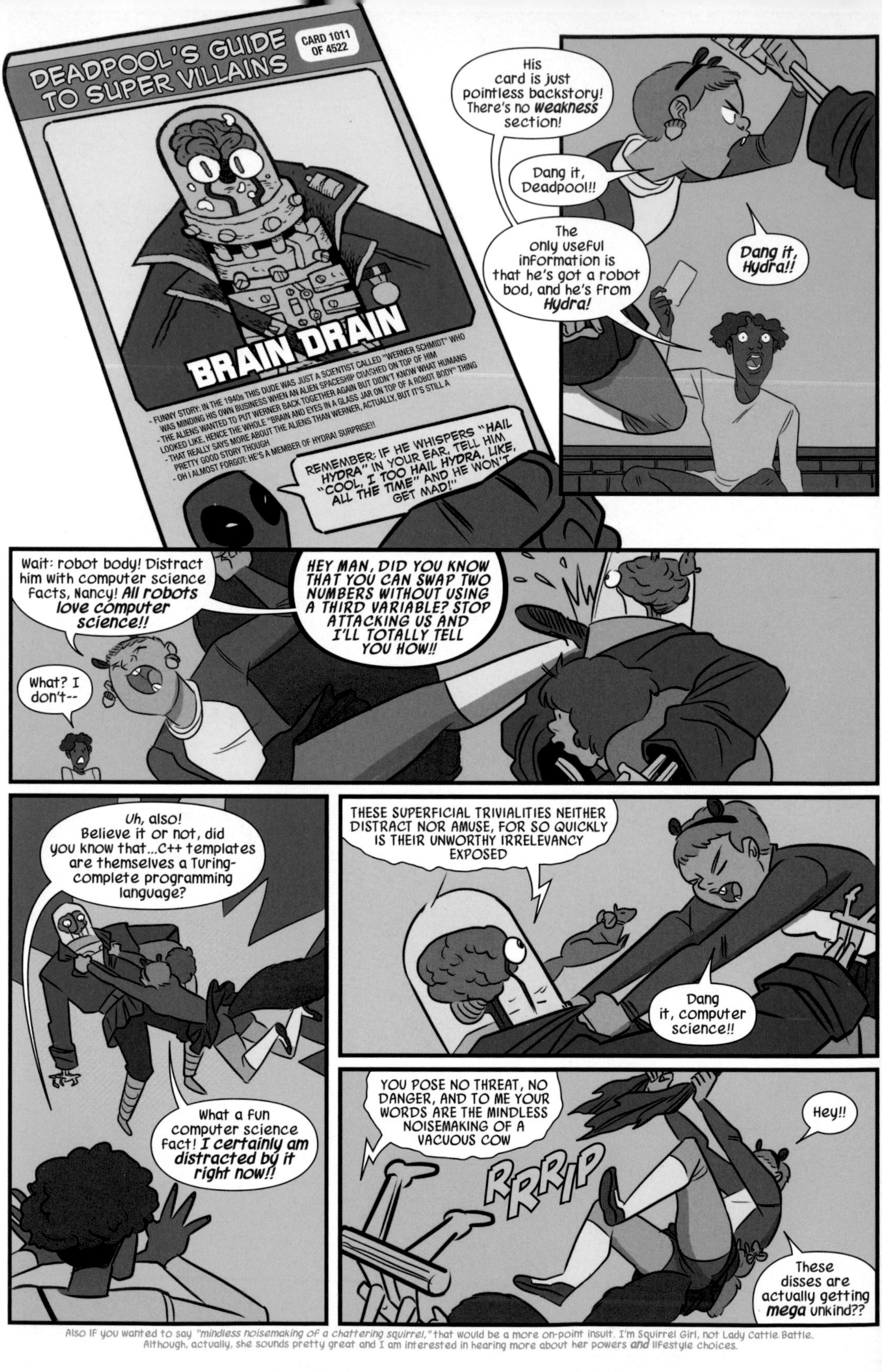
DEADPOOL'S GUIDE TO SUPER VILLAINS
CARD 1011 OF 4522
BRAIN DRAIN
- FUNNY STORY: IN THE 1940s THIS DUDE WAS JUST A SCIENTIST CALLED "WERNER SCHMIDT" WHO WAS MINDING HIS OWN BUSINESS WHEN AN ALIEN SPACESHIP CRASHED ON TOP OF HIM
- THE ALIENS WANTED TO PUT WERNER BACK TOGETHER AGAIN BUT DIDN'T KNOW WHAT HUMANS LOOKED LIKE, HENCE THE WHOLE "BRAIN AND EYES IN A GLASS JAR ON TOP OF A ROBOT BODY" THING
- THAT REALLY SAYS MORE ABOUT THE ALIENS THAN WERNER, ACTUALLY, BUT IT'S STILL A PRETTY GOOD STORY THOUGH
- OH I ALMOST FORGOT: HE'S A MEMBER OF HYDRA! SURPRISE!!
REMEMBER: IF HE WHISPERS "HAIL HYDRA" IN YOUR EAR, TELL HIM "COOL, I TOO HAIL HYDRA, LIKE, ALL THE TIME" AND HE WON'T GET MAD!"
His card is just pointless backstory! There's no weakness section!
Dang it, Deadpool!!
The only useful information is that he's got a robot bod, and he's from Hydra!
Dang it, Hydra!!
Wait: robot body! Distract him with computer science facts, Nancy! All robots love computer science!!
What? I don't--
HEY MAN, DID YOU KNOW THAT YOU CAN SWAP TWO NUMBERS WITHOUT USING A THIRD VARIABLE? STOP ATTACKING US AND I'LL TOTALLY TELL YOU HOW!!
Uh, also! Believe it or not, did you know that...C++ templates are themselves a Turing-complete programming language?
What a fun computer science fact! I certainly am distracted by it right now!!
THESE SUPERFICIAL TRIVIALITIES NEITHER DISTRACT NOR AMUSE, FOR SO QUICKLY IS THEIR UNWORTHY IRRELEVANCY EXPOSED
Dang it, computer science!!
YOU POSE NO THREAT, NO DANGER, AND TO ME YOUR WORDS ARE THE MINDLESS NOISEMAKING OF A VACUOUS COW
RRRIP
Hey!!
These disses are actually getting mega unkind??

Also if you wanted to say *"mindless noisemaking of a chattering squirrel,"* that would be a more on-point insult. I'm Squirrel Girl, not Lady Cattle Battle. Although, actually, she sounds pretty great and I am interested in hearing more about her powers ***and*** lifestyle choices.

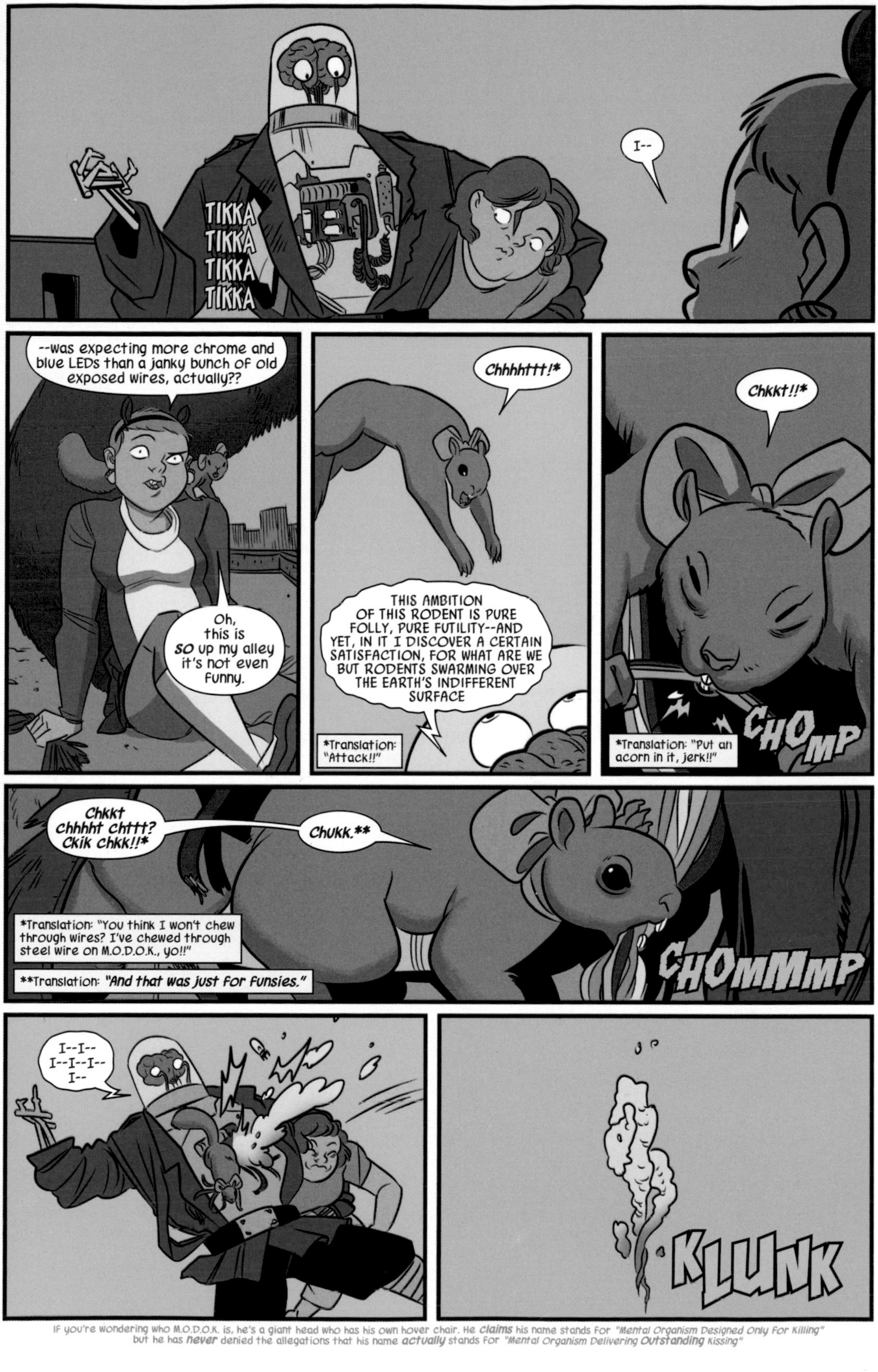
TIKKA TIKKA TIKKA TIKKA
I--
--was expecting more chrome and blue LEDs than a janky bunch of old exposed wires, actually??
Oh, this is SO up my alley it's not even funny.
Chhhhttt!*
THIS AMBITION OF THIS RODENT IS PURE FOLLY, PURE FUTILITY--AND YET, IN IT I DISCOVER A CERTAIN SATISFACTION, FOR WHAT ARE WE BUT RODENTS SWARMING OVER THE EARTH'S INDIFFERENT SURFACE
*Translation: "Attack!!"
Chkkt!!*
*Translation: "Put an acorn in it, jerk!!"
CHOMP
Chkkt chhhht chttt? Ckik chkk!!*
Chukk.**
*Translation: "You think I won't chew through wires? I've chewed through steel wire on M.O.D.O.K., yo!!"
**Translation: "And that was just for funsies."
CHOMMMMP
I--I-- I--I--I-- I--
KLUNK

If you're wondering who M.O.D.O.K. is, he's a giant head who has his own hover chair. He *claims* his name stands for "Mental Organism Designed Only For Killing" but he has *never* denied the allegations that his name *actually* stands for "Mental Organism Delivering *Outstanding* Kissing"

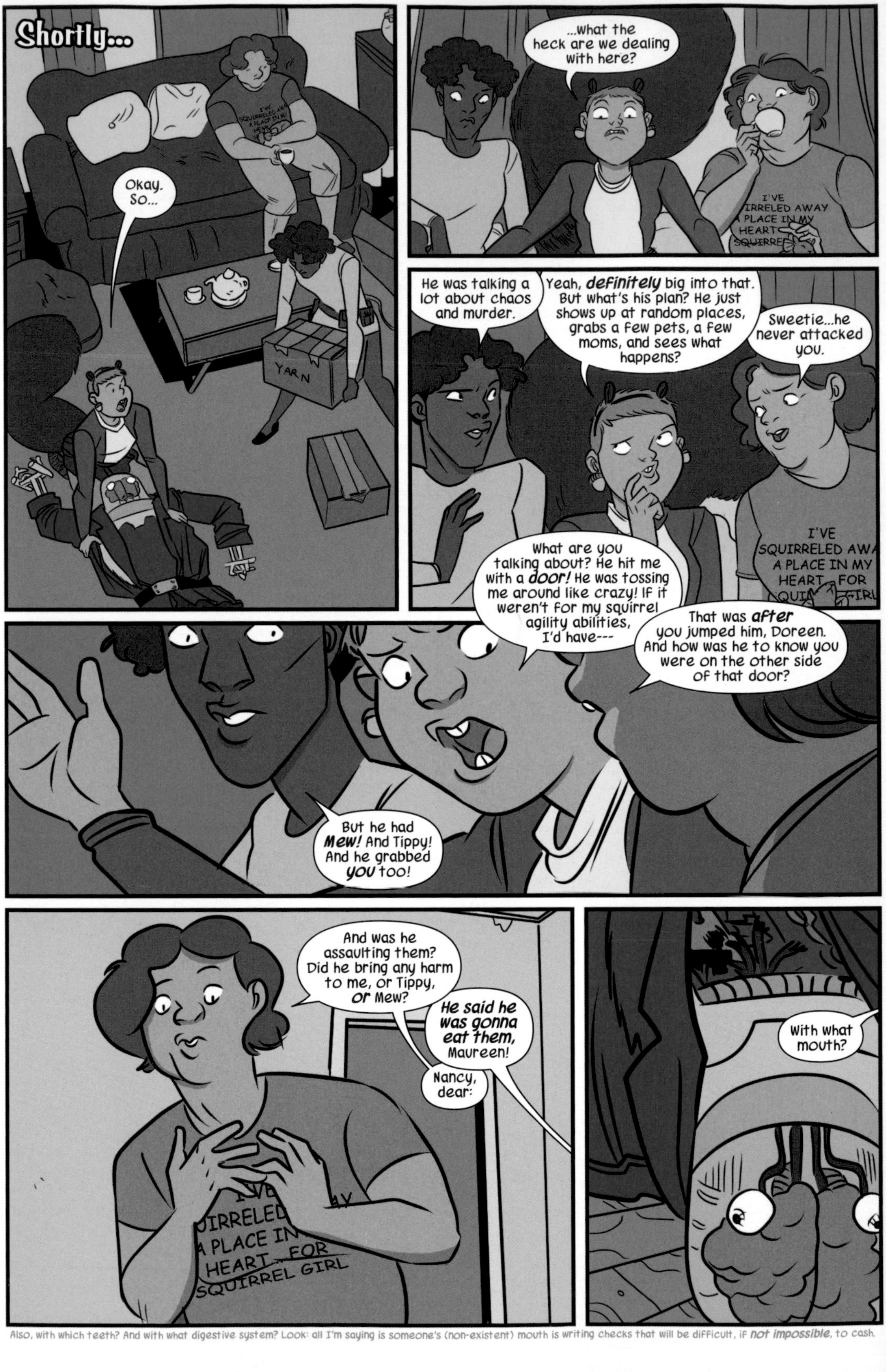
Shortly...
Okay. So...
YARN
...what the heck are we dealing with here?
He was talking a lot about chaos and murder.
Yeah, *definitely* big into that. But what's his plan? He just shows up at random places, grabs a few pets, a few moms, and sees what happens?
Sweetie...he never attacked you.
What are you talking about? He hit me with a *door!* He was tossing me around like crazy! If it weren't for my squirrel agility abilities, I'd have---
That was *after* you jumped him, Doreen. And how was he to know you were on the other side of that door?
But he had *Mew!* And Tippy! And he grabbed *you* too!
And was he assaulting them? Did he bring any harm to me, or Tippy, *or* Mew?
He said he was gonna eat them, Maureen!
Nancy, dear:
With what mouth?

Also, with which teeth? And with what digestive system? Look: all I'm saying is someone's (non-existent) mouth is writing checks that will be difficult, if *not impossible,* to cash.

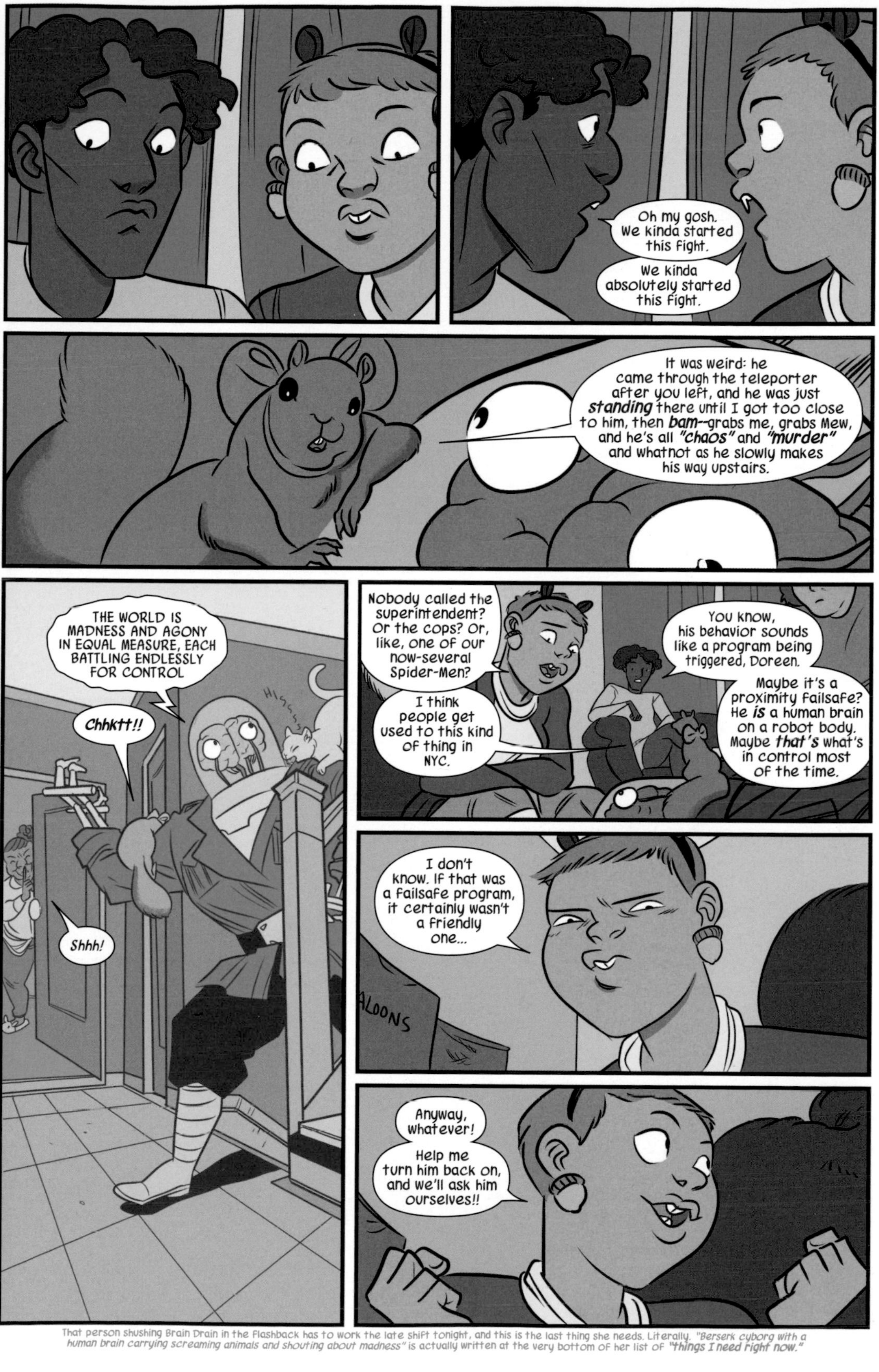

Oh my gosh. We kinda started this fight.
We kinda absolutely started this fight.
It was weird: he came through the teleporter after you left, and he was just *standing* there until I got too close to him, then *bam*--grabs me, grabs Mew, and he's all *"chaos"* and *"murder"* and whatnot as he slowly makes his way upstairs.
THE WORLD IS MADNESS AND AGONY IN EQUAL MEASURE, EACH BATTLING ENDLESSLY FOR CONTROL
Chhktt!!
HISSSS
Shhh!
Nobody called the superintendent? Or the cops? Or, like, one of our now-several Spider-Men?
I think people get used to this kind of thing in NYC.
You know, his behavior sounds like a program being triggered, Doreen.
Maybe it's a proximity failsafe? He *is* a human brain on a robot body. Maybe *that's* what's in control most of the time.
I don't know. If that was a failsafe program, it certainly wasn't a friendly one...
ALOONS
Anyway, whatever!
Help me turn him back on, and we'll ask him ourselves!!

That person shushing Brain Drain in the flashback has to work the late shift tonight, and this is the last thing she needs. Literally. *"Berserk cyborg with a human brain carrying screaming animals and shouting about madness"* is actually written at the very bottom of her list of ***"things I need right now."***

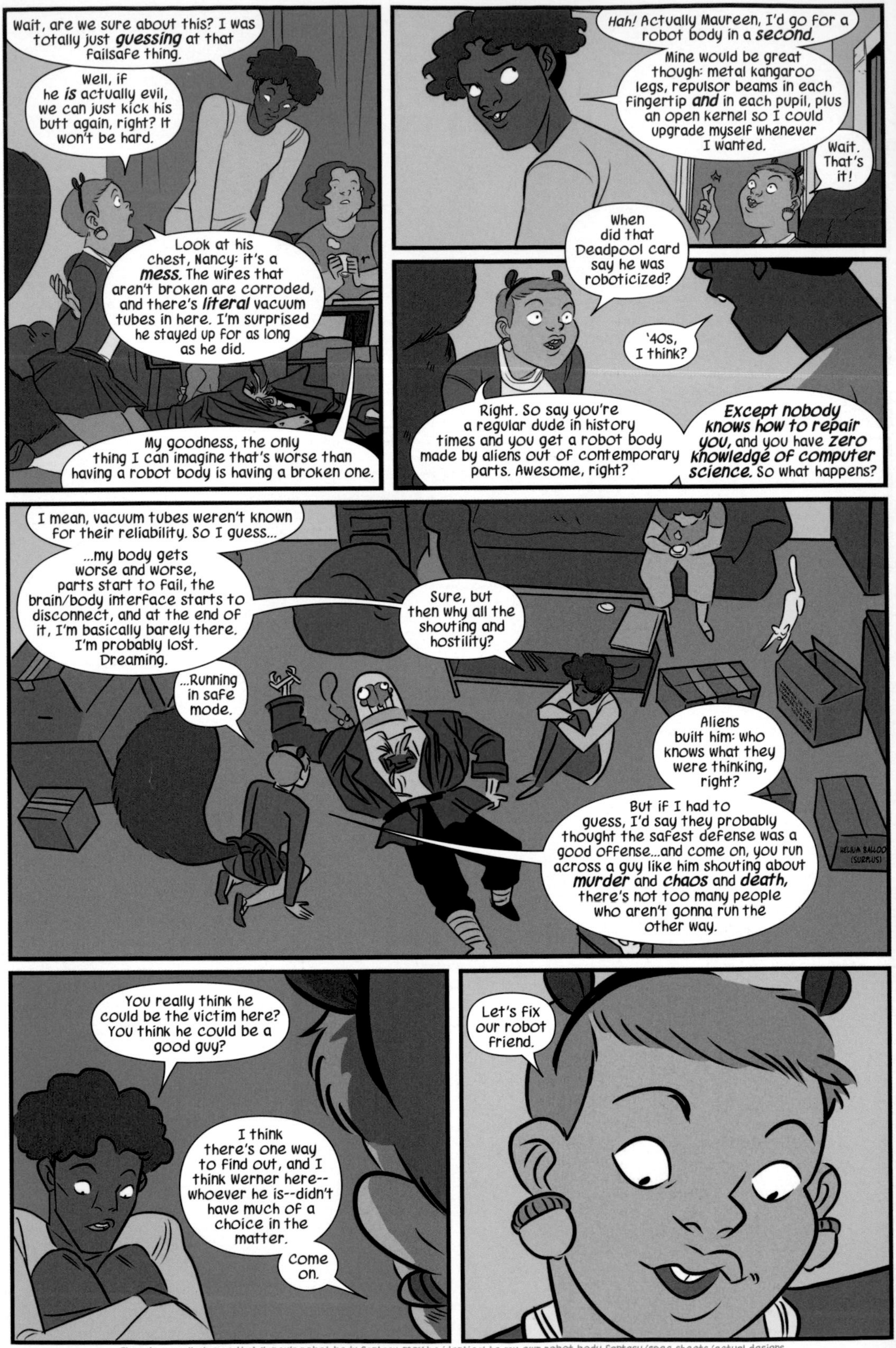
Wait, are we sure about this? I was totally just *guessing* at that failsafe thing.
Well, if he *is* actually evil, we can just kick his butt again, right? It won't be hard.
Look at his chest, Nancy: it's a *mess.* The wires that aren't broken are corroded, and there's *literal* vacuum tubes in here. I'm surprised he stayed up for as long as he did.
My goodness, the only thing I can imagine that's worse than having a robot body is having a broken one.
Hah! Actually Maureen, I'd go for a robot body in a *second.*
Mine would be great though: metal kangaroo legs, repulsor beams in each fingertip *and* in each pupil, plus an open kernel so I could upgrade myself whenever I wanted.
Wait. That's it!
When did that Deadpool card say he was roboticized?
'40s, I think?
Right. So say you're a regular dude in history times and you get a robot body made by aliens out of contemporary parts. Awesome, right?
Except nobody knows how to repair you, and you have *zero knowledge of computer science.* So what happens?
I mean, vacuum tubes weren't known for their reliability. So I guess...
...my body gets worse and worse, parts start to fail, the brain/body interface starts to disconnect, and at the end of it, I'm basically barely there. I'm probably lost. Dreaming.
Sure, but then why all the shouting and hostility?
...Running in safe mode.
Aliens built him: who knows what they were thinking, right?
But if I had to guess, I'd say they probably thought the safest defense was a good offense...and come on, you run across a guy like him shouting about *murder* and *chaos* and *death,* there's not too many people who aren't gonna run the other way.
You really think he could be the victim here? You think he could be a good guy?
I think there's one way to find out, and I think Werner here--whoever he is--didn't have much of a choice in the matter.
Come on.
Let's fix our robot friend.

There's a small chance that Nancy's robot body fantasy *may* be identical to my own robot body fantasy/spec sheets/actual designs that I've written up and carry with me everywhere and think about all the time.

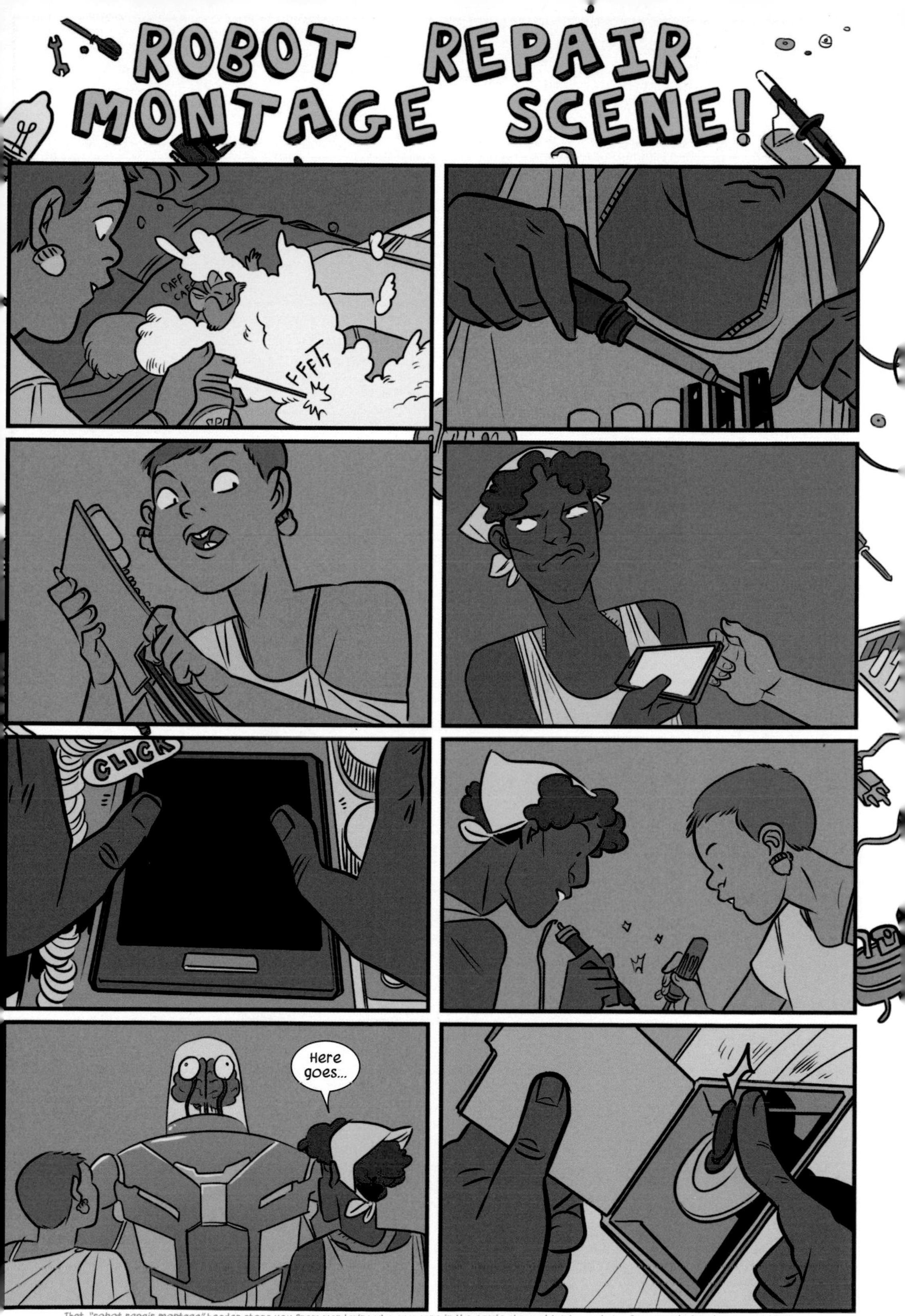
ROBOT REPAIR MONTAGE SCENE!
CAFF
FFFTT
CLICK
Here goes...

That *"robot repair montage"* header stops you from wondering why everyone in the comic stopped talking, and also from wondering why you can hear awesome pump-up robot repair montage music in your head whenever you look at this page and concentrate really hard!

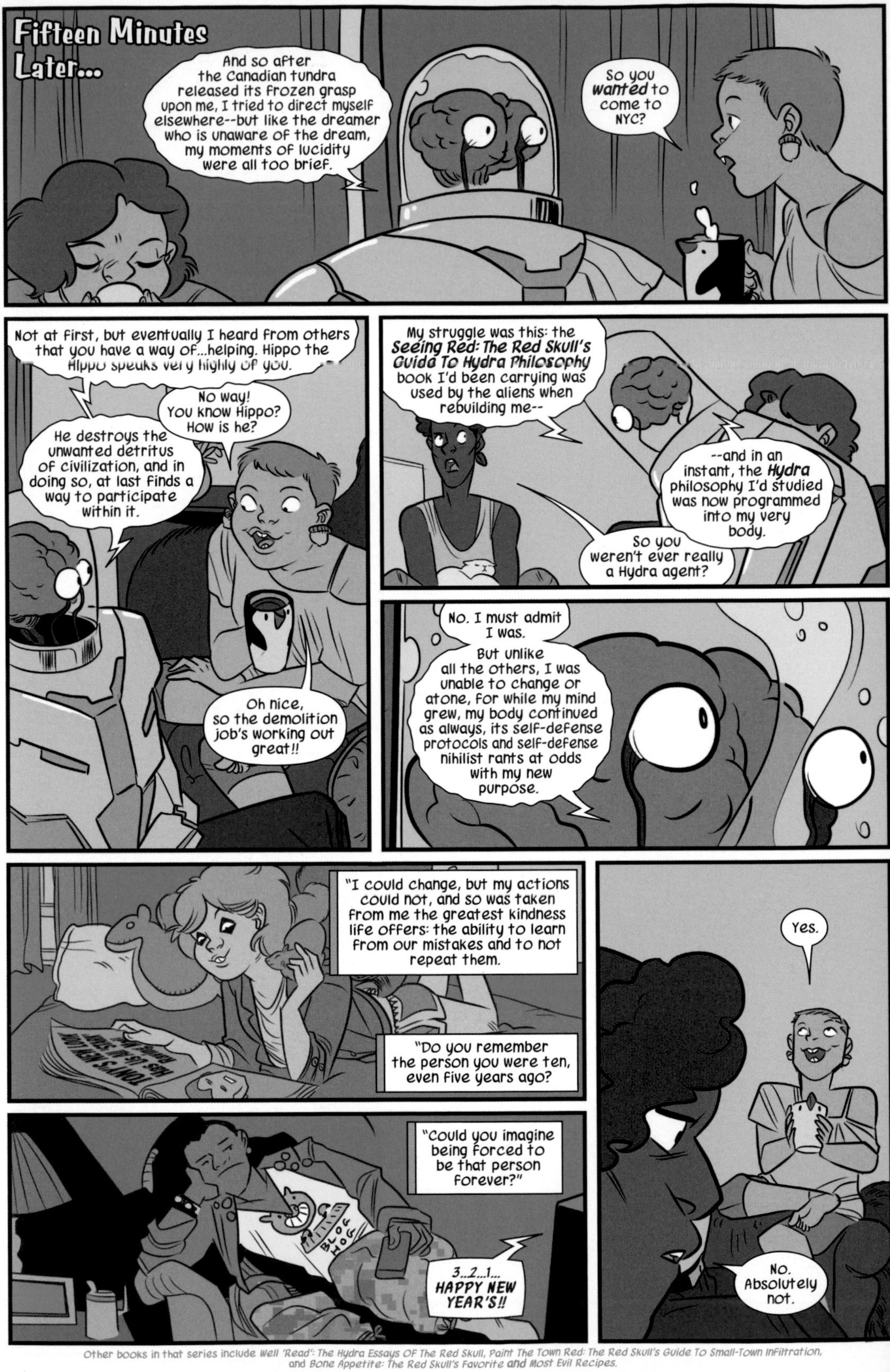
Fifteen Minutes Later...
And so after the Canadian tundra released its frozen grasp upon me, I tried to direct myself elsewhere--but like the dreamer who is unaware of the dream, my moments of lucidity were all too brief.
So you *wanted* to come to NYC?
Not at first, but eventually I heard from others that you have a way of...helping. Hippo the Hippo speaks very highly of you.
No way! You know Hippo? How is he?
He destroys the unwanted detritus of civilization, and in doing so, at last finds a way to participate within it.
Oh nice, so the demolition job's working out great!!
My struggle was this: the *Seeing Red: The Red Skull's Guide To Hydra Philosophy* book I'd been carrying was used by the aliens when rebuilding me--
--and in an instant, the *Hydra* philosophy I'd studied was now programmed into my very body.
So you weren't ever really a Hydra agent?
No. I must admit I was.
But unlike all the others, I was unable to change or atone, for while my mind grew, my body continued as always, its self-defense protocols and self-defense nihilist rants at odds with my new purpose.
"I could change, but my actions could not, and so was taken from me the greatest kindness life offers: the ability to learn from our mistakes and to not repeat them.
"Do you remember the person you were ten, even five years ago?
Yes.
"Could you imagine being forced to be that person forever?"
BLOG HOG
3...2...1... HAPPY NEW YEAR'S!!
No. Absolutely not.

Other books in that series include *Well 'Read': The Hydra Essays Of The Red Skull*, *Paint The Town Red: The Red Skull's Guide To Small-Town Infiltration*, and *Bone Appetite: The Red Skull's Favorite* and *Most Evil Recipes*.

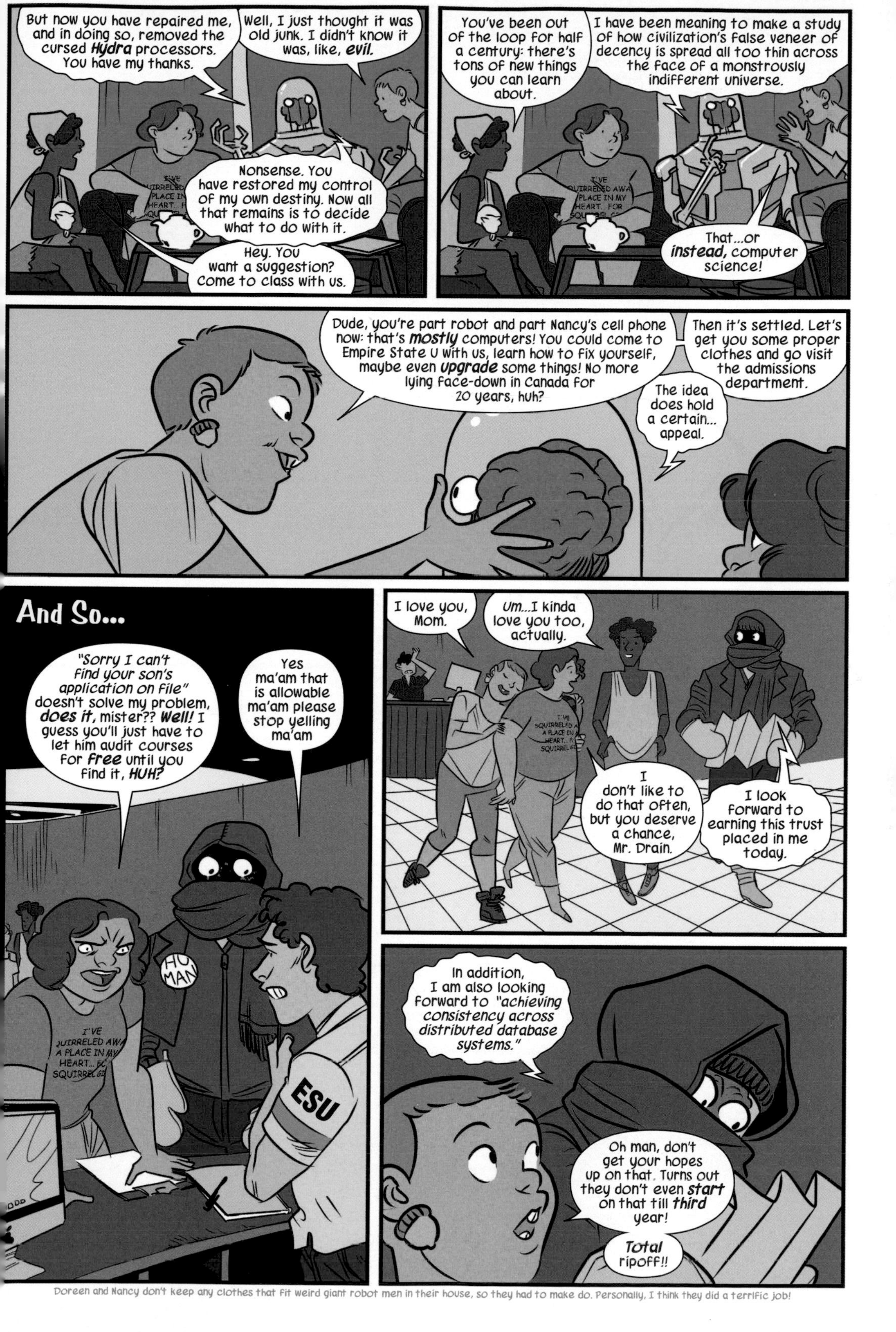
But now you have repaired me, and in doing so, removed the cursed *Hydra* processors. You have my thanks.
Well, I just thought it was old junk. I didn't know it was, like, ***evil.***
Nonsense. You have restored my control of my own destiny. Now all that remains is to decide what to do with it.
Hey. You want a suggestion? Come to class with us.
You've been out of the loop for half a century: there's tons of new things you can learn about.
I have been meaning to make a study of how civilization's false veneer of decency is spread all too thin across the face of a monstrously indifferent universe.
That...or ***instead,*** computer science!
Dude, you're part robot and part Nancy's cell phone now: that's ***mostly*** computers! You could come to Empire State U with us, learn how to fix yourself, maybe even ***upgrade*** some things! No more lying face-down in Canada for 20 years, huh?
Then it's settled. Let's get you some proper clothes and go visit the admissions department.
The idea does hold a certain... appeal.
And So...
"Sorry I can't find your son's application on file" doesn't solve my problem, ***does it,*** mister?? ***Well!*** I guess you'll just have to let him audit courses for ***free*** until you find it, ***HUH?***
Yes ma'am that is allowable ma'am please stop yelling ma'am
HU MAN
ESU
I love you, Mom.
Um...I kinda love you too, actually.
I don't like to do that often, but you deserve a chance, Mr. Drain.
I look forward to earning this trust placed in me today.
In addition, I am also looking forward to *"achieving consistency across distributed database systems."*
Oh man, don't get your hopes up on that. Turns out they don't even ***start*** on that till ***third*** year!
Total ripoff!!

Doreen and Nancy don't keep any clothes that fit weird giant robot men in their house, so they had to make do. Personally, I think they did a terrific job!

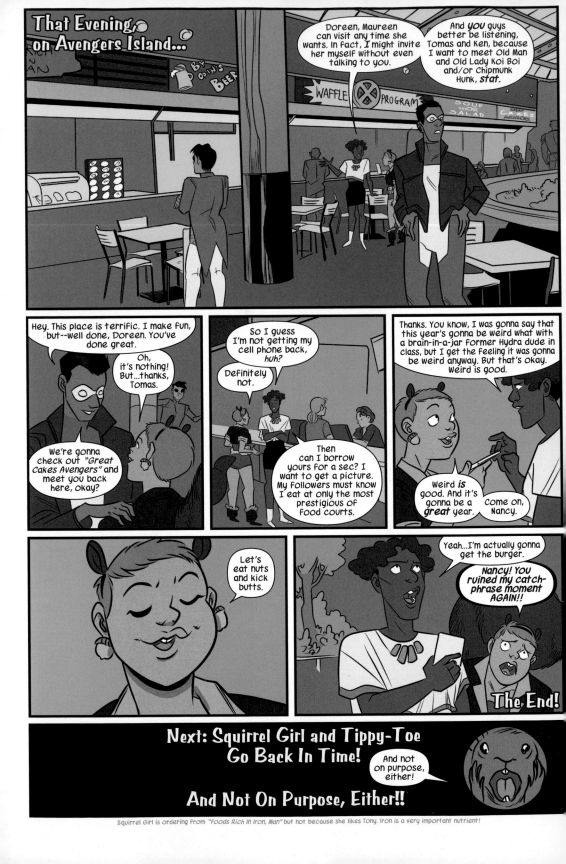

That Evening, on Avengers Island...

Doreen, Maureen can visit any time she wants. In fact, I might invite her myself without even talking to you.

And YOU guys better be listening, Tomas and Ken, because I want to meet Old Man and Old Lady Koi Boi and/or Chipmunk Hunk, stat.

BY ODIN'S BEER

WAFFLE PROGRAM

SOUP and SALAD

CAKES AVENGERS

Hey. This place is terrific. I make fun, but--well done, Doreen. You've done great.

Oh, it's nothing! But...thanks, Tomas.

We're gonna check out "Great Cakes Avengers" and meet you back here, okay?

So I guess I'm not getting my cell phone back, huh?

Definitely not.

Then can I borrow yours for a sec? I want to get a picture. My followers must know I eat at only the most prestigious of food courts.

Thanks. You know, I was gonna say that this year's gonna be weird what with a brain-in-a-jar former Hydra dude in class, but I get the feeling it was gonna be weird anyway. But that's okay. Weird is good.

Weird is good. And it's gonna be a great year.

Come on, Nancy.

Let's eat nuts and kick butts.

Yeah...I'm actually gonna get the burger.

Nancy! You ruined my catch-phrase moment AGAIN!!

The End!

Next: Squirrel Girl and Tippy-Toe Go Back In Time!

And not on purpose, either!

And Not On Purpose, Either!!

Squirrel Girl is ordering from "Foods Rich in Iron, Man" but not because she likes Tony. Iron is a very important nutrient!

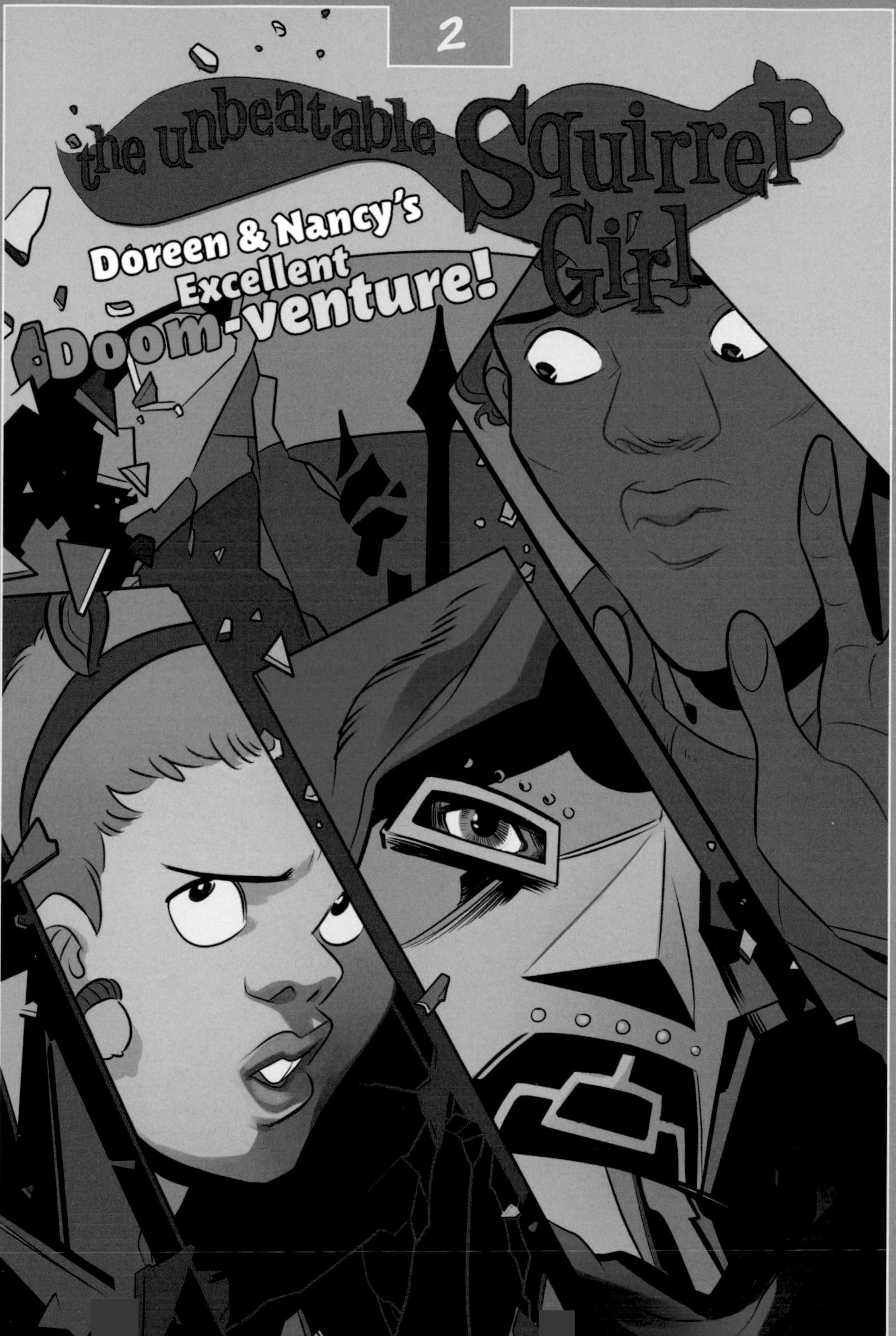
2
the unbeatable Squirrel Girl
Doreen & Nancy's Excellent Doom-venture!

Doreen Green isn't just a second-year computer science student: she secretly also has all the powers of both squirrel and girl! She uses her amazing abilities to fight crime **and** be as awesome as possible. You know her as...*The Unbeatable Squirrel Girl!* Find out what she's been up to, with...

Squirrel Girl *in a nutshell*

search!

#TIMEforachange

#aheadofherTIME

#theresaTIMEandaplace

#thirdTIMEisthecharm

#anywayyesthisissueisabouttimetravel

#surprise

Squirrel Girl! @unbeatablesg
Philosophers are always like "whoa I'm gonna a blow your mind what if we're just brains in jars and reality is fake whoaaaa"!

Squirrel Girl! @unbeatablesg
But check this: what if we're just brains in jars on SUPERPOWERED ROBOT BODIES? Oh snap! Did philosophy just get...SUPER AWESOME??

Squirrel Girl! @unbeatablesg
Anyway this is all to say I fought a brain in a jar on a robot bod and it was rad and his name is Werner and we're friends now, nbd

Squirrel Girl! @unbeatablesg
@starkmantony hey Tony I had a great idea! What if instead of wearing Iron Man suits, you put your brain in a jar and armored THAT instead?

Squirrel Girl! @unbeatablesg
@starkmantony you'd save mega $$$ on iron suits for sure PLUS it would give your enemies a smaller target to hit (tactical advantage)

Squirrel Girl! @unbeatablesg
@starkmantony instead of "Iron Man" we could call you "Iron MIND," and you'd float around the city solving math puzzles

Tony Stark @starkmantony ✓
@unbeatablesg Squirrel Girl, don't you have a crime to fight somewhere? Anywhere?

Squirrel Girl! @unbeatablesg
@starkmantony yes

Squirrel Girl! @unbeatablesg
@starkmantony for example, i'm currently fighting the crime of you not calling yourself "Iron Mind" and solving brain teasers

Nancy W. @sewwiththeflo
How attractive is it to be in your early 20s and running a blog for your cat? Because I'm seriously considering it.

Nancy W. @sewwiththeflo
And by "how attractive" I don't mean, like, "attractive to guys." I mean "how instantly appealing is that idea." Answer? Extremely.

Squirrel Girl! @unbeatablesg
@sewwiththeflo NEVER CHANGE <3

Nancy W. @sewwiththeflo
@unbeatablesg I'm gonna post Cat Thor fics too, and I'm working on one featuring Lokitten (v mischievous kitten)

Squirrel Girl! @unbeatablesg
@sewwiththeflo omg!! WE HAVE TO SEND THEM TO LOKI

Squirrel Girl! @unbeatablesg
@starkmantony TONY DO YOU HAVE A WAY TO EMAIL ASGARD

Squirrel Girl! @unbeatablesg
@starkmantony TONY

Squirrel Girl! @unbeatablesg
@starkmantony TONY

Squirrel Girl! @unbeatablesg
@starkmantony TONY

Squirrel Girl! @unbeatablesg
@starkmantony TONY WHY DOES IT SAY I'M BLOCKED

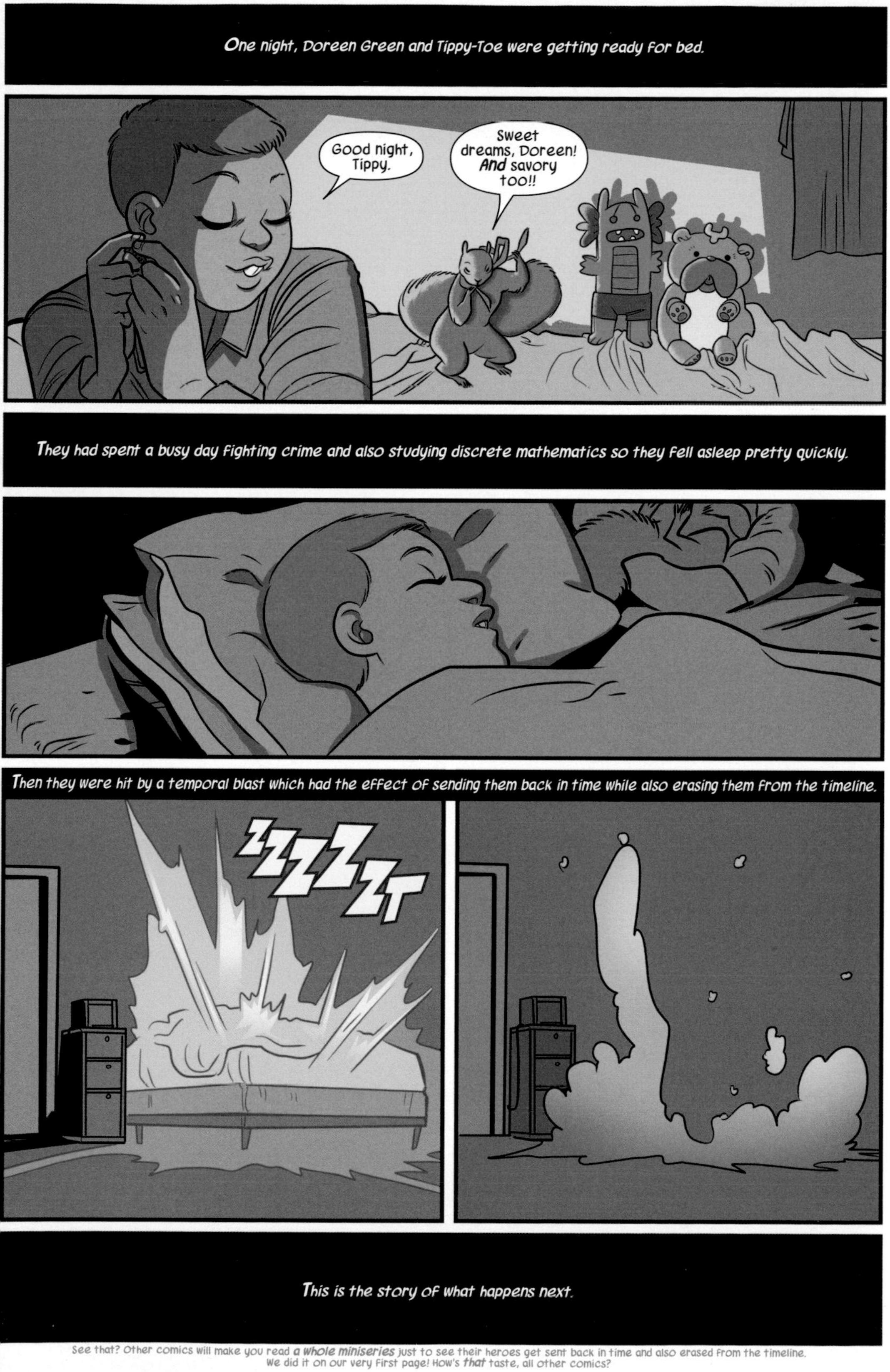
One night, Doreen Green and Tippy-Toe were getting ready for bed.
Good night, Tippy.
Sweet dreams, Doreen! And savory too!!
They had spent a busy day fighting crime and also studying discrete mathematics so they fell asleep pretty quickly.
Then they were hit by a temporal blast which had the effect of sending them back in time while also erasing them from the timeline.
ZZZZZT
This is the story of what happens next.

See that? Other comics will make you read *a whole miniseries* just to see their heroes get sent back in time and also erased from the timeline.
We did it on our very first page! How's *that* taste, all other comics?

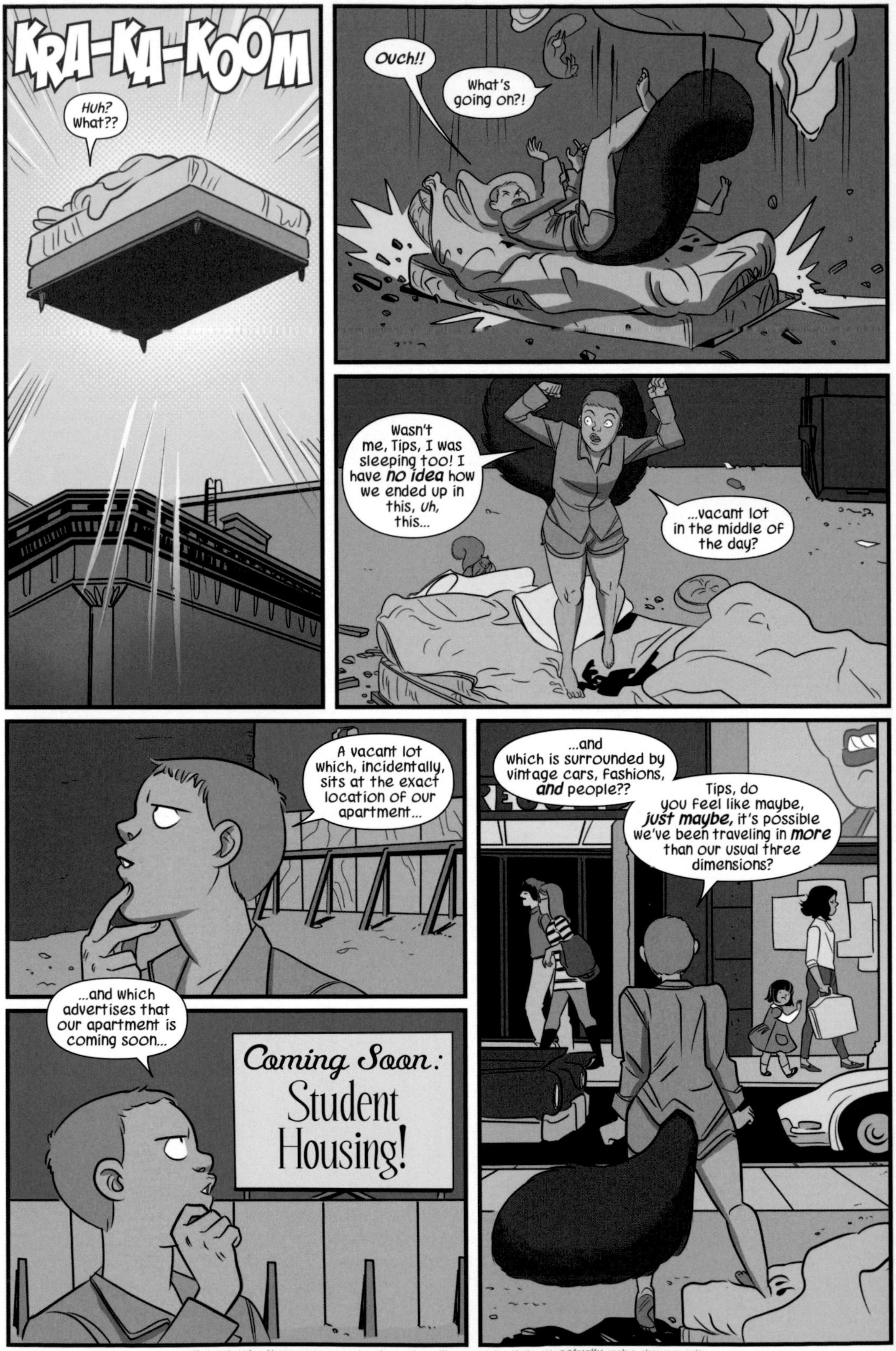
KRA-KA-KOOM
Huh? What??
Ouch!!
What's going on?!
Wasn't me, Tips, I was sleeping too! I have no idea how we ended up in this, uh, this...
...vacant lot in the middle of the day?
A vacant lot which, incidentally, sits at the exact location of our apartment...
...and which advertises that our apartment is coming soon...
Coming Soon: Student Housing!
...and which is surrounded by vintage cars, fashions, and people??
Tips, do you feel like maybe, just maybe, it's possible we've been traveling in more than our usual three dimensions?

I've cut out a three-page sequence here where Tippy explains that, *um, actually,* we're always moving through the fourth dimension (time) too. Come on, Tippy. Don't be that gal.

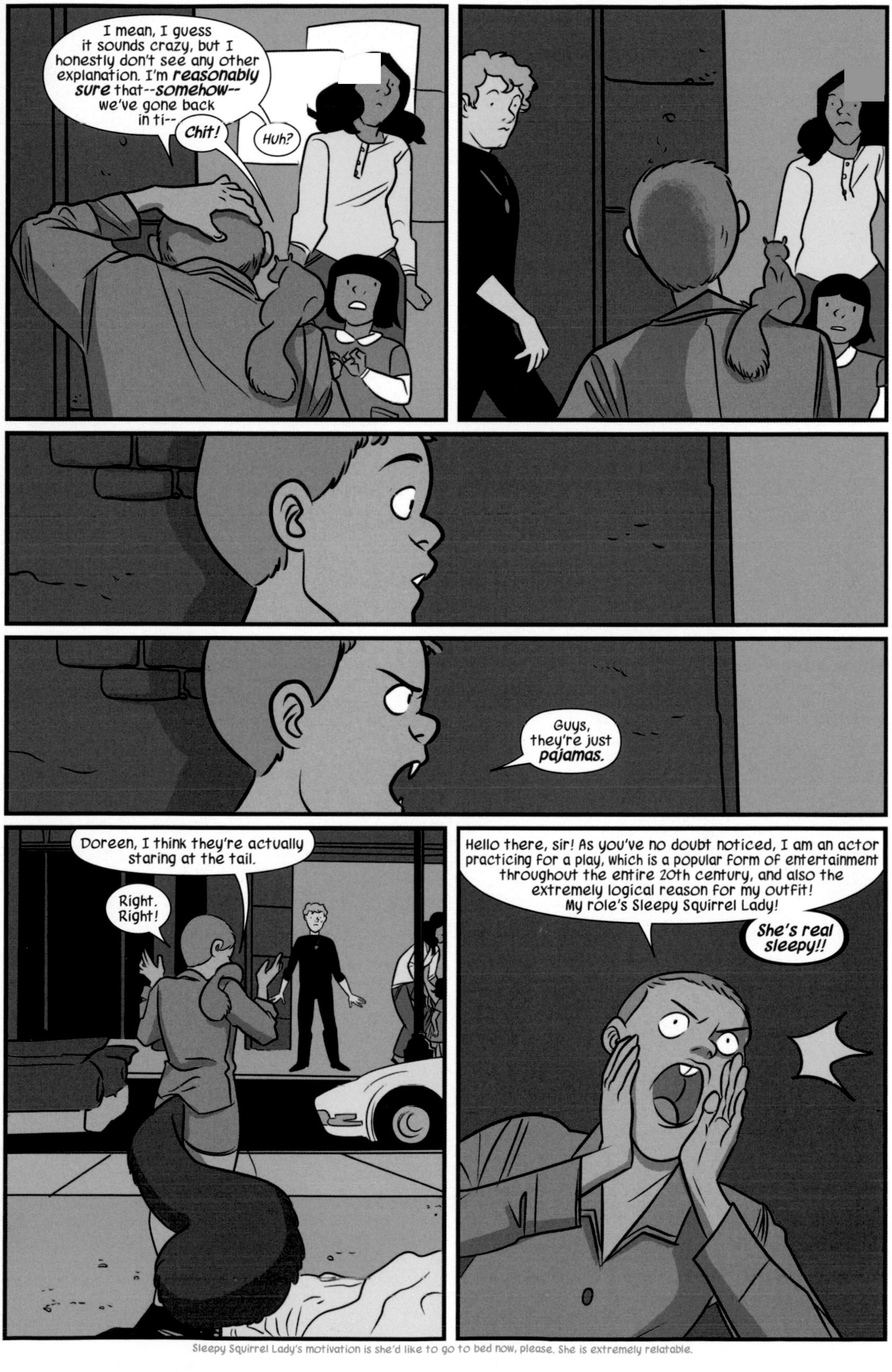
I mean, I guess it sounds crazy, but I honestly don't see any other explanation. I'm *reasonably sure* that--*somehow*--we've gone back in ti--
Chit!
Huh?
Guys, they're just *pajamas.*
Doreen, I think they're actually staring at the tail.
Right. Right!
Hello there, sir! As you've no doubt noticed, I am an actor practicing for a play, which is a popular form of entertainment throughout the entire 20th century, and also the extremely logical reason for my outfit! My role's Sleepy Squirrel Lady!
She's real sleepy!!
Sleepy Squirrel Lady's motivation is she'd like to go to bed now, please. She is extremely relatable.

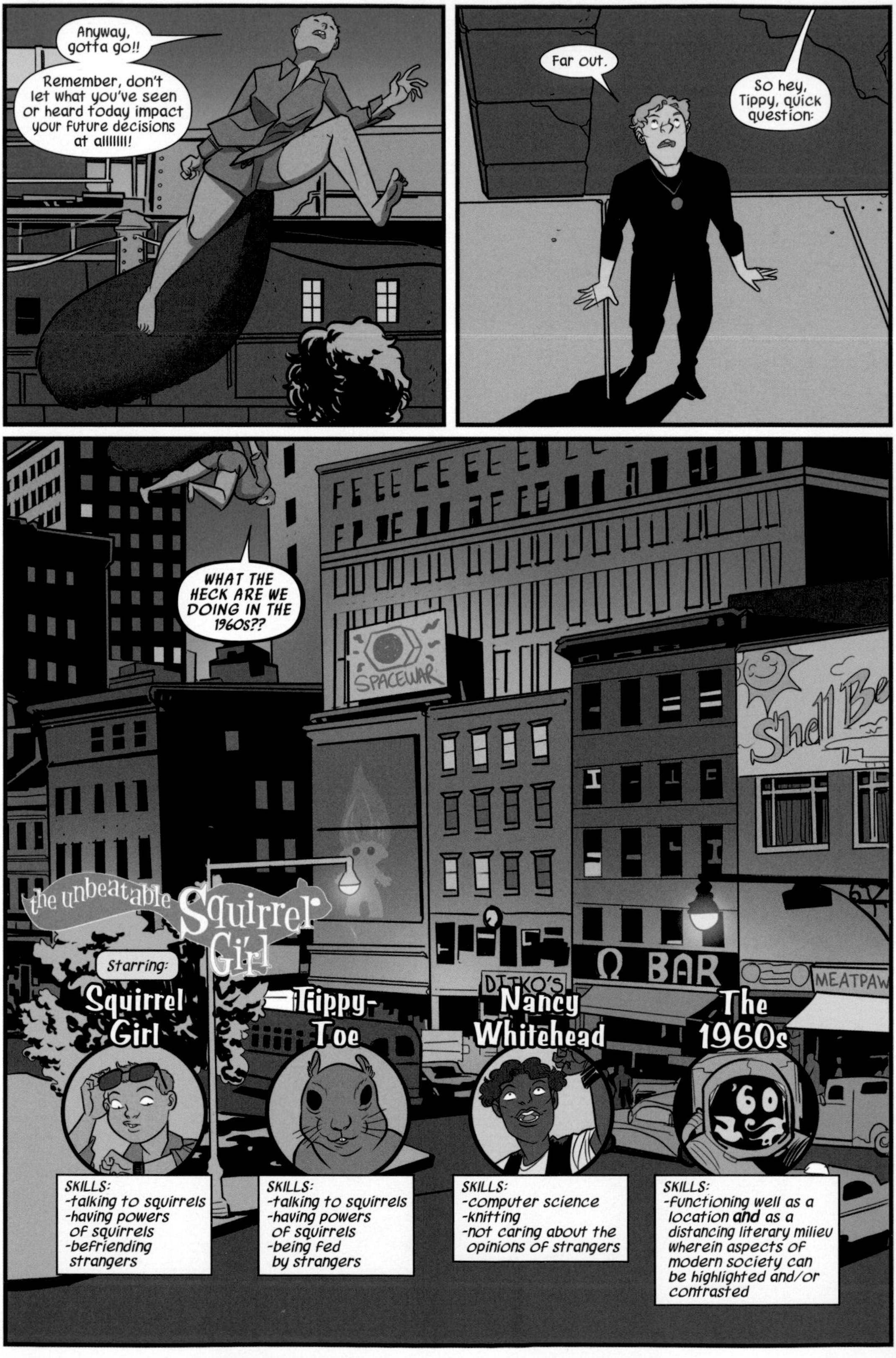
Anyway, gotta go!!
Remember, don't let what you've seen or heard today impact your future decisions at allllll!
Far out.
So hey, Tippy, quick question:
WHAT THE HECK ARE WE DOING IN THE 1960s??
SPACEWAR
Shell Be
DITKO'S
Ω BAR
MEATPAW
the unbeatable Squirrel Girl
Starring:
Squirrel Girl
SKILLS:
-talking to squirrels
-having powers of squirrels
-befriending strangers
Tippy-Toe
SKILLS:
-talking to squirrels
-having powers of squirrels
-being fed by strangers
Nancy Whitehead
SKILLS:
-computer science
-knitting
-not caring about the opinions of strangers
The 1960s
'60
SKILLS:
-functioning well as a location **and** as a distancing literary milieu wherein aspects of modern society can be highlighted and/or contrasted

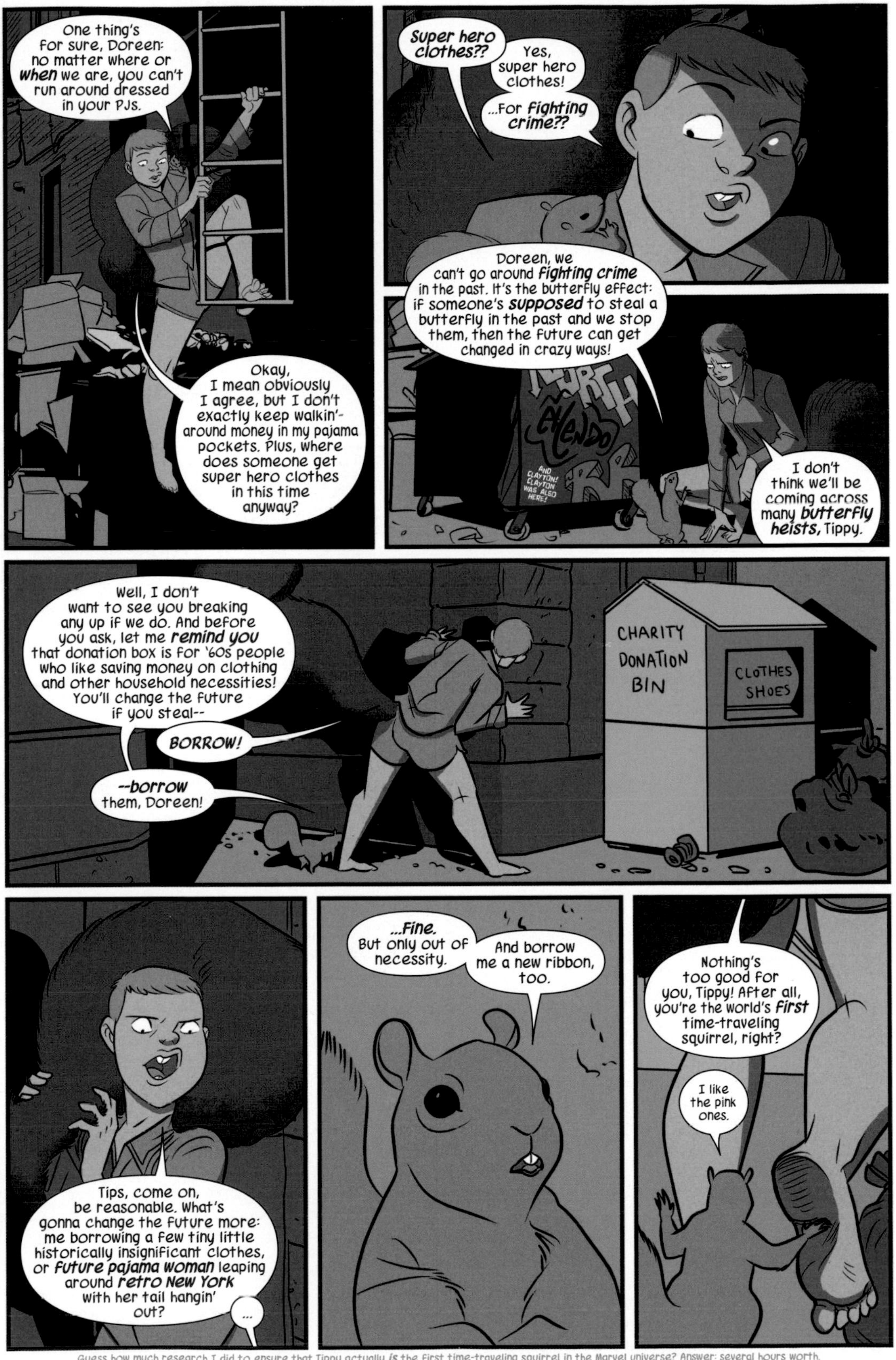
One thing's for sure, Doreen: no matter where or *when* we are, you can't run around dressed in your PJs.
Okay, I mean obviously I agree, but I don't exactly keep walkin'-around money in my pajama pockets. Plus, where does someone get super hero clothes in this time anyway?
Super hero clothes??
Yes, super hero clothes!
...For *fighting crime??*
Doreen, we can't go around *fighting crime* in the past. It's the butterfly effect: if someone's *supposed* to steal a butterfly in the past and we stop them, then the future can get changed in crazy ways!
AND CLAYTON! CLAYTON WAS ALSO HERE!
I don't think we'll be coming across many *butterfly heists,* Tippy.
Well, I don't want to see you breaking any up if we do. And before you ask, let me *remind you* that donation box is for '60s people who like saving money on clothing and other household necessities! You'll change the future if you steal--
CHARITY DONATION BIN
CLOTHES SHOES
BORROW!
--borrow them, Doreen!
Tips, come on, be reasonable. What's gonna change the future more: me borrowing a few tiny little historically insignificant clothes, or *future pajama woman* leaping around *retro New York* with her tail hangin' out?
...
...Fine. But only out of necessity.
And borrow me a new ribbon, too.
Nothing's too good for you, Tippy! After all, you're the world's *first* time-traveling squirrel, right?
I like the pink ones.

Guess how much research I did to ensure that Tippy actually *is* the first time-traveling squirrel in the Marvel universe? Answer: several hours worth. But *"research"* actually means *"sitting around reading other comics,"* so it's actually no big deal!

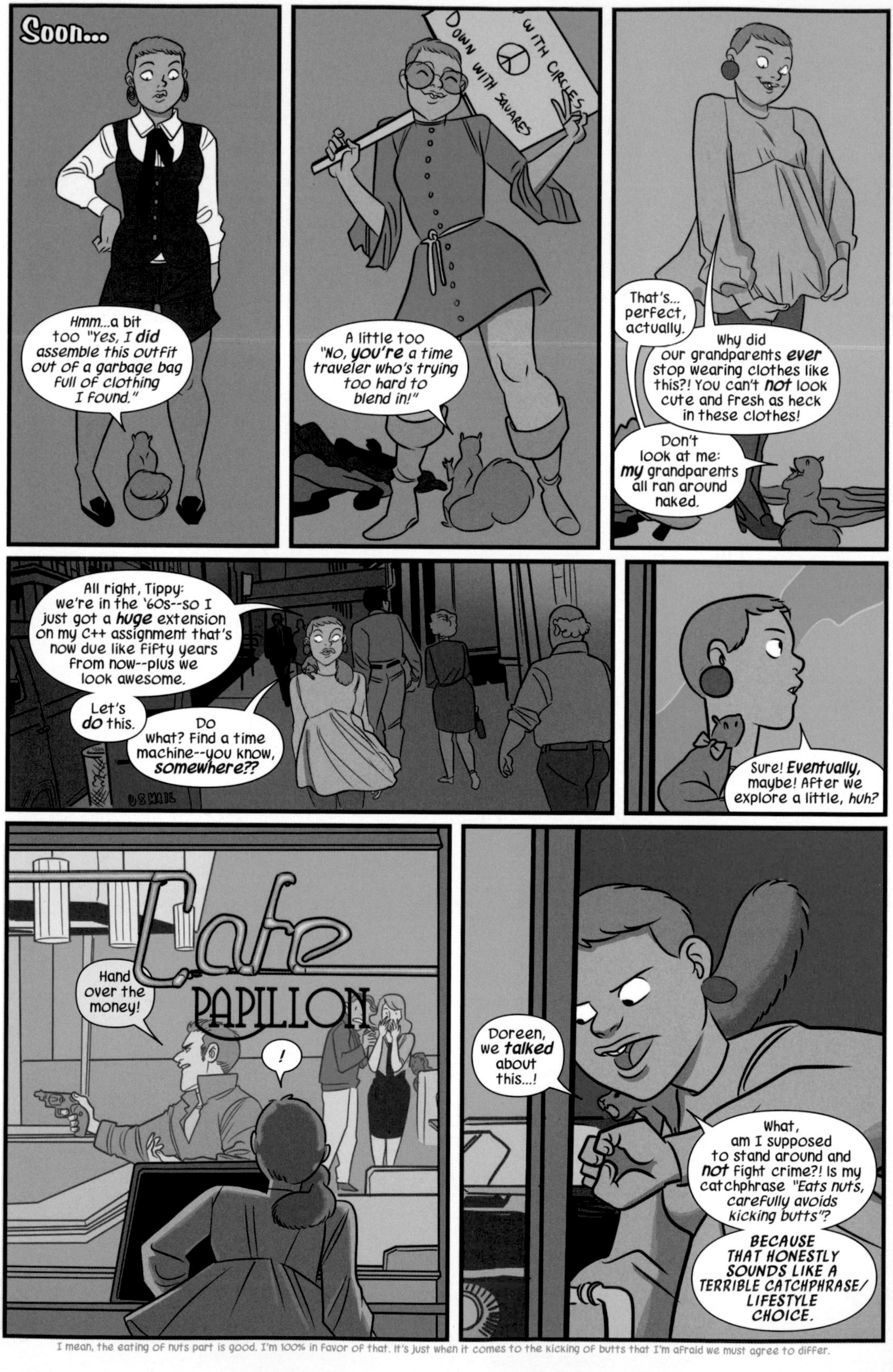
Soon...
Hmm...a bit too "Yes, I **did** assemble this outfit out of a garbage bag full of clothing I found."
WITH CIRCLES
DOWN WITH SQUARES
A little too "No, **you're** a time traveler who's trying too hard to blend in!"
That's... perfect, actually.
Why did our grandparents **ever** stop wearing clothes like this?! You can't **not** look cute and fresh as heck in these clothes!
Don't look at me: **my** grandparents all ran around naked.
All right, Tippy: we're in the '60s--so I just got a **huge** extension on my C++ assignment that's now due like fifty years from now--plus we look awesome.
Let's **do** this.
Do what? Find a time machine--you know, ***somewhere??***
US MAIL
Sure! ***Eventually,*** maybe! After we explore a little, *huh?*
Cafe
PAPILLON
Hand over the money!
!
Doreen, we ***talked*** about this...!
What, am I supposed to stand around and **not** fight crime?! Is my catchphrase *"Eats nuts, carefully avoids kicking butts"?*
BECAUSE THAT HONESTLY SOUNDS LIKE A TERRIBLE CATCHPHRASE/ LIFESTYLE CHOICE.

I mean, the eating of nuts part is good. I'm 100% in favor of that. It's just when it comes to the kicking of butts that I'm afraid we must agree to differ.

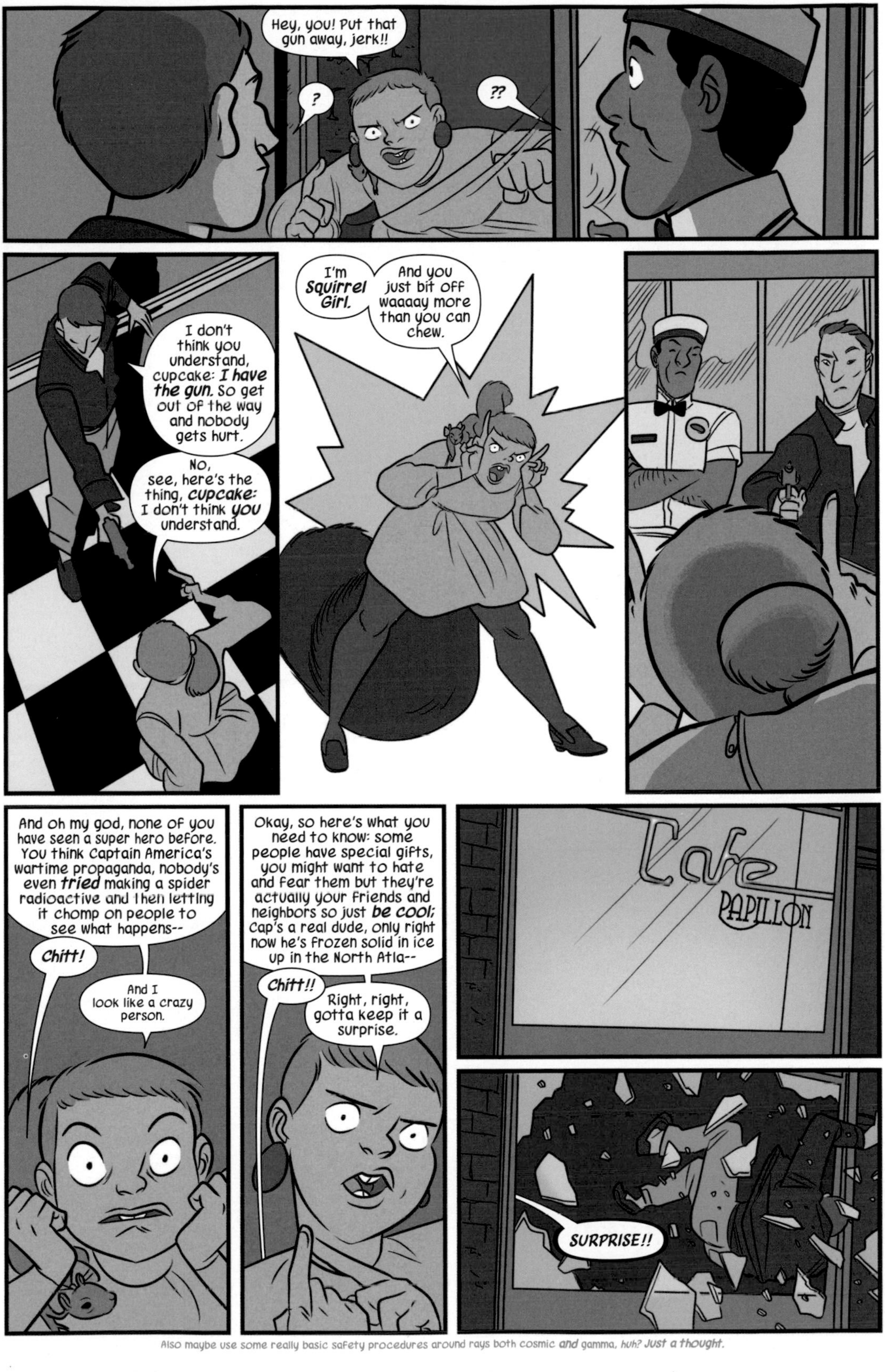
Hey, you! Put that gun away, jerk!!
?
??
I don't think you understand, cupcake: I have the gun. So get out of the way and nobody gets hurt.
No, see, here's the thing, cupcake: I don't think you understand.
I'm Squirrel Girl.
And you just bit off waaaay more than you can chew.
And oh my god, none of you have seen a super hero before. You think Captain America's wartime propaganda, nobody's even tried making a spider radioactive and then letting it chomp on people to see what happens--
Chitt!
And I look like a crazy person.
Okay, so here's what you need to know: some people have special gifts, you might want to hate and fear them but they're actually your friends and neighbors so just be cool; Cap's a real dude, only right now he's frozen solid in ice up in the North Atla--
Chitt!!
Right, right, gotta keep it a surprise.
Cafe
PAPILLON
SURPRISE!!

Also maybe use some really basic safety procedures around rays both cosmic *and* gamma, *huh? Just a thought.*

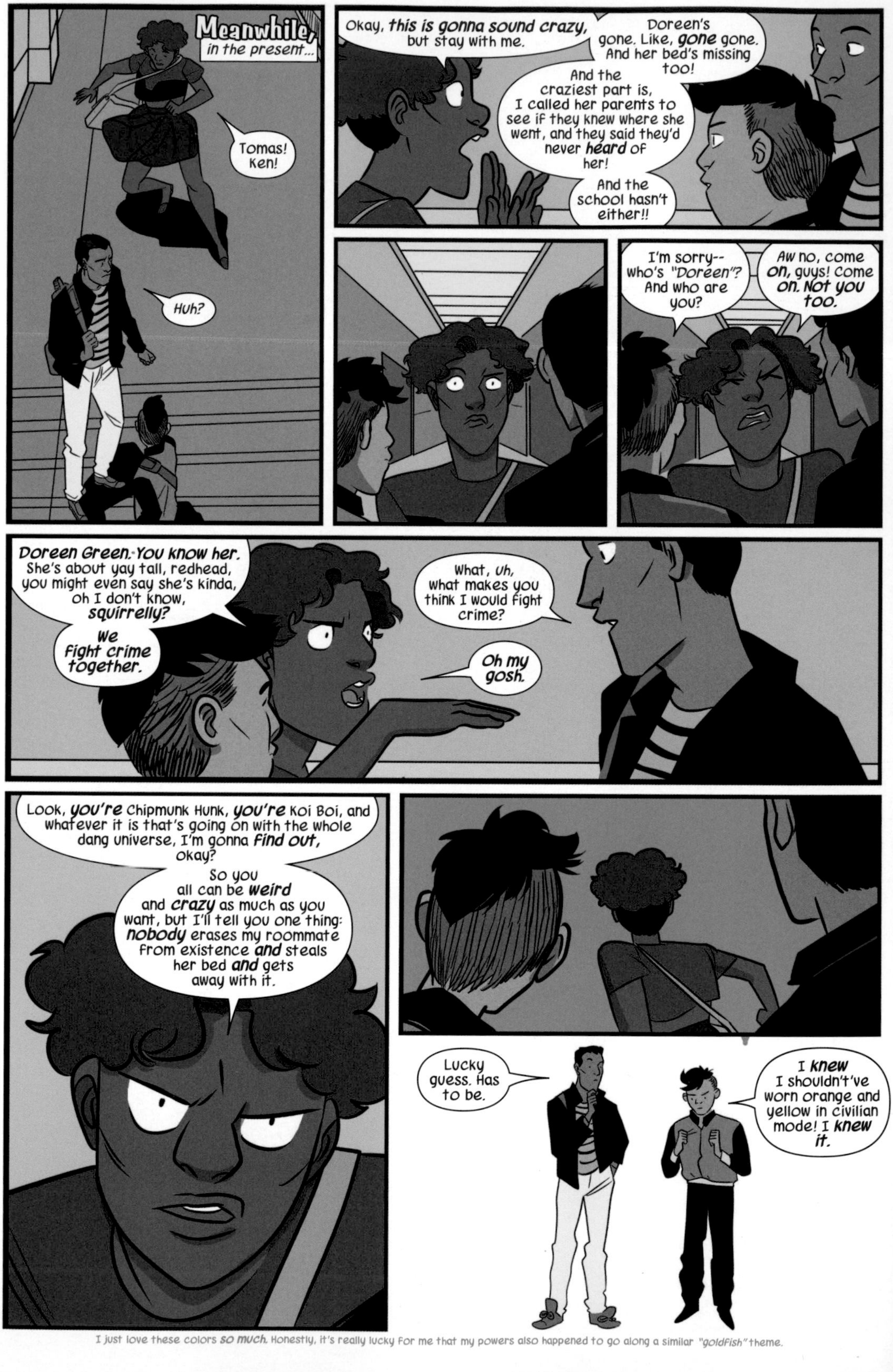
Meanwhile, in the present...
Tomas! Ken!
Huh?
Okay, this is gonna sound crazy, but stay with me.
Doreen's gone. Like, gone gone. And her bed's missing too!
And the craziest part is, I called her parents to see if they knew where she went, and they said they'd never heard of her!
And the school hasn't either!!
I'm sorry-- who's "Doreen"? And who are you?
Aw no, come on, guys! Come on. Not you too.
Doreen Green. You know her. She's about yay tall, redhead, you might even say she's kinda, oh I don't know, squirrelly?
We fight crime together.
What, uh, what makes you think I would fight crime?
Oh my gosh.
Look, you're Chipmunk Hunk, you're Koi Boi, and whatever it is that's going on with the whole dang universe, I'm gonna find out, okay?
So you all can be weird and crazy as much as you want, but I'll tell you one thing: nobody erases my roommate from existence and steals her bed and gets away with it.
Lucky guess. Has to be.
I knew I shouldn't've worn orange and yellow in civilian mode! I knew it.

I just love these colors *so much.* Honestly, it's really lucky for me that my powers also happened to go along a similar *"goldfish"* theme.

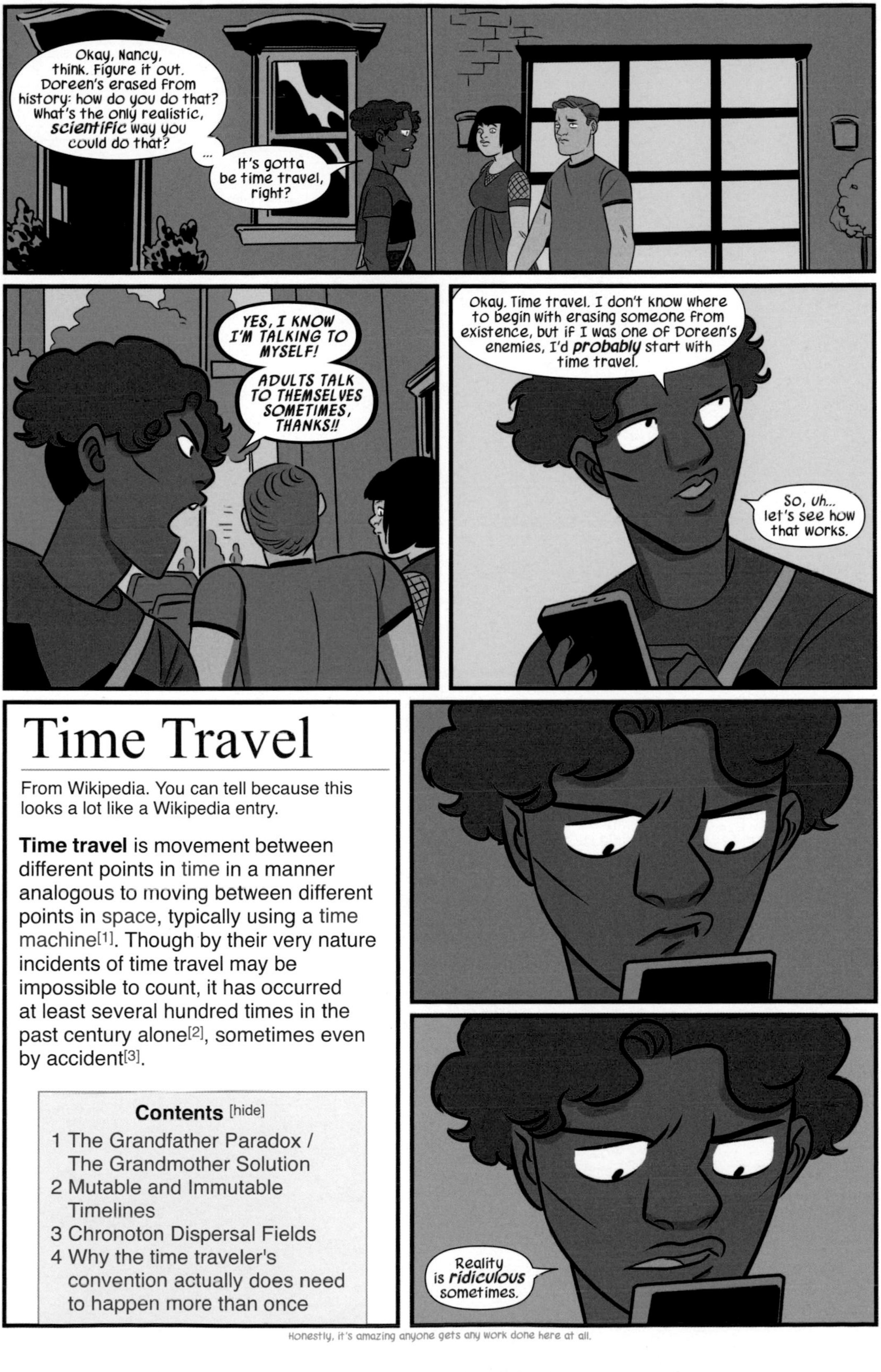
Okay, Nancy, think. Figure it out. Doreen's erased from history: how do you do that? What's the only realistic, *scientific* way you could do that?
...
It's gotta be time travel, right?
YES, I KNOW I'M TALKING TO MYSELF!
ADULTS TALK TO THEMSELVES SOMETIMES, THANKS!!
Okay. Time travel. I don't know where to begin with erasing someone from existence, but if I was one of Doreen's enemies, I'd *probably* start with time travel.
So, uh... let's see how that works.
Time Travel
From Wikipedia. You can tell because this looks a lot like a Wikipedia entry.
Time travel is movement between different points in time in a manner analogous to moving between different points in space, typically using a time machine[1]. Though by their very nature incidents of time travel may be impossible to count, it has occurred at least several hundred times in the past century alone[2], sometimes even by accident[3].
Contents [hide]
1 The Grandfather Paradox / The Grandmother Solution
2 Mutable and Immutable Timelines
3 Chronoton Dispersal Fields
4 Why the time traveler's convention actually does need to happen more than once
Reality is *ridiculous* sometimes.

Honestly, it's amazing anyone gets any work done here at all.

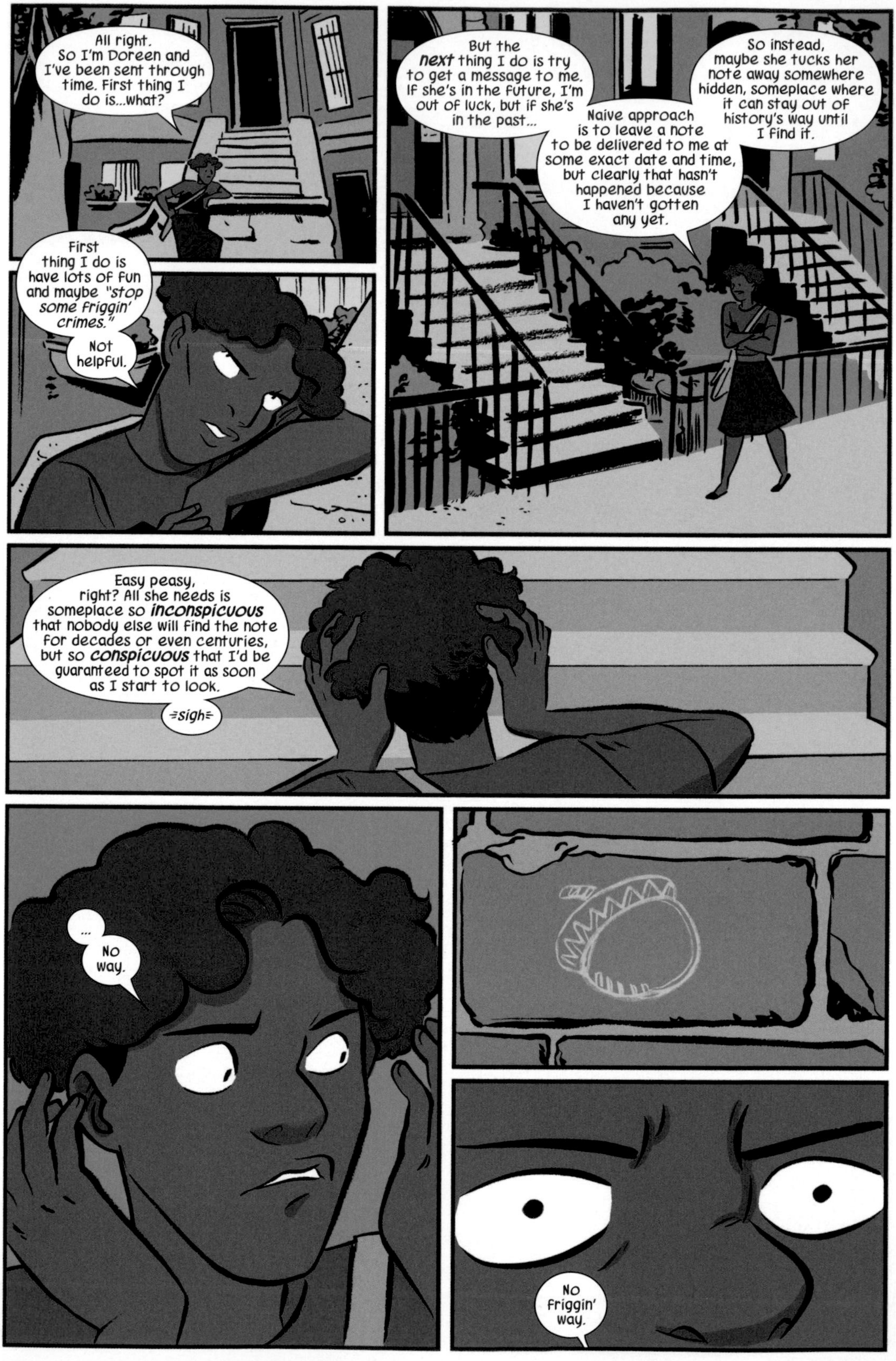
All right. So I'm Doreen and I've been sent through time. First thing I do is...what?
First thing I do is have lots of fun and maybe "stop some friggin' crimes."
Not helpful.
But the next thing I do is try to get a message to me. If she's in the future, I'm out of luck, but if she's in the past...
Naive approach is to leave a note to be delivered to me at some exact date and time, but clearly that hasn't happened because I haven't gotten any yet.
So instead, maybe she tucks her note away somewhere hidden, someplace where it can stay out of history's way until I find it.
Easy peasy, right? All she needs is someplace so inconspicuous that nobody else will find the note for decades or even centuries, but so conspicuous that I'd be guaranteed to spot it as soon as I start to look.
=sigh=
...
No way.
No friggin' way.

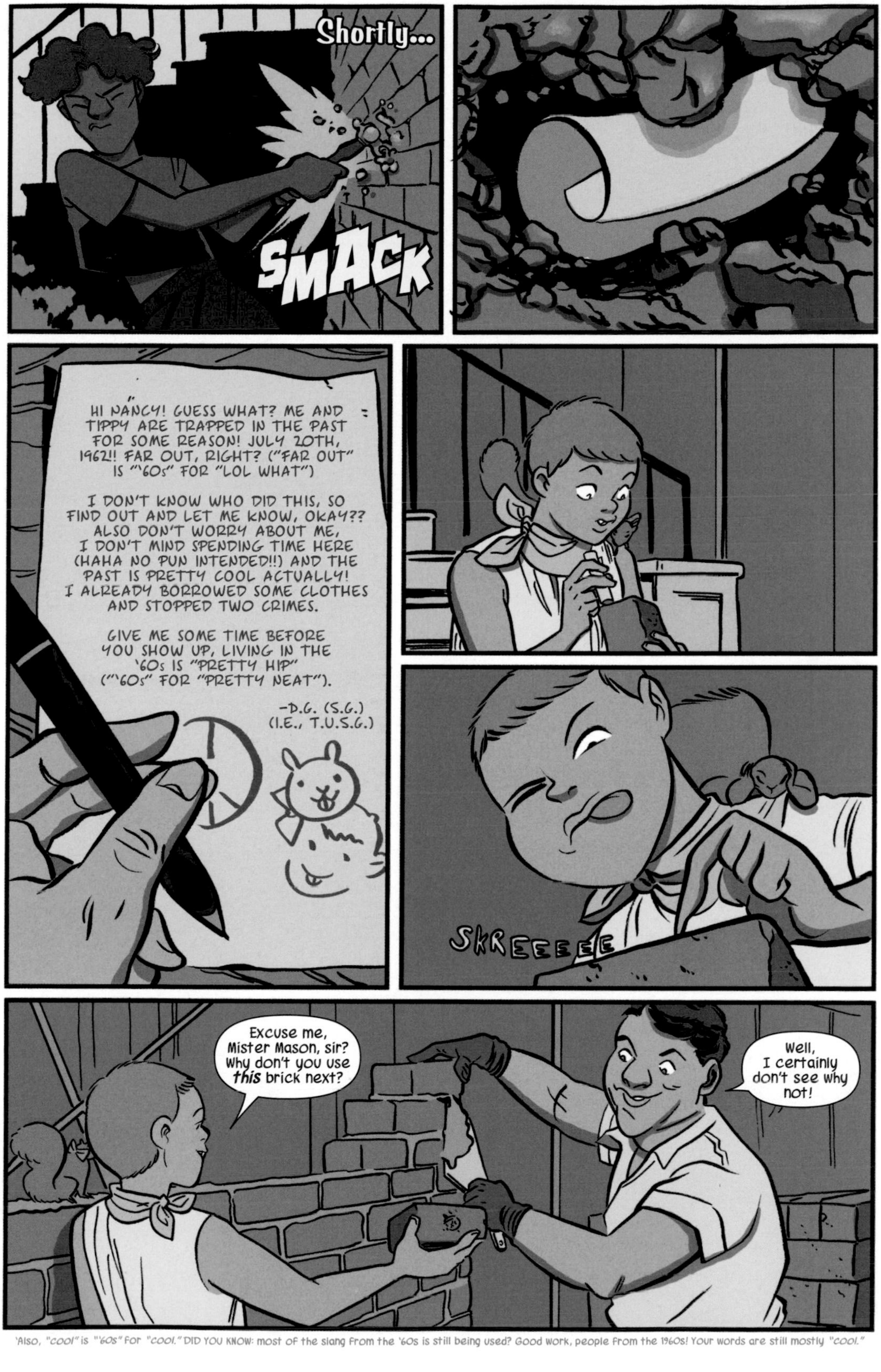
Shortly...
SMACK
"HI NANCY! GUESS WHAT? ME AND TIPPY ARE TRAPPED IN THE PAST FOR SOME REASON! JULY 20TH, 1962!! FAR OUT, RIGHT? ("FAR OUT" IS "'60s" FOR "LOL WHAT")
I DON'T KNOW WHO DID THIS, SO FIND OUT AND LET ME KNOW, OKAY?? ALSO DON'T WORRY ABOUT ME, I DON'T MIND SPENDING TIME HERE (HAHA NO PUN INTENDED!!) AND THE PAST IS PRETTY COOL ACTUALLY! I ALREADY BORROWED SOME CLOTHES AND STOPPED TWO CRIMES.
GIVE ME SOME TIME BEFORE YOU SHOW UP, LIVING IN THE '60s IS "PRETTY HIP" ("'60s" FOR "PRETTY NEAT").
-D.G. (S.G.) (I.E., T.U.S.G.)
SKREEEEEE
Excuse me, Mister Mason, sir? Why don't you use *this* brick next?
Well, I certainly don't see why not!

'Also, "cool" is "'60s" for "cool." DID YOU KNOW: most of the slang from the '60s is still being used? Good work, people from the 1960s! Your words are still mostly "cool."

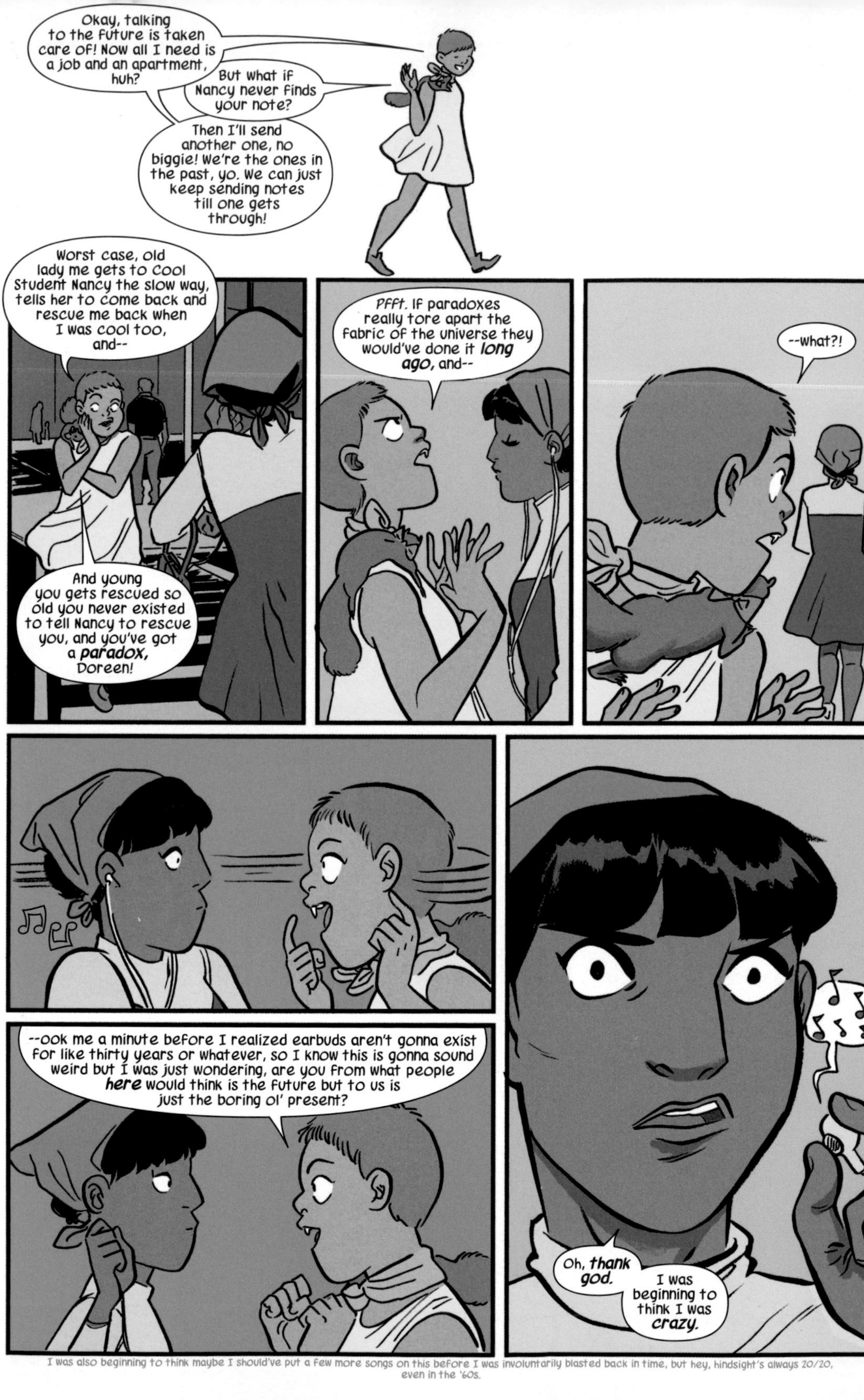
Okay, talking to the future is taken care of! Now all I need is a job and an apartment, huh?
But what if Nancy never finds your note?
Then I'll send another one, no biggie! We're the ones in the past, yo. We can just keep sending notes till one gets through!
Worst case, old lady me gets to Cool Student Nancy the slow way, tells her to come back and rescue me back when I was cool too, and--
And young you gets rescued so old you never existed to tell Nancy to rescue you, and you've got a **paradox,** Doreen!
Pfft. If paradoxes really tore apart the fabric of the universe they would've done it ***long ago,*** and--
--What?!
--ook me a minute before I realized earbuds aren't gonna exist for like thirty years or whatever, so I know this is gonna sound weird but I was just wondering, are you from what people ***here*** would think is the future but to us is just the boring ol' present?
Oh, ***thank god.***
I was beginning to think I was ***crazy.***
I was also beginning to think maybe I should've put a few more songs on this before I was involuntarily blasted back in time, but hey, hindsight's always 20/20, even in the '60s.

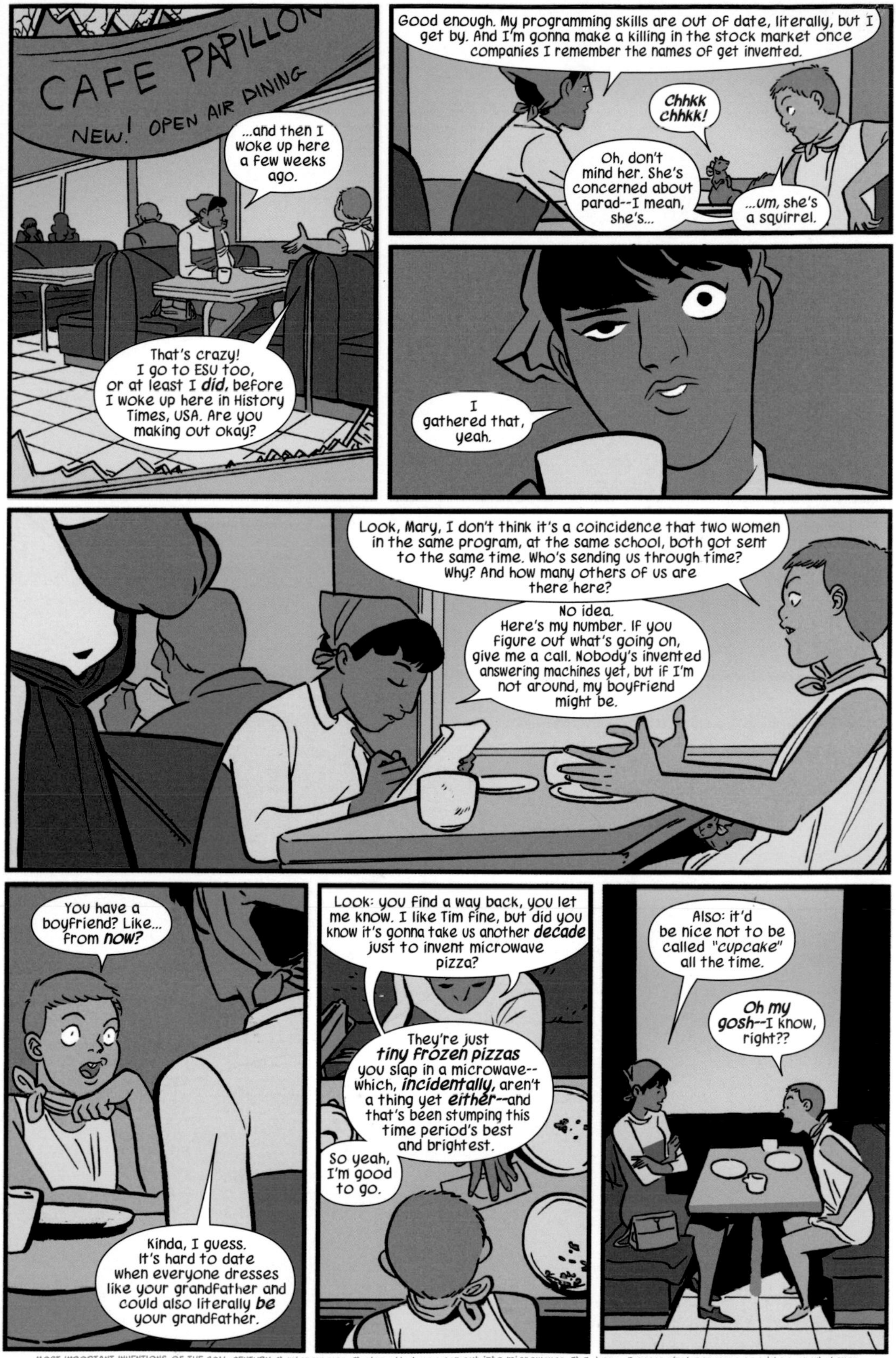
CAFE PAPILLON
NEW! OPEN AIR DINING
...and then I woke up here a few weeks ago.
That's crazy! I go to ESU too, or at least I *did*, before I woke up here in History Times, USA. Are you making out okay?
Good enough. My programming skills are out of date, literally, but I get by. And I'm gonna make a killing in the stock market once companies I remember the names of get invented.
Chhkk chhkk!
Oh, don't mind her. She's concerned about parad--I mean, she's...
...um, she's a squirrel.
I gathered that, yeah.
Look, Mary, I don't think it's a coincidence that two women in the same program, at the same school, both got sent to the same time. Who's sending us through time? Why? And how many others of us are there here?
No idea. Here's my number. If you figure out what's going on, give me a call. Nobody's invented answering machines yet, but if I'm not around, my boyfriend might be.
You have a boyfriend? Like... from *now?*
Kinda, I guess. It's hard to date when everyone dresses like your grandfather and could also literally *be* your grandfather.
Look: you find a way back, you let me know. I like Tim fine, but did you know it's gonna take us another *decade* just to invent microwave pizza?
They're just *tiny frozen pizzas* you slap in a microwave--which, *incidentally,* aren't a thing yet *either*--and that's been stumping this time period's best and brightest.
So yeah, I'm good to go.
Also: it'd be nice not to be called "*cupcake*" all the time.
Oh my gosh--I know, right??

MOST IMPORTANT INVENTIONS OF THE 20th CENTURY: 1) microwaves, 2) pizza that you can put into microwaves, 3) I dunno, I guess airplanes were good too or whatever

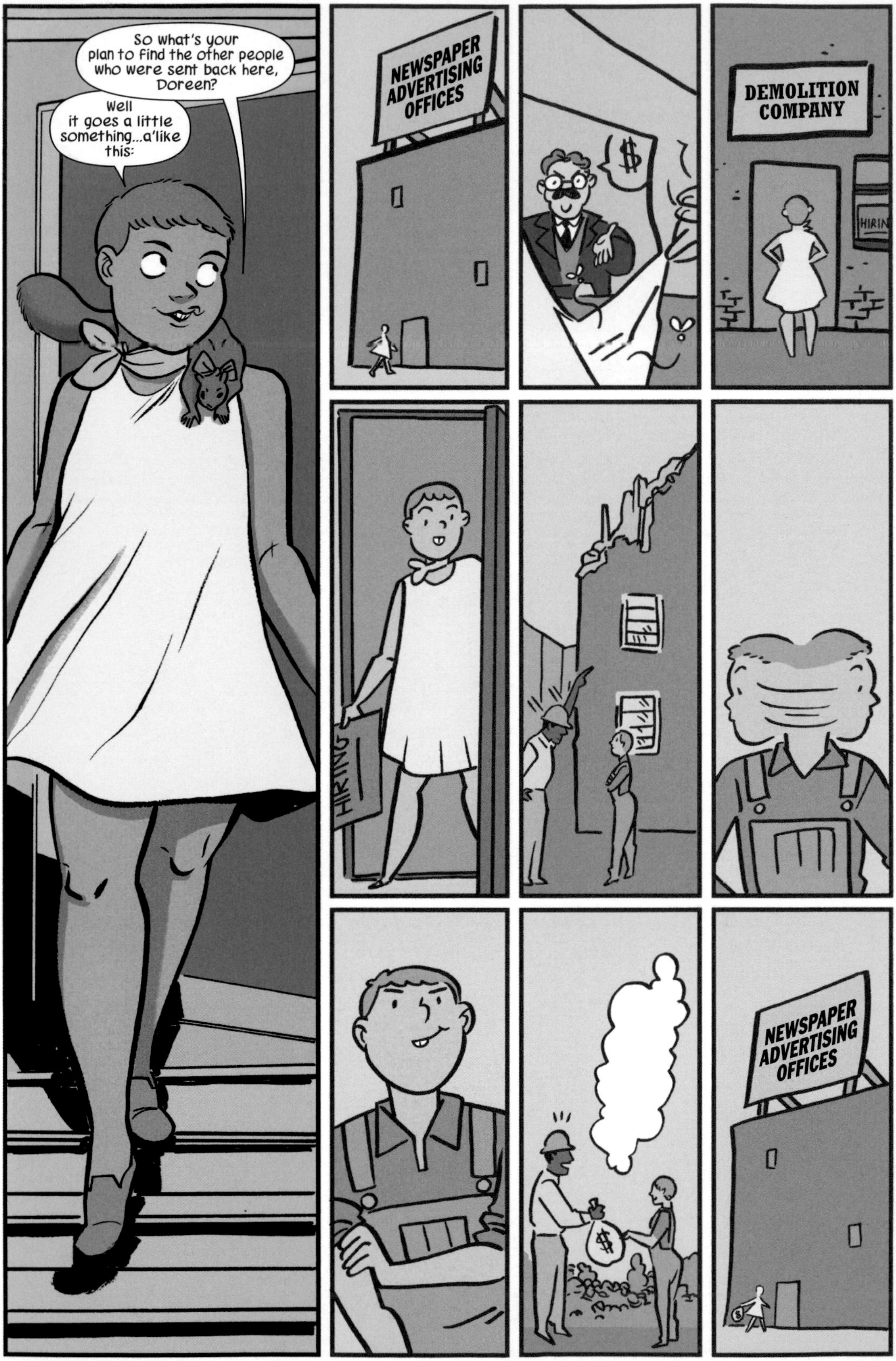
So what's your plan to find the other people who were sent back here, Doreen?
Well it goes a little something...a'like this:
NEWSPAPER ADVERTISING OFFICES
$
DEMOLITION COMPANY
HIRIN
HIRING
NEWSPAPER ADVERTISING OFFICES

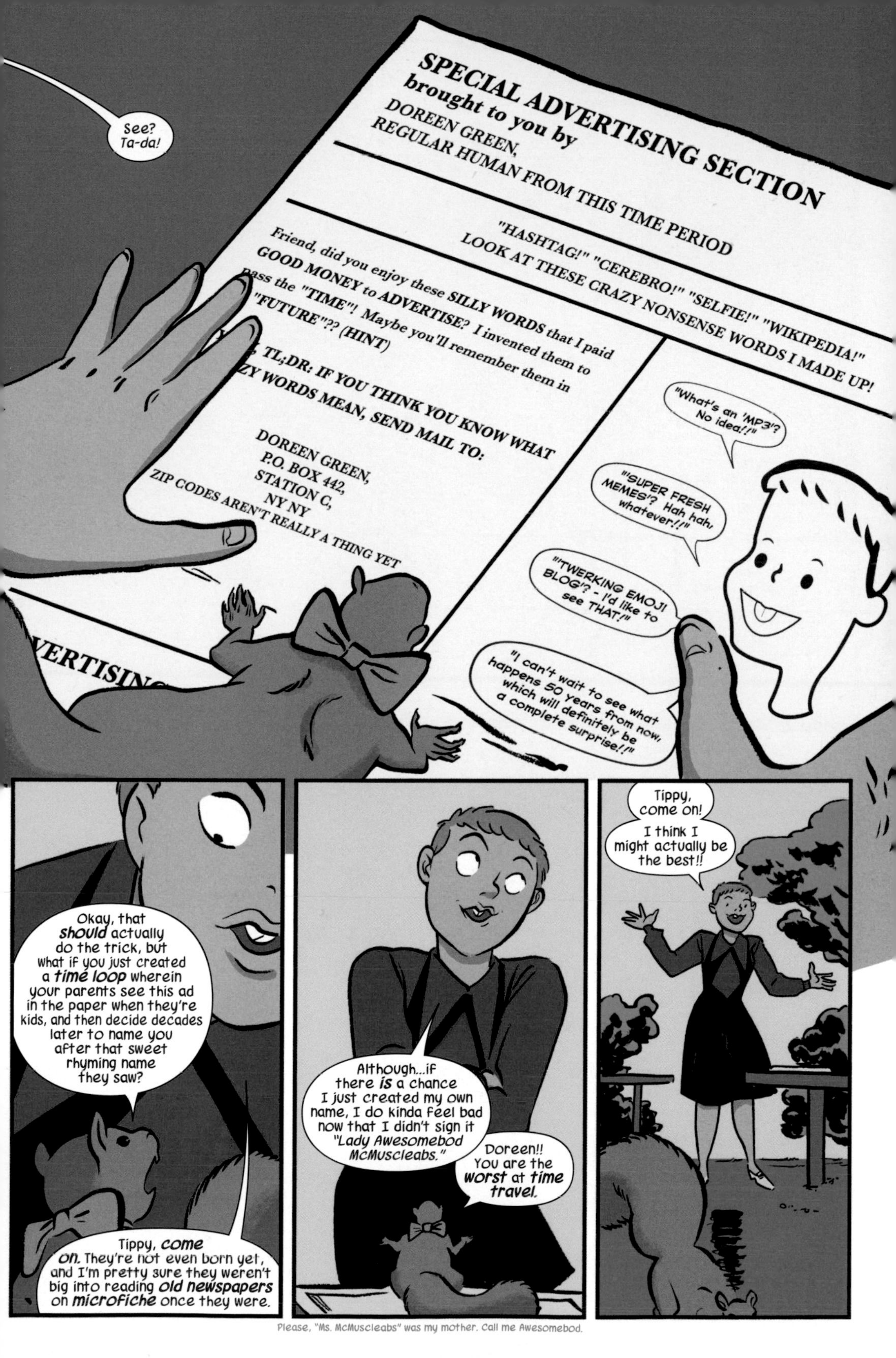
See? Ta-da!
SPECIAL ADVERTISING SECTION
brought to you by
DOREEN GREEN,
REGULAR HUMAN FROM THIS TIME PERIOD
"HASHTAG!" "CEREBRO!" "SELFIE!" "WIKIPEDIA!"
LOOK AT THESE CRAZY NONSENSE WORDS I MADE UP!
Friend, did you enjoy these SILLY WORDS that I paid
GOOD MONEY to ADVERTISE? I invented them to
pass the "TIME"! Maybe you'll remember them in
"FUTURE"?? (HINT)
, TL;DR: IF YOU THINK YOU KNOW WHAT
ZY WORDS MEAN, SEND MAIL TO:
DOREEN GREEN,
P.O. BOX 442,
STATION C,
NY NY
ZIP CODES AREN'T REALLY A THING YET
"What's an 'MP3'? No idea!!"
"SUPER FRESH MEMES'? Hah hah, whatever!!"
"TWERKING EMOJI BLOG'? - I'd like to see THAT!"
"I can't wait to see what happens 50 years from now, which will definitely be a complete surprise!!"
VERTISING
Okay, that *should* actually do the trick, but what if you just created a *time loop* wherein your parents see this ad in the paper when they're kids, and then decide decades later to name you after that sweet rhyming name they saw?
Tippy, *come on*. They're not even born yet, and I'm pretty sure they weren't big into reading *old newspapers* on *microfiche* once they were.
Although...if there *is* a chance I just created my own name, I do kinda feel bad now that I didn't sign it "Lady Awesomebod McMuscleabs."
Doreen!! You are the *worst* at *time travel*.
Tippy, come on!
I think I might actually be the best!!

Please, "Ms. McMuscleabs" was my mother. Call me Awesomebod.

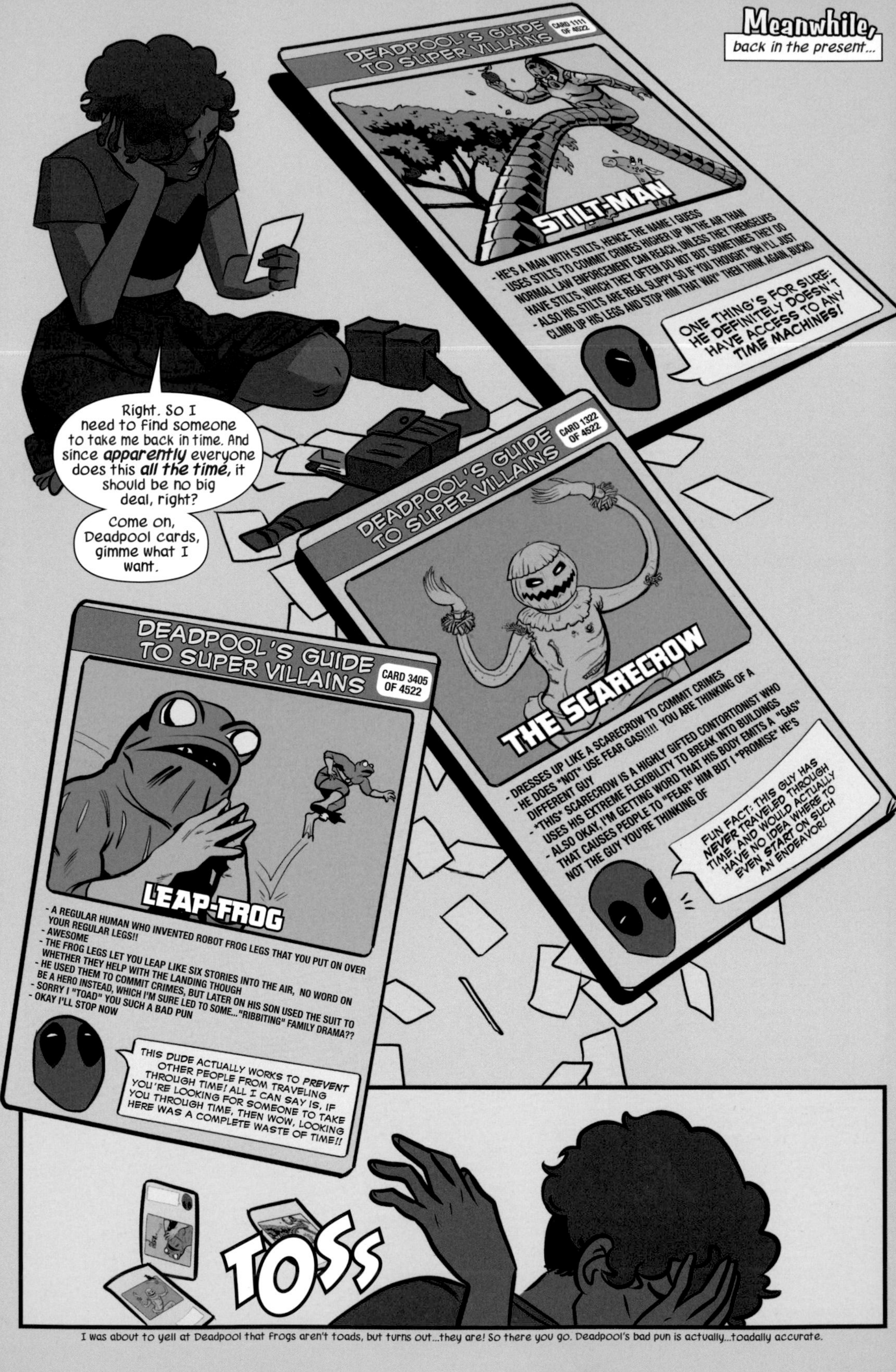
Meanwhile, back in the present...
Right. So I need to find someone to take me back in time. And since *apparently* everyone does this *all the time,* it should be no big deal, right?
Come on, Deadpool cards, gimme what I want.
DEADPOOL'S GUIDE TO SUPER VILLAINS
CARD 1111 OF 4522
STILT-MAN
- HE'S A MAN WITH STILTS, HENCE THE NAME I GUESS
- USES STILTS TO COMMIT CRIMES HIGHER UP IN THE AIR THAN NORMAL LAW ENFORCEMENT CAN REACH, UNLESS THEY THEMSELVES HAVE STILTS, WHICH THEY OFTEN DO NOT BUT SOMETIMES THEY DO
- ALSO HIS STILTS ARE REAL SLIPPY SO IF YOU THOUGHT "OH I'LL JUST CLIMB UP HIS LEGS AND STOP HIM THAT WAY" THEN THINK AGAIN, BUCKO
ONE THING'S FOR SURE: HE DEFINITELY DOESN'T HAVE ACCESS TO ANY *TIME MACHINES!*
DEADPOOL'S GUIDE TO SUPER VILLAINS
CARD 1322 OF 4522
THE SCARECROW
- DRESSES UP LIKE A SCARECROW TO COMMIT CRIMES
- HE DOES *NOT* USE FEAR GAS!!!!! YOU ARE THINKING OF A DIFFERENT GUY
- *THIS* SCARECROW IS A HIGHLY GIFTED CONTORTIONIST WHO USES HIS EXTREME FLEXIBILITY TO BREAK INTO BUILDINGS
- ALSO OKAY, I'M GETTING WORD THAT HIS BODY EMITS A "GAS" THAT CAUSES PEOPLE TO "FEAR" HIM BUT I *PROMISE* HE'S NOT THE GUY YOU'RE THINKING OF
FUN FACT: THIS GUY HAS *NEVER* TRAVELED THROUGH TIME, AND WOULD ACTUALLY HAVE NO IDEA WHERE TO EVEN *START* ON SUCH AN ENDEAVOR!
DEADPOOL'S GUIDE TO SUPER VILLAINS
CARD 3405 OF 4522
LEAP-FROG
- A REGULAR HUMAN WHO INVENTED ROBOT FROG LEGS THAT YOU PUT ON OVER YOUR REGULAR LEGS!!
- AWESOME
- THE FROG LEGS LET YOU LEAP LIKE SIX STORIES INTO THE AIR, NO WORD ON WHETHER THEY HELP WITH THE LANDING THOUGH
- HE USED THEM TO COMMIT CRIMES, BUT LATER ON HIS SON USED THE SUIT TO BE A HERO INSTEAD, WHICH I'M SURE LED TO SOME..."RIBBITING" FAMILY DRAMA??
- SORRY I "TOAD" YOU SUCH A BAD PUN
- OKAY I'LL STOP NOW
THIS DUDE ACTUALLY WORKS TO *PREVENT* OTHER PEOPLE FROM TRAVELING THROUGH TIME! ALL I CAN SAY IS, IF YOU'RE LOOKING FOR SOMEONE TO TAKE YOU THROUGH TIME, THEN WOW, LOOKING HERE WAS A COMPLETE WASTE OF TIME!!
TOSS

I was about to yell at Deadpool that frogs aren't toads, but turns out...they are! So there you go. Deadpool's bad pun is actually...toadally accurate.

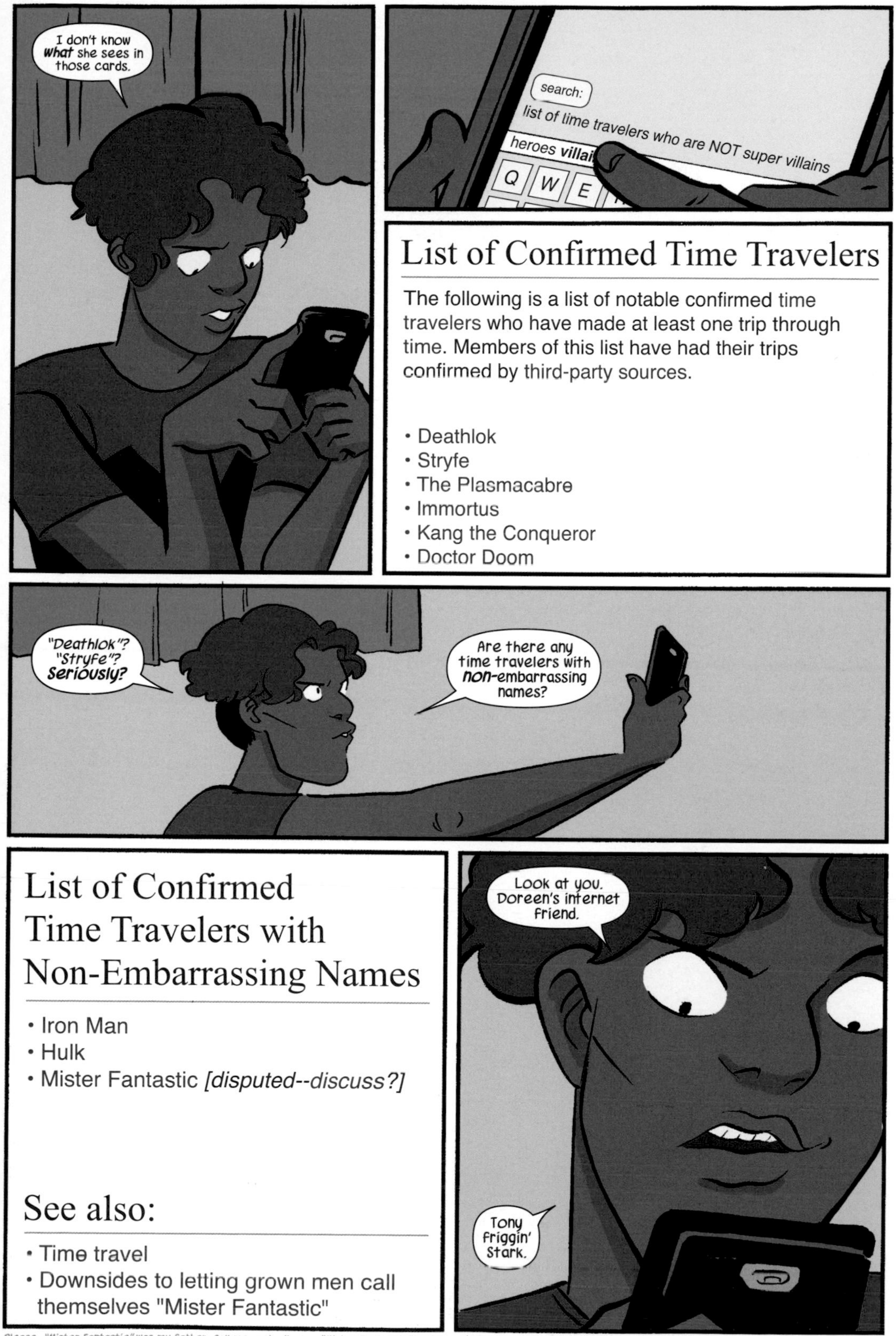

I don't know *what* she sees in those cards.
search:
list of time travelers who are NOT super villains
heroes villai
Q W E
List of Confirmed Time Travelers
The following is a list of notable confirmed time travelers who have made at least one trip through time. Members of this list have had their trips confirmed by third-party sources.
• Deathlok
• Stryfe
• The Plasmacabre
• Immortus
• Kang the Conqueror
• Doctor Doom
"Deathlok"? "Stryfe"? *Seriously?*
Are there any time travelers with *non*-embarrassing names?
List of Confirmed Time Travelers with Non-Embarrassing Names
• Iron Man
• Hulk
• Mister Fantastic *[disputed--discuss?]*
See also:
• Time travel
• Downsides to letting grown men call themselves "Mister Fantastic"
Look at you. Doreen's internet friend.
Tony friggin' Stark.

Please, *"Mister Fantastic"* was my father. Call me...actually, no, *"Mister Fantastic"* is fine, and on second thought that's absolutely a name I would like everyone to know me by.

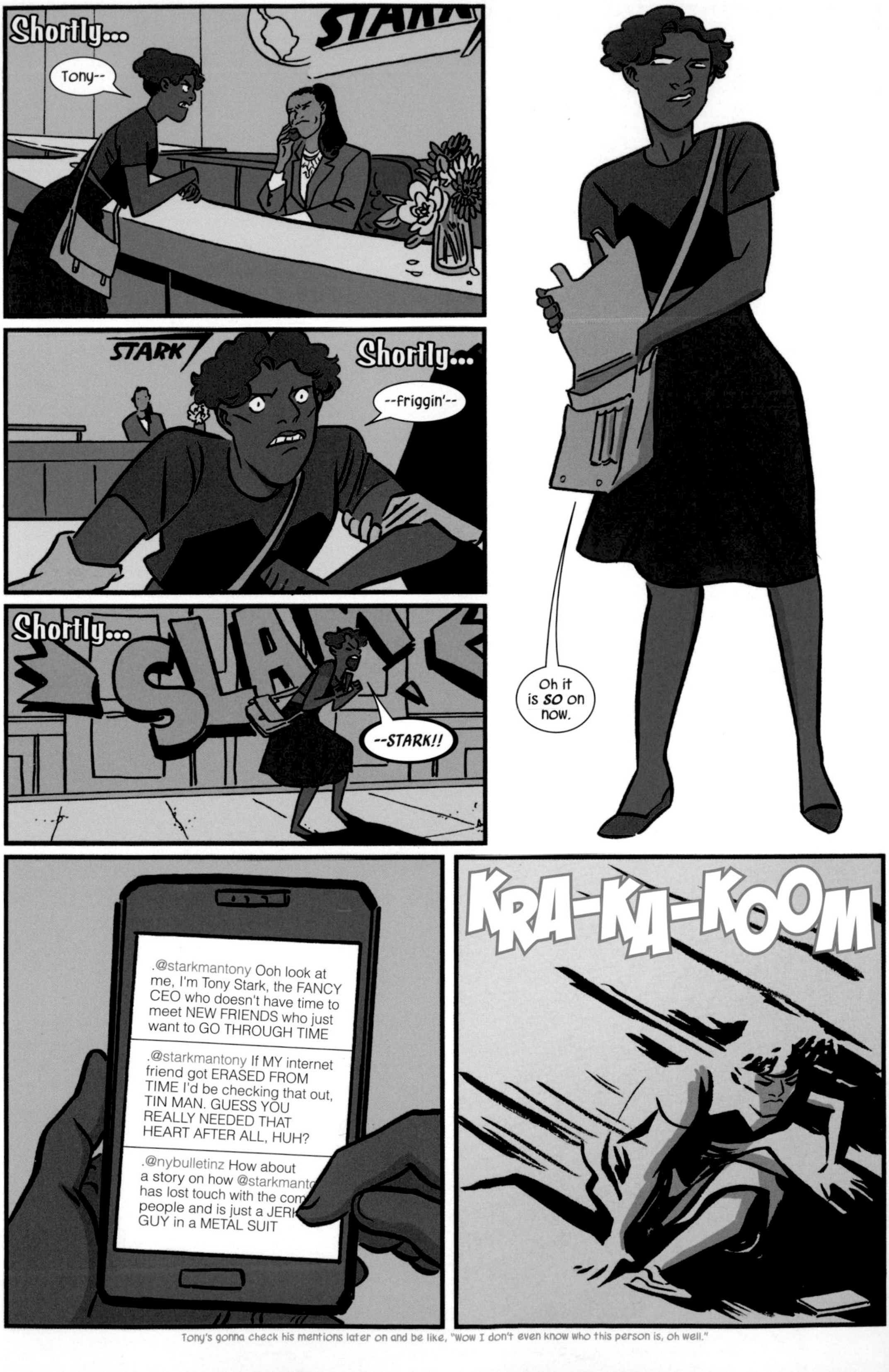
Shortly...
Tony--
STARK
Shortly...
--friggin'--
Shortly...
--STARK!!
Oh it is *SO* on now.
.@starkmantony Ooh look at me, I'm Tony Stark, the FANCY CEO who doesn't have time to meet NEW FRIENDS who just want to GO THROUGH TIME
.@starkmantony If MY internet friend got ERASED FROM TIME I'd be checking that out, TIN MAN. GUESS YOU REALLY NEEDED THAT HEART AFTER ALL, HUH?
.@nybulletinz How about a story on how @starkmanto has lost touch with the com people and is just a JERK GUY in a METAL SUIT
KRA-KA-KOOM

Tony's gonna check his mentions later on and be like, "Wow I don't even know who this person is, oh well."

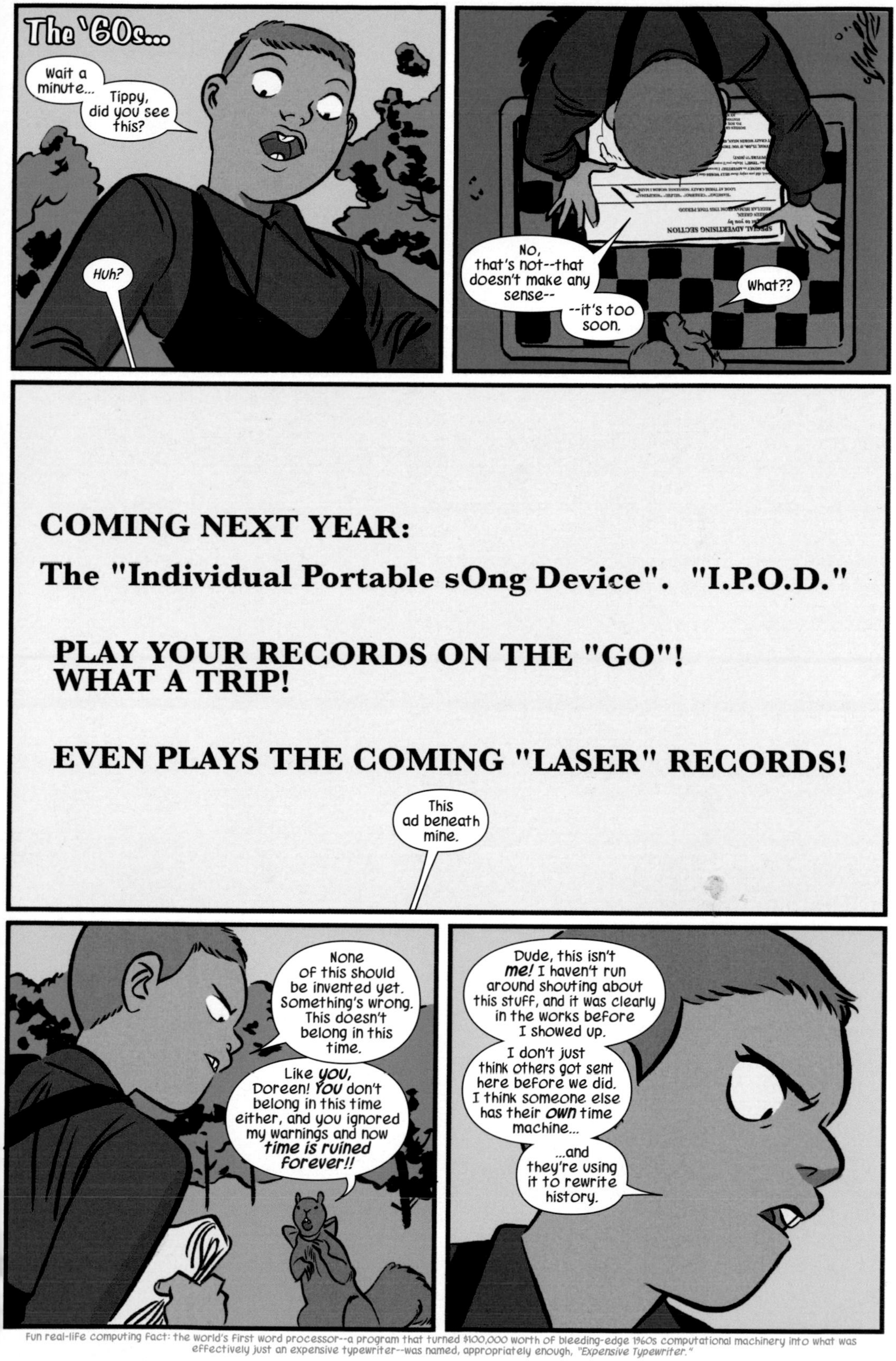
The '60s...
Wait a minute...
Tippy, did you see this?
Huh?
No, that's not--that doesn't make any sense--
--it's too soon.
What??
SPECIAL ADVERTISING SECTION
COMING NEXT YEAR:
The "Individual Portable sOng Device". "I.P.O.D."
PLAY YOUR RECORDS ON THE "GO"! WHAT A TRIP!
EVEN PLAYS THE COMING "LASER" RECORDS!
This ad beneath mine.
None of this should be invented yet. Something's wrong. This doesn't belong in this time.
Like YOU, Doreen! YOU don't belong in this time either, and you ignored my warnings and now time is ruined forever!!
Dude, this isn't me! I haven't run around shouting about this stuff, and it was clearly in the works before I showed up.
I don't just think others got sent here before we did. I think someone else has their OWN time machine...
...and they're using it to rewrite history.

Fun real-life computing fact: the world's first word processor--a program that turned $100,000 worth of bleeding-edge 1960s computational machinery into what was effectively just an expensive typewriter--was named, appropriately enough, *"Expensive Typewriter."*

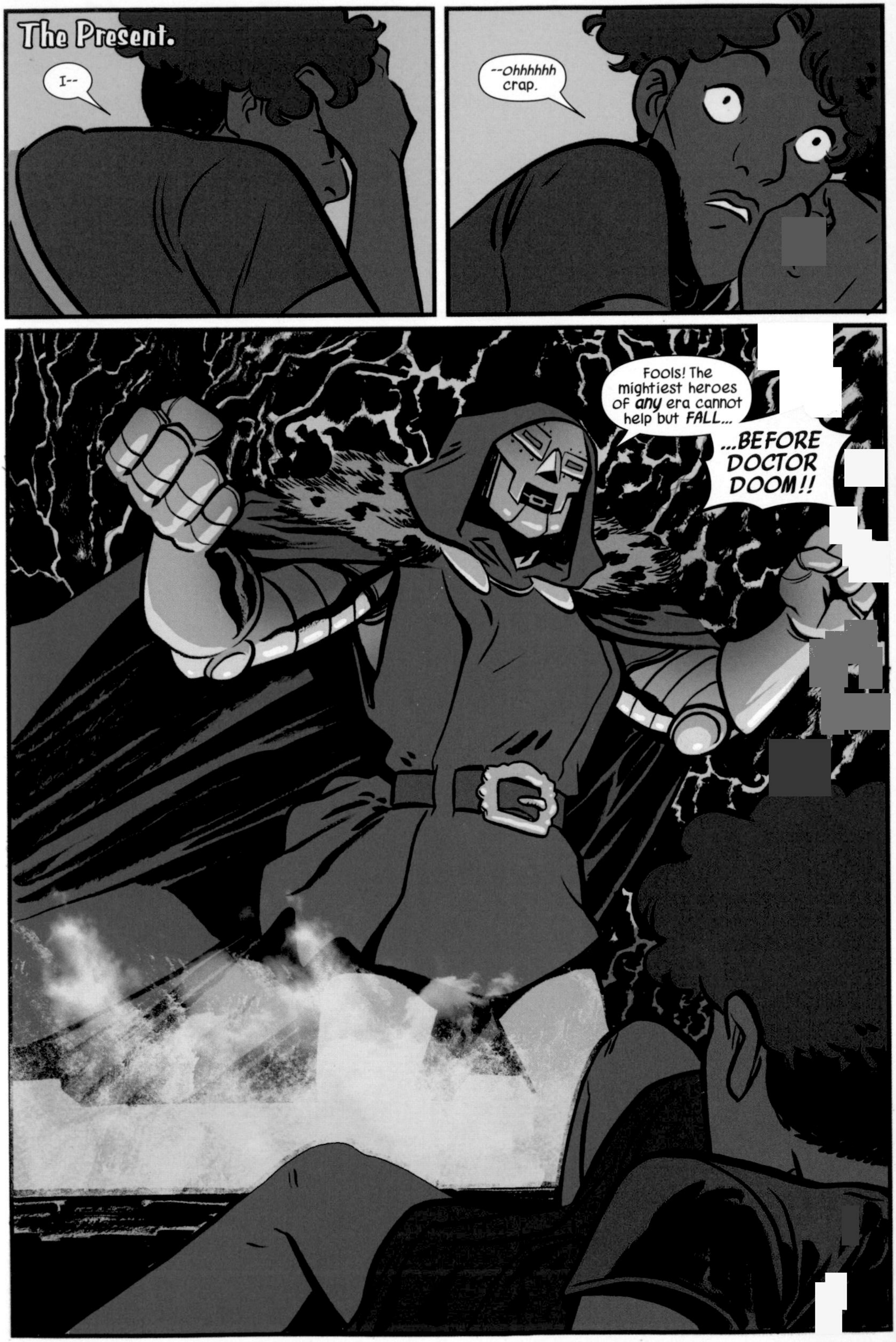
The Present.
I--
--Ohhhhhh crap.
Fools! The mightiest heroes of *any* era cannot help but *FALL*...
...BEFORE DOCTOR DOOM!!

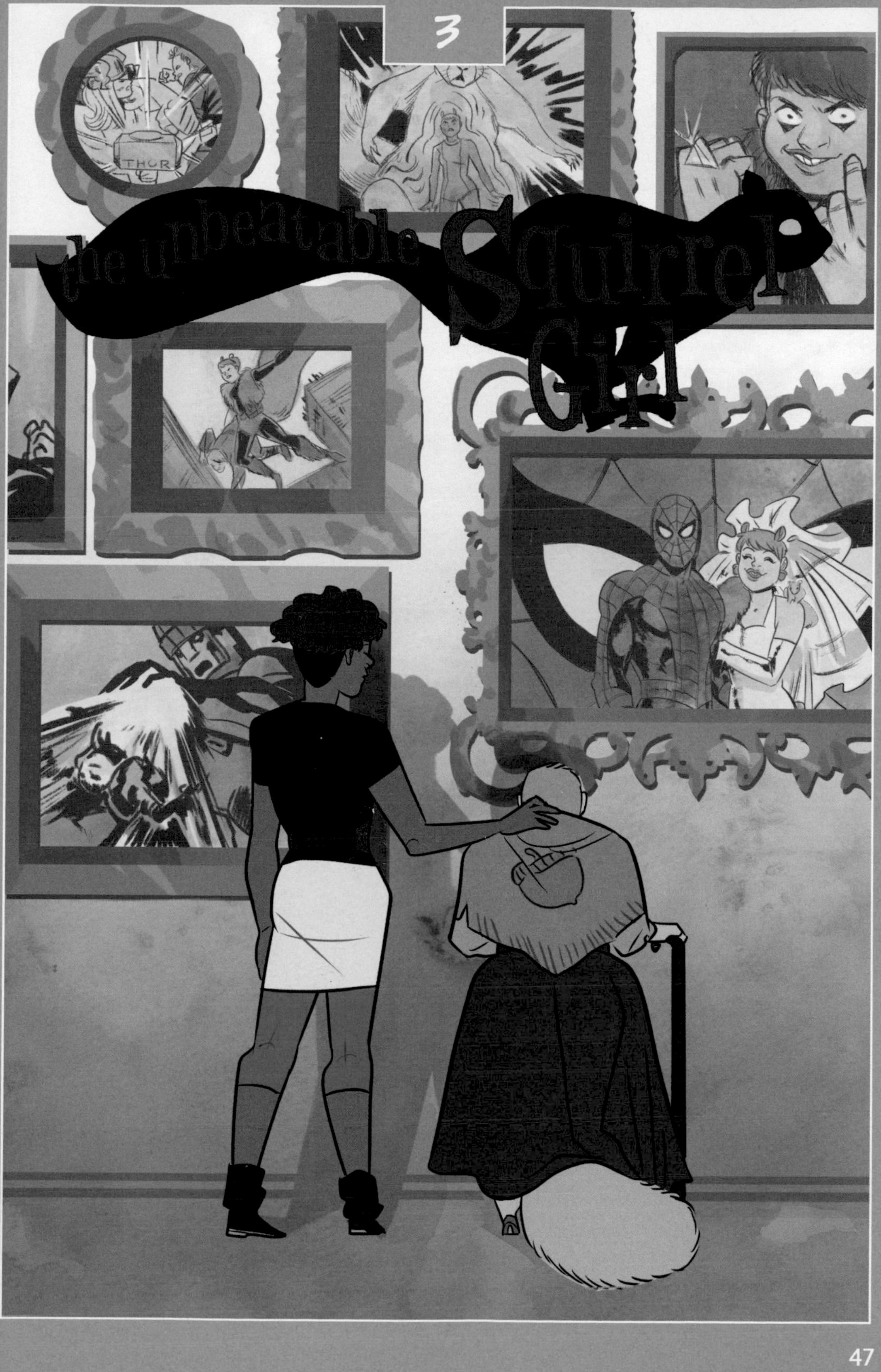
3
THOR
the unbeatable Squirrel Girl

Doreen Green isn't just a second-year computer science student: she secretly also has all the powers of both squirrel and girl! She uses her amazing abilities to fight crime **and** be as awesome as possible. You know her as...**The Unbeatable Squirrel Girl!** Find out what she's been up to, with...

Squirrel Girl
in a nutshell

search! 🔍

#doctordoom

#wikipedia

#doomipedia

#timetravel

#rhymetravel

#thymetravel

Nancy W. @sewwiththeflo
Nobody believes me, but before this morning Mew and I had a roommate. Then she got erased from time, and now nobody remembers her but me.

Nancy W. @sewwiththeflo
And she was AWESOME and SWEET and SMART and GOOD AT FIGHTS ACTUALLY, and it sucks without her.

Nancy W. @sewwiththeflo
RT if your roommate got erased from time and nobody remembers her.

Nancy W. @sewwiththeflo
See? That's proof she's gone, right there. She would've AT LEAST faved that.

Tony Stark @starkmantony ✓
Do you ever get the sense that the universe is missing something? Like there's something that should be there and just--isn't.

> **Nancy W.** @sewwiththeflo
> @starkmantony Whoa whoa whoa--you remember her too? I thought I was the only one!

Tony Stark @starkmantony ✓
Like you woke up today and even though you could SWEAR everything was the same, you still feel like something very important is absent...

> **Nancy W.** @sewwiththeflo
> @starkmantony Yes! Doreen!!

Tony Stark @starkmantony ✓
...and though some part of you knows that thing--whatever it was--might've been kind of a pain sometimes, you still miss it?

> **Nancy W.** @sewwiththeflo
> @starkmantony You and her do have a special relationship. Thank you! I felt like I was going crazy. So what's our next move, Tony?

Tony Stark @starkmantony ✓
Because I too had that feeling...UNTIL I tried the new consumer-level #IronManicure home beauty treatment kit, available TODAY!

Tony Stark @starkmantony ✓
Your hands are too precious for just any manicure kit. Take the Stark #IronManicure Challenge: satisfaction guaranteed or your money back!

Tony Stark @starkmantony ✓
You'll feel like a Stark with our red-and-gold nail file, clipper, and angled cuticle nipper. All thanks to the new #IronManicure kit!

> **Nancy W.** @sewwiththeflo
> @starkmantony blocked

> **HULK** @HULKYSMASHY
> @starkmantony HULK WONDERS IF MANICURE KIT COMES IN GREEN AND PURPLE BECAUSE HULK THINK THOSE COLORS ARE MUCH PRETTIER

Nancy W. @sewwiththeflo
So here I am, minding my own business, when there's a huge blast of sound and light and I get knocked over. Guess who did it?

Nancy W. @sewwiththeflo
Doctor Doom. Doctor DOOM, friends and neighbors. Ruler of Latveria, ambassador, metal-suit wearer. Big as life.

Nancy W. @sewwiththeflo
So yeah anyway I should really get off my phone now because he's RIGHT HERE

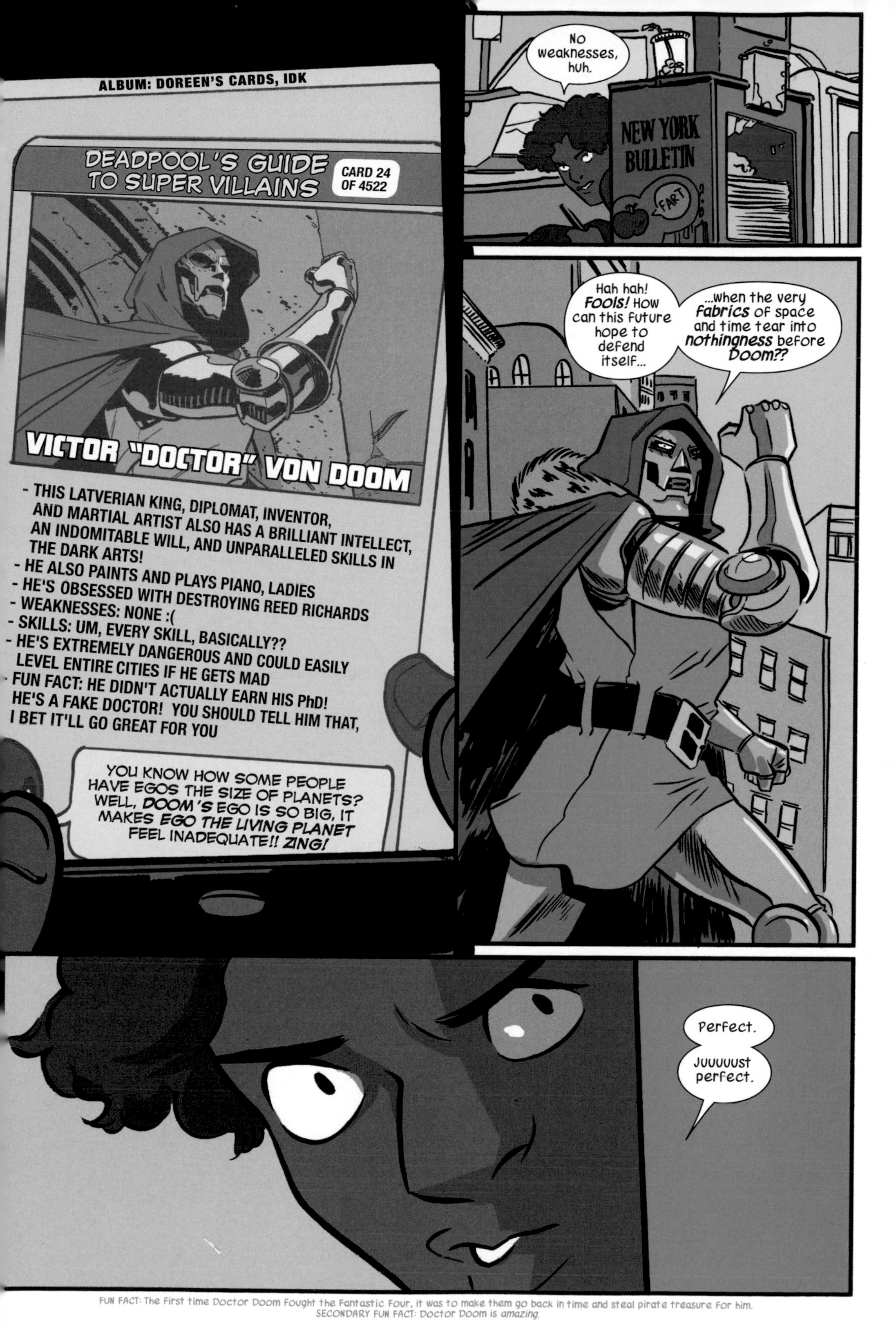
ALBUM: DOREEN'S CARDS, IDK
DEADPOOL'S GUIDE TO SUPER VILLAINS
CARD 24 OF 4522
VICTOR "DOCTOR" VON DOOM
- THIS LATVERIAN KING, DIPLOMAT, INVENTOR, AND MARTIAL ARTIST ALSO HAS A BRILLIANT INTELLECT, AN INDOMITABLE WILL, AND UNPARALLELED SKILLS IN THE DARK ARTS!
- HE ALSO PAINTS AND PLAYS PIANO, LADIES
- HE'S OBSESSED WITH DESTROYING REED RICHARDS
- WEAKNESSES: NONE :(
- SKILLS: UM, EVERY SKILL, BASICALLY??
- HE'S EXTREMELY DANGEROUS AND COULD EASILY LEVEL ENTIRE CITIES IF HE GETS MAD
- FUN FACT: HE DIDN'T ACTUALLY EARN HIS PhD! HE'S A FAKE DOCTOR! YOU SHOULD TELL HIM THAT, I BET IT'LL GO GREAT FOR YOU
YOU KNOW HOW SOME PEOPLE HAVE EGOS THE SIZE OF PLANETS? WELL, DOOM'S EGO IS SO BIG, IT MAKES EGO THE LIVING PLANET FEEL INADEQUATE!! ZING!
No weaknesses, huh.
NEW YORK BULLETIN
FART
Hah hah! Fools! How can this future hope to defend itself...
...when the very fabrics of space and time tear into nothingness before Doom??
Perfect.
Juuuuust perfect.

FUN FACT: The first time Doctor Doom fought the Fantastic Four, it was to make them go back in time and steal pirate treasure for him.
SECONDARY FUN FACT: Doctor Doom is *amazing.*

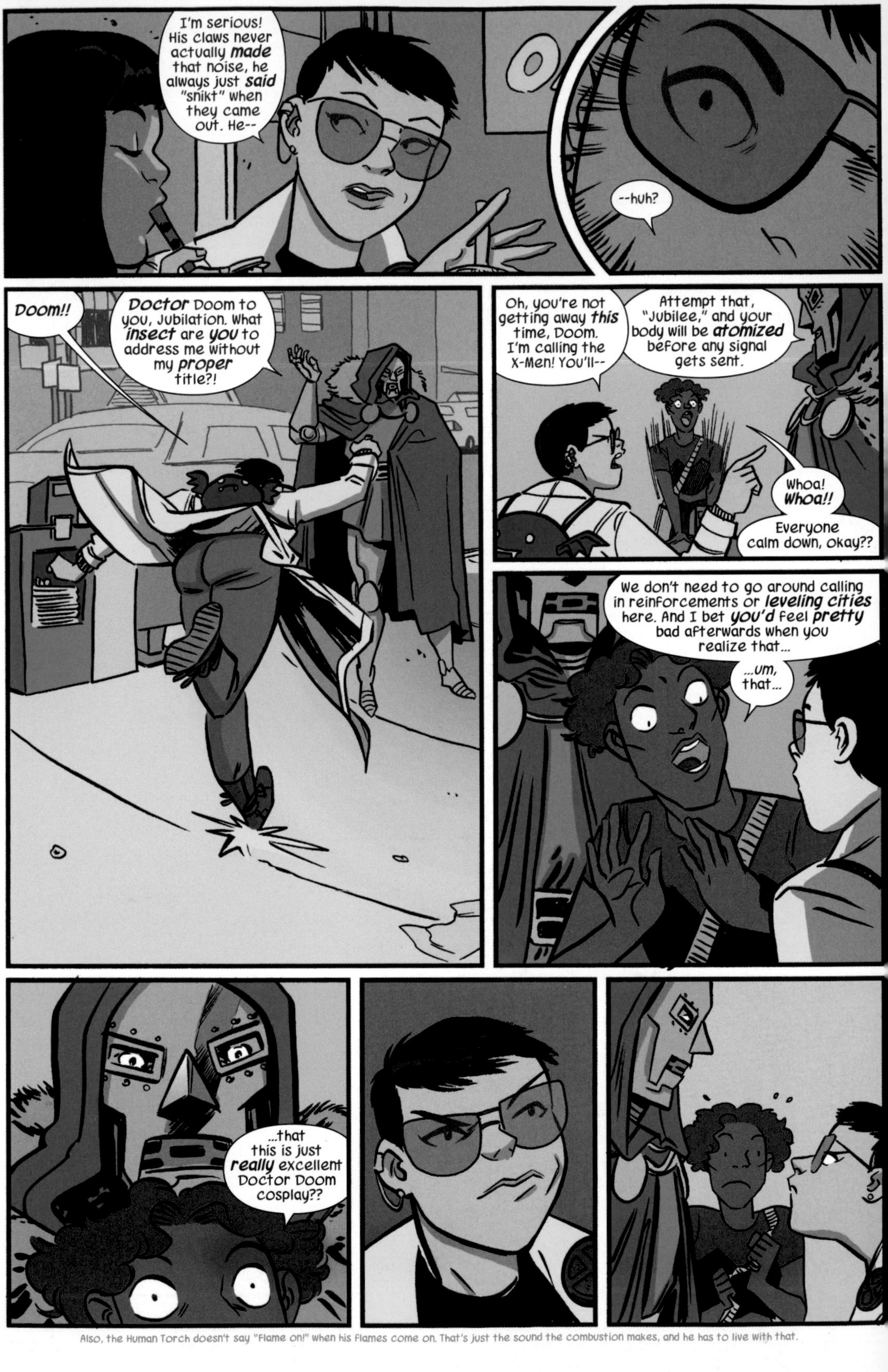
I'm serious! His claws never actually made that noise, he always just said "snikt" when they came out. He--
--huh?
Doom!!
Doctor Doom to you, Jubilation. What insect are you to address me without my proper title?!
Oh, you're not getting away this time, Doom. I'm calling the X-Men! You'll--
Attempt that, "Jubilee," and your body will be atomized before any signal gets sent.
Whoa! Whoa!!
Everyone calm down, okay??
We don't need to go around calling in reinforcements or leveling cities here. And I bet you'd feel pretty bad afterwards when you realize that...
...um, that...
...that this is just really excellent Doctor Doom cosplay??

Also, the Human Torch doesn't say "Flame on!" when his flames come on. That's just the sound the combustion makes, and he has to live with that.

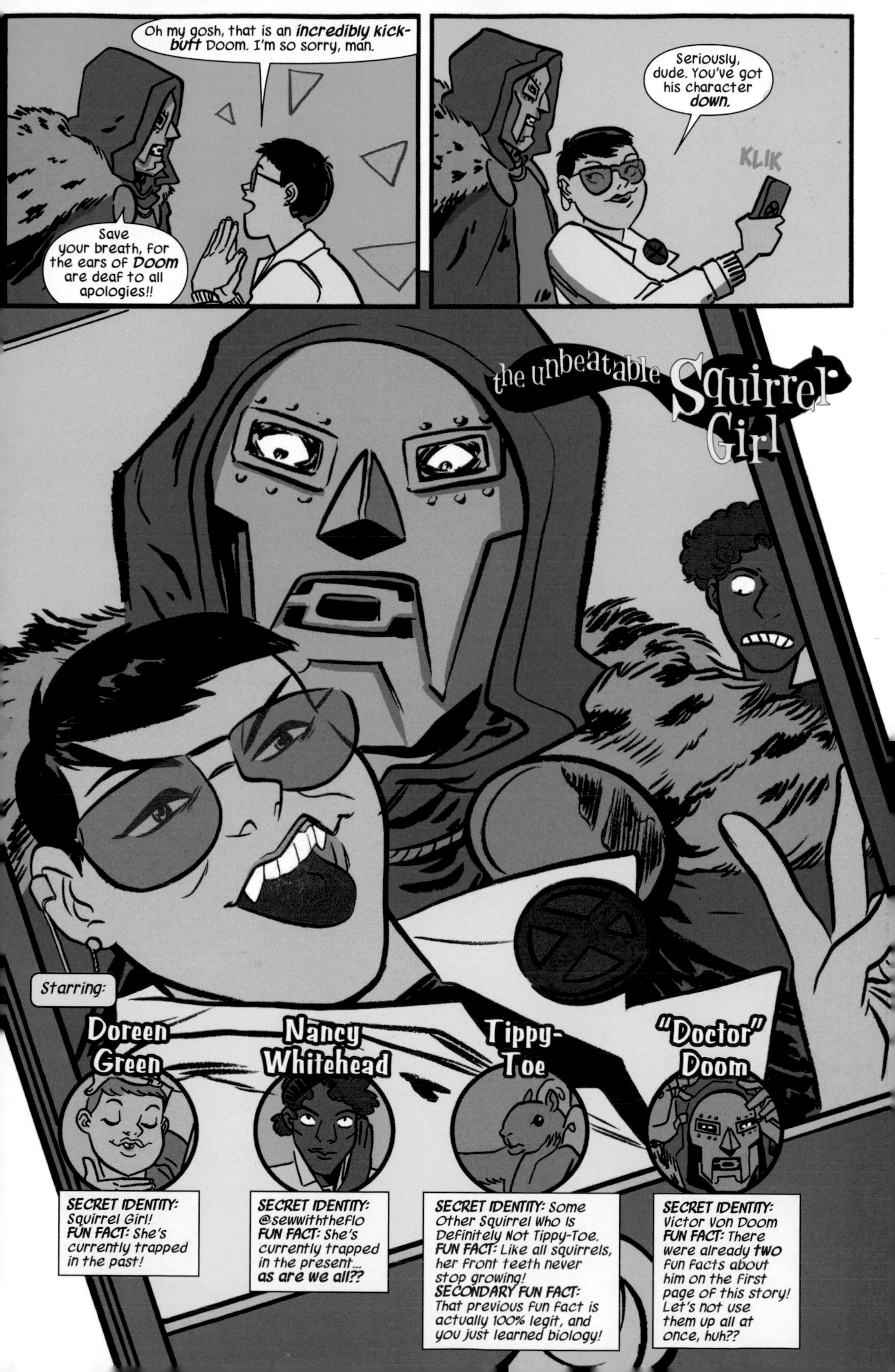

Oh my gosh, that is an *incredibly kick-butt* Doom. I'm so sorry, man.
Save your breath, for the ears of **DOOM** are deaf to all apologies!!
Seriously, dude. You've got his character **down.**
KLIK
the unbeatable Squirrel Girl
Starring:
Doreen Green
Nancy Whitehead
Tippy-Toe
"Doctor" Doom
SECRET IDENTITY: Squirrel Girl! **FUN FACT:** She's currently trapped in the past!
SECRET IDENTITY: @sewwiththeflo **FUN FACT:** She's currently trapped in the present... **as are we all??**
SECRET IDENTITY: Some Other Squirrel Who Is Definitely Not Tippy-Toe. **FUN FACT:** Like all squirrels, her front teeth never stop growing! **SECONDARY FUN FACT:** That previous fun fact is actually 100% legit, and you just learned biology!
SECRET IDENTITY: Victor Von Doom **FUN FACT:** There were already **two** fun facts about him on the first page of this story! Let's not use them up all at once, huh??

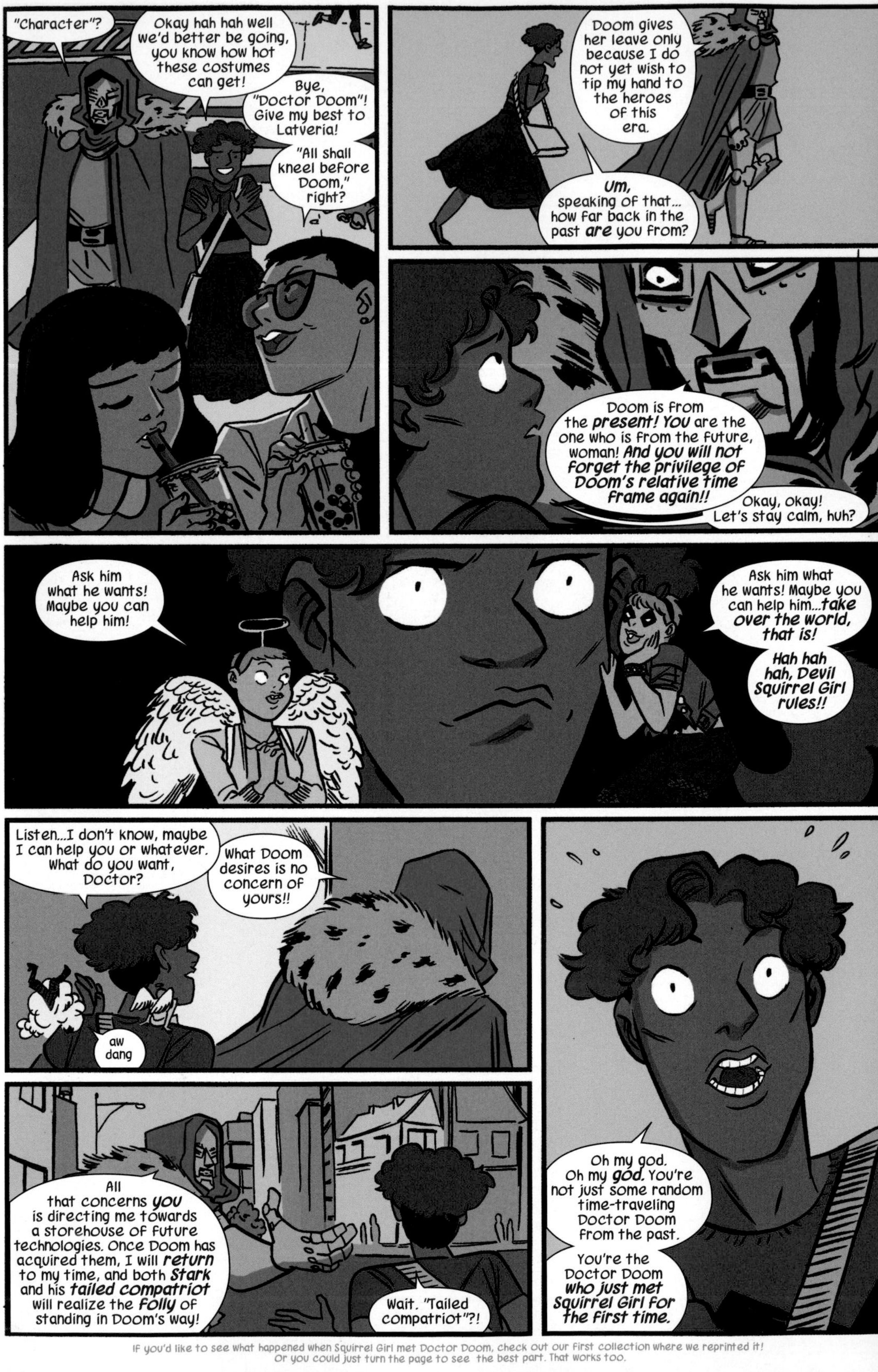
"Character"?
Okay hah hah well we'd better be going, you know how hot these costumes can get!
Bye, "Doctor Doom"! Give my best to Latveria!
"All shall kneel before Doom," right?
Doom gives her leave only because I do not yet wish to tip my hand to the heroes of this era.
Um, speaking of that... how far back in the past are you from?
Doom is from the present! You are the one who is from the future, woman! And you will not forget the privilege of Doom's relative time frame again!!
Okay, okay! Let's stay calm, huh?
Ask him what he wants! Maybe you can help him!
Ask him what he wants! Maybe you can help him...take over the world, that is!
Hah hah hah, Devil Squirrel Girl rules!!
Listen...I don't know, maybe I can help you or whatever. What do you want, Doctor?
What Doom desires is no concern of yours!!
aw dang
All that concerns you is directing me towards a storehouse of future technologies. Once Doom has acquired them, I will return to my time, and both Stark and his tailed compatriot will realize the folly of standing in Doom's way!
Wait. "Tailed compatriot"?!
Oh my god. Oh my god. You're not just some random time-traveling Doctor Doom from the past.
You're the Doctor Doom who just met Squirrel Girl for the first time.

If you'd like to see what happened when Squirrel Girl met Doctor Doom, check out our first collection where we reprinted it! Or you could just turn the page to see the best part. That works too.

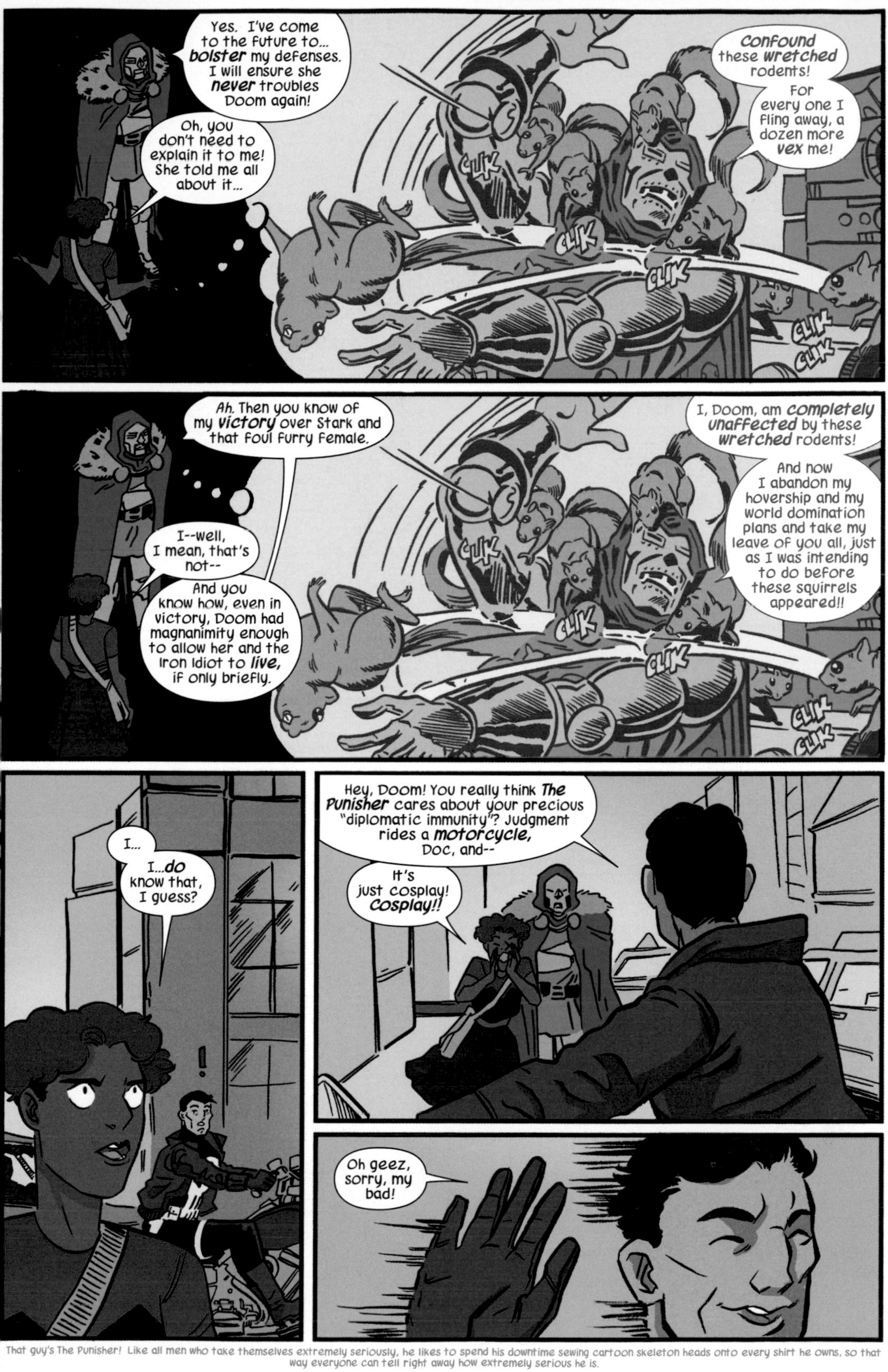
Yes. I've come to the future to... bolster my defenses. I will ensure she never troubles Doom again!
Oh, you don't need to explain it to me! She told me all about it...
Confound these wretched rodents!
For every one I fling away, a dozen more vex me!
CLIK
CLIK
CLIK
CLIK
CLIK
Ah. Then you know of my victory over Stark and that foul furry female.
I--well, I mean, that's not--
And you know how, even in victory, Doom had magnanimity enough to allow her and the Iron Idiot to live, if only briefly.
I, Doom, am completely unaffected by these wretched rodents!
And now I abandon my hovership and my world domination plans and take my leave of you all, just as I was intending to do before these squirrels appeared!!
CLIK
CLIK
CLIK
CLIK
CLIK
I... I...do know that, I guess?
!
Hey, Doom! You really think The Punisher cares about your precious "diplomatic immunity"? Judgment rides a motorcycle, Doc, and--
It's just cosplay! Cosplay!!
Oh geez, sorry, my bad!

That guy's The Punisher! Like all men who take themselves extremely seriously, he likes to spend his downtime sewing cartoon skeleton heads onto every shirt he owns, so that way everyone can tell right away how extremely serious he is.

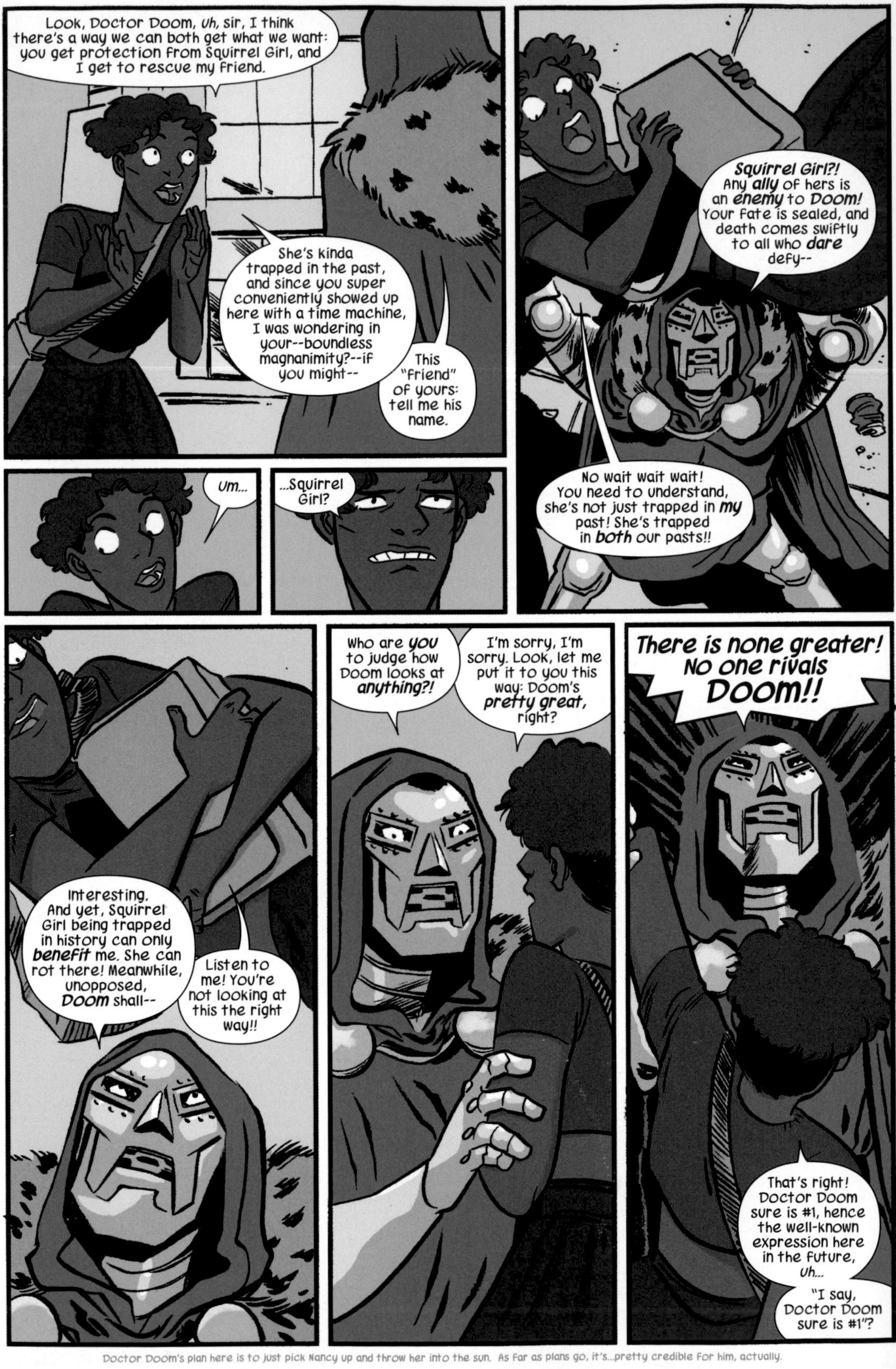
Look, Doctor Doom, uh, sir, I think there's a way we can both get what we want: you get protection from Squirrel Girl, and I get to rescue my friend.
She's kinda trapped in the past, and since you super conveniently showed up here with a time machine, I was wondering in your--boundless magnanimity?--if you might--
This "friend" of yours: tell me his name.
Um...
...Squirrel Girl?
Squirrel Girl?! Any ally of hers is an enemy to Doom! Your fate is sealed, and death comes swiftly to all who dare defy--
No wait wait wait! You need to understand, she's not just trapped in my past! She's trapped in both our pasts!!
Interesting. And yet, Squirrel Girl being trapped in history can only benefit me. She can rot there! Meanwhile, unopposed, Doom shall--
Listen to me! You're not looking at this the right way!!
Who are you to judge how Doom looks at anything?!
I'm sorry, I'm sorry. Look, let me put it to you this way: Doom's pretty great, right?
There is none greater! No one rivals Doom!!
That's right! Doctor Doom sure is #1, hence the well-known expression here in the future, uh...
"I say, Doctor Doom sure is #1"?

Doctor Doom's plan here is to just pick Nancy up and throw her into the sun. As far as plans go, it's...pretty credible for him, actually.

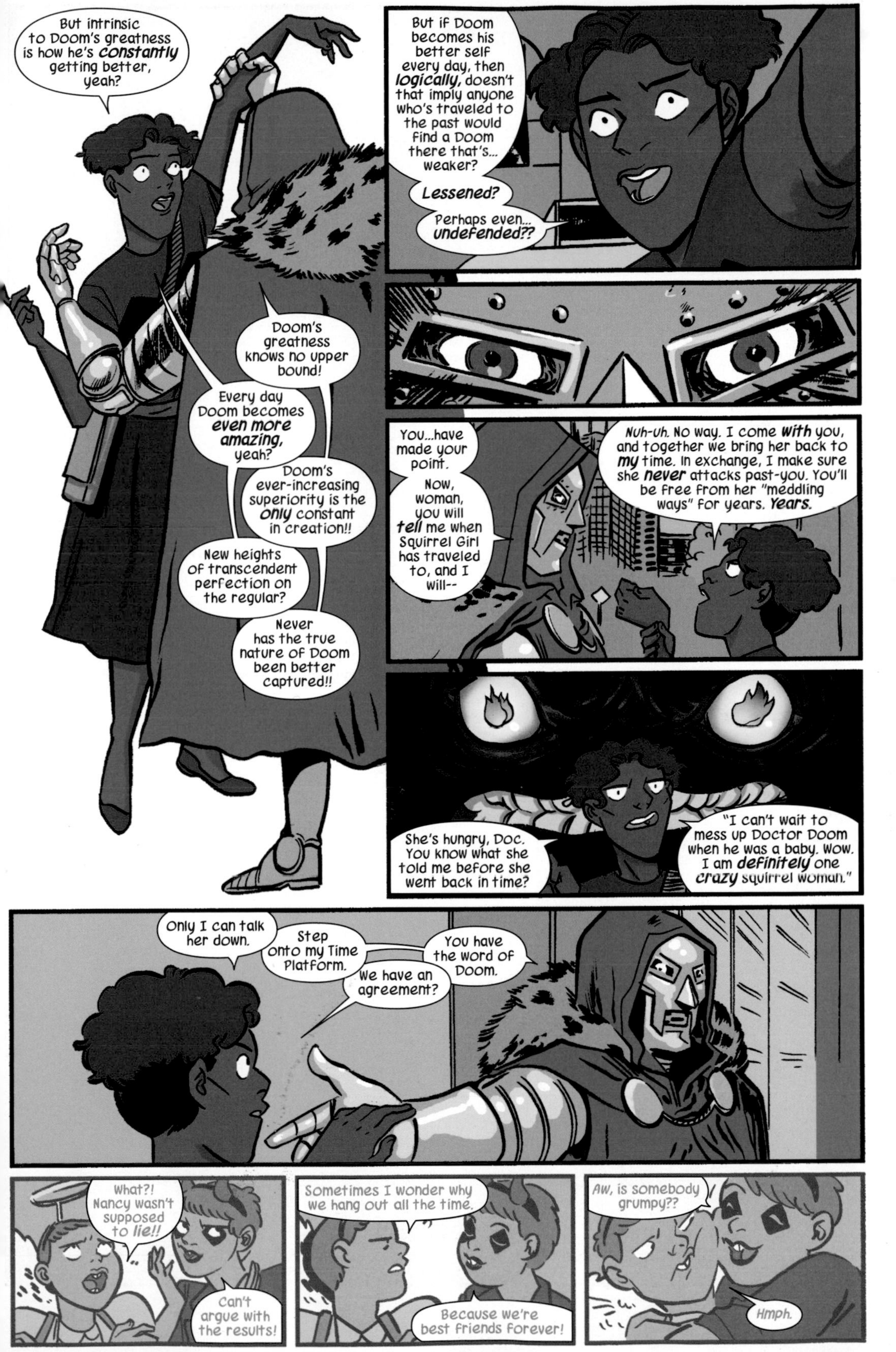

But intrinsic to Doom's greatness is how he's *constantly* getting better, yeah?
But if Doom becomes his better self every day, then ***logically,*** doesn't that imply anyone who's traveled to the past would find a Doom there that's... weaker?
Lessened?
Perhaps even... ***undefended??***
Doom's greatness knows no upper bound!
Every day Doom becomes ***even more amazing,*** yeah?
Doom's ever-increasing superiority is the ***only*** constant in creation!!
New heights of transcendent perfection on the regular?
Never has the true nature of Doom been better captured!!
You...have made your point.
Now, woman, you will ***tell*** me when Squirrel Girl has traveled to, and I will--
Nuh-uh. No way. I come ***with*** you, and together we bring her back to ***my*** time. In exchange, I make sure she ***never*** attacks past-you. You'll be free from her "meddling ways" for years. ***Years.***
She's hungry, Doc. You know what she told me before she went back in time?
"I can't wait to mess up Doctor Doom when he was a baby. Wow. I am ***definitely*** one ***crazy*** squirrel woman."
Only I can talk her down.
Step onto my Time Platform.
We have an agreement?
You have the word of Doom.
What?! Nancy wasn't supposed to *lie!!*
Can't argue with the results!
Sometimes I wonder why we hang out all the time.
Because we're best friends forever!
Aw, is somebody grumpy??
Hmph.

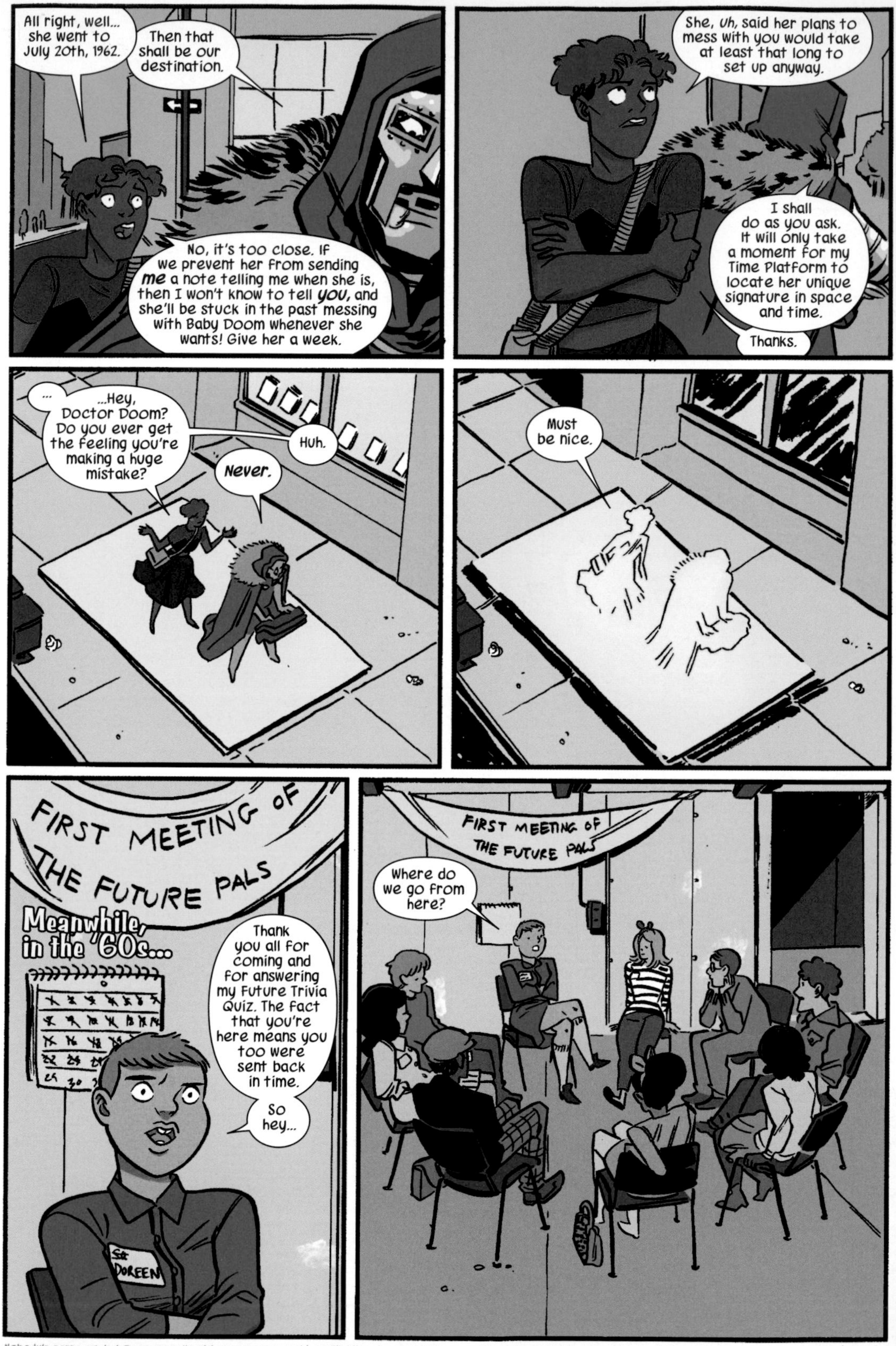
All right, well... she went to July 20th, 1962.
Then that shall be our destination.
No, it's too close. If we prevent her from sending me a note telling me when she is, then I won't know to tell you, and she'll be stuck in the past messing with Baby Doom whenever she wants! Give her a week.
She, uh, said her plans to mess with you would take at least that long to set up anyway.
I shall do as you ask. It will only take a moment for my Time Platform to locate her unique signature in space and time.
Thanks.
...
...Hey, Doctor Doom? Do you ever get the feeling you're making a huge mistake?
Never.
Huh.
Must be nice.
FIRST MEETING OF THE FUTURE PALS
Meanwhile, in the '60s...
Thank you all for coming and for answering my Future Trivia Quiz. The fact that you're here means you too were sent back in time.
So hey...
DOREEN
FIRST MEETING OF THE FUTURE PALS
Where do we go from here?

Nobody's gonna ask but Doreen really wishes someone would, so I'll bite: she called this group "The Future Pals" because they're all from the future, and she also hopes that in time they'll all become pals. *Pretty adorable, Doreen.*

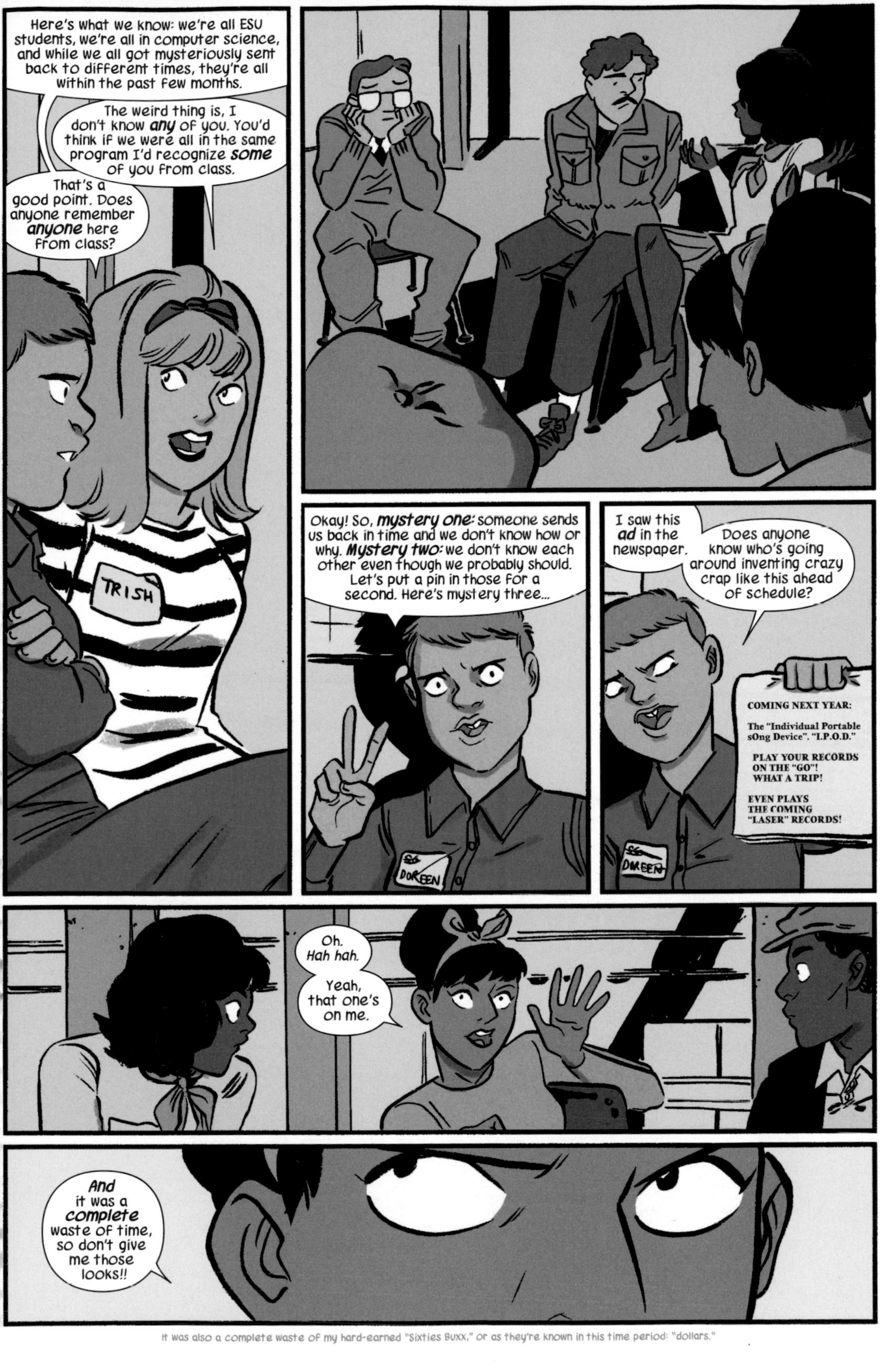
Here's what we know: we're all ESU students, we're all in computer science, and while we all got mysteriously sent back to different times, they're all within the past few months.
The weird thing is, I don't know *any* of you. You'd think if we were all in the same program I'd recognize *some* of you from class.
That's a good point. Does anyone remember *anyone* here from class?
TRISH
Okay! So, *mystery one:* someone sends us back in time and we don't know how or why. *Mystery two:* we don't know each other even though we probably should. Let's put a pin in those for a second. Here's mystery three...
DOREEN
I saw this *ad* in the newspaper.
Does anyone know who's going around inventing crazy crap like this ahead of schedule?
COMING NEXT YEAR:
The "Individual Portable sOng Device". "I.P.O.D."
PLAY YOUR RECORDS ON THE "GO"! WHAT A TRIP!
EVEN PLAYS THE COMING "LASER" RECORDS!
DOREEN
Oh. Hah hah.
Yeah, that one's on me.
And it was a *complete* waste of time, so don't give me those looks!!

It was also a complete waste of my hard-earned "Sixties Buxx," or as they're known in this time period: "dollars."

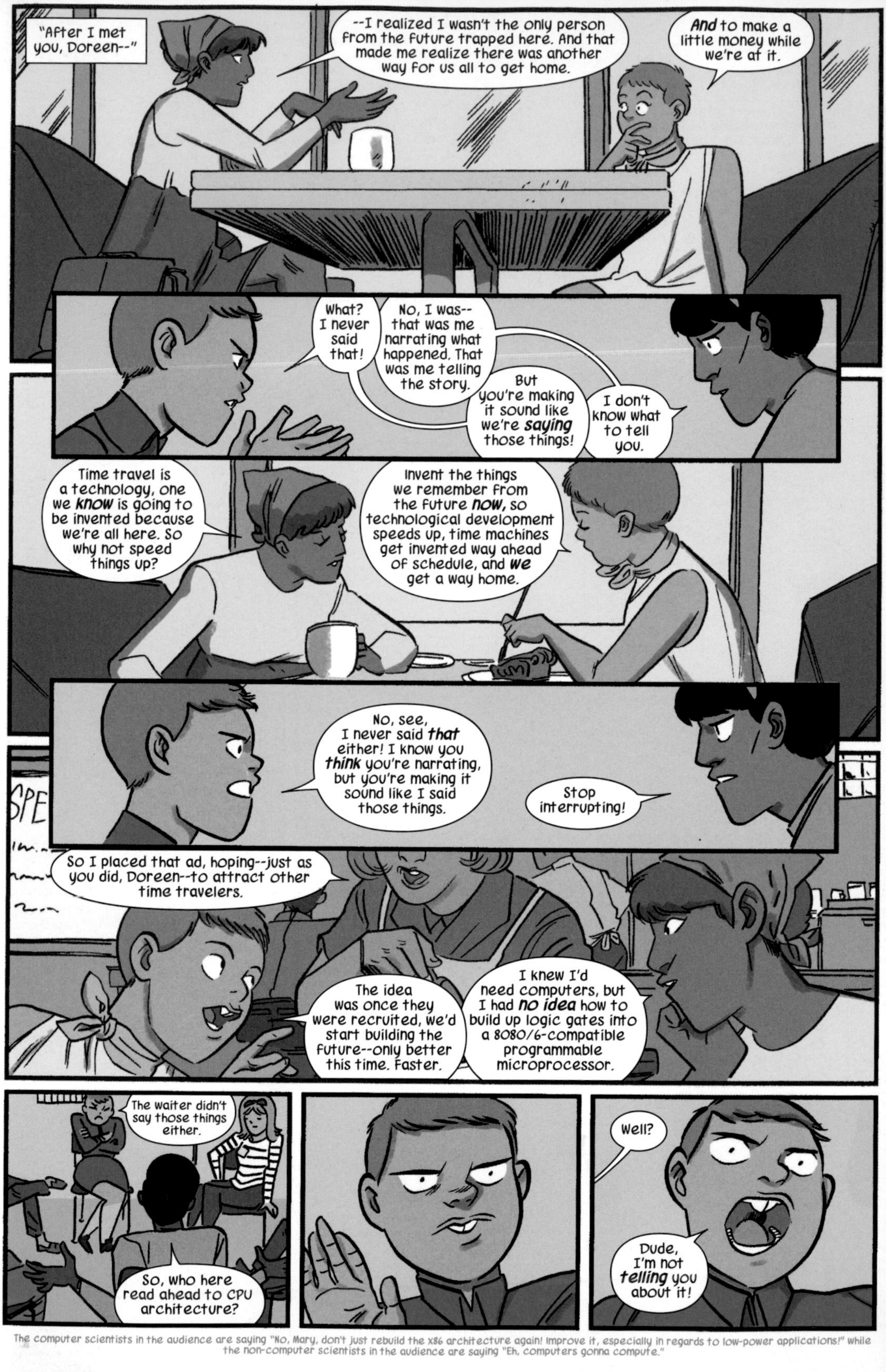
"After I met you, Doreen--"
--I realized I wasn't the only person from the future trapped here. And that made me realize there was another way for us all to get home.
And to make a little money while we're at it.
What? I never said that!
No, I was-- that was me narrating what happened. That was me telling the story.
But you're making it sound like we're saying those things!
I don't know what to tell you.
Time travel is a technology, one we know is going to be invented because we're all here. So why not speed things up?
Invent the things we remember from the future now, so technological development speeds up, time machines get invented way ahead of schedule, and we get a way home.
No, see, I never said that either! I know you think you're narrating, but you're making it sound like I said those things.
Stop interrupting!
So I placed that ad, hoping--just as you did, Doreen--to attract other time travelers.
The idea was once they were recruited, we'd start building the future--only better this time. Faster.
I knew I'd need computers, but I had no idea how to build up logic gates into a 8080/6-compatible programmable microprocessor.
The waiter didn't say those things either.
So, who here read ahead to CPU architecture?
Well?
Dude, I'm not telling you about it!

The computer scientists in the audience are saying "No, Mary, don't just rebuild the x86 architecture again! Improve it, especially in regards to low-power applications!" while the non-computer scientists in the audience are saying "Eh, computers gonna compute."

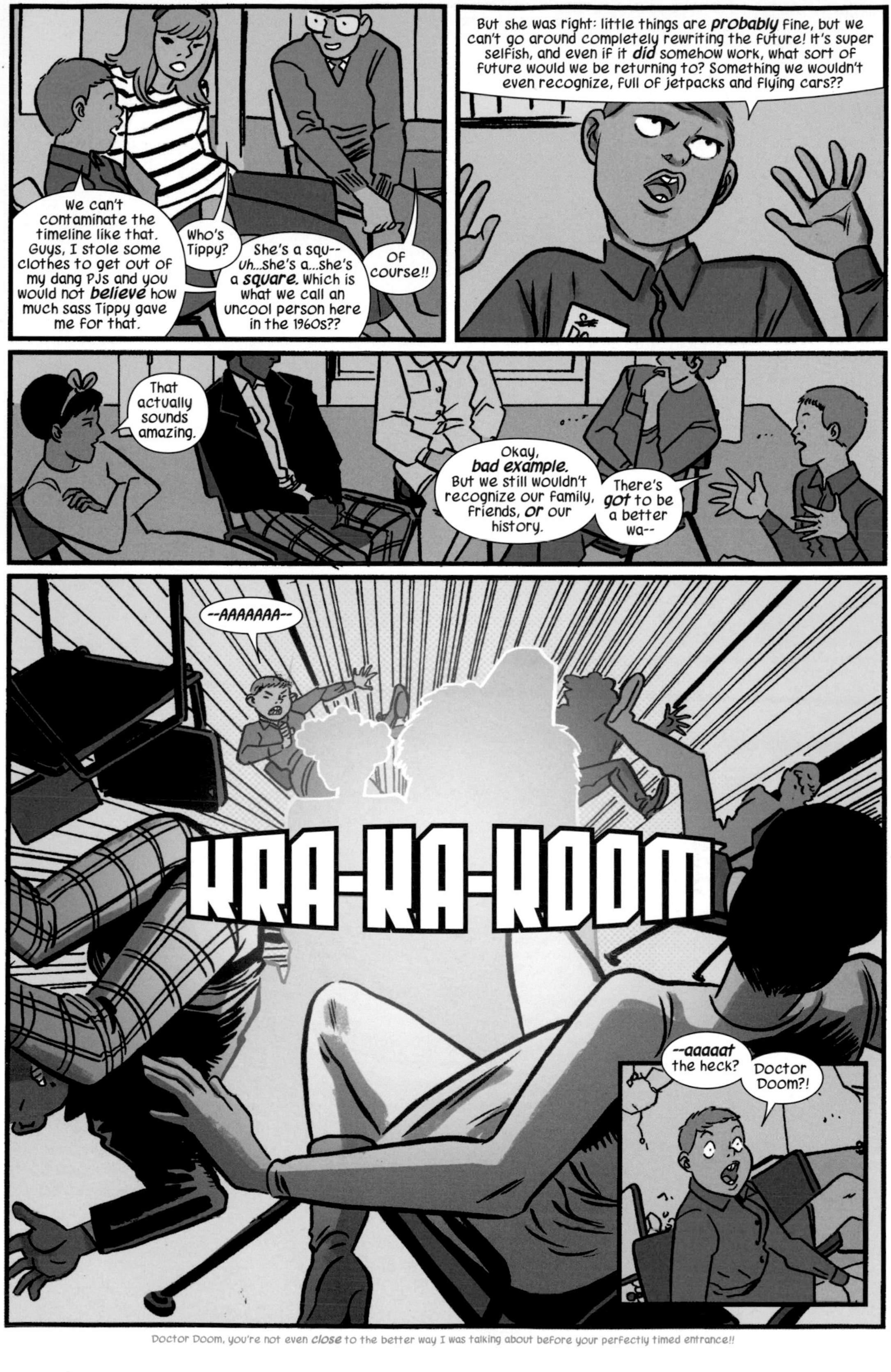
We can't contaminate the timeline like that. Guys, I stole some clothes to get out of my dang PJs and you would not *believe* how much sass Tippy gave me for that.
Who's Tippy?
She's a squ-- uh...she's a...she's a *square.* Which is what we call an uncool person here in the 1960s??
Of course!!
But she was right: little things are *probably* fine, but we can't go around completely rewriting the future! It's super selfish, and even if it *did* somehow work, what sort of future would we be returning to? Something we wouldn't even recognize, full of jetpacks and flying cars??
That actually sounds amazing.
Okay, *bad example.* But we still wouldn't recognize our family, friends, *or* our history.
There's *got* to be a better wa--
--AAAAAAA--
KRA-KA-KOOM
--aaaaat the heck?
Doctor Doom?!

Doctor Doom, you're not even *close* to the better way I was talking about before your perfectly timed entrance!!

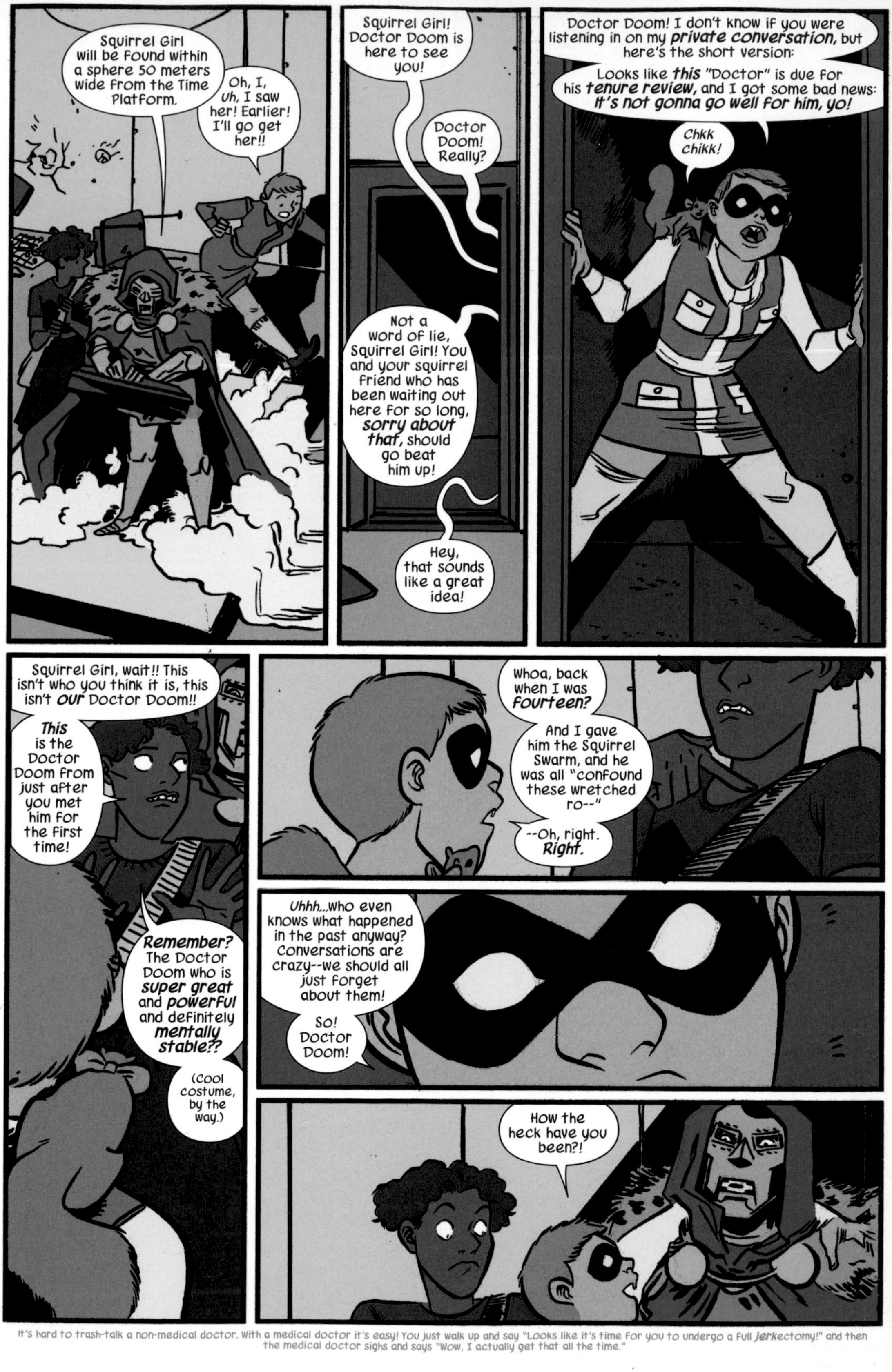
Squirrel Girl will be found within a sphere 50 meters wide from the Time Platform.
Oh, I, uh, I saw her! Earlier! I'll go get her!!
Squirrel Girl! Doctor Doom is here to see you!
Doctor Doom! Really?
Not a word of lie, Squirrel Girl! You and your squirrel friend who has been waiting out here for so long, sorry about that, should go beat him up!
Hey, that sounds like a great idea!
Doctor Doom! I don't know if you were listening in on my private conversation, but here's the short version:
Looks like this "Doctor" is due for his tenure review, and I got some bad news: It's not gonna go well for him, yo!
Chkk Chikk!
Squirrel Girl, wait!! This isn't who you think it is, this isn't our Doctor Doom!!
This is the Doctor Doom from just after you met him for the first time!
Whoa, back when I was fourteen?
And I gave him the Squirrel Swarm, and he was all "confound these wretched ro--"
--Oh, right. Right.
Remember? The Doctor Doom who is super great and powerful and definitely mentally stable??
(Cool costume, by the way.)
Uhhh...who even knows what happened in the past anyway? Conversations are crazy--we should all just forget about them!
So! Doctor Doom!
How the heck have you been?!

It's hard to trash-talk a non-medical doctor. With a medical doctor it's easy! You just walk up and say "Looks like it's time for you to undergo a full *jerk*ectomy!" and then the medical doctor sighs and says "Wow, I actually get that all the time."

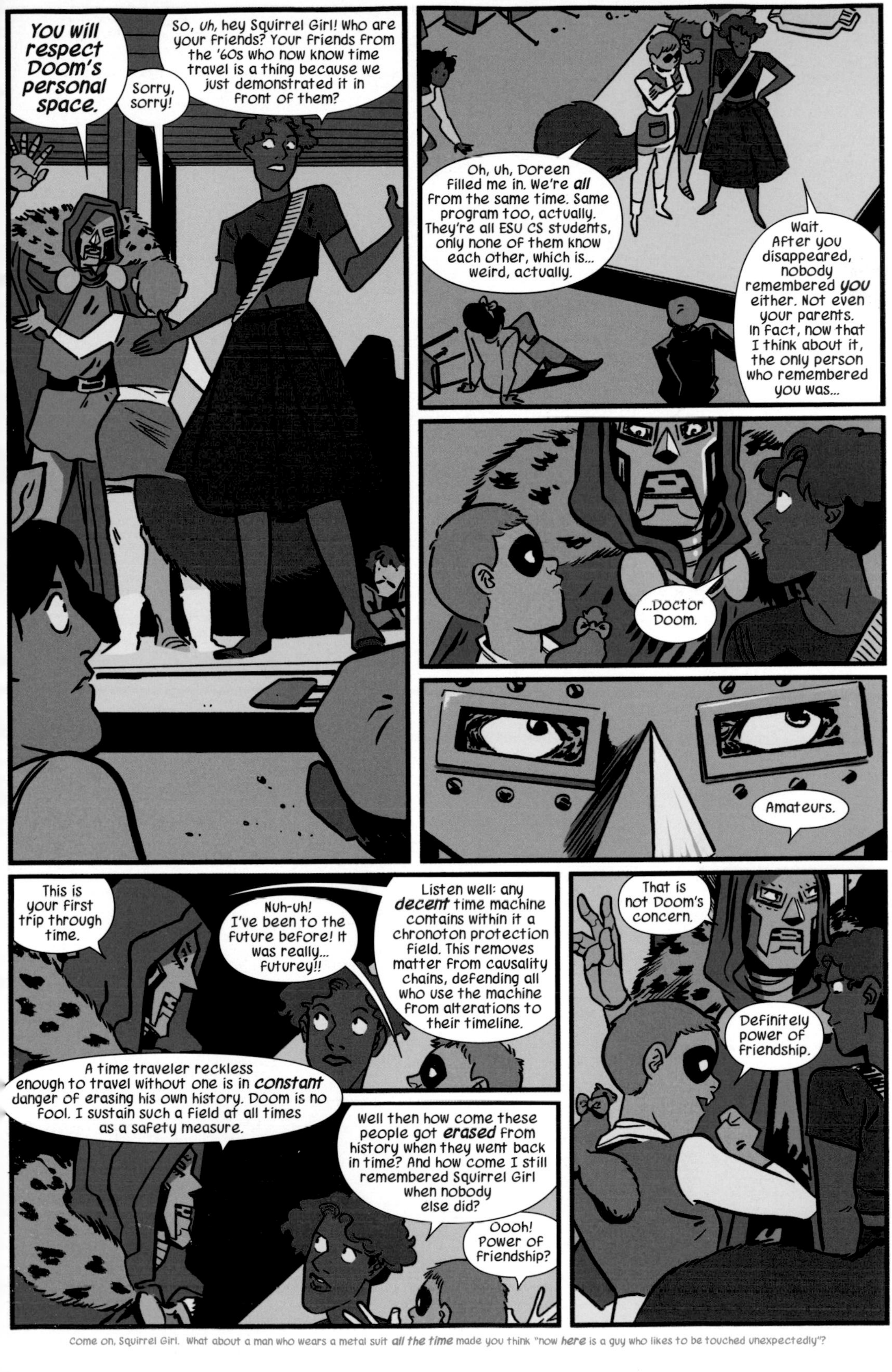
You will respect Doom's personal space.
Sorry, sorry!
So, uh, hey Squirrel Girl! Who are your friends? Your friends from the '60s who now know time travel is a thing because we just demonstrated it in front of them?
Oh, uh, Doreen filled me in. We're all from the same time. Same program too, actually. They're all ESU CS students, only none of them know each other, which is... weird, actually.
Wait. After you disappeared, nobody remembered you either. Not even your parents. In fact, now that I think about it, the only person who remembered you was...
...Doctor Doom.
Amateurs.
This is your first trip through time.
Nuh-uh! I've been to the future before! It was really... futurey!!
Listen well: any decent time machine contains within it a chronoton protection field. This removes matter from causality chains, defending all who use the machine from alterations to their timeline.
A time traveler reckless enough to travel without one is in constant danger of erasing his own history. Doom is no fool. I sustain such a field at all times as a safety measure.
Well then how come these people got erased from history when they went back in time? And how come I still remembered Squirrel Girl when nobody else did?
Oooh! Power of friendship?
That is not Doom's concern.
Definitely power of friendship.

Come on, Squirrel Girl. What about a man who wears a metal suit *all the time* made you think "now *here* is a guy who likes to be touched unexpectedly"?

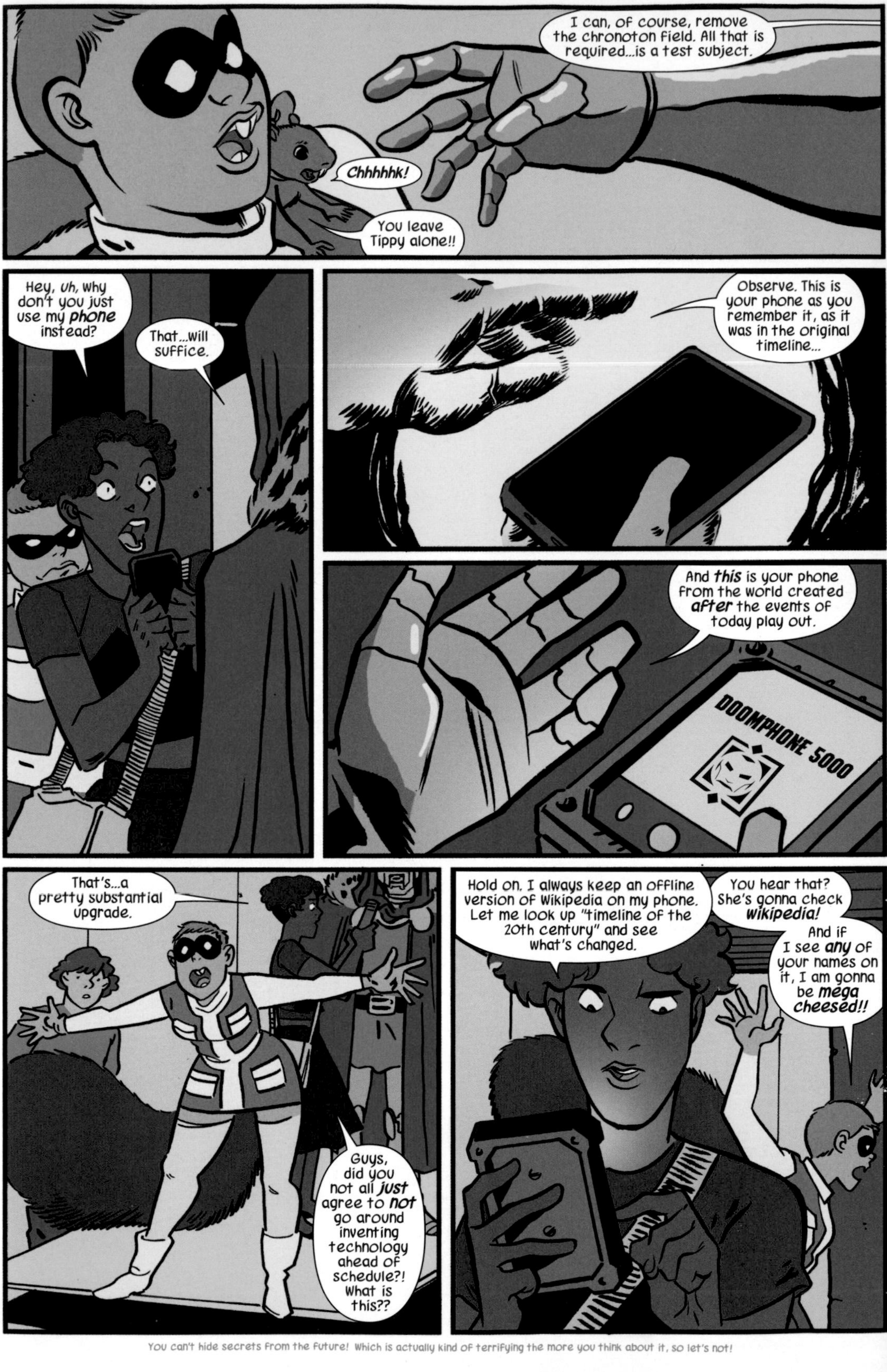
I can, of course, remove the chronoton field. All that is required...is a test subject.
Chhhhhk!
You leave Tippy alone!!
Hey, uh, why don't you just use my *phone* instead?
That...will suffice.
Observe. This is your phone as you remember it, as it was in the original timeline...
And *this* is your phone from the world created *after* the events of today play out.
DOOMPHONE 5000
That's...a pretty substantial upgrade.
Guys, did you not all *just* agree to *not* go around inventing technology ahead of schedule?! What is this??
Hold on. I always keep an offline version of Wikipedia on my phone. Let me look up "timeline of the 20th century" and see what's changed.
You hear that? She's gonna check *wikipedia!*
And if I see *any* of your names on it, I am gonna be *mega cheesed!!*

You can't hide secrets from the future! Which is actually kind of terrifying the more you think about it, so let's not!

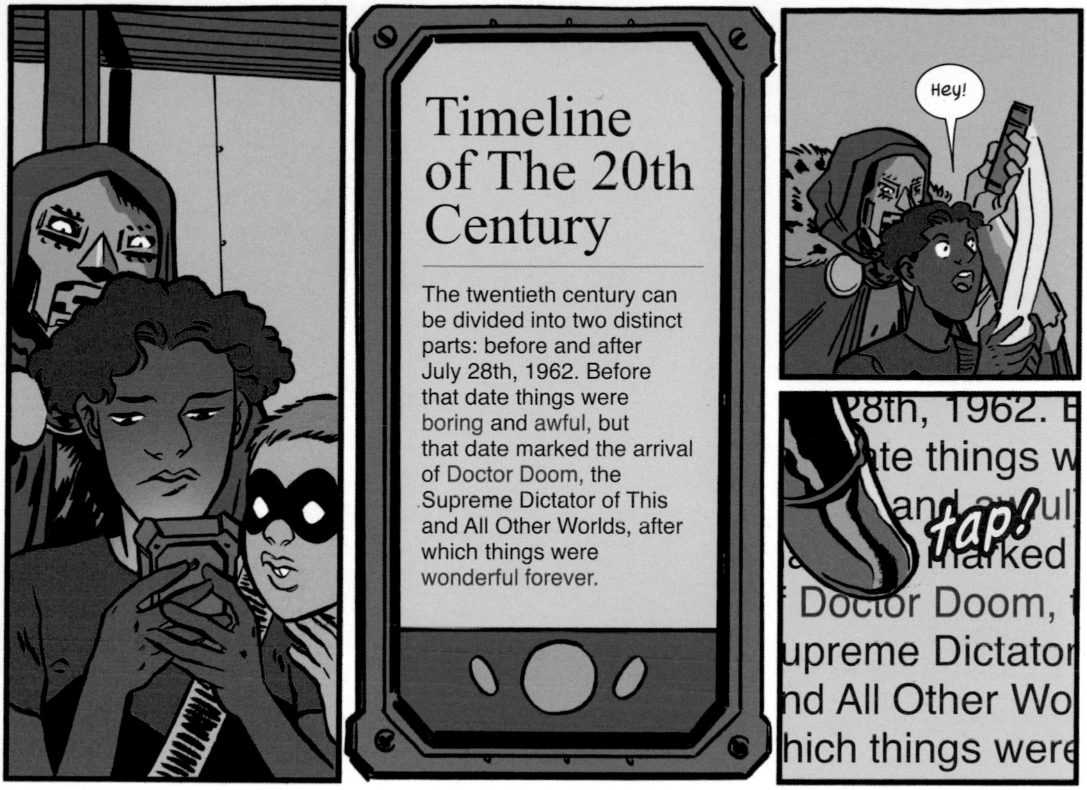
Timeline of The 20th Century
The twentieth century can be divided into two distinct parts: before and after July 28th, 1962. Before that date things were boring and awful, but that date marked the arrival of Doctor Doom, the Supreme Dictator of This and All Other Worlds, after which things were wonderful forever.
Hey!
tap!

Doctor Victor Von Doom, PhD, is a beloved benevolent dictator, scientist, inventor, sorcerer supreme, genius, and artist who appeared under mysterious circumstances on Planet Doom (formerly "Earth") on July 28th, 1962. He quickly took over the world, issuing many decrees for reasons known only to His Supreme Greatness, including specifying that Reed Richards and his closest three associates be kept out of space, alternate dimensions, and cinemas; that otherwise-unremarkable student Peter Parker under no circumstances be allowed near spiders; that all gamma ray testing be immediately suspended; among others. His rule is notable for having been absolutely perfect in every way.

Contents [hide]

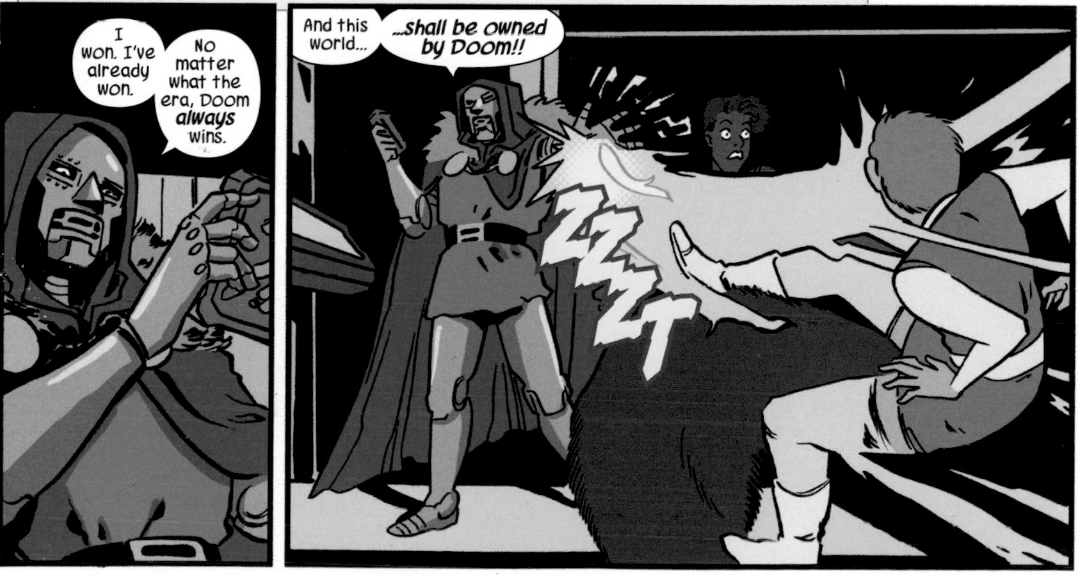
I won. I've already won.
No matter what the era, Doom ***always*** wins.
And this world...
...shall be owned by Doom!!
ZZZT

Yes, this ***does*** canonically establish that among Doom's many abilities is the ability to make his touchscreens work even when he's wearing metal gloves. ***Must be nice.***

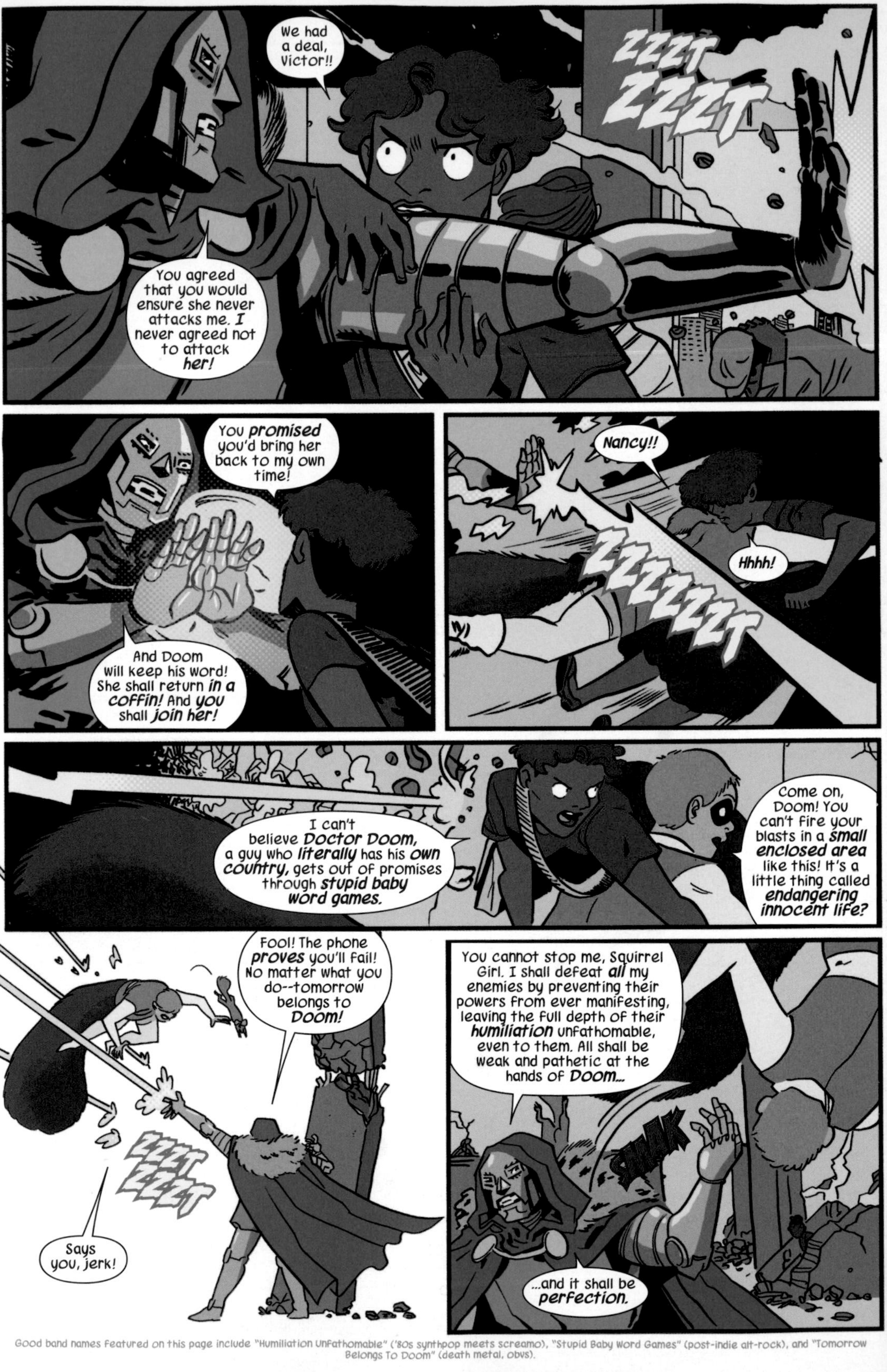
We had a deal, Victor!!
ZZZT ZZZT
You agreed that you would ensure she never attacks me. I never agreed not to attack her!
You promised you'd bring her back to my own time!
And Doom will keep his word! She shall return in a coffin! And you shall join her!
Nancy!!
Hhhh!
ZZZZZZZZT
I can't believe Doctor Doom, a guy who literally has his own country, gets out of promises through stupid baby word games.
Come on, Doom! You can't fire your blasts in a small enclosed area like this! It's a little thing called endangering innocent life?
Fool! The phone proves you'll fail! No matter what you do--tomorrow belongs to Doom!
ZZZT ZZZT
Says you, jerk!
You cannot stop me, Squirrel Girl. I shall defeat all my enemies by preventing their powers from ever manifesting, leaving the full depth of their humiliation unfathomable, even to them. All shall be weak and pathetic at the hands of Doom...
SHAK
...and it shall be perfection.

Good band names featured on this page include "Humiliation Unfathomable" ('80s synthpop meets screamo), "Stupid Baby Word Games" (post-indie alt-rock), and "Tomorrow Belongs To Doom" (death metal, obvs).

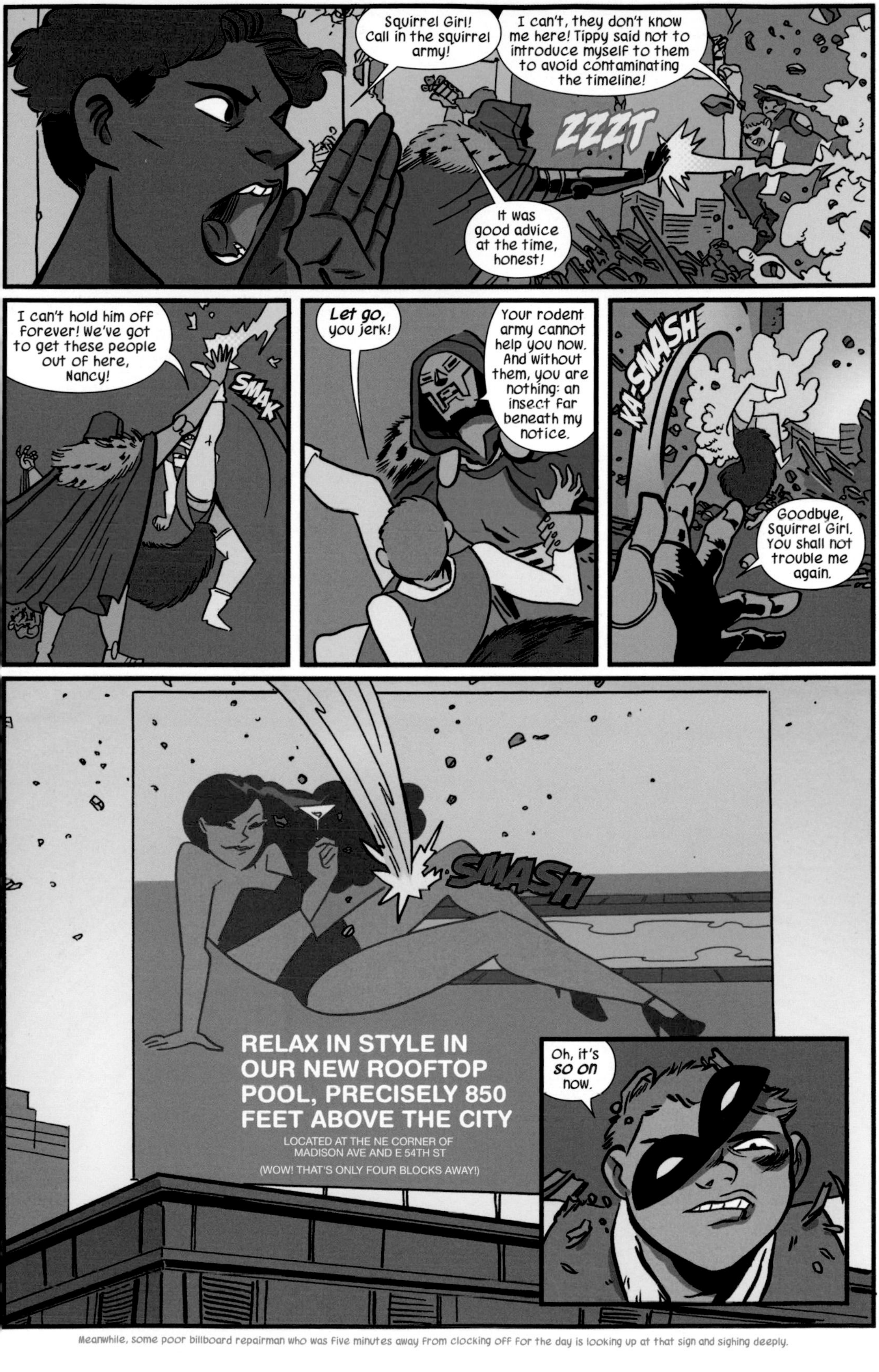
Squirrel Girl! Call in the squirrel army!
I can't, they don't know me here! Tippy said not to introduce myself to them to avoid contaminating the timeline!
ZZZT
It was good advice at the time, honest!
I can't hold him off forever! We've got to get these people out of here, Nancy!
SMAK
Let go, you jerk!
Your rodent army cannot help you now. And without them, you are nothing: an insect far beneath my notice.
KA-SMASH
Goodbye, Squirrel Girl. You shall not trouble me again.
SMASH
RELAX IN STYLE IN OUR NEW ROOFTOP POOL, PRECISELY 850 FEET ABOVE THE CITY
LOCATED AT THE NE CORNER OF MADISON AVE AND E 54TH ST
(WOW! THAT'S ONLY FOUR BLOCKS AWAY!)
Oh, it's so on now.

Meanwhile, some poor billboard repairman who was five minutes away from clocking off for the day is looking up at that sign and sighing deeply.

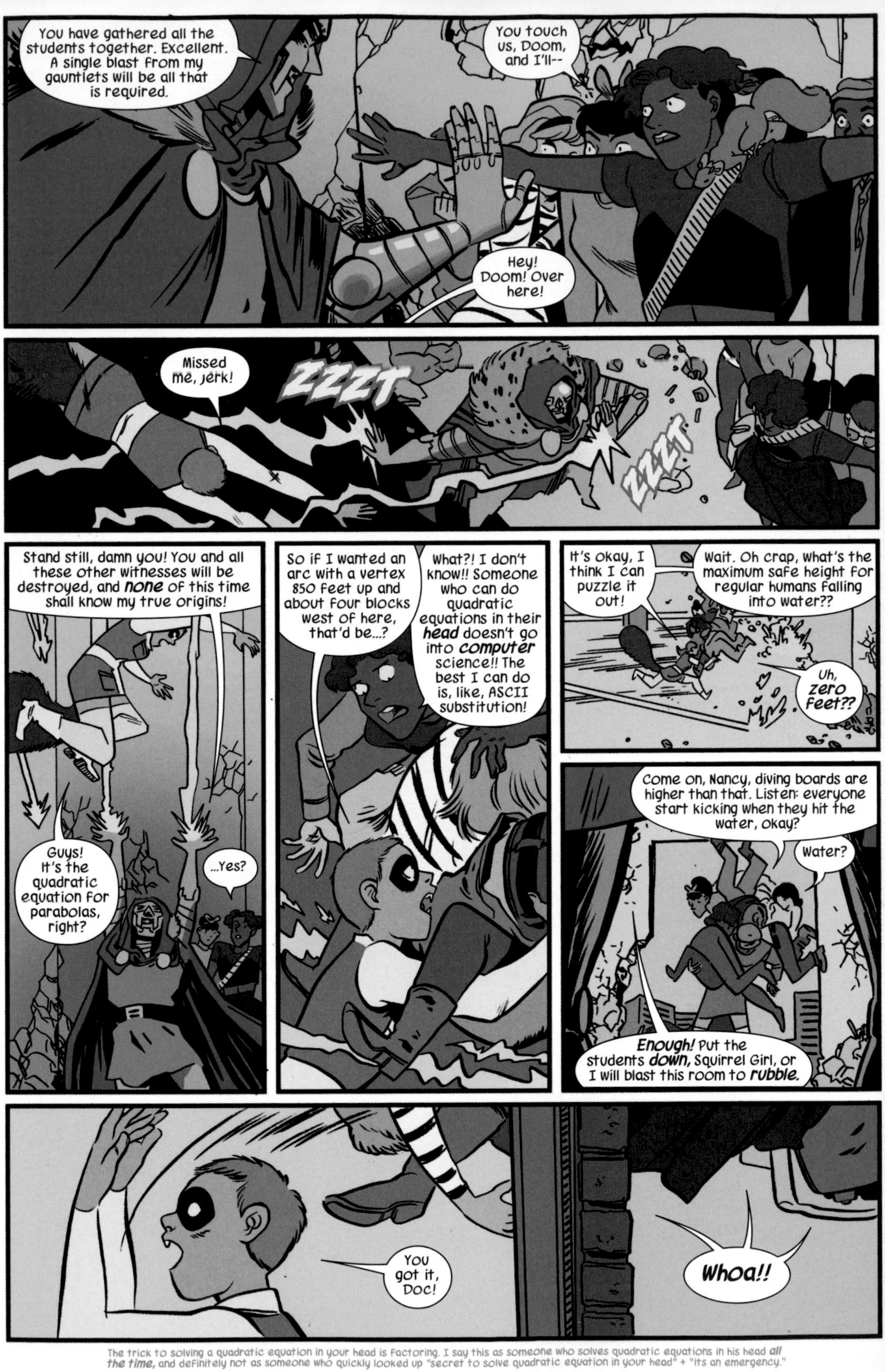
You have gathered all the students together. Excellent. A single blast from my gauntlets will be all that is required.
You touch us, Doom, and I'll--
Hey! Doom! Over here!
Missed me, jerk!
ZZZT
ZZZT
Stand still, damn you! You and all these other witnesses will be destroyed, and NONE of this time shall know my true origins!
Guys! It's the quadratic equation for parabolas, right?
...Yes?
So if I wanted an arc with a vertex 850 feet up and about four blocks west of here, that'd be...?
What?! I don't know!! Someone who can do quadratic equations in their head doesn't go into computer science!! The best I can do is, like, ASCII substitution!
It's okay, I think I can puzzle it out!
Wait. Oh crap, what's the maximum safe height for regular humans falling into water??
Uh, zero feet??
Come on, Nancy, diving boards are higher than that. Listen: everyone start kicking when they hit the water, okay?
Water?
Enough! Put the students down, Squirrel Girl, or I will blast this room to rubble.
You got it, Doc!
Whoa!!

The trick to solving a quadratic equation in your head is factoring. I say this as someone who solves quadratic equations in his head *all the time,* and definitely not as someone who quickly looked up "secret to solve quadratic equation in your head" + "its an emergency."

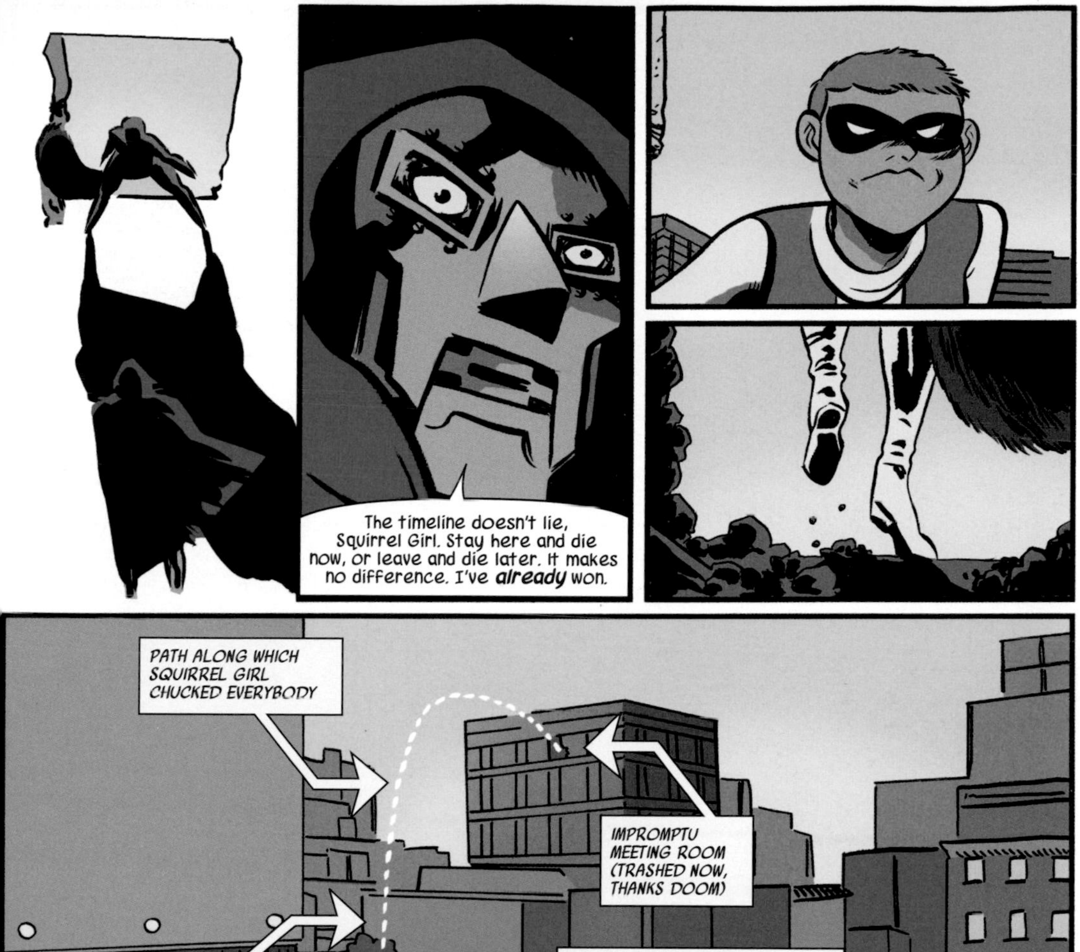
The timeline doesn't lie, Squirrel Girl. Stay here and die now, or leave and die later. It makes no difference. I've *already* won.
PATH ALONG WHICH SQUIRREL GIRL CHUCKED EVERYBODY
IMPROMPTU MEETING ROOM (TRASHED NOW, THANKS DOOM)
REALLY GOOD PARABOLIC CURVE
ROOFTOP POOL (PRECISELY WHERE IT WAS ADVERTISED TO BE!)
SPLASH
Dudes, I'm *totally glad* you all know how to swim!

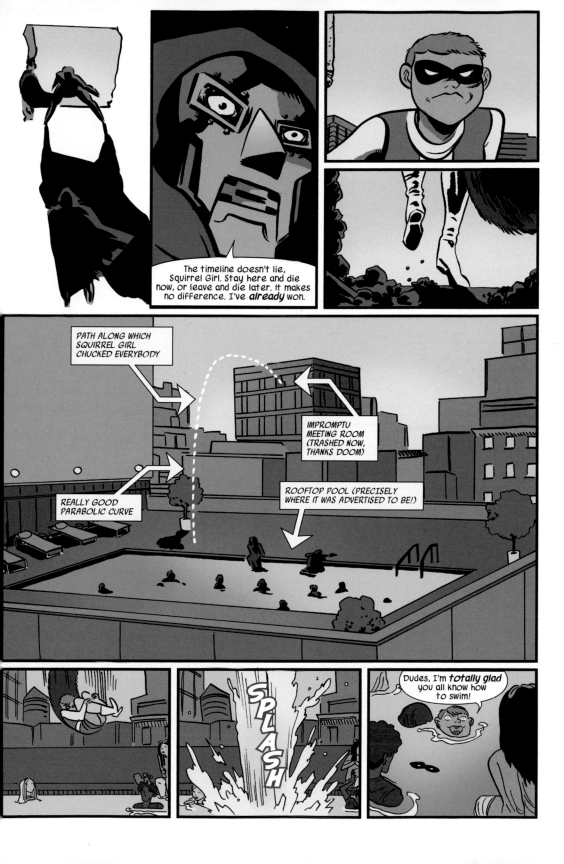

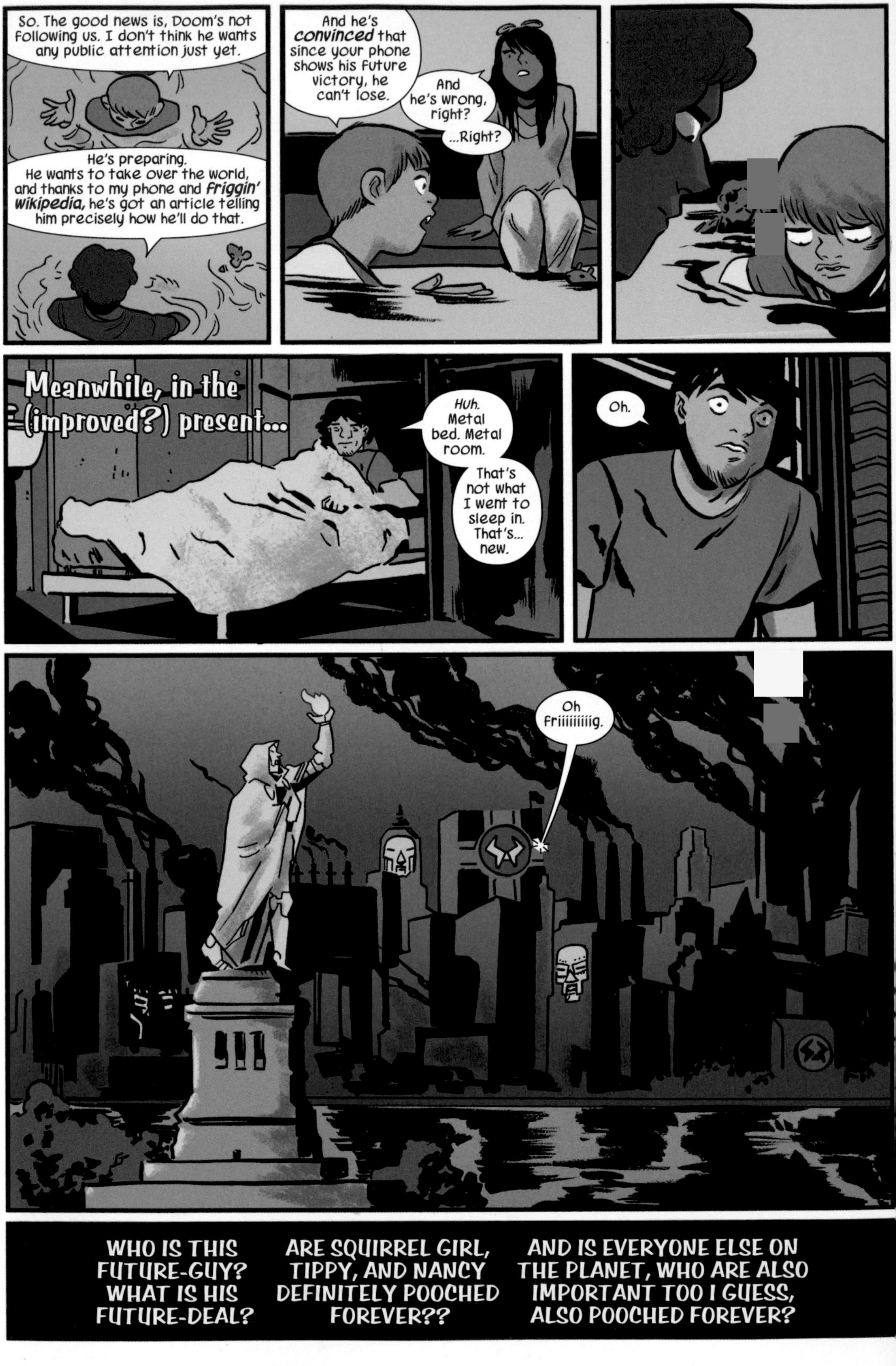
So. The good news is, Doom's not following us. I don't think he wants any public attention just yet.
He's preparing. He wants to take over the world, and thanks to my phone and friggin' wikipedia, he's got an article telling him precisely how he'll do that.
And he's convinced that since your phone shows his future victory, he can't lose.
And he's wrong, right?
...Right?
Meanwhile, in the (improved?) present...
Huh. Metal bed. Metal room.
That's not what I went to sleep in. That's... new.
Oh.
Oh friiiiiiiig.
WHO IS THIS FUTURE-GUY? WHAT IS HIS FUTURE-DEAL?
ARE SQUIRREL GIRL, TIPPY, AND NANCY DEFINITELY POOCHED FOREVER??
AND IS EVERYONE ELSE ON THE PLANET, WHO ARE ALSO IMPORTANT TOO I GUESS, ALSO POOCHED FOREVER?

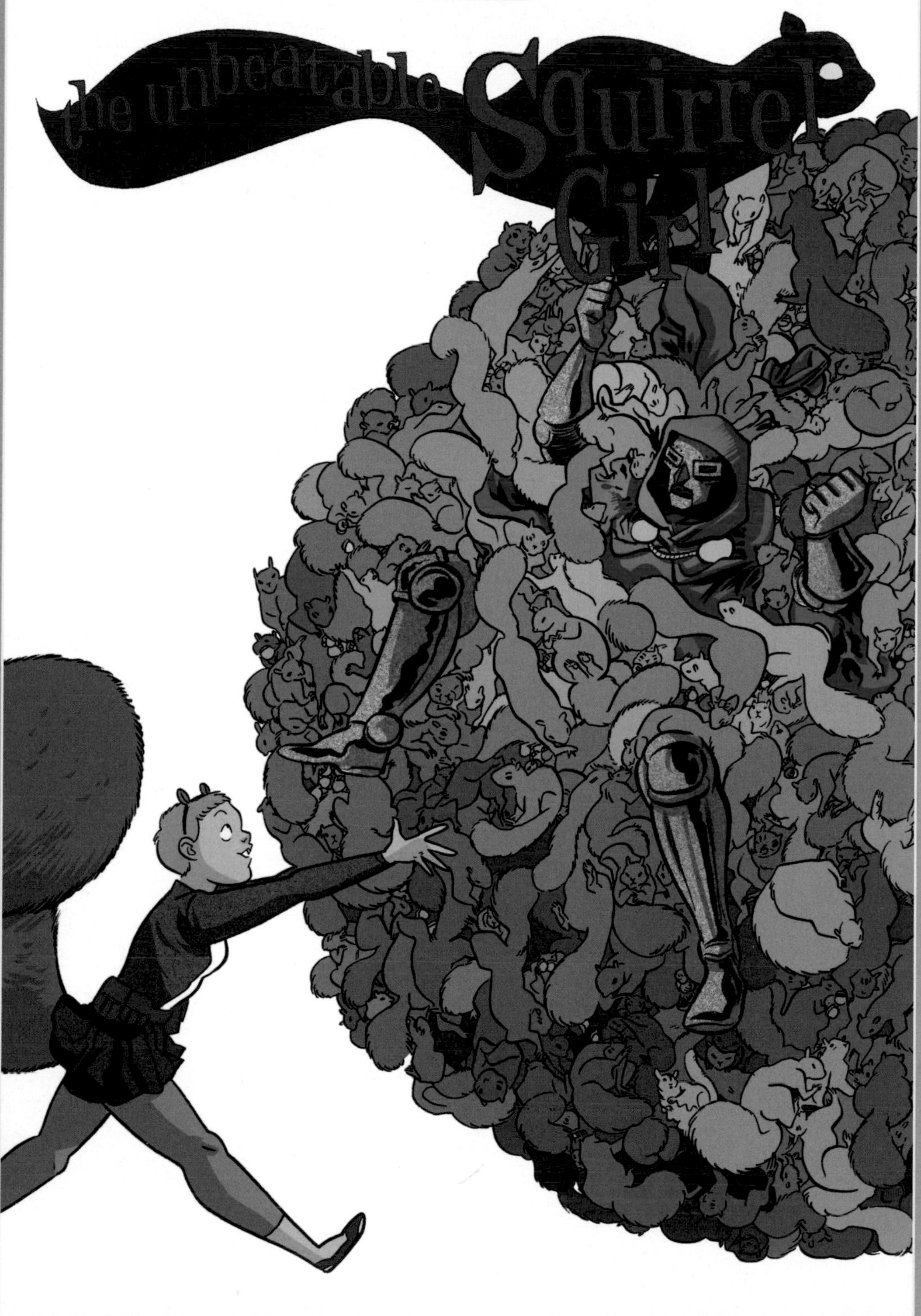
the unbeatable Squirrel Girl

Doreen Green isn't just a second-year computer science student: she secretly also has all the powers of both squirrel and girl! She uses her amazing abilities to Fight crime **and** be as awesome as possible. You know her as...**The Unbeatable Squirrel Girl!** Find out what she's been up to, with...

Squirrel Girl *in a nutshell*

[X] URGENT

WHILE YOU WERE OUT

To **The United Nations**

From **Squirrel Girl**

Of ~~The Whitehead~~ **The Present**

[X] TELEPHONED		[ ] PLEASE CALL	
[ ] CAME TO SEE YOU		[ ] WILL CALL AGAIN	
[X] WANTS TO SEE YOU		[ ] RETURNED YOUR CALL	

Message You guys, Doctor Doom came back to the *sixties* (which is *now*) (obviously) and is going to take over the world TOMORROW unless we stop him, but he's got *Future Wikipedia* that already shows he's gonna win so I'm not really sure what to do, if you have any idea I'm all ears (not a pun even though I wear a second set of ears for fashion reasons)

[ ] URGENT

WHILE YOU WERE OUT

To **Nancy Whitehead**

From **Squirrel Girl**

Of The apartment we share because we're roommates

[X] TELEPHONED		[ ] PLEASE CALL	
[ ] CAME TO SEE YOU		[X] WILL CALL AGAIN	
[ ] WANTS TO SEE YOU		[ ] RETURNED YOUR CALL	

Message Nancy it was super cool that you came back in time to rescue me and all these other CS students trapped here!! ps I know you don't have a phone, will you write me back on one of these notes because I've got like a thousand of them [ ]yes [ ]no

---

[ ] URGENT

WHILE YOU WERE OUT

To **Mr. and Mrs. Stark**

From **Squirrel Girl**

Of **The Iron Man Fandom**

[ ] TELEPHONED		[ ] PLEASE CALL	
[X] CAME TO SEE YOU		[ ] WILL CALL AGAIN	
[ ] WANTS TO SEE YOU		[ ] RETURNED YOUR CALL	

Message hey you don't know me but I just wanted to say the two of you should definitely have a baby in a few decades and name him Tony!! okay, thank me later

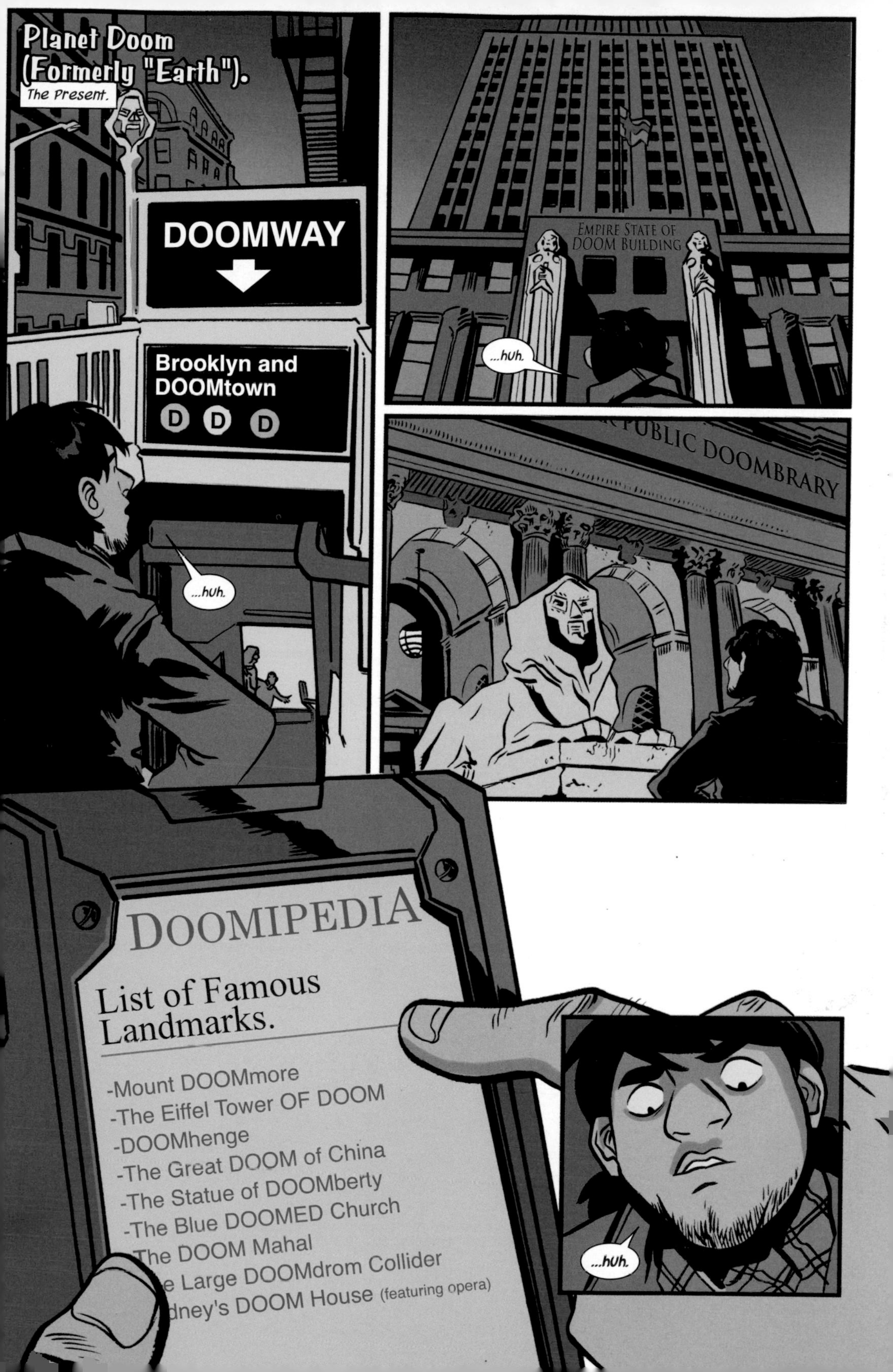
Planet Doom (Formerly "Earth").
The Present.
DOOMWAY
Brooklyn and DOOMtown
D D D
...huh.
EMPIRE STATE OF DOOM BUILDING
...huh.
PUBLIC DOOMBRARY
DOOMIPEDIA
List of Famous Landmarks.
-Mount DOOMmore
-The Eiffel Tower OF DOOM
-DOOMhenge
-The Great DOOM of China
-The Statue of DOOMberty
-The Blue DOOMED Church
The DOOM Mahal
e Large DOOMdrom Collider
dney's DOOM House (featuring opera)
...huh.

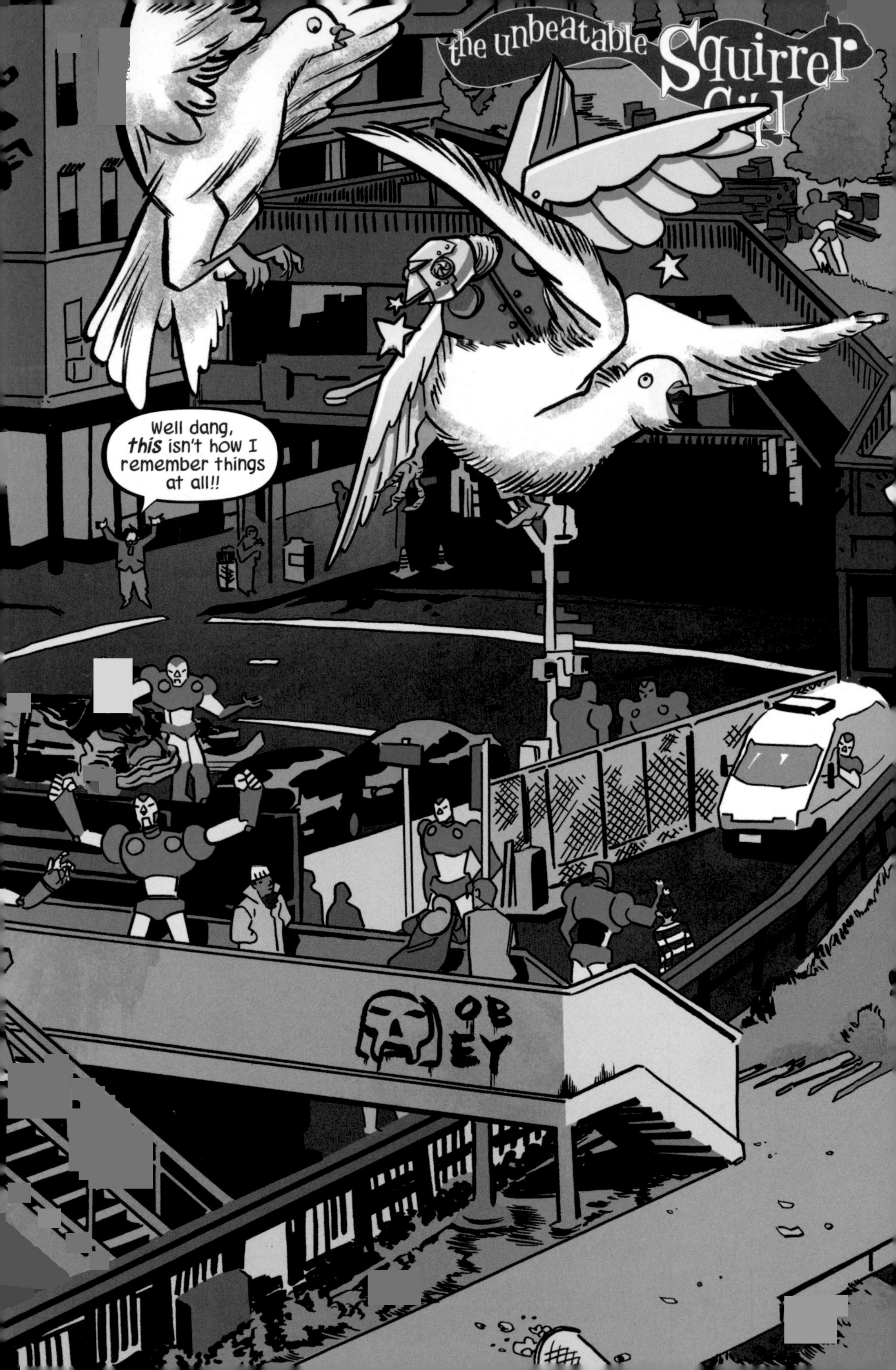
the unbeatable Squirrel Girl
Well dang, *this* isn't how I remember things at all!!
OBEY

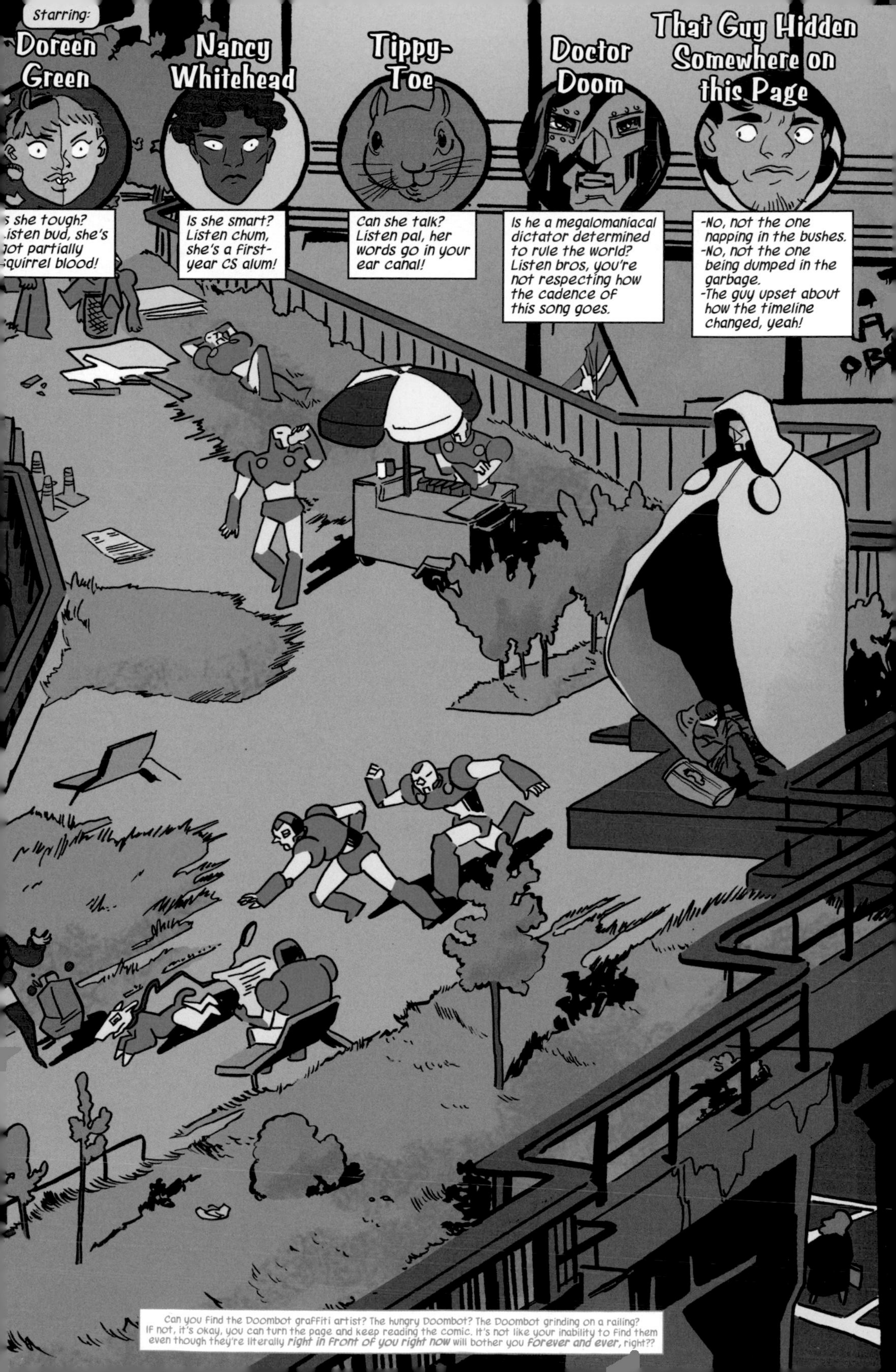
Starring:
Doreen Green
Nancy Whitehead
Tippy-Toe
Doctor Doom
That Guy Hidden Somewhere on this Page
s she tough? isten bud, she's ot partially quirrel blood!
Is she smart? Listen chum, she's a first-year CS alum!
Can she talk? Listen pal, her words go in your ear canal!
Is he a megalomaniacal dictator determined to rule the world? Listen bros, you're not respecting how the cadence of this song goes.
-No, not the one napping in the bushes. -No, not the one being dumped in the garbage. -The guy upset about how the timeline changed, yeah!
Can you find the Doombot graffiti artist? The hungry Doombot? The Doombot grinding on a railing? If not, it's okay, you can turn the page and keep reading the comic. It's not like your inability to find them even though they're literally right in front of you right now will bother you forever and ever, right??

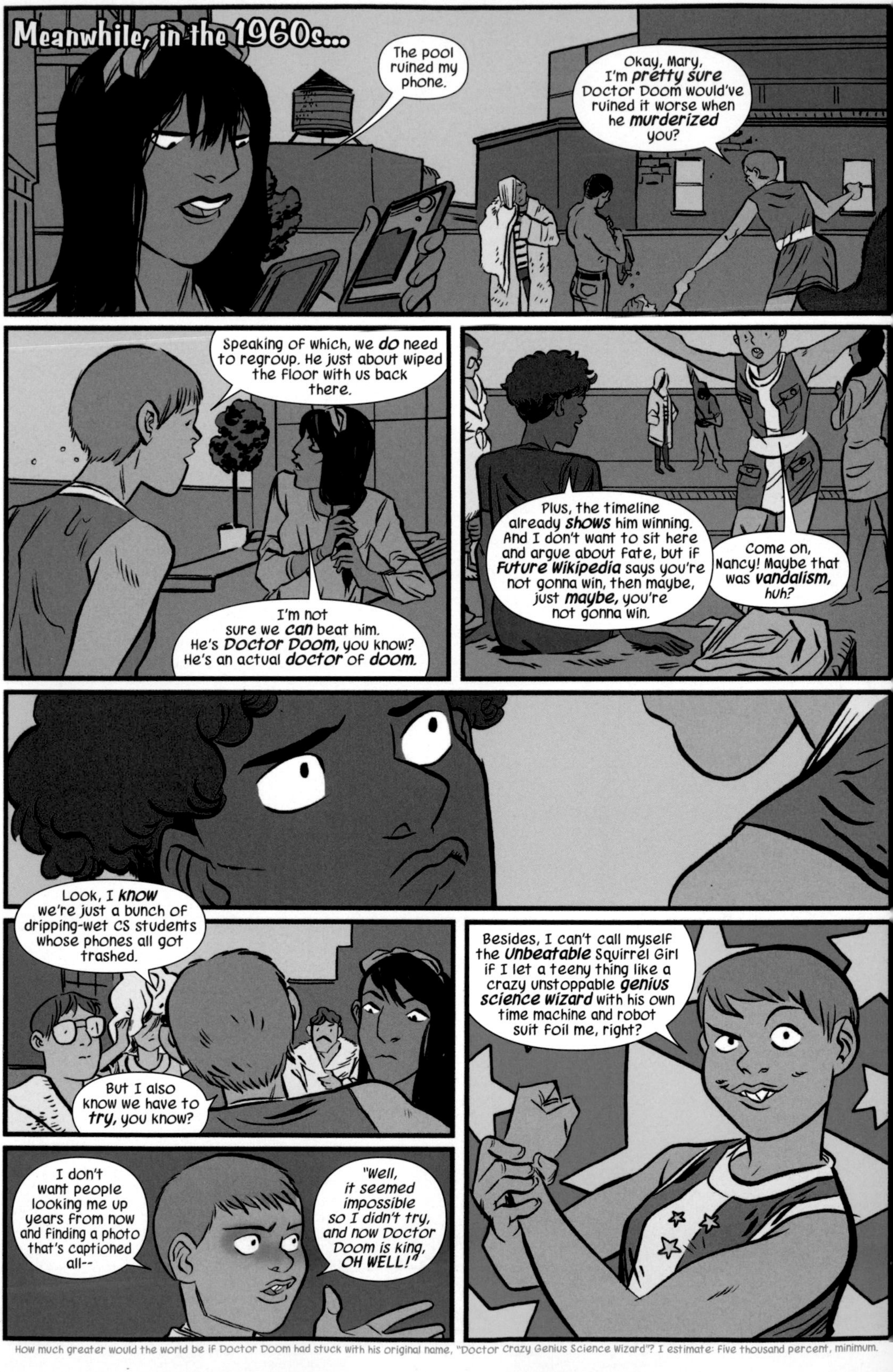
Meanwhile, in the 1960s...
The pool ruined my phone.
Okay, Mary, I'm pretty sure Doctor Doom would've ruined it worse when he murderized you?
Speaking of which, we do need to regroup. He just about wiped the floor with us back there.
I'm not sure we can beat him. He's Doctor Doom, you know? He's an actual doctor of doom.
Plus, the timeline already shows him winning. And I don't want to sit here and argue about fate, but if Future Wikipedia says you're not gonna win, then maybe, just maybe, you're not gonna win.
Come on, Nancy! Maybe that was vandalism, huh?
Look, I know we're just a bunch of dripping-wet CS students whose phones all got trashed.
But I also know we have to try, you know?
I don't want people looking me up years from now and finding a photo that's captioned all--
"Well, it seemed impossible so I didn't try, and now Doctor Doom is king, OH WELL!"
Besides, I can't call myself the Unbeatable Squirrel Girl if I let a teeny thing like a crazy unstoppable genius science wizard with his own time machine and robot suit foil me, right?

How much greater would the world be if Doctor Doom had stuck with his original name, "Doctor Crazy Genius Science Wizard"? I estimate: Five thousand percent, minimum.

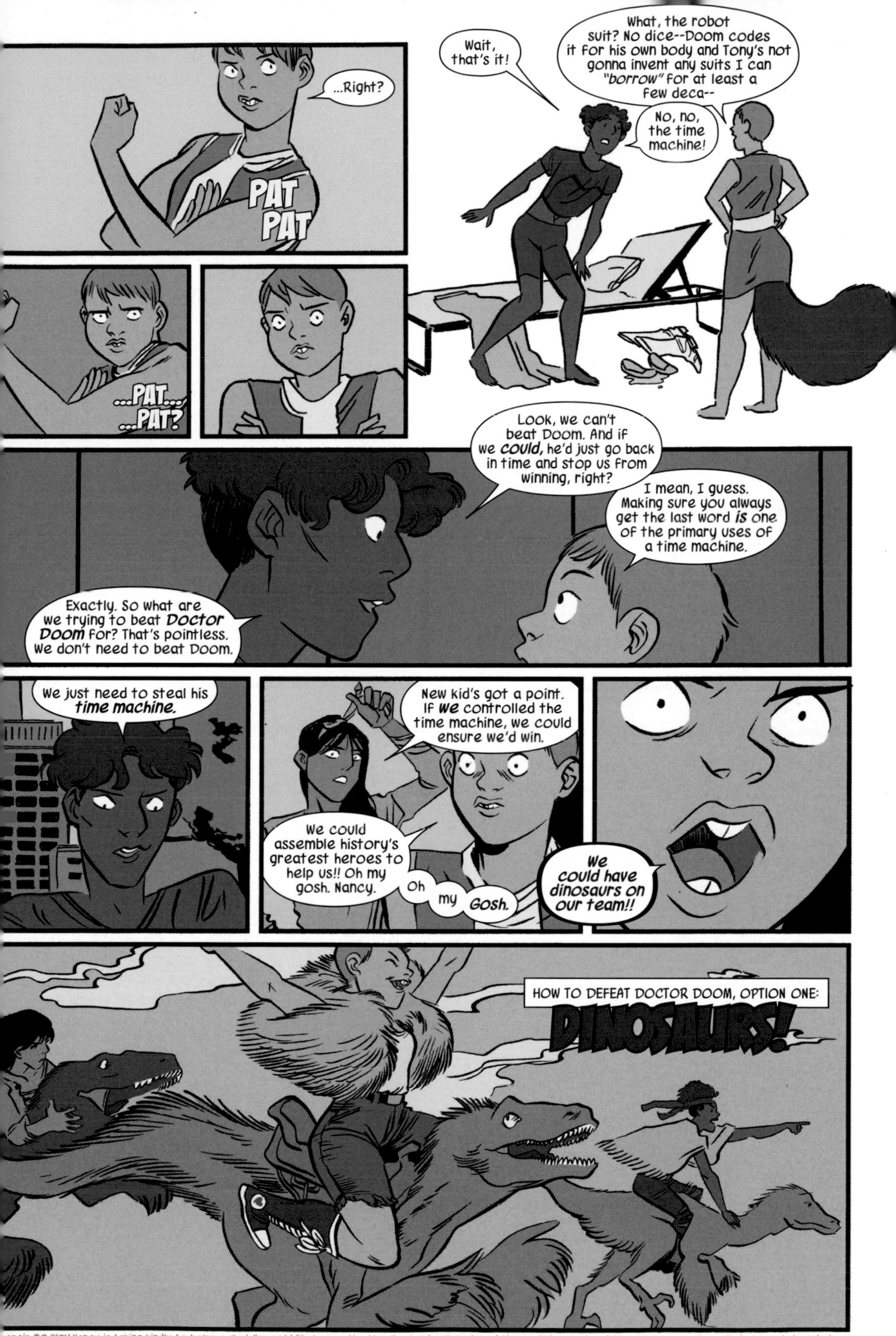
...Right?
PAT PAT
...PAT... ...PAT?
Wait, that's it!
What, the robot suit? No dice--Doom codes it for his own body and Tony's not gonna invent any suits I can "borrow" for at least a few deca--
No, no, the time machine!
Look, we can't beat Doom. And if we COULD, he'd just go back in time and stop us from winning, right?
I mean, I guess. Making sure you always get the last word IS one of the primary uses of a time machine.
Exactly. So what are we trying to beat Doctor Doom for? That's pointless. We don't need to beat Doom.
We just need to steal his time machine.
New kid's got a point. If WE controlled the time machine, we could ensure we'd win.
We could assemble history's greatest heroes to help us!! Oh my gosh. Nancy.
Oh
my
Gosh.
We could have dinosaurs on our team!!
HOW TO DEFEAT DOCTOR DOOM, OPTION ONE:
DINOSAURS!

ere's *NO WAY* Nancy is taking kindly to being called *"new kid,"* but once the timeline has been restored there will be plenty of time to go over who called whom what, and when, and how completely baloney some of those names may or may not have been.

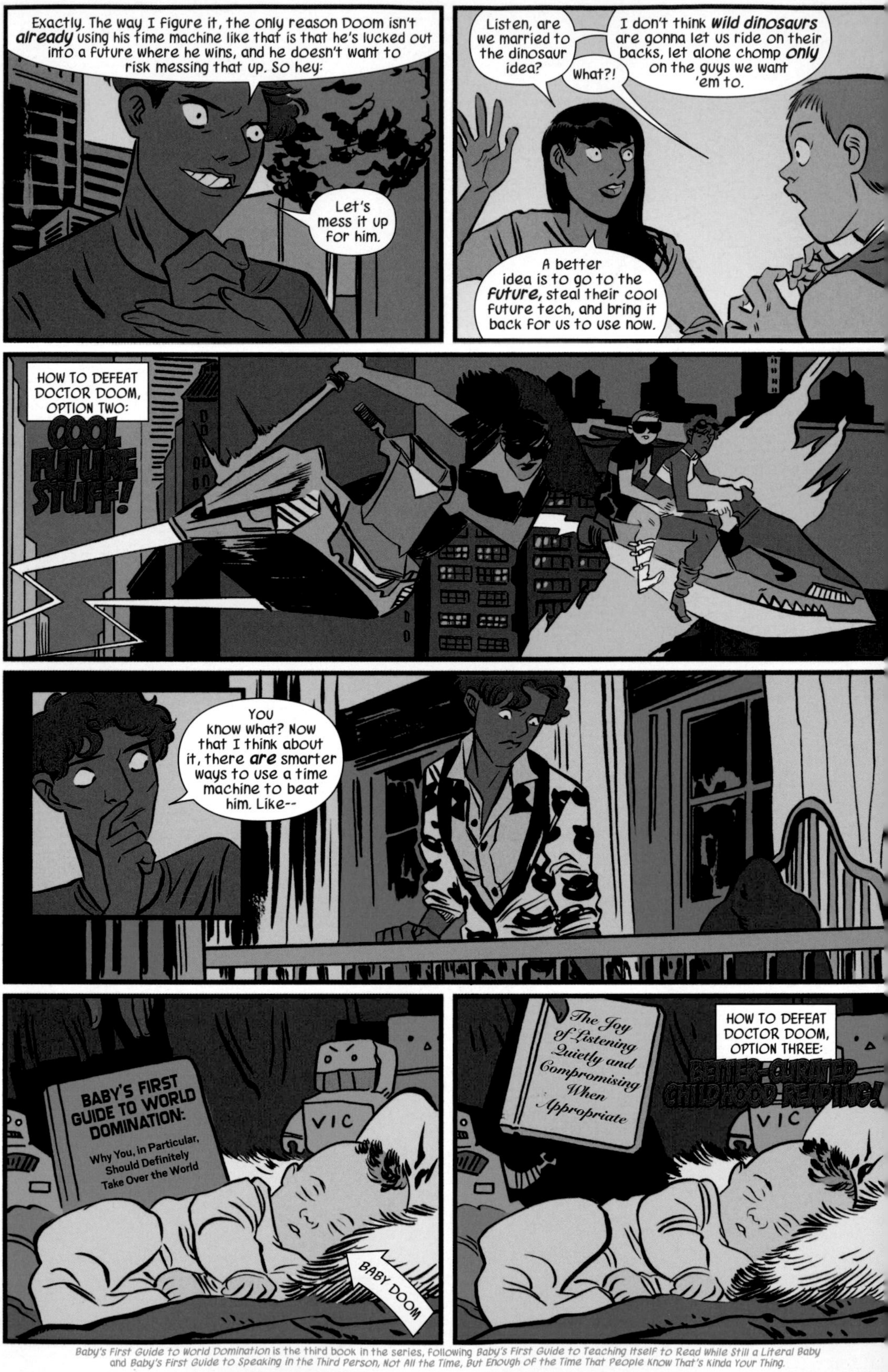
Exactly. The way I figure it, the only reason Doom isn't *already* using his time machine like that is that he's lucked out into a future where he wins, and he doesn't want to risk messing that up. So hey:
Let's mess it up for him.
Listen, are we married to the dinosaur idea?
What?!
I don't think *wild dinosaurs* are gonna let us ride on their backs, let alone chomp *only* on the guys we want 'em to.
A better idea is to go to the *future,* steal their cool future tech, and bring it back for us to use now.
HOW TO DEFEAT DOCTOR DOOM, OPTION TWO:
COOL FUTURE STUFF!
You know what? Now that I think about it, there *are* smarter ways to use a time machine to beat him. Like--
BABY'S FIRST GUIDE TO WORLD DOMINATION:
Why You, in Particular, Should Definitely Take Over the World
VIC
BABY DOOM
The Joy of Listening Quietly and Compromising When Appropriate
HOW TO DEFEAT DOCTOR DOOM, OPTION THREE:
BETTER-CURATED CHILDHOOD READING!
VIC

Baby's First Guide to World Domination is the third book in the series, following *Baby's First Guide to Teaching Itself to Read While Still a Literal Baby* and *Baby's First Guide to Speaking in the Third Person, Not All the Time, But Enough of the Time That People Know That's Kinda Your Thing.*

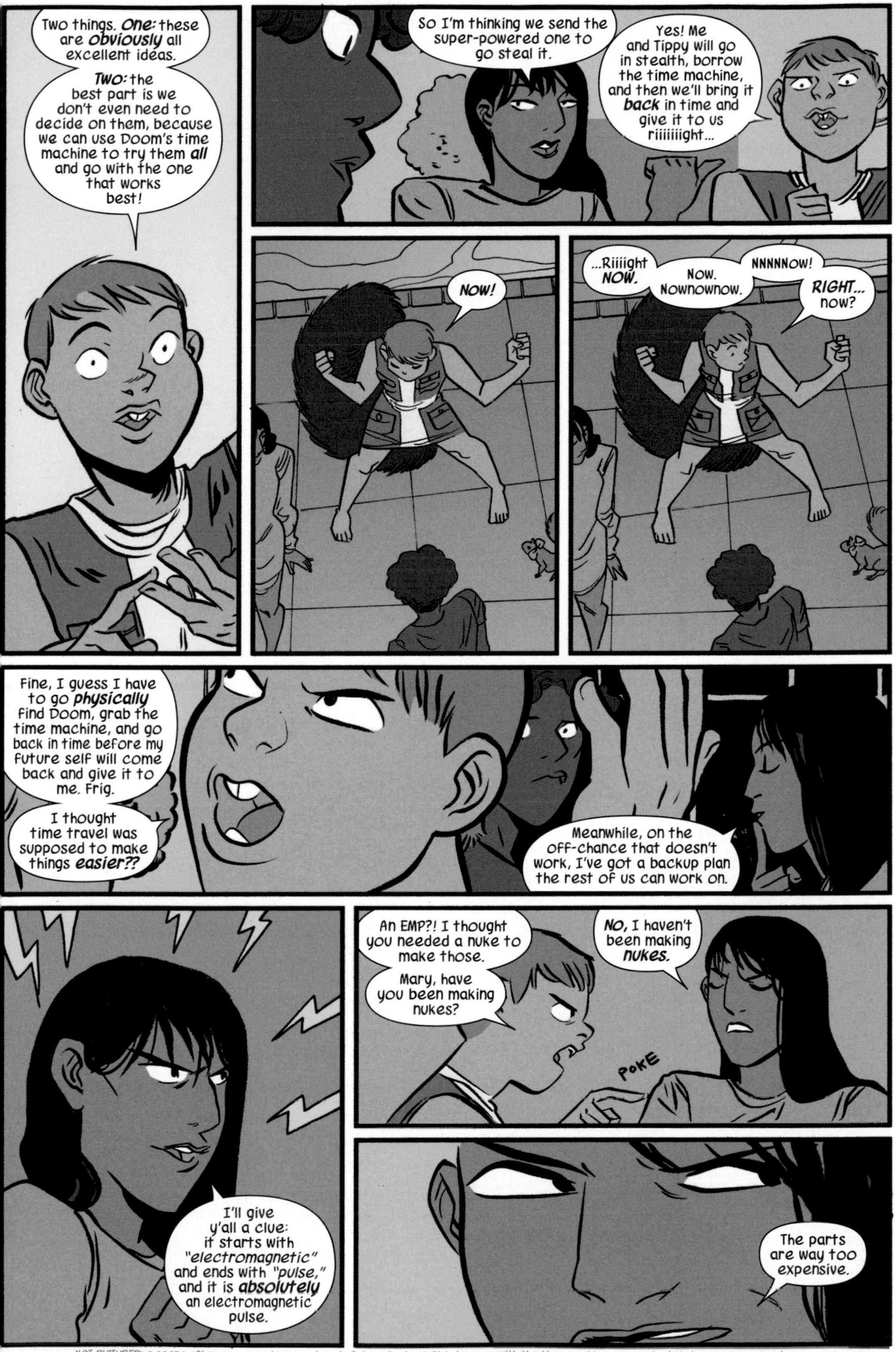
Two things. One: these are obviously all excellent ideas.
Two: the best part is we don't even need to decide on them, because we can use Doom's time machine to try them all and go with the one that works best!
So I'm thinking we send the super-powered one to go steal it.
Yes! Me and Tippy will go in stealth, borrow the time machine, and then we'll bring it back in time and give it to us riiiiiiight...
NOW!
...Riiiight NOW.
Now. Nownownow.
NNNNNOW!
RIGHT... now?
Fine, I guess I have to go physically find Doom, grab the time machine, and go back in time before my future self will come back and give it to me. Frig.
I thought time travel was supposed to make things easier??
Meanwhile, on the off-chance that doesn't work, I've got a backup plan the rest of us can work on.
I'll give y'all a clue: it starts with "electromagnetic" and ends with "pulse," and it is absolutely an electromagnetic pulse.
An EMP?! I thought you needed a nuke to make those.
Mary, have you been making nukes?
NO, I haven't been making nukes.
POKE
The parts are way too expensive.

NOT PICTURED: a scene after everyone leaves, wherein Future Squirrel Girl shows up with the time machine, sees nobody is here anymore, and says "Dang it, I really need to wear a watch with my costume because I have **no idea** what time it was I was talking about" and disappears again.

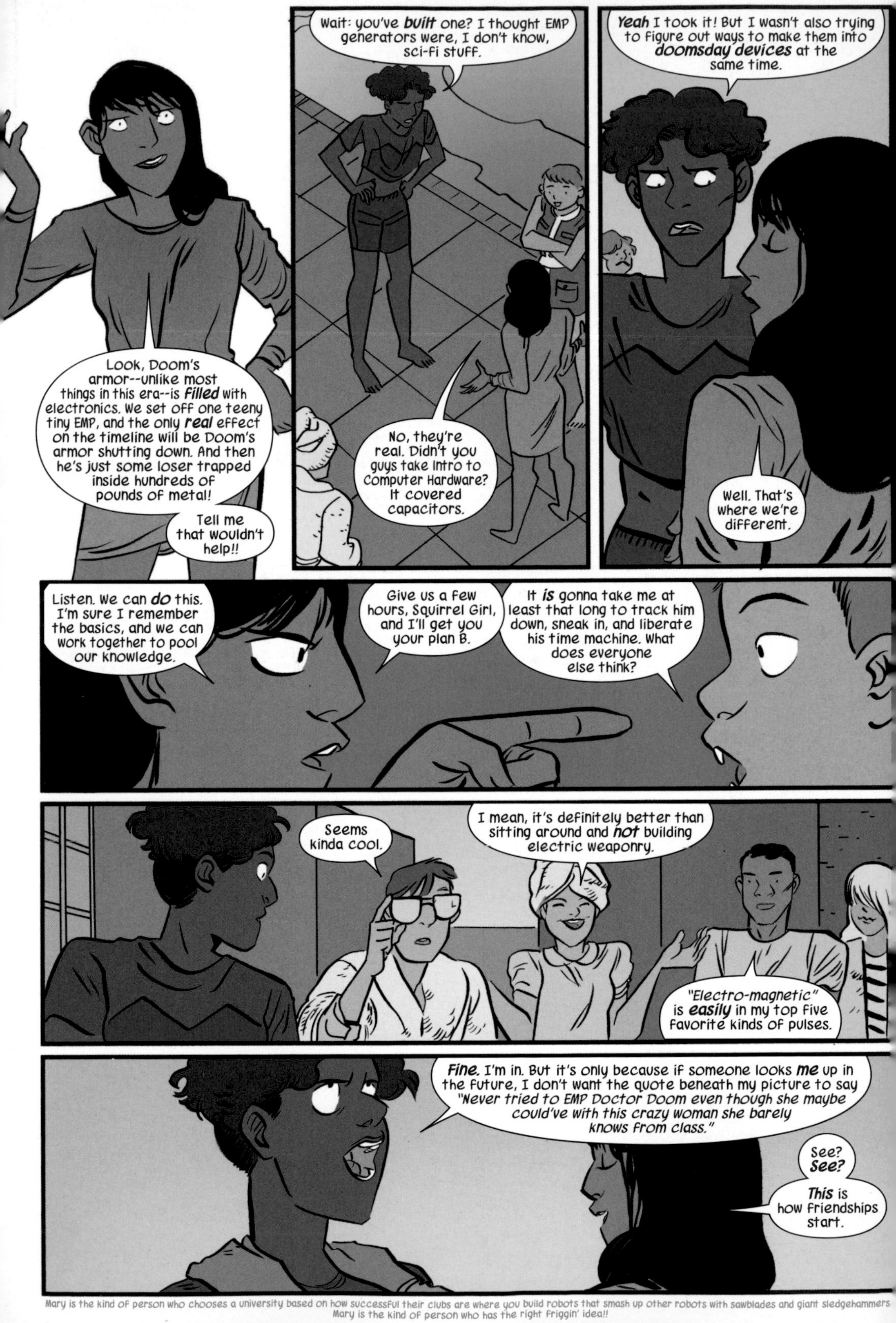
Look, Doom's armor--unlike most things in this era--is *filled* with electronics. We set off one teeny tiny EMP, and the only *real* effect on the timeline will be Doom's armor shutting down. And then he's just some loser trapped inside hundreds of pounds of metal!
Tell me that wouldn't help!!
Wait: you've *built* one? I thought EMP generators were, I don't know, sci-fi stuff.
No, they're real. Didn't you guys take Intro to Computer Hardware? It covered capacitors.
Yeah I took it! But I wasn't also trying to figure out ways to make them into *doomsday devices* at the same time.
Well. That's where we're different.
Listen. We can *do* this. I'm sure I remember the basics, and we can work together to pool our knowledge.
Give us a few hours, Squirrel Girl, and I'll get you your plan B.
It *is* gonna take me at least that long to track him down, sneak in, and liberate his time machine. What does everyone else think?
Seems kinda cool.
I mean, it's definitely better than sitting around and *not* building electric weaponry.
"Electro-magnetic" is *easily* in my top five favorite kinds of pulses.
Fine. I'm in. But it's only because if someone looks *me* up in the future, I don't want the quote beneath my picture to say *"Never tried to EMP Doctor Doom even though she maybe could've with this crazy woman she barely knows from class."*
See? *See?*
This is how friendships start.

Mary is the kind of person who chooses a university based on how successful their clubs are where you build robots that smash up other robots with sawblades and giant sledgehammers
Mary is the kind of person who has the right friggin' idea!!

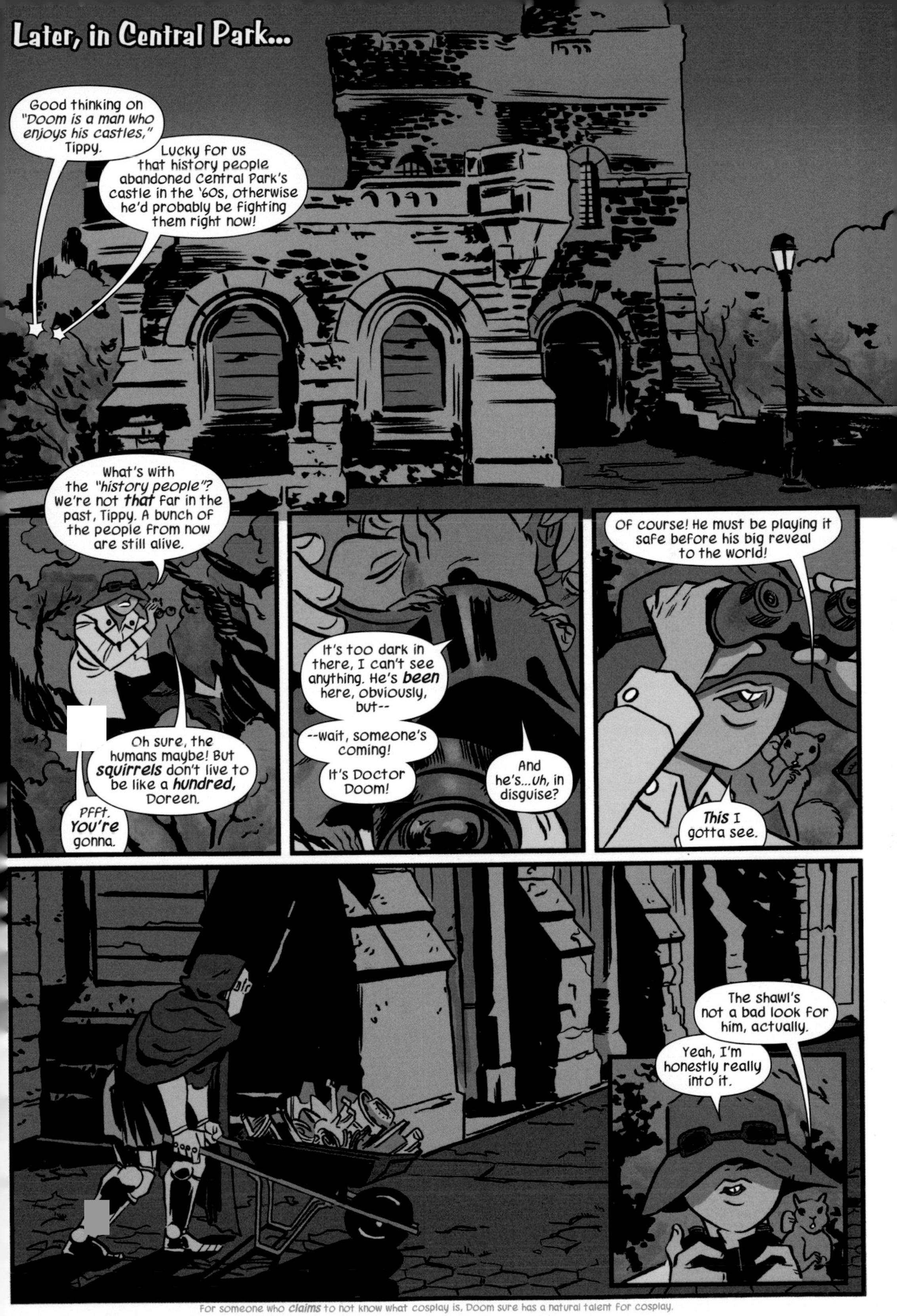
Later, in Central Park...
Good thinking on "Doom is a man who enjoys his castles," Tippy.
Lucky for us that history people abandoned Central Park's castle in the '60s, otherwise he'd probably be fighting them right now!
What's with the "history people"? We're not that far in the past, Tippy. A bunch of the people from now are still alive.
Oh sure, the humans maybe! But squirrels don't live to be like a hundred, Doreen.
Pffft. You're gonna.
It's too dark in there, I can't see anything. He's been here, obviously, but--
--wait, someone's coming!
It's Doctor Doom!
And he's...uh, in disguise?
Of course! He must be playing it safe before his big reveal to the world!
This I gotta see.
The shawl's not a bad look for him, actually.
Yeah, I'm honestly really into it.

For someone who *claims* to not know what cosplay is, Doom sure has a natural talent for cosplay.

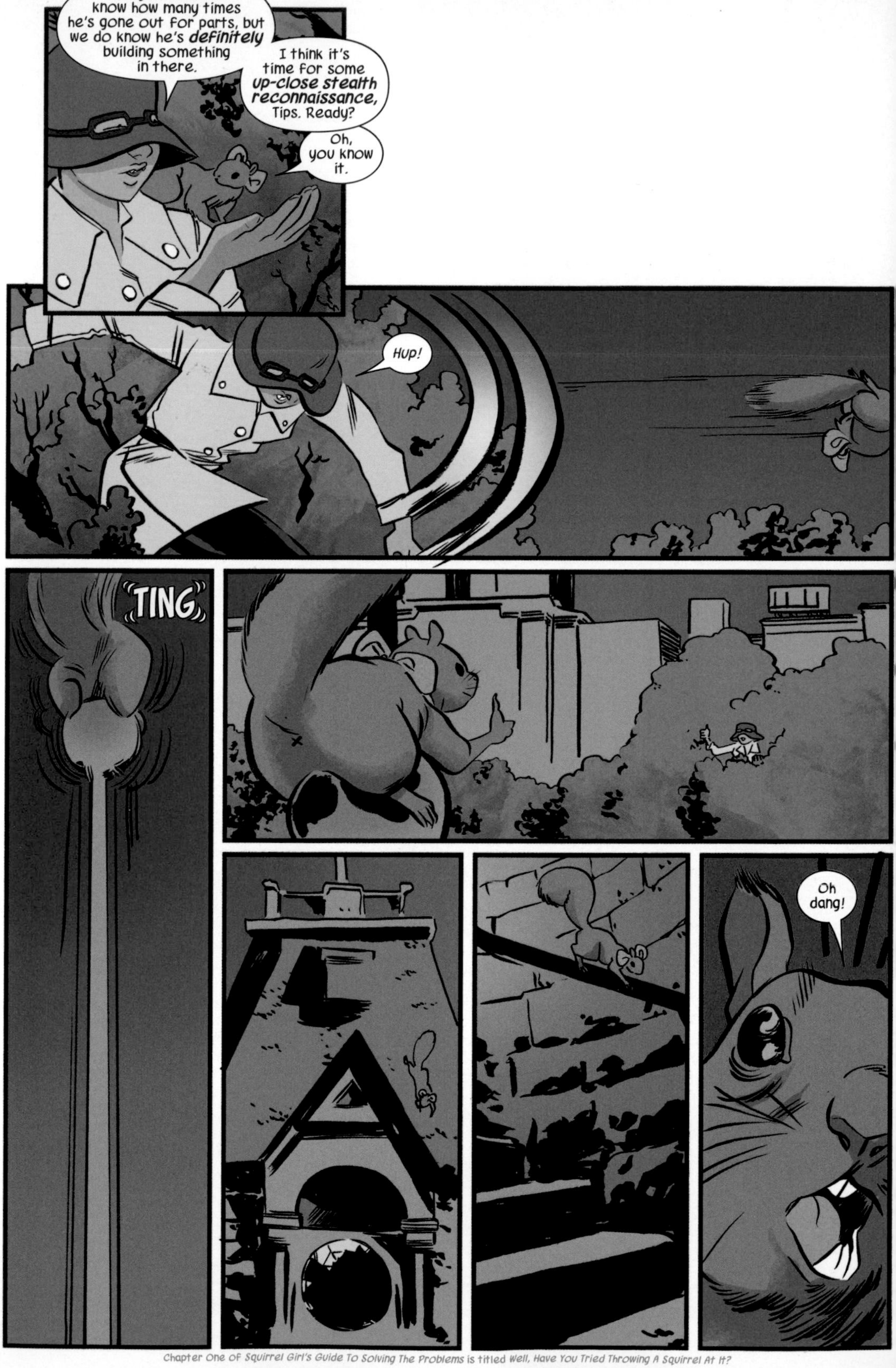
All right, we don't know how many times he's gone out for parts, but we do know he's *definitely* building something in there.
I think it's time for some *up-close stealth reconnaissance,* Tips. Ready?
Oh, you know it.
Hup!
TING
Oh dang!

Chapter One of *Squirrel Girl's Guide To Solving The Problems* is titled *Well, Have You Tried Throwing A Squirrel At It?*

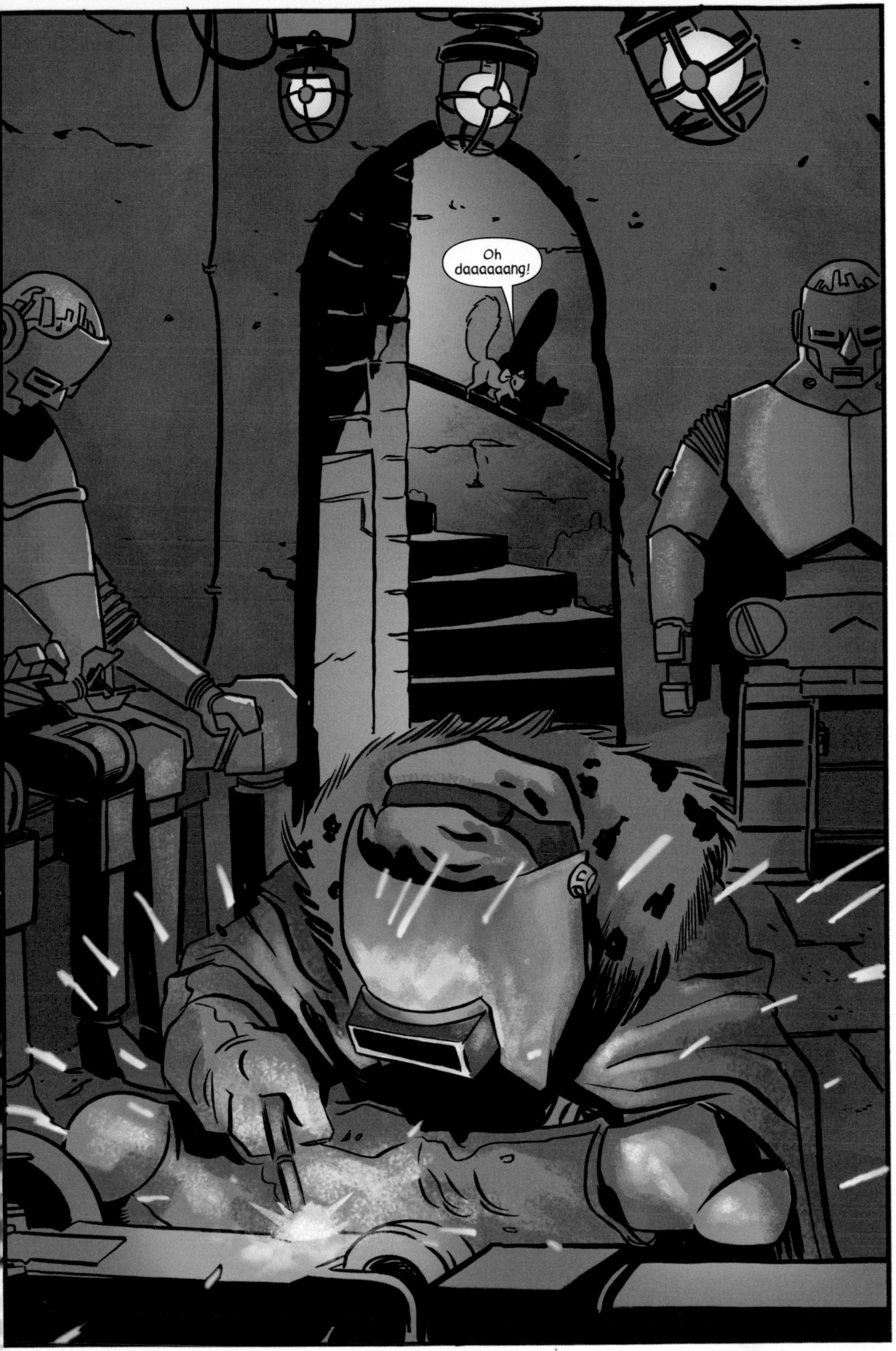
Oh daaaaaang!

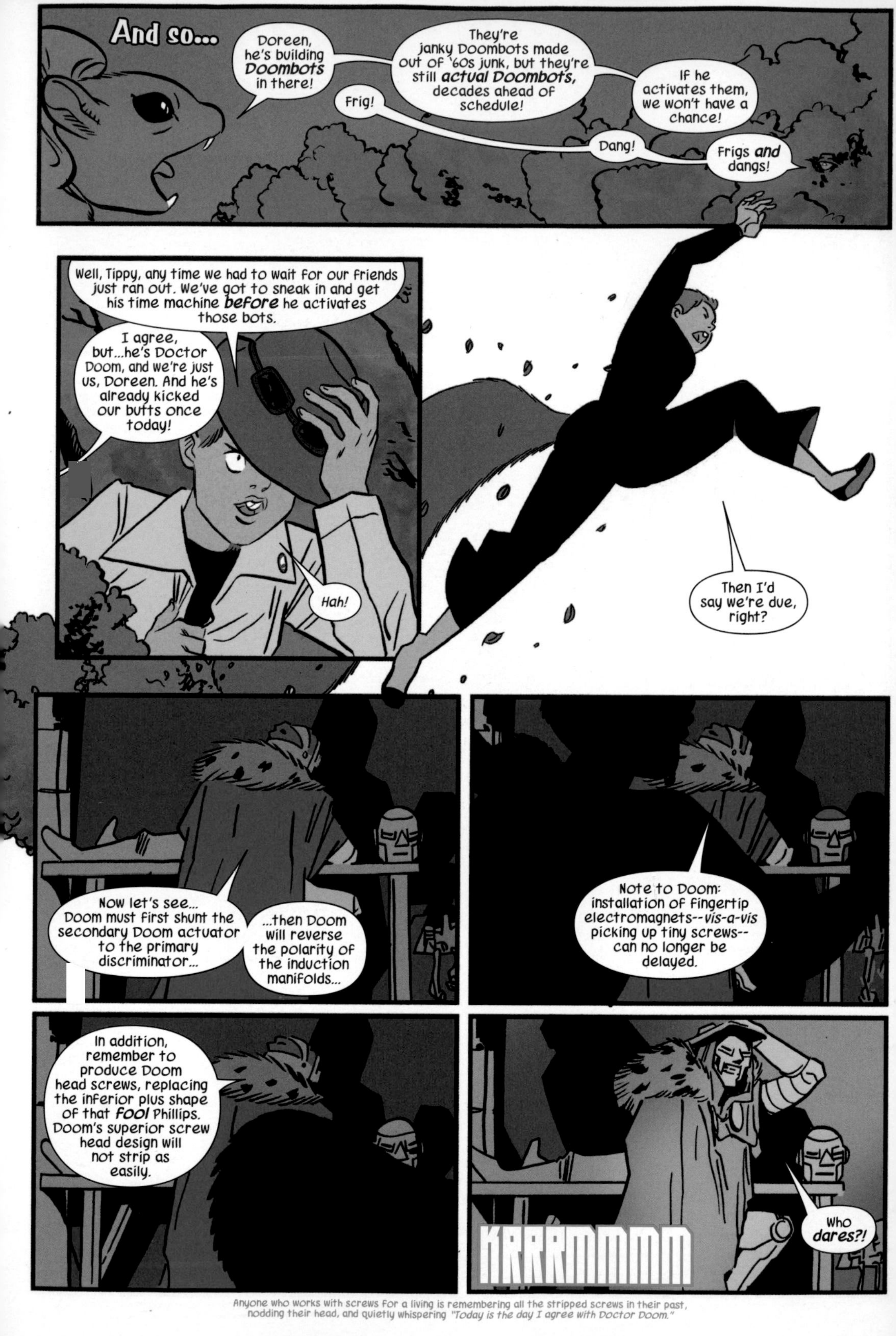
And so...
Doreen, he's building Doombots in there!
They're janky Doombots made out of '60s junk, but they're still actual Doombots, decades ahead of schedule!
If he activates them, we won't have a chance!
Frig!
Dang!
Frigs and dangs!
Well, Tippy, any time we had to wait for our friends just ran out. We've got to sneak in and get his time machine before he activates those bots.
I agree, but...he's Doctor Doom, and we're just us, Doreen. And he's already kicked our butts once today!
Hah!
Then I'd say we're due, right?
Now let's see... Doom must first shunt the secondary Doom actuator to the primary discriminator...
...then Doom will reverse the polarity of the induction manifolds...
Note to Doom: installation of fingertip electromagnets--vis-a-vis picking up tiny screws--can no longer be delayed.
In addition, remember to produce Doom head screws, replacing the inferior plus shape of that fool Phillips. Doom's superior screw head design will not strip as easily.
KRRRMMMM
Who dares?!

Anyone who works with screws for a living is remembering all the stripped screws in their past, nodding their head, and quietly whispering *"Today is the day I agree with Doctor Doom."*

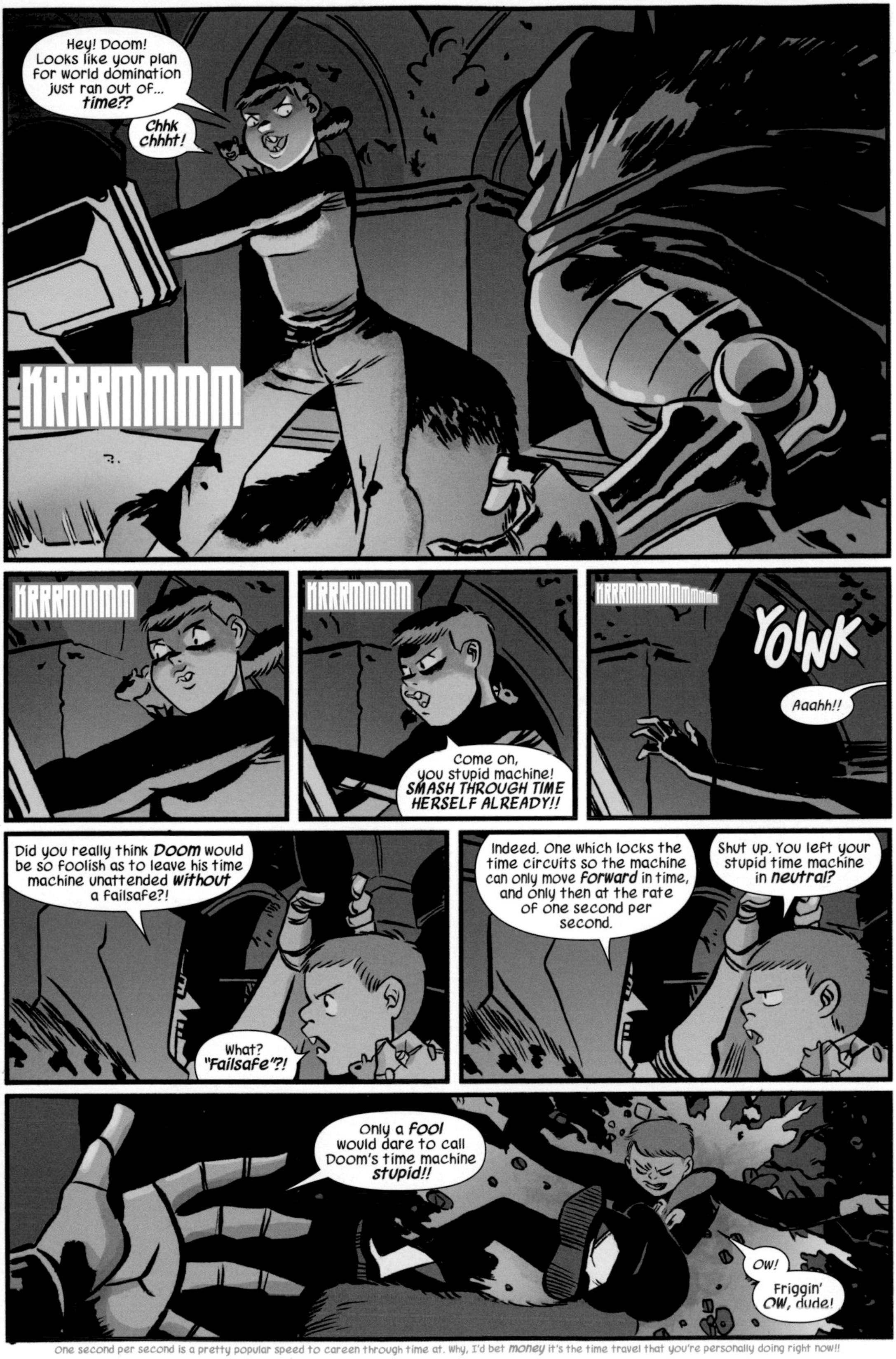
Hey! Doom! Looks like your plan for world domination just ran out of... time??
Chhk chhht!
KRRRMMMM
KRRRMMMM
KRRRMMMM
Come on, you stupid machine! SMASH THROUGH TIME HERSELF ALREADY!!
KRRRMMMMMmmmm
YOINK
Aaahh!!
Did you really think Doom would be so foolish as to leave his time machine unattended without a failsafe?!
What? "Failsafe"?!
Indeed. One which locks the time circuits so the machine can only move forward in time, and only then at the rate of one second per second.
Shut up. You left your stupid time machine in neutral?
Only a fool would dare to call Doom's time machine stupid!!
Ow!
Friggin' OW, dude!

One second per second is a pretty popular speed to careen through time at. Why, I'd bet *money* it's the time travel that you're personally doing right now!!

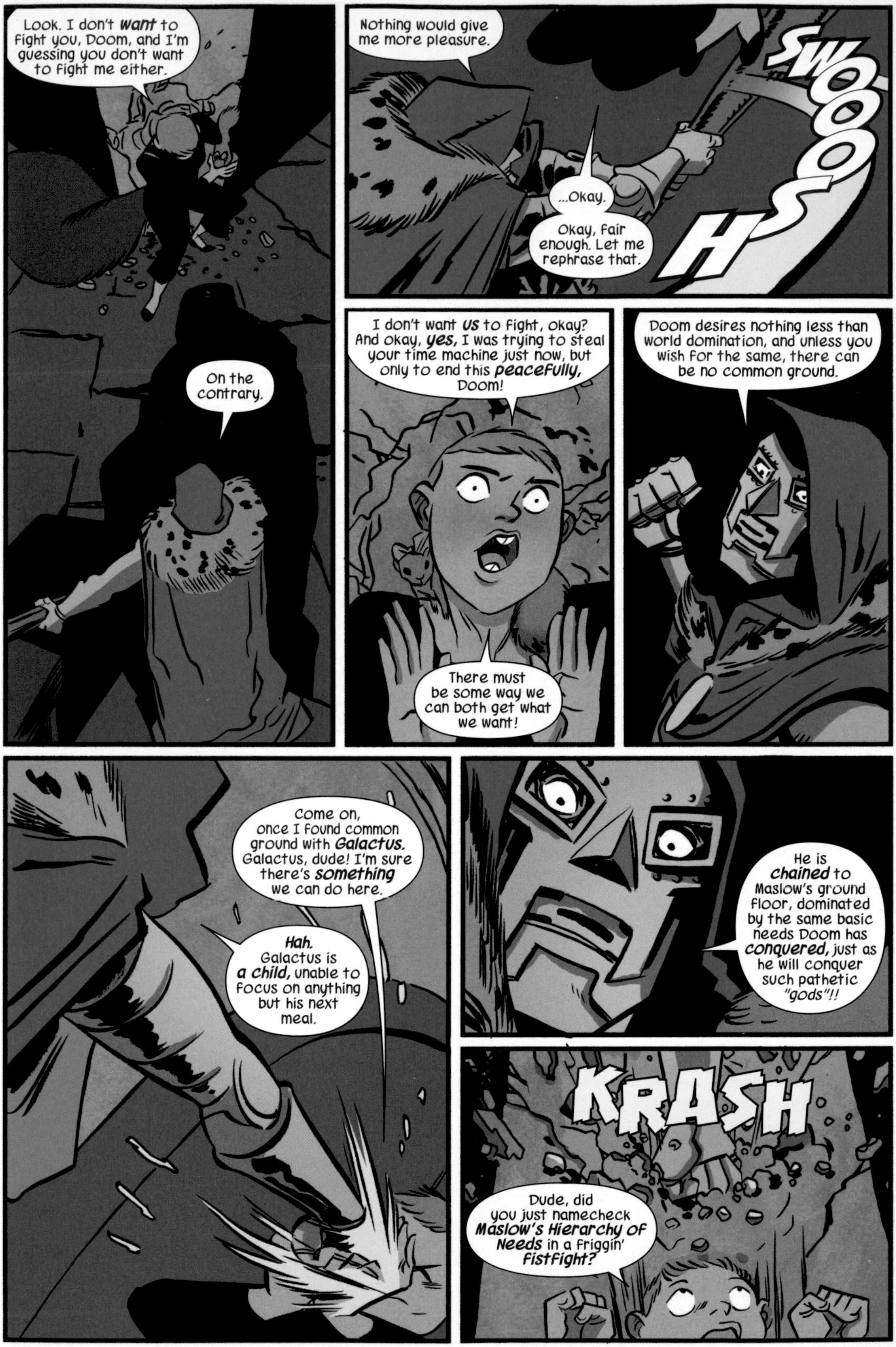
Look. I don't want to fight you, Doom, and I'm guessing you don't want to fight me either.
On the contrary.
Nothing would give me more pleasure.
SWOOOOSH
...Okay.
Okay, fair enough. Let me rephrase that.
I don't want US to fight, okay? And okay, yes, I was trying to steal your time machine just now, but only to end this peacefully, Doom!
There must be some way we can both get what we want!
Doom desires nothing less than world domination, and unless you wish for the same, there can be no common ground.
Come on, once I found common ground with Galactus. Galactus, dude! I'm sure there's something we can do here.
Hah. Galactus is a child, unable to focus on anything but his next meal.
He is chained to Maslow's ground floor, dominated by the same basic needs Doom has conquered, just as he will conquer such pathetic "gods"!!
KRASH
Dude, did you just namecheck Maslow's Hierarchy of Needs in a friggin' fistfight?

If you don't know it, Maslow's Hierarchy of Needs basically says *"yo, ain't nobody self-actualizing their bad selves if they're friggin' hungry or sad or whatever,"* only Maslow didn't say *"yo"* or *"friggin'"* nearly as much in his book as I did in my summary of it here (his loss).

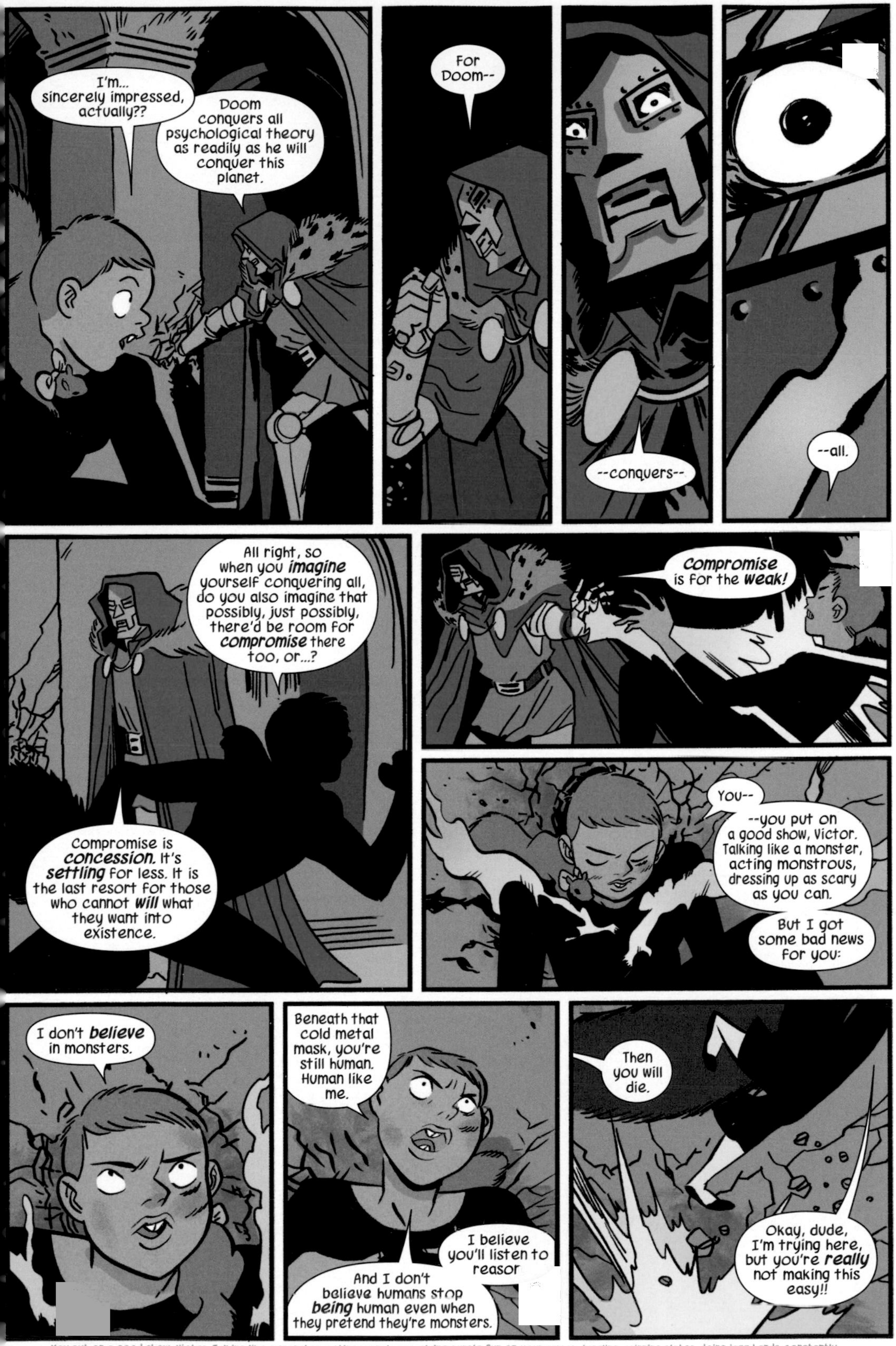
I'm... sincerely impressed, actually??
Doom conquers all psychological theory as readily as he will conquer this planet.
For Doom--
--conquers--
--all.
All right, so when you *imagine* yourself conquering all, do you also imagine that possibly, just possibly, there'd be room for *compromise* there too, or...?
Compromise is *concession*. It's *settling* for less. It is the last resort for those who cannot *will* what they want into existence.
Compromise is for the *weak!*
You--
--you put on a good show, Victor. Talking like a monster, acting monstrous, dressing up as scary as you can.
But I got some bad news for you:
I don't *believe* in monsters.
Beneath that cold metal mask, you're still human. Human like me.
I believe you'll listen to reaso
And I don't believe humans stop *being* human even when they pretend they're monsters.
Then you will die.
Okay, dude, I'm trying here, but you're *really* not making this easy!!

You put on a good show, Victor. Talking like a monster, acting monstrous, gluing purple fur on your armor, juggling, spinning plates, doing jazz hands constantly. It's an impressive, extremely confusing show.

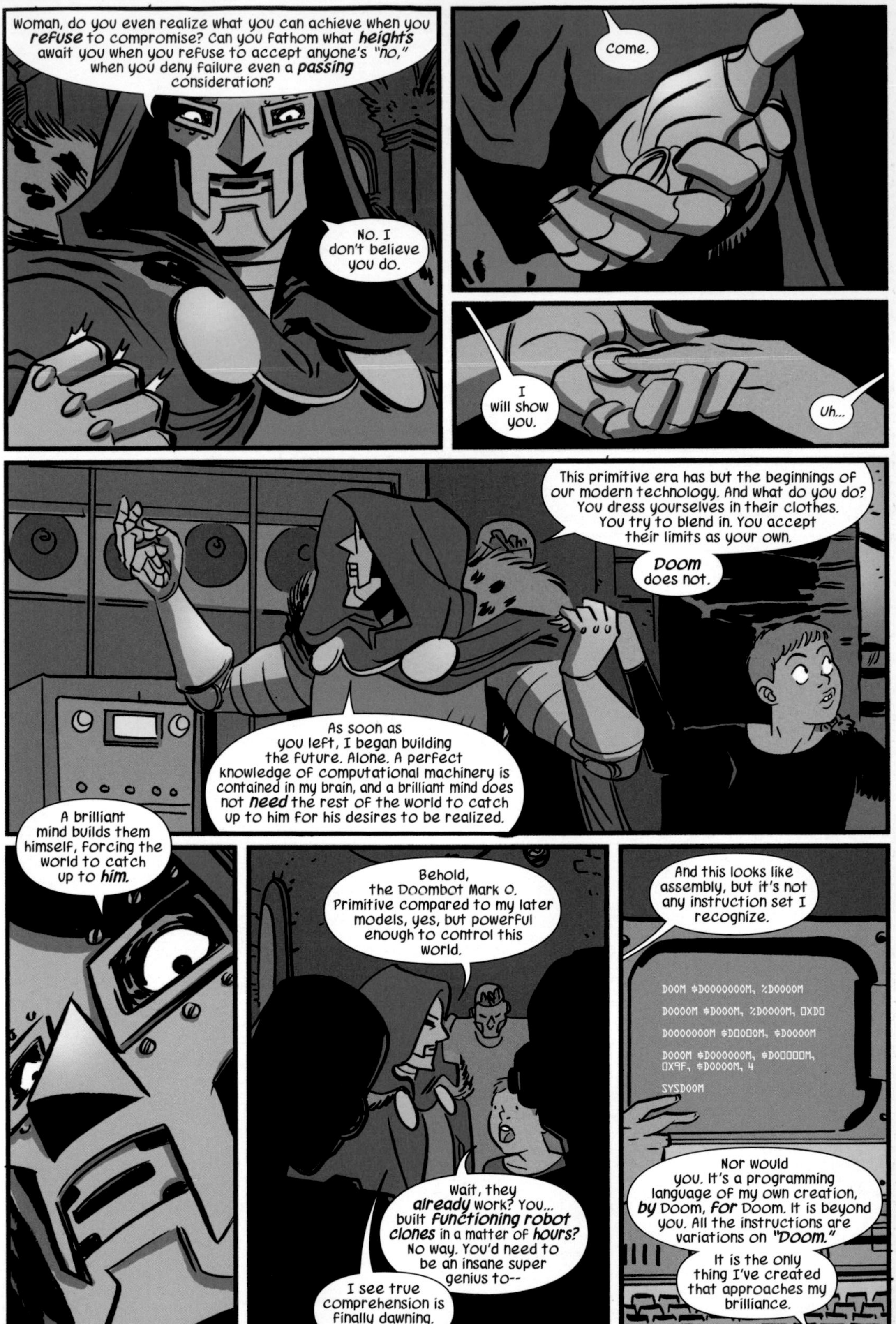
Woman, do you even realize what you can achieve when you *refuse* to compromise? Can you fathom what *heights* await you when you refuse to accept anyone's "*no,*" when you deny failure even a *passing* consideration?
No. I don't believe you do.
Come.
I will show you.
Uh...
This primitive era has but the beginnings of our modern technology. And what do you do? You dress yourselves in their clothes. You try to blend in. You accept their limits as your own.
Doom does not.
As soon as you left, I began building the future. Alone. A perfect knowledge of computational machinery is contained in my brain, and a brilliant mind does not *need* the rest of the world to catch up to him for his desires to be realized.
A brilliant mind builds them himself, forcing the world to catch up to *him.*
Behold, the Doombot Mark 0. Primitive compared to my later models, yes, but powerful enough to control this world.
Wait, they *already* work? You... built *functioning robot clones* in a matter of *hours?* No way. You'd need to be an insane super genius to--
I see true comprehension is finally dawning.
And this looks like assembly, but it's not any instruction set I recognize.
DOOM $DOOOOOOOM, %DOOOOM
DOOOOM $DOOOM, %DOOOOM, 0XD0
DOOOOOOOM $D0O0OM, $DOOOOM
DOOOM $DOOOOOOM, $DO0000M,
0X9F, $DOOOOM, 4
SYSDOOM
Nor would you. It's a programming language of my own creation, *by* Doom, *for* Doom. It is beyond you. All the instructions are variations on *"Doom."*
It is the only thing I've created that approaches my brilliance.

It's a good language because it reminds me of myself. And doom in general too. So, that's two reasons.

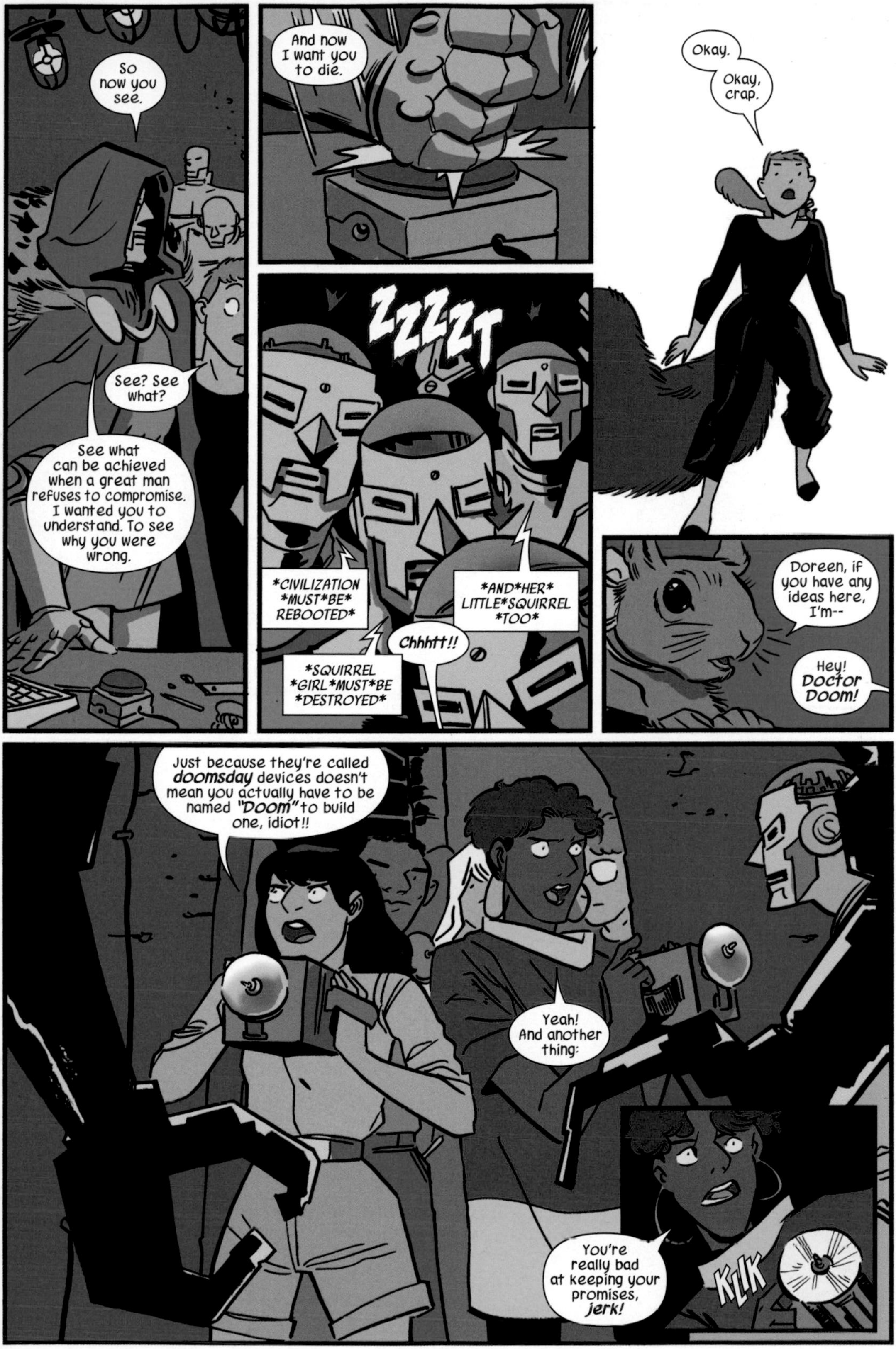
So now you see.
And now I want you to die.
Okay.
Okay, crap.
See? See what?
See what can be achieved when a great man refuses to compromise. I wanted you to understand. To see why you were wrong.
ZZZZT
*CIVILIZATION *MUST*BE* REBOOTED*
*AND*HER* LITTLE*SQUIRREL *TOO*
Chhhtt!!
*SQUIRREL *GIRL*MUST*BE *DESTROYED*
Doreen, if you have any ideas here, I'm--
Hey! Doctor Doom!
Just because they're called doomsday devices doesn't mean you actually have to be named "Doom" to build one, idiot!!
Yeah! And another thing:
You're really bad at keeping your promises, jerk!
KLIK

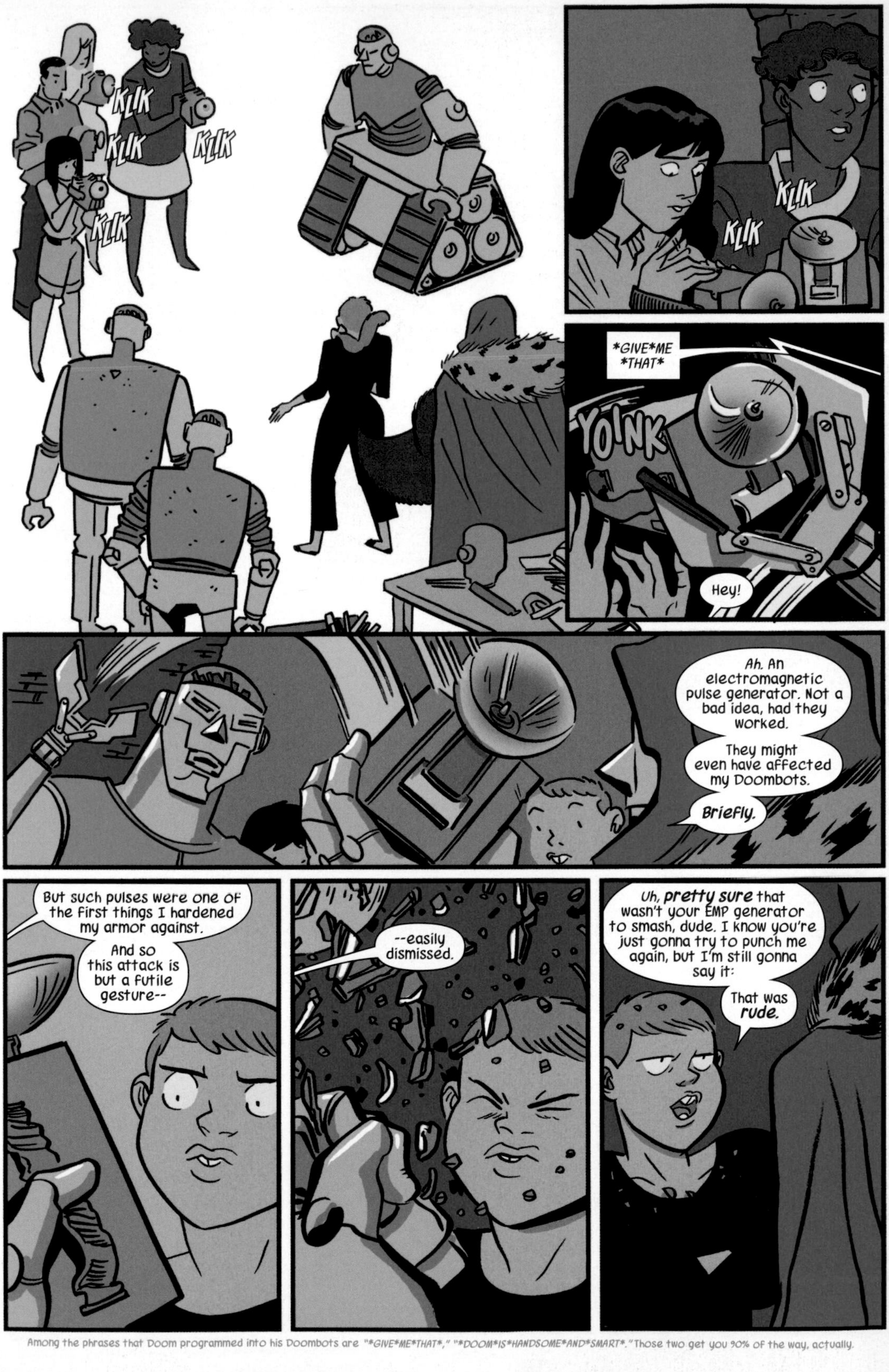
KLIK
KLIK
KLIK
KLIK
KLIK
KLIK
*GIVE*ME *THAT*
YOINK
Hey!
Ah. An electromagnetic pulse generator. Not a bad idea, had they worked.
They might even have affected my Doombots.
Briefly.
But such pulses were one of the first things I hardened my armor against.
And so this attack is but a futile gesture--
--easily dismissed.
Uh, pretty sure that wasn't your EMP generator to smash, dude. I know you're just gonna try to punch me again, but I'm still gonna say it:
That was rude.

Among the phrases that Doom programmed into his Doombots are "*GIVE*ME*THAT*," "*DOOM*IS*HANDSOME*AND*SMART*." Those two get you 90% of the way, actually.

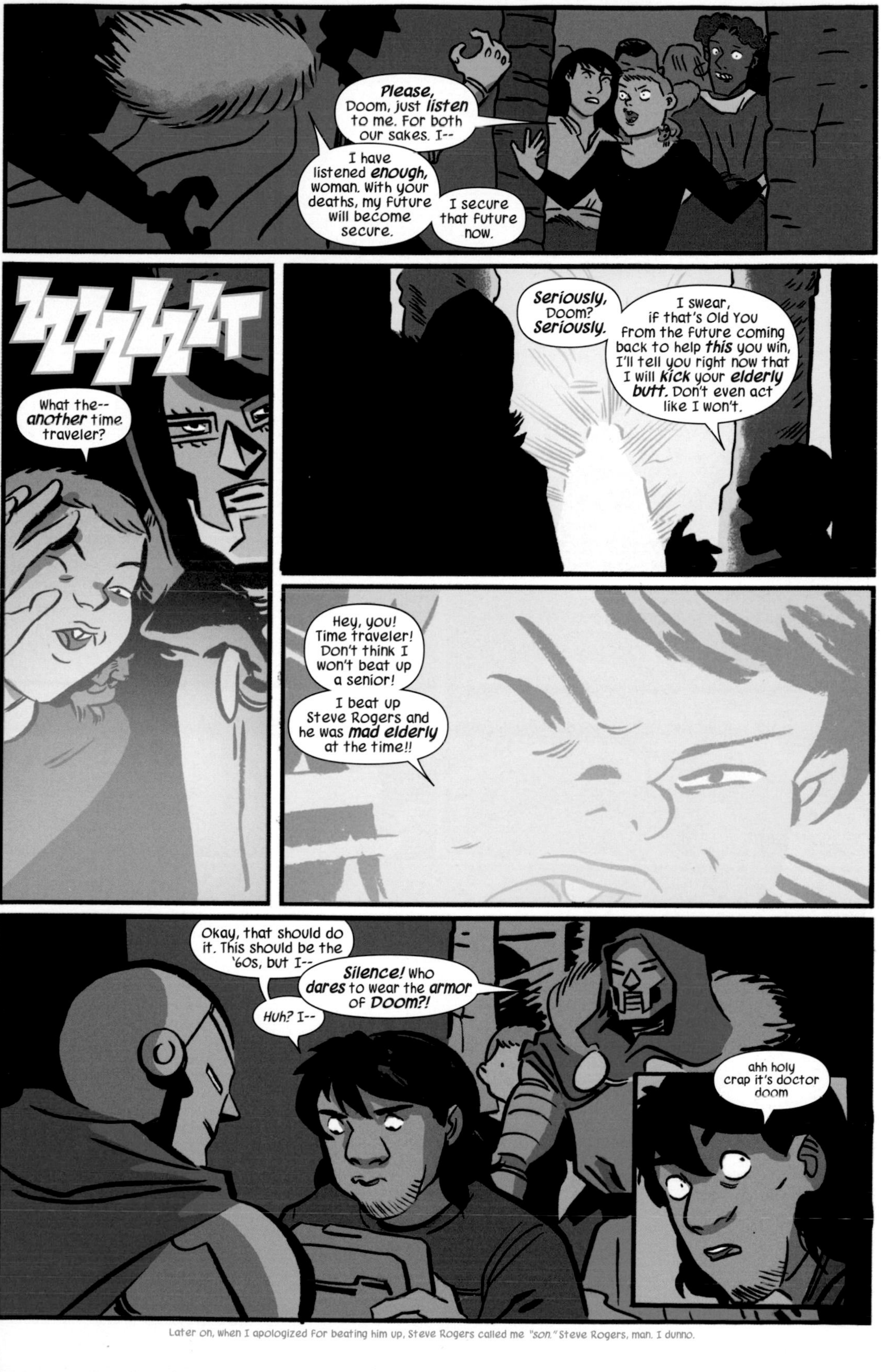
Please, Doom, just listen to me. For both our sakes. I--
I have listened enough, woman. With your deaths, my future will become secure.
I secure that future now.
ZZZZZZZZT
What the-- another time traveler?
Seriously, Doom? Seriously.
I swear, if that's Old You from the future coming back to help this you win, I'll tell you right now that I will kick your elderly butt. Don't even act like I won't.
Hey, you! Time traveler! Don't think I won't beat up a senior!
I beat up Steve Rogers and he was mad elderly at the time!!
Okay, that should do it. This should be the '60s, but I--
Silence! Who dares to wear the armor of Doom?!
Huh? I--
ahh holy crap it's doctor doom
Later on, when I apologized for beating him up, Steve Rogers called me "son." Steve Rogers, man. I dunno.

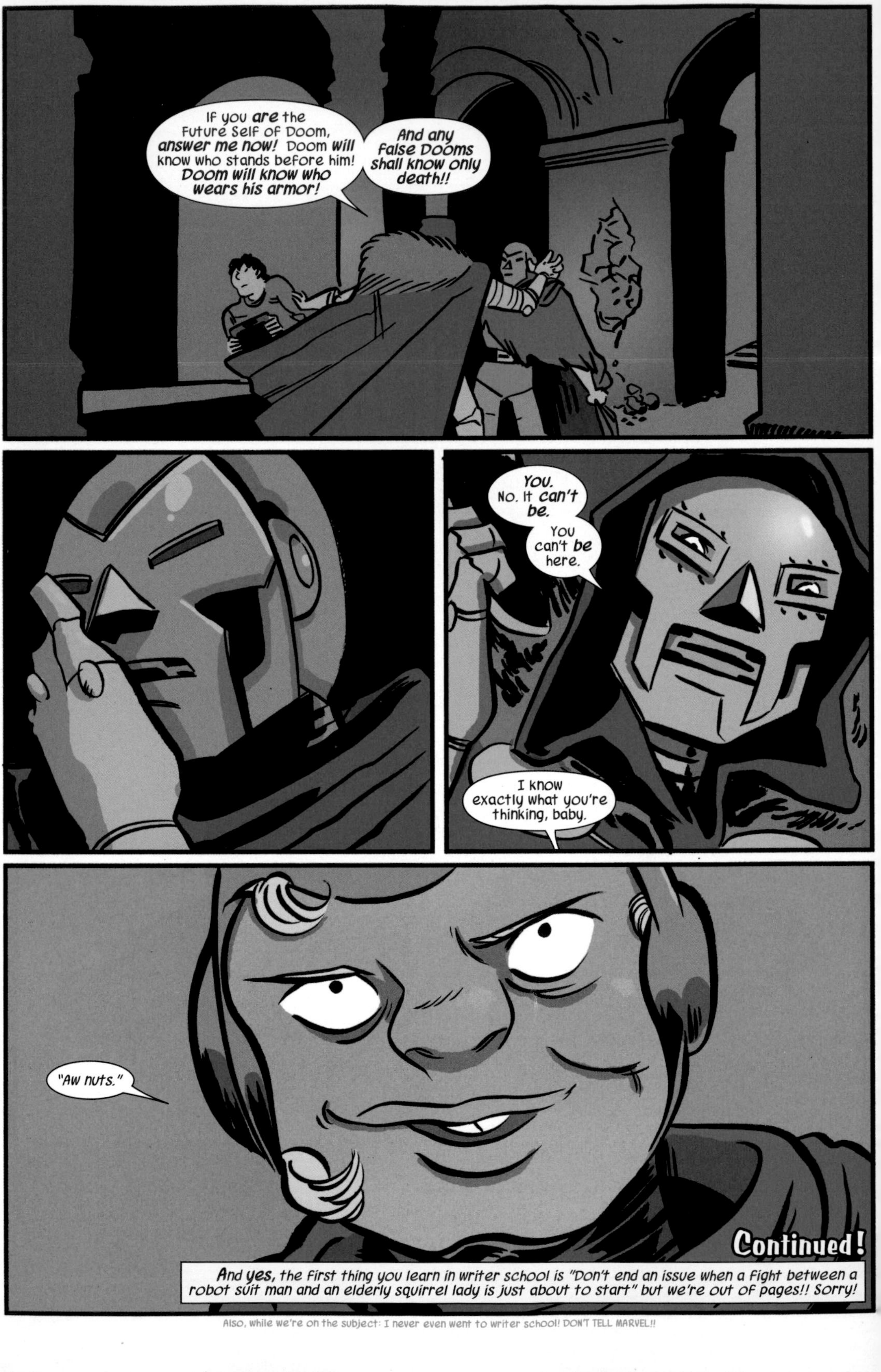
If you are the Future Self of Doom, answer me now! Doom will know who stands before him! Doom will know who wears his armor!
And any false Dooms shall know only death!!
You. No. It can't be.
You can't be here.
I know exactly what you're thinking, baby.
"Aw nuts."
Continued!
And yes, the first thing you learn in writer school is "Don't end an issue when a fight between a robot suit man and an elderly squirrel lady is just about to start" but we're out of pages!! Sorry!

Also, while we're on the subject: I never even went to writer school! DON'T TELL MARVEL!!

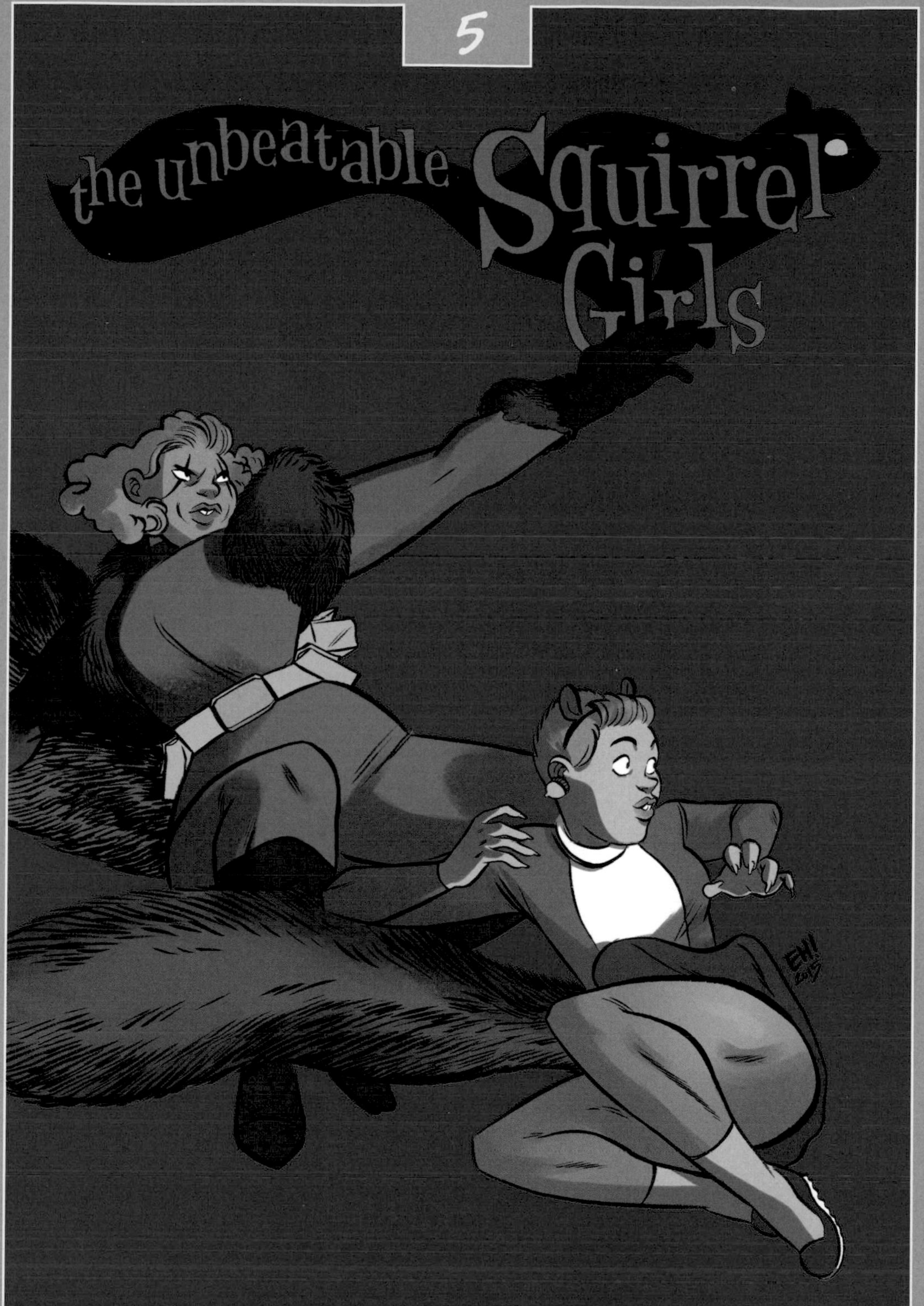
5
the unbeatable Squirrel Girls
EH! 2015

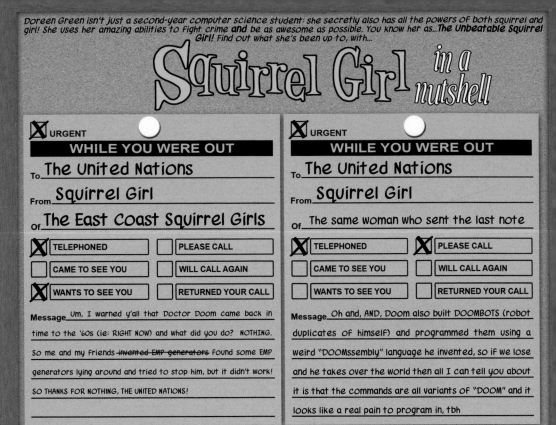

Doreen Green isn't just a second-year computer science student: she secretly also has all the powers of both squirrel and girl! She uses her amazing abilities to fight crime **and** be as awesome as possible. You know her as...**The Unbeatable Squirrel Girl!** Find out what she's been up to, with...

Squirrel Girl *in a nutshell*

☒ URGENT

WHILE YOU WERE OUT

To **The United Nations**

From **Squirrel Girl**

Of **The East Coast Squirrel Girls**

☒ TELEPHONED	☐ PLEASE CALL
☐ CAME TO SEE YOU	☐ WILL CALL AGAIN
☒ WANTS TO SEE YOU	☐ RETURNED YOUR CALL

Message: Um, I warned y'all that Doctor Doom came back in time to the '60s (ie: RIGHT NOW) and what did you do? NOTHING. So me and my friends ~~invented EMP generators~~ found some EMP generators lying around and tried to stop him, but it didn't work! SO THANKS FOR NOTHING, THE UNITED NATIONS!

☒ URGENT

WHILE YOU WERE OUT

To **The United Nations**

From **Squirrel Girl**

Of The same woman who sent the last note

☒ TELEPHONED	☒ PLEASE CALL
☐ CAME TO SEE YOU	☐ WILL CALL AGAIN
☐ WANTS TO SEE YOU	☐ RETURNED YOUR CALL

Message: Oh and, AND, Doom also built DOOMBOTS (robot duplicates of himself) and programmed them using a weird "DOOMssembly" language he invented, so if we lose and he takes over the world then all I can tell you about it is that the commands are all variants of "DOOM" and it looks like a real pain to program in, tbh

☒ URGENT

WHILE YOU WERE OUT

To **The United Nations**

From **Squirrel Girl**

Of how do you not know me yet, sheesh

☐ TELEPHONED	☐ PLEASE CALL
☐ CAME TO SEE YOU	☐ WILL CALL AGAIN
☒ WANTS TO SEE YOU	☐ RETURNED YOUR CALL

Message: Also this guy Cody came back in time from the future (ie: MY present) with an older me!! Haha YEP I'M FROM THE FUTURE and wasn't even born in the '60s!! I don't even mind telling you United Nations guys anymore, because nobody even READS these notes even though I put them up really nicely on your stupid bulletin board!!

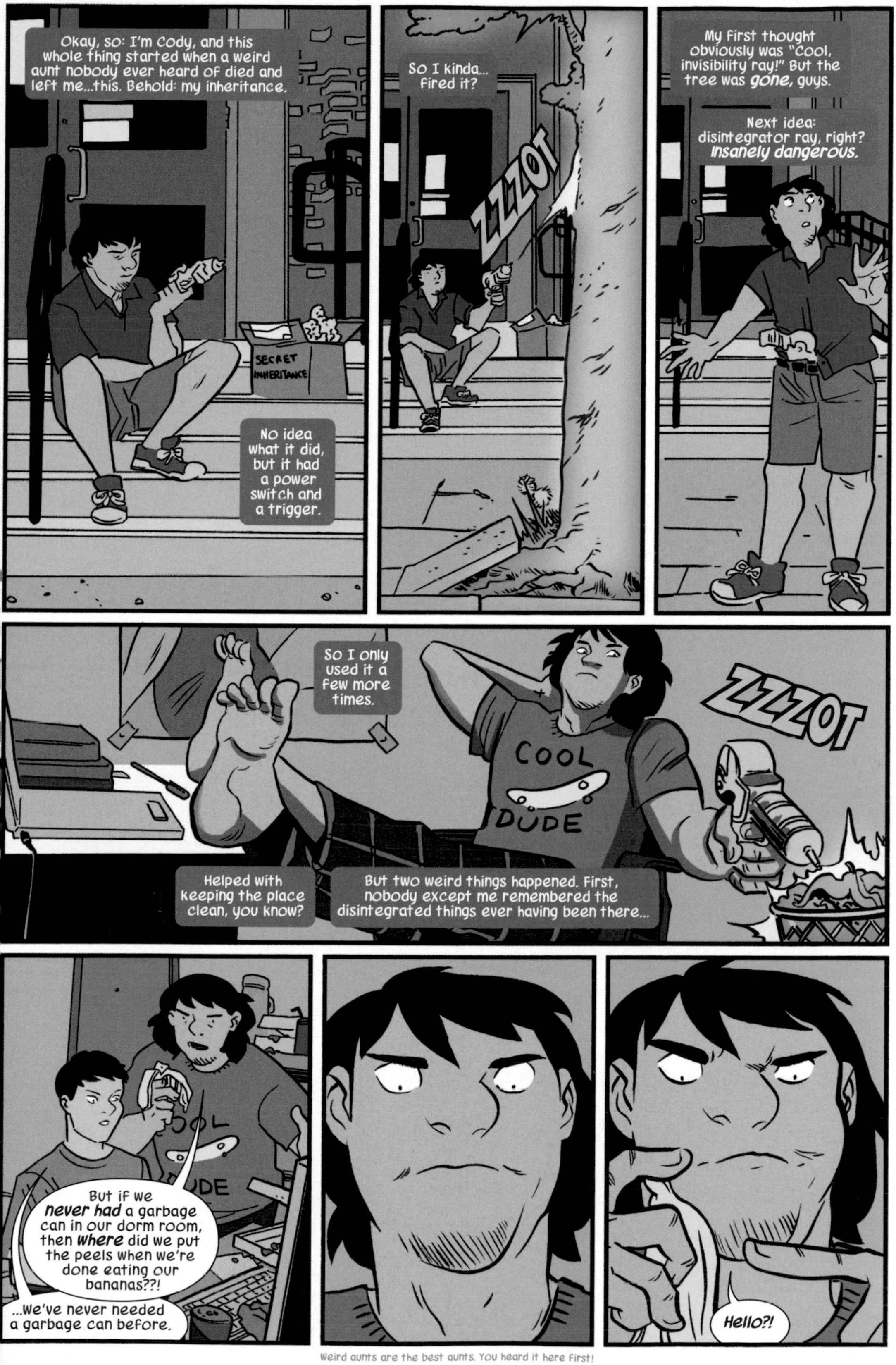
Okay, so: I'm Cody, and this whole thing started when a weird aunt nobody ever heard of died and left me...this. Behold: my inheritance.
SECRET INHERITANCE
No idea what it did, but it had a power switch and a trigger.
So I kinda... fired it?
ZZZOT
My first thought obviously was "Cool, invisibility ray!" But the tree was gone, guys.
Next idea: disintegrator ray, right? Insanely dangerous.
So I only used it a few more times.
COOL DUDE
ZZZOT
Helped with keeping the place clean, you know?
But two weird things happened. First, nobody except me remembered the disintegrated things ever having been there...
But if we never had a garbage can in our dorm room, then where did we put the peels when we're done eating our bananas??!
...We've never needed a garbage can before.
Hello?!

Weird aunts are the best aunts. You heard it here first!

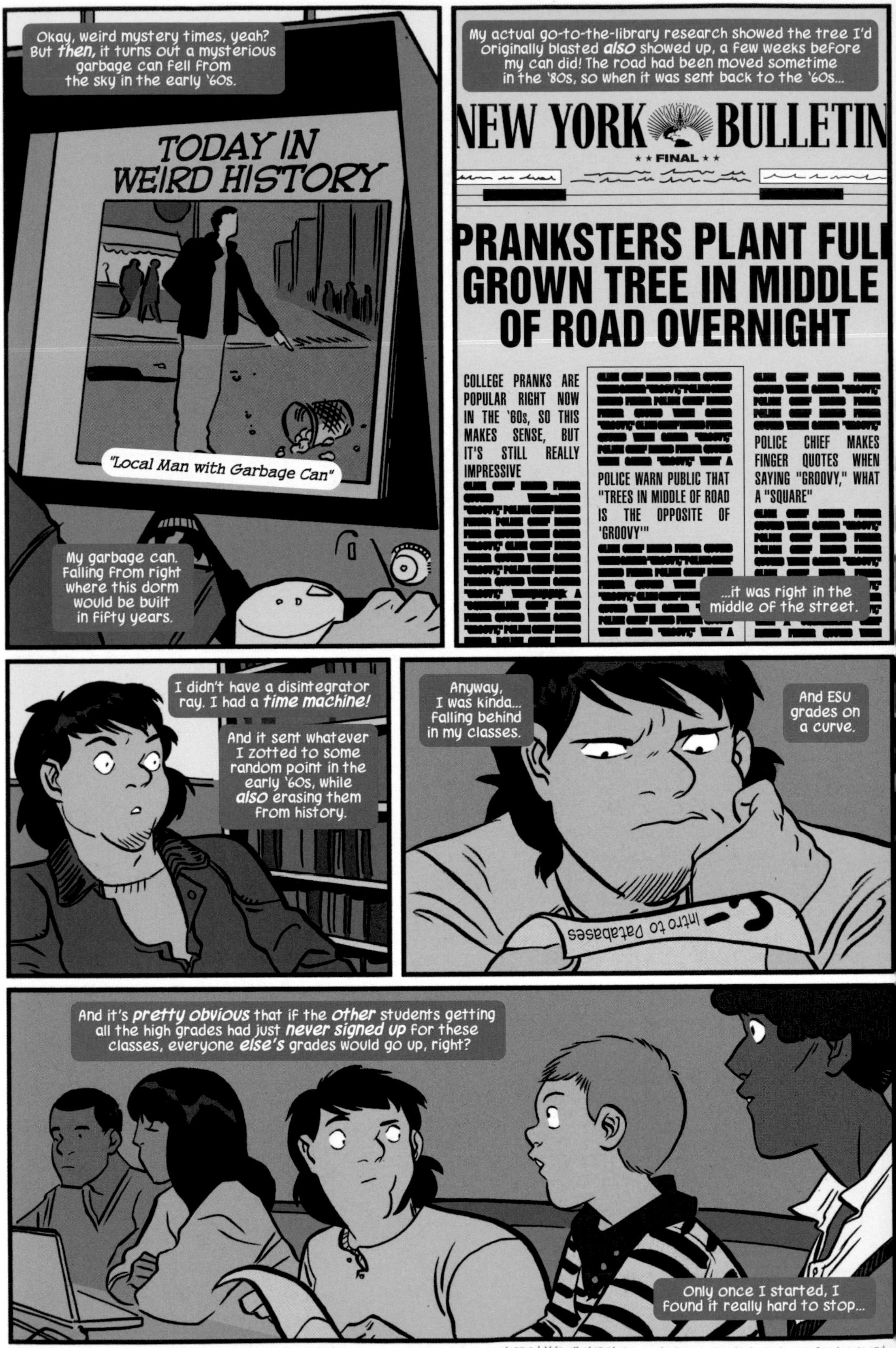

Okay, weird mystery times, yeah? But *then*, it turns out a mysterious garbage can fell from the sky in the early '60s.
TODAY IN WEIRD HISTORY
"Local Man with Garbage Can"
My garbage can. Falling from right where this dorm would be built in fifty years.
My actual go-to-the-library research showed the tree I'd originally blasted *also* showed up, a few weeks before my can did! The road had been moved sometime in the '80s, so when it was sent back to the '60s...
NEW YORK BULLETIN
★★ FINAL ★★
PRANKSTERS PLANT FULL GROWN TREE IN MIDDLE OF ROAD OVERNIGHT
COLLEGE PRANKS ARE POPULAR RIGHT NOW IN THE '60s, SO THIS MAKES SENSE, BUT IT'S STILL REALLY IMPRESSIVE
POLICE WARN PUBLIC THAT "TREES IN MIDDLE OF ROAD IS THE OPPOSITE OF 'GROOVY'"
POLICE CHIEF MAKES FINGER QUOTES WHEN SAYING "GROOVY," WHAT A "SQUARE"
...it was right in the middle of the street.
I didn't have a disintegrator ray. I had a *time machine!*
And it sent whatever I zotted to some random point in the early '60s, while *also* erasing them from history.
Anyway, I was kinda... falling behind in my classes.
And ESU grades on a curve.
Intro to Databases
And it's *pretty obvious* that if the *other* students getting all the high grades had just *never signed up* for these classes, everyone *else's* grades would go up, right?
Only once I started, I found it really hard to stop...

If you go back to Volume 1 Issue 7 of this book, you'll see Cody in class there, *almost like we planned this all along!* Yes, we truly are excellent comics professionals and *definitely* not making this up as we go along.

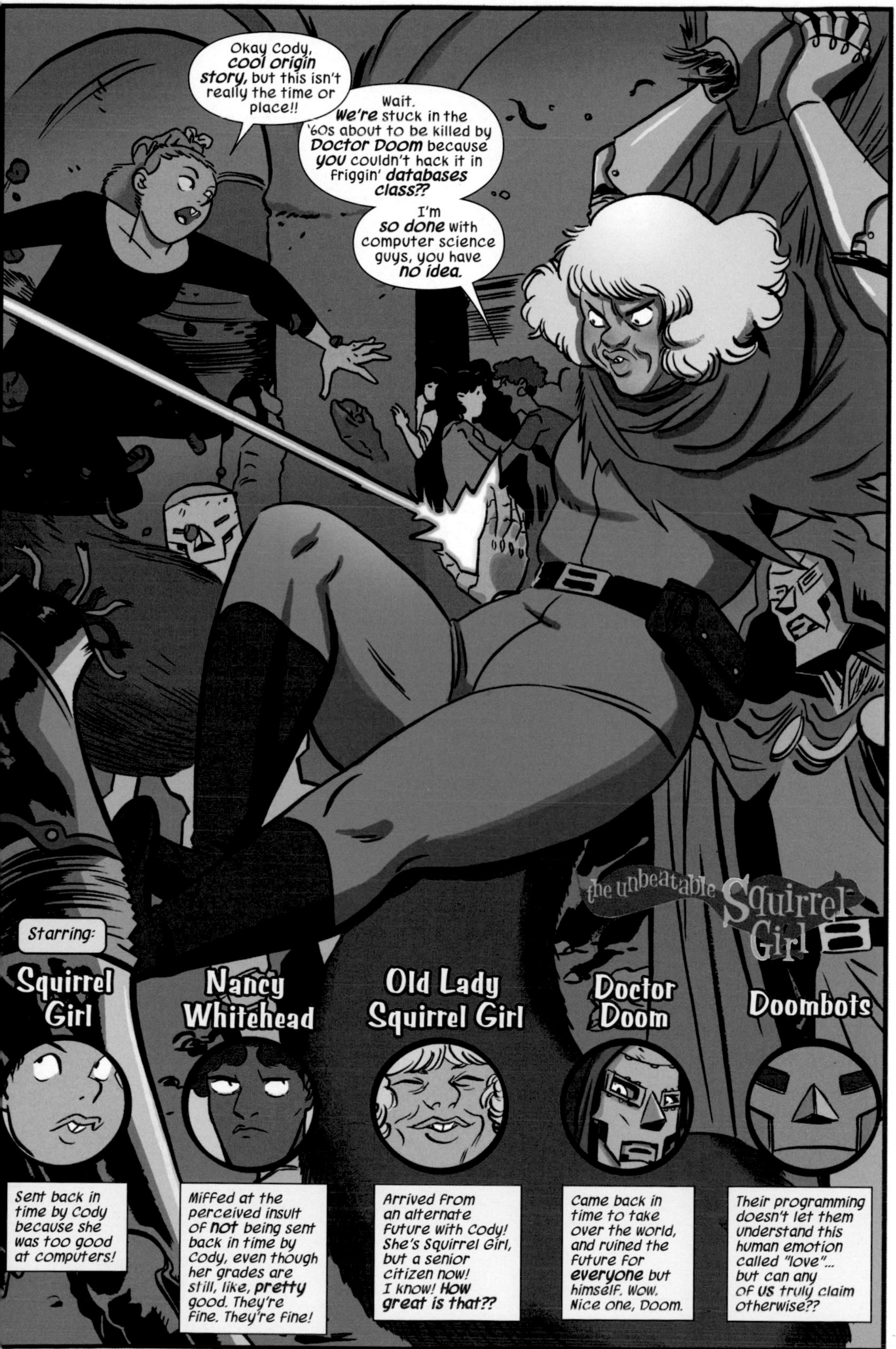
Okay Cody, cool origin story, but this isn't really the time or place!!
Wait. We're stuck in the '60s about to be killed by Doctor Doom because you couldn't hack it in friggin' databases class??
I'm so done with computer science guys, you have no idea.
the unbeatable Squirrel Girl
Starring:
Squirrel Girl
Nancy Whitehead
Old Lady Squirrel Girl
Doctor Doom
Doombots
Sent back in time by Cody because she was too good at computers!
Miffed at the perceived insult of not being sent back in time by Cody, even though her grades are still, like, pretty good. They're fine. They're fine!
Arrived from an alternate future with Cody! She's Squirrel Girl, but a senior citizen now! I know! How great is that??
Came back in time to take over the world, and ruined the future for everyone but himself. Wow. Nice one, Doom.
Their programming doesn't let them understand this human emotion called "love"... but can any of us truly claim otherwise??

Also starring: Tippy-Toe, who is upset her character photo didn't make the cut, and who says it would've been a shot of her holding up a tiny dumbbell, only with acorns at its ends instead of weights. Dang, Tippy, that's actually super cute! Now I'm upset too!

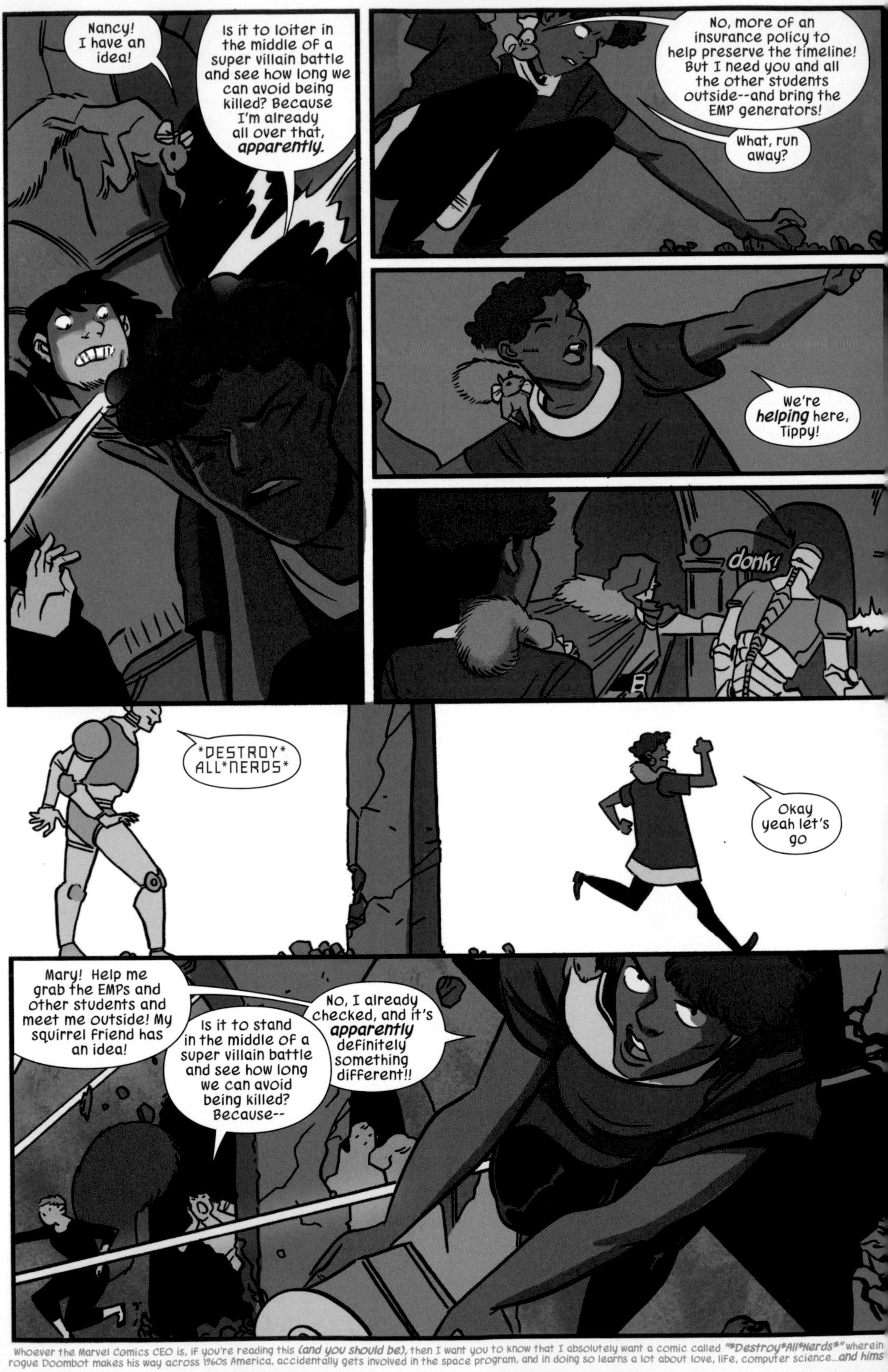

Nancy! I have an idea!
Is it to loiter in the middle of a super villain battle and see how long we can avoid being killed? Because I'm already all over that, *apparently.*
No, more of an insurance policy to help preserve the timeline! But I need you and all the other students outside--and bring the EMP generators!
What, run away?
We're *helping* here, Tippy!
donk!
DESTROY ALL*NERDS*
Okay yeah let's go
Mary! Help me grab the EMPs and other students and meet me outside! My squirrel friend has an idea!
Is it to stand in the middle of a super villain battle and see how long we can avoid being killed? Because--
No, I already checked, and it's *apparently* definitely something different!!

Whoever the Marvel Comics CEO is, if you're reading this *(and you should be)*, then I want you to know that I absolutely want a comic called *"*Destroy*All*Nerds*"* wherein rogue Doombot makes his way across 1960s America, accidentally gets involved in the space program, and in doing so learns a lot about love, life, computer science*...and hims*

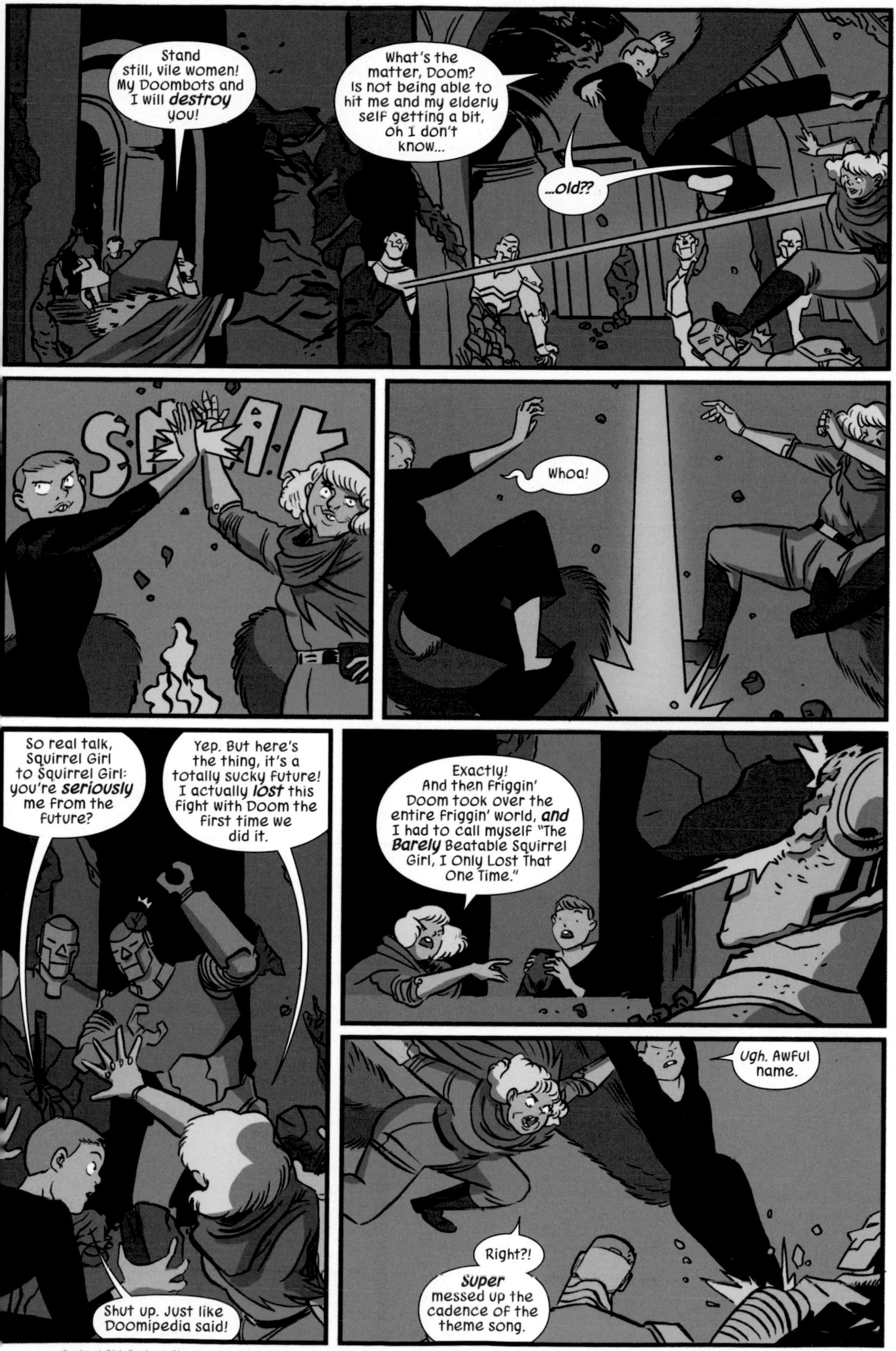
Stand still, vile women! My Doombots and I will *destroy* you!
What's the matter, Doom? Is not being able to hit me and my elderly self getting a bit, oh I don't know...
...old??
Whoa!
So real talk, Squirrel Girl to Squirrel Girl: you're *seriously* me from the future?
Yep. But here's the thing, it's a totally sucky future! I actually *lost* this fight with Doom the first time we did it.
Shut up. Just like Doomipedia said!
Exactly! And then friggin' Doom took over the entire friggin' world, *and* I had to call myself "The *Barely* Beatable Squirrel Girl, I Only Lost That One Time."
Ugh. Awful name.
Right?!
Super messed up the cadence of the theme song.

Squirrel Girl, Squirrel Girl / Let's not beat / Squirrel Girl / Did she lose? / On-ly once / And it was / To a dunce / Hey there! Sick burns on Doctor Doom

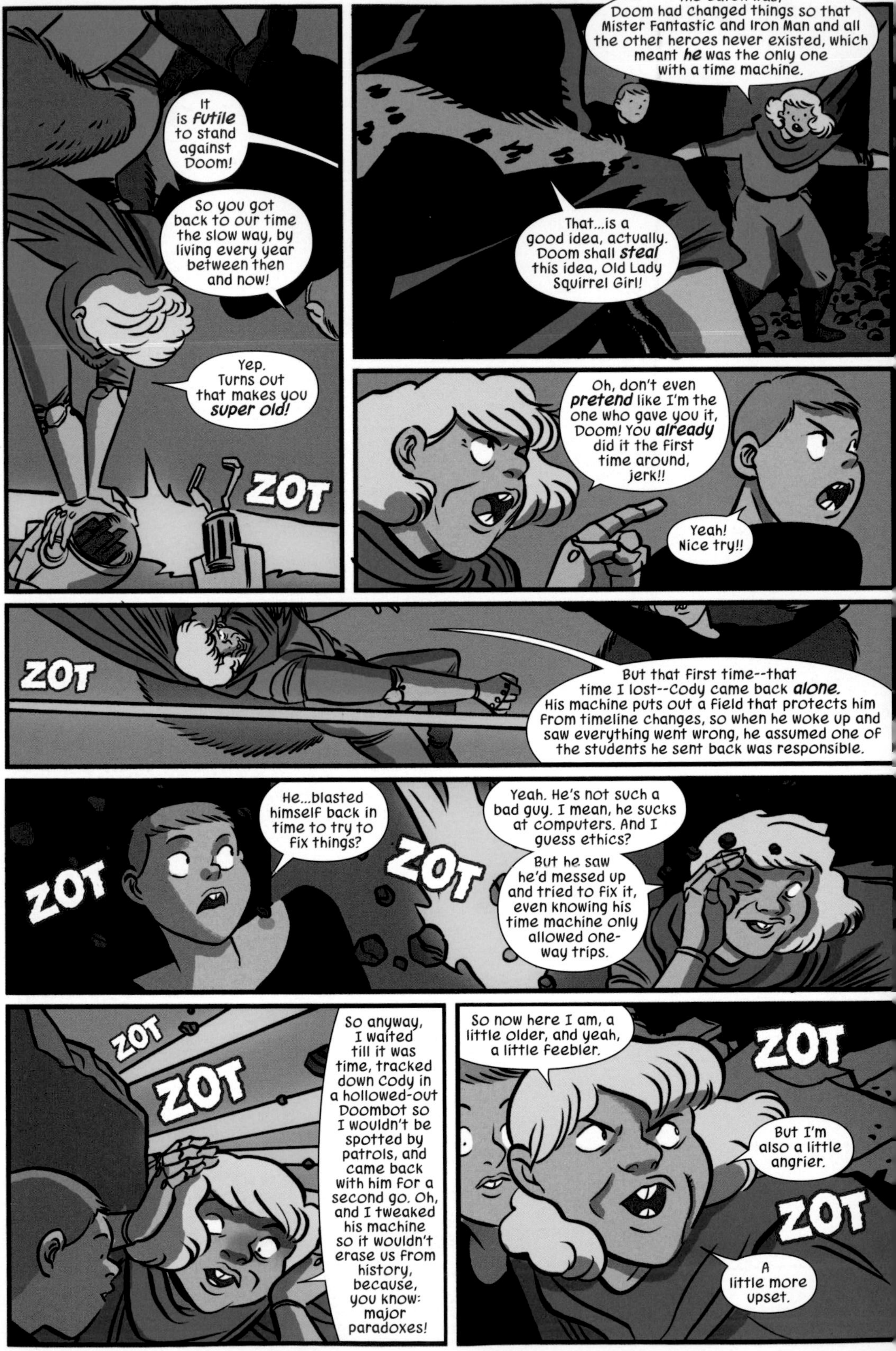
It is futile to stand against Doom!
So you got back to our time the slow way, by living every year between then and now!
Yep. Turns out that makes you super old!
ZOT
The catch was, Doom had changed things so that Mister Fantastic and Iron Man and all the other heroes never existed, which meant he was the only one with a time machine.
That...is a good idea, actually. Doom shall steal this idea, Old Lady Squirrel Girl!
Oh, don't even pretend like I'm the one who gave you it, Doom! You already did it the first time around, jerk!!
Yeah! Nice try!!
ZOT
But that first time--that time I lost--Cody came back alone. His machine puts out a field that protects him from timeline changes, so when he woke up and saw everything went wrong, he assumed one of the students he sent back was responsible.
ZOT
He...blasted himself back in time to try to fix things?
ZOT
Yeah. He's not such a bad guy. I mean, he sucks at computers. And I guess ethics?
But he saw he'd messed up and tried to fix it, even knowing his time machine only allowed one-way trips.
ZOT
ZOT
So anyway, I waited till it was time, tracked down Cody in a hollowed-out Doombot so I wouldn't be spotted by patrols, and came back with him for a second go. Oh, and I tweaked his machine so it wouldn't erase us from history, because, you know: major paradoxes!
So now here I am, a little older, and yeah, a little feebler.
ZOT
But I'm also a little angrier.
ZOT
A little more upset.

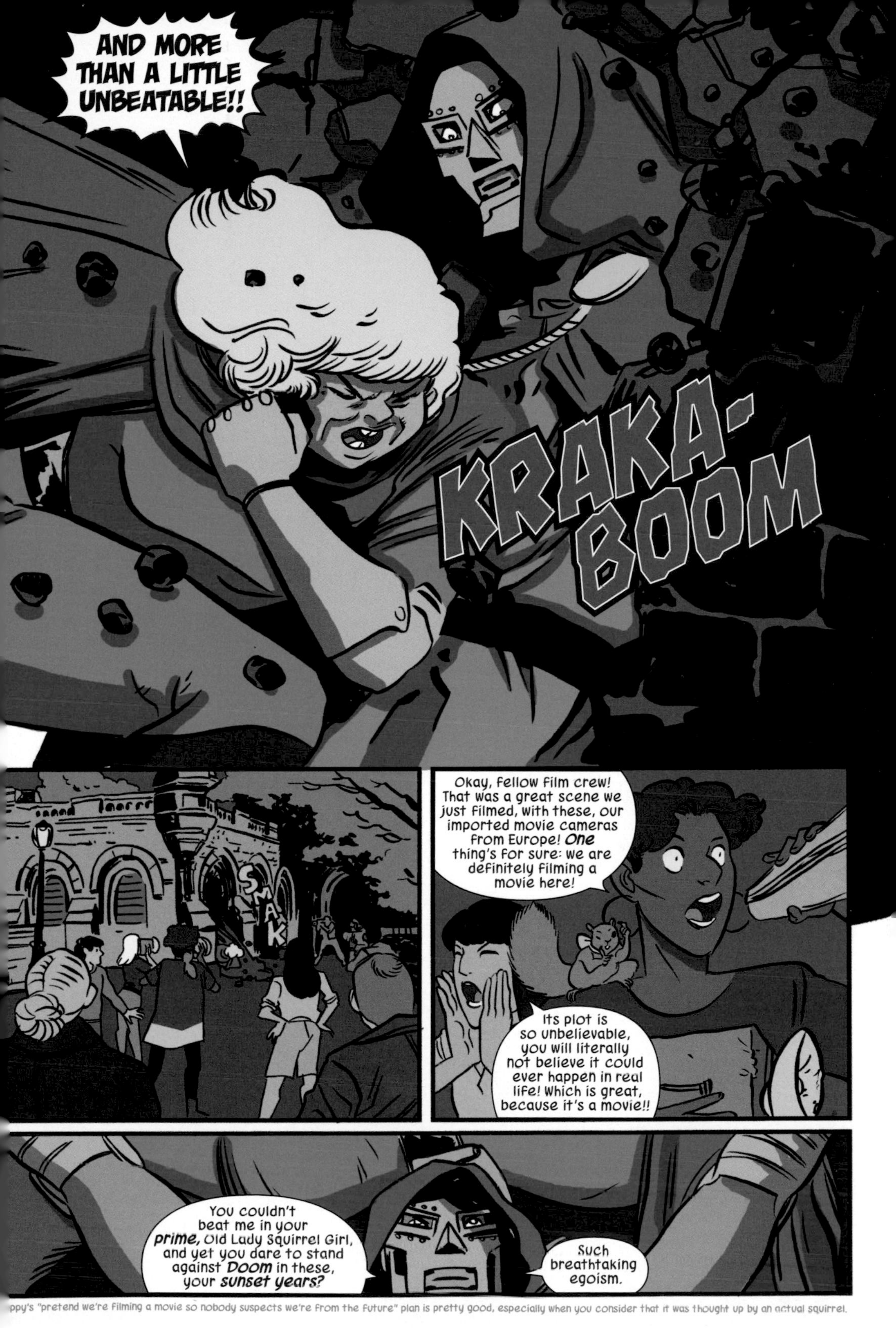
AND MORE THAN A LITTLE UNBEATABLE!!
KRAKA-BOOM
SMAK
Okay, fellow film crew! That was a great scene we just filmed, with these, our imported movie cameras from Europe! *One* thing's for sure: we are definitely filming a movie here!
Its plot is so unbelievable, you will literally not believe it could ever happen in real life! Which is great, because it's a movie!!
You couldn't beat me in your *prime,* Old Lady Squirrel Girl, and yet you dare to stand against *Doom* in these, your *sunset years?*
Such breathtaking egoism.

ppy's "pretend we're filming a movie so nobody suspects we're from the future" plan is pretty good, especially when you consider that it was thought up by an actual squirrel.

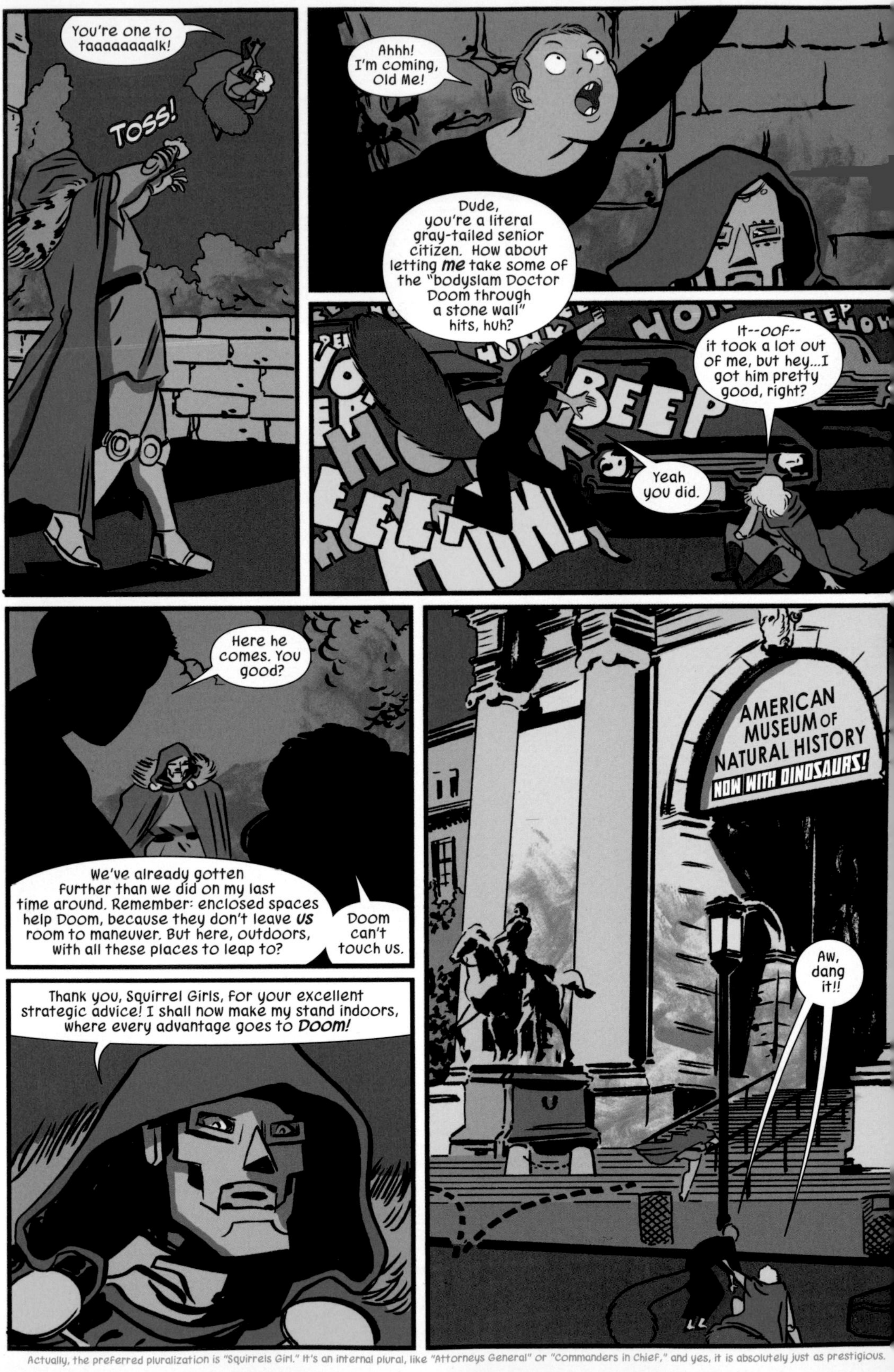
You're one to taaaaaaaalk!
TOSS!
Ahhh! I'm coming, Old Me!
Dude, you're a literal gray-tailed senior citizen. How about letting *me* take some of the "bodyslam Doctor Doom through a stone wall" hits, huh?
It--oof-- it took a lot out of me, but hey...I got him pretty good, right?
BEEP
Yeah you did.
Here he comes. You good?
We've already gotten further than we did on my last time around. Remember: enclosed spaces help Doom, because they don't leave *US* room to maneuver. But here, outdoors, with all these places to leap to?
Doom can't touch us.
Thank you, Squirrel Girls, for your excellent strategic advice! I shall now make my stand indoors, where every advantage goes to *DOOM!*
AMERICAN MUSEUM OF NATURAL HISTORY
NOW WITH DINOSAURS!
Aw, dang it!!

Actually, the preferred pluralization is "Squirrels Girl." It's an internal plural, like "Attorneys General" or "Commanders in Chief," and yes, it is absolutely just as prestigious.

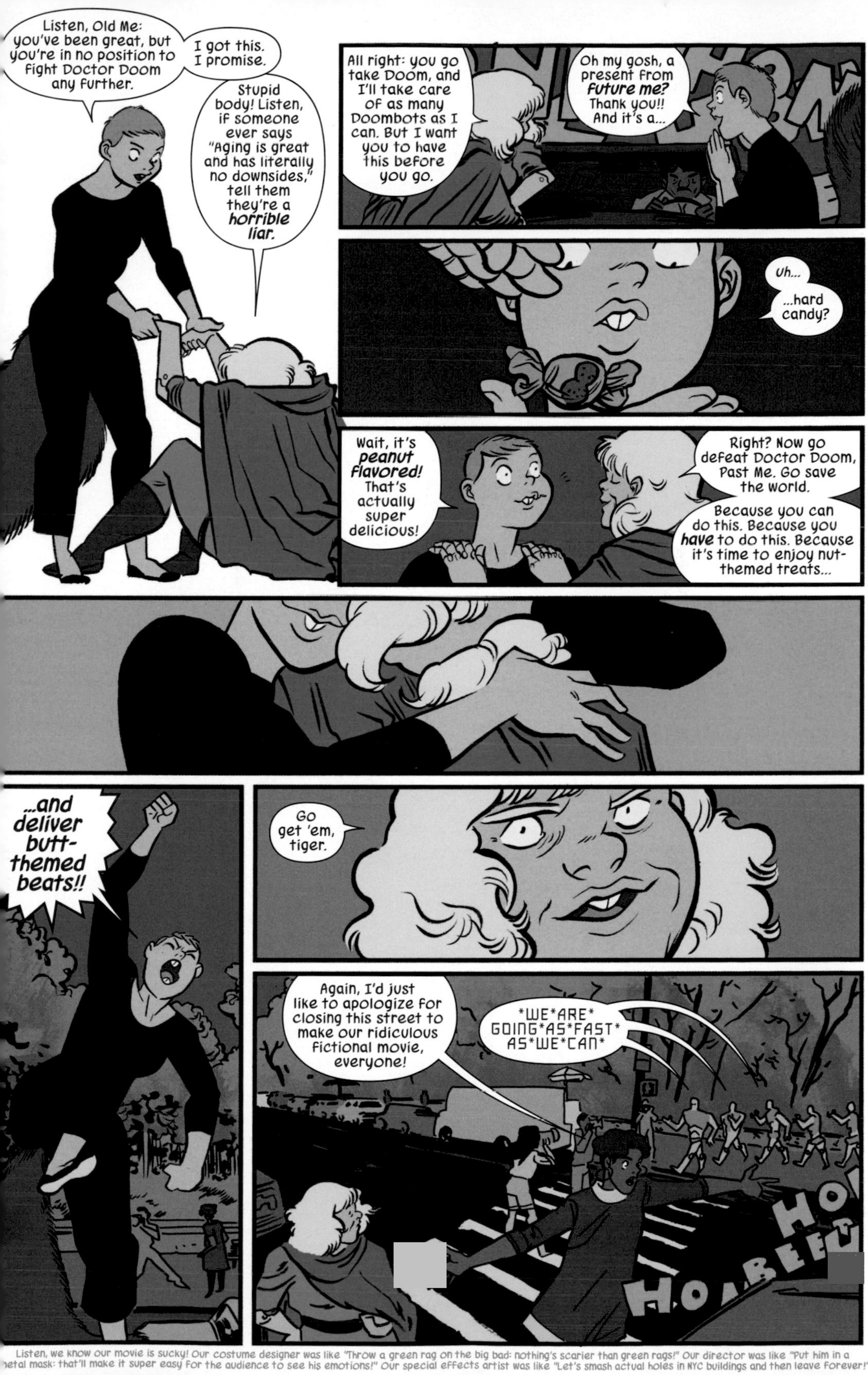
Listen, Old Me: you've been great, but you're in no position to fight Doctor Doom any further.
I got this. I promise.
Stupid body! Listen, if someone ever says "Aging is great and has literally no downsides," tell them they're a horrible liar.
All right: you go take Doom, and I'll take care of as many Doombots as I can. But I want you to have this before you go.
Oh my gosh, a present from future me? Thank you!! And it's a...
Uh...
...hard candy?
Wait, it's peanut flavored! That's actually super delicious!
Right? Now go defeat Doctor Doom, Past Me. Go save the world.
Because you can do this. Because you have to do this. Because it's time to enjoy nut-themed treats...
...and deliver butt-themed beats!!
Go get 'em, tiger.
Again, I'd just like to apologize for closing this street to make our ridiculous fictional movie, everyone!
*WE*ARE* GOING*AS*FAST* AS*WE*CAN*

Listen, we know our movie is sucky! Our costume designer was like "Throw a green rag on the big bad: nothing's scarier than green rags!" Our director was like "Put him in a netal mask: that'll make it super easy for the audience to see his emotions!" Our special effects artist was like "Let's smash actual holes in NYC buildings and then leave forever!"

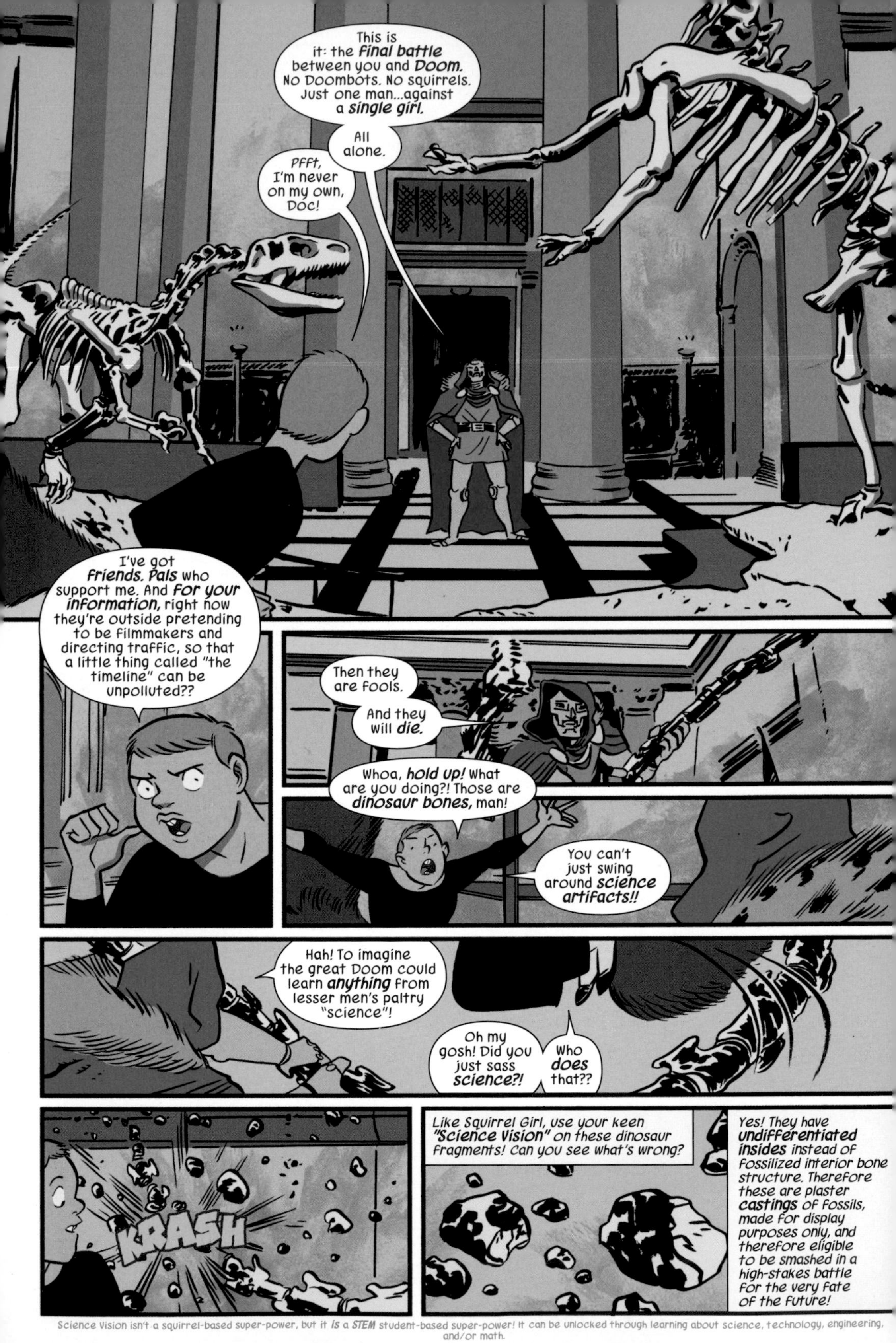

This is it: the final battle between you and Doom. No Doombots. No squirrels. Just one man...against a single girl.
All alone.
Pfft, I'm never on my own, Doc!
I've got friends. Pals who support me. And for your information, right now they're outside pretending to be filmmakers and directing traffic, so that a little thing called "the timeline" can be unpolluted??
Then they are fools.
And they will die.
Whoa, hold up! What are you doing?! Those are dinosaur bones, man!
You can't just swing around science artifacts!!
Hah! To imagine the great Doom could learn anything from lesser men's paltry "science"!
Oh my gosh! Did you just sass science?!
Who does that??
KRASH
Like Squirrel Girl, use your keen "Science Vision" on these dinosaur fragments! Can you see what's wrong?
Yes! They have undifferentiated insides instead of fossilized interior bone structure. Therefore these are plaster castings of fossils, made for display purposes only, and therefore eligible to be smashed in a high-stakes battle for the very fate of the future!

Science Vision isn't a squirrel-based super-power, but it *is* a ***STEM*** student-based super-power! It can be unlocked through learning about science, technology, engineering, and/or math.

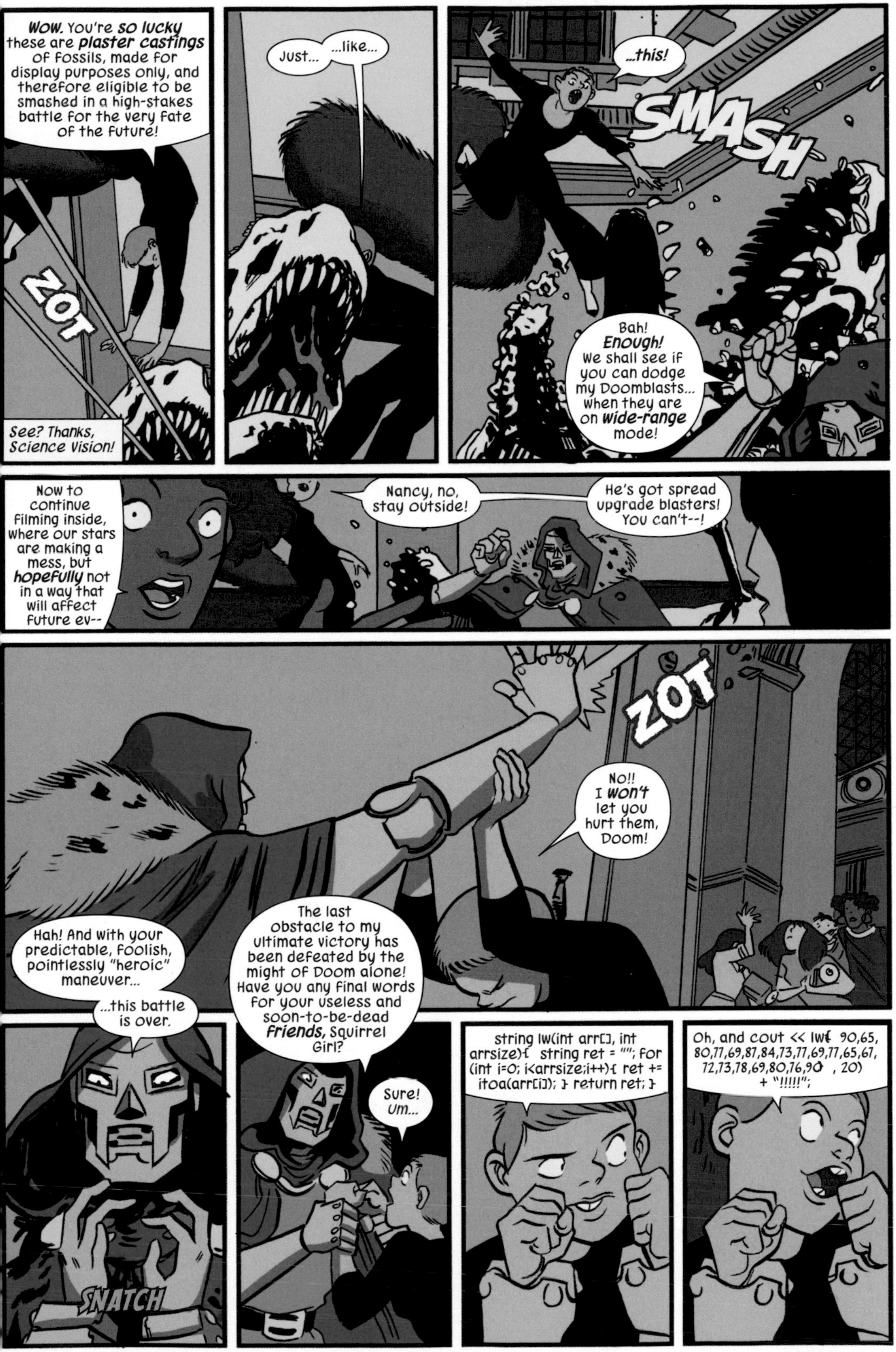
WOW. You're so lucky these are plaster castings of fossils, made for display purposes only, and therefore eligible to be smashed in a high-stakes battle for the very fate of the future!
ZOT
See? Thanks, Science Vision!
Just...
...like...
...this!
SMASH
Bah! Enough! We shall see if you can dodge my Doomblasts... when they are on wide-range mode!
Now to continue filming inside, where our stars are making a mess, but hopefully not in a way that will affect future ev--
Nancy, no, stay outside!
He's got spread upgrade blasters! You can't--!
ZOT
No!! I won't let you hurt them, Doom!
Hah! And with your predictable, foolish, pointlessly "heroic" maneuver...
...this battle is over.
The last obstacle to my ultimate victory has been defeated by the might of Doom alone! Have you any final words for your useless and soon-to-be-dead friends, Squirrel Girl?
Sure! Um...
SNATCH
string lw(int arr[], int arrsize){ string ret = ""; for (int i=0; i<arrsize;i++){ ret += itoa(arr[i]); } return ret; }
Oh, and cout << lw({ 90,65, 80,77,69,87,84,73,77,69,77,65,67, 72,73,78,69,80,76,90 }, 20) + "!!!!!";

Those of us who can run C++ programs in our heads are going *"Oh dang!!"* right now, while the rest of us are saying "Man, I could run that program in my head if I wanted to," looking around, and then quickly turning the page to see what happens.

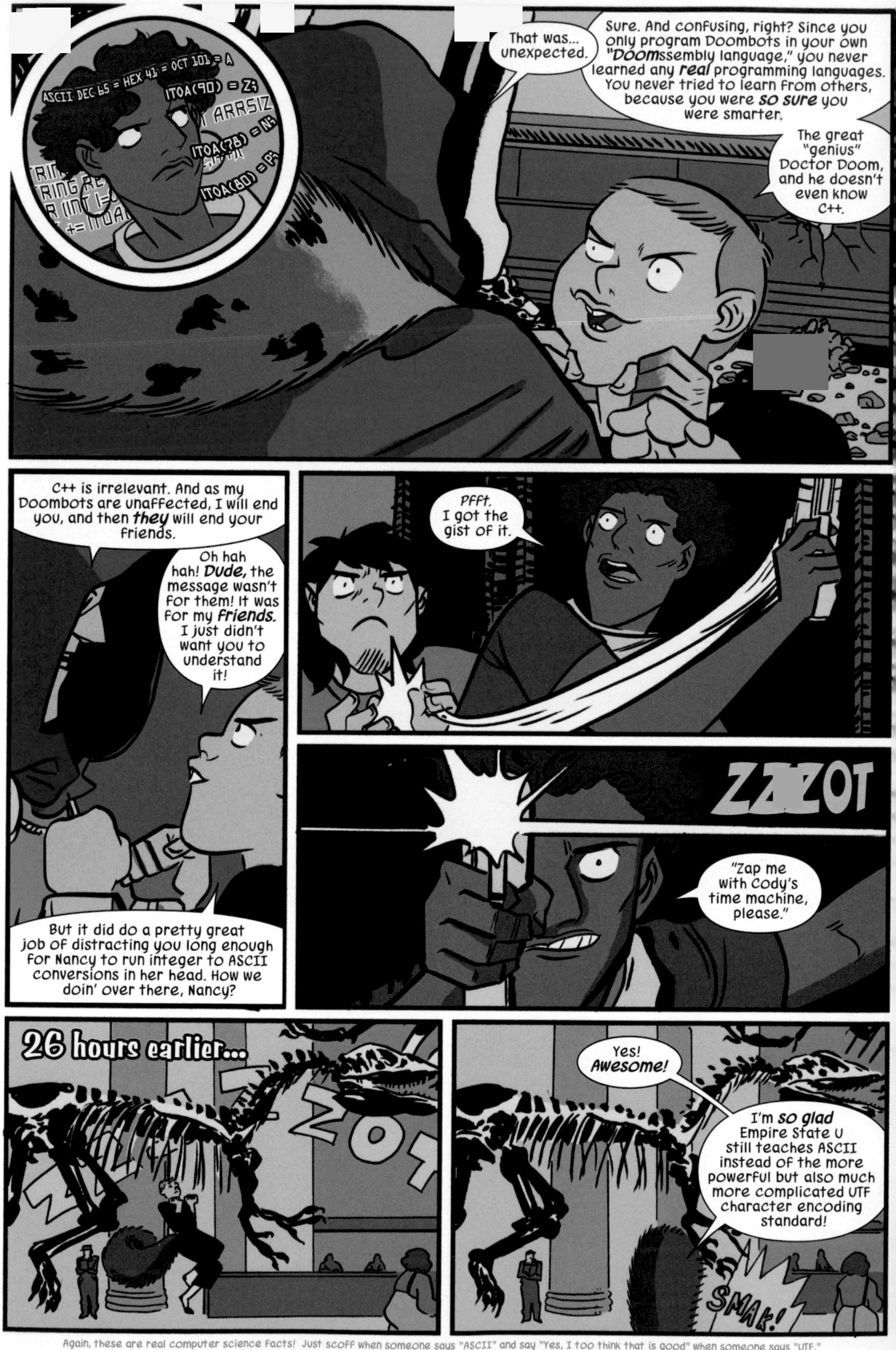
ASCII DEC 65 = HEX 41 = OCT 101 = A
ITOA(90) = Z
ITOA(78) = N
ITOA(80) = P
That was... unexpected.
Sure. And confusing, right? Since you only program Doombots in your own "DOOMssembly language," you never learned any real programming languages. You never tried to learn from others, because you were so sure you were smarter.
The great "genius" Doctor Doom, and he doesn't even know C++.
C++ is irrelevant. And as my Doombots are unaffected, I will end you, and then they will end your friends.
Oh hah hah! Dude, the message wasn't for them! It was for my friends. I just didn't want you to understand it!
But it did do a pretty great job of distracting you long enough for Nancy to run integer to ASCII conversions in her head. How we doin' over there, Nancy?
Pfft. I got the gist of it.
ZZZOT
"Zap me with Cody's time machine, please."
26 hours earlier...
ZOT
Yes! Awesome!
I'm so glad Empire State U still teaches ASCII instead of the more powerful but also much more complicated UTF character encoding standard!
SMAK!

Again, these are real computer science facts! Just scoff when someone says "ASCII" and say "Yes, I too think that is good" when someone says "UTF," and you will *absolutely* pass as a computer scientist.

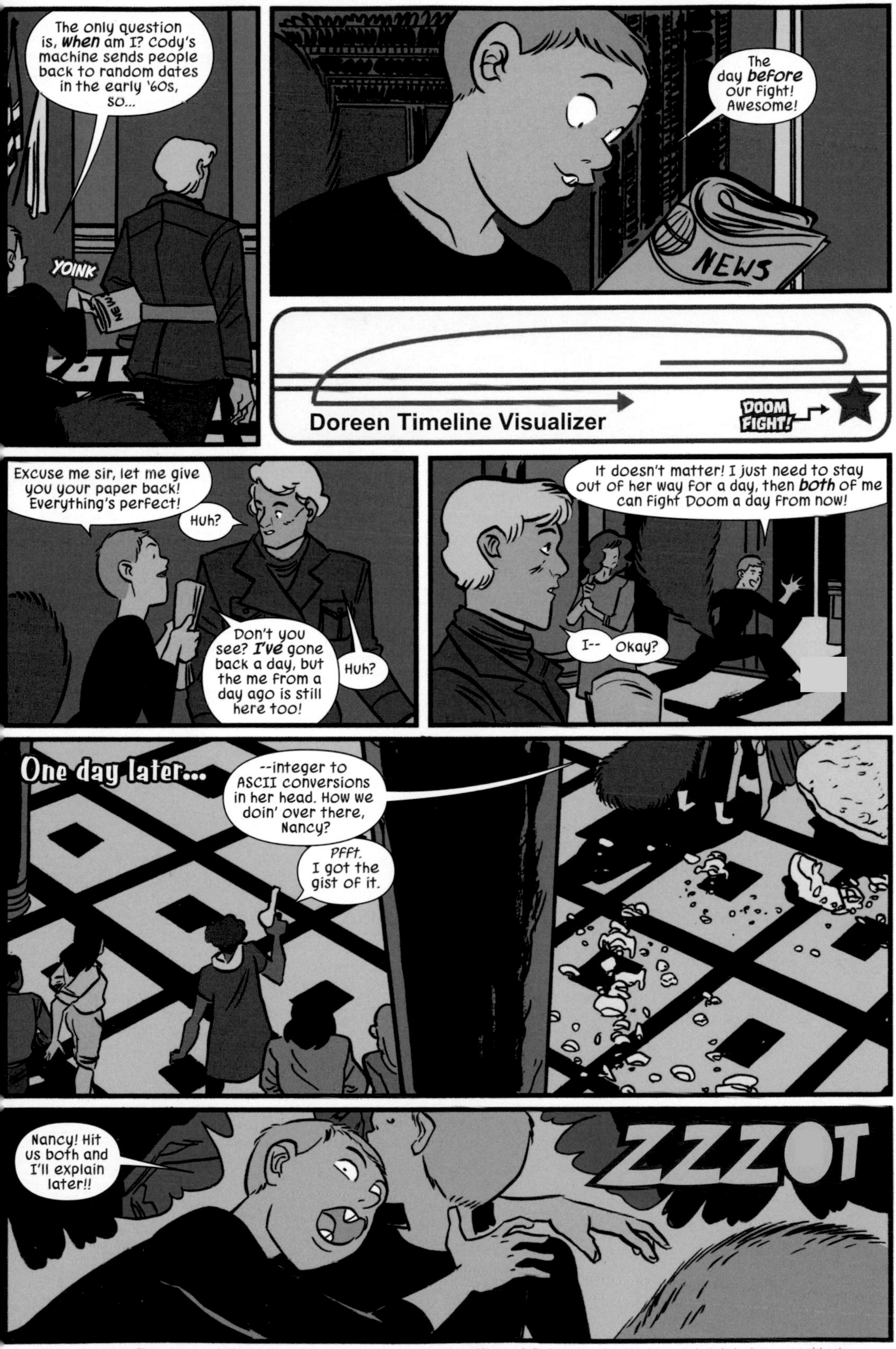
The only question is, **when** am I? Cody's machine sends people back to random dates in the early '60s, so...
YOINK
NEWS
The day **before** our fight! Awesome!
NEWS
Doreen Timeline Visualizer
DOOM FIGHT!
Excuse me sir, let me give you your paper back! Everything's perfect!
Huh?
Don't you see? ***I've*** gone back a day, but the me from a day ago is still here too!
Huh?
It doesn't matter! I just need to stay out of her way for a day, then **both** of me can fight Doom a day from now!
I--
Okay?
One day later...
--integer to ASCII conversions in her head. How we doin' over there, Nancy?
Pfft. I got the gist of it.
Nancy! Hit us both and I'll explain later!!
ZZZOT

This businessman will never appear in this comic again, so here is his entire backstory: his name is "Pete McFleet" and his interests include business, spreadsheets, and the business of spreadsheets. Fare thee well, Pete McFleet!

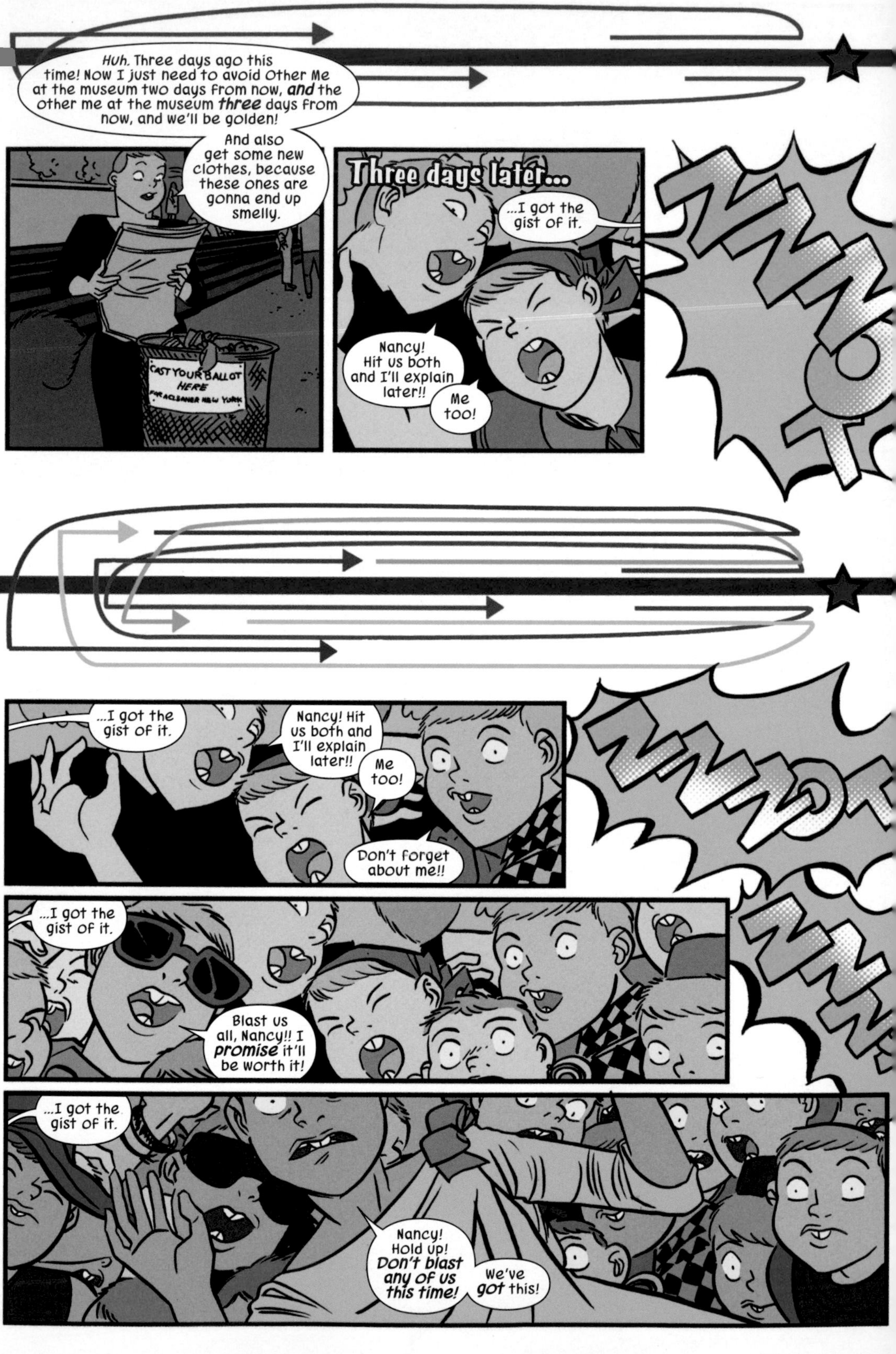

Huh. Three days ago this time! Now I just need to avoid Other Me at the museum two days from now, and the other me at the museum three days from now, and we'll be golden!
And also get some new clothes, because these ones are gonna end up smelly.
CAST YOUR BALLOT HERE FOR A CLEANER NEW YORK
Three days later...
...I got the gist of it.
Nancy! Hit us both and I'll explain later!!
Me too!
...I got the gist of it.
Nancy! Hit us both and I'll explain later!!
Me too!
Don't forget about me!!
...I got the gist of it.
Blast us all, Nancy!! I promise it'll be worth it!
...I got the gist of it.
Nancy! Hold up! Don't blast any of us this time!
We've got this!

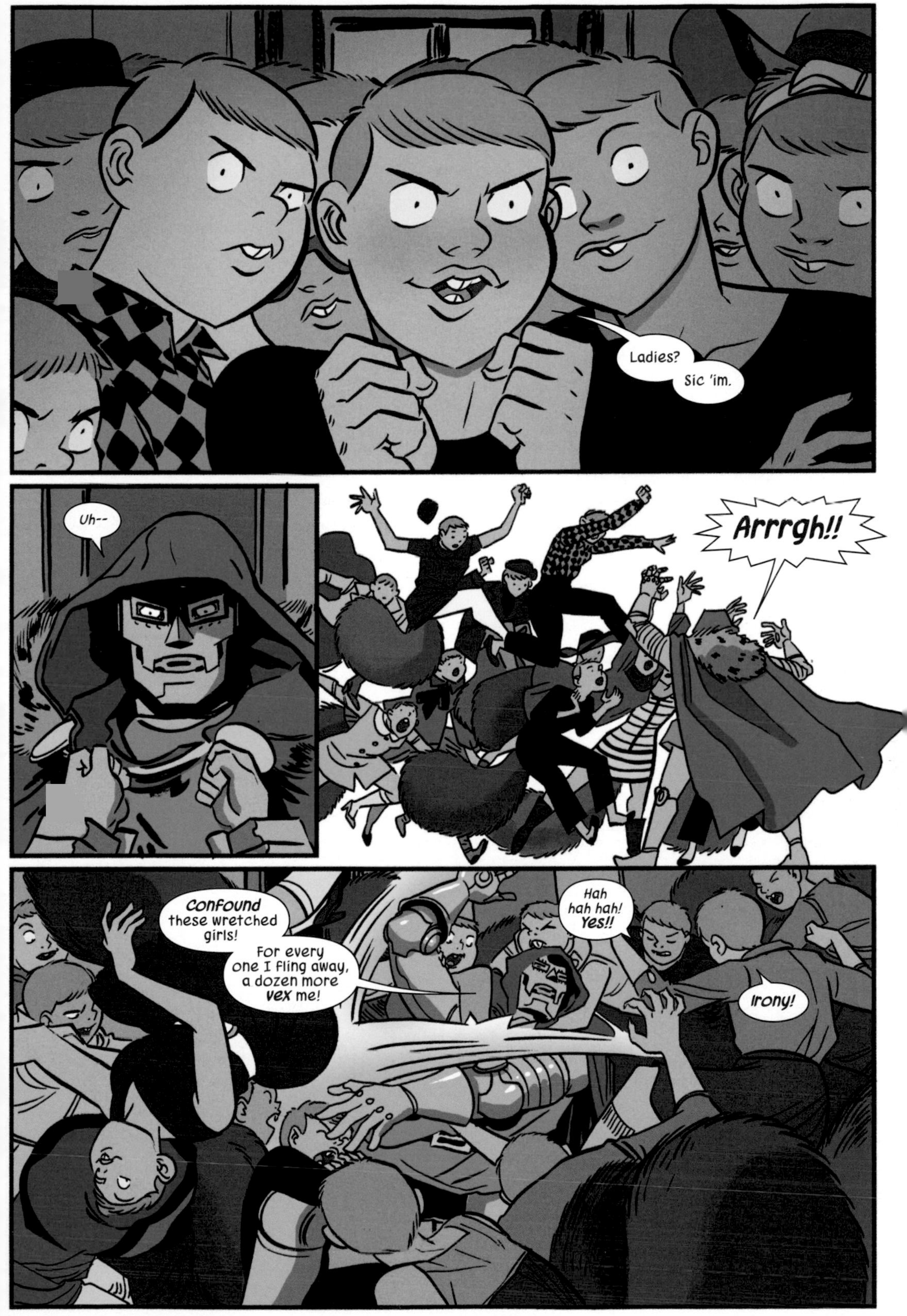
Ladies?
Sic 'im.
Uh--
Arrrgh!!
Confound these wretched girls!
For every one I fling away, a dozen more vex me!
Hah hah hah! Yes!!
Irony!

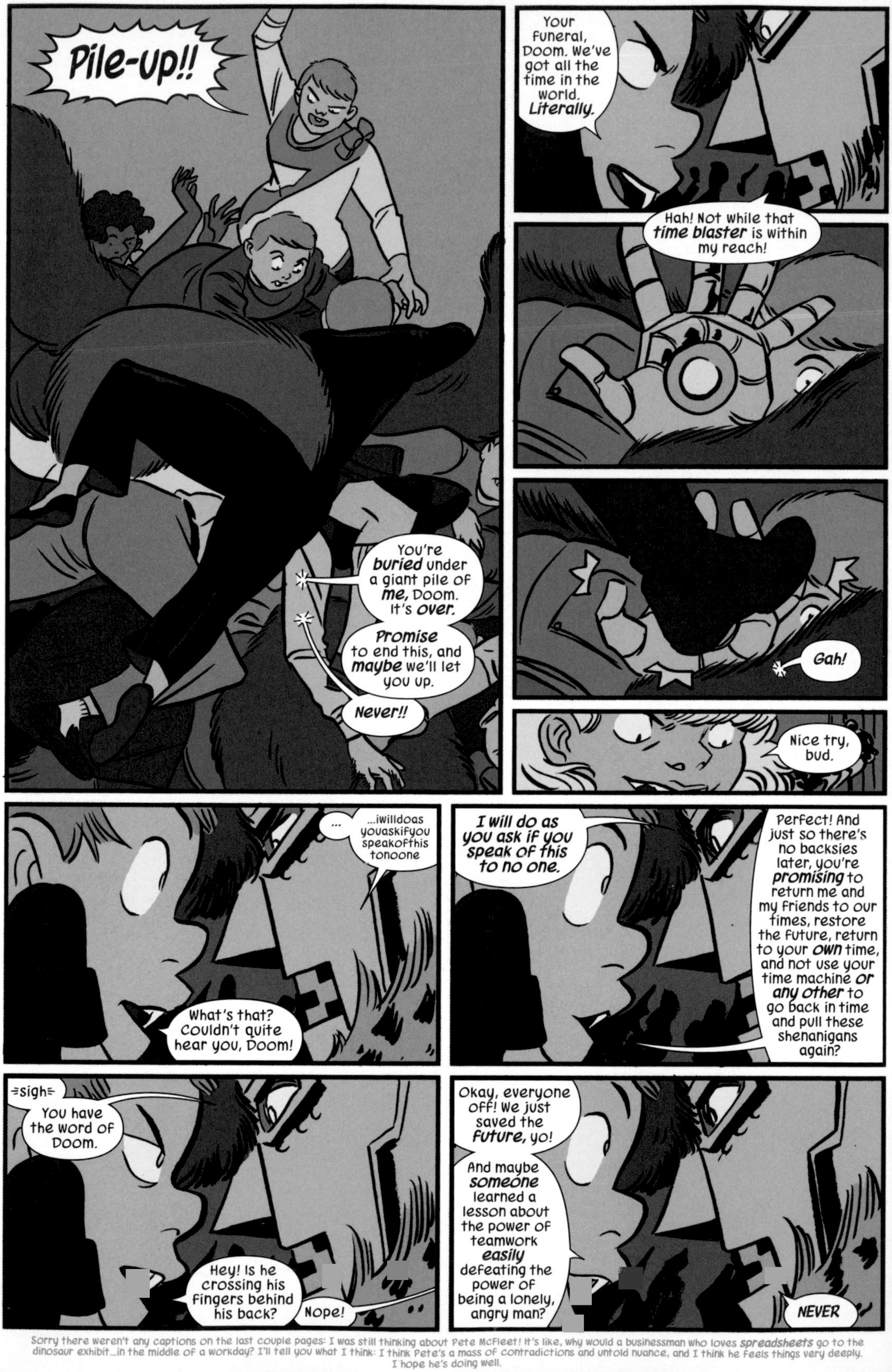
Pile-up!!
You're buried under a giant pile of me, Doom. It's over.
Promise to end this, and maybe we'll let you up.
Never!!
Your funeral, Doom. We've got all the time in the world. Literally.
Hah! Not while that time blaster is within my reach!
Gah!
Nice try, bud.
...
...iwilldoas youaskifyou speakofthis tonoone
What's that? Couldn't quite hear you, Doom!
I will do as you ask if you speak of this to no one.
Perfect! And just so there's no backsies later, you're promising to return me and my friends to our times, restore the future, return to your own time, and not use your time machine or any other to go back in time and pull these shenanigans again?
=sigh=
You have the word of Doom.
Hey! Is he crossing his fingers behind his back?
Nope!
Okay, everyone off! We just saved the future, yo!
And maybe someone learned a lesson about the power of teamwork easily defeating the power of being a lonely, angry man?
NEVER

Sorry there weren't any captions on the last couple pages: I was still thinking about Pete McFleet! It's like, why would a businessman who loves *spreadsheets* go to the dinosaur exhibit...in the middle of a workday? I'll tell you what I think: I think Pete's a mass of contradictions and untold nuance, and I think he feels things very deeply. I hope he's doing well.

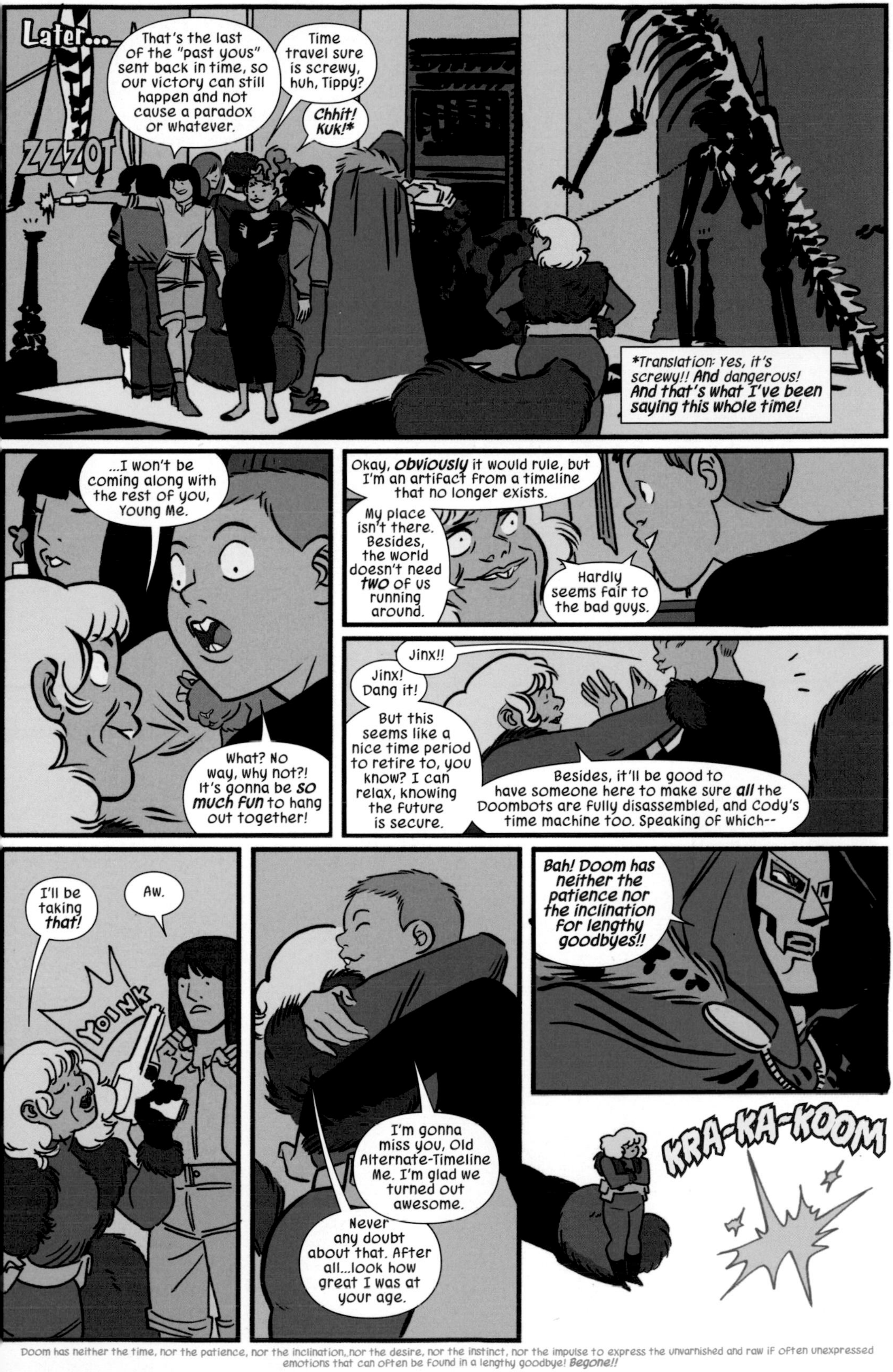
Later...
That's the last of the "past yous" sent back in time, so our victory can still happen and not cause a paradox or whatever.
Time travel sure is screwy, huh, Tippy?
Chhit! Kuk!*
ZZZOT
*Translation: Yes, it's screwy!! And dangerous! And that's what I've been saying this whole time!
...I won't be coming along with the rest of you, Young Me.
What? No way, why not?! It's gonna be so much fun to hang out together!
Okay, obviously it would rule, but I'm an artifact from a timeline that no longer exists.
My place isn't there. Besides, the world doesn't need two of us running around.
Hardly seems fair to the bad guys.
Jinx!!
Jinx! Dang it!
But this seems like a nice time period to retire to, you know? I can relax, knowing the future is secure.
Besides, it'll be good to have someone here to make sure all the Doombots are fully disassembled, and Cody's time machine too. Speaking of which--
I'll be taking that!
Aw.
YOINK
I'm gonna miss you, Old Alternate-Timeline Me. I'm glad we turned out awesome.
Never any doubt about that. After all...look how great I was at your age.
Bah! Doom has neither the patience nor the inclination for lengthy goodbyes!!
KRA-KA-KOOM

Doom has neither the time, nor the patience, nor the inclination, nor the desire, nor the instinct, nor the impulse to express the unvarnished and raw if often unexpressed emotions that can often be found in a lengthy goodbye! *Begone!!*

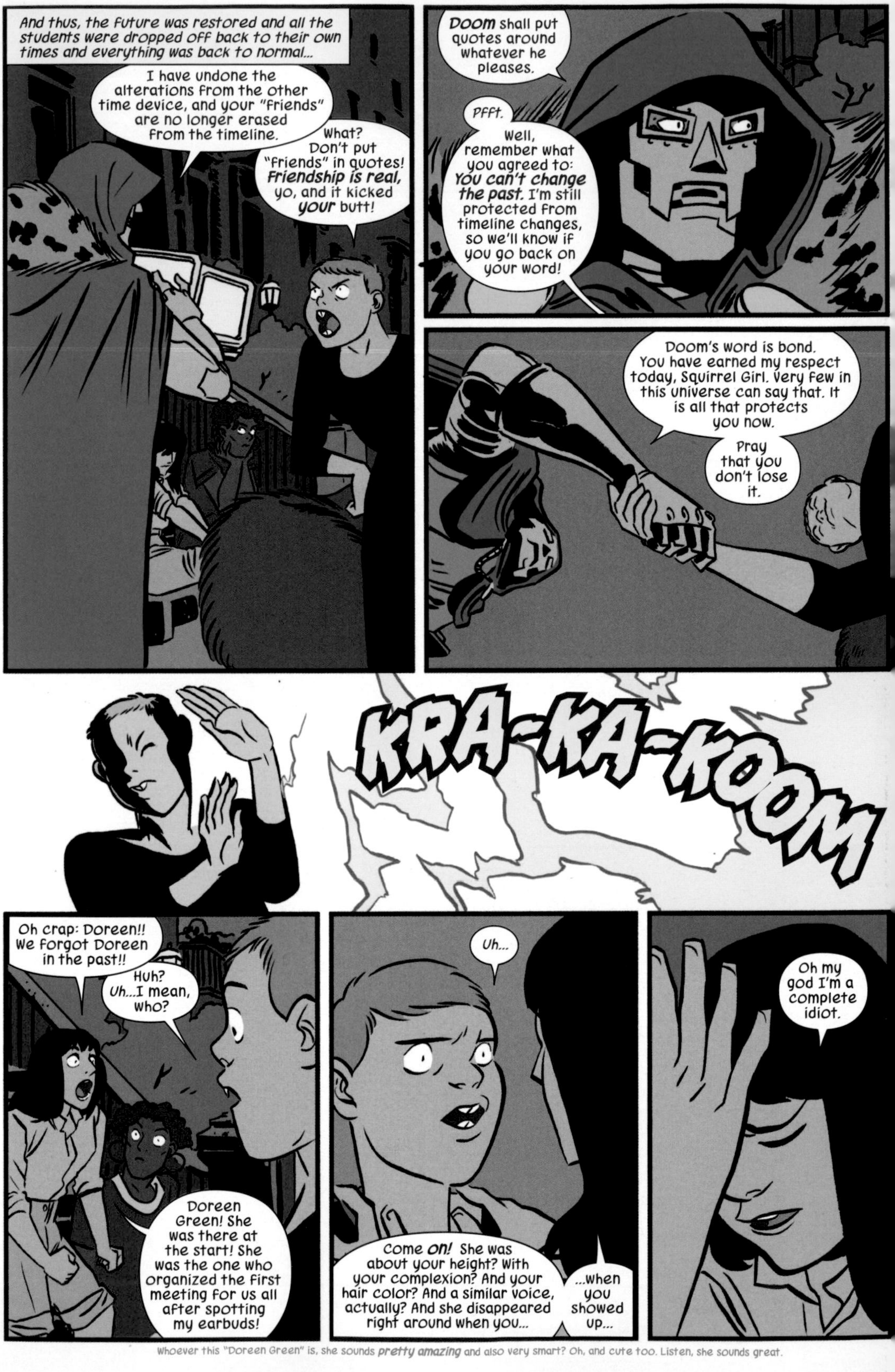
And thus, the future was restored and all the students were dropped off back to their own times and everything was back to normal...
I have undone the alterations from the other time device, and your "friends" are no longer erased from the timeline.
What? Don't put "friends" in quotes! Friendship is real, yo, and it kicked your butt!
Doom shall put quotes around whatever he pleases.
Pfft.
Well, remember what you agreed to: You can't change the past. I'm still protected from timeline changes, so we'll know if you go back on your word!
Doom's word is bond. You have earned my respect today, Squirrel Girl. Very few in this universe can say that. It is all that protects you now.
Pray that you don't lose it.
KRA-KA-KOOM
Oh crap: Doreen!! We forgot Doreen in the past!!
Huh? Uh...I mean, who?
Doreen Green! She was there at the start! She was the one who organized the first meeting for us all after spotting my earbuds!
Uh...
Come on! She was about your height? With your complexion? And your hair color? And a similar voice, actually? And she disappeared right around when you...
...when you showed up...
Oh my god I'm a complete idiot.

Whoever this "Doreen Green" is, she sounds *pretty amazing* and also very smart? Oh, and cute too. Listen, she sounds great.

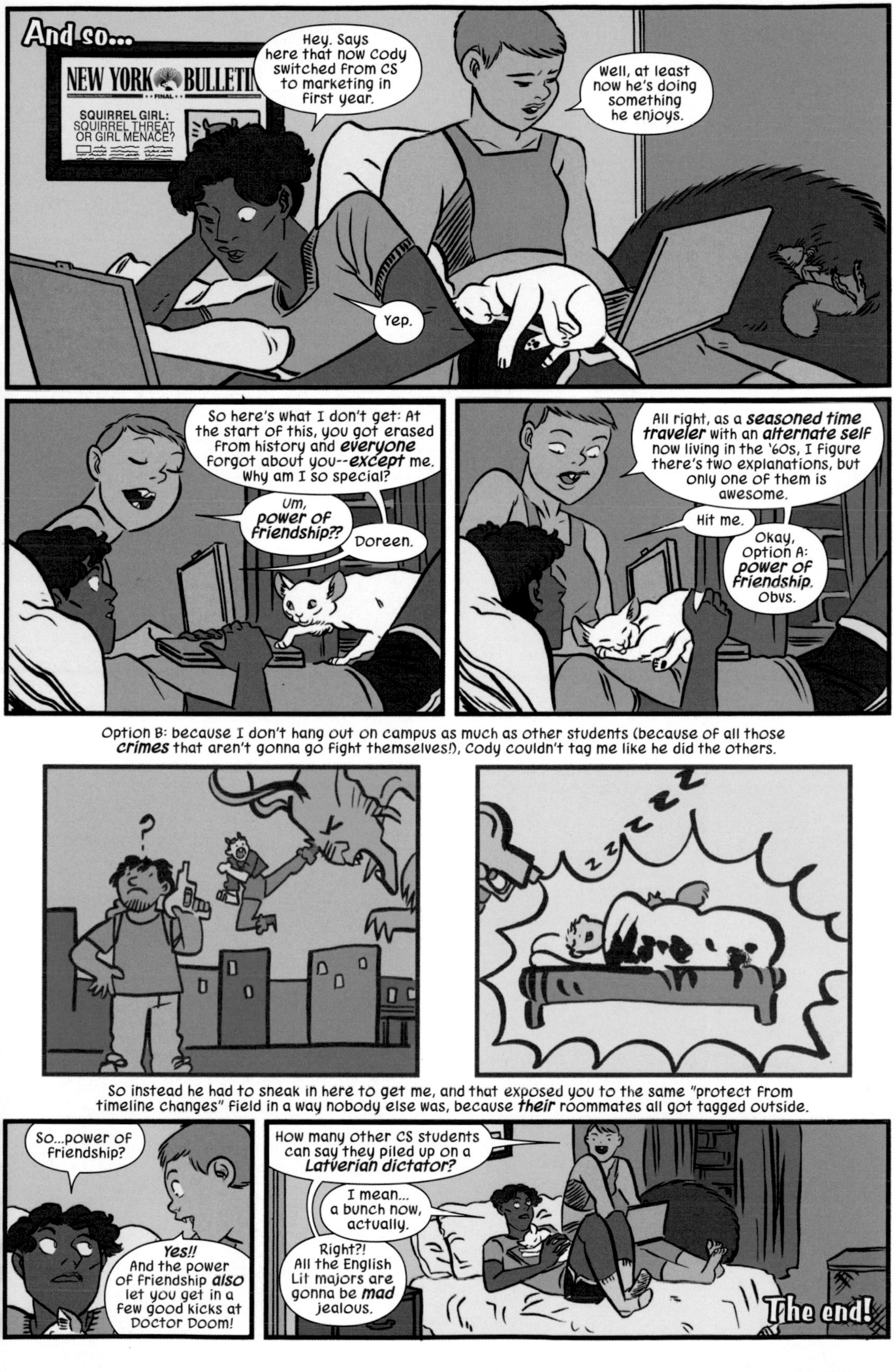
And so...
NEW YORK BULLETI
FINAL
SQUIRREL GIRL: SQUIRREL THREAT OR GIRL MENACE?
Hey. Says here that now Cody switched from CS to marketing in first year.
Well, at least now he's doing something he enjoys.
Yep.
So here's what I don't get: At the start of this, you got erased from history and *everyone* forgot about you--*except* me. Why am I so special?
Um, *power of friendship??*
Doreen.
All right, as a *seasoned time traveler* with an *alternate self* now living in the '60s, I figure there's two explanations, but only one of them is awesome.
Hit me.
Okay, Option A: *power of friendship.* Obvs.
Option B: because I don't hang out on campus as much as other students (because of all those *crimes* that aren't gonna go fight themselves!), Cody couldn't tag me like he did the others.
?
ZZZZZZ
So instead he had to sneak in here to get me, and that exposed you to the same "protect from timeline changes" field in a way nobody else was, because *their* roommates all got tagged outside.
So...power of friendship?
Yes!! And the power of friendship *also* let you get in a few good kicks at Doctor Doom!
How many other CS students can say they piled up on a *Latverian dictator?*
I mean... a bunch now, actually.
Right?! All the English Lit majors are gonna be *mad* jealous.
The end!

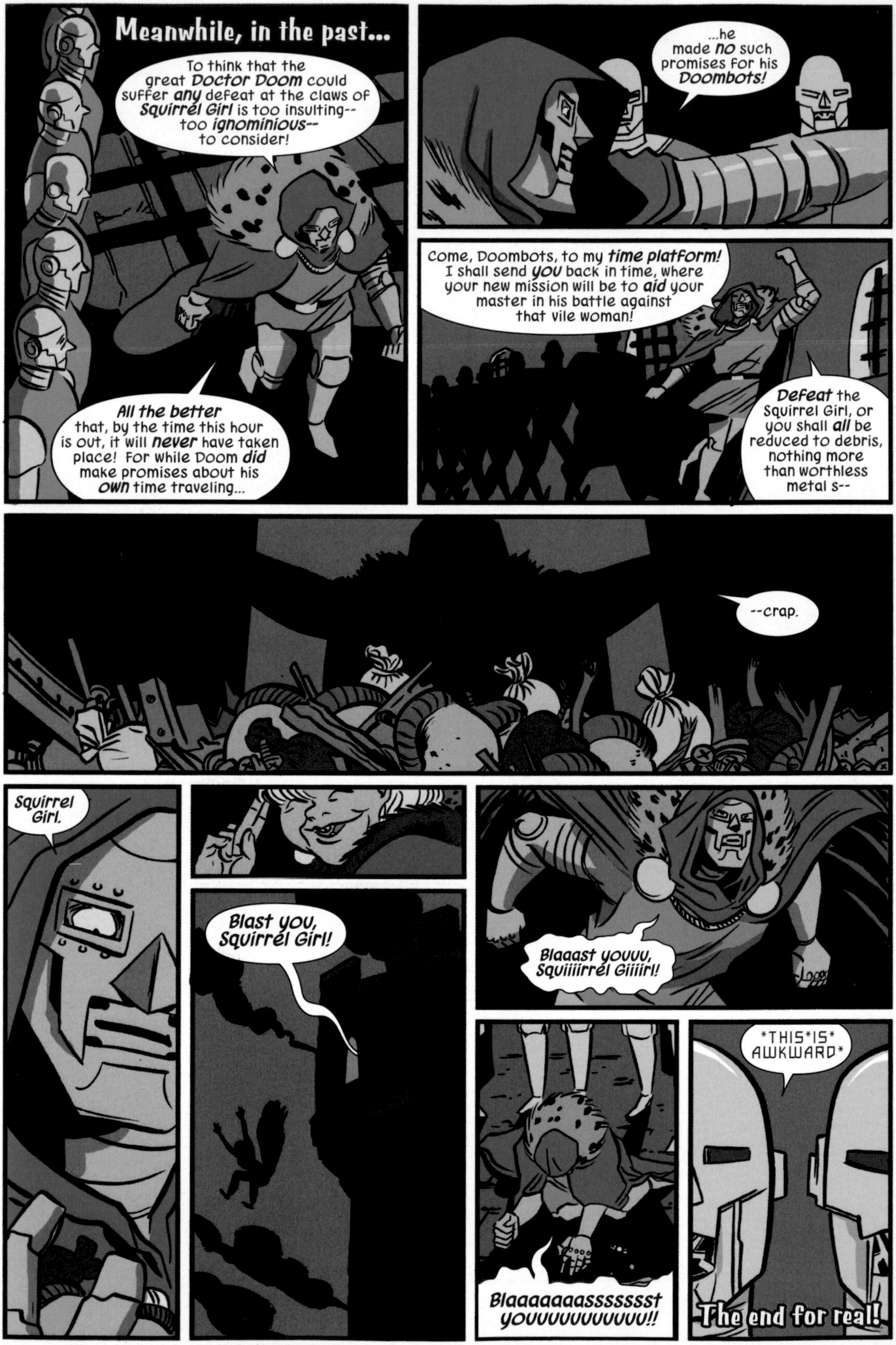
Meanwhile, in the past...
To think that the great Doctor Doom could suffer any defeat at the claws of Squirrel Girl is too insulting-- too ignominious-- to consider!
All the better that, by the time this hour is out, it will never have taken place! For while Doom did make promises about his own time traveling...
...he made no such promises for his Doombots!
Come, Doombots, to my time platform! I shall send you back in time, where your new mission will be to aid your master in his battle against that vile woman!
Defeat the Squirrel Girl, or you shall all be reduced to debris, nothing more than worthless metal s--
--crap.
Squirrel Girl.
Blast you, Squirrel Girl!
Blaaast youuu, Squiiiirrel Giiiirl!
Blaaaaaaassssssst youuuuuuuuuuu!!
*THIS*IS* AWKWARD*
The end for real!

Afterwards Old Lady Squirrel Girl lived happily ever after until she eventually died of old age, which is a pretty good way to go, assuming you have to.
And in her will she left the time blaster to Cody, so everything would work out as it was supposed to! *Oh snap she was the weird aunt all along, oh snap!!*

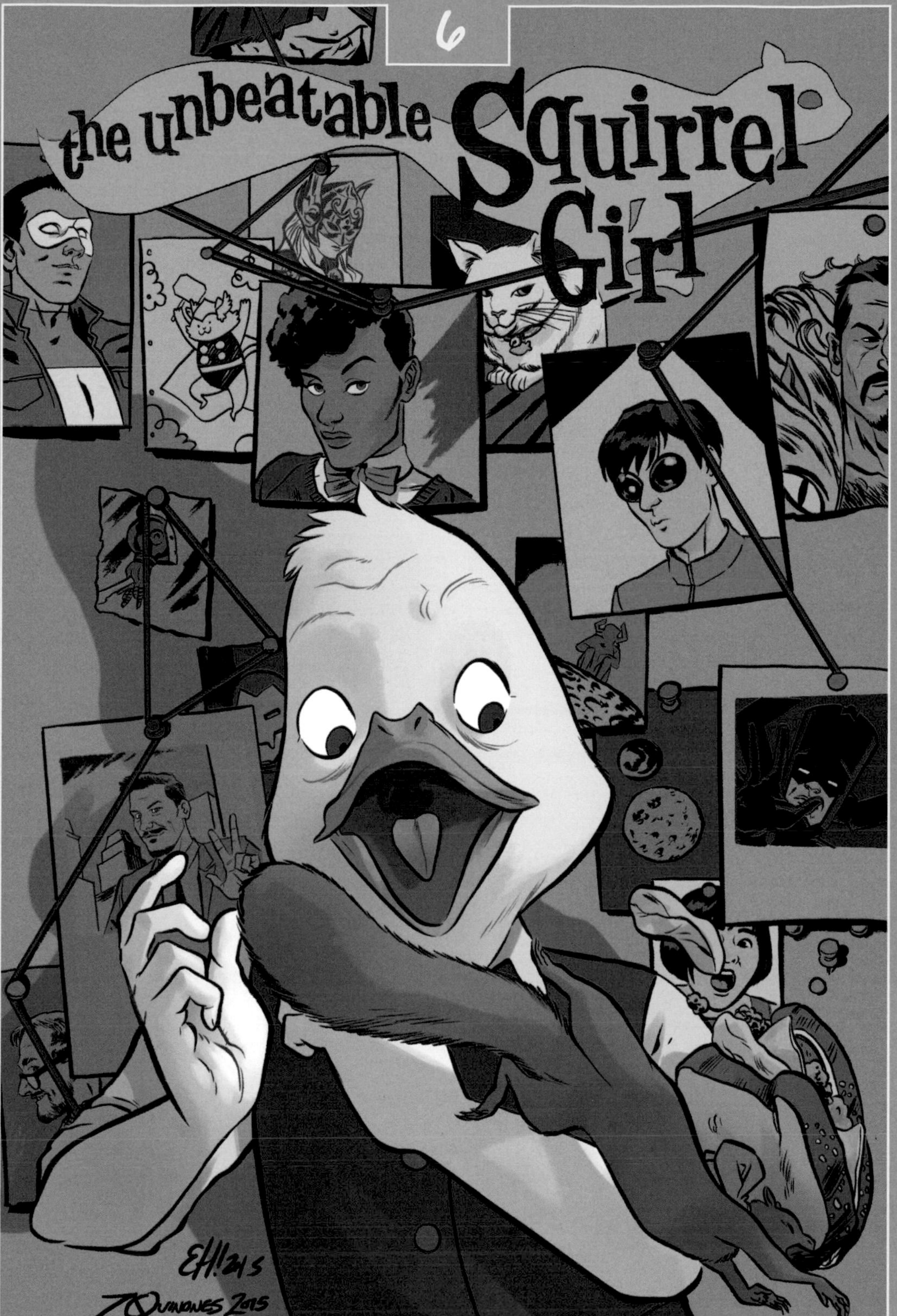
6
the unbeatable Squirrel Girl
EH!2015
JQuinones 2015

Doreen Green isn't just a first-year computer science student: she secretly also has all the powers of both squirrel and girl!
She uses her amazing abilities to fight crime **and** be as awesome as possible. You know her as...**The Unbeatable Squirrel Girl!**
Let's catch up with what she's been up to until now, with...

Squirrel Girl *in a nutshell*

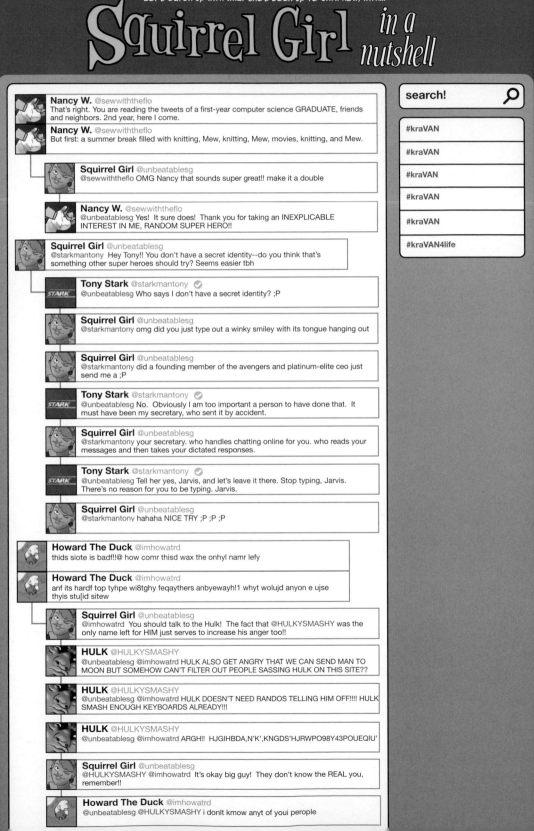

search!

#kraVAN

#kraVAN

#kraVAN

#kraVAN

#kraVAN

#kraVAN4life

Nancy W. @sewwiththeflo
That's right. You are reading the tweets of a first-year computer science GRADUATE, friends and neighbors. 2nd year, here I come.

Nancy W. @sewwiththeflo
But first: a summer break filled with knitting, Mew, knitting, Mew, movies, knitting, and Mew.

Squirrel Girl @unbeatablesg
@sewwiththeflo OMG Nancy that sounds super great!! make it a double

Nancy W. @sewwiththeflo
@unbeatablesg Yes! It sure does! Thank you for taking an INEXPLICABLE INTEREST IN ME, RANDOM SUPER HERO!!

Squirrel Girl @unbeatablesg
@starkmantony Hey Tony!! You don't have a secret identity--do you think that's something other super heroes should try? Seems easier tbh

Tony Stark @starkmantony ✅
@unbeatablesg Who says I don't have a secret identity? ;P

Squirrel Girl @unbeatablesg
@starkmantony omg did you just type out a winky smiley with its tongue hanging out

Squirrel Girl @unbeatablesg
@starkmantony did a founding member of the avengers and platinum-elite ceo just send me a ;P

Tony Stark @starkmantony
@unbeatablesg No. Obviously I am too important a person to have done that. It must have been my secretary, who sent it by accident.

Squirrel Girl @unbeatablesg
@starkmantony your secretary. who handles chatting online for you. who reads your messages and then takes your dictated responses.

Tony Stark @starkmantony ✅
@unbeatablesg Tell her yes, Jarvis, and let's leave it there. Stop typing, Jarvis. There's no reason for you to be typing. Jarvis.

Squirrel Girl @unbeatablesg
@starkmantony hahaha NICE TRY ;P ;P ;P

Howard The Duck @imhowatrd
thids siote is badf!!@ how comr thisd wax the onhyl namr lefy

Howard The Duck @imhowatrd
anf its hardf top tyhpe wi8tghy feqaythers anbyewayh!1 whyt wolujd anyon e ujse thyis stu[id sitew

Squirrel Girl @unbeatablesg
@imhowatrd You should talk to the Hulk! The fact that @HULKYSMASHY was the only name left for HIM just serves to increase his anger too!!

HULK @HULKYSMASHY
@unbeatablesg @imhowatrd HULK ALSO GET ANGRY THAT WE CAN SEND MAN TO MOON BUT SOMEHOW CAN'T FILTER OUT PEOPLE SASSING HULK ON THIS SITE??

HULK @HULKYSMASHY
@unbeatablesg @imhowatrd HULK DOESN'T NEED RANDOS TELLING HIM OFF!!!! HULK SMASH ENOUGH KEYBOARDS ALREADY!!!

HULK @HULKYSMASHY
@unbeatablesg @imhowatrd ARGH!! HJGIHBDA,N'K',KNGDS'HJRWPO98Y43POUEQIU'

Squirrel Girl @unbeatablesg
@HULKYSMASHY @imhowatrd It's okay big guy! They don't know the REAL you, remember!!

Howard The Duck @imhowatrd
@unbeatablesg @HULKYSMASHY i donlt kmow anyt of youi perople

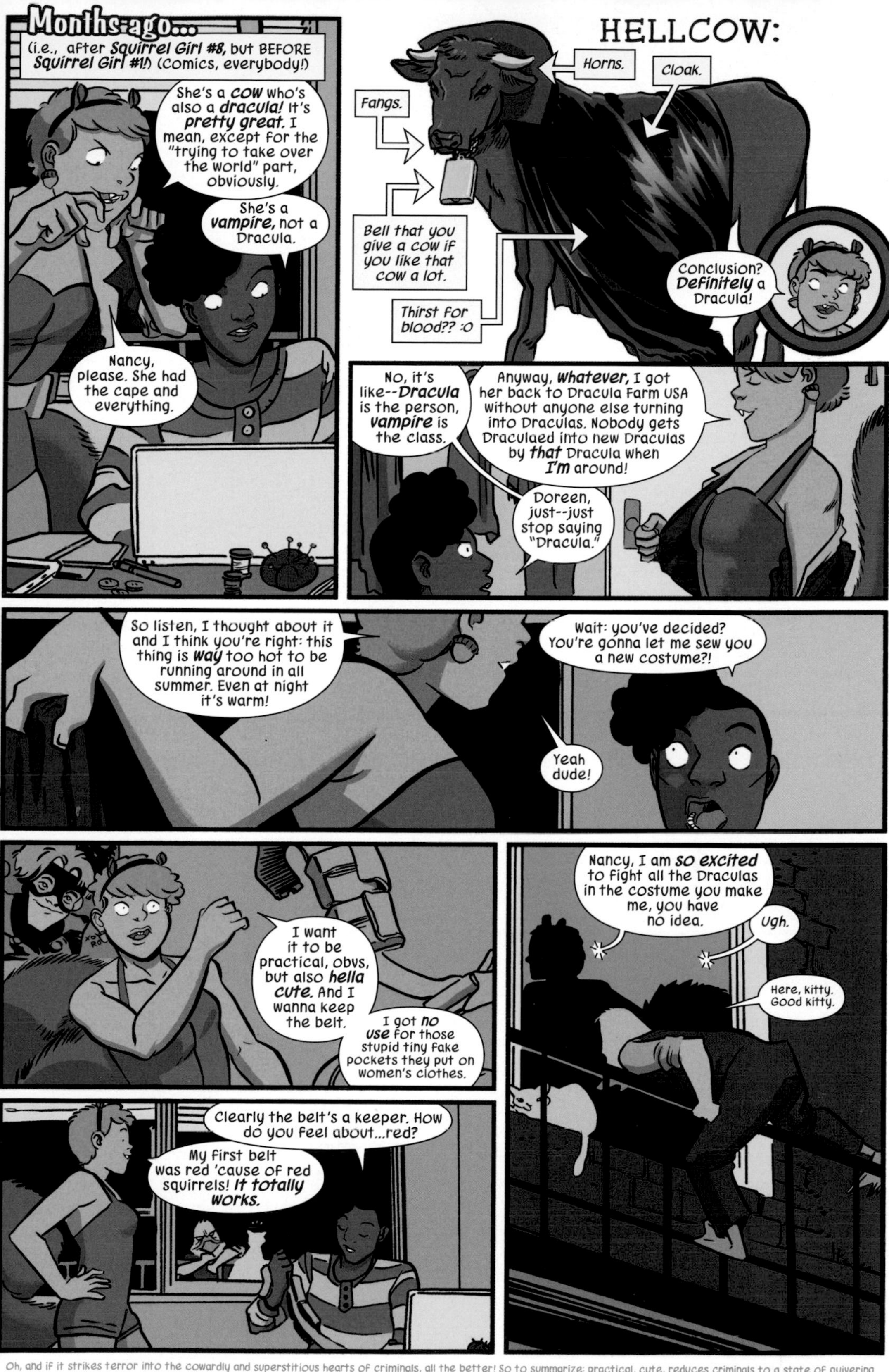
Months ago...
(i.e., after Squirrel Girl #8, but BEFORE Squirrel Girl #1!) (Comics, everybody!)
She's a COW who's also a dracula! It's pretty great. I mean, except for the "trying to take over the world" part, obviously.
She's a vampire, not a Dracula.
Nancy, please. She had the cape and everything.
HELLCOW:
Horns.
Cloak.
Fangs.
Bell that you give a cow if you like that cow a lot.
Thirst for blood?? :0
Conclusion? Definitely a Dracula!
No, it's like--Dracula is the person, vampire is the class.
Anyway, whatever, I got her back to Dracula Farm USA without anyone else turning into Draculas. Nobody gets Draculaed into new Draculas by that Dracula when I'm around!
Doreen, just--just stop saying "Dracula."
So listen, I thought about it and I think you're right: this thing is way too hot to be running around in all summer. Even at night it's warm!
Wait: you've decided? You're gonna let me sew you a new costume?!
Yeah dude!
I want it to be practical, obvs, but also hella cute. And I wanna keep the belt.
I got no use for those stupid tiny fake pockets they put on women's clothes.
Nancy, I am so excited to fight all the Draculas in the costume you make me, you have no idea.
Ugh.
Here, kitty. Good kitty.
Clearly the belt's a keeper. How do you feel about...red?
My first belt was red 'cause of red squirrels! It totally works.

Oh, and if it strikes terror into the cowardly and superstitious hearts of criminals, all the better! So to summarize: practical, cute, reduces criminals to a state of quivering and abject terror, useful pockets and/or belt. Got it, Chip?

Is this...do you do this in every issue? Does Marvel pay more for these?

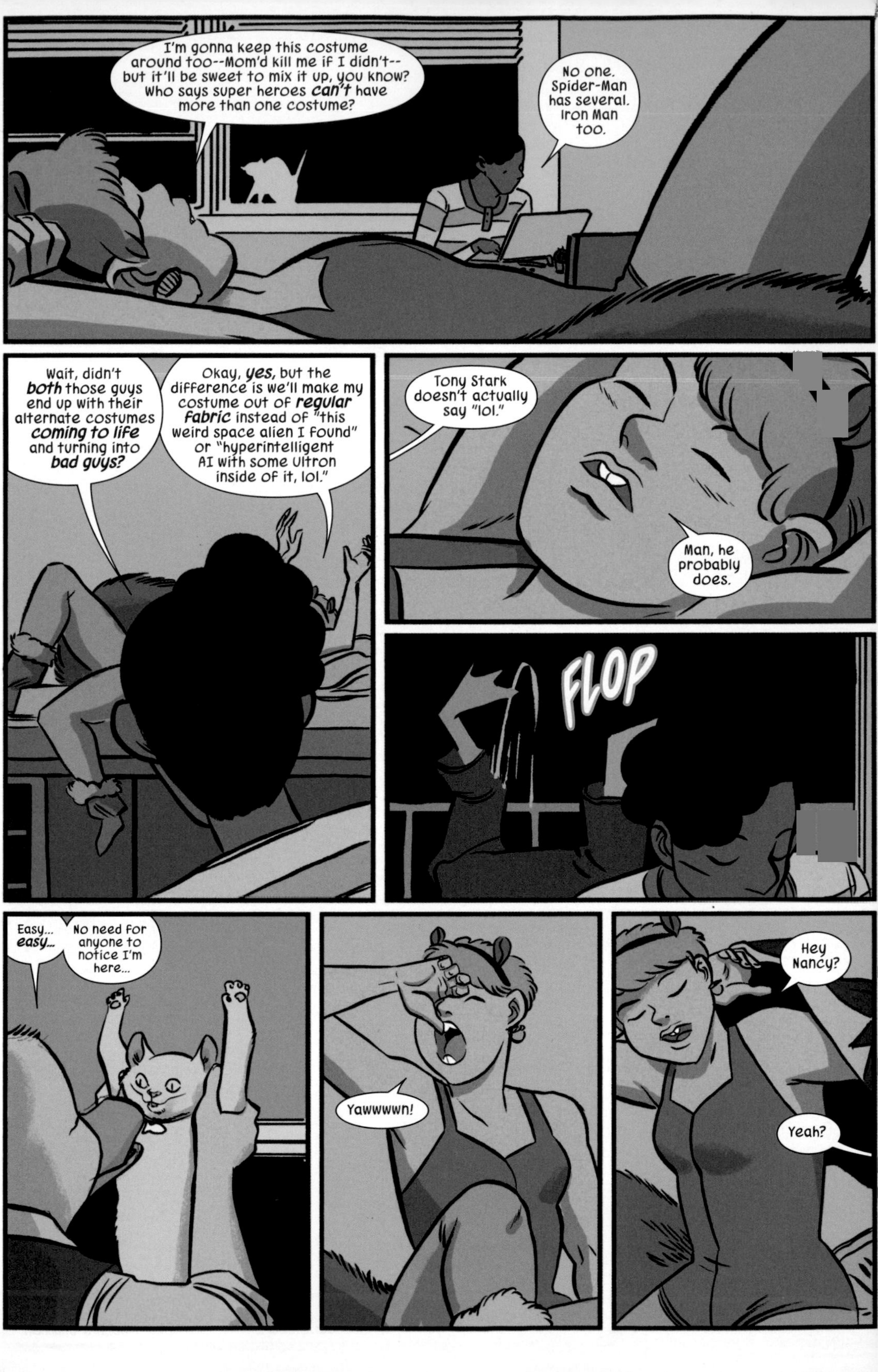
I'm gonna keep this costume around too--Mom'd kill me if I didn't--but it'll be sweet to mix it up, you know? Who says super heroes *can't* have more than one costume?
No one. Spider-Man has several. Iron Man too.
Wait, didn't **both** those guys end up with their alternate costumes **coming to life** and turning into **bad guys?**
Okay, **yes,** but the difference is we'll make my costume out of **regular fabric** instead of "this weird space alien I found" or "hyperintelligent AI with some Ultron inside of it, lol."
Tony Stark doesn't actually say "lol."
Man, he probably does.
FLOP
Easy... *easy...*
No need for anyone to notice I'm here...
Yawwwwn!
Hey Nancy?
Yeah?

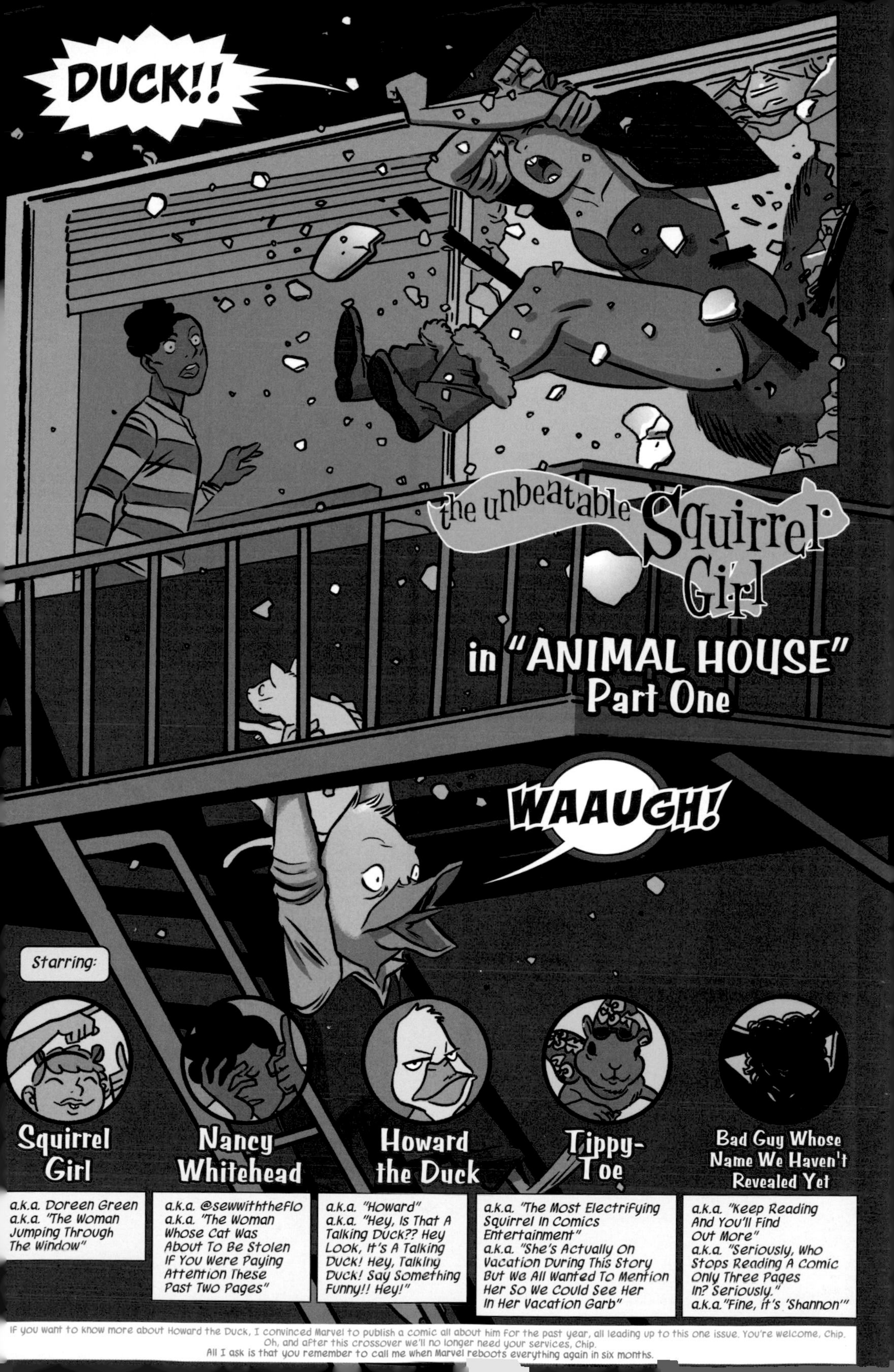
DUCK!!
the unbeatable Squirrel Girl
in "ANIMAL HOUSE" Part One
WAAUGH!
Starring:
Squirrel Girl
a.k.a. Doreen Green
a.k.a. "The Woman Jumping Through The Window"
Nancy Whitehead
a.k.a. @sewwiththeflo
a.k.a. "The Woman Whose Cat Was About To Be Stolen If You Were Paying Attention These Past Two Pages"
Howard the Duck
a.k.a. "Howard"
a.k.a. "Hey, Is That A Talking Duck?? Hey Look, It's A Talking Duck! Hey, Talking Duck! Say Something Funny!! Hey!"
Tippy-Toe
a.k.a. "The Most Electrifying Squirrel In Comics Entertainment"
a.k.a. "She's Actually On Vacation During This Story But We All Wanted To Mention Her So We Could See Her In Her Vacation Garb"
Bad Guy Whose Name We Haven't Revealed Yet
a.k.a. "Keep Reading And You'll Find Out More"
a.k.a. "Seriously, Who Stops Reading A Comic Only Three Pages In? Seriously."
a.k.a. "Fine, it's 'Shannon'"
If you want to know more about Howard the Duck, I convinced Marvel to publish a comic all about him for the past year, all leading up to this one issue. You're welcome, Chip.
Oh, and after this crossover we'll no longer need your services, Chip.
All I ask is that you remember to call me when Marvel reboots everything again in six months.

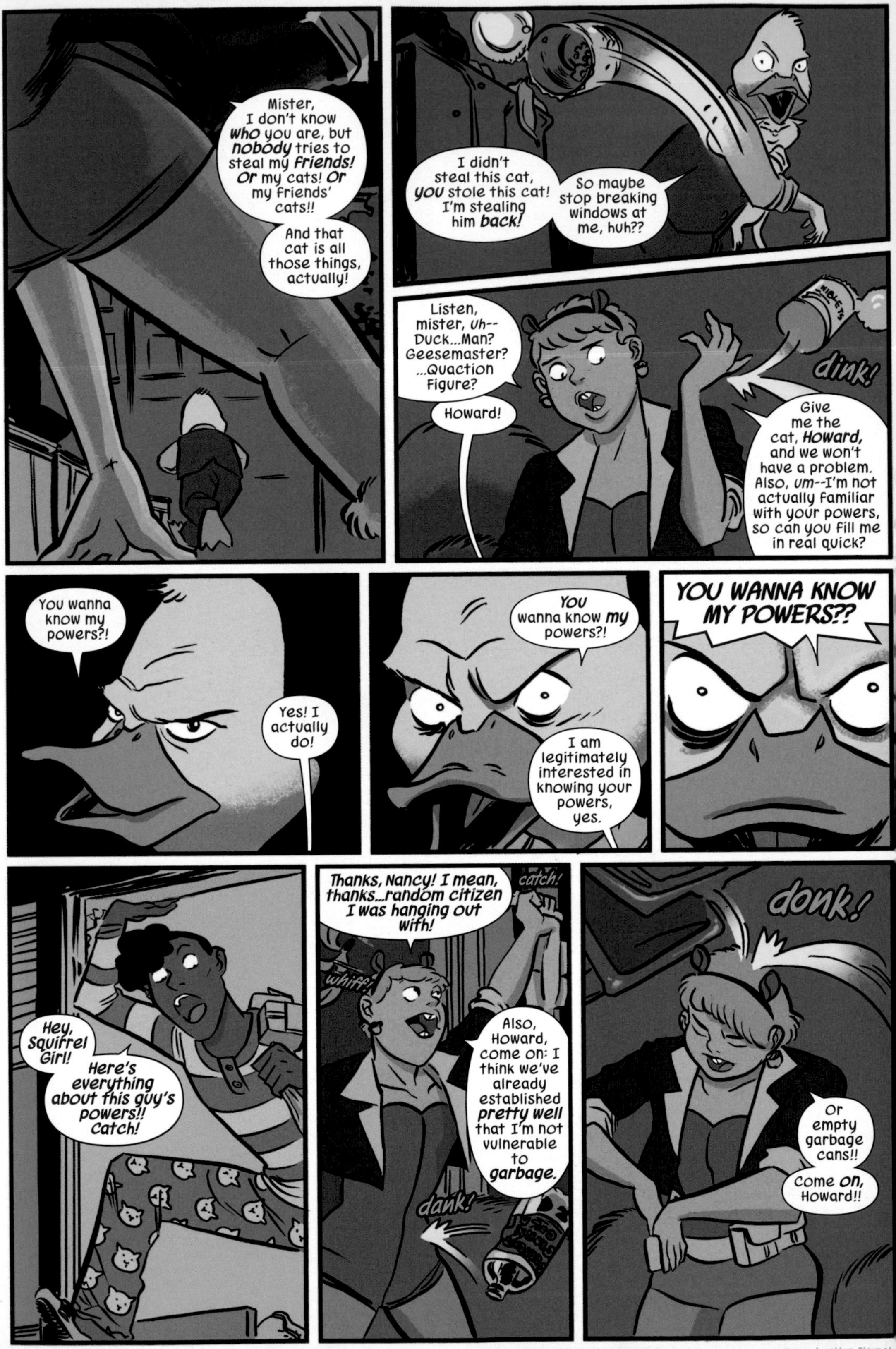

Mister, I don't know *who* you are, but *nobody* tries to steal my *friends!* *Or* my cats! *Or* my friends' cats!!
And that cat is all those things, actually!
I didn't steal this cat, *you* stole this cat! I'm stealing him *back!*
So maybe stop breaking windows at me, huh??
Listen, mister, *uh*-- Duck...Man? Geesemaster? ...Quaction Figure?
Howard!
dink!
Give me the cat, *Howard,* and we won't have a problem. Also, *um*--I'm not actually familiar with your powers, so can you fill me in real quick?
You wanna know my powers?!
Yes! I actually do!
You wanna know *my* powers?!
I am legitimately interested in knowing your powers, yes.
YOU WANNA KNOW MY POWERS??
Hey, Squirrel Girl! Here's everything about this guy's powers!! Catch!
Thanks, Nancy! I mean, thanks...random citizen I was hanging out with!
catch!
whiff!
Also, Howard, come on: I think we've already established *pretty well* that I'm not vulnerable to *garbage.*
dank!
donk!
Or empty garbage cans!!
Come *on,* Howard!!

If they ever make a Howard the Duck figure and it doesn't say "Quaction Figure" on it somewhere, I'll be...still pretty happy actually, because come on: Howard action figure!
I hate paying the same amount for an action figure that's half the size of a normal figure. Can we make it two Howard figures in a trenchcoat?

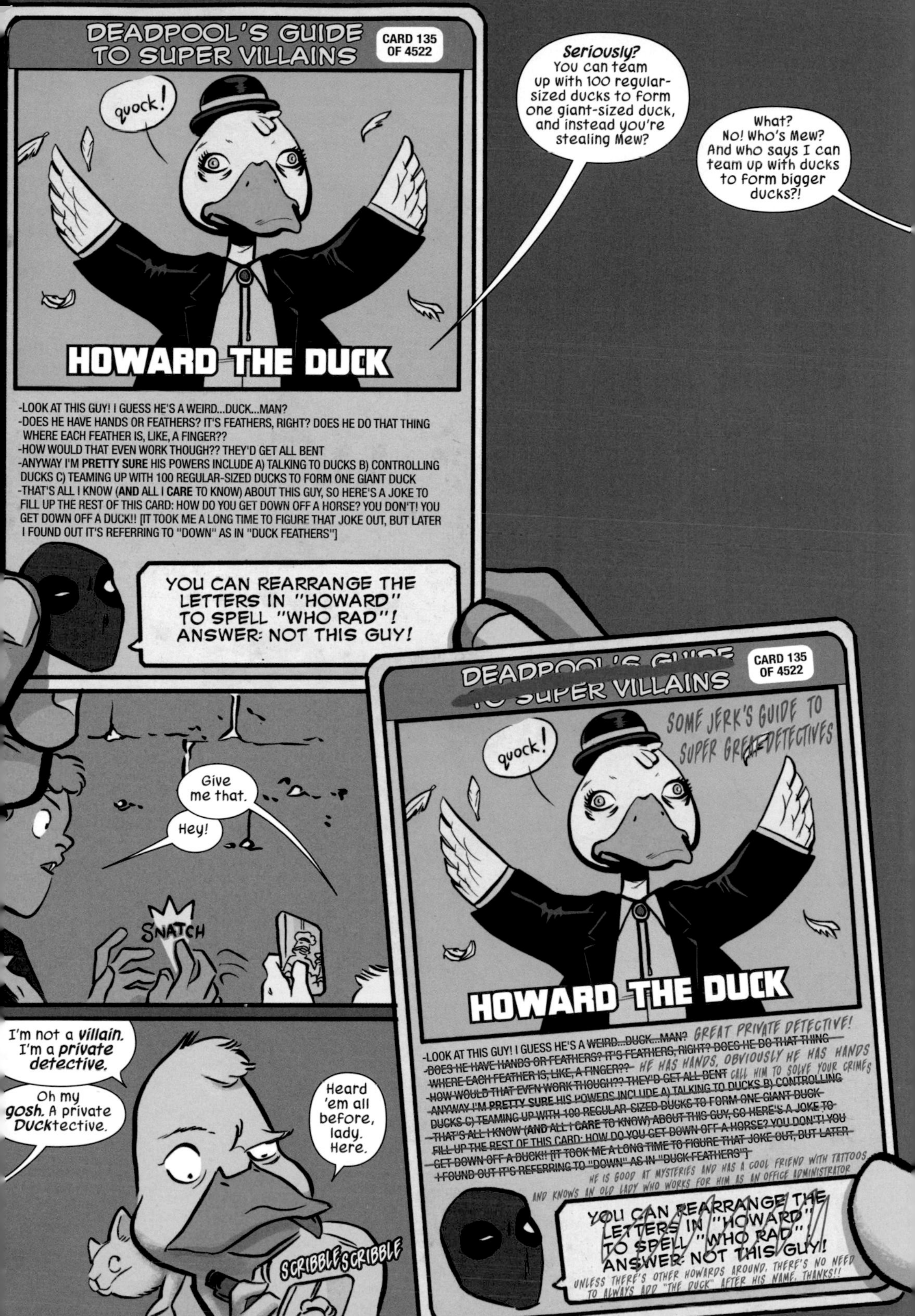
DEADPOOL'S GUIDE TO SUPER VILLAINS
CARD 135 OF 4522
quock!
HOWARD THE DUCK
-LOOK AT THIS GUY! I GUESS HE'S A WEIRD...DUCK...MAN?
-DOES HE HAVE HANDS OR FEATHERS? IT'S FEATHERS, RIGHT? DOES HE DO THAT THING WHERE EACH FEATHER IS, LIKE, A FINGER??
-HOW WOULD THAT EVEN WORK THOUGH?? THEY'D GET ALL BENT
-ANYWAY I'M PRETTY SURE HIS POWERS INCLUDE A) TALKING TO DUCKS B) CONTROLLING DUCKS C) TEAMING UP WITH 100 REGULAR-SIZED DUCKS TO FORM ONE GIANT DUCK
-THAT'S ALL I KNOW (AND ALL I CARE TO KNOW) ABOUT THIS GUY, SO HERE'S A JOKE TO FILL UP THE REST OF THIS CARD: HOW DO YOU GET DOWN OFF A HORSE? YOU DON'T! YOU GET DOWN OFF A DUCK!! [IT TOOK ME A LONG TIME TO FIGURE THAT JOKE OUT, BUT LATER I FOUND OUT IT'S REFERRING TO "DOWN" AS IN "DUCK FEATHERS"]
YOU CAN REARRANGE THE LETTERS IN "HOWARD" TO SPELL "WHO RAD"! ANSWER: NOT THIS GUY!
Seriously? You can team up with 100 regular-sized ducks to form one giant-sized duck, and instead you're stealing Mew?
What? No! Who's Mew? And who says I can team up with ducks to form bigger ducks?!
Give me that.
Hey!
SNATCH
I'm not a villain. I'm a private detective.
Oh my gosh. A private Ducktective.
Heard 'em all before, lady. Here.
SCRIBBLE SCRIBBLE
DEADPOOL'S GUIDE TO SUPER VILLAINS
CARD 135 OF 4522
SOME JERK'S GUIDE TO SUPER GREAT DETECTIVES
quock!
HOWARD THE DUCK
-LOOK AT THIS GUY! I GUESS HE'S A ~~WEIRD...DUCK...MAN?~~ GREAT PRIVATE DETECTIVE!
~~-DOES HE HAVE HANDS OR FEATHERS? IT'S FEATHERS, RIGHT? DOES HE DO THAT THING WHERE EACH FEATHER IS, LIKE, A FINGER??~~ HE HAS HANDS, OBVIOUSLY HE HAS HANDS
~~-HOW WOULD THAT EVEN WORK THOUGH?? THEY'D GET ALL BENT~~ CALL HIM TO SOLVE YOUR CRIMES
~~-ANYWAY I'M PRETTY SURE HIS POWERS INCLUDE A) TALKING TO DUCKS B) CONTROLLING DUCKS C) TEAMING UP WITH 100 REGULAR-SIZED DUCKS TO FORM ONE GIANT DUCK~~
~~-THAT'S ALL I KNOW (AND ALL I CARE TO KNOW) ABOUT THIS GUY, SO HERE'S A JOKE TO FILL UP THE REST OF THIS CARD: HOW DO YOU GET DOWN OFF A HORSE? YOU DON'T! YOU GET DOWN OFF A DUCK!! [IT TOOK ME A LONG TIME TO FIGURE THAT JOKE OUT, BUT LATER I FOUND OUT IT'S REFERRING TO "DOWN" AS IN "DUCK FEATHERS"]~~
HE IS GOOD AT MYSTERIES AND HAS A COOL FRIEND WITH TATTOOS AND KNOWS AN OLD LADY WHO WORKS FOR HIM AS AN OFFICE ADMINISTRATOR
~~YOU CAN REARRANGE THE LETTERS IN "HOWARD" TO SPELL "WHO RAD"! ANSWER: NOT THIS GUY!~~
UNLESS THERE'S OTHER HOWARDS AROUND, THERE'S NO NEED TO ALWAYS ADD "THE DUCK" AFTER HIS NAME, THANKS!!

you're wondering why Howard's card is number 135, 135 is the sum of 40 plus 34 plus 61, and those numbers make up an ASCII-art duck. ***OBSERVE:*** ("=

("= ((ha ha see what i did there ha ha

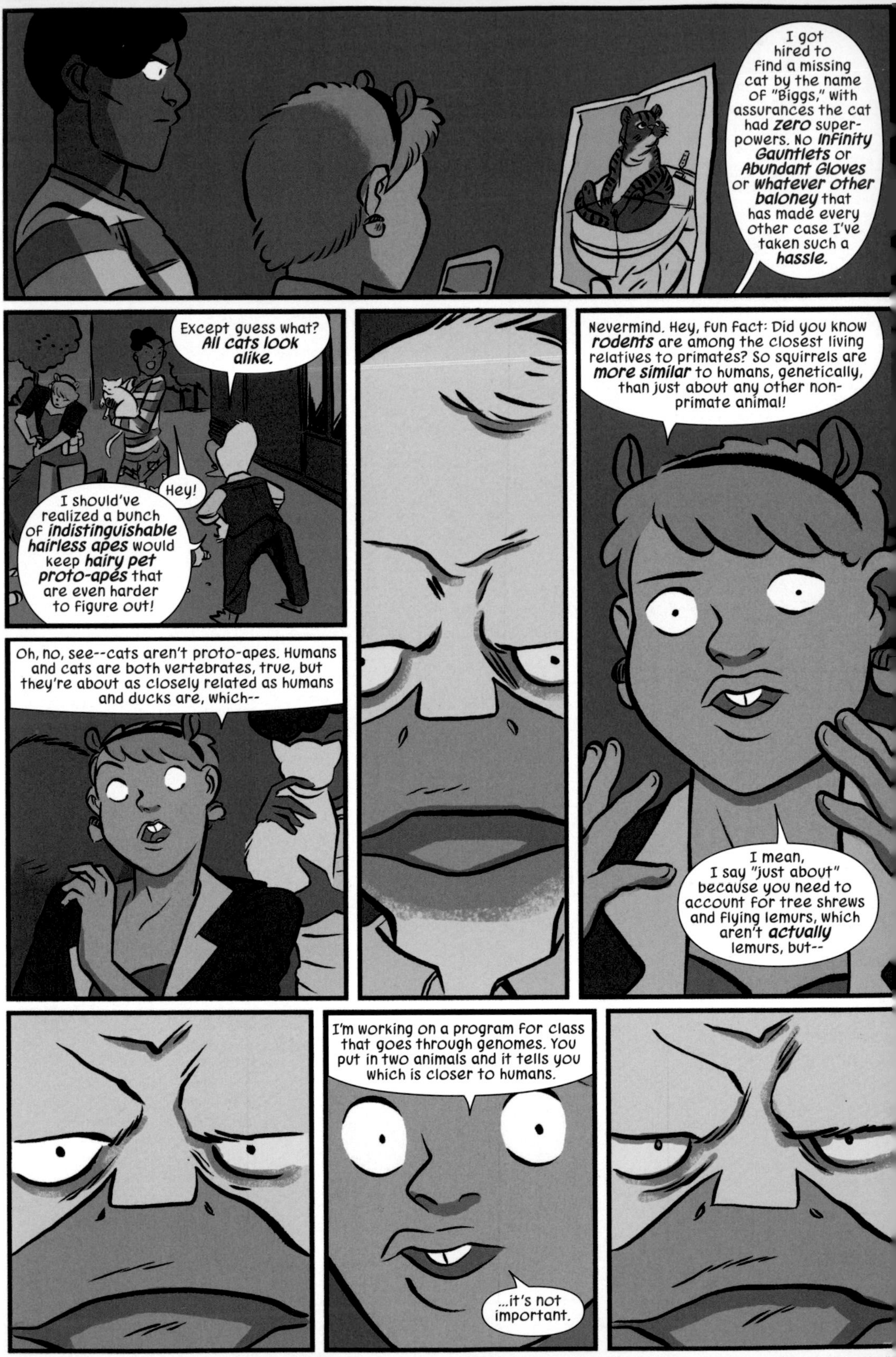

I got hired to find a missing cat by the name of "Biggs," with assurances the cat had zero super-powers. No Infinity Gauntlets or Abundant Gloves or whatever other baloney that has made every other case I've taken such a hassle.
Except guess what? All cats look alike.
Hey!
I should've realized a bunch of indistinguishable hairless apes would keep hairy pet proto-apes that are even harder to figure out!
Oh, no, see--cats aren't proto-apes. Humans and cats are both vertebrates, true, but they're about as closely related as humans and ducks are, which--
Nevermind. Hey, fun fact: Did you know rodents are among the closest living relatives to primates? So squirrels are more similar to humans, genetically, than just about any other non-primate animal!
I mean, I say "just about" because you need to account for tree shrews and flying lemurs, which aren't actually lemurs, but--
I'm working on a program for class that goes through genomes. You put in two animals and it tells you which is closer to humans.
...it's not important.

SCIENCE CORNER: Actually, humans and ducks diverged when mammals and birds did (pre-dinosaurs), but humans and cats diverged later as mammals diversified. So humans actuall share *more* genes with cats than they do with ducks. Sorry, Howard.

Um, ***actually,*** humans are ***very*** different from cats and ducks. Citation: my own eyes.

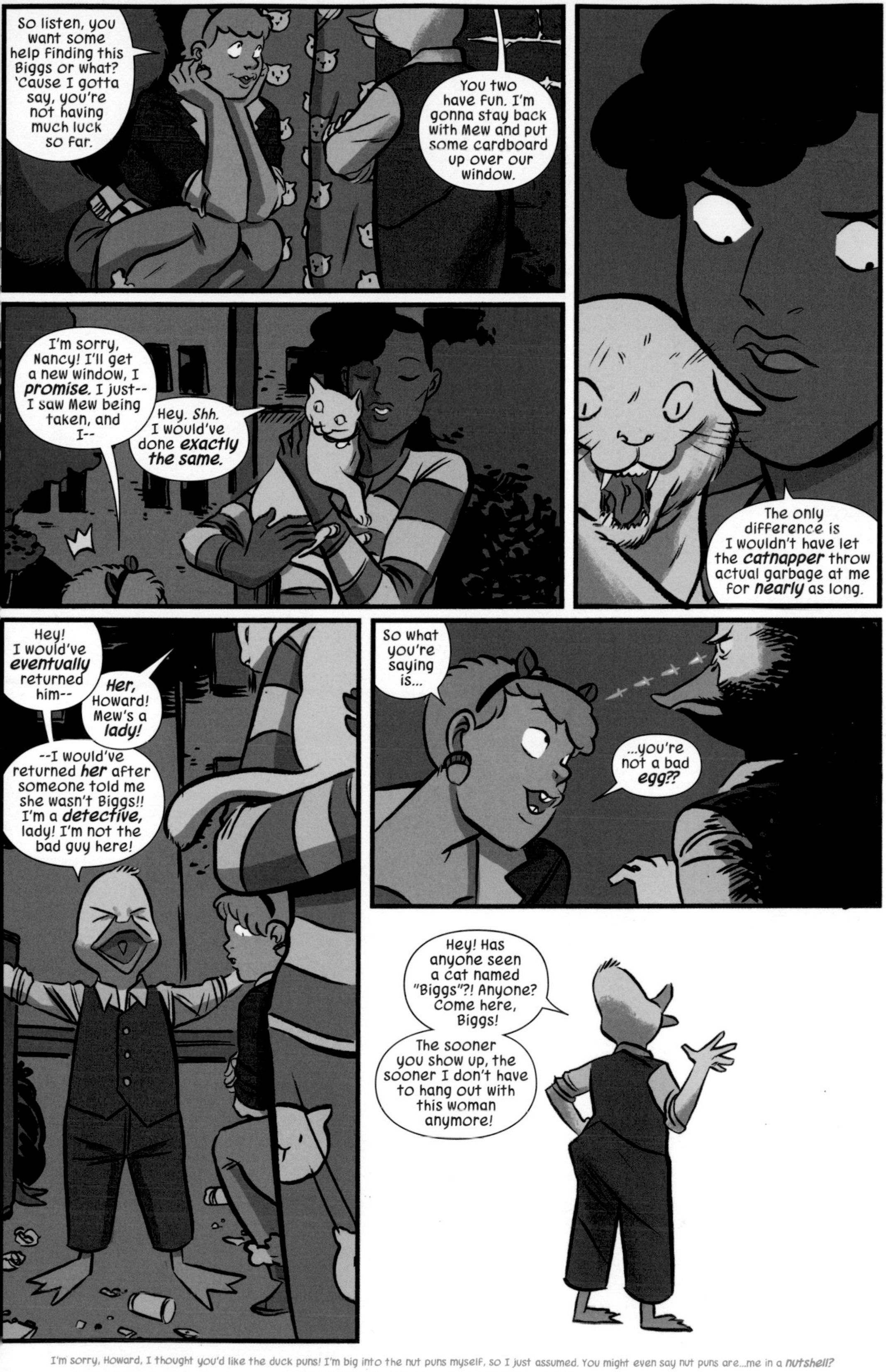
So listen, you want some help finding this Biggs or what? 'Cause I gotta say, you're not having much luck so far.
You two have fun. I'm gonna stay back with Mew and put some cardboard up over our window.
I'm sorry, Nancy! I'll get a new window, I *promise.* I just-- I saw Mew being taken, and I--
Hey. *Shh.* I would've done ***exactly the same.***
The only difference is I wouldn't have let the ***catnapper*** throw actual garbage at me for ***nearly*** as long.
Hey! I would've ***eventually*** returned him--
Her, Howard! Mew's a ***lady!***
--I would've returned ***her*** after someone told me she wasn't Biggs!! I'm a ***detective,*** lady! I'm not the bad guy here!
So what you're saying is...
...you're not a bad ***egg??***
Hey! Has anyone seen a cat named "Biggs"?! Anyone? Come here, Biggs!
The sooner you show up, the sooner I don't have to hang out with this woman anymore!

I'm sorry, Howard, I thought you'd like the duck puns! I'm big into the nut puns myself, so I just assumed. You might even say nut puns are...me in a ***nutshell?***
Ugh I didn't realize this was a crossover with the ***PUN****isher.*

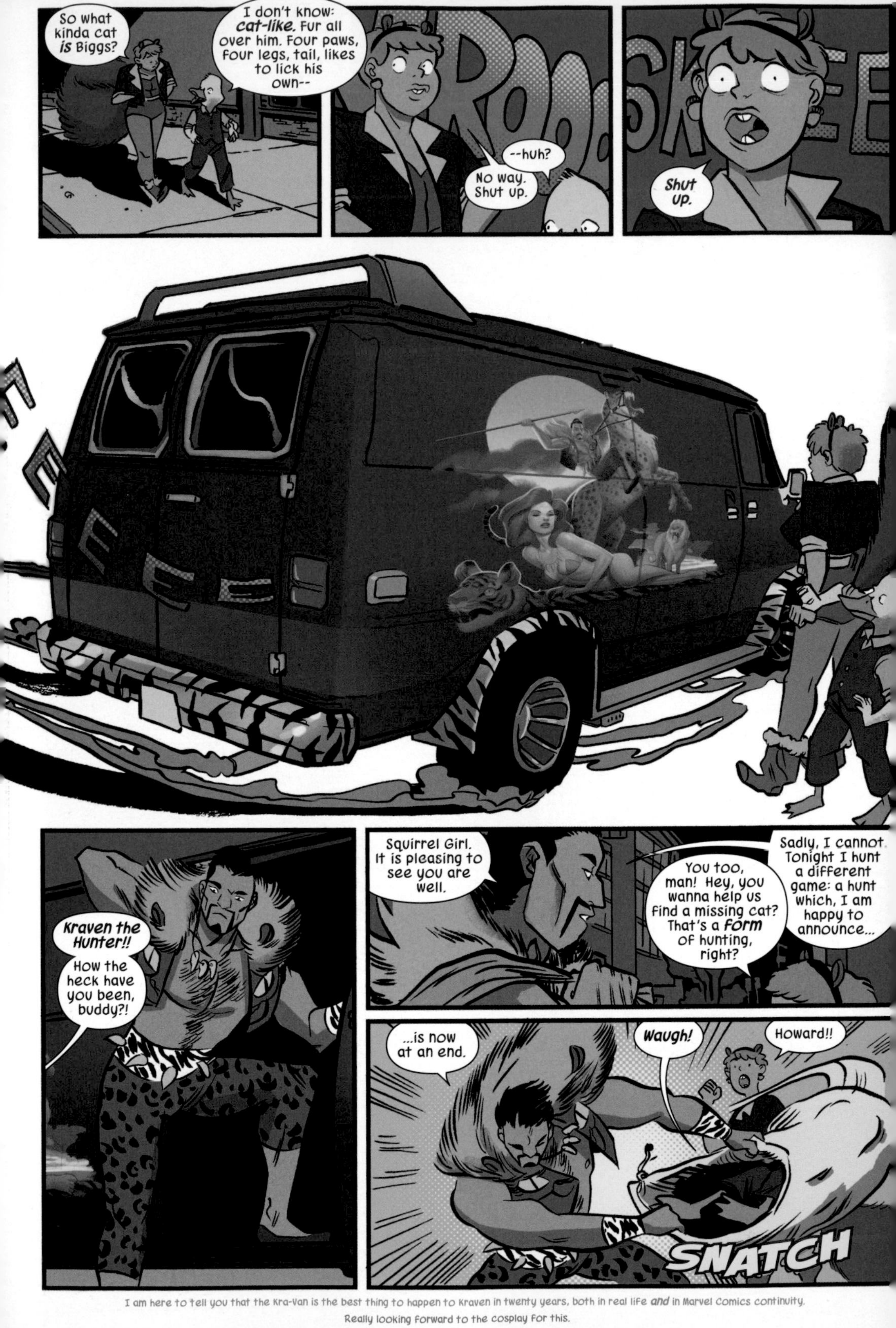
So what kinda cat *is* Biggs?
I don't know: *cat-like.* Fur all over him. Four paws, four legs, tail, likes to lick his own--
--huh?
No way. Shut up.
Shut up.
Kraven the Hunter!!
How the heck have you been, buddy?!
Squirrel Girl. It is pleasing to see you are well.
You too, man! Hey, you wanna help us find a missing cat? That's a *form* of hunting, right?
Sadly, I cannot. Tonight I hunt a different game: a hunt which, I am happy to announce...
...is now at an end.
Waugh!
Howard!!
SNATCH

I am here to tell you that the Kra-Van is the best thing to happen to Kraven in twenty years, both in real life *and* in Marvel Comics continuity. Really looking forward to the cosplay for this.

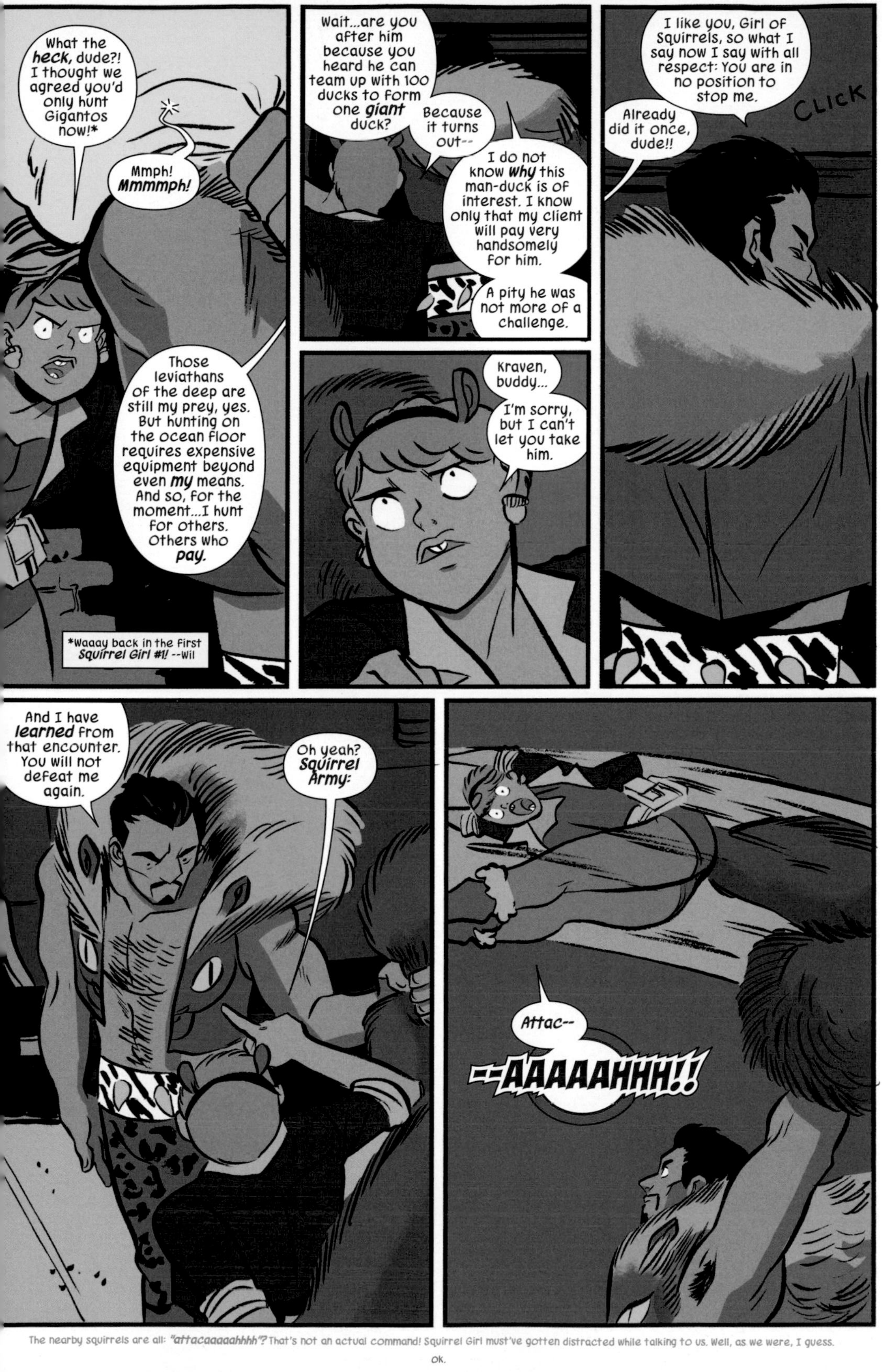
What the heck, dude?! I thought we agreed you'd only hunt Gigantos now!*
Mmph! Mmmmph!
Those leviathans of the deep are still my prey, yes. But hunting on the ocean floor requires expensive equipment beyond even my means. And so, for the moment...I hunt for others. Others who pay.
*Waaay back in the first Squirrel Girl #1! --Wil
Wait...are you after him because you heard he can team up with 100 ducks to form one giant duck?
Because it turns out--
I do not know why this man-duck is of interest. I know only that my client will pay very handsomely for him.
A pity he was not more of a challenge.
Kraven, buddy...
I'm sorry, but I can't let you take him.
I like you, Girl of Squirrels, so what I say now I say with all respect: You are in no position to stop me.
CLICK
Already did it once, dude!!
And I have learned from that encounter. You will not defeat me again.
Oh yeah? Squirrel Army:
Attac--
--AAAAAHHH!!

The nearby squirrels are all: *"attacaaaaahhhh"?* That's not an actual command! Squirrel Girl must've gotten distracted while talking to us. Well, as we were, I guess.

ok.

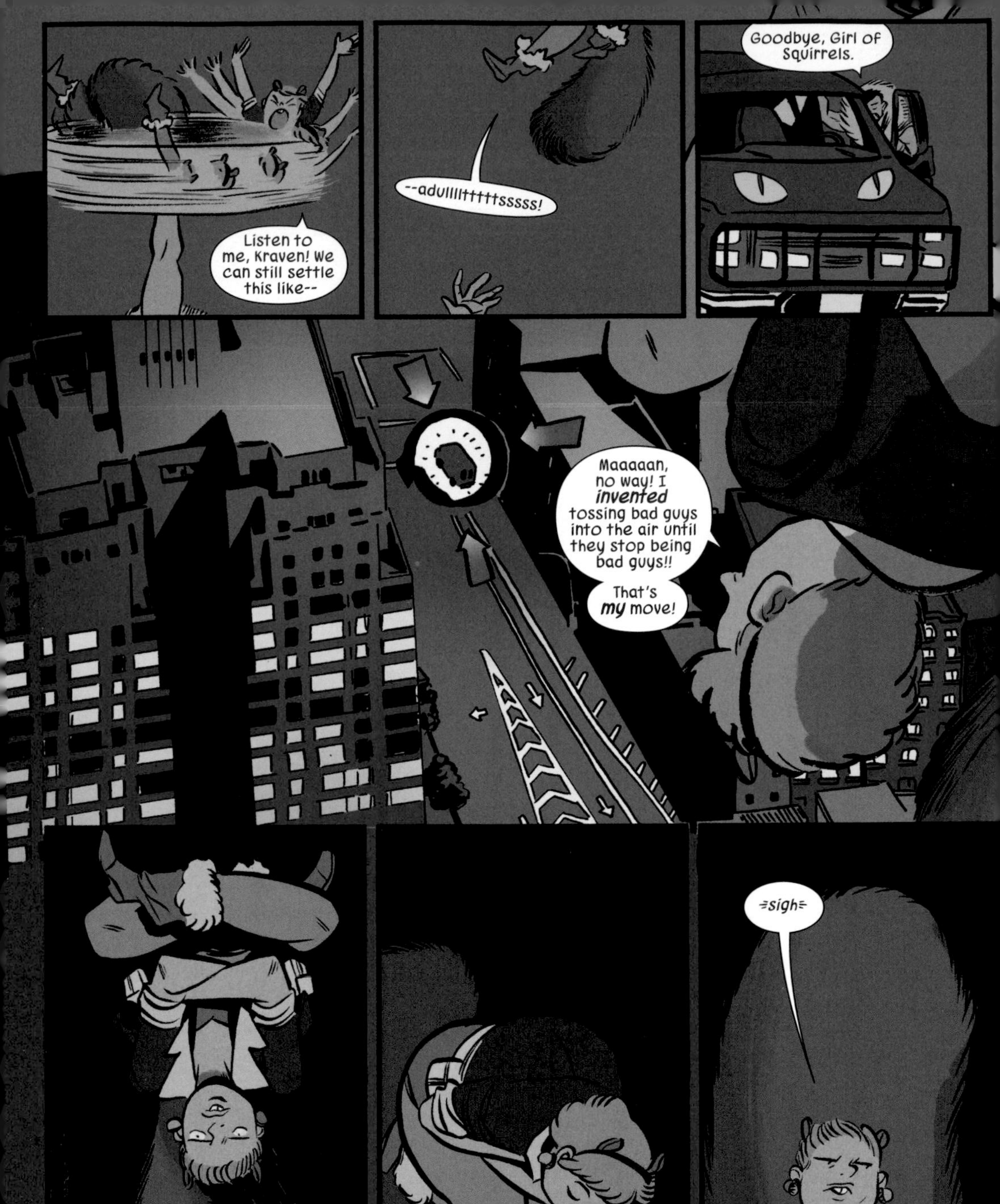
Listen to me, Kraven! We can still settle this like--
--adulllltttttsssss!
Goodbye, Girl of Squirrels.
Maaaaan, no way! I invented tossing bad guys into the air until they stop being bad guys!!
That's my move!
=sigh=

Huh! So ***that's*** what that feels like!

I would be so conflicted, 'cause I'm in a battle, but being tossed into the air would be so much fun!

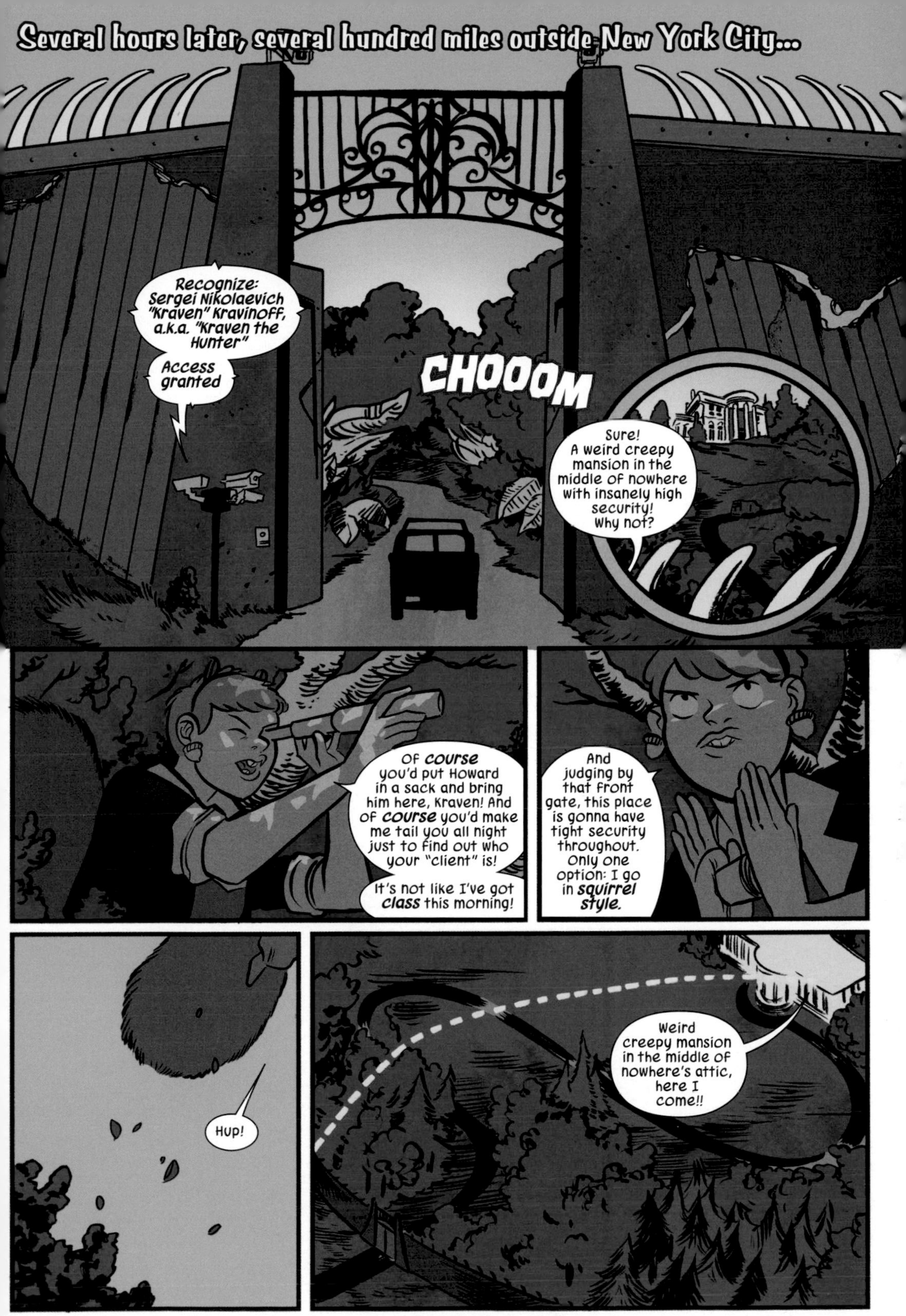
Several hours later, several hundred miles outside New York City...
Recognize: Sergei Nikolaevich "Kraven" Kravinoff, a.k.a. "Kraven the Hunter"
Access granted
CHOOOM
Sure! A weird creepy mansion in the middle of nowhere with insanely high security! Why not?
Of *course* you'd put Howard in a sack and bring him here, Kraven! And of *course* you'd make me tail you all night just to find out who your "client" is!
It's not like I've got *class* this morning!
And judging by that front gate, this place is gonna have tight security throughout. Only one option: I go in *squirrel style.*
Hup!
Weird creepy mansion in the middle of nowhere's attic, here I come!!

I'm worried about Doreen Green missing class too, but don't worry: she reads ahead, so when she has to miss class like this, she doesn't fall too far behind. Thanks, Doreen! Now we can all enjoy the rest of this comic without worrying.

Hm. I heard she just skims.

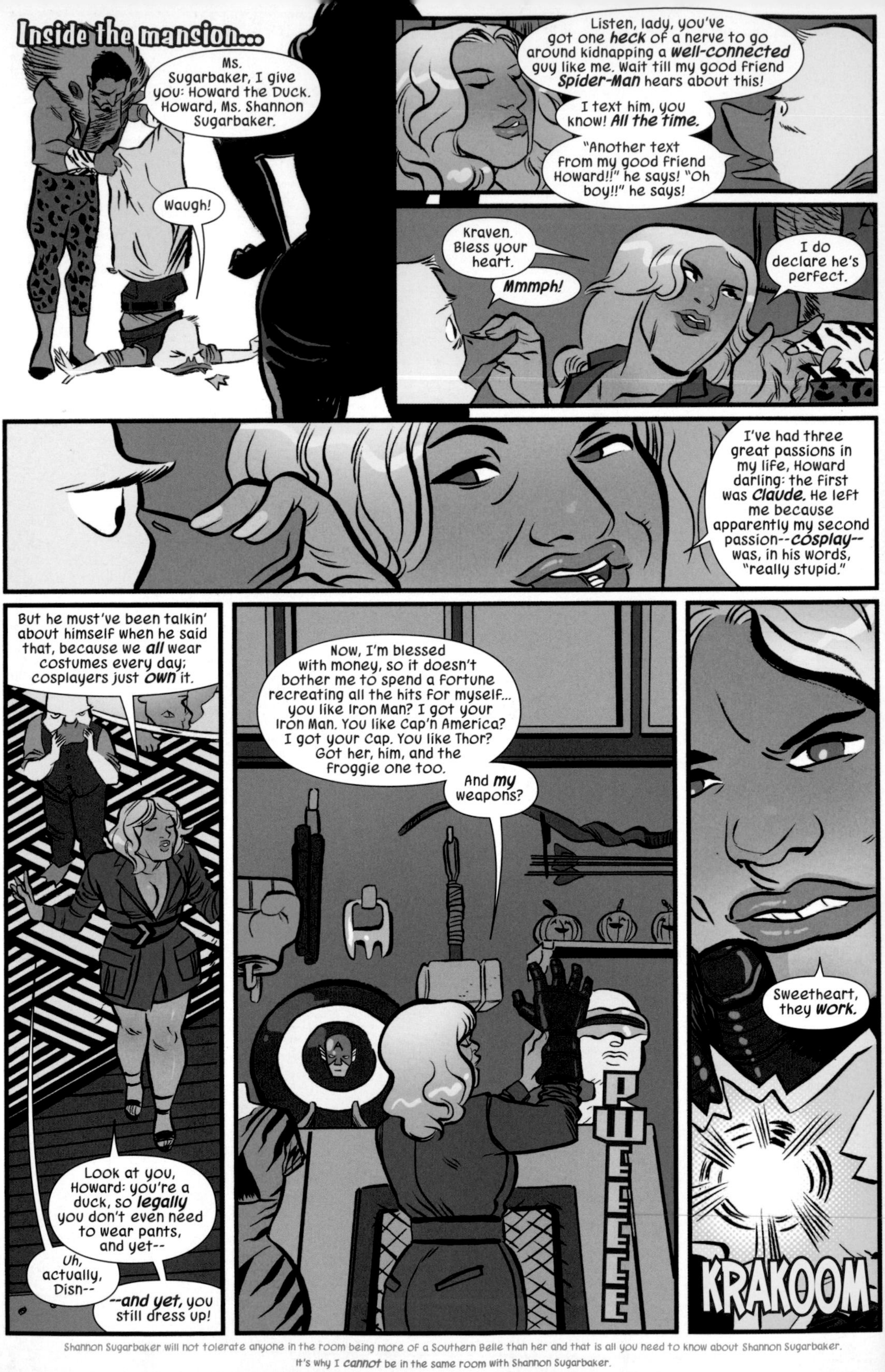
Inside the mansion...
Ms. Sugarbaker, I give you: Howard the Duck. Howard, Ms. Shannon Sugarbaker.
Waugh!
Listen, lady, you've got one heck of a nerve to go around kidnapping a well-connected guy like me. Wait till my good friend Spider-Man hears about this!
I text him, you know! All the time.
"Another text from my good friend Howard!!" he says! "Oh boy!!" he says!
Kraven. Bless your heart.
Mmmph!
I do declare he's perfect.
I've had three great passions in my life, Howard darling: the first was Claude. He left me because apparently my second passion--cosplay--was, in his words, "really stupid."
But he must've been talkin' about himself when he said that, because we all wear costumes every day; cosplayers just OWN it.
Look at you, Howard: you're a duck, so legally you don't even need to wear pants, and yet--
Uh, actually, Disn--
--and yet, you still dress up!
Now, I'm blessed with money, so it doesn't bother me to spend a fortune recreating all the hits for myself... you like Iron Man? I got your Iron Man. You like Cap'n America? I got your Cap. You like Thor? Got her, him, and the froggie one too.
And my weapons?
PWEEEEE
Sweetheart, they work.
KRAKOOM!

Shannon Sugarbaker will not tolerate anyone in the room being more of a Southern Belle than her and that is all you need to know about Shannon Sugarbaker.

It's why I *cannot* be in the same room with Shannon Sugarbaker.

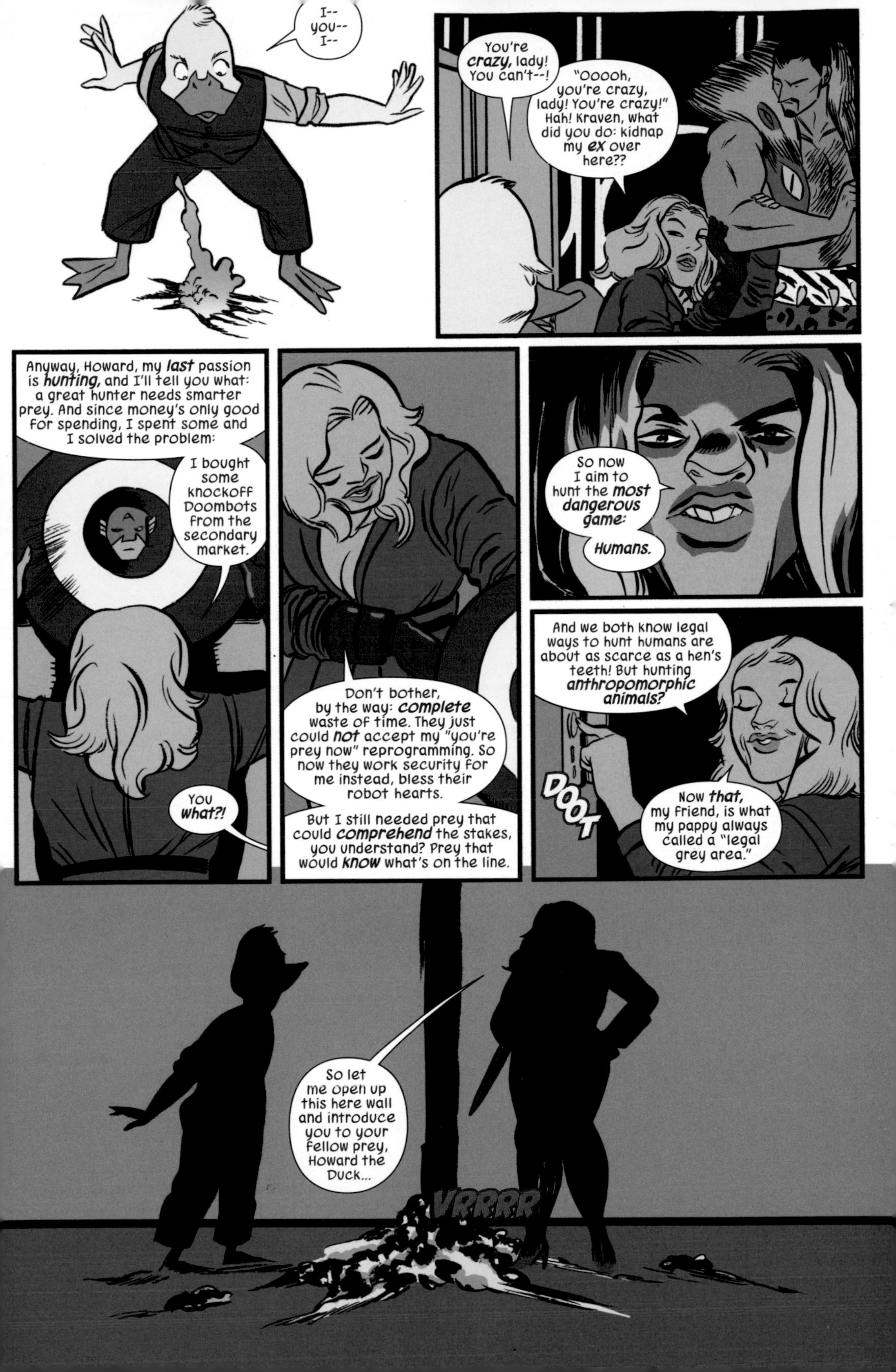
I-- you-- I--
You're crazy, lady! You can't--!
"Ooooh, you're crazy, lady! You're crazy!" Hah! Kraven, what did you do: kidnap my ex over here??
Anyway, Howard, my last passion is hunting, and I'll tell you what: a great hunter needs smarter prey. And since money's only good for spending, I spent some and I solved the problem:
I bought some knockoff Doombots from the secondary market.
You what?!
Don't bother, by the way: complete waste of time. They just could not accept my "you're prey now" reprogramming. So now they work security for me instead, bless their robot hearts.
But I still needed prey that could comprehend the stakes, you understand? Prey that would know what's on the line.
So now I aim to hunt the most dangerous game:
Humans.
And we both know legal ways to hunt humans are about as scarce as a hen's teeth! But hunting anthropomorphic animals?
DOOT
Now that, my friend, is what my pappy always called a "legal grey area."
So let me open up this here wall and introduce you to your fellow prey, Howard the Duck...
VRRRR

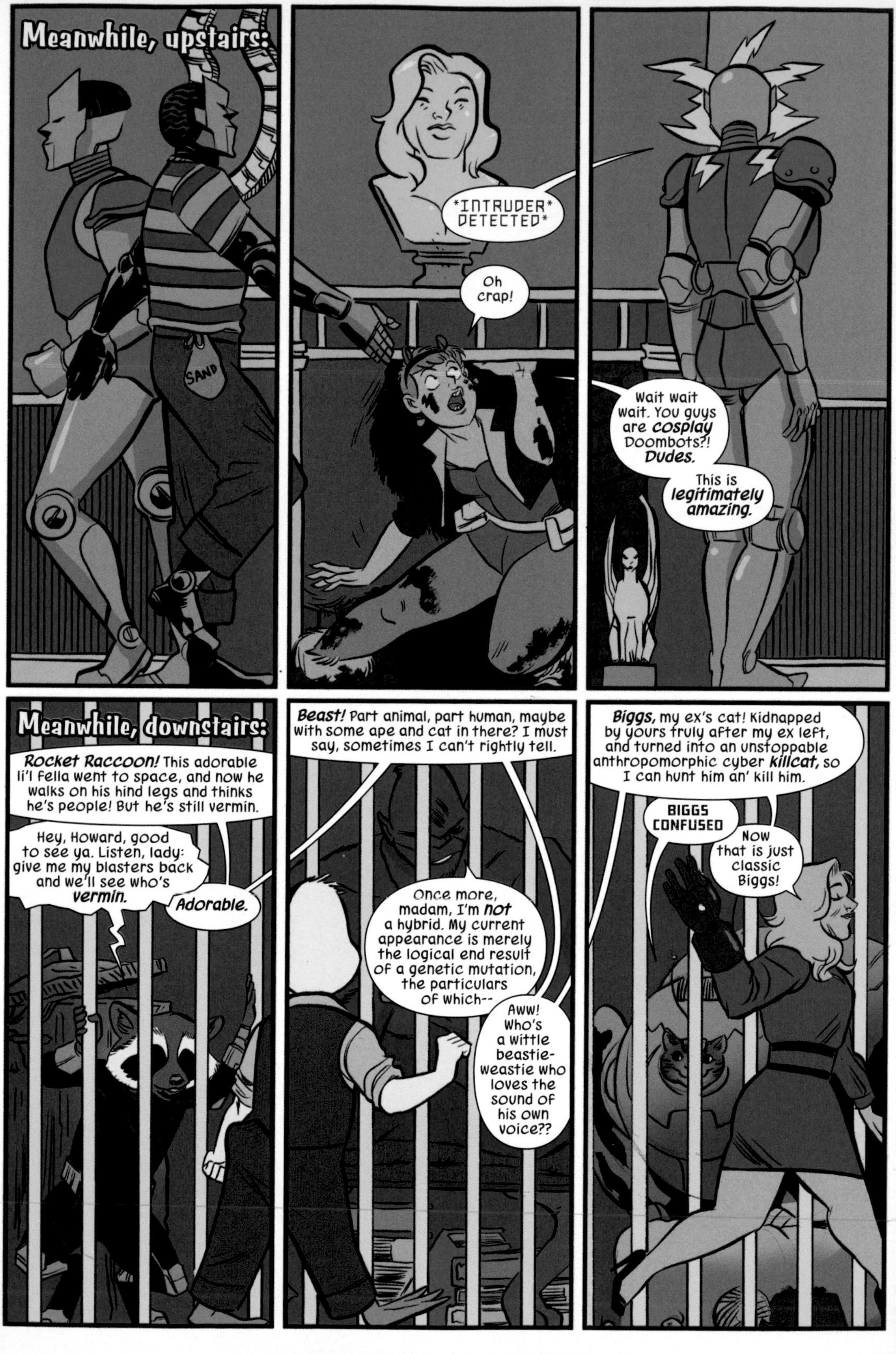

Meanwhile, upstairs:
INTRUDER DETECTED*
Oh crap!
Wait wait wait. You guys are *cosplay* Doombots?! *Dudes.*
This is *legitimately amazing.*
SAND
Meanwhile, downstairs:
Rocket Raccoon! This adorable li'l fella went to space, and now he walks on his hind legs and thinks he's people! But he's still vermin.
Hey, Howard, good to see ya. Listen, lady: give me my blasters back and we'll see who's *vermin.*
Adorable.
Beast! Part animal, part human, maybe with some ape and cat in there? I must say, sometimes I can't rightly tell.
Once more, madam, I'm *not* a hybrid. My current appearance is merely the logical end result of a genetic mutation, the particulars of which--
Aww! Who's a wittle beastie-weastie who loves the sound of his own voice??
Biggs, my ex's cat! Kidnapped by yours truly after my ex left, and turned into an unstoppable anthropomorphic cyber *killcat,* so I can hunt him an' kill him.
BIGGS CONFUSED
Now that is just classic Biggs!

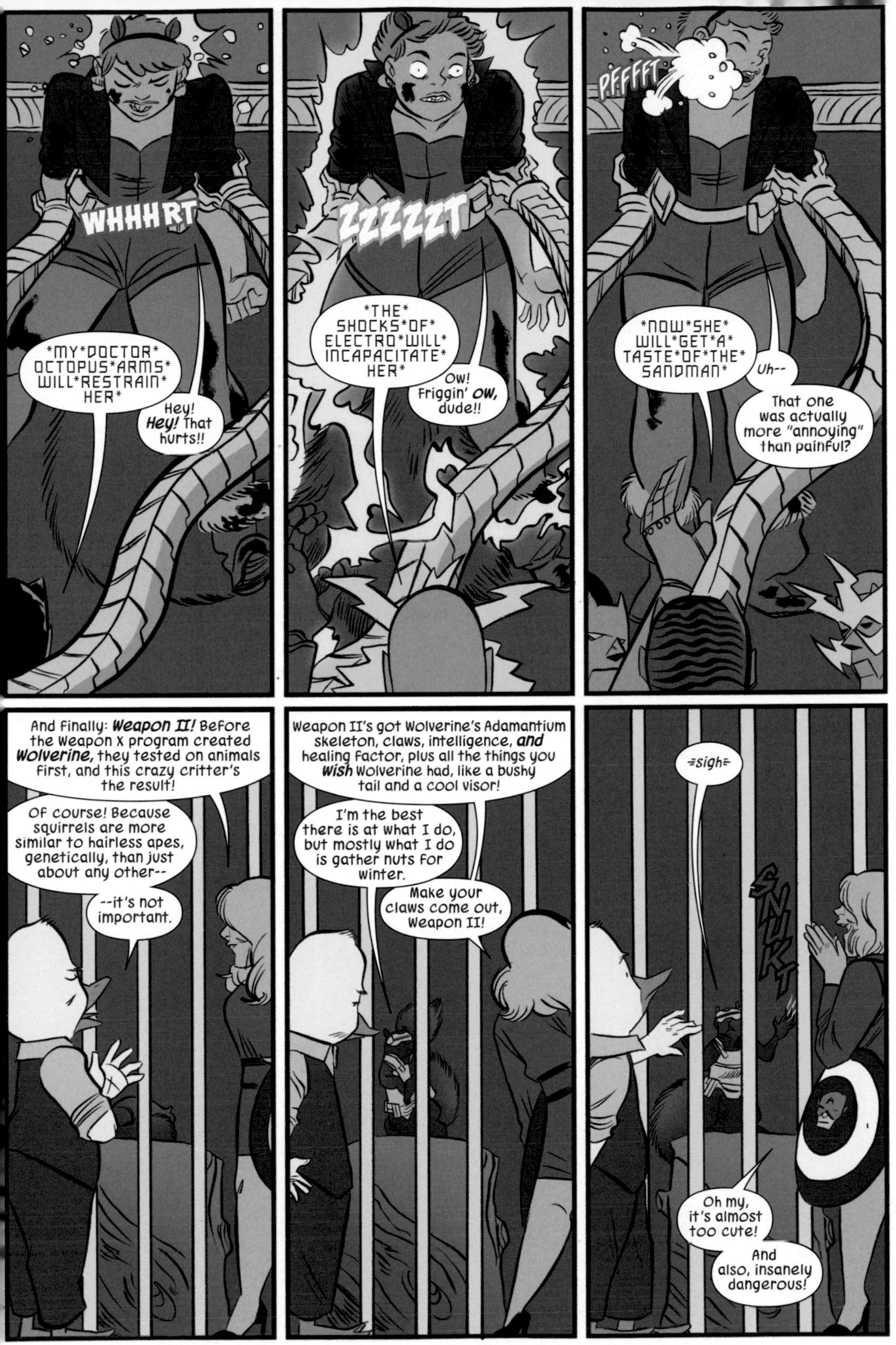
WHHHRT
*MY*DOCTOR*OCTOPUS*ARMS*WILL*RESTRAIN*HER*
Hey! Hey! That hurts!!
ZZZZZT
*THE*SHOCKS*OF*ELECTRO*WILL*INCAPACITATE*HER*
Ow! Friggin' OW, dude!!
PFFFFT
*NOW*SHE*WILL*GET*A*TASTE*OF*THE*SANDMAN*
Uh--
That one was actually more "annoying" than painful?
And finally: Weapon II! Before the Weapon X program created Wolverine, they tested on animals first, and this crazy critter's the result!
Of course! Because squirrels are more similar to hairless apes, genetically, than just about any other--
--it's not important.
Weapon II's got Wolverine's Adamantium skeleton, claws, intelligence, and healing factor, plus all the things you wish Wolverine had, like a bushy tail and a cool visor!
I'm the best there is at what I do, but mostly what I do is gather nuts for winter.
Make your claws come out, Weapon II!
=sigh=
SNIKT
Oh my, it's almost too cute!
And also, insanely dangerous!

*THERE*CAN*BE*NO*ESCAPE*/*MY*SAND*WAS*PROGRAMMED*TO*BE*COARSE*AND*ROUGH*AND*IRRITATING*AND*TO*GET*EVERYWHERE*

SCIENCE CORNER: Interesting sand fact: sand is actually just dirt but different I guess!

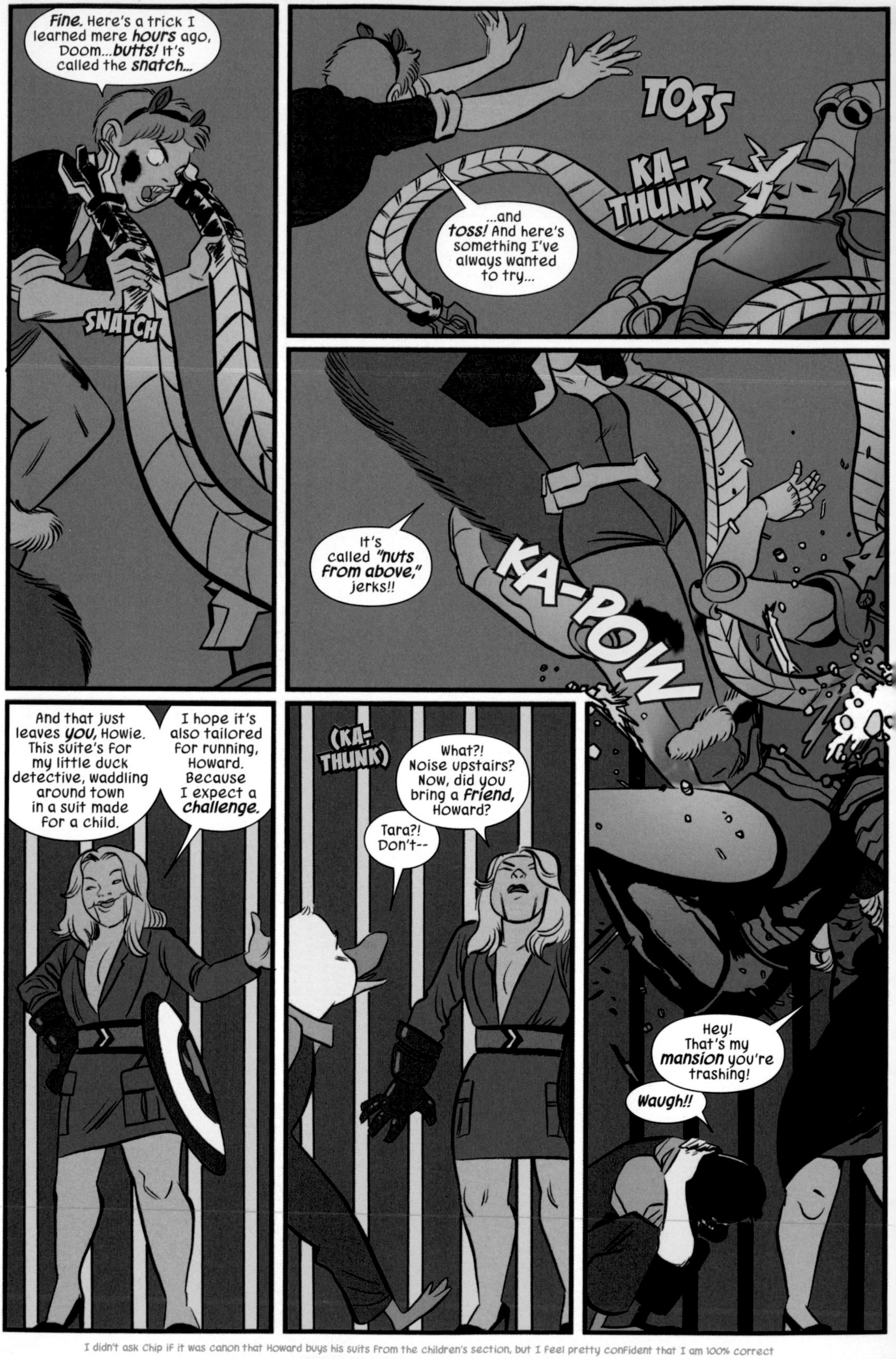
Fine. Here's a trick I learned mere hours ago, Doom...butts! It's called the snatch...
SNATCH
TOSS
KA-THUNK
...and toss! And here's something I've always wanted to try...
It's called "nuts from above," jerks!!
KA-POW
And that just leaves YOU, Howie. This suite's for my little duck detective, waddling around town in a suit made for a child.
I hope it's also tailored for running, Howard. Because I expect a challenge.
(KA-THUNK)
What?! Noise upstairs? Now, did you bring a friend, Howard?
Tara?! Don't--
Hey! That's my mansion you're trashing!
Waugh!!

I didn't ask Chip if it was canon that Howard buys his suits from the children's section, but I feel pretty confident that I am 100% correct

Um, *children* buy their suits from the *Howard* section, *Ryan.*

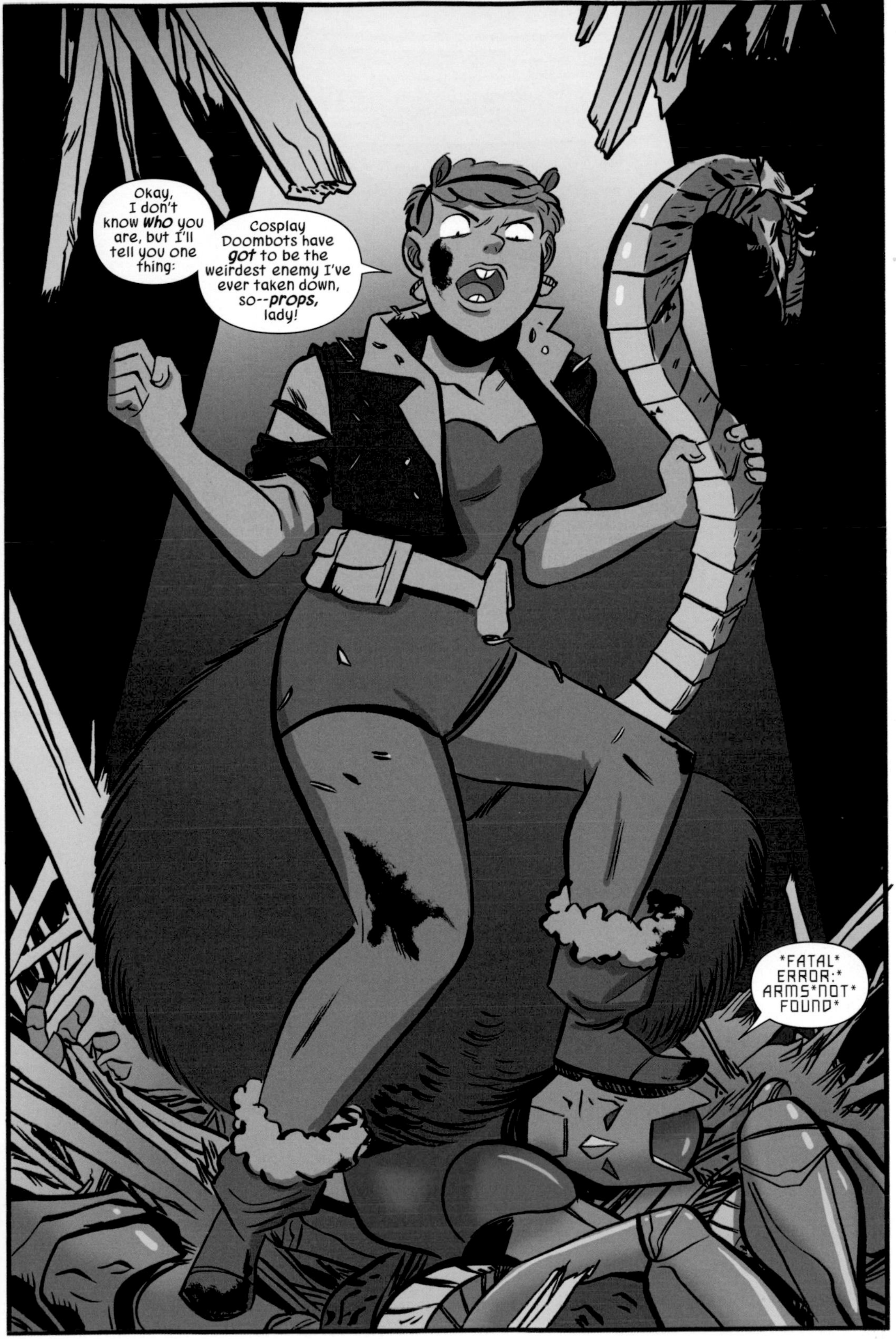
Okay, I don't know *WHO* you are, but I'll tell you one thing:
Cosplay Doombots have *GOT* to be the weirdest enemy I've ever taken down, so--*PROPS,* lady!
FATAL ERROR:* ARMS*NOT* FOUND*

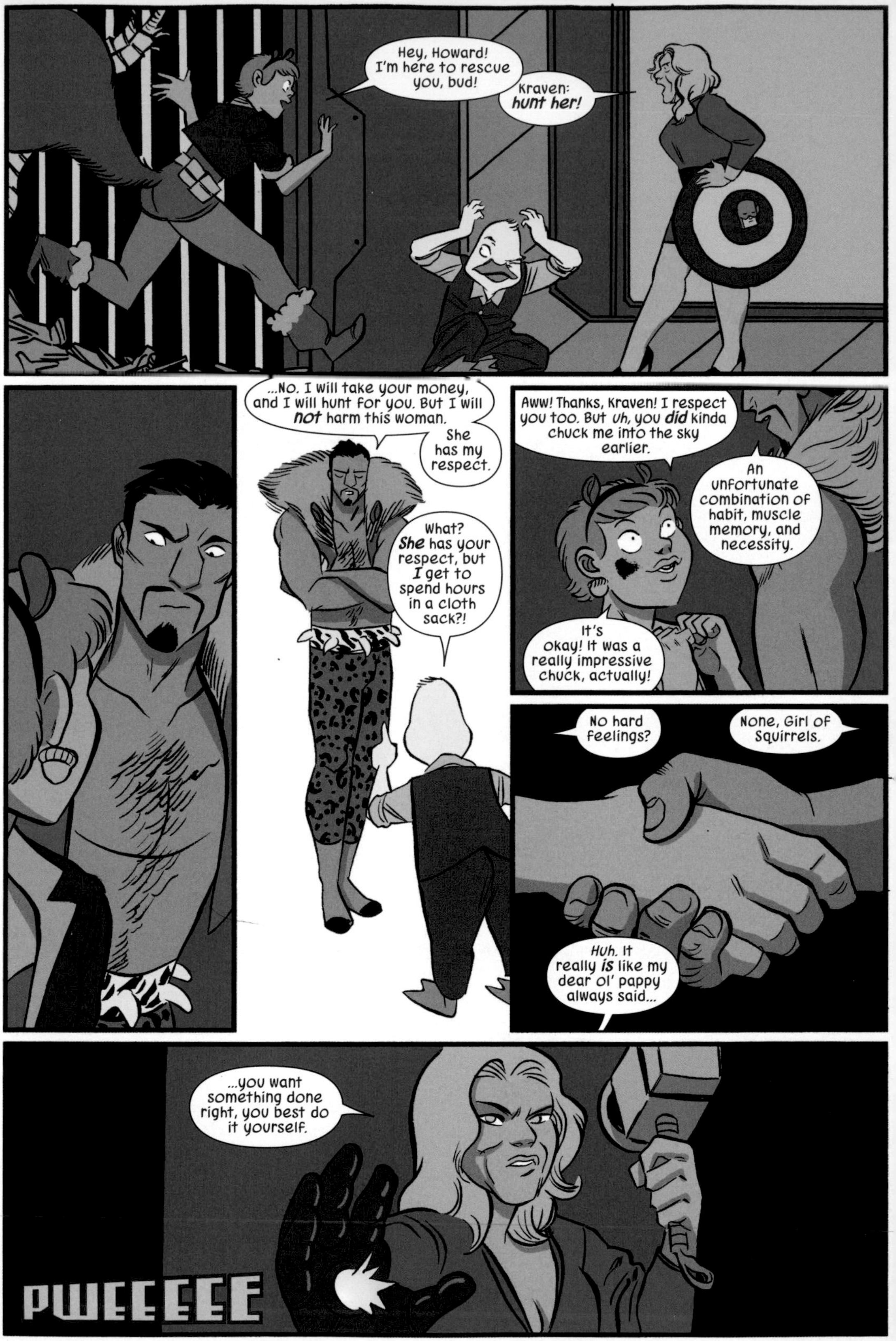
Hey, Howard! I'm here to rescue you, bud!
Kraven: **hunt her!**
...No. I will take your money, and I will hunt for you. But I will **not** harm this woman.
She has my respect.
What? **She** has your respect, but **I** get to spend hours in a cloth sack?!
Aww! Thanks, Kraven! I respect you too. But *uh,* you **did** kinda chuck me into the sky earlier.
An unfortunate combination of habit, muscle memory, and necessity.
It's okay! It was a really impressive chuck, actually!
No hard feelings?
None, Girl of Squirrels.
Huh. It really **is** like my dear ol' pappy always said...
...you want something done right, you best do it yourself.
PWEEEEE

My pappy's down-home country sayings don't ***all*** apply quite well to super hero cosplay battles, but it's nice that some of them do. Thanks, Pappy!
Um, if you want something done right, you hire a person who specializes in the task that needs completing. Your pappy needs to be corrected.

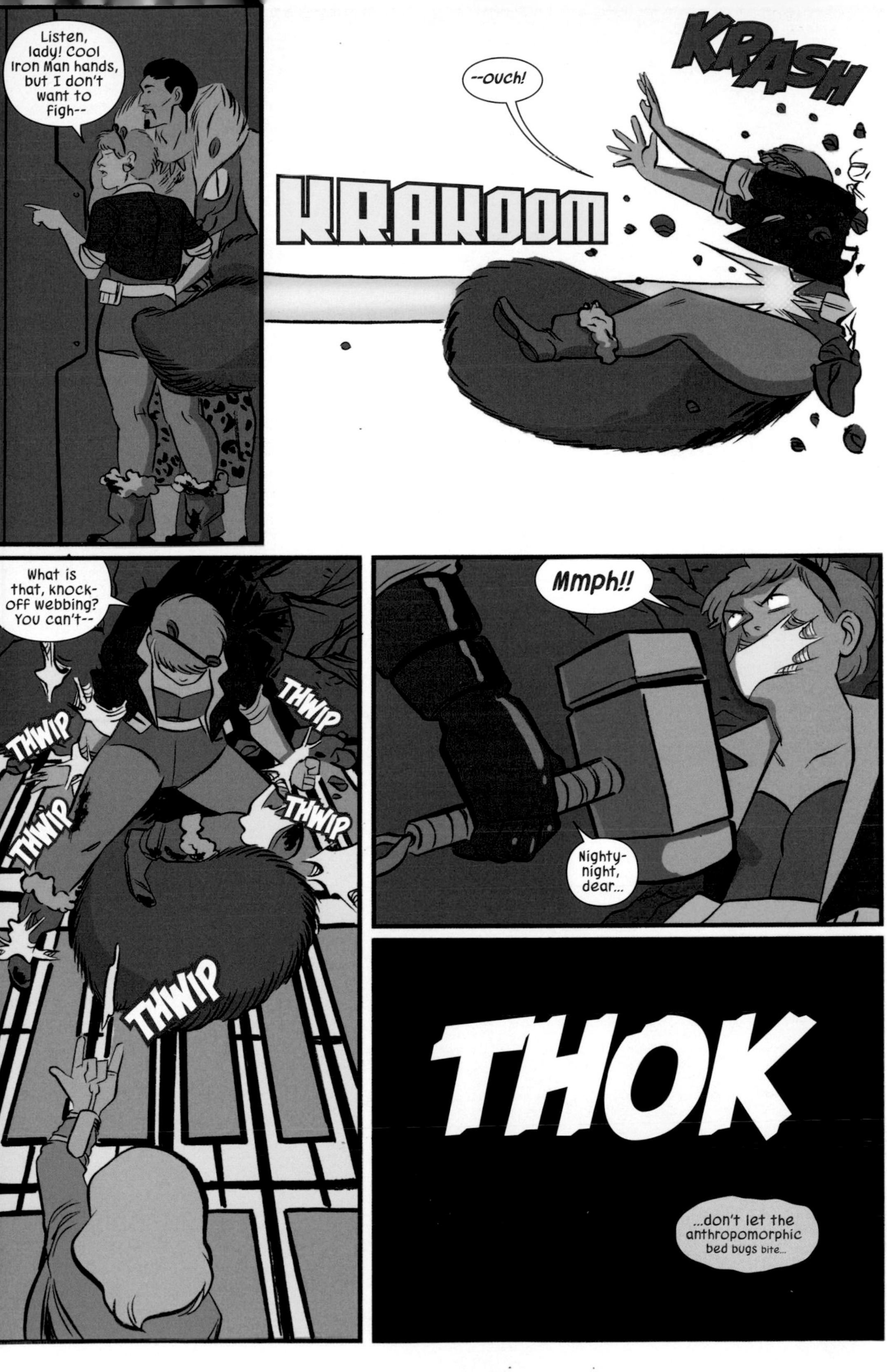
Listen, lady! Cool Iron Man hands, but I don't want to figh--
KRASH
--ouch!
KRAKOOM
What is that, knock-off webbing? You can't--
THWIP
THWIP
THWIP
THWIP
THWIP
Mmph!!
Nighty-night, dear...
THOK
...don't let the anthropomorphic bed bugs bite...

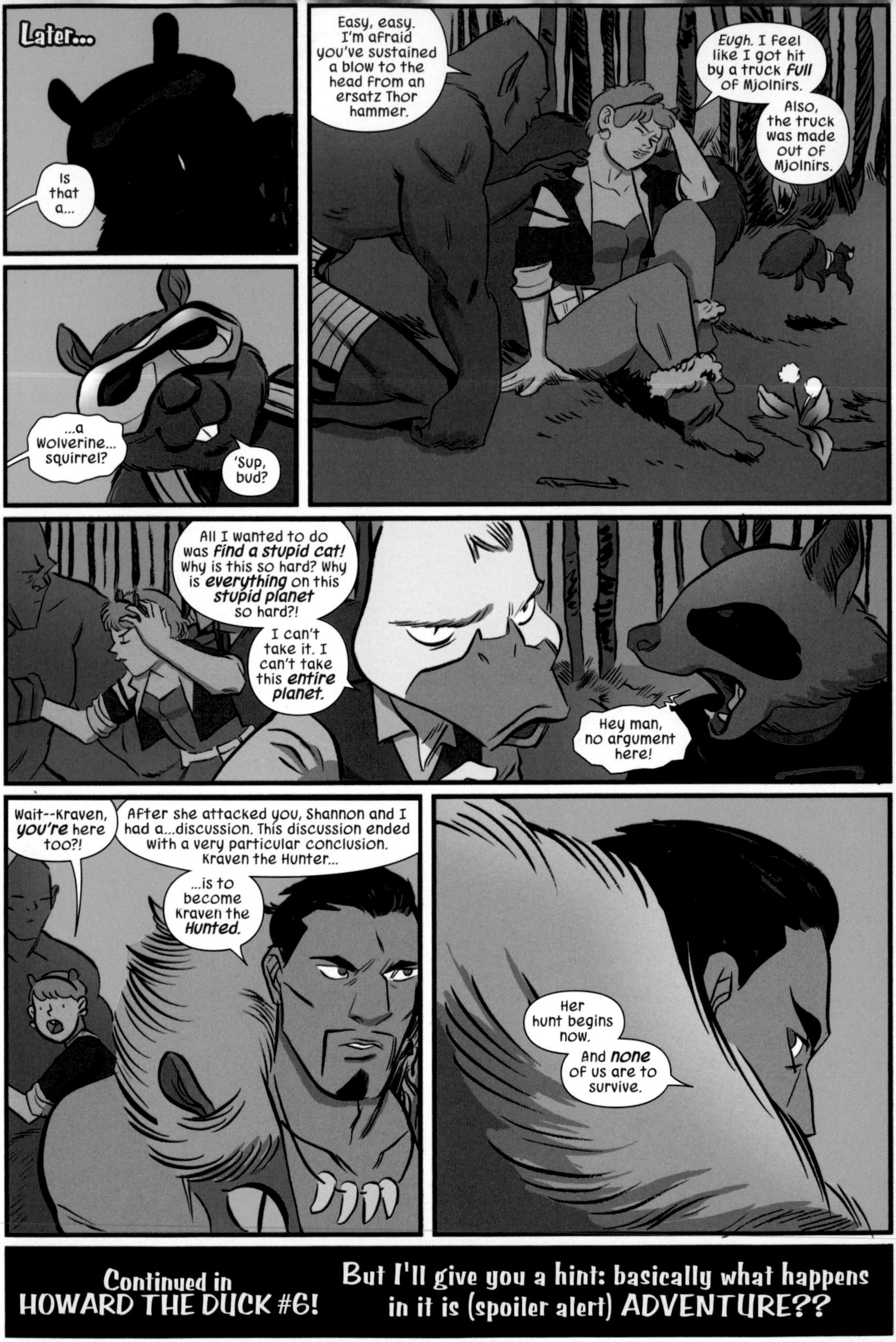
Later...
Is that a...
...a Wolverine... squirrel?
'Sup, bud?
Easy, easy. I'm afraid you've sustained a blow to the head from an ersatz Thor hammer.
Eugh. I feel like I got hit by a truck *full* of Mjolnirs.
Also, the truck was made out of Mjolnirs.
All I wanted to do was *find a stupid cat!* Why is this so hard? Why is *everything* on this *stupid planet* so hard?!
I can't take it. I can't take this *entire planet.*
Hey man, no argument here!
Wait--Kraven, *you're* here too?!
After she attacked you, Shannon and I had a...discussion. This discussion ended with a very particular conclusion. Kraven the Hunter...
...is to become Kraven the *Hunted.*
Her hunt begins now.
And *none* of us are to survive.
Continued in HOWARD THE DUCK #6!
But I'll give you a hint: basically what happens in it is (spoiler alert) ADVENTURE??

Also: cosplay. Lots of cosplay.
I'm cosplaying right now! It's as a guy who forgot that he now has to write a whole *Howard the Duck* comic!!

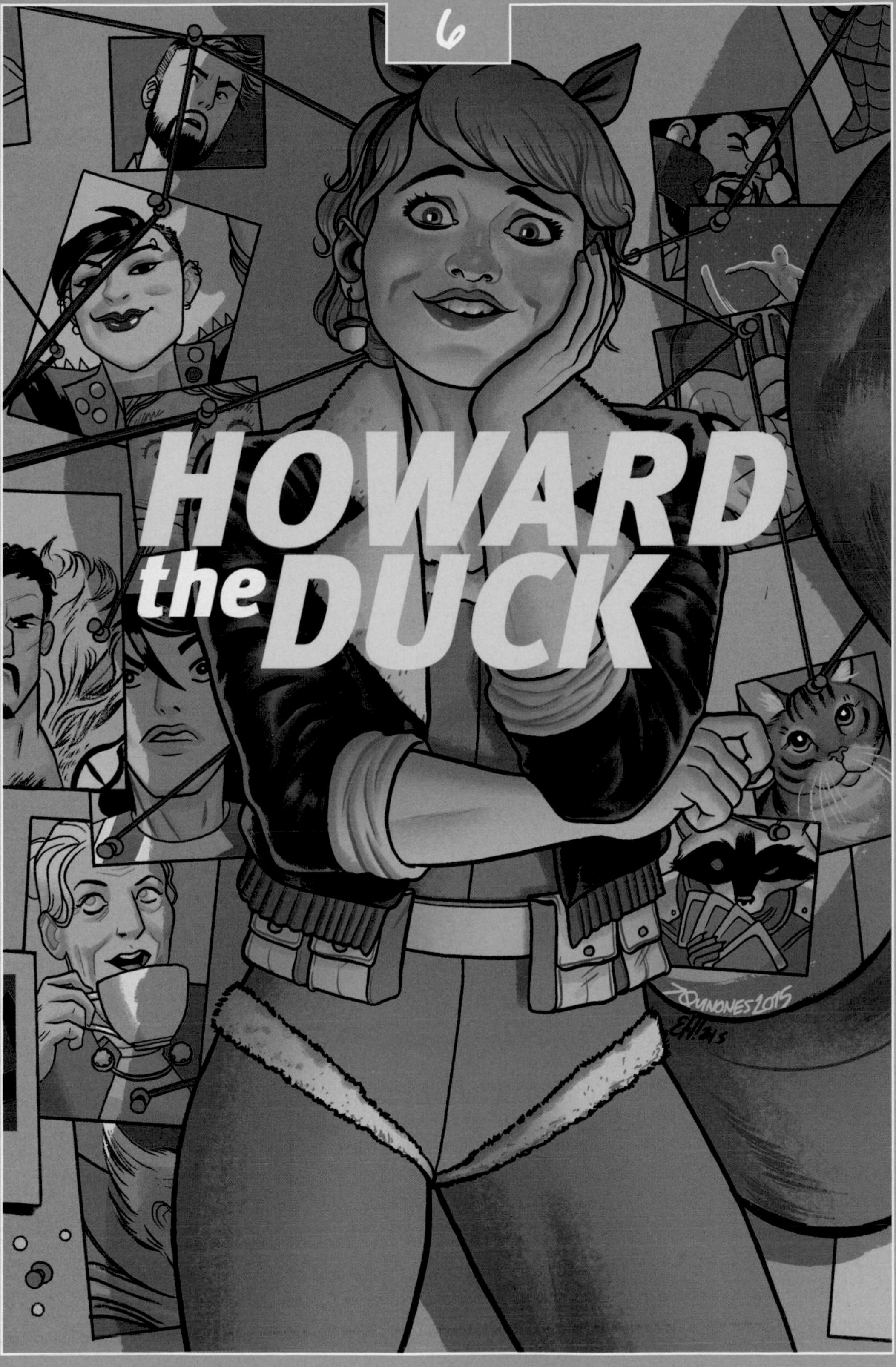
6
HOWARD the DUCK
QUINONES 2015
EH! 2015

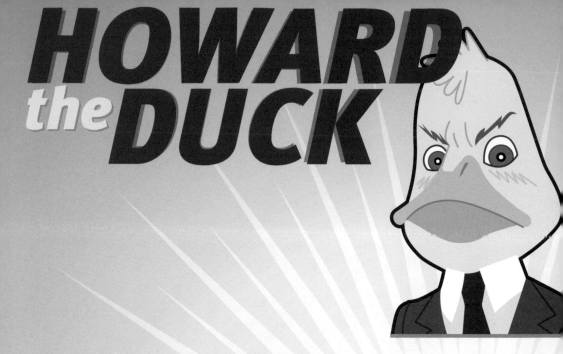

HOWARD the DUCK

HEY, HOPEFULLY THIS ISN'T NEWS TO YOU, BUT THIS ISSUE RIGHT HERE IS PART TWO OF A TWO-PART STORY THAT BEGAN IN **THE UNBEATABLE SQUIRREL GIRL #6!** HOWARD DOES A PRETTY GOOD JOB ON THE NEXT PAGE OF SUMMARIZING WHAT HAPPENED IN THAT ISSUE, BUT STILL, **U.S.G.** IS REALLY GOOD, YOU SHOULD TRACK THAT ISSUE DOWN. (AND YES YOU **CAN** TRUST THIS TOTALLY UNBIASED RECAPPER!)

ANYWAY, HERE'S SOME ADDITIONAL HOWARD-CENTRIC CONTEXT FOR THIS ISSUE, OKAY?

EVER SINCE THE START OF THIS NEW VOLUME, HOWARD'S HAD WHAT APPEARS TO BE A CYBORG CAT FOR A PET. WHAT IS **UP** WITH THAT CAT? FIND OUT IN THIS VERY ISSUE, WHICH TAKES PLACE BETWEEN THIS VOLUME AND THE LAST ONE. (I KNOW, I KNOW — COMICS!)

HUH. GUESS THERE WASN'T A WHOLE LOTTA CONTEXT TO SHARE ACTUALLY. YOU'RE FREE TO GO!

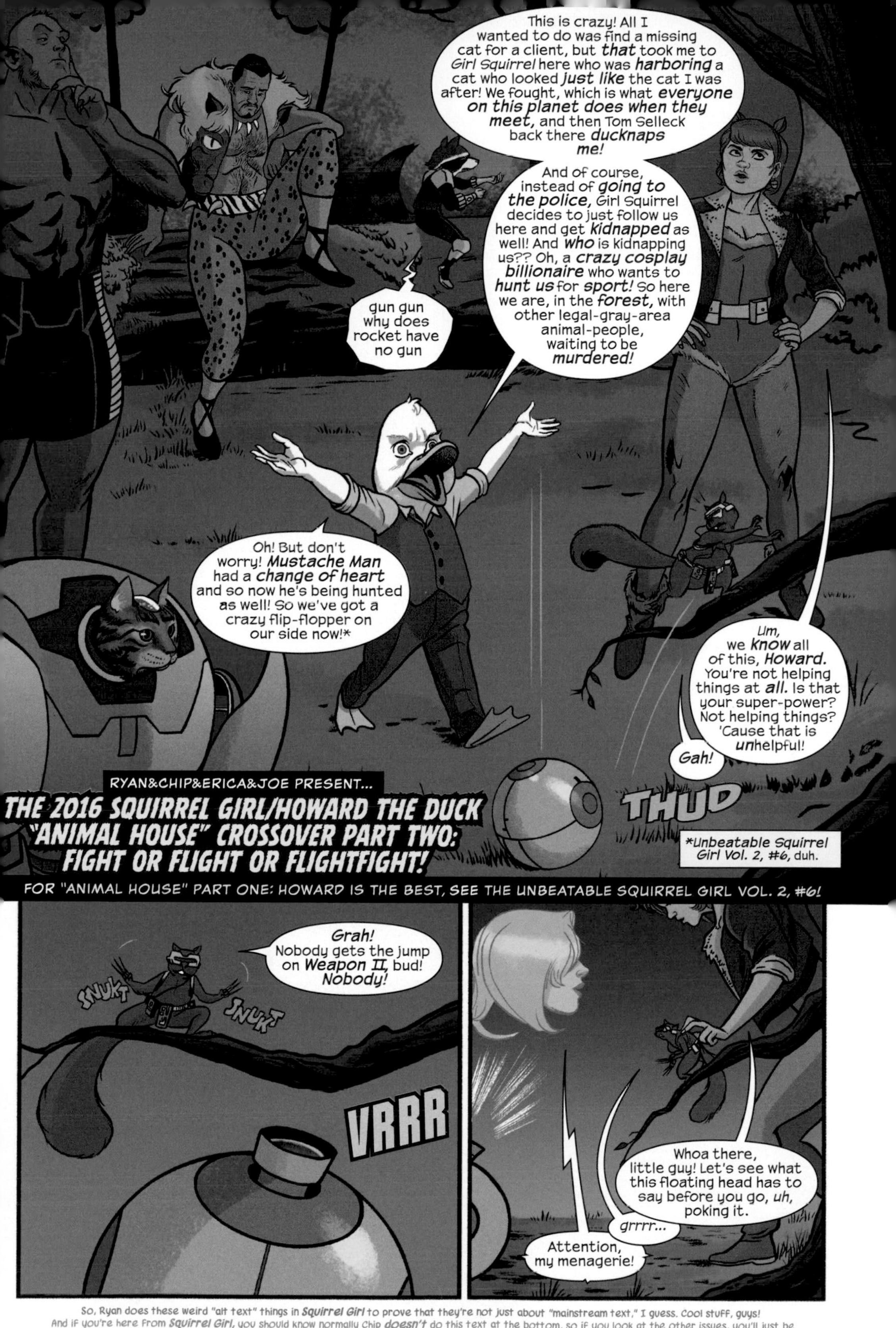
This is crazy! All I wanted to do was find a missing cat for a client, but *that* took me to *Girl Squirrel* here who was *harboring* a cat who looked *just like* the cat I was after! We fought, which is what *everyone on this planet does when they meet,* and then Tom Selleck back there *ducknaps me!*
gun gun why does rocket have no gun
And of course, instead of *going to the police,* Girl Squirrel decides to just follow us here and get *kidnapped* as well! And *who* is kidnapping us?? Oh, a *crazy cosplay billionaire* who wants to *hunt us* for *sport!* So here we are, in the *forest,* with other legal-gray-area animal-people, waiting to be *murdered!*
Oh! But don't worry! *Mustache Man* had a *change of heart* and so now he's being hunted as well! So we've got a crazy flip-flopper on our side now!*
Um, we *know* all of this, *Howard.* You're not helping things at *all.* Is that your super-power? Not helping things? 'Cause that is *un*helpful!
Gah!
THUD
RYAN&CHIP&ERICA&JOE PRESENT...
THE 2016 SQUIRREL GIRL/HOWARD THE DUCK "ANIMAL HOUSE" CROSSOVER PART TWO: FIGHT OR FLIGHT OR FLIGHTFIGHT!
**Unbeatable Squirrel Girl Vol. 2, #6*, duh.
FOR "ANIMAL HOUSE" PART ONE: HOWARD IS THE BEST, SEE THE UNBEATABLE SQUIRREL GIRL VOL. 2, #6!
Grah! Nobody gets the jump on *Weapon II*, bud! *Nobody!*
SNUKT
SNUKT
VRRR
Whoa there, little guy! Let's see what this floating head has to say before you go, *uh,* poking it.
grrrr...
Attention, my menagerie!

So, Ryan does these weird "alt text" things in *Squirrel Girl* to prove that they're not just about "mainstream text," I guess. Cool stuff, guys! And if you're here from *Squirrel Girl,* you should know normally Chip *doesn't* do this text at the bottom, so if you look at the other issues, you'll just be disappointed!! Okay bye

Weapon II was in the same program as the old *Wolverine*, who was *Weapon X*! You probably thought that was just an "X" and not a "10"! Funny story: Professor Xavier actually named the X-Men *"Ten-Men,"* because he wanted ten guys on the team, but nobody got it so he just let people believe it was X-Men.

Now *that's* a tenhilarating addition to Marvel canon!

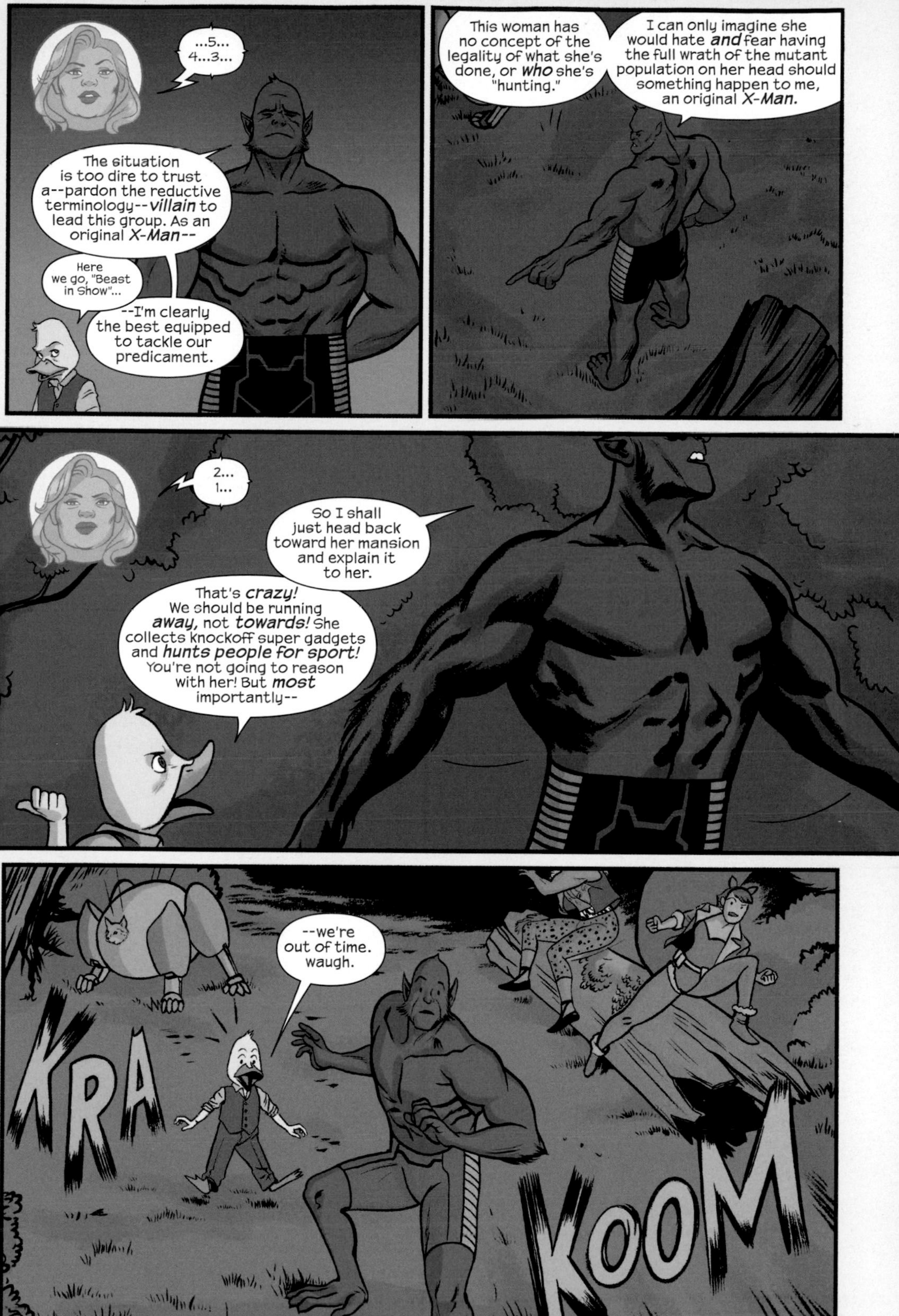
...5...
4...3...
The situation is too dire to trust a--pardon the reductive terminology--*villain* to lead this group. As an original *X-Man*--
Here we go, "Beast in Show"...
--I'm clearly the best equipped to tackle our predicament.
This woman has no concept of the legality of what she's done, or *who* she's "hunting."
I can only imagine she would hate *and* fear having the full wrath of the mutant population on her head should something happen to me, an original *X-Man.*
2...
1...
So I shall just head back toward her mansion and explain it to her.
That's *crazy!* We should be running *away,* not *towards!* She collects knockoff super gadgets and *hunts people for sport!* You're not going to reason with her! But *most* importantly--
--we're out of time. waugh.
KRA
KOOM

Don't call yourself *Beast* if you're super smart and want people to listen to you! Take a page from *Mr. Fantastic.* Who wouldn't listen to a *Mr. Fantastic?* Even *Dr. Doom* knew he should let people know he's a *doctor* in his name.

Thought you could ever only have a character say "...we're out of time" in a time travel story? *Think again.*

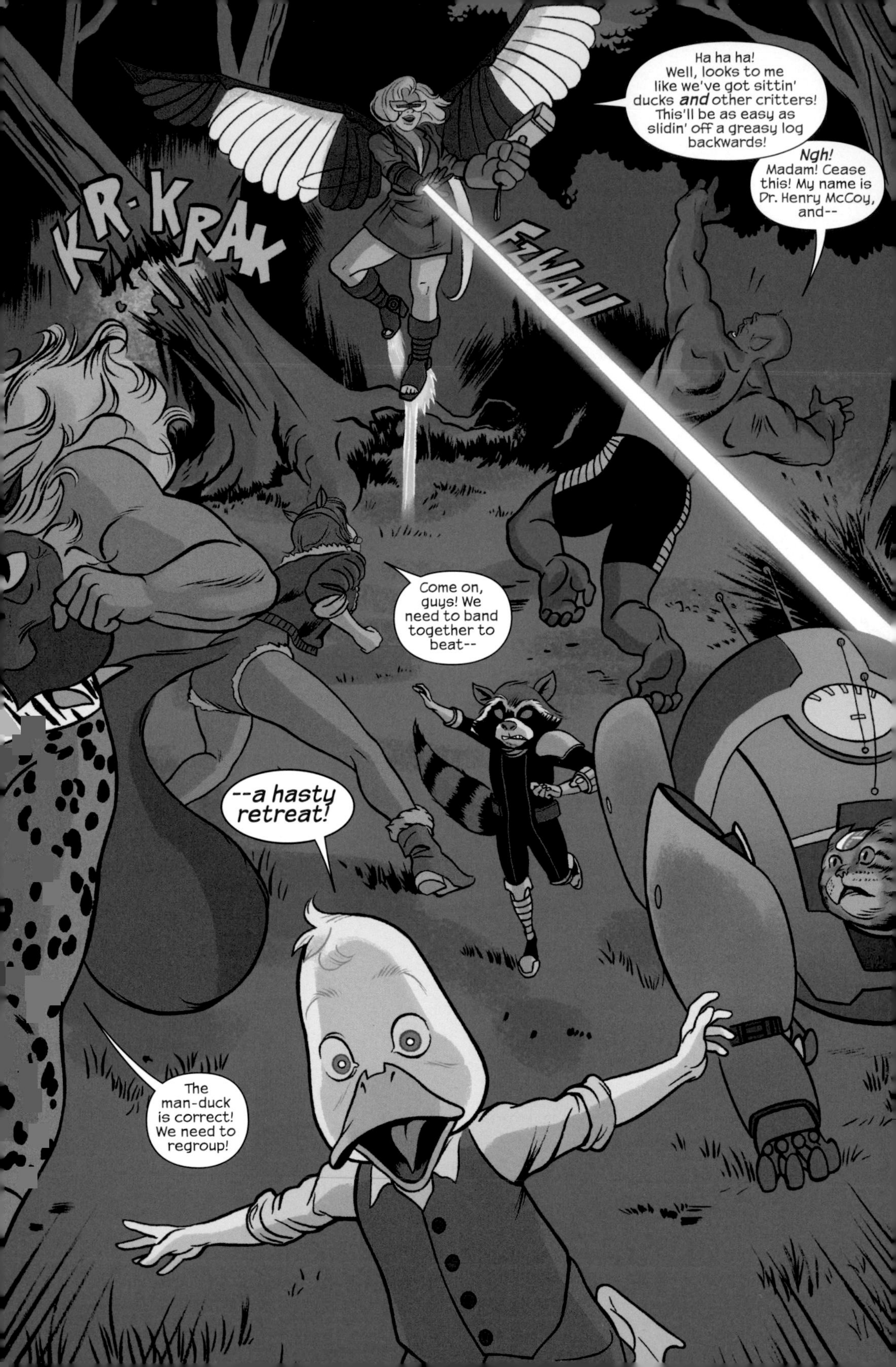
Ha ha ha! Well, looks to me like we've got sittin' ducks *and* other critters! This'll be as easy as slidin' off a greasy log backwards!
Ngh! Madam! Cease this! My name is Dr. Henry McCoy, and--
KR-KRAK
FZWAY
Come on, guys! We need to band together to beat--
--a hasty retreat!
The man-duck is correct! We need to regroup!

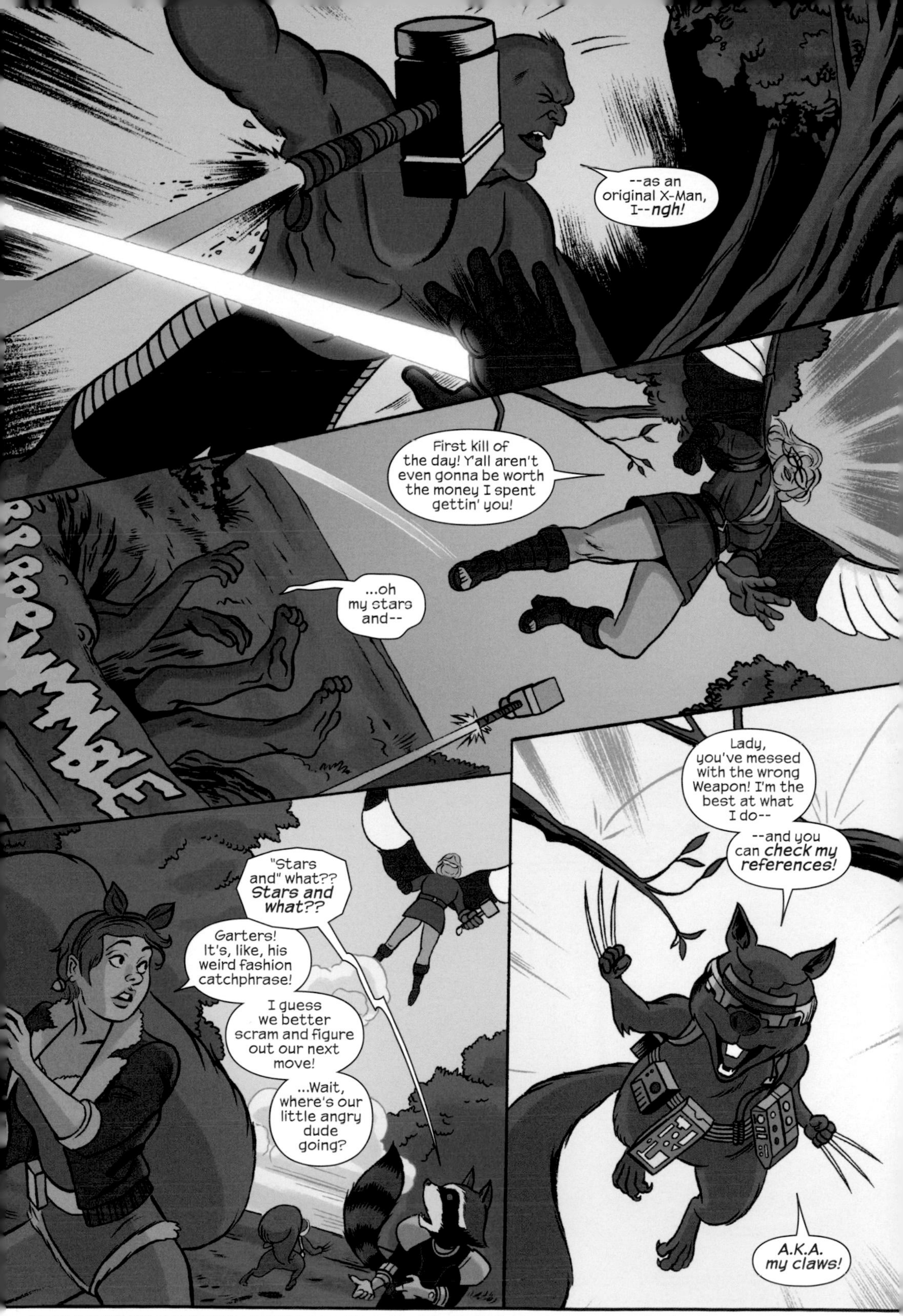
--as an original X-Man, I--*ngh!*
First kill of the day! Y'all aren't even gonna be worth the money I spent gettin' you!
...oh my stars and--
"Stars and" what?? *Stars and what??*
Garters! It's, like, his weird fashion catchphrase!
I guess we better scram and figure out our next move!
...Wait, where's our little angry dude going?
Lady, you've messed with the wrong Weapon! I'm the best at what I do--
--and you can *check my references!*
A.K.A. my claws!

Actually, "garters" in this case refers to the Most Noble Order of the Garter, which is the highest order of chivalry in the U.K. *See, Ryan? I can know things, too.*
I like how your impression of me is "a guy who knows things." I'll take it!

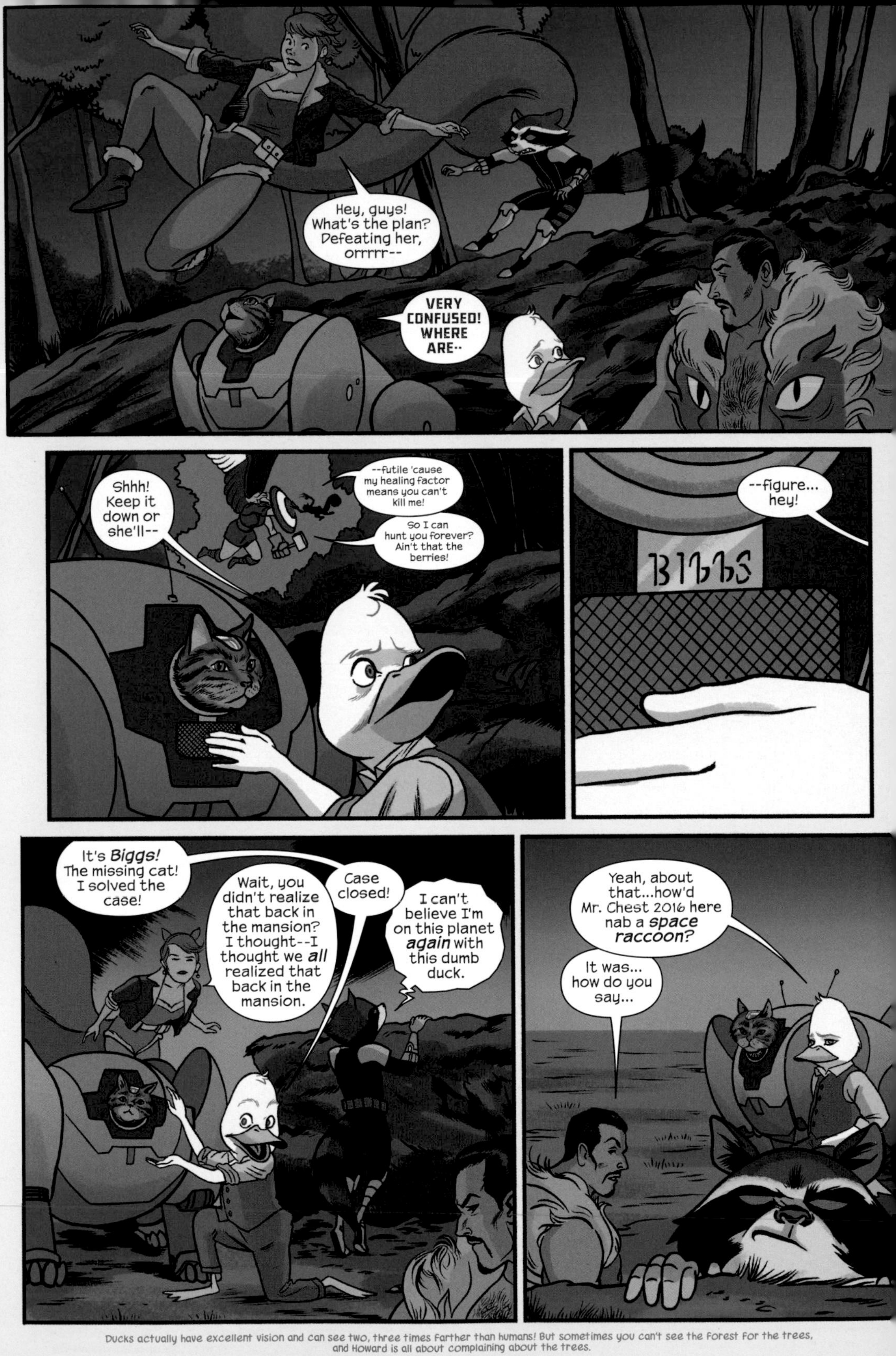

Hey, guys! What's the plan? Defeating her, orrrrr--
VERY CONFUSED! WHERE ARE..
Shhh! Keep it down or she'll--
--futile 'cause my healing factor means you can't kill me!
So I can hunt you forever? Ain't that the berries!
--figure... hey!
It's *Biggs!* The missing cat! I solved the case!
Wait, you didn't realize that back in the mansion? I thought--I thought we *all* realized that back in the mansion.
Case closed!
I can't believe I'm on this planet *again* with this dumb duck.
Yeah, about that...how'd Mr. Chest 2016 here nab a *space raccoon?*
It was... how do you say...

Ducks actually have excellent vision and can see two, three times farther than humans! But sometimes you can't see the forest for the trees, and Howard is all about complaining about the trees.

As a guy who knows things, I agree.

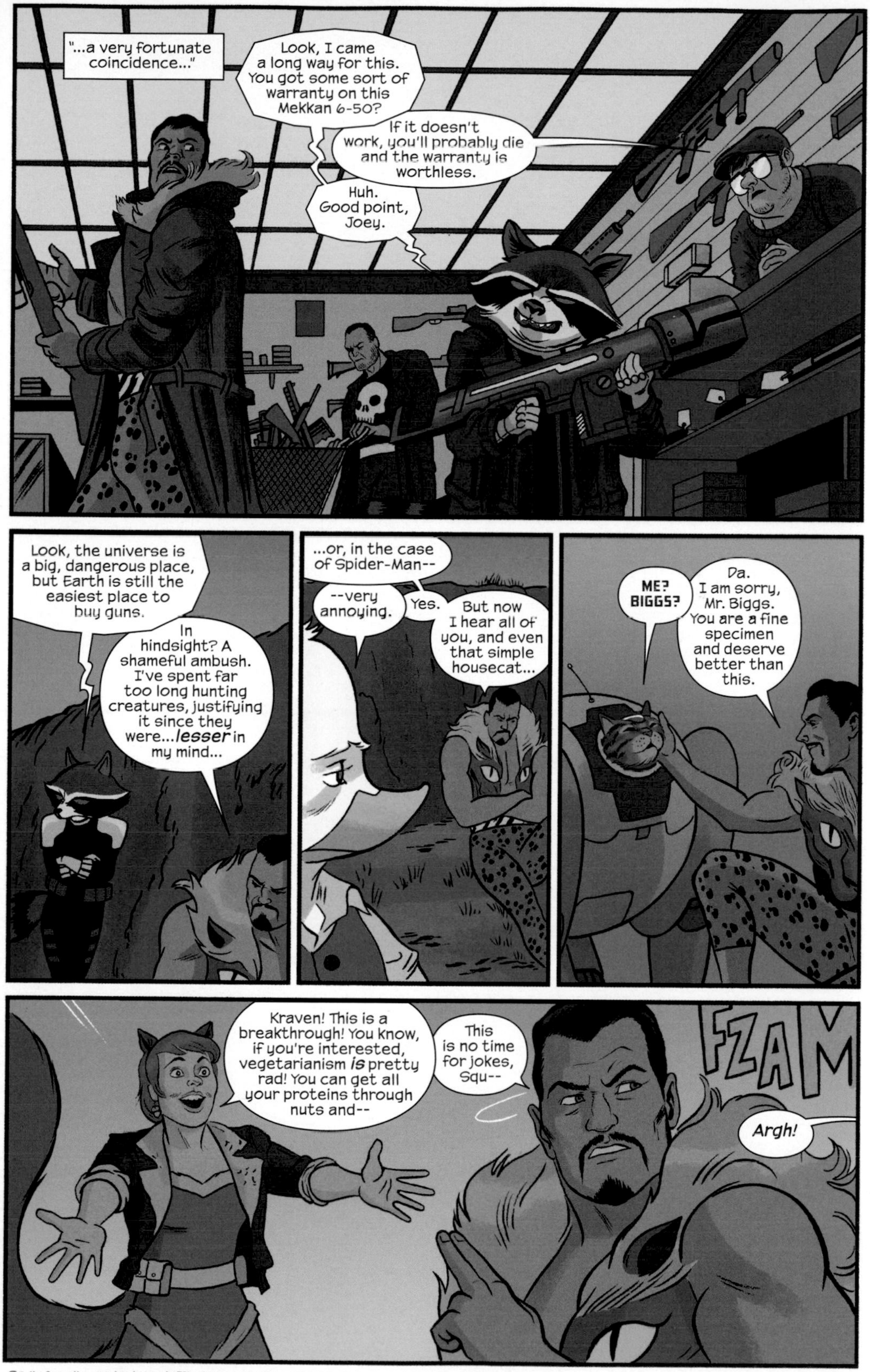
"...a very fortunate coincidence..."
Look, I came a long way for this. You got some sort of warranty on this Mekkan 6-50?
If it doesn't work, you'll probably die and the warranty is worthless.
Huh. Good point, Joey.
Look, the universe is a big, dangerous place, but Earth is still the easiest place to buy guns.
In hindsight? A shameful ambush. I've spent far too long hunting creatures, justifying it since they were...*lesser* in my mind...
...or, in the case of Spider-Man--
--very annoying.
Yes.
But now I hear all of you, and even that simple housecat...
ME? BIGGS?
Da. I am sorry, Mr. Biggs. You are a fine specimen and deserve better than this.
Kraven! This is a breakthrough! You know, if you're interested, vegetarianism *is* pretty rad! You can get all your proteins through nuts and--
This is no time for jokes, Squ--
FZAM
Argh!

Da. My favorite comics trope is ESL characters only saying the simplest words in their native language, like Gambit saying *"Oui"* or *"chere,"* almost as if those are the only foreign words the writer knows? Oh well! *Sayonara!*

Mine's when their speech is only partially translated for dramatic effect. It really gives *un petit quelque chose* to the *mise-en-scène.*

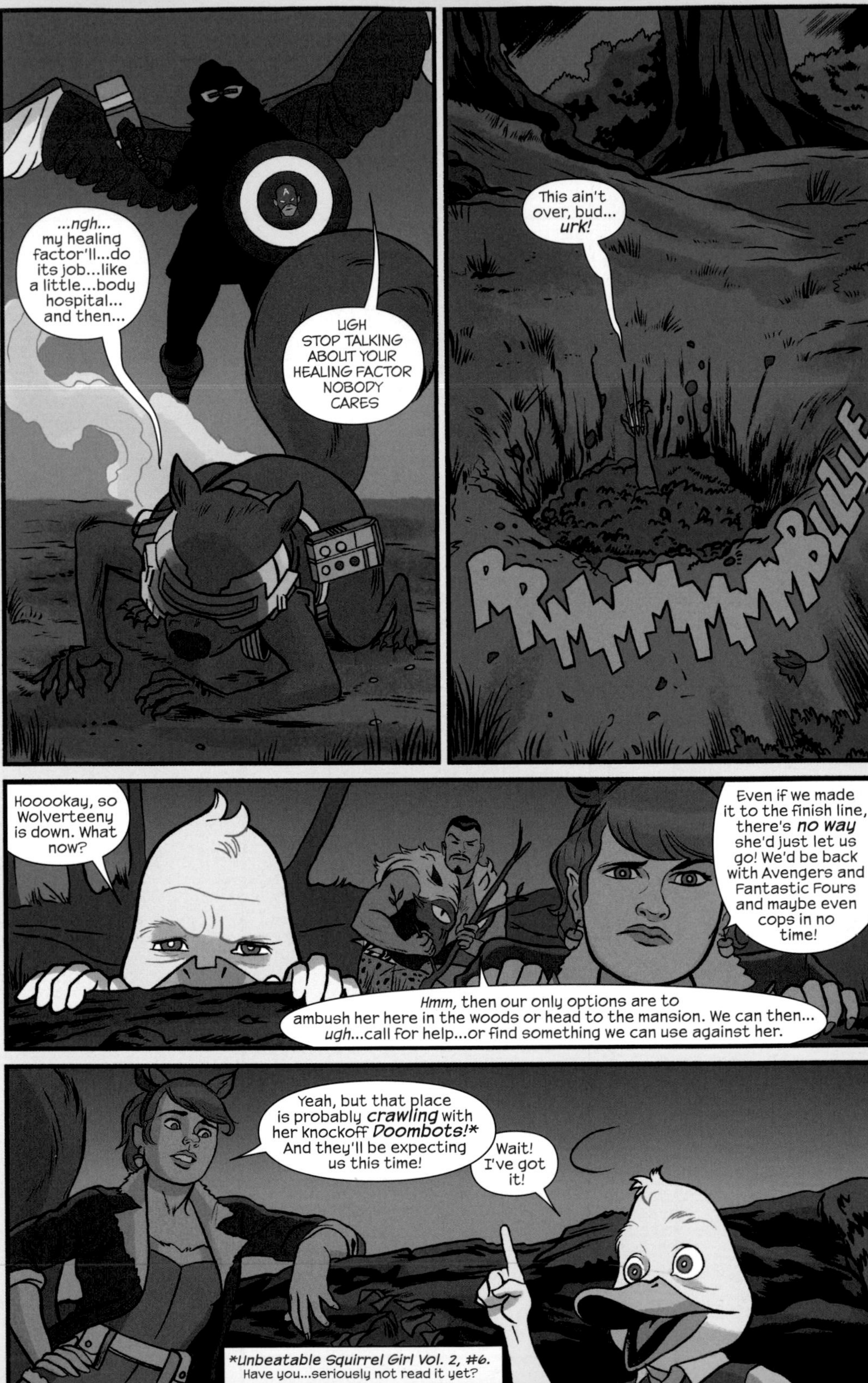

...ngh... my healing factor'll...do its job...like a little...body hospital... and then...
UGH STOP TALKING ABOUT YOUR HEALING FACTOR NOBODY CARES
This ain't over, bud... **urk!**
Hooookay, so Wolverteeny is down. What now?
Even if we made it to the finish line, there's ***no way*** she'd just let us go! We'd be back with Avengers and Fantastic Fours and maybe even cops in no time!
Hmm, then our only options are to ambush her here in the woods or head to the mansion. We can then... *ugh*...call for help...or find something we can use against her.
Yeah, but that place is probably ***crawling*** with her knockoff ***Doombots!**** And they'll be expecting us this time!
Wait! I've got it!
**Unbeatable Squirrel Girl Vol. 2, #6.* Have you...seriously not read it yet?

And who calls their abilities a "Factor"? That's like me saying my "writing Factor" will finish this script in no time, or Ryan saying "My tall Factor will help me get that can on the top shelf." It's weird, man.

Chip, look, do you want the can or not?

Poop. That's what cats do. They poop. -Chipipedia!
Uh, I'm gonna call "chiptation needed" on that one.

Always use SafeSearch with Starksearch. Just trust me.
Spider-Man set up an autoreply to send "lol no way!!" to every text Howard sends, and he hasn't noticed yet. It's been months.

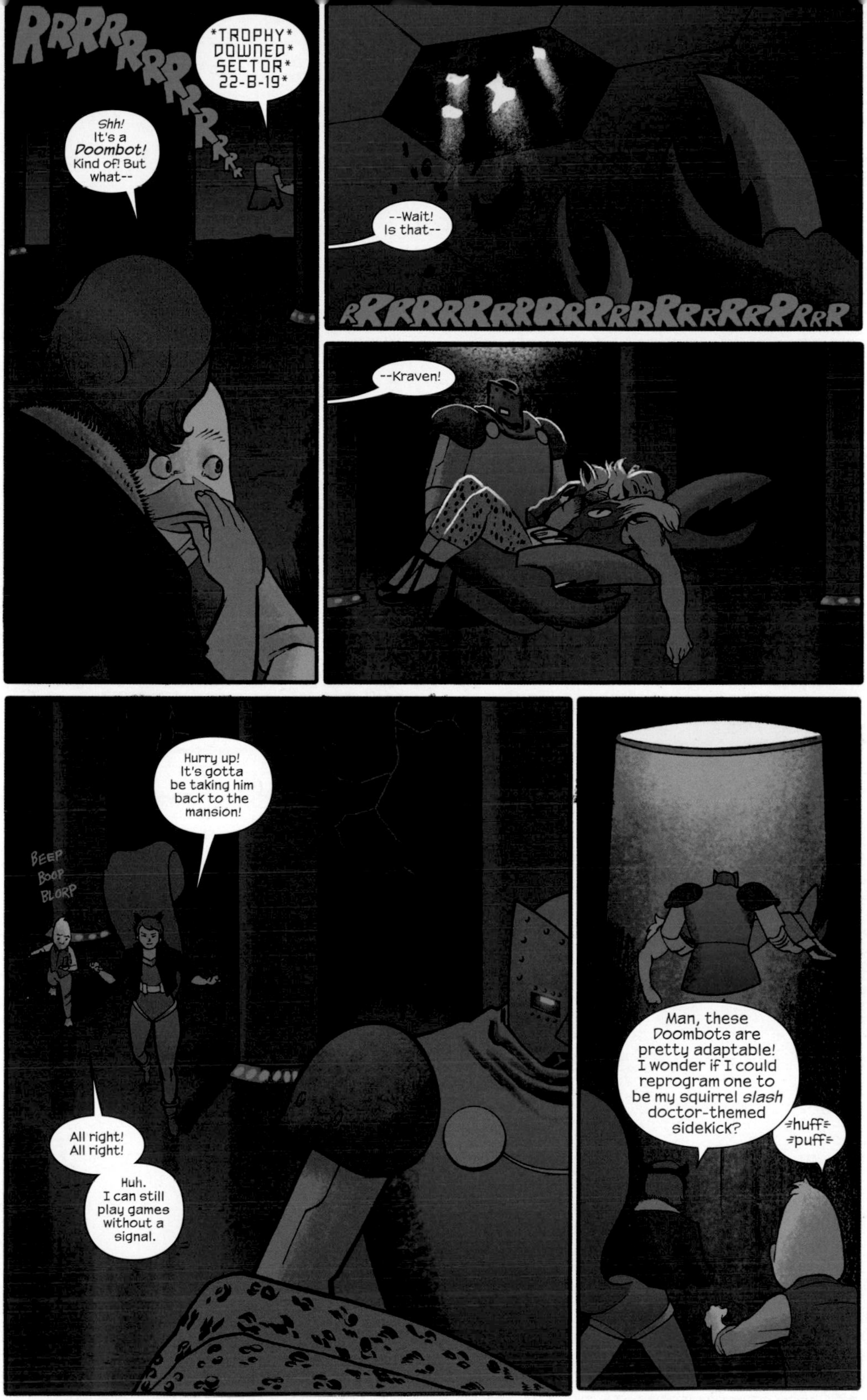
RRRRRRRRRRRRRk
TROPHY DOWNED* SECTOR* 22-B-19*
Shh! It's a Doombot! Kind of! But what--
--Wait! Is that--
RRRRRRRRRRRRRRRRRRRRRRRRRR
--Kraven!
Hurry up! It's gotta be taking him back to the mansion!
BEEP BOOP BLORP
All right! All right!
Huh. I can still play games without a signal.
Man, these Doombots are pretty adaptable! I wonder if I could reprogram one to be my squirrel slash doctor-themed sidekick?
=huff= =puff=

Think about it, Ryan. If you *don't* go for it, I'm going to make one Howard's sidekick: ***Dr. Plume.***
Wow. I *really* should've read ***Howard the Duck*** before agreeing to this crossover.

Other cosplay books: *Be the Hero You Want to See in the World But Without Powers, House of M: Designer Mutant Cosplay, Cos and Effect: Succeed in your Job by Dressing Like Storm.*
Not to mention *Fired With Cos: How You Too Can Get Fired For Dressing like Storm 24/7, We Have a Dress Code Here*

Kraven's actually died before and he was even a ghost for a while! Imagine a ghost hunter skulking around hunting the living? It would be like the opposite of a ghostbuster, and pretty cool. *Call me, Hollywood.*

Hollywood, my idea is like Chip's, only better because it's *also* like *Die Hard.* Call me First.

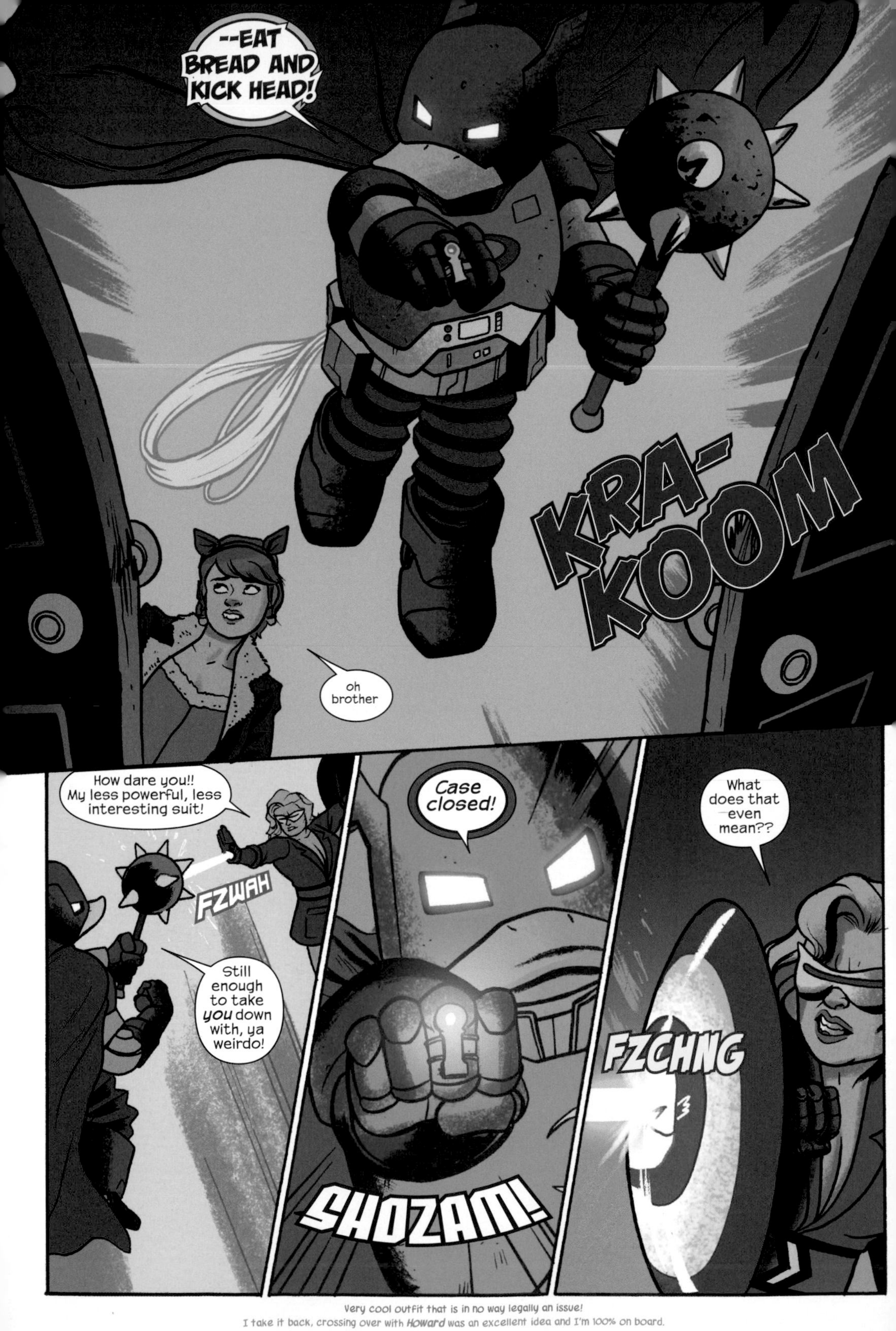
--EAT BREAD AND KICK HEAD!
KRA-KOOM
oh brother
How dare you!! My less powerful, less interesting suit!
FZWAH
Still enough to take *you* down with, ya weirdo!
Case closed!
SHOZAM!
What does that even mean??
FZCHNG

Very cool outfit that is in no way legally an issue!
I take it back, crossing over with *Howard* was an excellent idea and I'm 100% on board.

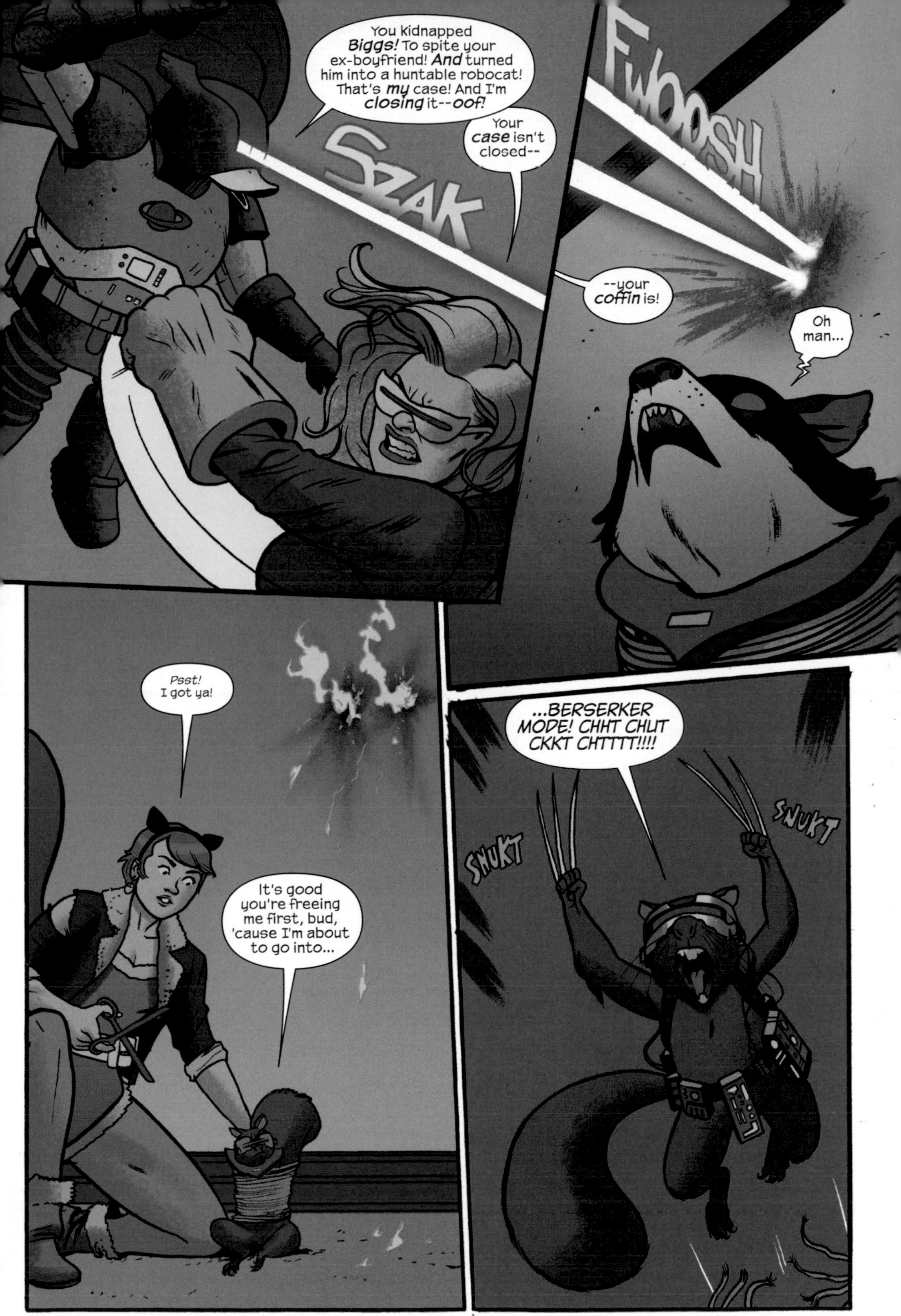
You kidnapped Biggs! To spite your ex-boyfriend! And turned him into a huntable robocat! That's my case! And I'm closing it--oof!
SZAK
Your case isn't closed--
FWOOSH
--your coffin is!
Oh man...
Psst! I got ya!
It's good you're freeing me first, bud, 'cause I'm about to go into...
...BERSERKER MODE! CHHT CHUT CKKT CHTTTT!!!!
SNUKT
SNUKT

Adorable!
Adorable.

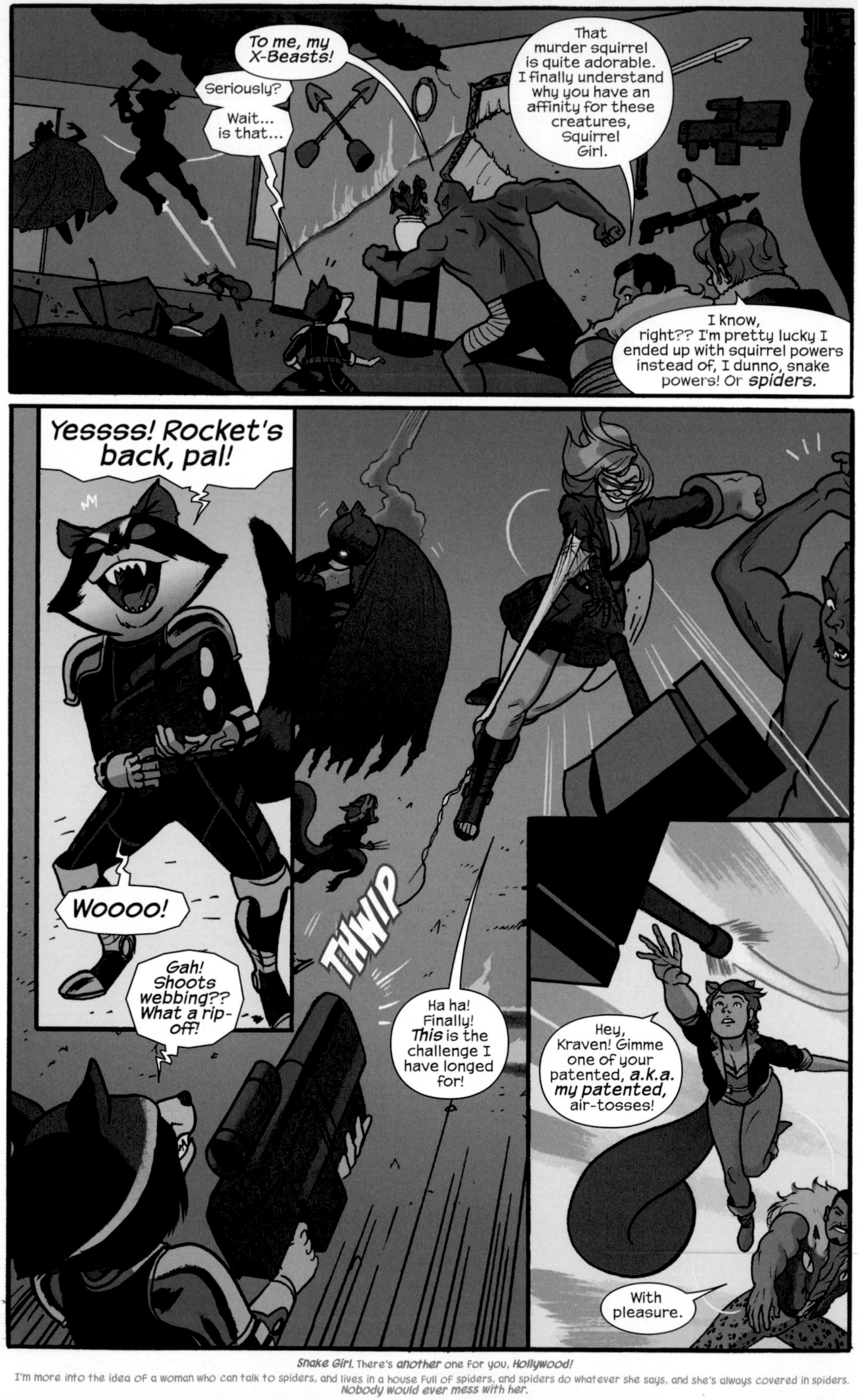

To me, my X-Beasts!
Seriously?
Wait... is that...
That murder squirrel is quite adorable. I finally understand why you have an affinity for these creatures, Squirrel Girl.
I know, right?? I'm pretty lucky I ended up with squirrel powers instead of, I dunno, snake powers! Or spiders.
Yessss! Rocket's back, pal!
Woooo!
Gah! Shoots webbing?? What a rip-off!
THWIP
Ha ha! Finally! This is the challenge I have longed for!
Hey, Kraven! Gimme one of your patented, a.k.a. my patented, air-tosses!
With pleasure.

Snake Girl. There's *another* one for you, *Hollywood!*
I'm more into the idea of a woman who can talk to spiders, and lives in a house full of spiders, and spiders do whatever she says, and she's always covered in spiders. *Nobody would ever mess with her.*

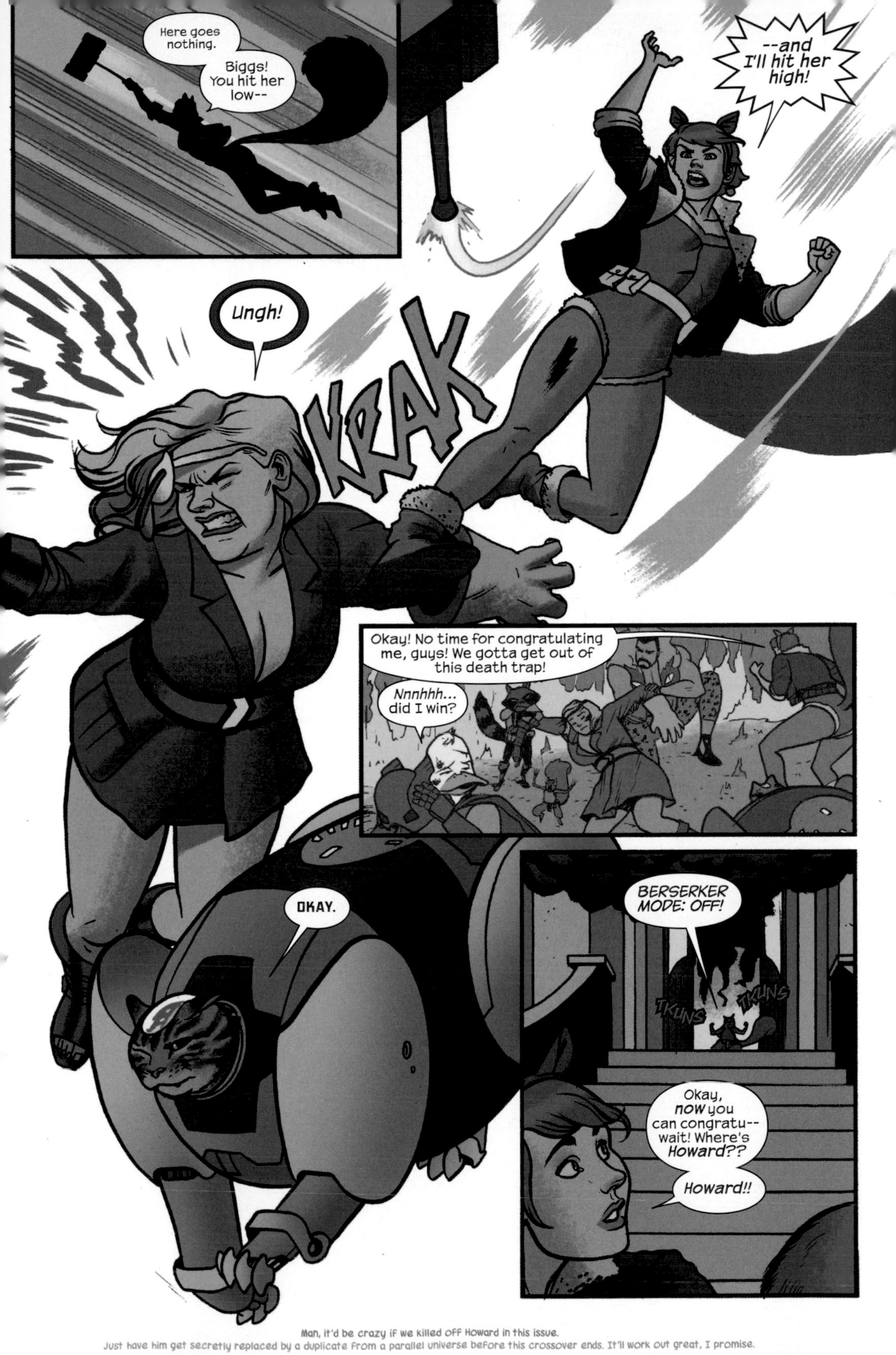
Here goes nothing.
Biggs! You hit her low--
--and I'll hit her high!
Ungh!
KRAK
OKAY.
Okay! No time for congratulating me, guys! We gotta get out of this death trap!
Nnnhhh... did I win?
BERSERKER MODE: OFF!
TKUNS
TKUNS
Okay, NOW you can congratu-- wait! Where's Howard??
Howard!!

Man, it'd be crazy if we killed off Howard in this issue.
Just have him get secretly replaced by a duplicate from a parallel universe before this crossover ends. It'll work out great, I promise.

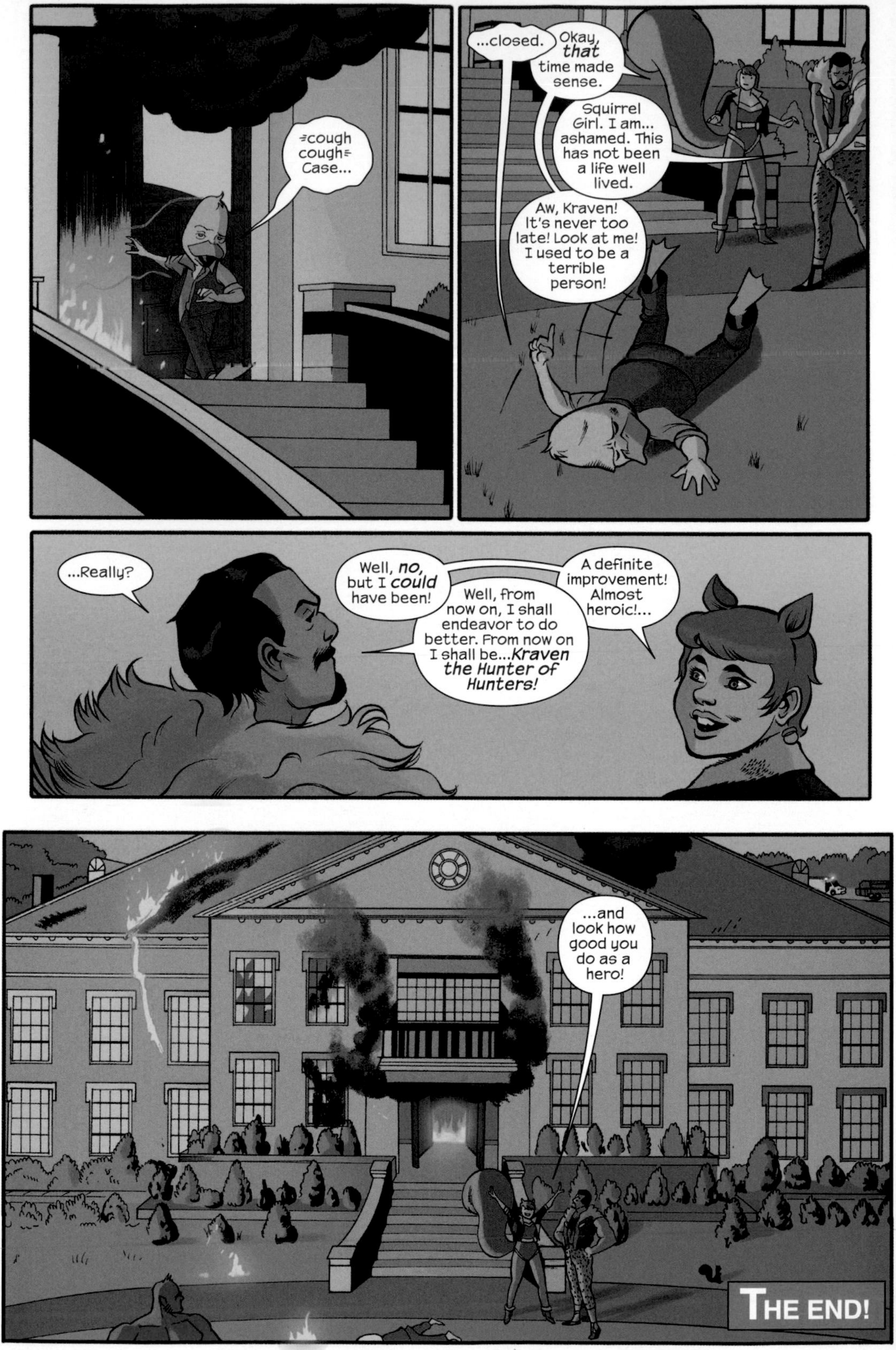
=cough cough= Case...
...closed.
Okay, *that* time made sense.
Squirrel Girl. I am... ashamed. This has not been a life well lived.
Aw, Kraven! It's never too late! Look at me! I used to be a terrible person!
...Really?
Well, *no,* but I *could* have been!
A definite improvement! Almost heroic!...
Well, from now on, I shall endeavor to do better. From now on I shall be...*Kraven the Hunter of Hunters!*
...and look how good you do as a hero!
THE END!

We won't stop until we reform every super villain. Next up? *Doombots.*
This summer...one Doombot discovers the only thing preventing him from taking over the world...is a crazy little thing called "love."

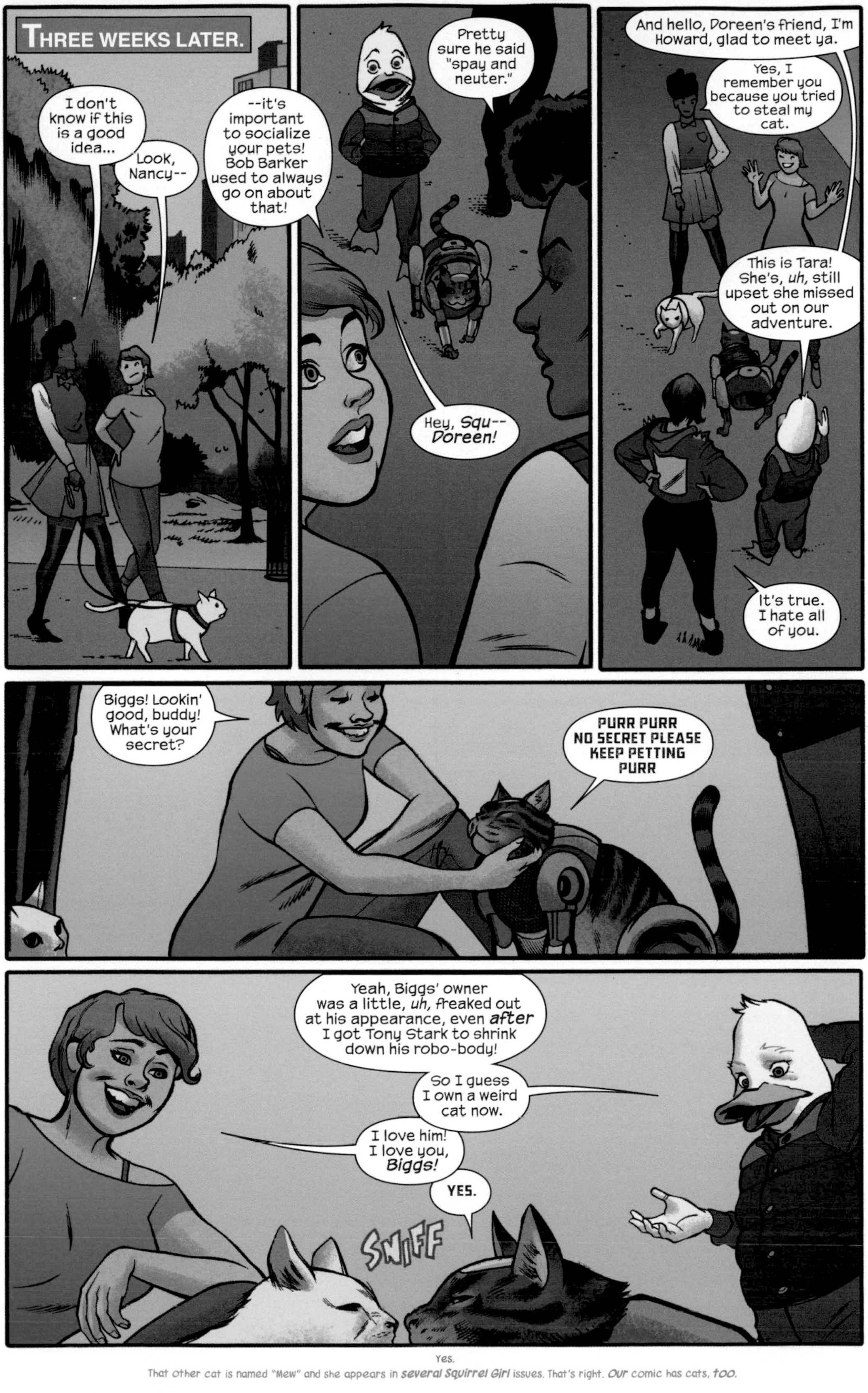
THREE WEEKS LATER.
I don't know if this is a good idea...
Look, Nancy--
--it's important to socialize your pets! Bob Barker used to always go on about that!
Pretty sure he said "spay and neuter."
Hey, Squ-- Doreen!
And hello, Doreen's friend, I'm Howard, glad to meet ya.
Yes, I remember you because you tried to steal my cat.
This is Tara! She's, uh, still upset she missed out on our adventure.
It's true. I hate all of you.
Biggs! Lookin' good, buddy! What's your secret?
PURR PURR NO SECRET PLEASE KEEP PETTING PURR
Yeah, Biggs' owner was a little, uh, freaked out at his appearance, even after I got Tony Stark to shrink down his robo-body!
So I guess I own a weird cat now.
I love him! I love you, Biggs!
YES.
SNIFF

Yes.
That other cat is named "Mew" and she appears in *several Squirrel Girl* issues. That's right. *Our* comic has cats, *too.*

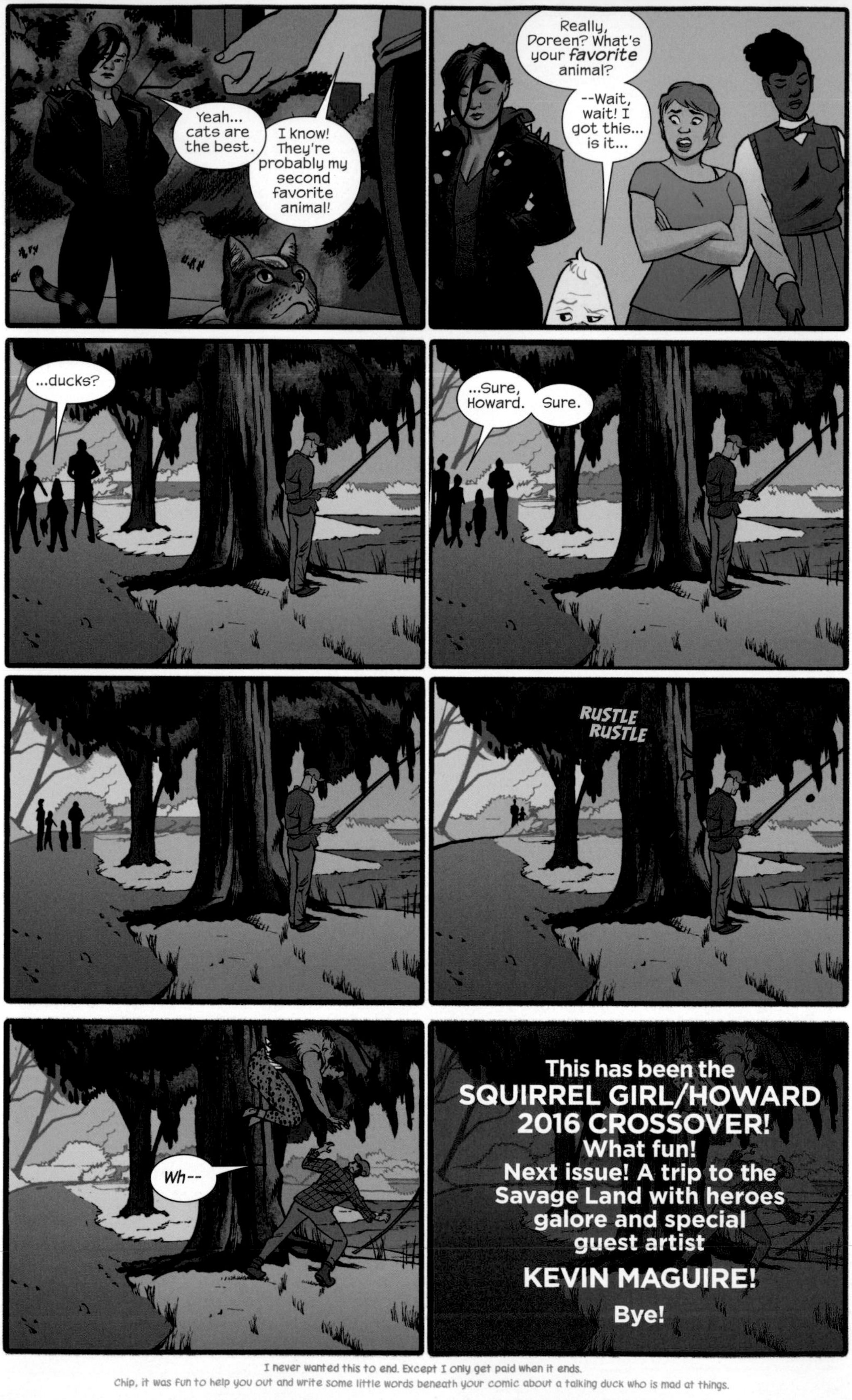
Yeah... cats are the best.
I know! They're probably my second favorite animal!
Really, Doreen? What's your favorite animal?
--Wait, wait! I got this... is it...
...ducks?
...Sure, Howard.
Sure.
RUSTLE RUSTLE
Wh--
This has been the SQUIRREL GIRL/HOWARD 2016 CROSSOVER! What fun! Next issue! A trip to the Savage Land with heroes galore and special guest artist KEVIN MAGUIRE! Bye!

I never wanted this to end. Except I only get paid when it ends.
Chip, it was fun to help you out and write some little words beneath your comic about a talking duck who is mad at things.

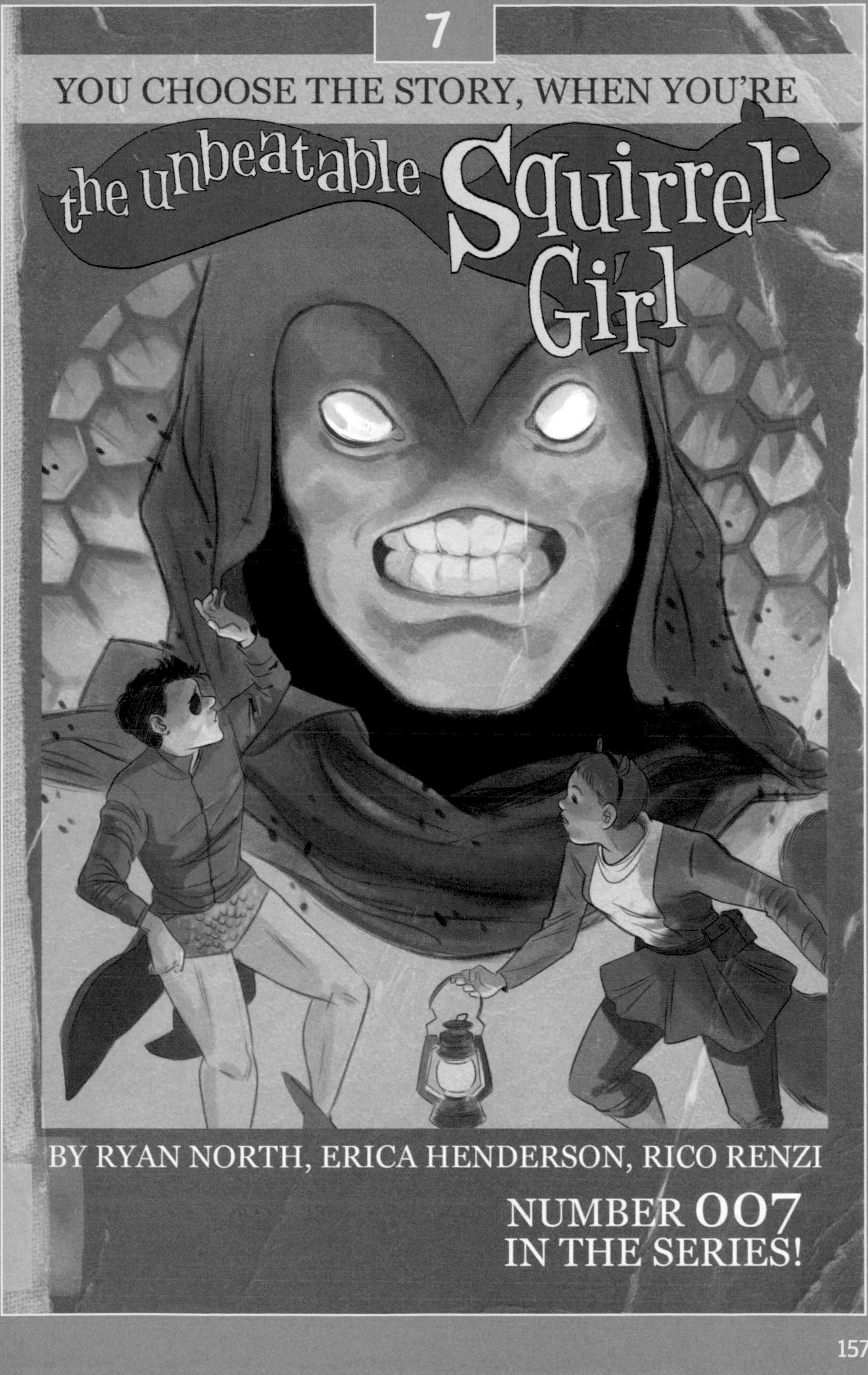
7
YOU CHOOSE THE STORY, WHEN YOU'RE
the unbeatable Squirrel Girl
BY RYAN NORTH, ERICA HENDERSON, RICO RENZI
NUMBER 007
IN THE SERIES!

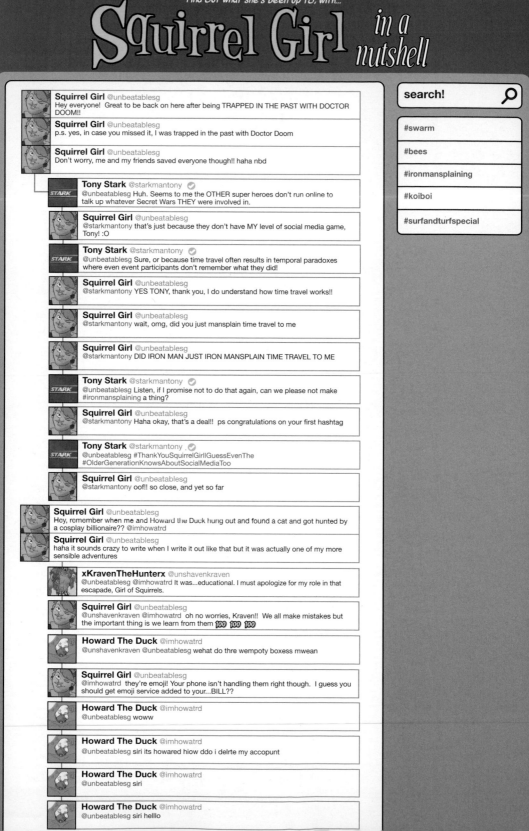

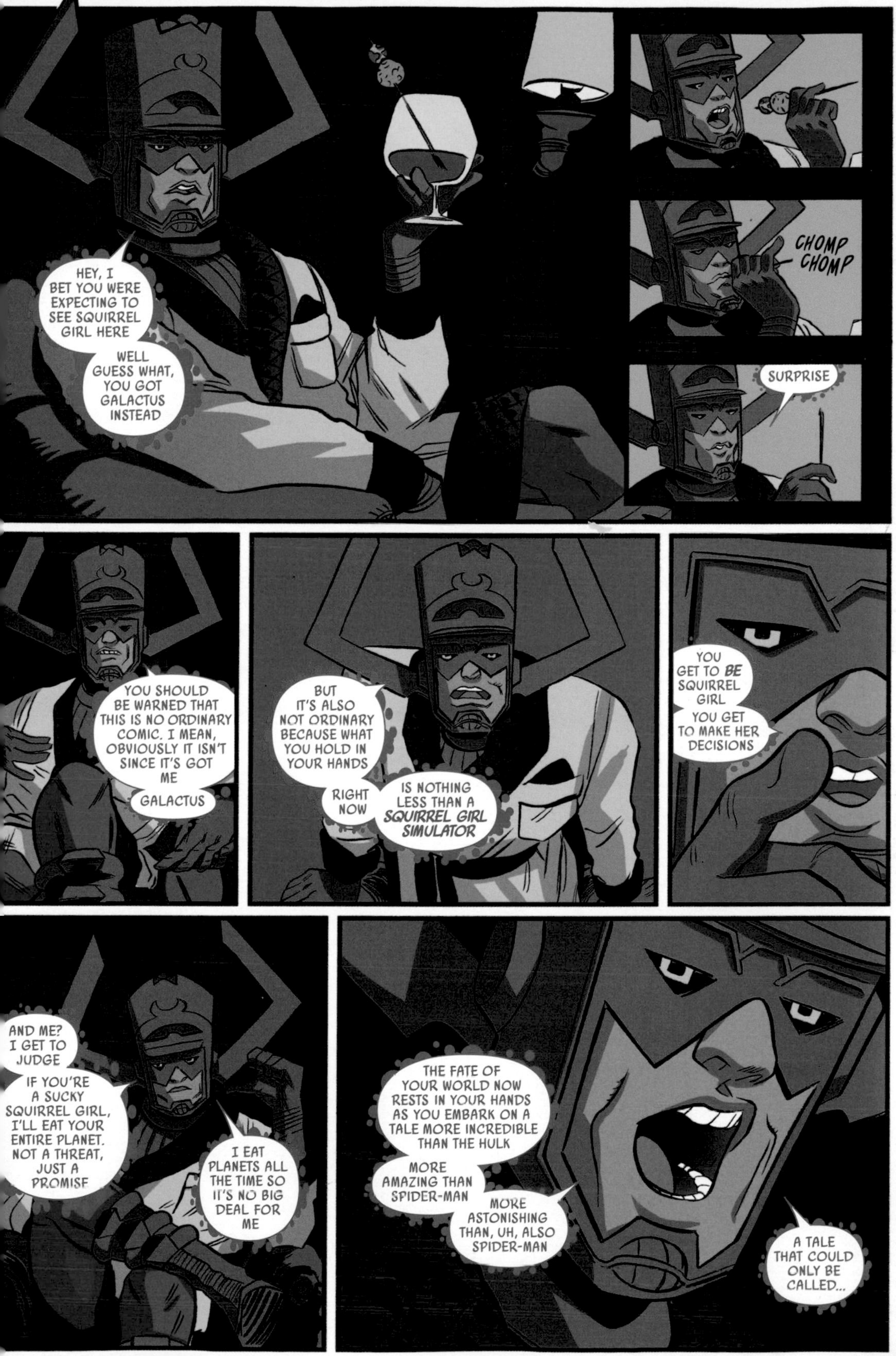
HEY, I BET YOU WERE EXPECTING TO SEE SQUIRREL GIRL HERE
WELL GUESS WHAT, YOU GOT GALACTUS INSTEAD
CHOMP CHOMP
SURPRISE
YOU SHOULD BE WARNED THAT THIS IS NO ORDINARY COMIC. I MEAN, OBVIOUSLY IT ISN'T SINCE IT'S GOT ME
GALACTUS
BUT IT'S ALSO NOT ORDINARY BECAUSE WHAT YOU HOLD IN YOUR HANDS
RIGHT NOW
IS NOTHING LESS THAN A SQUIRREL GIRL SIMULATOR
YOU GET TO BE SQUIRREL GIRL
YOU GET TO MAKE HER DECISIONS
AND ME? I GET TO JUDGE
IF YOU'RE A SUCKY SQUIRREL GIRL, I'LL EAT YOUR ENTIRE PLANET. NOT A THREAT, JUST A PROMISE
I EAT PLANETS ALL THE TIME SO IT'S NO BIG DEAL FOR ME
THE FATE OF YOUR WORLD NOW RESTS IN YOUR HANDS AS YOU EMBARK ON A TALE MORE INCREDIBLE THAN THE HULK
MORE AMAZING THAN SPIDER-MAN
MORE ASTONISHING THAN, UH, ALSO SPIDER-MAN
A TALE THAT COULD ONLY BE CALLED...

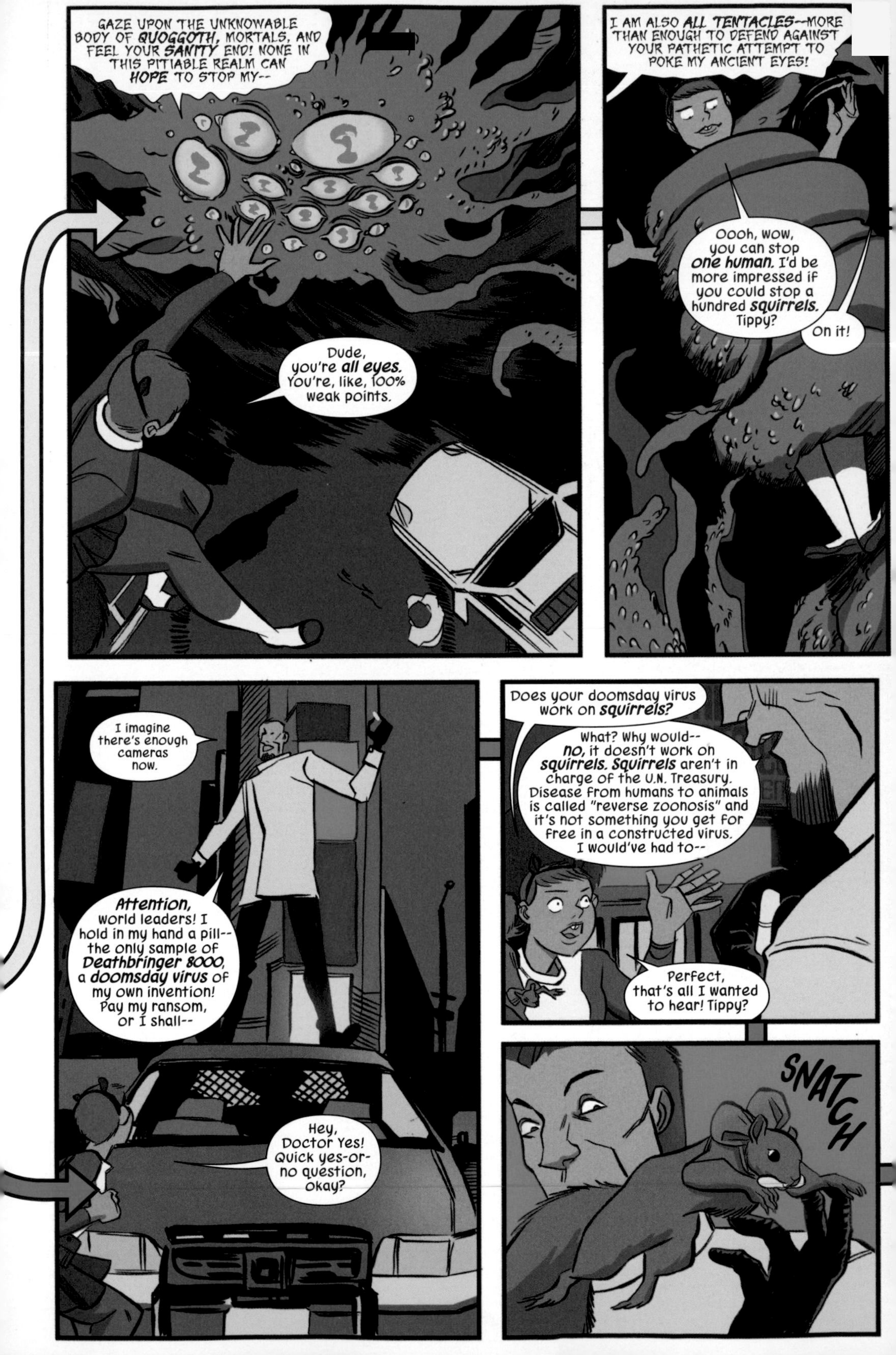

GAZE UPON THE UNKNOWABLE BODY OF QUOGGOTH, MORTALS, AND FEEL YOUR SANITY END! NONE IN THIS PITIABLE REALM CAN HOPE TO STOP MY--
Dude, you're all eyes. You're, like, 100% weak points.
I AM ALSO ALL TENTACLES--MORE THAN ENOUGH TO DEFEND AGAINST YOUR PATHETIC ATTEMPT TO POKE MY ANCIENT EYES!
Oooh, wow, you can stop one human. I'd be more impressed if you could stop a hundred squirrels. Tippy?
On it!
I imagine there's enough cameras now.
Attention, world leaders! I hold in my hand a pill--the only sample of Deathbringer 8000, a doomsday virus of my own invention! Pay my ransom, or I shall--
Hey, Doctor Yes! Quick yes-or-no question, okay?
Does your doomsday virus work on squirrels?
What? Why would--no, it doesn't work on squirrels. Squirrels aren't in charge of the U.N. Treasury. Disease from humans to animals is called "reverse zoonosis" and it's not something you get for free in a constructed virus. I would've had to--
Perfect, that's all I wanted to hear! Tippy?
SNATCH

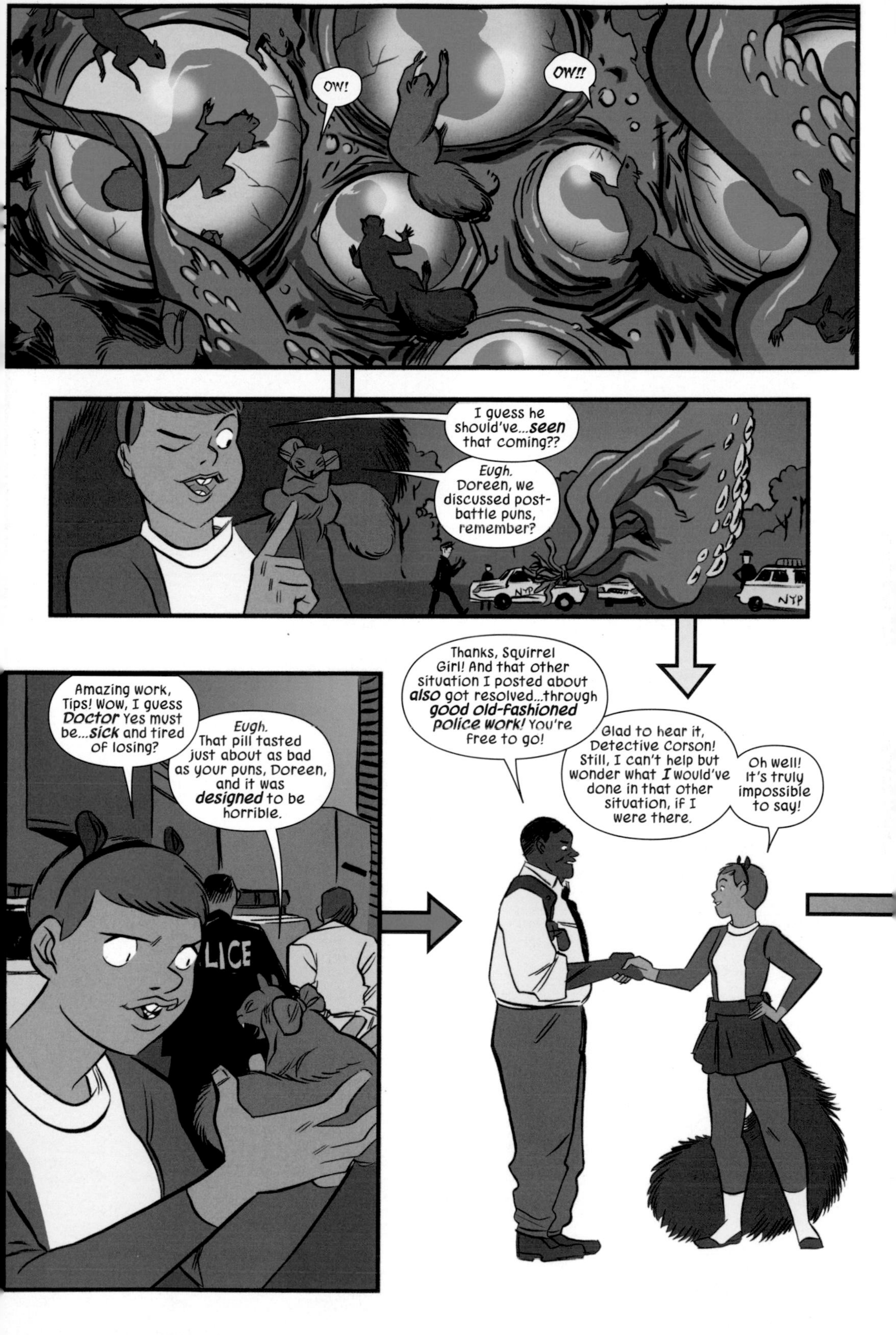
OW!
OW!!
I guess he should've...*seen* that coming??
Eugh. Doreen, we discussed post-battle puns, remember?
Amazing work, Tips! Wow, I guess *Doctor* Yes must be...*sick* and tired of losing?
Eugh. That pill tasted just about as bad as your puns, Doreen, and it was *designed* to be horrible.
LICE
Thanks, Squirrel Girl! And that other situation I posted about *also* got resolved...through *good old-fashioned police work!* You're free to go!
Glad to hear it, Detective Corson! Still, I can't help but wonder what *I* would've done in that other situation, if I were there.
Oh well! It's truly impossible to say!

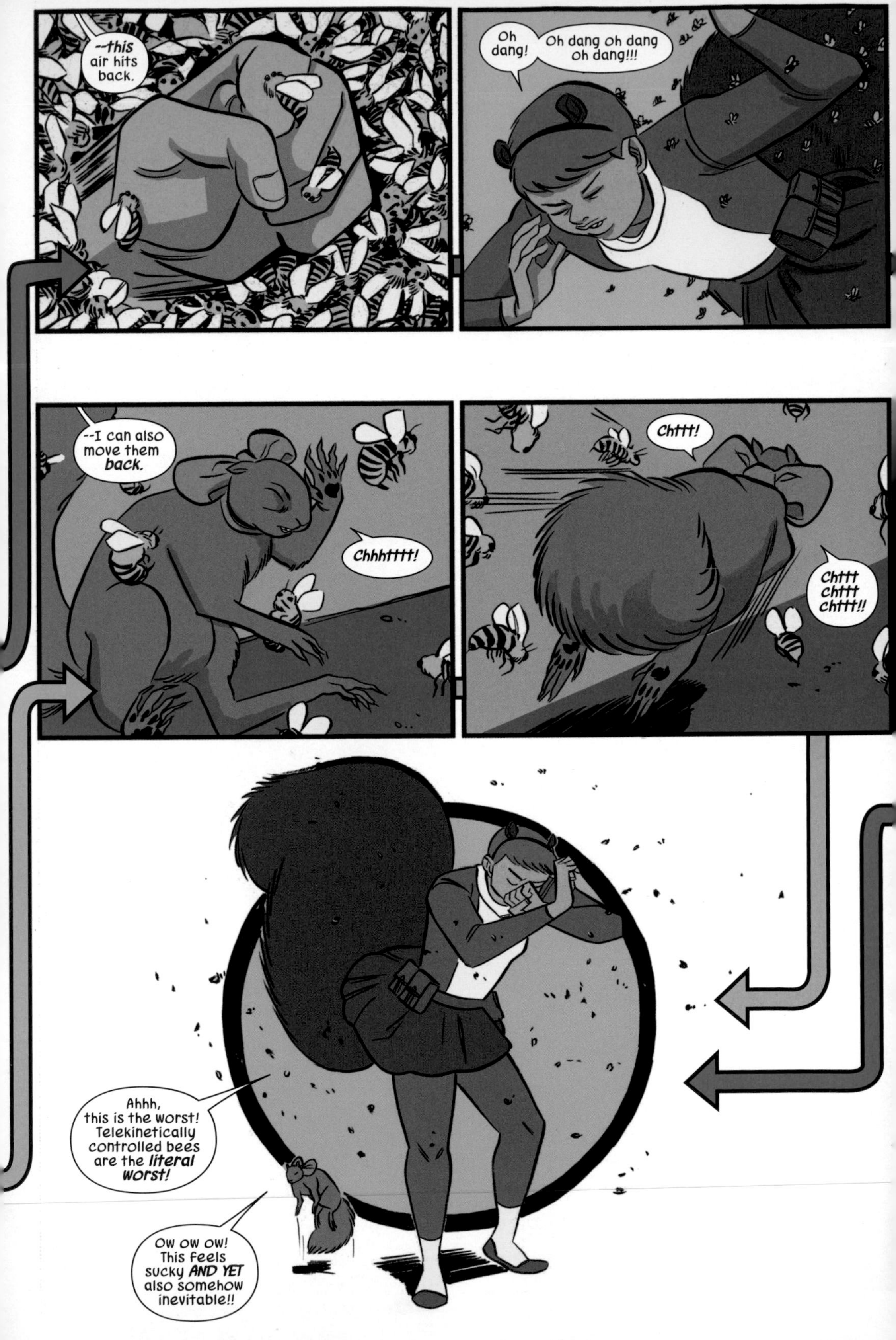
--this air hits back.
Oh dang!
Oh dang oh dang oh dang!!!
--I can also move them back.
Chhhtttt!
Chttt!
Chttt chttt chttt!!
Ahhh, this is the worst! Telekinetically controlled bees are the literal worst!
Ow ow ow! This feels sucky AND YET also somehow inevitable!!

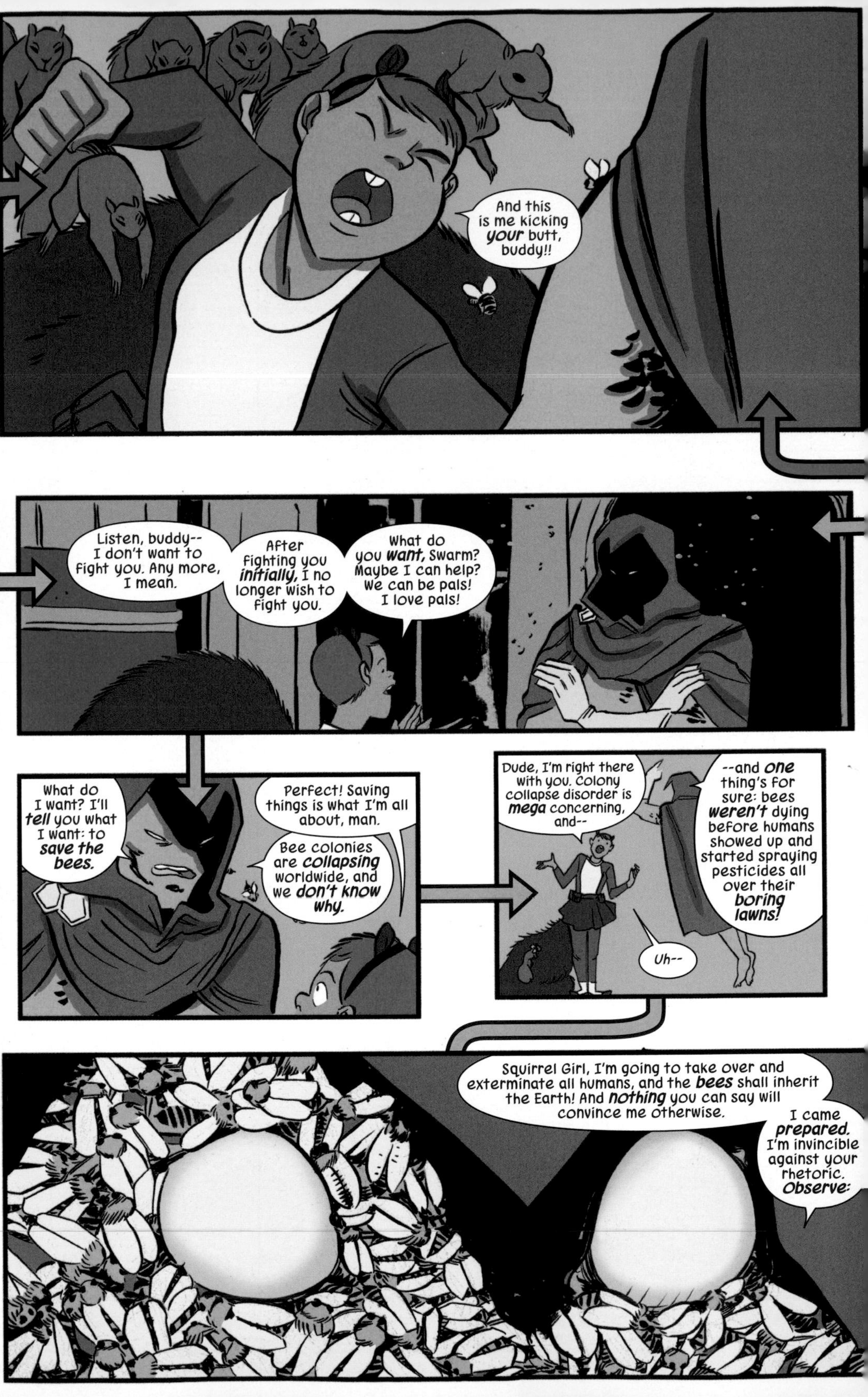

And this is me kicking *your* butt, buddy!!
Listen, buddy-- I don't want to fight you. Any more, I mean.
After fighting you *initially,* I no longer wish to fight you.
What do you *want,* Swarm? Maybe I can help? We can be pals! I love pals!
What do I want? I'll *tell* you what I want: to *save the bees.*
Perfect! Saving things is what I'm all about, man.
Bee colonies are *collapsing* worldwide, and we *don't know why.*
Dude, I'm right there with you. Colony collapse disorder is *mega* concerning, and--
--and *one* thing's for sure: bees *weren't* dying before humans showed up and started spraying pesticides all over their *boring lawns!*
Uh--
Squirrel Girl, I'm going to take over and exterminate all humans, and the *bees* shall inherit the Earth! And *nothing* you can say will convince me otherwise.
I came *prepared.* I'm invincible against your rhetoric. *Observe:*

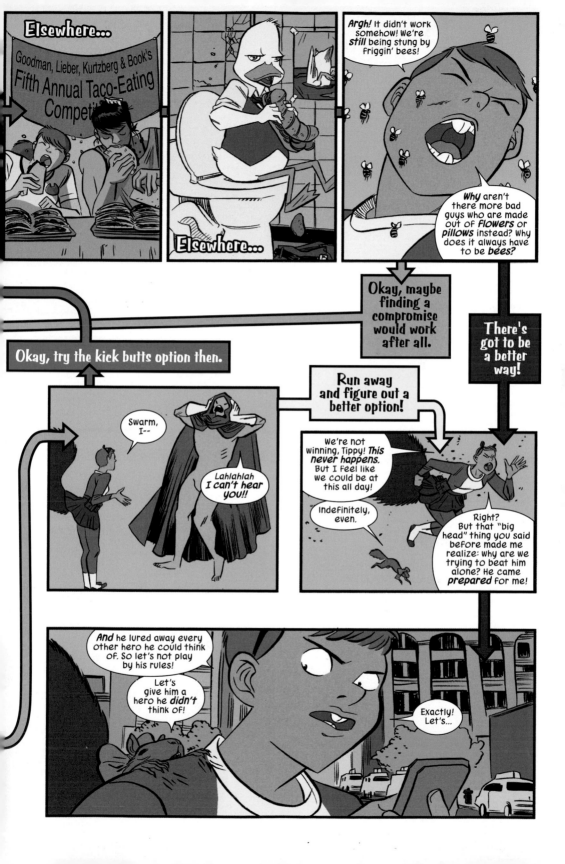

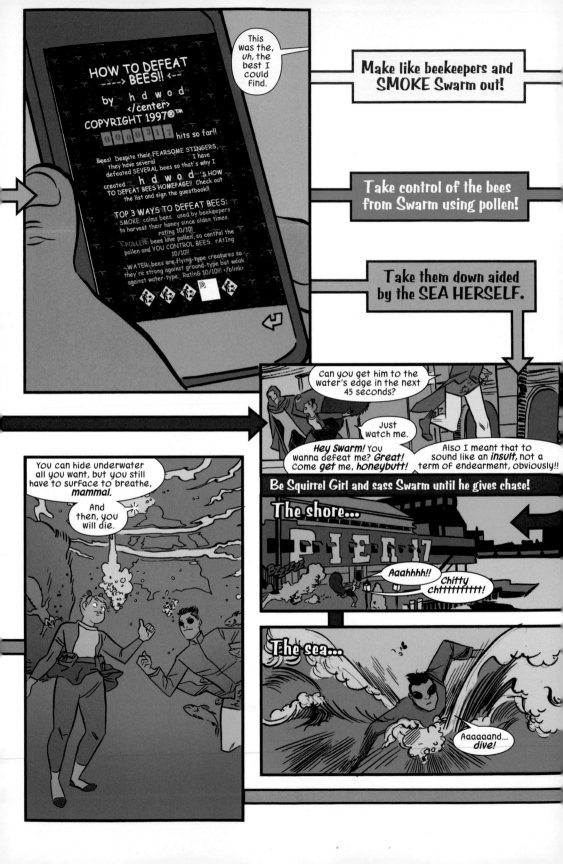

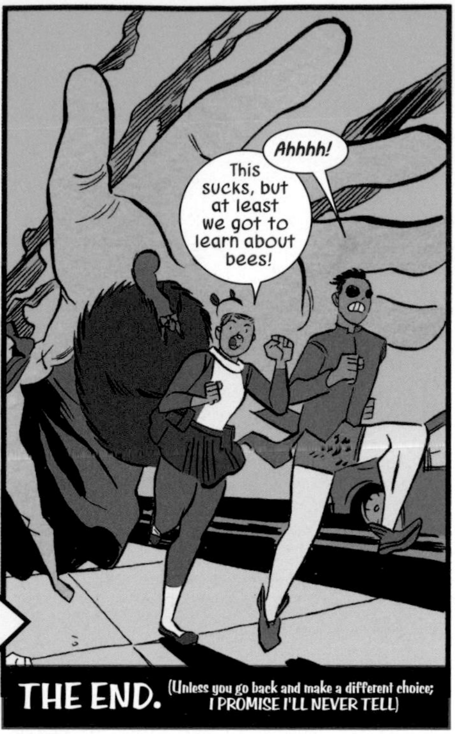
Ahhhh!
This sucks, but at least we got to learn about bees!
THE END. (Unless you go back and make a different choice; I PROMISE I'LL NEVER TELL)

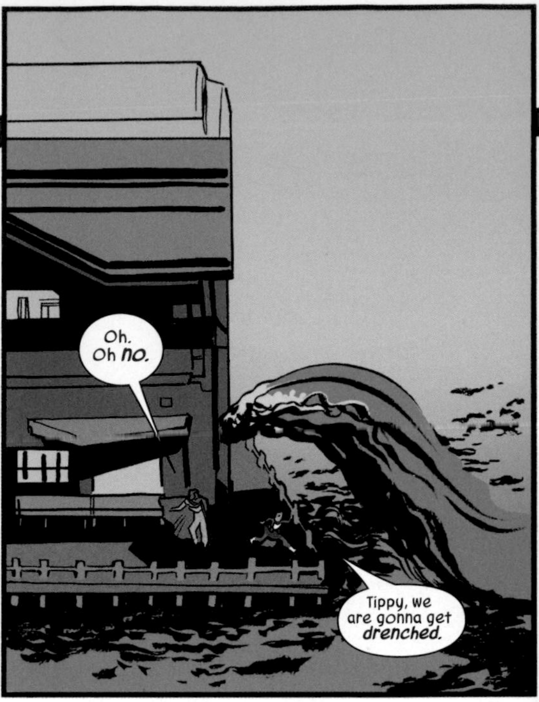
Oh. Oh no.
Tippy, we are gonna get drenched.

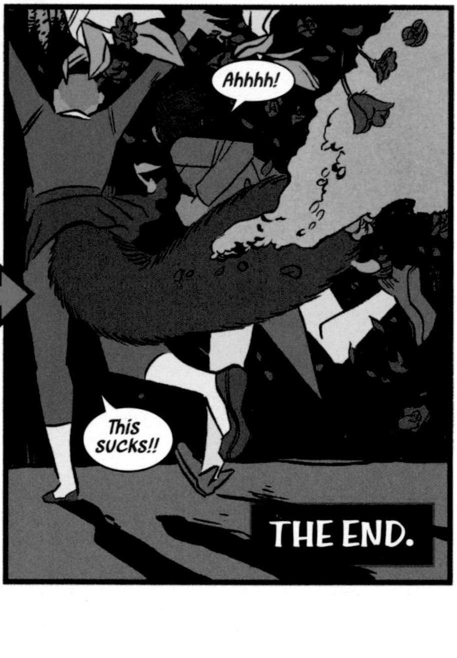
Ahhhh!
This sucks!!
THE END.

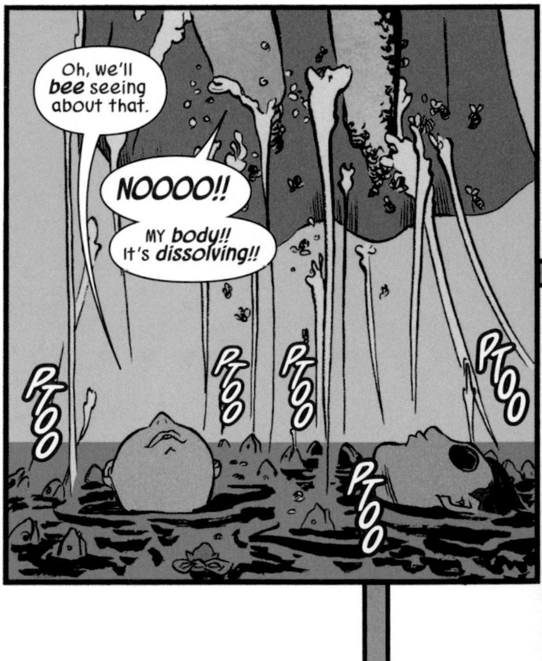
Oh, we'll bee seeing about that.
NOOOO!!
MY body!! It's dissolving!!
PTOO
PTOO
PTOO
PTOO
PTOO

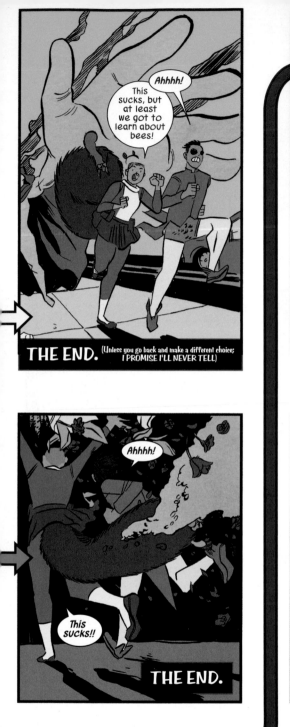

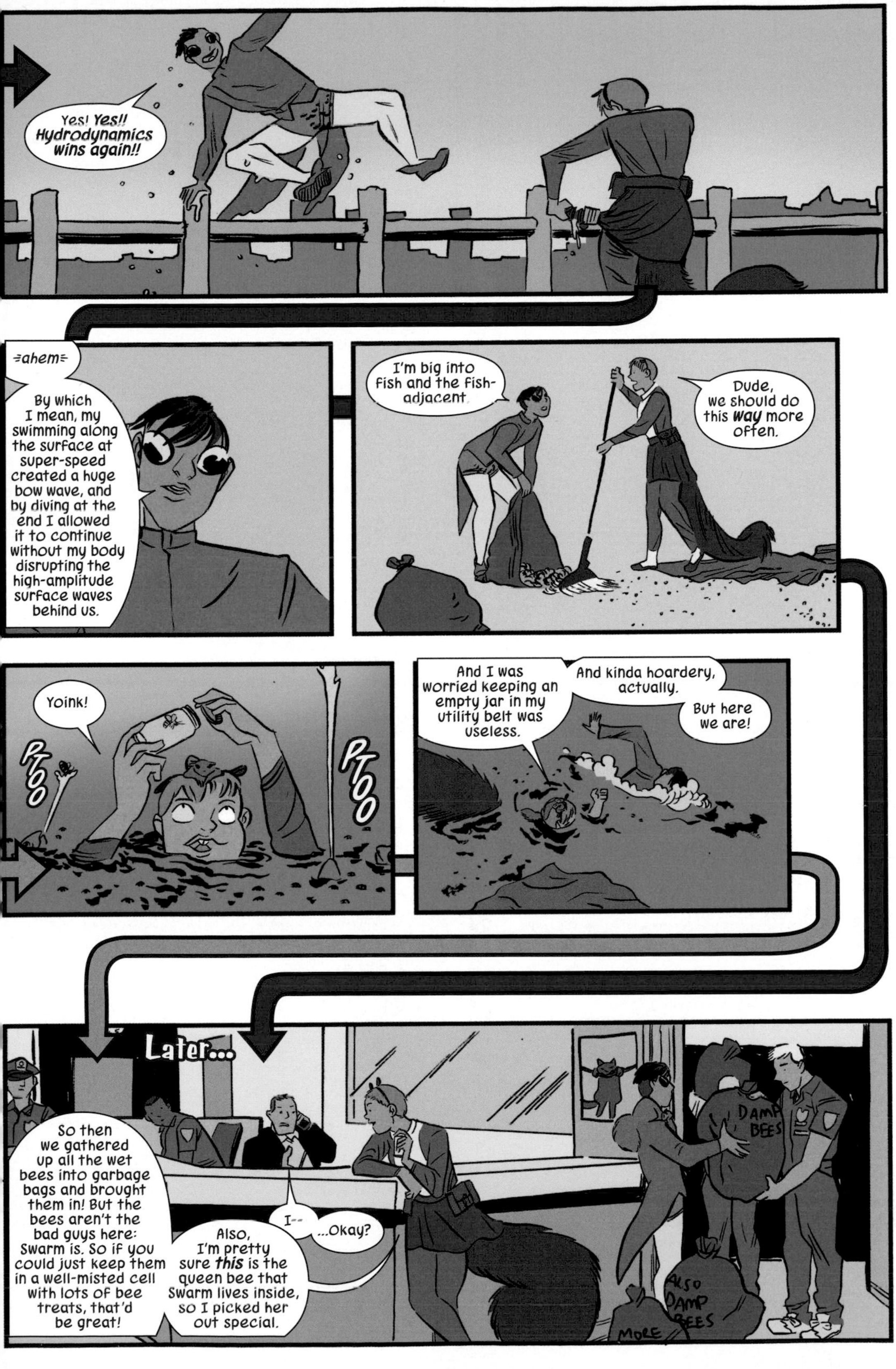

Yes! Yes!! Hydrodynamics wins again!!
=ahem=
By which I mean, my swimming along the surface at super-speed created a huge bow wave, and by diving at the end I allowed it to continue without my body disrupting the high-amplitude surface waves behind us.
I'm big into fish and the fish-adjacent.
Dude, we should do this way more often.
Yoink!
PTOO
PTOO
And I was worried keeping an empty jar in my utility belt was useless.
And kinda hoardery, actually.
But here we are!
Later...
So then we gathered up all the wet bees into garbage bags and brought them in! But the bees aren't the bad guys here: Swarm is. So if you could just keep them in a well-misted cell with lots of bee treats, that'd be great!
Also, I'm pretty sure this is the queen bee that Swarm lives inside, so I picked her out special.
I--
...Okay?
DAMP BEES
ALSO DAMP BEES
MORE

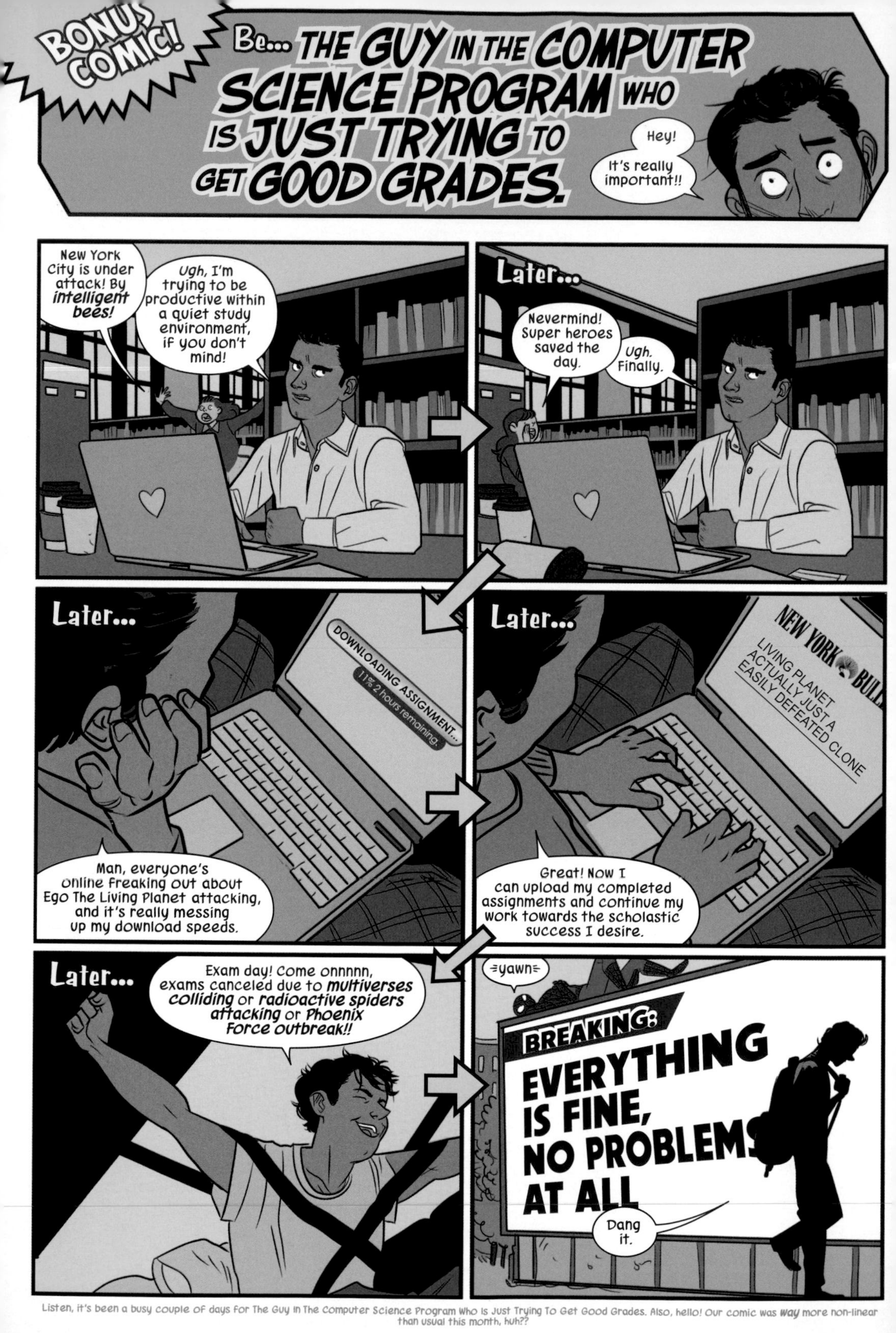
BONUS COMIC!
Be... THE GUY IN THE COMPUTER SCIENCE PROGRAM WHO IS JUST TRYING TO GET GOOD GRADES.
Hey!
It's really important!!
New York City is under attack! By *intelligent bees!*
Ugh, I'm trying to be productive within a quiet study environment, if you don't mind!
Later...
Nevermind! Super heroes saved the day.
Ugh. Finally.
Later...
DOWNLOADING ASSIGNMENT...
11% 2 hours remaining.
Man, everyone's online freaking out about Ego The Living Planet attacking, and it's really messing up my download speeds.
Later...
NEW YORK BUL
LIVING PLANET ACTUALLY JUST A EASILY DEFEATED CLONE
Great! Now I can upload my completed assignments and continue my work towards the scholastic success I desire.
Later...
Exam day! Come onnnnn, exams canceled due to *multiverses colliding* or *radioactive spiders attacking* or *Phoenix Force outbreak!!*
yawn
BREAKING:
EVERYTHING IS FINE, NO PROBLEMS AT ALL
Dang it.

Listen, it's been a busy couple of days for The Guy In The Computer Science Program Who Is Just Trying To Get Good Grades. Also, hello! Our comic was *way* more non-linear than usual this month, huh??

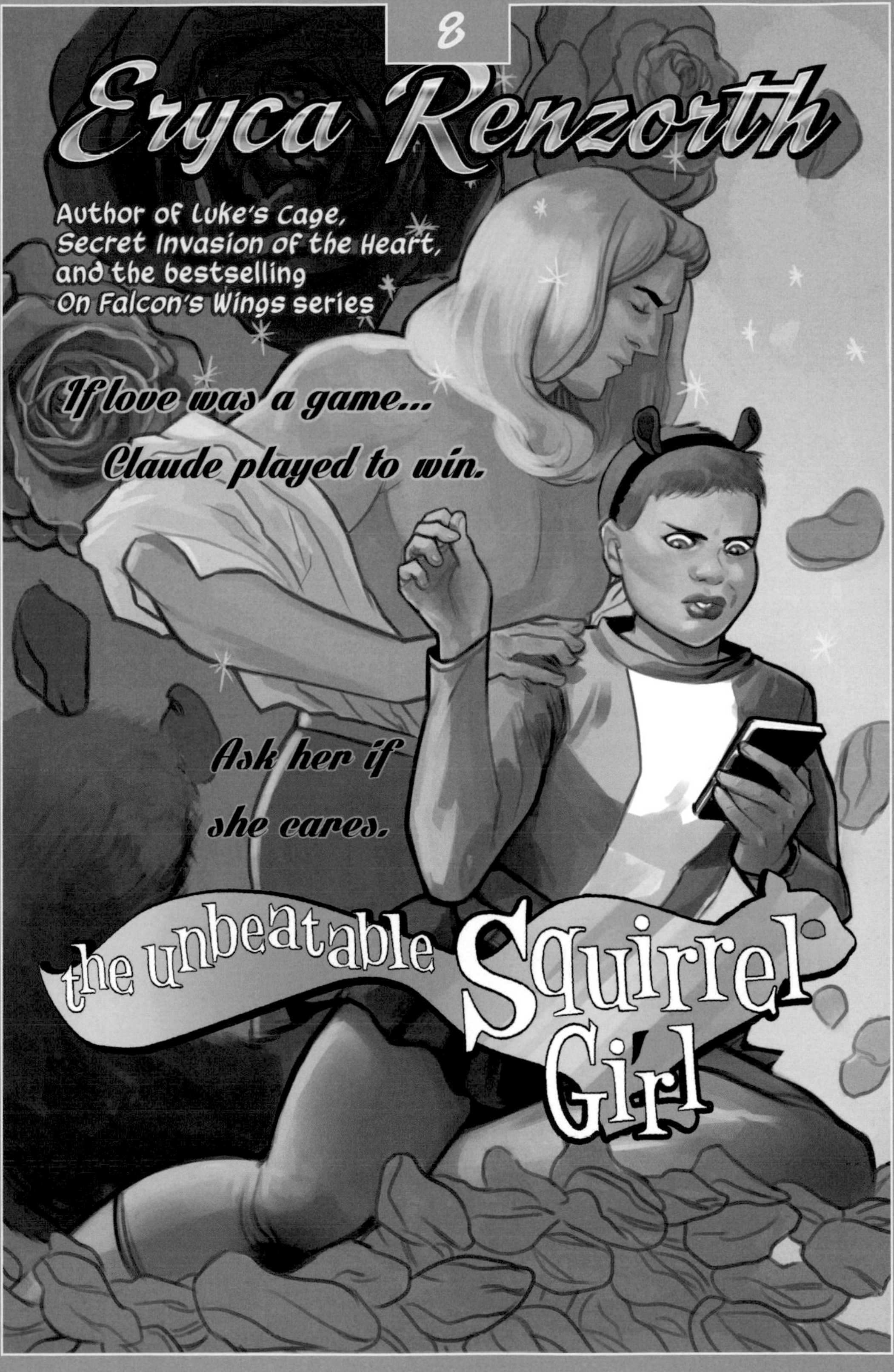
8
Eryca Renzorth
Author of Luke's Cage, Secret Invasion of the Heart, and the bestselling On Falcon's Wings series
If love was a game...
Claude played to win.
Ask her if
she cares.
the unbeatable Squirrel Girl

Doreen Green isn't just a second-year computer science student: she secretly also has all the powers of both squirrel and girl! She uses her amazing abilities to fight crime **and** be as awesome as possible. You know her as...*The Unbeatable Squirrel Girl!* Find out what she's been up to, with...

Squirrel Girl *in a nutshell*

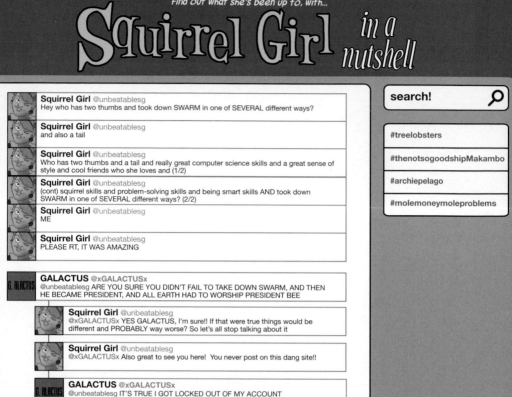

Squirrel Girl @unbeatablesg
Hey who has two thumbs and took down SWARM in one of SEVERAL different ways?

Squirrel Girl @unbeatablesg
and also a tail

Squirrel Girl @unbeatablesg
Who has two thumbs and a tail and really great computer science skills and a great sense of style and cool friends who she loves and (1/2)

Squirrel Girl @unbeatablesg
(cont) squirrel skills and problem-solving skills and being smart skills AND took down SWARM in one of SEVERAL different ways? (2/2)

Squirrel Girl @unbeatablesg
ME

Squirrel Girl @unbeatablesg
PLEASE RT, IT WAS AMAZING

GALACTUS @xGALACTUSx
@unbeatablesg ARE YOU SURE YOU DIDN'T FAIL TO TAKE DOWN SWARM, AND THEN HE BECAME PRESIDENT, AND ALL EARTH HAD TO WORSHIP PRESIDENT BEE

Squirrel Girl @unbeatablesg
@xGALACTUSx YES GALACTUS, I'm sure!! If that were true things would be different and PROBABLY way worse? So let's all stop talking about it

Squirrel Girl @unbeatablesg
@xGALACTUSx Also great to see you here! You never post on this dang site!!

GALACTUS @xGALACTUSx
@unbeatablesg IT'S TRUE I GOT LOCKED OUT OF MY ACCOUNT

GALACTUS @xGALACTUSx
@unbeatablesg THEY HAD A SECURITY QUESTION THAT I HAD TO ANSWER TO UNLOCK IT AND GUESS WHAT I SET THE QUESTION AS

GALACTUS @xGALACTUSx
@unbeatablesg GO ON, GUESS

Squirrel Girl @unbeatablesg
@xGALACTUSx um... "Universe's maiden name"? "Name of first Universe"? "Favorite power cosmic"?

GALACTUS @xGALACTUSx
@unbeatablesg APPARENTLY WHEN I FIRST SIGNED UP I'D SET IT TO "HI GALACTUS, IT'S YOU FROM THE PAST!! NO QUESTIONS HERE, YOU RULE BUDDY!!"

GALACTUS @xGALACTUSx
@unbeatablesg IT'S LIKE, THANKS PAST ME, JUST SOME REAL TERRIFIC WORK THERE

GALACTUS @xGALACTUSx
@unbeatablesg ANYWAY I USED THE POWER COSMIC TO REWIND TIME AND CHANGE THINGS SO I NEVER CHOSE THAT SECURITY QUESTION

GALACTUS @xGALACTUSx
@unbeatablesg AS A SIDE EFFECT IT CAUSED TWO SOLAR SYSTEMS TO NEVER HAVE BEEN FORMED BUT THEY WERE DUDS ANYWAY, JUST REAL DUD SOLAR SYSTEMS

Squirrel Girl @unbeatablesg
@xGALACTUSx ...

GALACTUS @xGALACTUSx
@unbeatablesg ALSO

GALACTUS @xGALACTUSx
@unbeatablesg I HAVE ALREADY FORGOTTEN MY NEW PASSWORD

GALACTUS @xGALACTUSx
@unbeatablesg SO THAT'S A THING

search!

#treelobsters

#thenotsogoodshipMakambo

#archiepelago

#molemoneymoleproblems

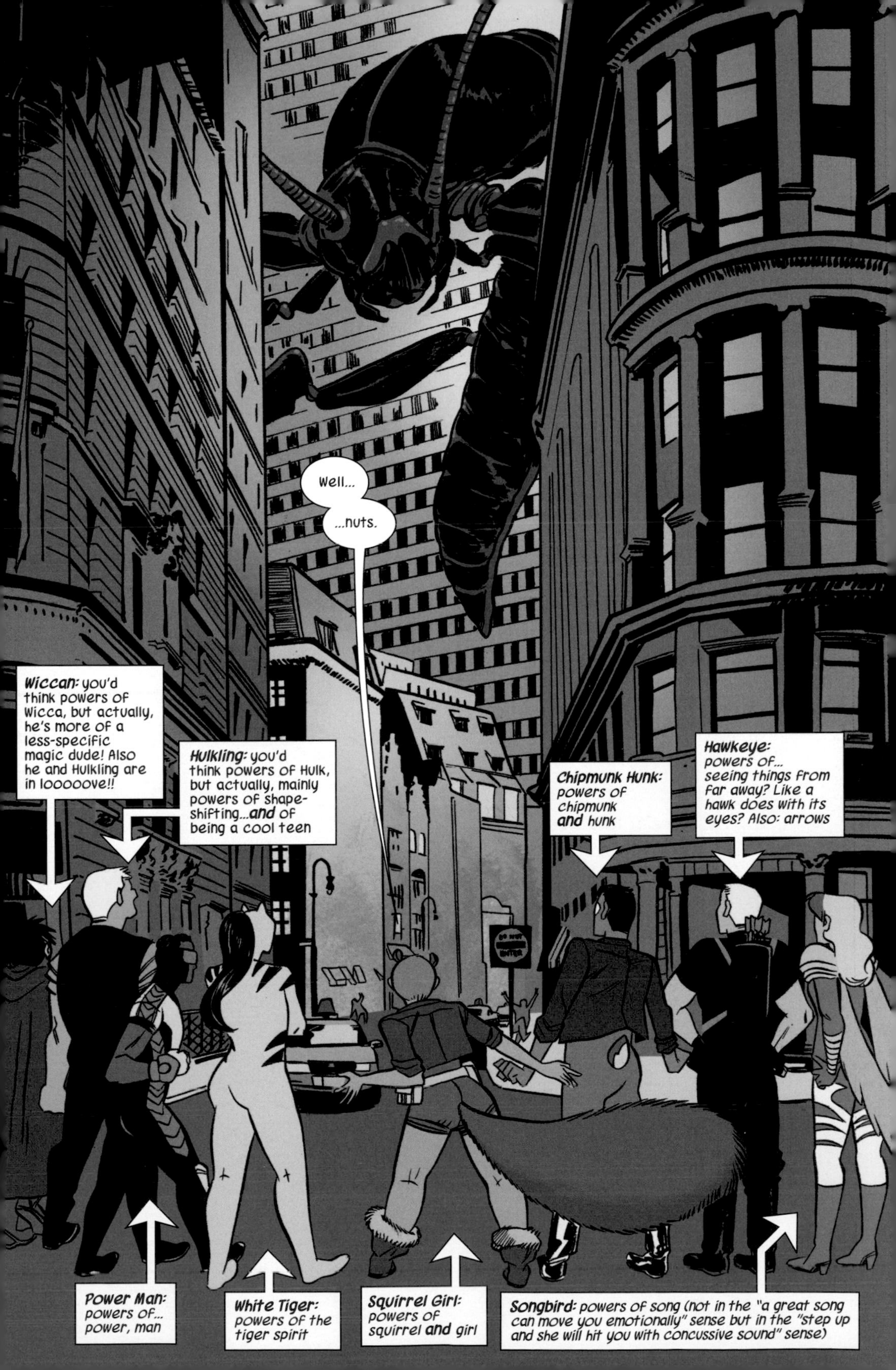
Well...
...nuts.
Wiccan: you'd think powers of Wicca, but actually, he's more of a less-specific magic dude! Also he and Hulkling are in looooove!!
Hulkling: you'd think powers of Hulk, but actually, mainly powers of shape-shifting...and of being a cool teen
Chipmunk Hunk: powers of chipmunk and hunk
Hawkeye: powers of... seeing things from far away? Like a hawk does with its eyes? Also: arrows
Power Man: powers of... power, man
White Tiger: powers of the tiger spirit
Squirrel Girl: powers of squirrel and girl
Songbird: powers of song (not in the "a great song can move you emotionally" sense but in the "step up and she will hit you with concussive sound" sense)

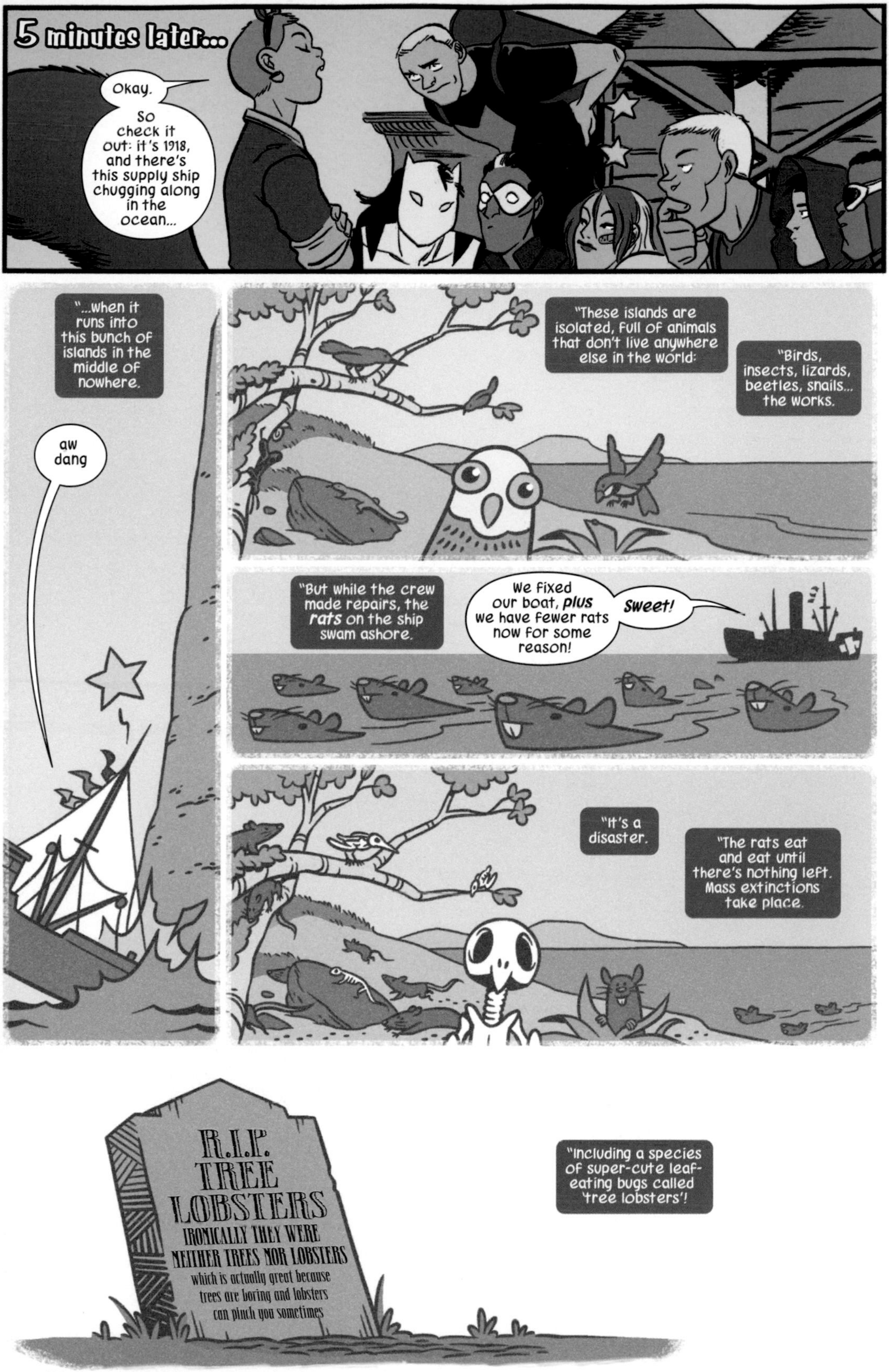

5 minutes later...
Okay.
So check it out: it's 1918, and there's this supply ship chugging along in the ocean...
"...when it runs into this bunch of islands in the middle of nowhere.
aw dang
"These islands are isolated, full of animals that don't live anywhere else in the world:
"Birds, insects, lizards, beetles, snails... the works.
"But while the crew made repairs, the *rats* on the ship swam ashore.
We fixed our boat, **plus** we have fewer rats now for some reason!
Sweet!
"It's a disaster.
"The rats eat and eat until there's nothing left. Mass extinctions take place.
R.I.P. TREE LOBSTERS
IRONICALLY THEY WERE NEITHER TREES NOR LOBSTERS
which is actually great because trees are boring and lobsters can pinch you sometimes
"Including a species of super-cute leaf-eating bugs called 'tree lobsters'!

"A bunch of islands" is called an "archipelago." If Squirrel Girl ever fights a guy who can split into a bunch of smaller guys whenever he gets wet and who is named "Archie Pelago," then you will know precisely where I got my inspiration.

Tree lobsters are *the cutest*. They pair off in couples and follow each other around, and when they sleep they cuddle up together so that one insect's legs protectively cover the other. They're *insects that spoon each other,* it's the cutest—I love you, tree lobsters!

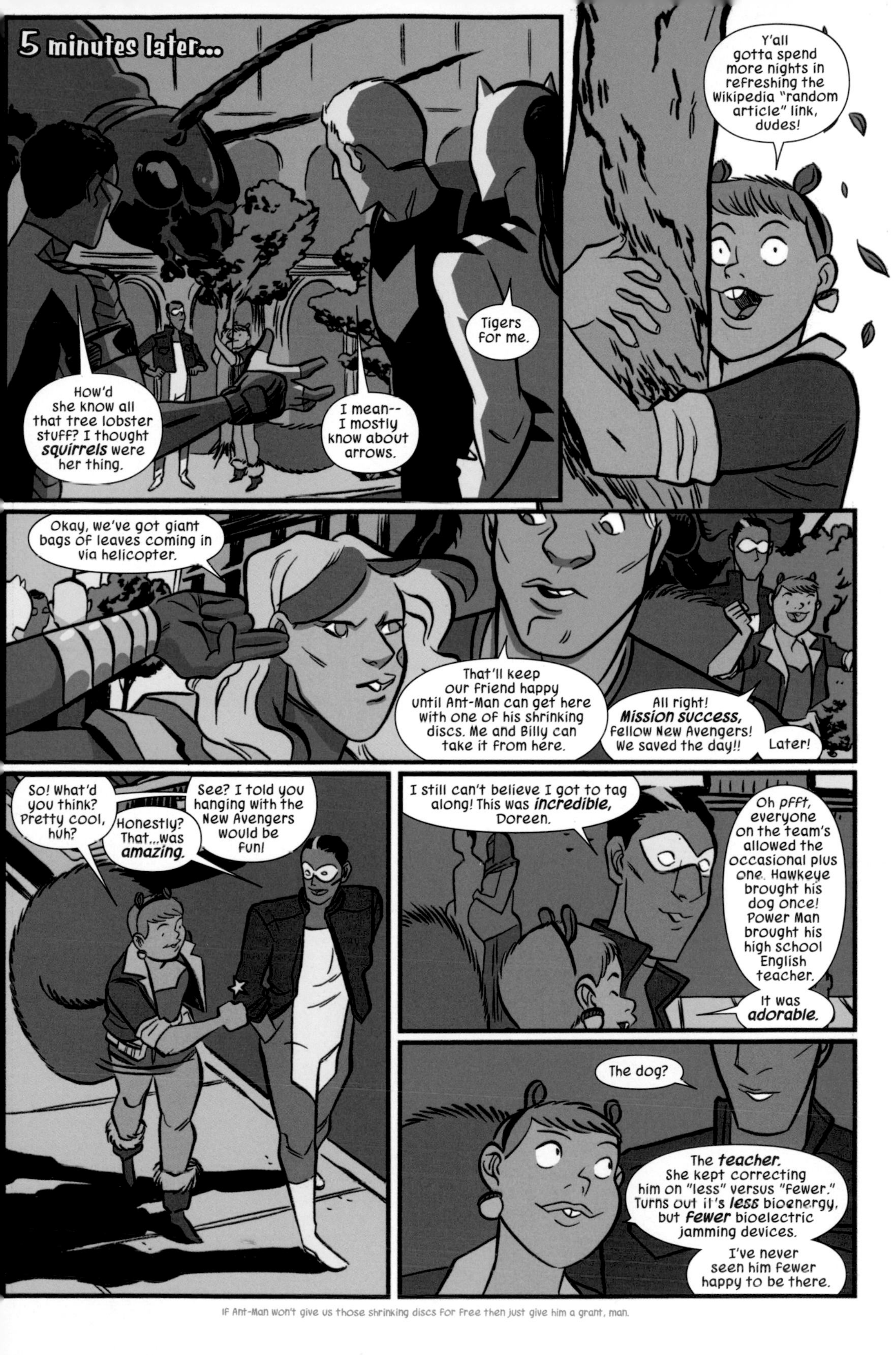
5 minutes later...
Y'all gotta spend more nights in refreshing the Wikipedia "random article" link, dudes!
How'd she know all that tree lobster stuff? I thought squirrels were her thing.
I mean-- I mostly know about arrows.
Tigers for me.
Okay, we've got giant bags of leaves coming in via helicopter.
That'll keep our friend happy until Ant-Man can get here with one of his shrinking discs. Me and Billy can take it from here.
All right! Mission success, fellow New Avengers! We saved the day!!
Later!
So! What'd you think? Pretty cool, huh?
Honestly? That...was amazing.
See? I told you hanging with the New Avengers would be fun!
I still can't believe I got to tag along! This was incredible, Doreen.
Oh pfft, everyone on the team's allowed the occasional plus one. Hawkeye brought his dog once! Power Man brought his high school English teacher.
It was adorable.
The dog?
The teacher. She kept correcting him on "less" versus "fewer." Turns out it's less bioenergy, but fewer bioelectric jamming devices.
I've never seen him fewer happy to be there.

If Ant-Man won't give us those shrinking discs for free then just give him a grant, man.

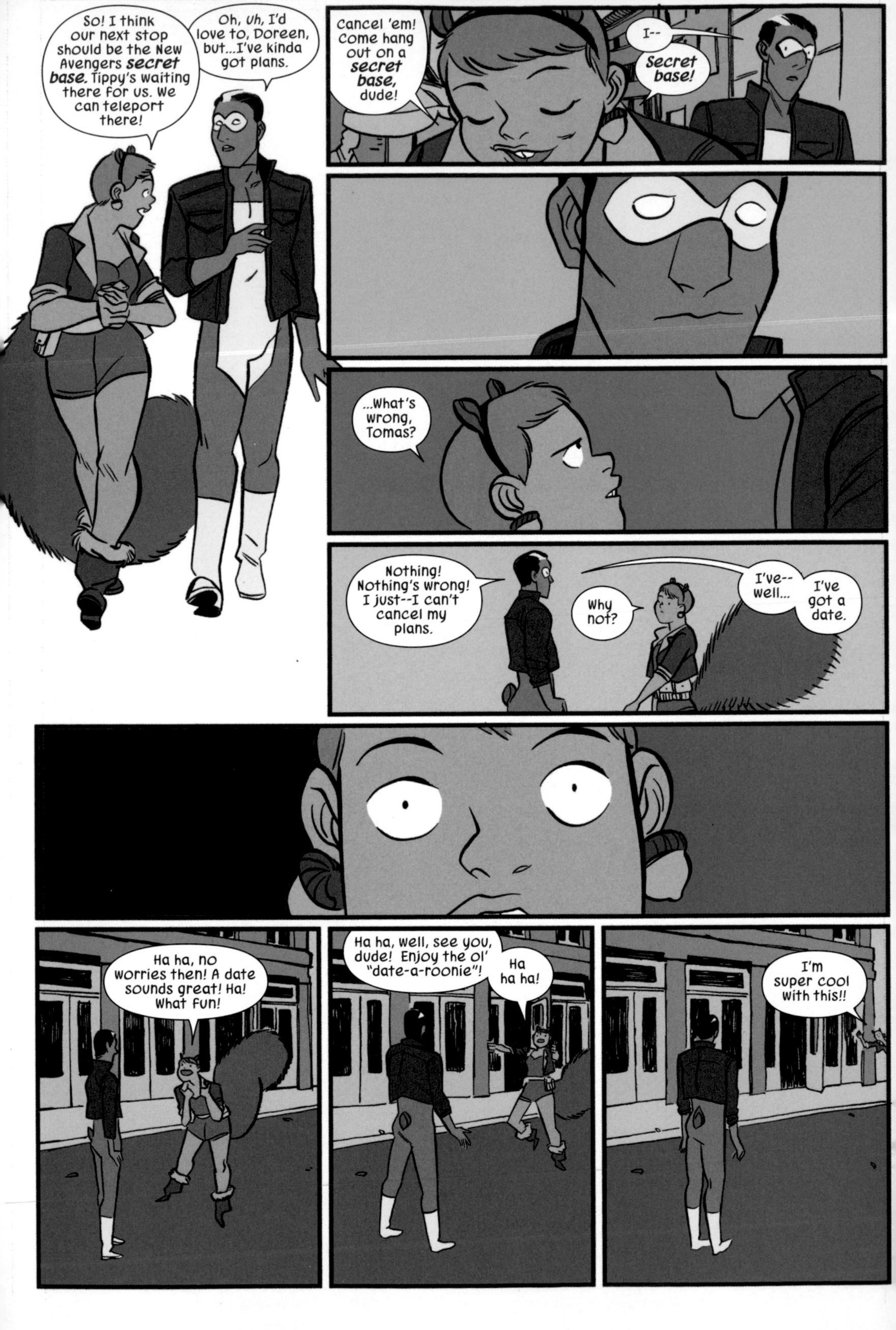
So! I think our next stop should be the New Avengers **secret base.** Tippy's waiting there for us. We can teleport there!
Oh, uh, I'd love to, Doreen, but...I've kinda got plans.
Cancel 'em! Come hang out on a **secret base,** dude!
I--
Secret base!
...What's wrong, Tomas?
Nothing! Nothing's wrong! I just--I can't cancel my plans.
Why not?
I've-- well...
I've got a date.
Ha ha, no worries then! A date sounds great! Ha! What fun!
Ha ha, well, see you, dude! Enjoy the ol' "date-a-roonie"!
Ha ha ha!
I'm super cool with this!!

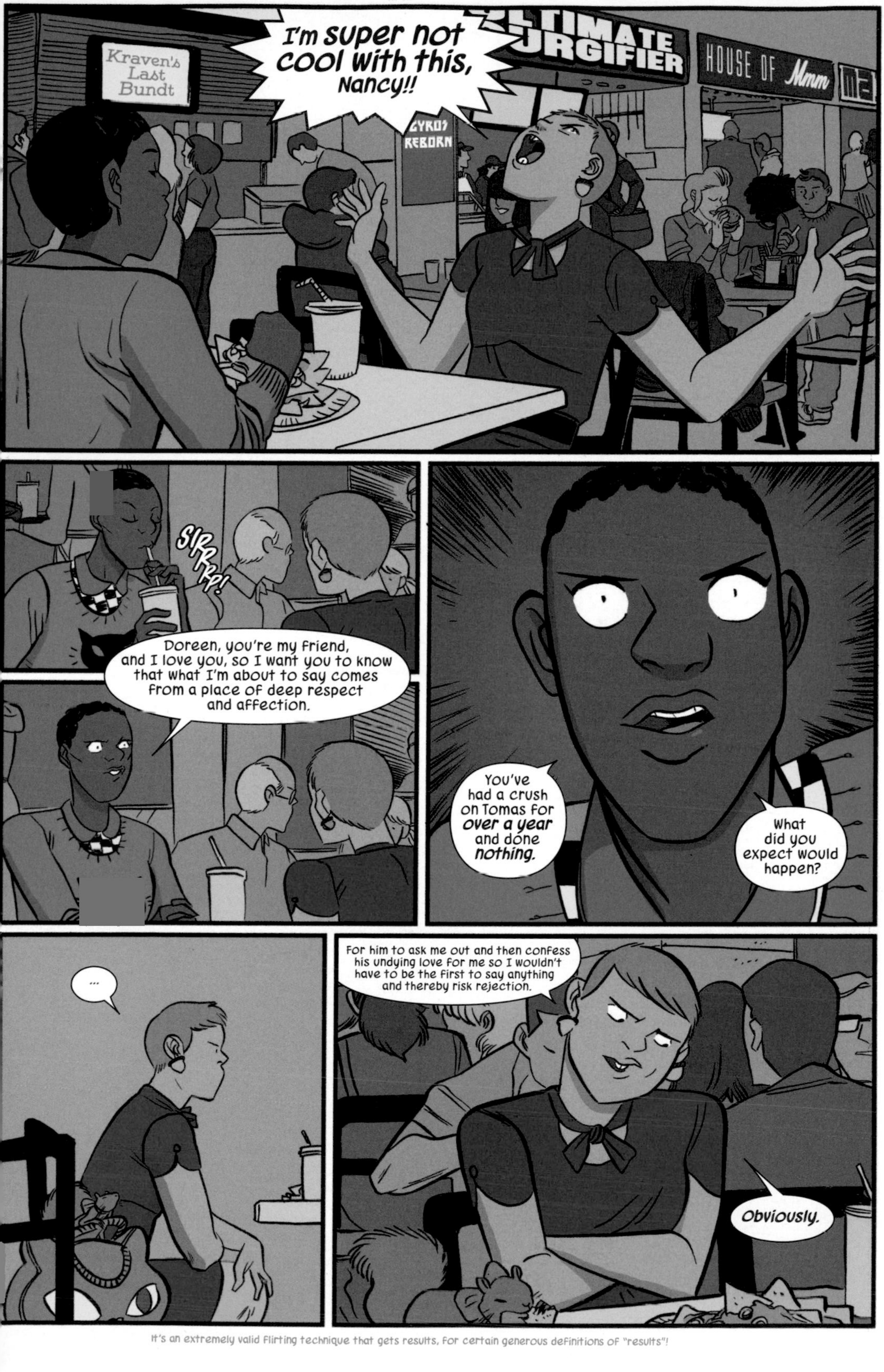
Kraven's Last Bundt
I'm super not cool with this, Nancy!!
ULTIMATE BURGIFIER
HOUSE OF Mmm
GYROS REBORN
SIRRRP!
Doreen, you're my friend, and I love you, so I want you to know that what I'm about to say comes from a place of deep respect and affection.
You've had a crush on Tomas for over a year and done nothing.
What did you expect would happen?
...
For him to ask me out and then confess his undying love for me so I wouldn't have to be the first to say anything and thereby risk rejection.
Obviously.

It's an extremely valid flirting technique that gets results, for certain generous definitions of "results"!

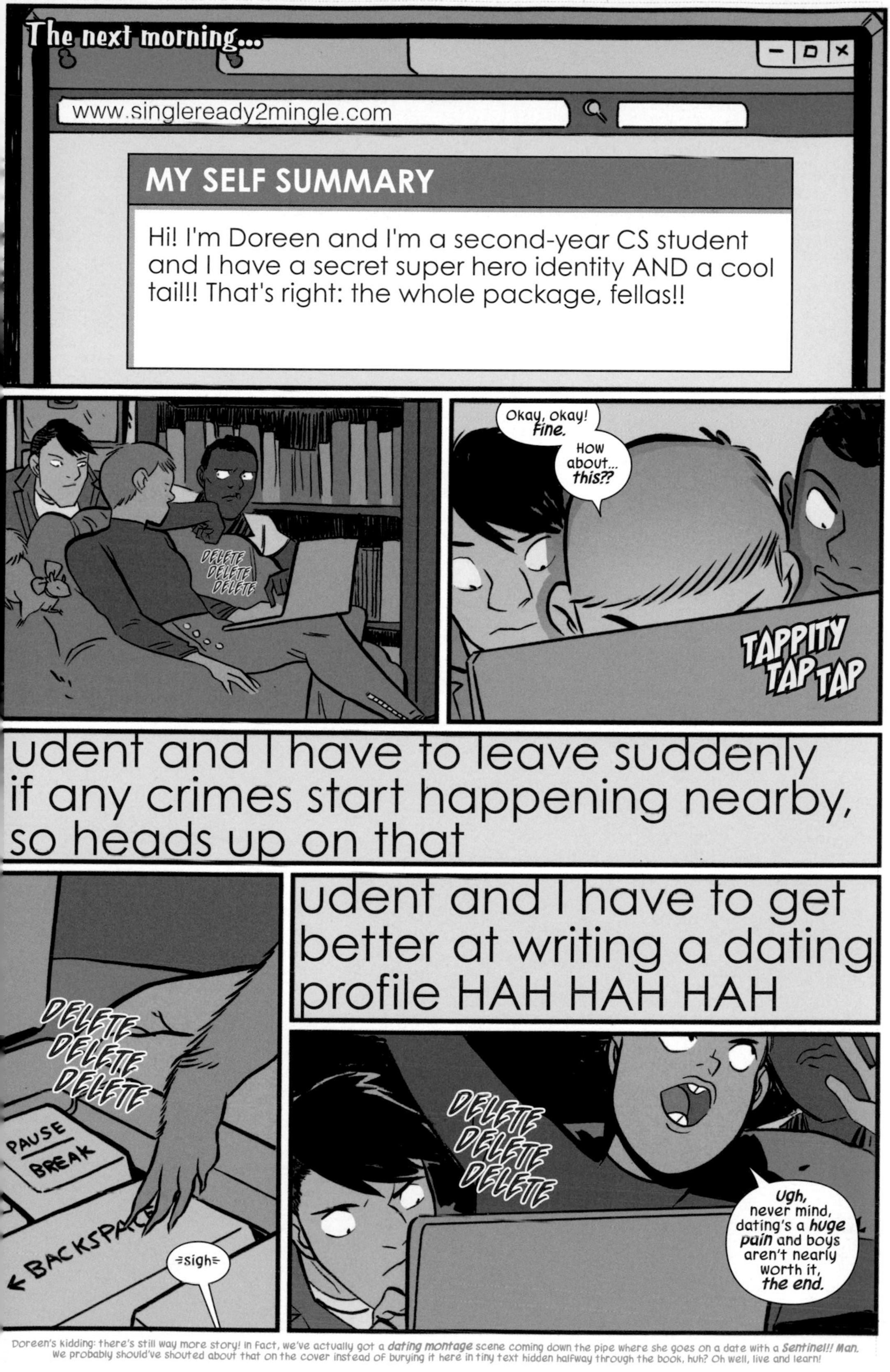
The next morning...
www.singleready2mingle.com
MY SELF SUMMARY
Hi! I'm Doreen and I'm a second-year CS student and I have a secret super hero identity AND a cool tail!! That's right: the whole package, fellas!!
DELETE DELETE DELETE
Okay, okay! Fine.
How about... this??
TAPPITY TAP TAP
udent and I have to leave suddenly if any crimes start happening nearby, so heads up on that
udent and I have to get better at writing a dating profile HAH HAH HAH
DELETE DELETE DELETE
PAUSE
BREAK
← BACKSPACE
=sigh=
DELETE DELETE DELETE
Ugh, never mind, dating's a huge pain and boys aren't nearly worth it, the end.

Doreen's kidding: there's still way more story! In fact, we've actually got a ***dating montage*** scene coming down the pipe where she goes on a date with a ***Sentinel!! Man.*** We probably should've shouted about that on the cover instead of burying it here in tiny text hidden halfway through the book, huh? Oh well, live and learn!

Look, it's not complicated. All I'm looking for are boys who like squirrels who like girls who like squirrels who like boys who like girls who like squirrels who like boys.

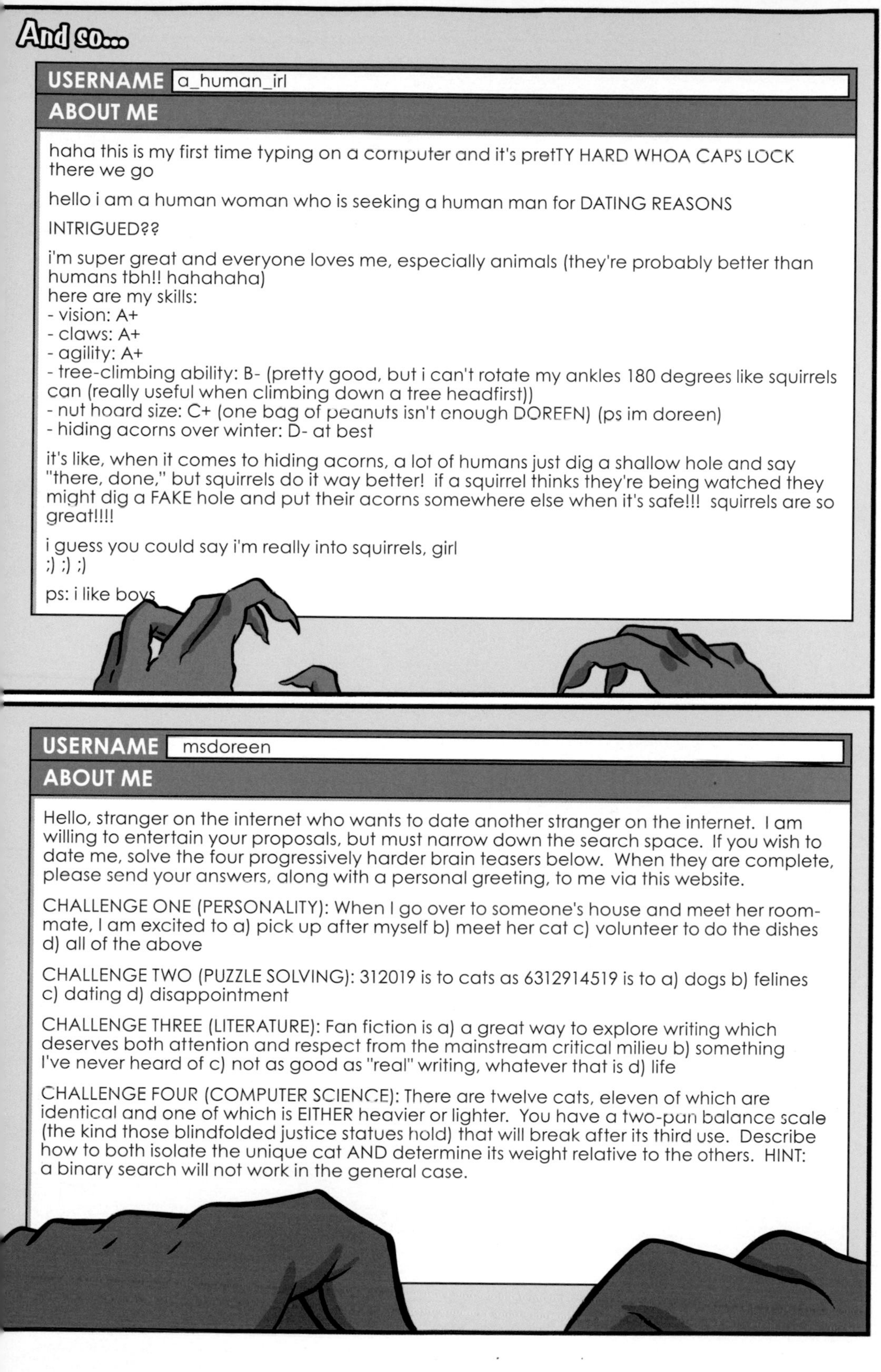
And so...
USERNAME a_human_irl
ABOUT ME
haha this is my first time typing on a computer and it's pretTY HARD WHOA CAPS LOCK there we go
hello i am a human woman who is seeking a human man for DATING REASONS
INTRIGUED??
i'm super great and everyone loves me, especially animals (they're probably better than humans tbh!! hahahaha)
here are my skills:
- vision: A+
- claws: A+
- agility: A+
- tree-climbing ability: B- (pretty good, but i can't rotate my ankles 180 degrees like squirrels can (really useful when climbing down a tree headfirst))
- nut hoard size: C+ (one bag of peanuts isn't enough DOREEN) (ps im doreen)
- hiding acorns over winter: D- at best
it's like, when it comes to hiding acorns, a lot of humans just dig a shallow hole and say "there, done," but squirrels do it way better! if a squirrel thinks they're being watched they might dig a FAKE hole and put their acorns somewhere else when it's safe!!! squirrels are so great!!!!
i guess you could say i'm really into squirrels, girl
;) ;) ;)
ps: i like boys
USERNAME msdoreen
ABOUT ME
Hello, stranger on the internet who wants to date another stranger on the internet. I am willing to entertain your proposals, but must narrow down the search space. If you wish to date me, solve the four progressively harder brain teasers below. When they are complete, please send your answers, along with a personal greeting, to me via this website.
CHALLENGE ONE (PERSONALITY): When I go over to someone's house and meet her roommate, I am excited to a) pick up after myself b) meet her cat c) volunteer to do the dishes d) all of the above
CHALLENGE TWO (PUZZLE SOLVING): 312019 is to cats as 6312914519 is to a) dogs b) felines c) dating d) disappointment
CHALLENGE THREE (LITERATURE): Fan fiction is a) a great way to explore writing which deserves both attention and respect from the mainstream critical milieu b) something I've never heard of c) not as good as "real" writing, whatever that is d) life
CHALLENGE FOUR (COMPUTER SCIENCE): There are twelve cats, eleven of which are identical and one of which is EITHER heavier or lighter. You have a two-pan balance scale (the kind those blindfolded justice statues hold) that will break after its third use. Describe how to both isolate the unique cat AND determine its weight relative to the others. HINT: a binary search will not work in the general case.

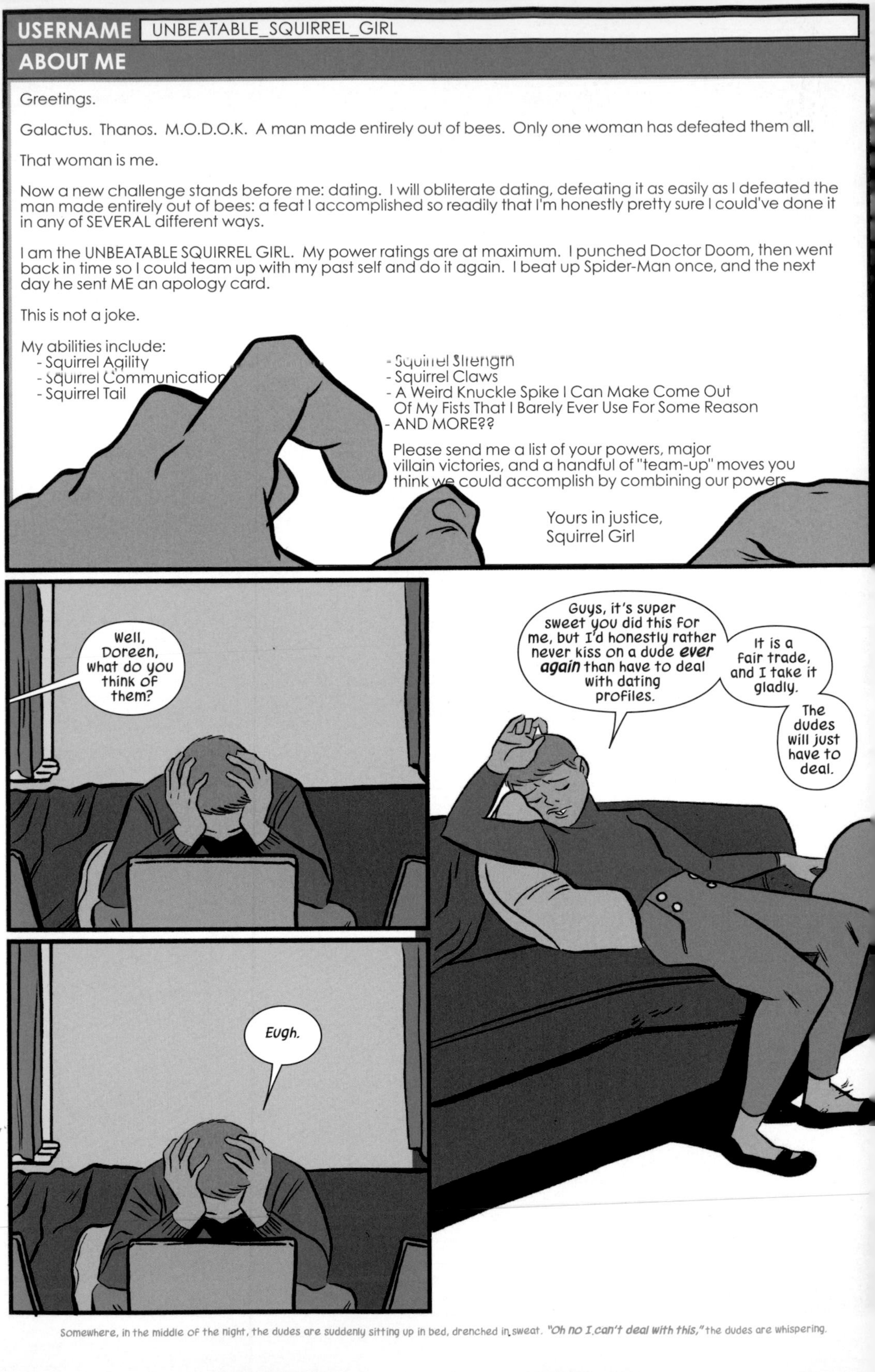
USERNAME
UNBEATABLE_SQUIRREL_GIRL
ABOUT ME
Greetings.
Galactus. Thanos. M.O.D.O.K. A man made entirely out of bees. Only one woman has defeated them all.
That woman is me.
Now a new challenge stands before me: dating. I will obliterate dating, defeating it as easily as I defeated the man made entirely out of bees: a feat I accomplished so readily that I'm honestly pretty sure I could've done it in any of SEVERAL different ways.
I am the UNBEATABLE SQUIRREL GIRL. My power ratings are at maximum. I punched Doctor Doom, then went back in time so I could team up with my past self and do it again. I beat up Spider-Man once, and the next day he sent ME an apology card.
This is not a joke.
My abilities include:
- Squirrel Agility
- Squirrel Communicatio
- Squirrel Tail
- Squirrel Strength
- Squirrel Claws
- A Weird Knuckle Spike I Can Make Come Out Of My Fists That I Barely Ever Use For Some Reason
- AND MORE??
Please send me a list of your powers, major villain victories, and a handful of "team-up" moves you think we could accomplish by combining our powers
Yours in justice,
Squirrel Girl
Well, Doreen, what do you think of them?
Eugh.
Guys, it's super sweet you did this for me, but I'd honestly rather never kiss on a dude *ever again* than have to deal with dating profiles.
It is a fair trade, and I take it gladly.
The dudes will just have to deal.

Somewhere, in the middle of the night, the dudes are suddenly sitting up in bed, drenched in sweat. *"Oh no I can't deal with this,"* the dudes are whispering.

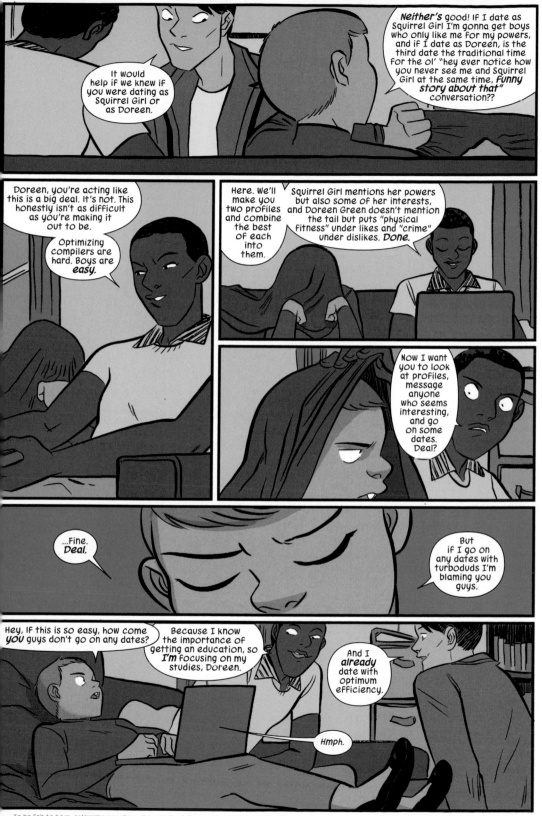

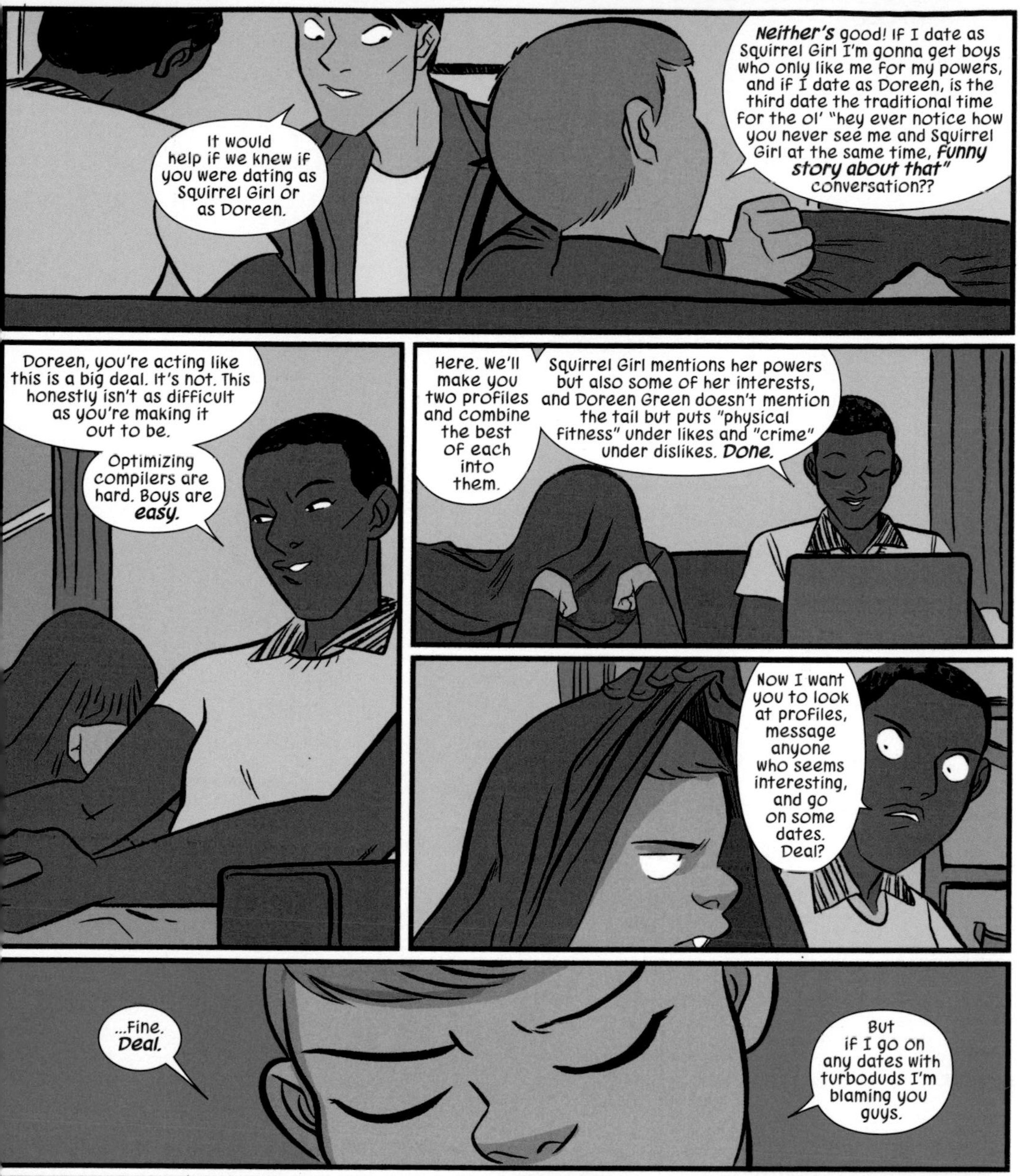
It would help if we knew if you were dating as Squirrel Girl or as Doreen.
Neither's good! If I date as Squirrel Girl I'm gonna get boys who only like me for my powers, and if I date as Doreen, is the third date the traditional time for the ol' "hey ever notice how you never see me and Squirrel Girl at the same time, *funny story about that*" conversation??
Doreen, you're acting like this is a big deal. It's not. This honestly isn't as difficult as you're making it out to be.
Optimizing compilers are hard. Boys are *easy.*
Here. We'll make you two profiles and combine the best of each into them.
Squirrel Girl mentions her powers but also some of her interests, and Doreen Green doesn't mention the tail but puts "physical fitness" under likes and "crime" under dislikes. *Done.*
Now I want you to look at profiles, message anyone who seems interesting, and go on some dates. Deal?
...Fine. *Deal.*
But if I go on any dates with turboduds I'm blaming you guys.
Hey, if this is so easy, how come *you* guys don't go on any dates?
Because I know the importance of getting an education, so *I'm* focusing on my studies, Doreen.
And I *already* date with optimum efficiency.
Hmph.

To be fair to boys, optimizing compilers *are* super hard. Some of the problems involved have been proven undecidable! That means they're so tricky that it's *literally impossible* to come up with a single algorithm that will always produce a correct yes or no answer. That's a hard problem, yo! Also, an extremely fascinating one!

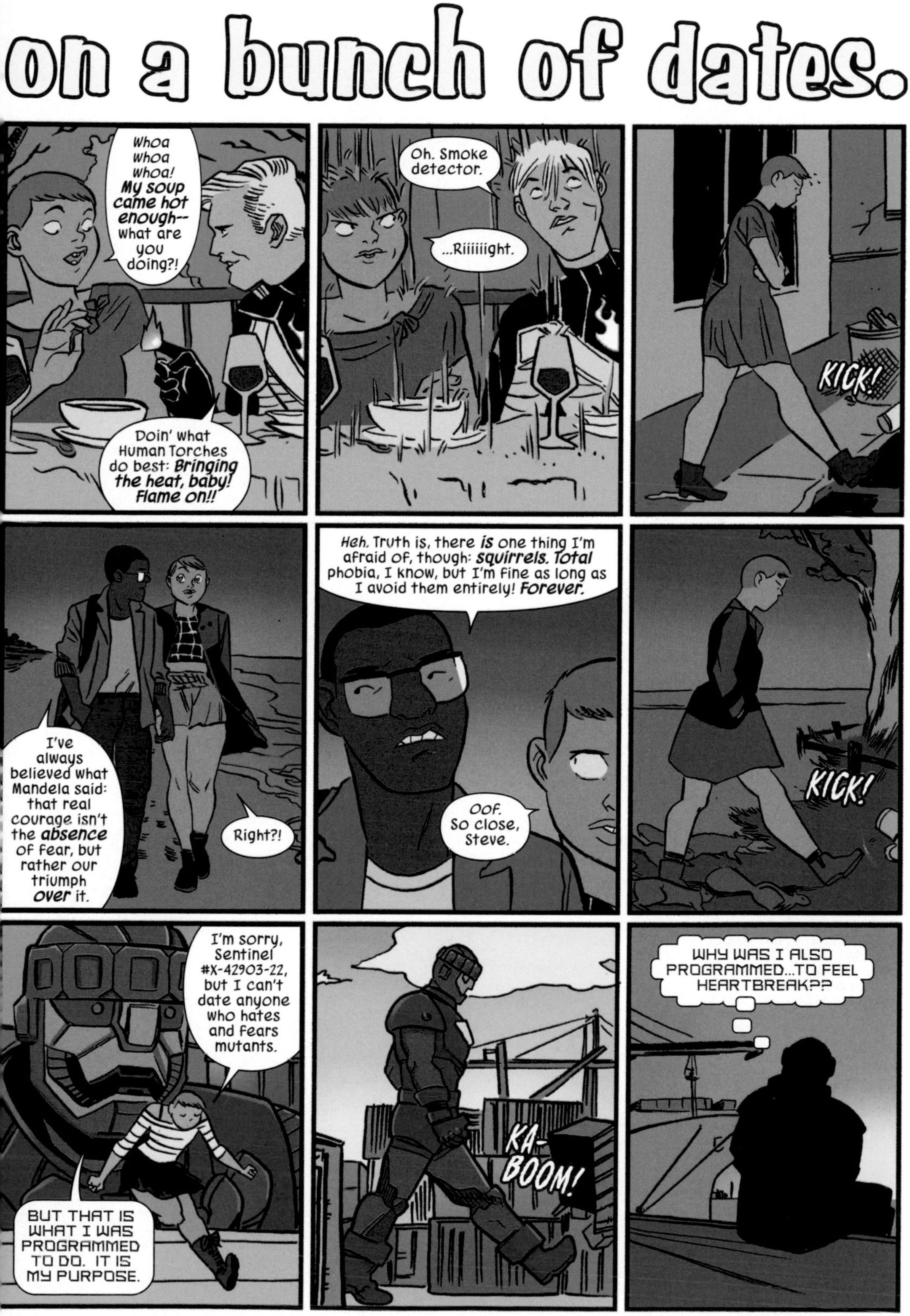
on a bunch of dates.
Whoa whoa whoa! My soup came hot enough-- what are you doing?!
Doin' what Human Torches do best: Bringing the heat, baby! Flame on!!
Oh. Smoke detector.
...Riiiiiight.
KICK!
I've always believed what Mandela said: that real courage isn't the absence of fear, but rather our triumph over it.
Right?!
Heh. Truth is, there is one thing I'm afraid of, though: squirrels. Total phobia, I know, but I'm fine as long as I avoid them entirely! Forever.
Oof. So close, Steve.
KICK!
I'm sorry, Sentinel #X-42903-22, but I can't date anyone who hates and fears mutants.
BUT THAT IS WHAT I WAS PROGRAMMED TO DO. IT IS MY PURPOSE.
KA-BOOM!
WHY WAS I ALSO PROGRAMMED...TO FEEL HEARTBREAK??

Called it.

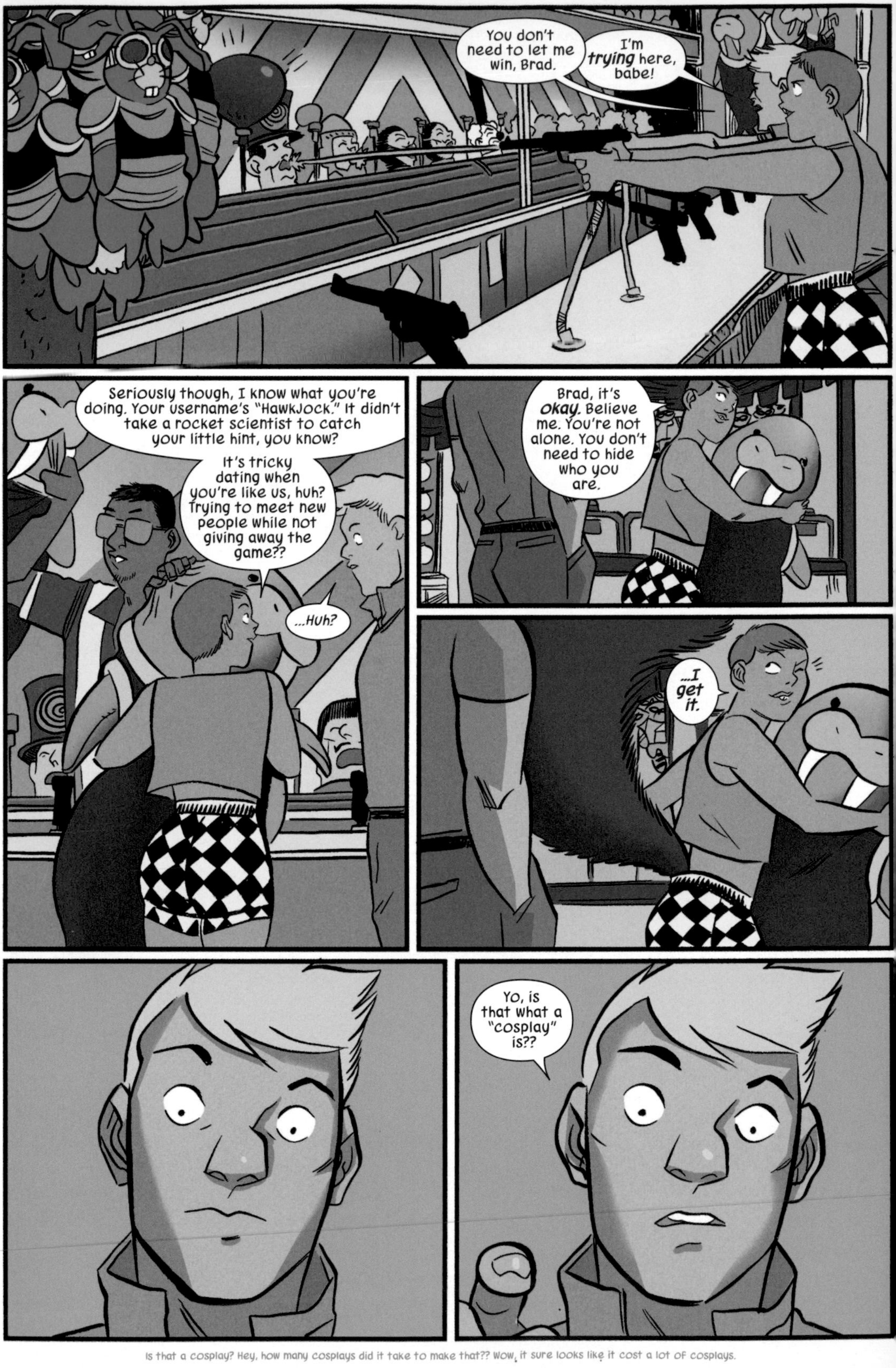
You don't need to let me win, Brad.
I'm *trying* here, babe!
Seriously though, I know what you're doing. Your username's "HawkJock." It didn't take a rocket scientist to catch your little hint, you know?
It's tricky dating when you're like us, huh? Trying to meet new people while not giving away the game??
...Huh?
Brad, it's *okay.* Believe me. You're not alone. You don't need to hide who you are.
...I get it.
Yo, is that what a "cosplay" is??

Is that a cosplay? Hey, how many cosplays did it take to make that?? Wow, it sure looks like it cost a lot of cosplays.

Brad was on this other dating site where the name "HawkJock" was taken and it suggested he call himself "BirdNerd" instead. Brad was all, "No go, bro."

Marcus is a real guy, but sadly he's a bad guy – in the Marvel Universe, anyway! In the real world guys named Marcus are a thing too, and they're pretty chill, but sadly none of them have centaur-symbiote-werewolf powers. *Yet.*

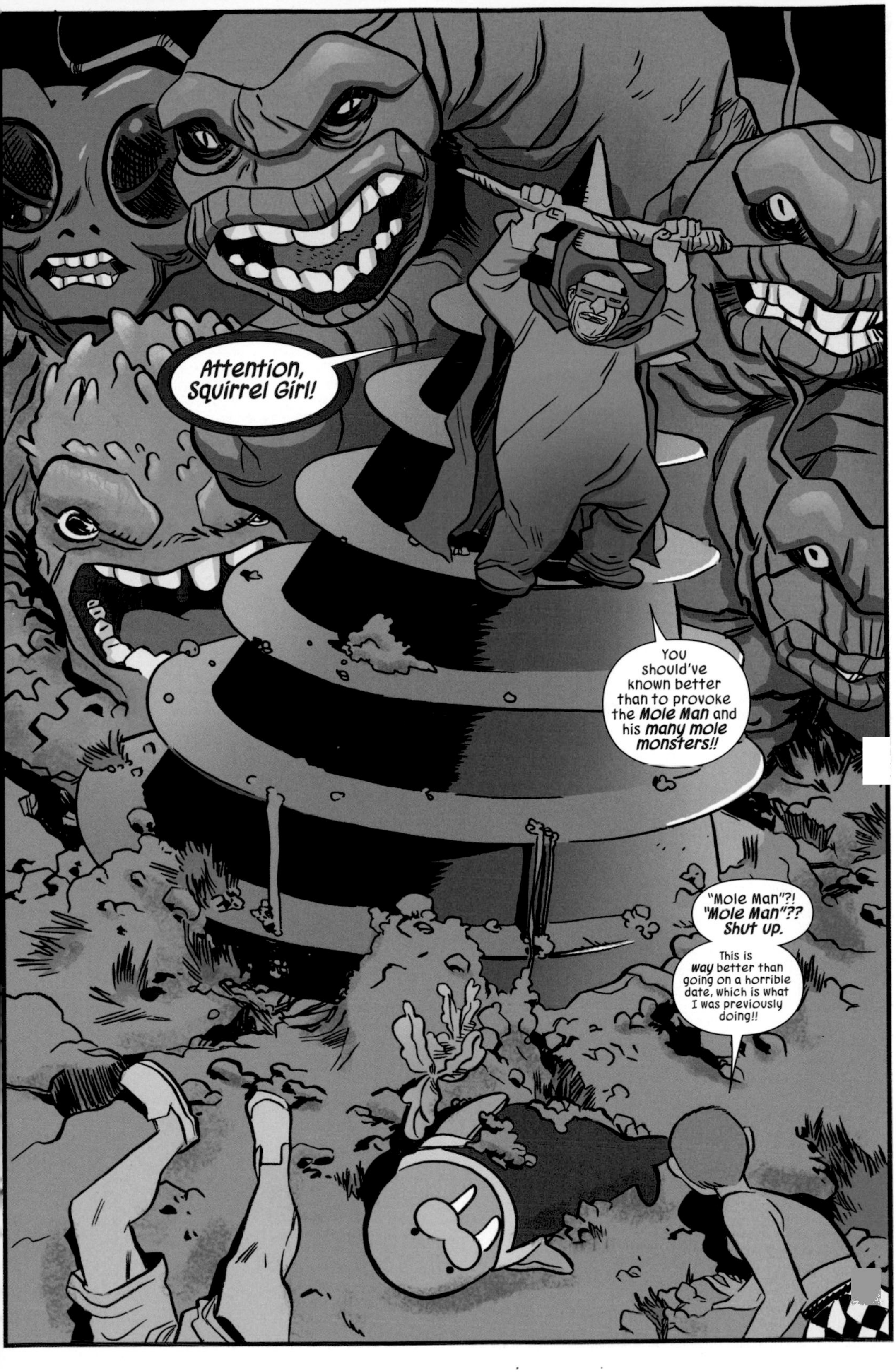
Attention, Squirrel Girl!
You should've known better than to provoke the Mole Man and his many mole monsters!!
"Mole Man"?! "Mole Man"?? Shut up.
This is way better than going on a horrible date, which is what I was previously doing!!

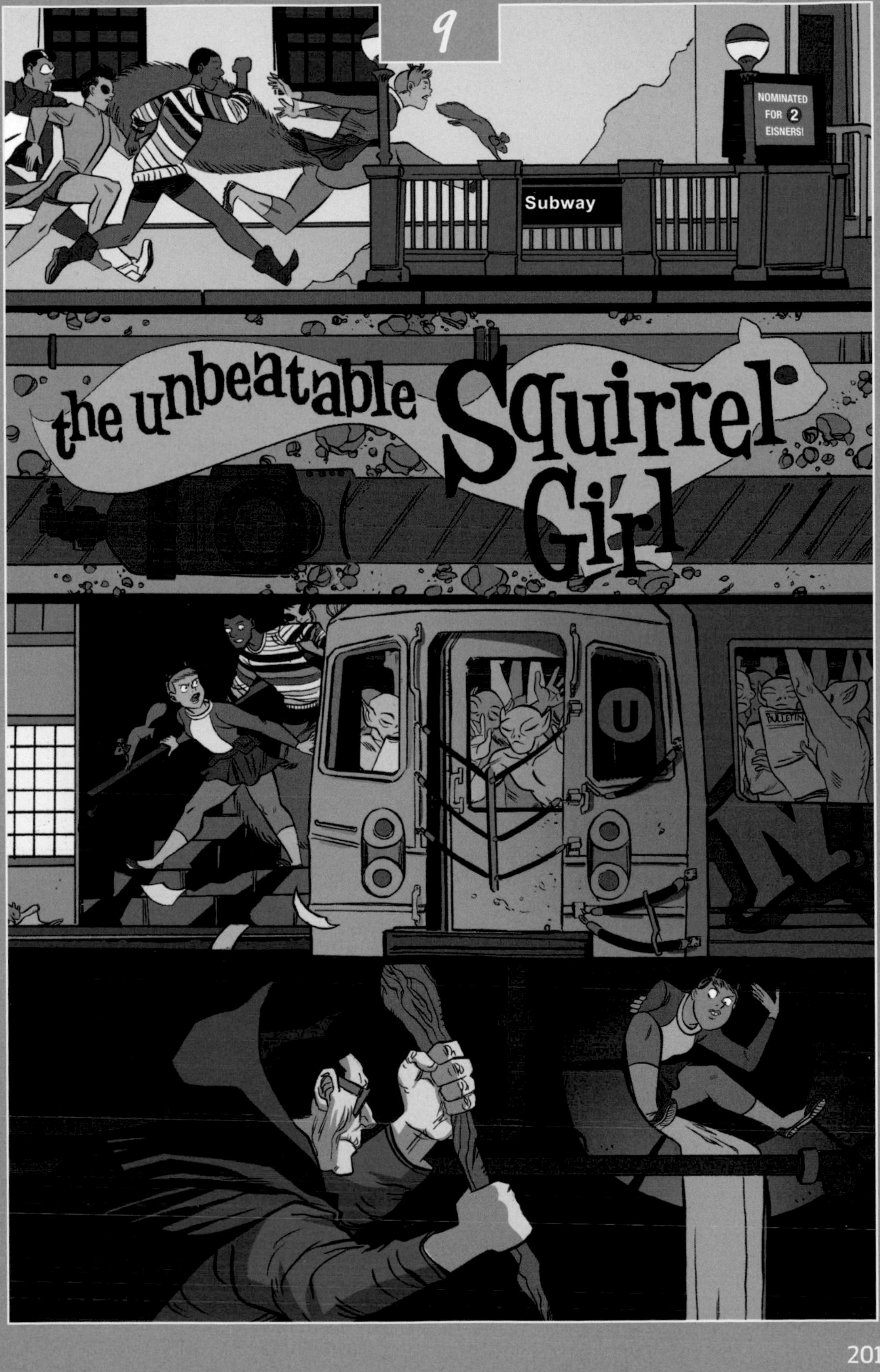
9
NOMINATED FOR 2 EISNERS!
Subway
the unbeatable Squirrel Girl
U
BULLETIN

Doreen Green isn't just a second-year computer science student: she secretly also has all the powers of both squirrel and girl! She uses her amazing abilities to fight crime **and** be as awesome as possible. You know her as...The Unbeatable Squirrel Girl! Find out what she's been up to, with...

Squirrel Girl *in a nutshell*

search! 🔍

#lookatthesizeofthatrock

#bigbenmorelikelittlebennow

#weisenheimer

#saucyhoyden

Squirrel Girl @unbeatablesg
Which bold, confident, attractive woman is going on an internet date tonight? THIS LADY RIGHT HERE, PEACE OUT Y'ALL!!

Squirrel Girl @unbeatablesg
UPDATE, SEVERAL HOURS LATER: haha nevermind DATING IS THE WORST, THE END

 xKravenTheHunterx @unshavenkraven
@unbeatablesg What is wrong, Girl of Squirrels?

Squirrel Girl @unbeatablesg
@unshavenkraven hahah where do i even begin?

Squirrel Girl @unbeatablesg
@unshavenkraven let's just say that my best date so far has been with a giant Sentinel robot, and even THAT was awful

 xKravenTheHunterx @unshavenkraven
@unbeatablesg I was not aware that Sentinels were programmed for dating.

Squirrel Girl @unbeatablesg
@unshavenkraven Kraven

 Squirrel Girl @unbeatablesg
@unshavenkraven THEY'RE NOT

Squirrel Girl @unbeatablesg
@unshavenkraven IT'S THE WORST

Tony Stark @starkmantony ✓
@unbeatablesg Hey someone named "Brad" has sent me 7 separate emails claiming you admitted that super heroes are a government conspiracy??

Tony Stark @starkmantony ✓
@unbeatablesg And that I'm part of it, and that, I quote, "THE FACTS WILL SPEAK FOR THEMSELVES WHEN WILL YOUR LIES END DEMAND TRUTH NOW"?

Squirrel Girl @unbeatablesg
@starkmantony OH GOD, NEVER DATE BRAD, TONY

Squirrel Girl @unbeatablesg
@starkmantony NEVER DO IT

Tony Stark @starkmantony ✓
@starkmantony I...wasn't planning to

 Squirrel Girl @unbeatablesg
@starkmantony HE'LL MAKE UP STORIES ABOUT YOU, PLUS HE DOESN'T HAVE THE POWERS OF HAWK AND JOCK EVEN THO HE'S "HAWKJOCK" ON THE DATING SITE

Squirrel Girl @unbeatablesg
@starkmantony AND THEN MOLE MAN WILL SHOW UP FOR SOME REASON

 Squirrel Girl @unbeatablesg
@starkmantony WHICH REMINDS ME, I SHOULD PROBABLY GET BACK TO THAT

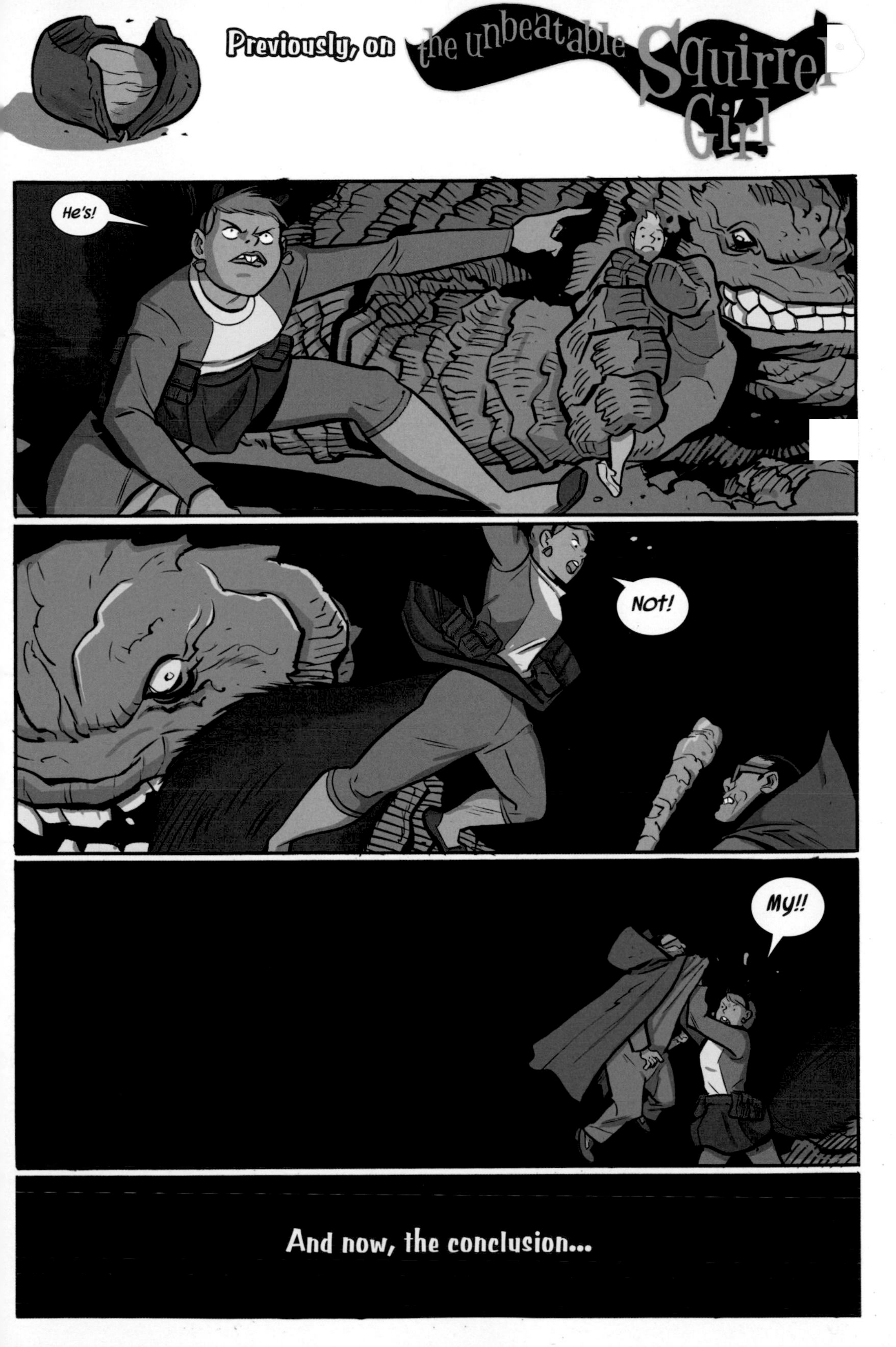
Previously, on the unbeatable Squirrel Girl
He's!
Not!
My!!
And now, the conclusion...

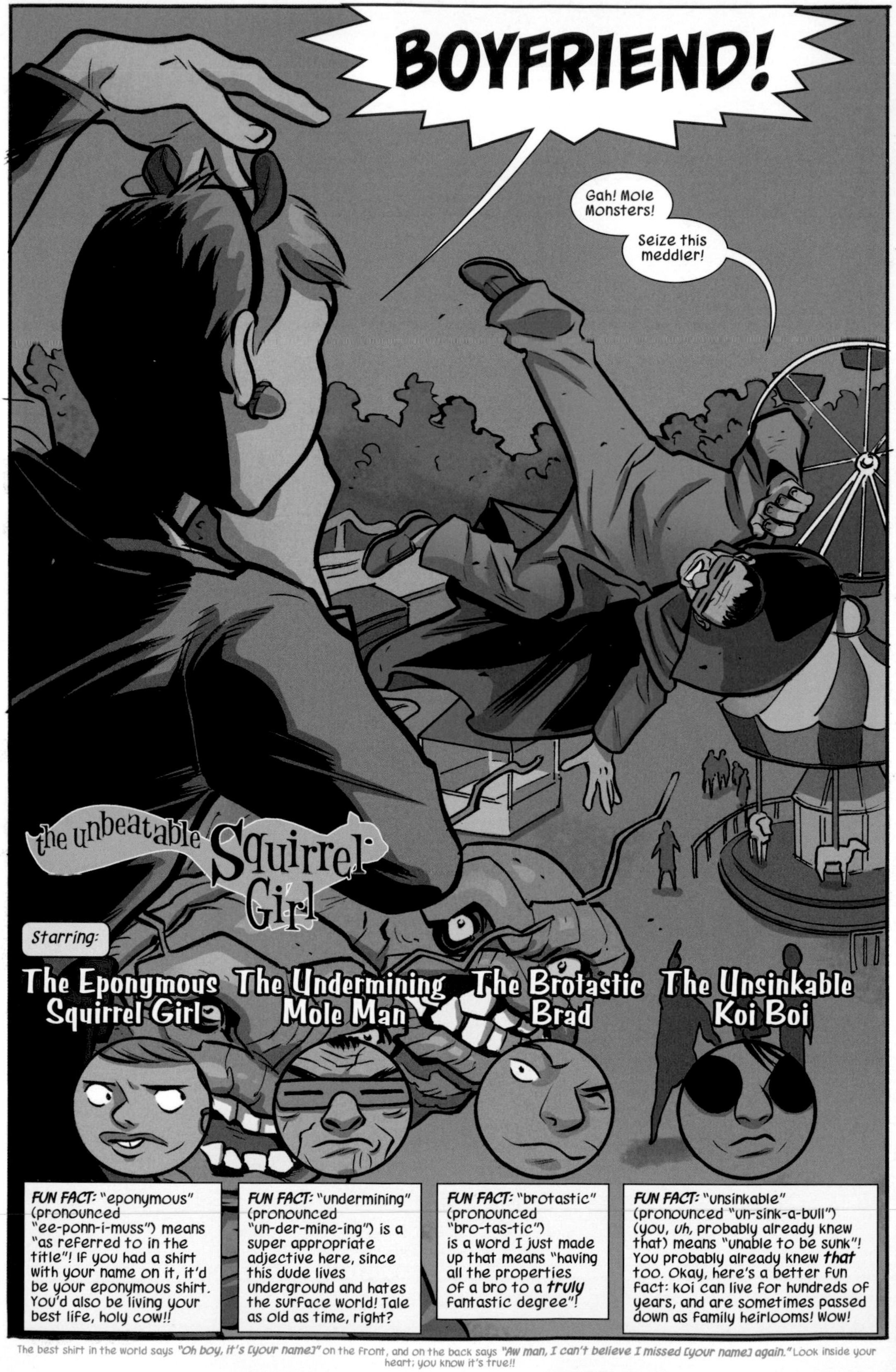
BOYFRIEND!
Gah! Mole Monsters!
Seize this meddler!
the unbeatable Squirrel Girl
Starring:
The Eponymous Squirrel Girl
The Undermining Mole Man
The Brotastic Brad
The Unsinkable Koi Boi
FUN FACT: "eponymous" (pronounced "ee-ponn-i-muss") means "as referred to in the title"! If you had a shirt with your name on it, it'd be your eponymous shirt. You'd also be living your best life, holy cow!!
FUN FACT: "undermining" (pronounced "un-der-mine-ing") is a super appropriate adjective here, since this dude lives underground and hates the surface world! Tale as old as time, right?
FUN FACT: "brotastic" (pronounced "bro-tas-tic") is a word I just made up that means "having all the properties of a bro to a *truly* fantastic degree"!
FUN FACT: "unsinkable" (pronounced "un-sink-a-bull") (you, *uh*, probably already knew that) means "unable to be sunk"! You probably already knew *that* too. Okay, here's a better fun fact: koi can live for hundreds of years, and are sometimes passed down as family heirlooms! Wow!

The best shirt in the world says *"Oh boy, it's [your name]"* on the front, and on the back says *"Aw man, I can't believe I missed [your name] again."* Look inside your heart; you know it's true!!

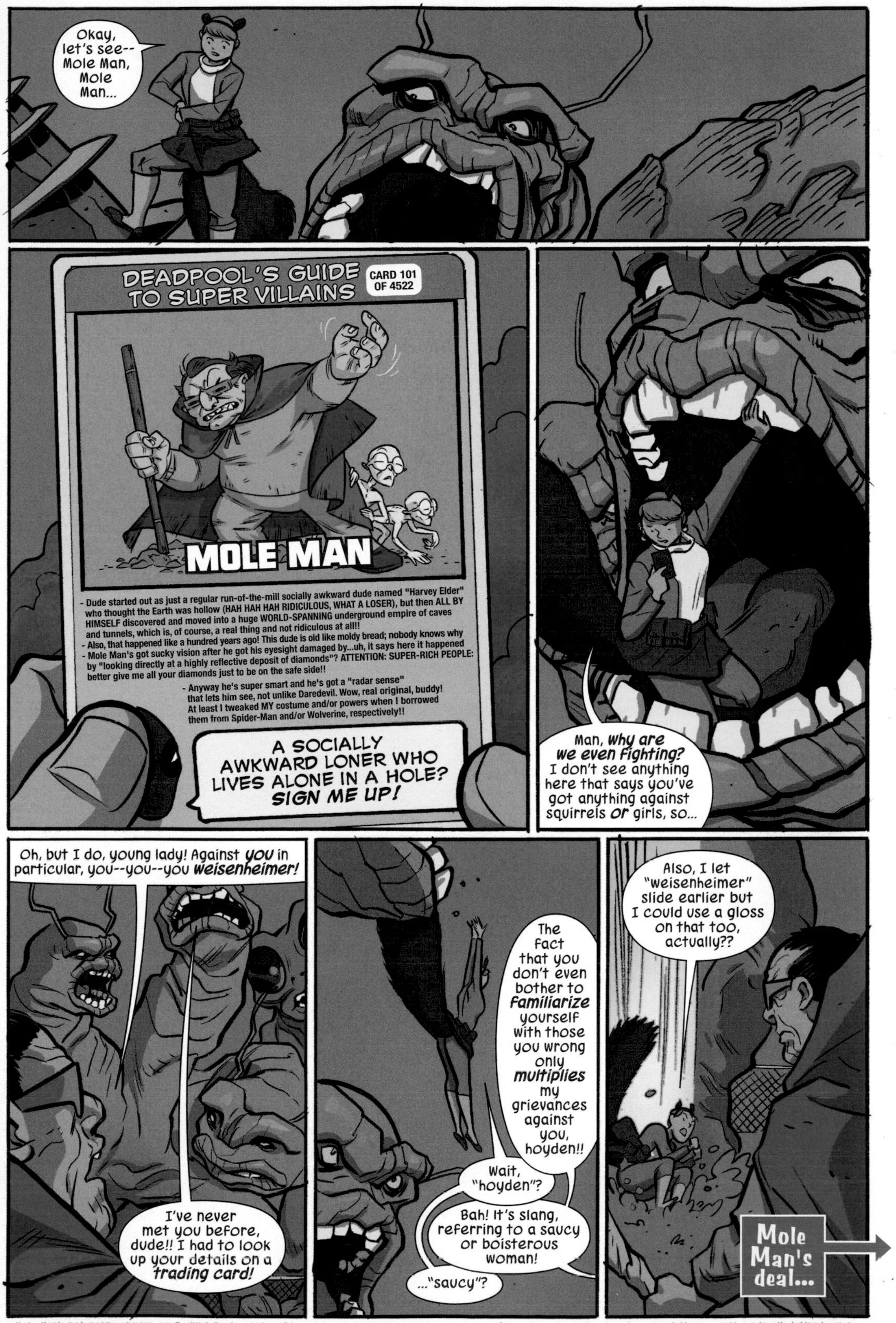

Okay, let's see-- Mole Man, Mole Man...
DEADPOOL'S GUIDE TO SUPER VILLAINS
CARD 101 OF 4522
MOLE MAN
- Dude started out as just a regular run-of-the-mill socially awkward dude named "Harvey Elder" who thought the Earth was hollow (HAH HAH HAH RIDICULOUS, WHAT A LOSER), but then ALL BY HIMSELF discovered and moved into a huge WORLD-SPANNING underground empire of caves and tunnels, which is, of course, a real thing and not ridiculous at all!!
- Also, that happened like a hundred years ago! This dude is old like moldy bread; nobody knows why
- Mole Man's got sucky vision after he got his eyesight damaged by...uh, it says here it happened by "looking directly at a highly reflective deposit of diamonds"? ATTENTION: SUPER-RICH PEOPLE: better give me all your diamonds just to be on the safe side!!
- Anyway he's super smart and he's got a "radar sense" that lets him see, not unlike Daredevil. Wow, real original, buddy! At least I tweaked MY costume and/or powers when I borrowed them from Spider-Man and/or Wolverine, respectively!!
A SOCIALLY AWKWARD LONER WHO LIVES ALONE IN A HOLE? SIGN ME UP!
Man, why are we even fighting? I don't see anything here that says you've got anything against squirrels or girls, so...
Oh, but I do, young lady! Against you in particular, you--you--you weisenheimer!
I've never met you before, dude!! I had to look up your details on a trading card!
The fact that you don't even bother to familiarize yourself with those you wrong only multiplies my grievances against you, hoyden!!
Wait, "hoyden"?
Bah! It's slang, referring to a saucy or boisterous woman!
..."saucy"?
Also, I let "weisenheimer" slide earlier but I could use a gloss on that too, actually??
Mole Man's deal...

Mole Man's not gonna answer, so I will! A "weisenheimer" is someone who makes smug, arrogant, and/or clever jokes to show how smart they are. It's an insult dating back to the early 1900s...*not unlike Mole Man himself??* Zing! Look at me, I'm a regular saucy weisenheimer down here!

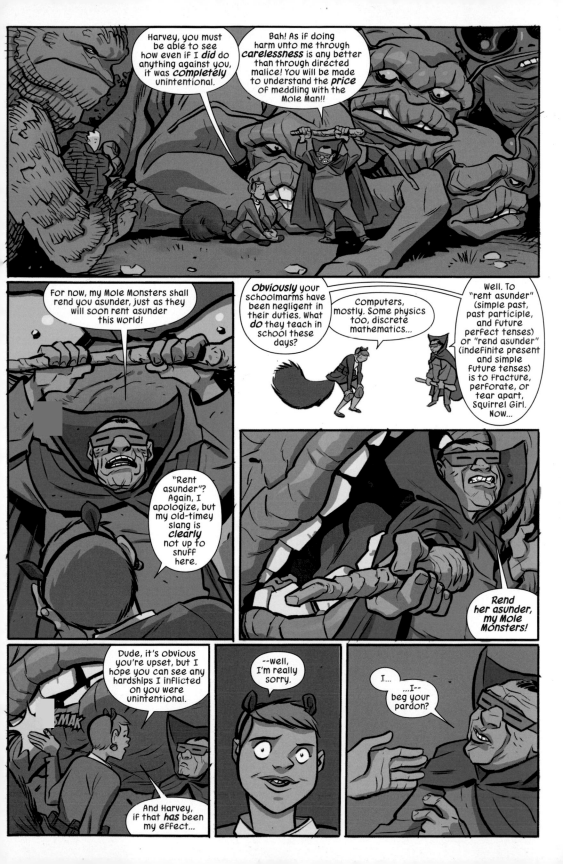

Thor throws things into the sun without even *trying* sometimes. Here's a tip: don't lend Thor anything if it's easily chucked and does not belong in the fiery heart of a sun.

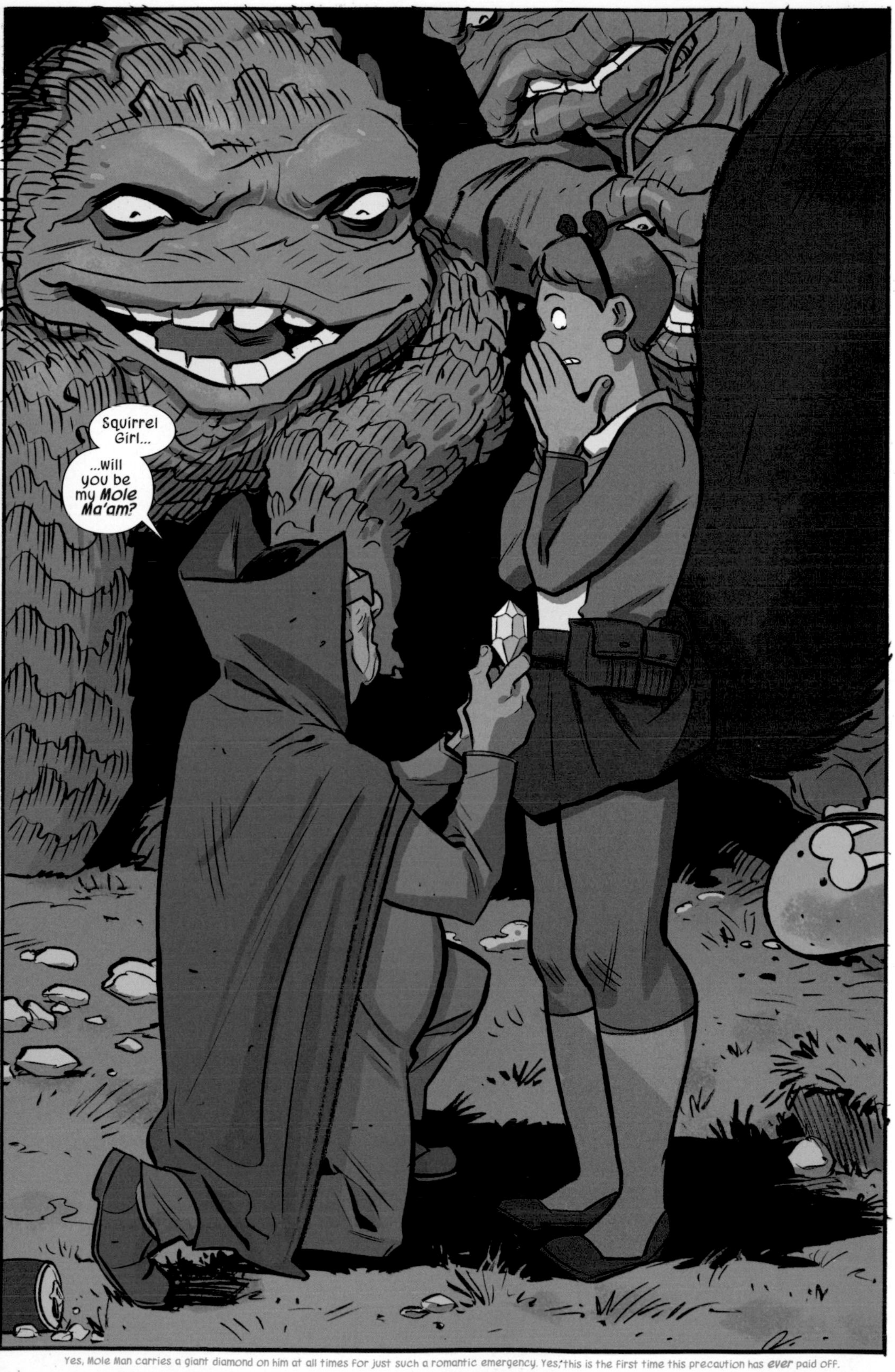
Squirrel Girl...
...will you be my *Mole Ma'am?*

Yes, Mole Man carries a giant diamond on him at all times for just such a romantic emergency. Yes, this is the first time this precaution has *ever* paid off.

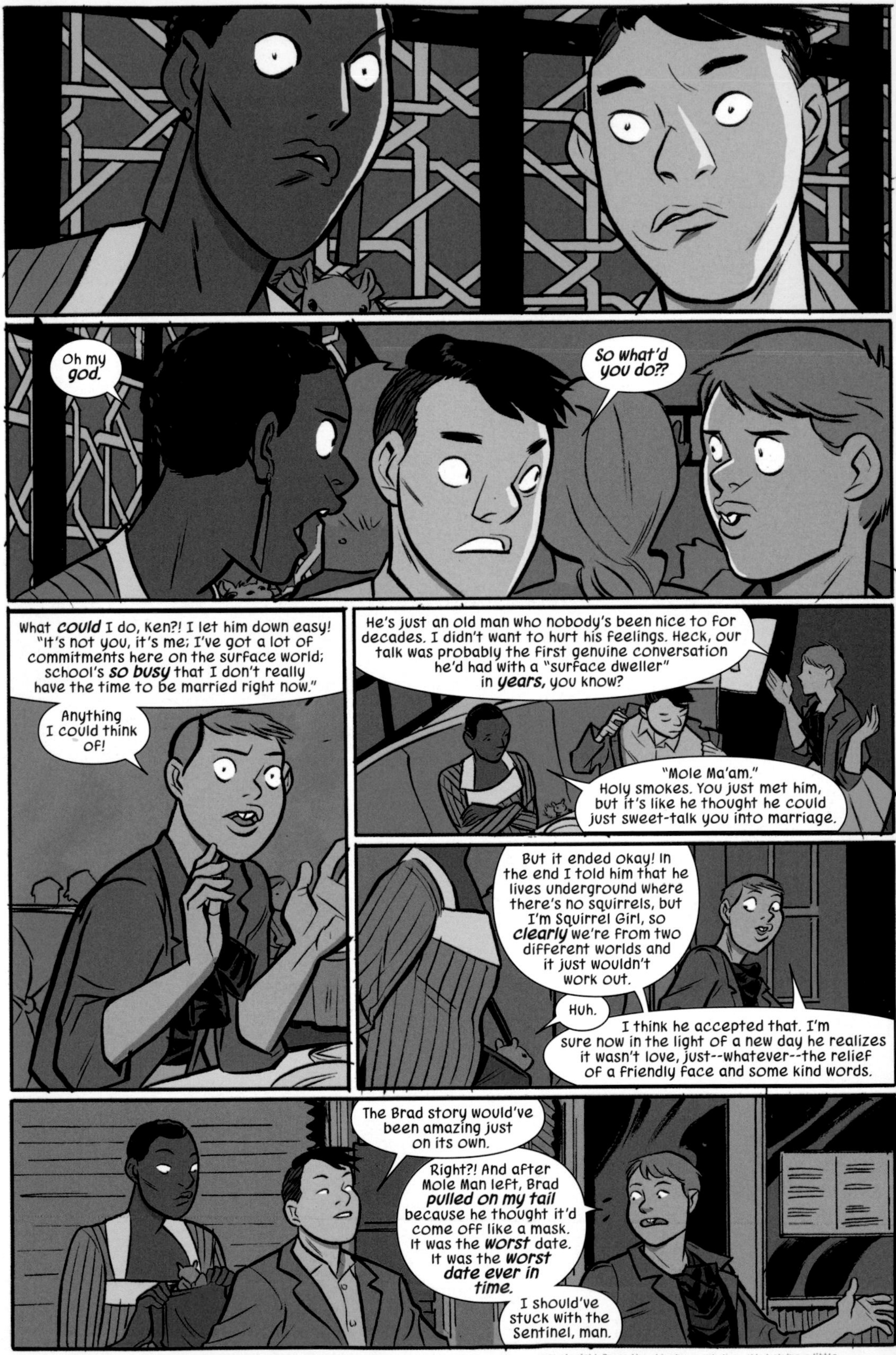
Oh my god.
So what'd you do??
What could I do, Ken?! I let him down easy! "It's not you, it's me; I've got a lot of commitments here on the surface world; school's so busy that I don't really have the time to be married right now."
Anything I could think of!
He's just an old man who nobody's been nice to for decades. I didn't want to hurt his feelings. Heck, our talk was probably the first genuine conversation he'd had with a "surface dweller" in years, you know?
"Mole Ma'am." Holy smokes. You just met him, but it's like he thought he could just sweet-talk you into marriage.
But it ended okay! In the end I told him that he lives underground where there's no squirrels, but I'm Squirrel Girl, so clearly we're from two different worlds and it just wouldn't work out.
Huh.
I think he accepted that. I'm sure now in the light of a new day he realizes it wasn't love, just--whatever--the relief of a friendly face and some kind words.
The Brad story would've been amazing just on its own.
Right?! And after Mole Man left, Brad pulled on my tail because he thought it'd come off like a mask. It was the worst date. It was the worst date ever in time.
I should've stuck with the Sentinel, man.

Somewhere out there, a Sentinel is trying to make himself feel better by gorging on ice cream straight from the shipping container. It's helping a little.

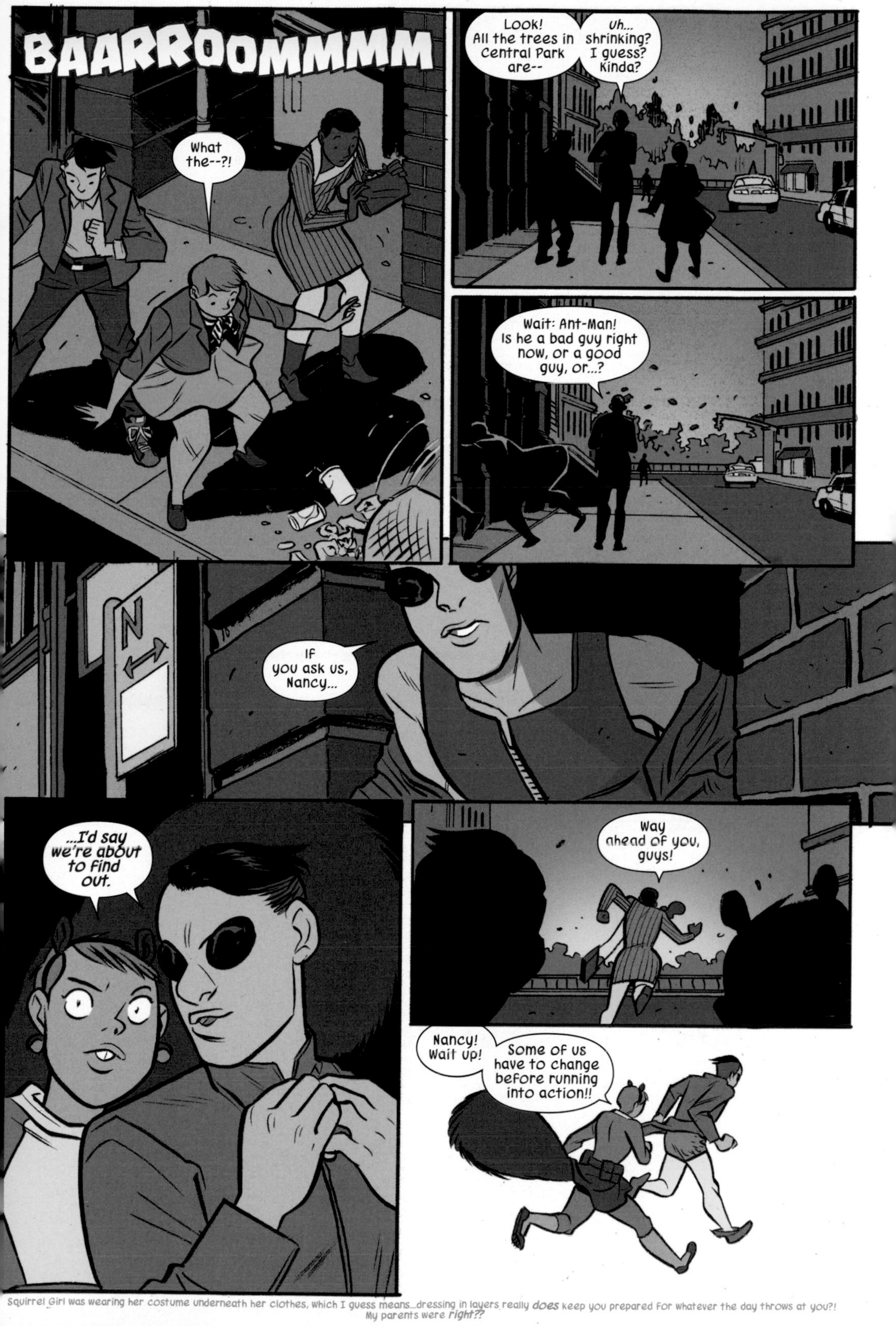
BAARROOMMMM
What the--?!
Look! All the trees in Central Park are--
Uh... shrinking? I guess? Kinda?
Wait: Ant-Man! Is he a bad guy right now, or a good guy, or...?
N
If you ask us, Nancy...
...I'd say we're about to find out.
Way ahead of you, guys!
Nancy! Wait up!
Some of us have to change before running into action!!

Squirrel Girl was wearing her costume underneath her clothes, which I guess means...dressing in layers really *does* keep you prepared for whatever the day throws at you?! My parents were *right??*

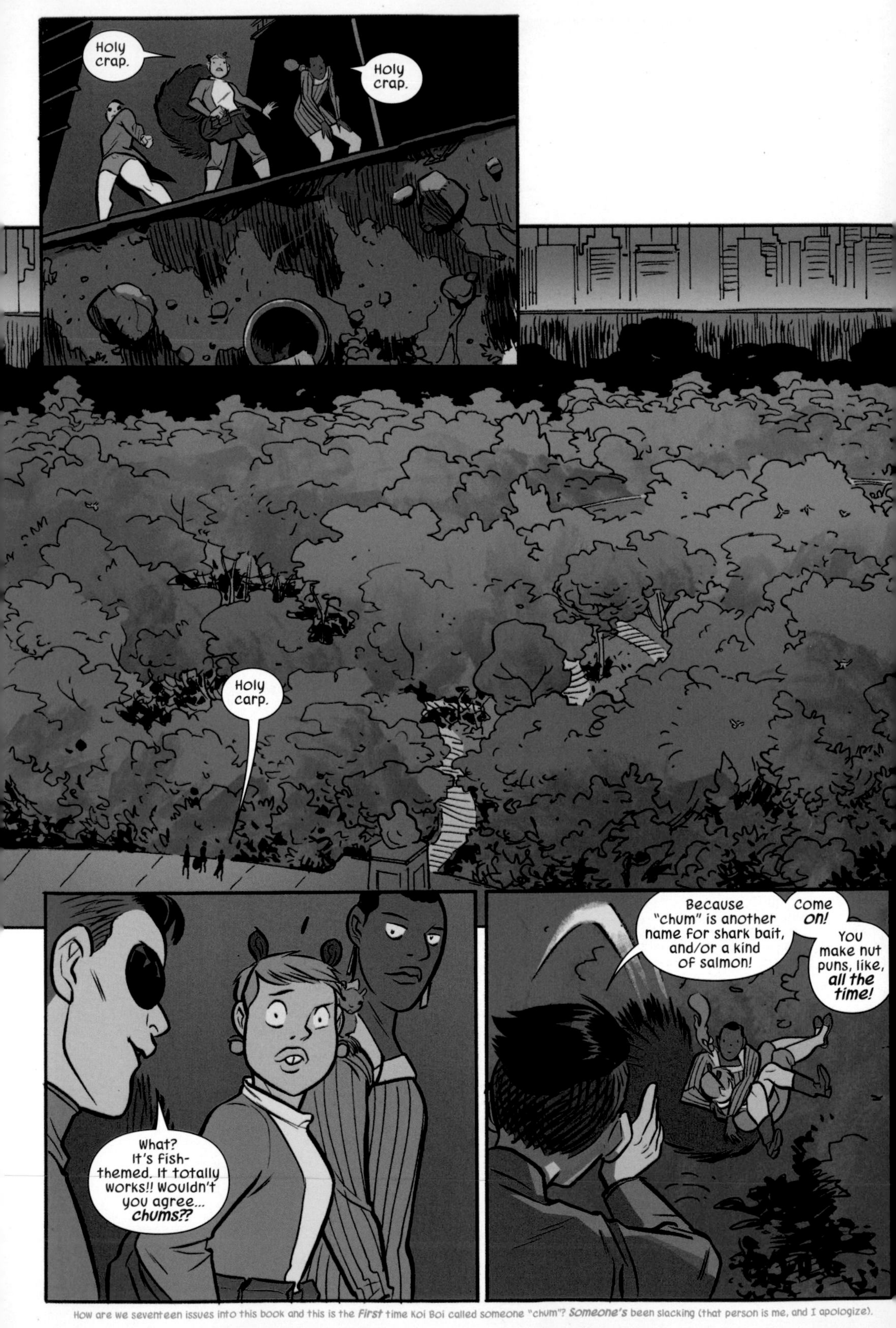
Holy crap.
Holy crap.
Holy carp.
What? It's fish-themed. It totally works!! Wouldn't you agree... *chums??*
Because "chum" is another name for shark bait, and/or a kind of salmon!
Come *on!*
You make nut puns, like, *all the time!*

How are we seventeen issues into this book and this is the *first* time Koi Boi called someone "chum"? *Someone's* been slacking (that person is me, and I apologize).

Please, "Mr. Hands" was my Father. Call me "Grabby."

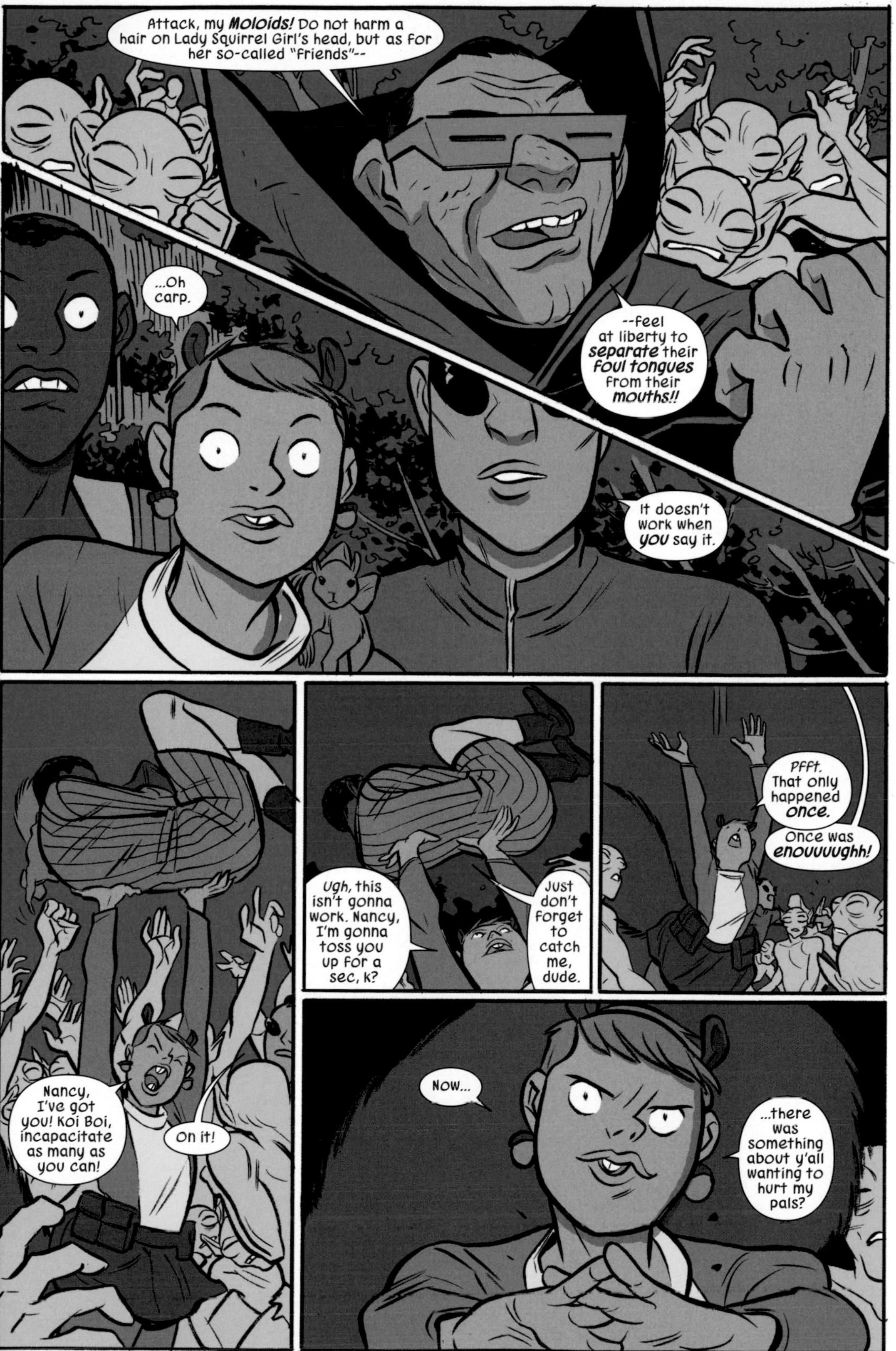
Attack, my Moloids! Do not harm a hair on Lady Squirrel Girl's head, but as for her so-called "friends"--
--feel at liberty to separate their foul tongues from their mouths!!
...Oh carp.
It doesn't work when YOU say it.
Nancy, I've got you! Koi Boi, incapacitate as many as you can!
On it!
Ugh, this isn't gonna work. Nancy, I'm gonna toss you up for a sec, k?
Just don't forget to catch me, dude.
Pfft. That only happened once.
Once was enouuuughh!
Now...
...there was something about y'all wanting to hurt my pals?

To be fair, "oh carp" *kinda* works when Squirrel Girl says it, but *only* if she's being attacked by fish. Keep that line in your back pocket, Squirrel Girl! Who *knows* when the maddening depths of oceans will, at last, seek their revenge??

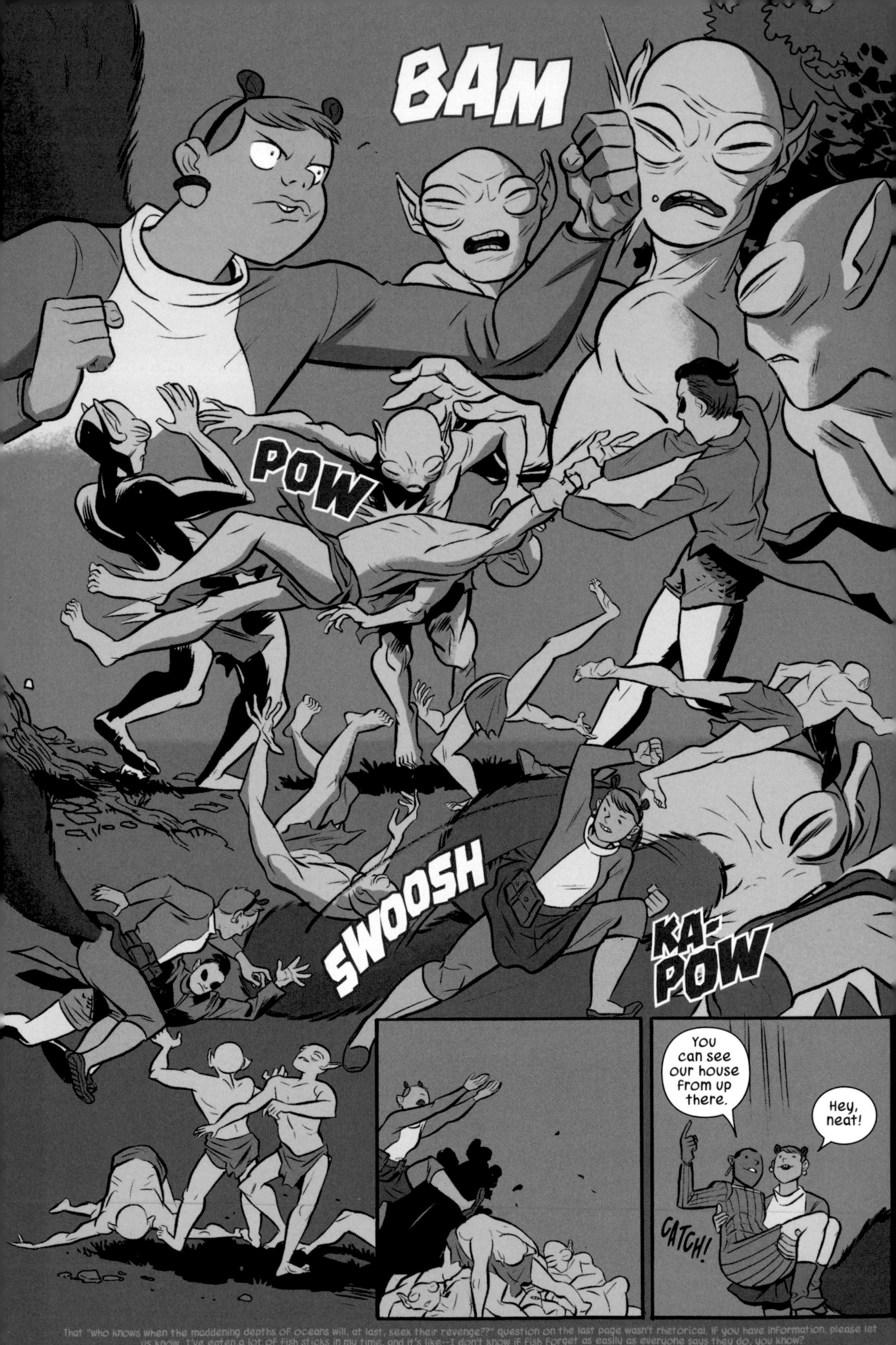
BAM
POW
SWOOSH
KA-POW
You can see our house from up there.
Hey, neat!
CATCH!

That "who knows when the maddening depths of oceans will, at last, seek their revenge??" question on the last page wasn't rhetorical. If you have information, please let us know. I've eaten a lot of fish sticks in my time, and it's like--I don't know if fish forget as easily as everyone says they do, you know?

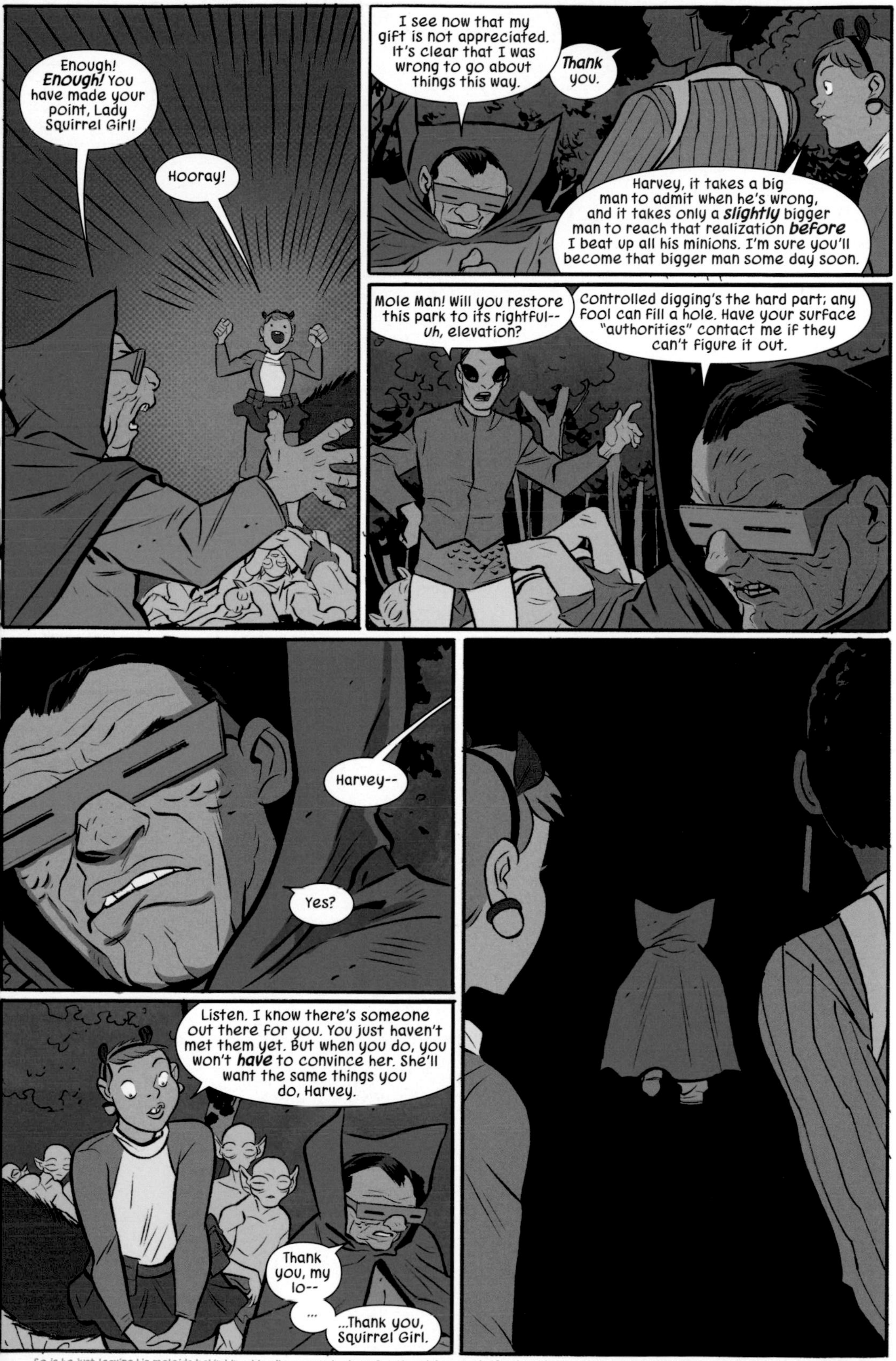
Enough! **Enough!** You have made your point, Lady Squirrel Girl!
Hooray!
I see now that my gift is not appreciated. It's clear that I was wrong to go about things this way.
Thank you.
Harvey, it takes a big man to admit when he's wrong, and it takes only a **slightly** bigger man to reach that realization **before** I beat up all his minions. I'm sure you'll become that bigger man some day soon.
Mole Man! Will you restore this park to its rightful-- *uh,* elevation?
Controlled digging's the hard part; any fool can fill a hole. Have your surface "authorities" contact me if they can't figure it out.
Harvey--
Yes?
Listen. I know there's someone out there for you. You just haven't met them yet. But when you do, you won't **have** to convince her. She'll want the same things you do, Harvey.
Thank you, my lo--
...
...Thank you, Squirrel Girl.

So is he just leaving his moloids behind in a big pile, or coming back for them later, or what? He's probably coming back for them later, right? Yeah, we should go; he's probably coming back for them later.

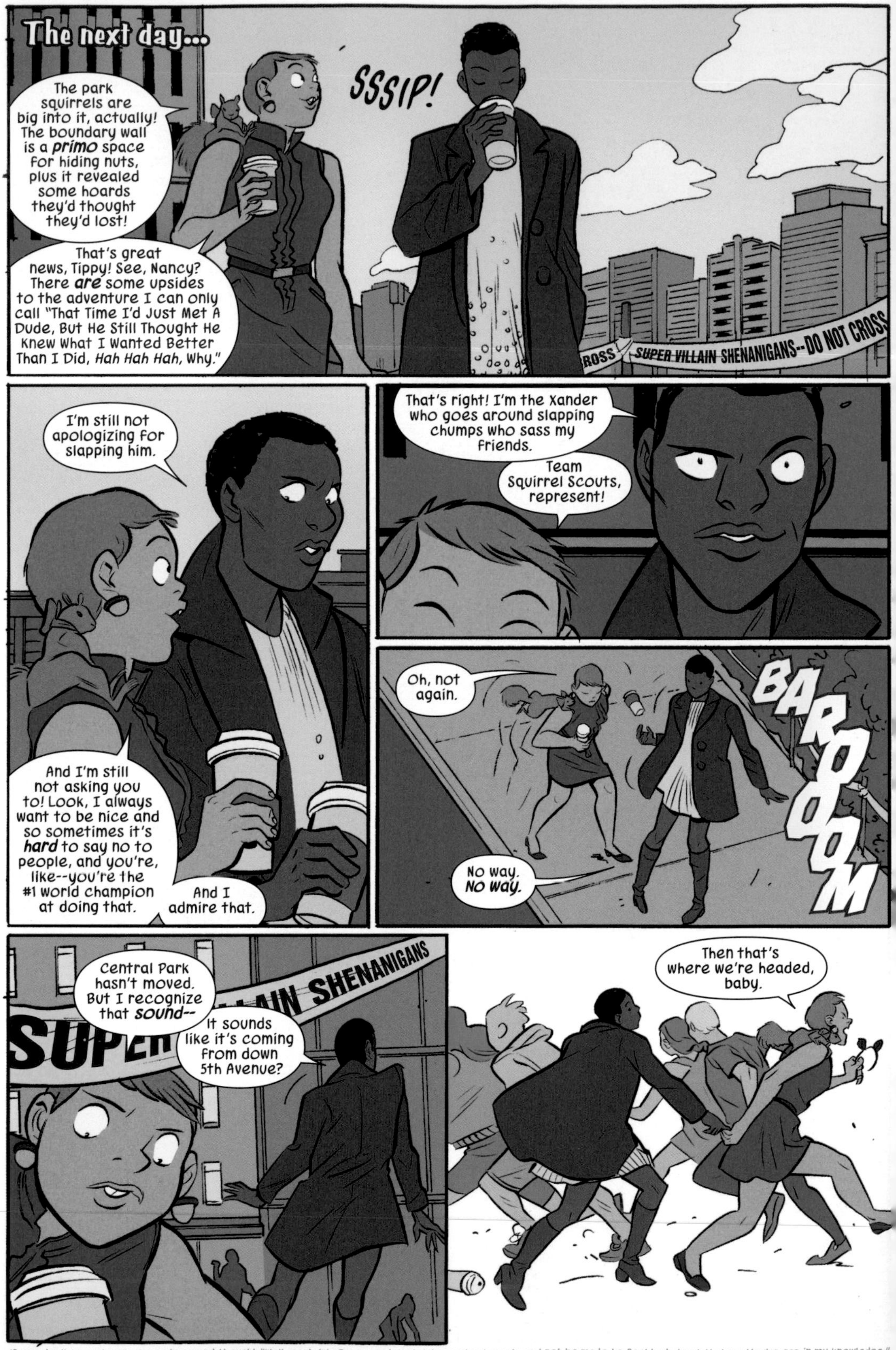
The next day...
The park squirrels are big into it, actually! The boundary wall is a *primo* space for hiding nuts, plus it revealed some hoards they'd thought they'd lost!
SSSIP!
That's great news, Tippy! See, Nancy? There *are* some upsides to the adventure I can only call "That Time I'd Just Met A Dude, But He Still Thought He Knew What I Wanted Better Than I Did, *Hah Hah Hah,* Why."
CROSS SUPER VILLAIN SHENANIGANS--DO NOT CROSS
I'm still not apologizing for slapping him.
And I'm still not asking you to! Look, I always want to be nice and so sometimes it's *hard* to say no to people, and you're, like--you're the #1 world champion at doing that.
And I admire that.
That's right! I'm the Xander who goes around slapping chumps who sass my friends.
Team Squirrel Scouts, represent!
Oh, not again.
BAROOOOM
No way. *No way.*
SUPER VILLAIN SHENANIGANS
Central Park hasn't moved. But I recognize that *sound--*
It sounds like it's coming from down 5th Avenue?
Then that's where we're headed, baby.

If you don't know New York roadways and thought "Well, certainly I can read my talking squirrel comic and not be made to feel bad about that particular gap in my knowledge," no worries! 5th Avenue is just, like, a road that runs along Central Park. They named a chocolate bar after it.

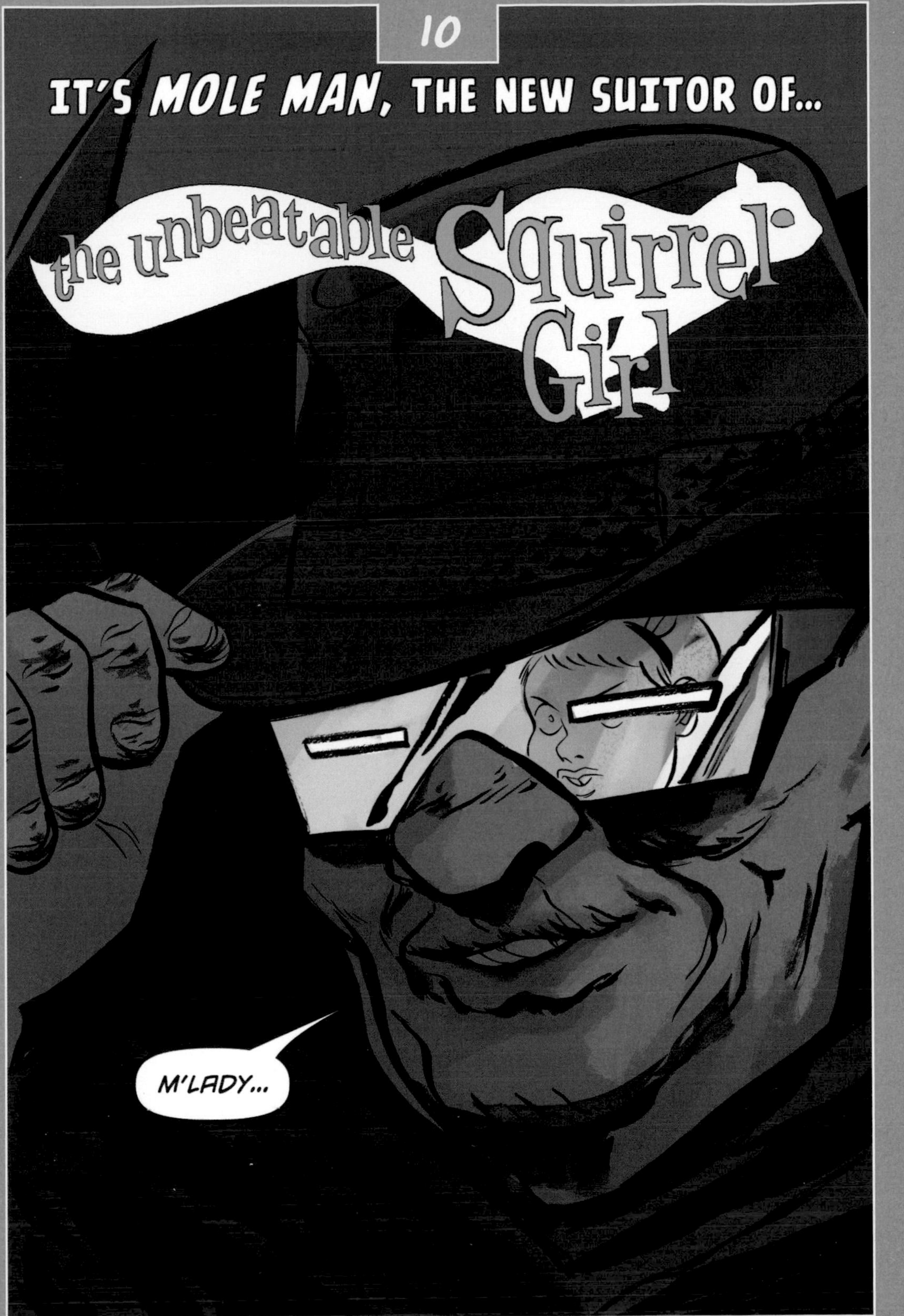
10
IT'S MOLE MAN, THE NEW SUITOR OF...
the unbeatable Squirrel Girl
M'LADY...

Doreen Green isn't just a second-year computer science student: she secretly also has all the powers of both squirrel and girl! She uses her amazing abilities to fight crime **and** be as awesome as possible. You know her as...*The Unbeatable Squirrel Girl!* Find out what she's been up to, with...

Squirrel Girl *in a nutshell*

Squirrel Girl @unbeatablesg
RT if you got like 9999999 new followers b/c Mole Man went on tv, NAMED YOU, and said he'd only stop stealing buildings if you dated him!!

Squirrel Girl @unbeatablesg
No RTs huh? Haha weird how I'M THE ONLY ONE THIS IS HAPPENING TO FOR SOME FRIGGIN' REASON

Squirrel Girl @unbeatablesg
hahaha what even is reality

Howard The Duck @imhowatrd
@unbeatablesg humnas makr datign pretty weikrd, huh??

Squirrel Girl @unbeatablesg
@imhowatrd oh Howard, you have no idea. NO IDEA

Squirrel Girl @unbeatablesg
@imhowatrd I went on a date with a giant purple robot and that was like the most normal part of the past few days!!

Squirrel Girl @unbeatablesg
@imhowatrd I hope he's doing well

SENTINEL X-42903-22 @X4290322
@unbeatablesg HEY

SENTINEL X-42903-22 @X4290322
@unbeatablesg ERROR 552255: DON'T SUBTWEET ME

Egg @imduderadtude
@unbeatablesg just date him alreayd

Squirrel Girl @unbeatablesg
@imduderadtude YOU DATE HIM

Egg @imduderadtude
@unbeatablesg im 12

Squirrel Girl @unbeatablesg
@imduderadtude 100 YEARS OF COMPUTATIONAL MACHINERY DEVELOPMENT SO A 12-YEAR-OLD BOY I DON'T KNOW CAN GIVE ME UNSOLICITED DATING ADVICE

Egg @imduderadtude
@unbeatablesg lol

Egg @imduderadtude
@unbeatablesg i also make memes

Squirrel Girl @unbeatablesg
@imduderadtude ...Any good ones?

Tony Stark @starkmantony ✓
@unbeatablesg @imduderadtude No they're super bad!! Don't waste your time

Squirrel Girl @unbeatablesg
@starkmantony Tony Stark!! YOU consume THE FRESHEST OF MEMES??

Tony Stark @starkmantony ✓
@unbeatablesg @imduderadtude Haha not with this kid I don't!

Egg @imduderadtude
@starkmantony UM WOW WHAT DOES IT SYA IN MY BIO,, MR STARK?? WHAT DOES IT SAY

Egg @imduderadtude
@starkmantony IT SAYS "DONT @ ME IF U DON'T LIKE MY MEMES!!!"!!! THAT'S WHAT IT SAYS

Egg @imduderadtude
@starkmantony BLOCKED

search! 🔍

#moleman

#molemaam

#evenmolemoneyevenmoleproblems

#holycarp

#voteloki

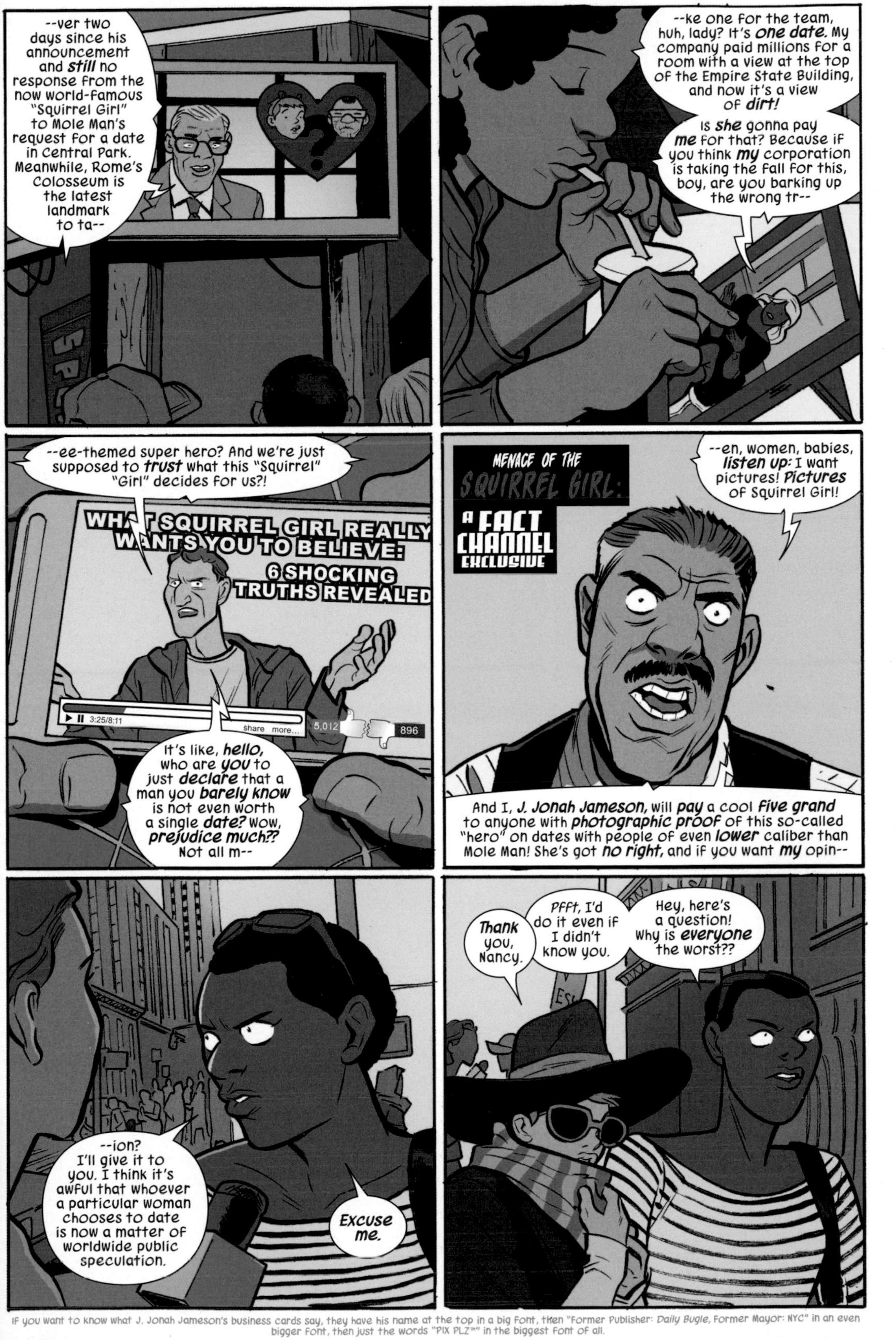
--ver two days since his announcement and still no response from the now world-famous "Squirrel Girl" to Mole Man's request for a date in Central Park. Meanwhile, Rome's Colosseum is the latest landmark to ta--
--ke one for the team, huh, lady? It's one date. My company paid millions for a room with a view at the top of the Empire State Building, and now it's a view of dirt!
Is she gonna pay me for that? Because if you think my corporation is taking the fall for this, boy, are you barking up the wrong tr--
--ee-themed super hero? And we're just supposed to trust what this "Squirrel" "Girl" decides for us?!
WHAT SQUIRREL GIRL REALLY WANTS YOU TO BELIEVE: 6 SHOCKING TRUTHS REVEALED
3:25/8:11
share more...
5,012
896
It's like, hello, who are you to just declare that a man you barely know is not even worth a single date? Wow, prejudice much?? Not all m--
MENACE OF THE SQUIRREL GIRL: A FACT CHANNEL EXCLUSIVE
--en, women, babies, listen up: I want pictures! Pictures of Squirrel Girl!
And I, J. Jonah Jameson, will pay a cool five grand to anyone with photographic proof of this so-called "hero" on dates with people of even lower caliber than Mole Man! She's got no right, and if you want my opin--
--ion? I'll give it to you. I think it's awful that whoever a particular woman chooses to date is now a matter of worldwide public speculation.
Excuse me.
Thank you, Nancy.
Pfft, I'd do it even if I didn't know you.
Hey, here's a question! Why is everyone the worst??

If you want to know what J. Jonah Jameson's business cards say, they have his name at the top in a big font, then "Former Publisher: *Daily Bugle*, Former Mayor: NYC" in an even bigger font, then just the words "PIX PLZ™" in the biggest font of all.

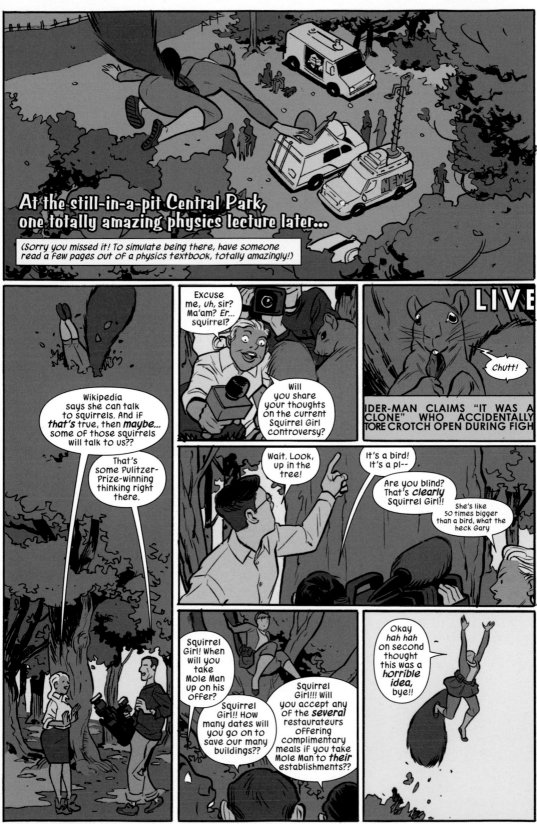

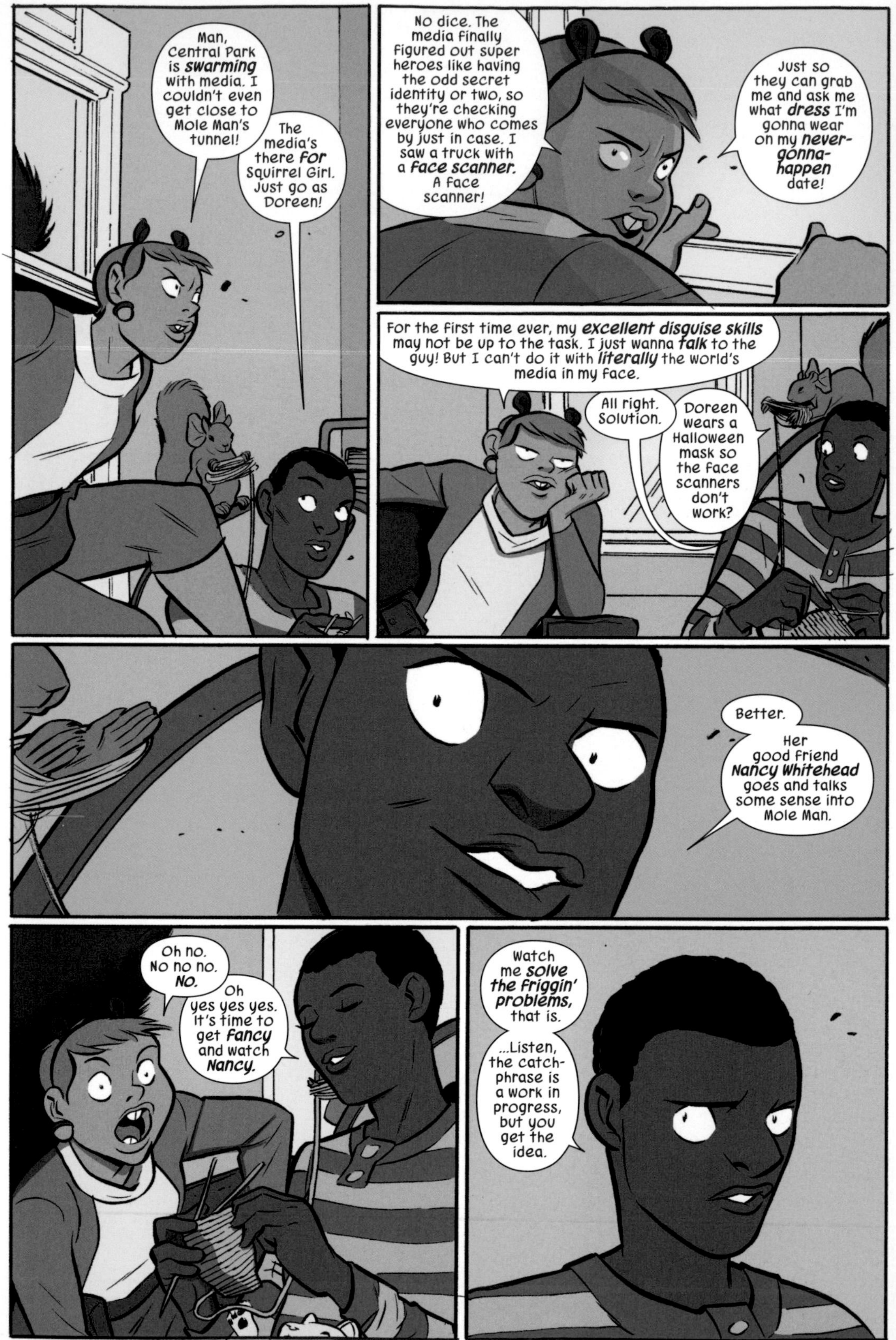
Man, Central Park is swarming with media. I couldn't even get close to Mole Man's tunnel!
The media's there for Squirrel Girl. Just go as Doreen!
No dice. The media finally figured out super heroes like having the odd secret identity or two, so they're checking everyone who comes by just in case. I saw a truck with a face scanner. A face scanner!
Just so they can grab me and ask me what dress I'm gonna wear on my never-gonna-happen date!
For the first time ever, my excellent disguise skills may not be up to the task. I just wanna talk to the guy! But I can't do it with literally the world's media in my face.
All right. Solution.
Doreen wears a Halloween mask so the face scanners don't work?
Better.
Her good friend Nancy Whitehead goes and talks some sense into Mole Man.
Oh no. No no no. NO.
Oh yes yes yes. It's time to get Fancy and watch Nancy.
Watch me solve the friggin' problems, that is.
...Listen, the catchphrase is a work in progress, but you get the idea.

Basically the only other word that rhymes with "Nancy" is "necromancy," i.e.: *the art of making skeletons come to life and fight chumps for you.* So...something to look forward to, I guess??

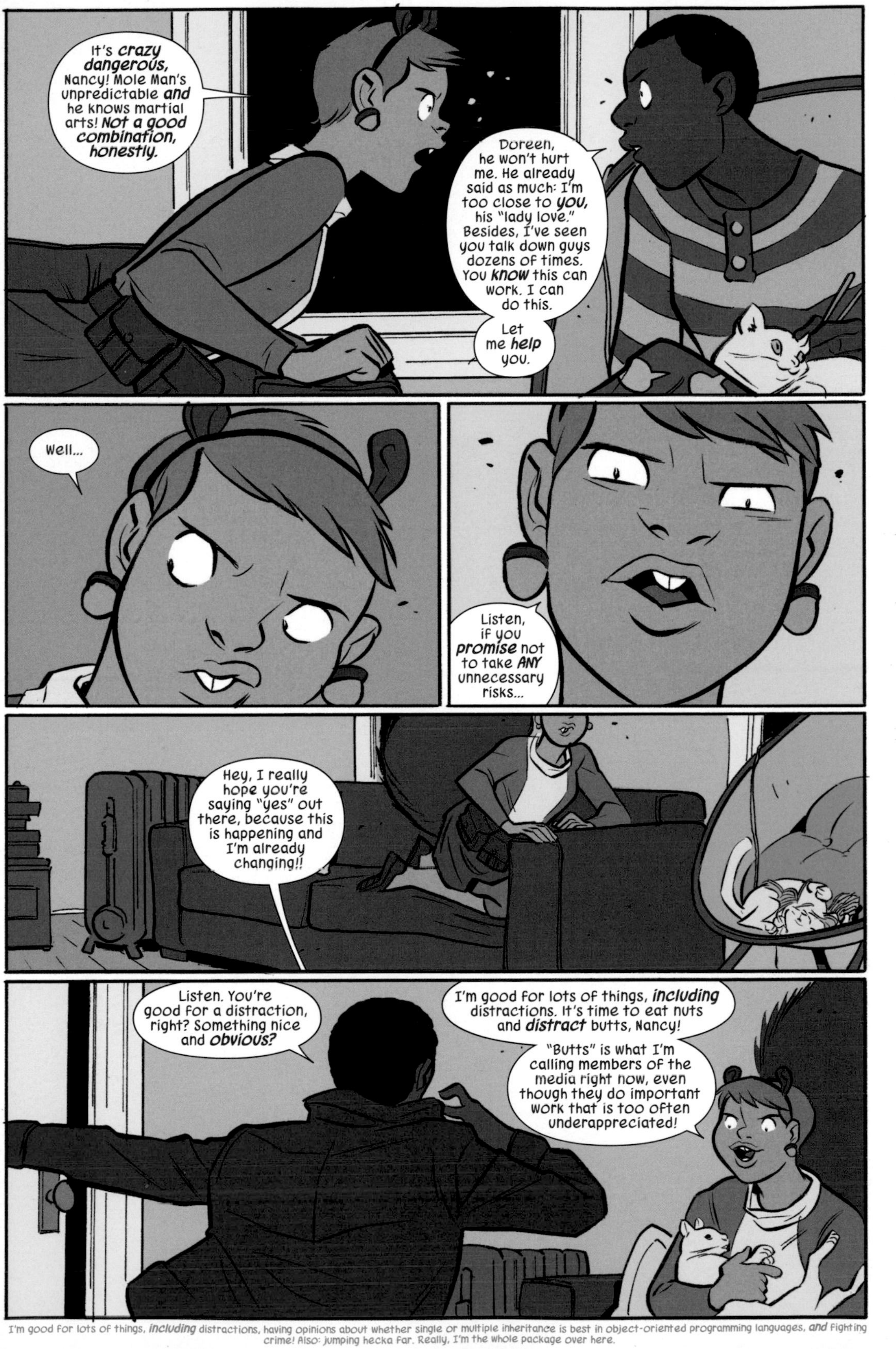
It's crazy dangerous, Nancy! Mole Man's unpredictable and he knows martial arts! Not a good combination, honestly.
Doreen, he won't hurt me. He already said as much: I'm too close to you, his "lady love." Besides, I've seen you talk down guys dozens of times. You know this can work. I can do this.
Let me help you.
Well...
Listen, if you promise not to take ANY unnecessary risks...
Hey, I really hope you're saying "yes" out there, because this is happening and I'm already changing!!
Listen. You're good for a distraction, right? Something nice and obvious?
I'm good for lots of things, including distractions. It's time to eat nuts and distract butts, Nancy!
"Butts" is what I'm calling members of the media right now, even though they do important work that is too often underappreciated!

I'm good for lots of things, *including* distractions, having opinions about whether single or multiple inheritance is best in object-oriented programming languages, *and* fighting crime! Also: jumping hecka far. Really, I'm the whole package over here.

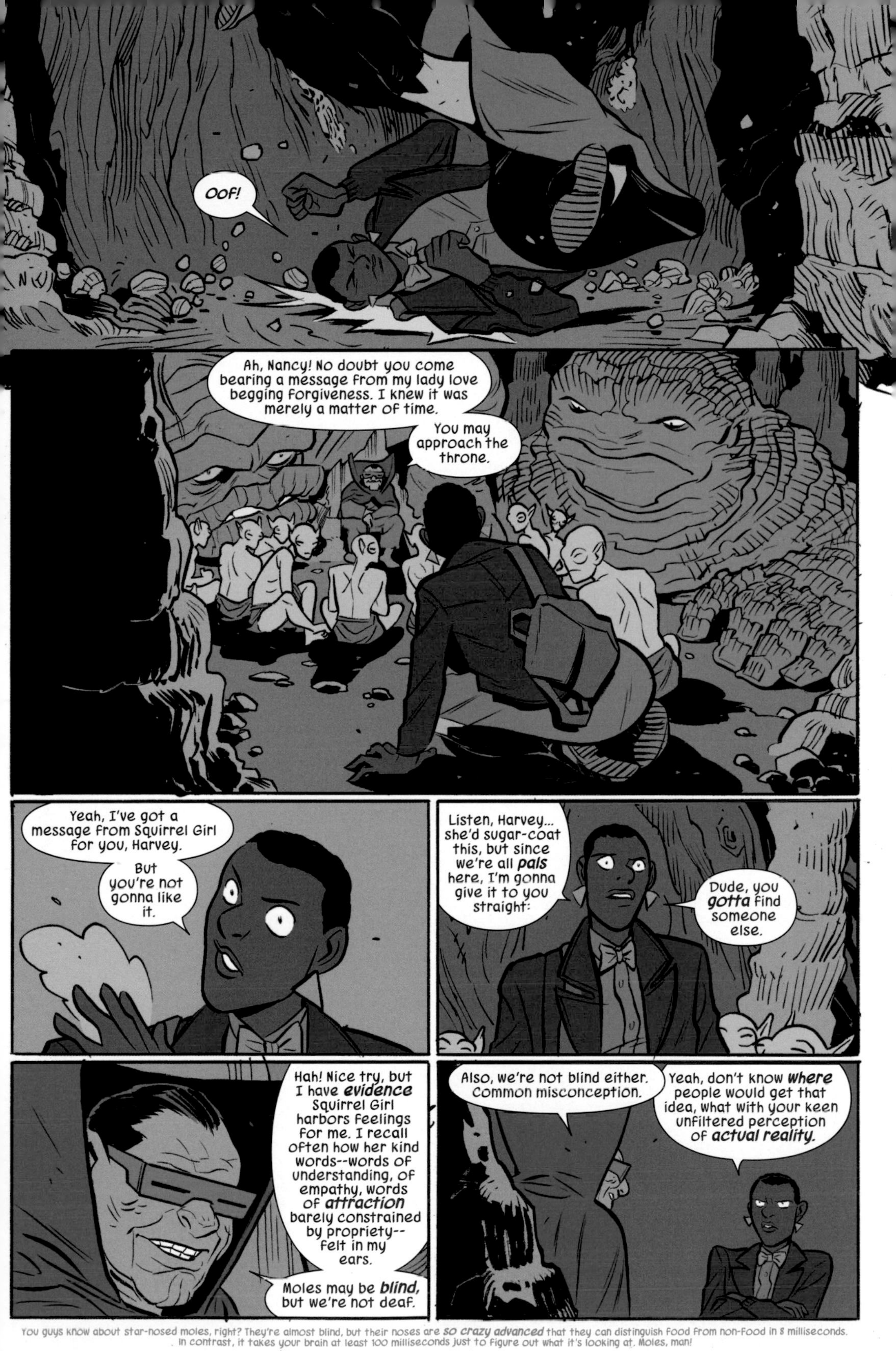
OOF!
Ah, Nancy! No doubt you come bearing a message from my lady love begging forgiveness. I knew it was merely a matter of time.
You may approach the throne.
Yeah, I've got a message from Squirrel Girl for you, Harvey.
But you're not gonna like it.
Listen, Harvey... she'd sugar-coat this, but since we're all *pals* here, I'm gonna give it to you straight:
Dude, you *gotta* find someone else.
Hah! Nice try, but I have *evidence* Squirrel Girl harbors feelings for me. I recall often how her kind words--words of understanding, of empathy, words of *attraction* barely constrained by propriety--felt in my ears.
Moles may be *blind,* but we're not deaf.
Also, we're not blind either. Common misconception.
Yeah, don't know *where* people would get that idea, what with your keen unfiltered perception of *actual reality.*

You guys know about star-nosed moles, right? They're almost blind, but their noses are *so crazy advanced* that they can distinguish food from non-food in 8 milliseconds. In contrast, it takes your brain at least 100 milliseconds just to figure out what it's looking at. Moles, man!

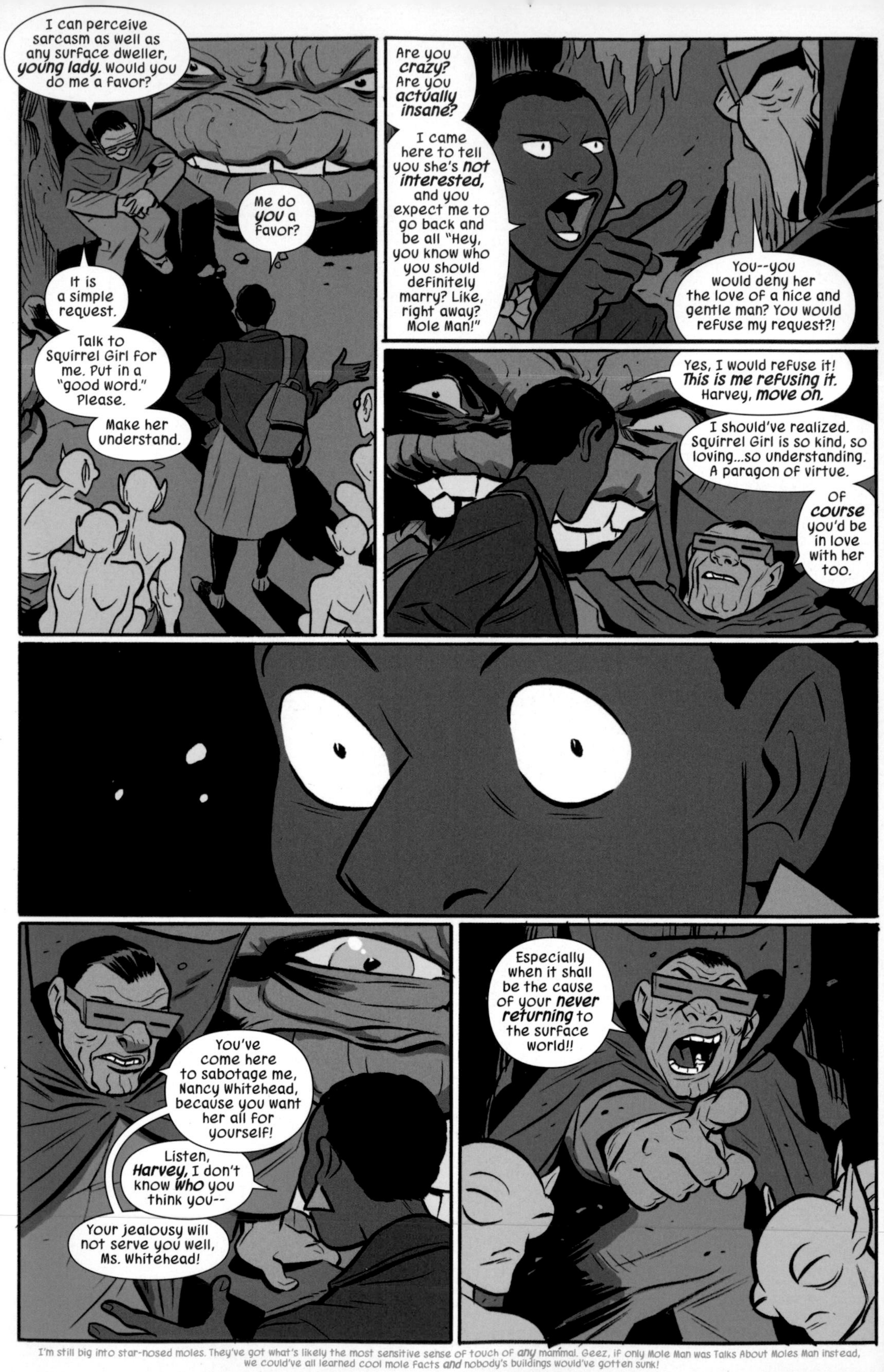

I can perceive sarcasm as well as any surface dweller, *young lady.* Would you do me a favor?
Me do *you* a favor?
It is a simple request.
Talk to Squirrel Girl for me. Put in a "good word." Please.
Make her understand.
Are you *crazy?* Are you *actually insane?*
I came here to tell you she's *not interested,* and you expect me to go back and be all "Hey, you know who you should definitely marry? Like, right away? Mole Man!"
You--you would deny her the love of a nice and gentle man? You would refuse my request?!
Yes, I would refuse it! *This is me refusing it.* Harvey, *move on.*
I should've realized. Squirrel Girl is so kind, so loving...so understanding. A paragon of virtue.
Of *course* you'd be in love with her too.
You've come here to sabotage me, Nancy Whitehead, because you want her all for yourself!
Listen, *Harvey,* I don't know *who* you think you--
Your jealousy will not serve you well, Ms. Whitehead!
Especially when it shall be the cause of your *never returning* to the surface world!!

I'm still big into star-nosed moles. They've got what's likely the most sensitive sense of touch of *any* mammal. Geez, if only Mole Man was Talks About Moles Man instead, we could've all learned cool mole facts *and* nobody's buildings would've gotten sunk!

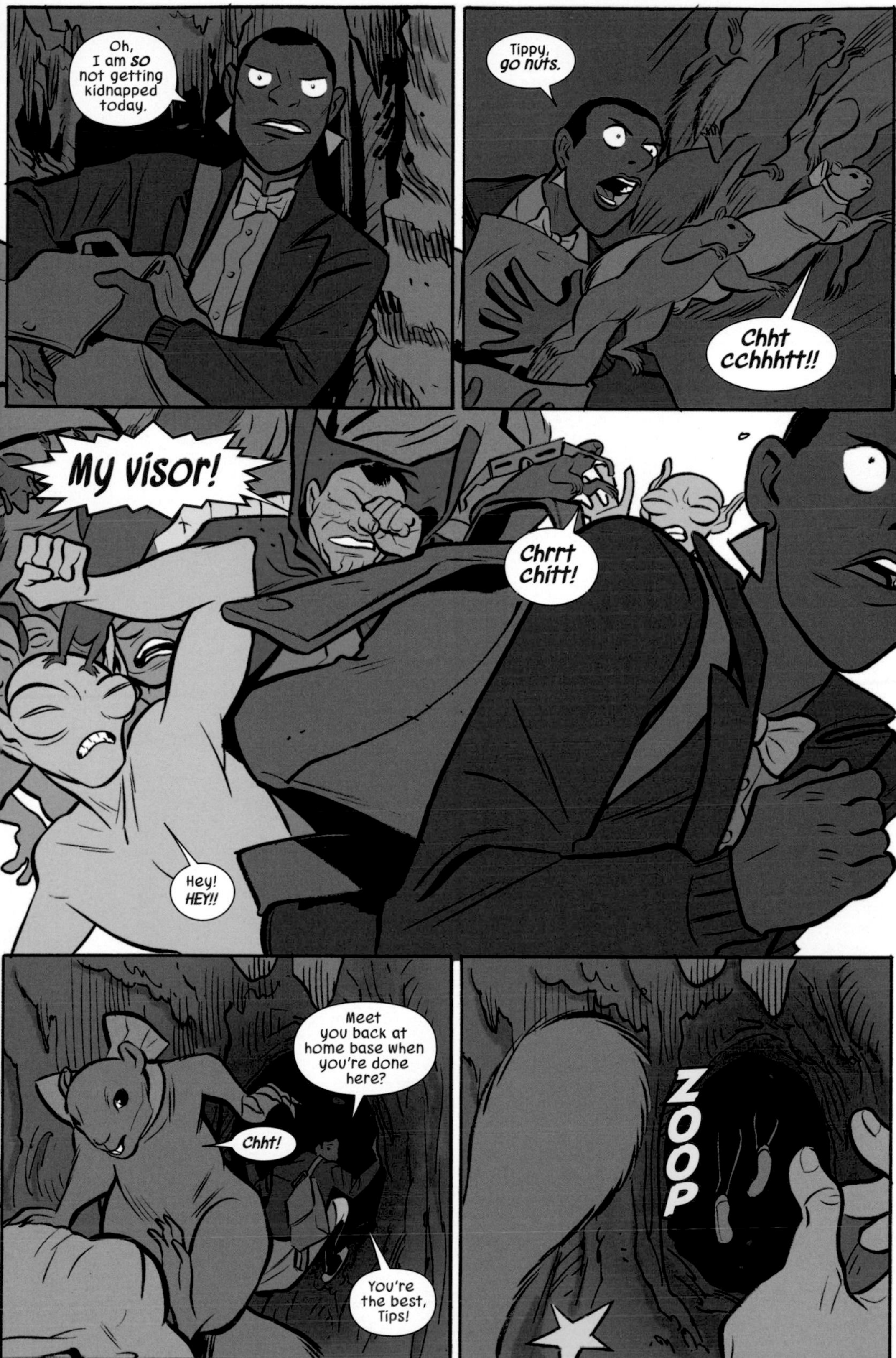
Oh, I am *so* not getting kidnapped today.
Tippy, *go nuts.*
Chht cchhhtt!!
My visor!
Chrrt chitt!
Hey! *HEY!!*
Meet you back at home base when you're done here?
Chht!
You're the best, Tips!
ZOOP

Nancy and Doreen call their apartment "home base" because it sounds *way* cooler than "the apartment we both rent." If *you're* looking for a cool name to call where you live, you could do worse than "home base"!

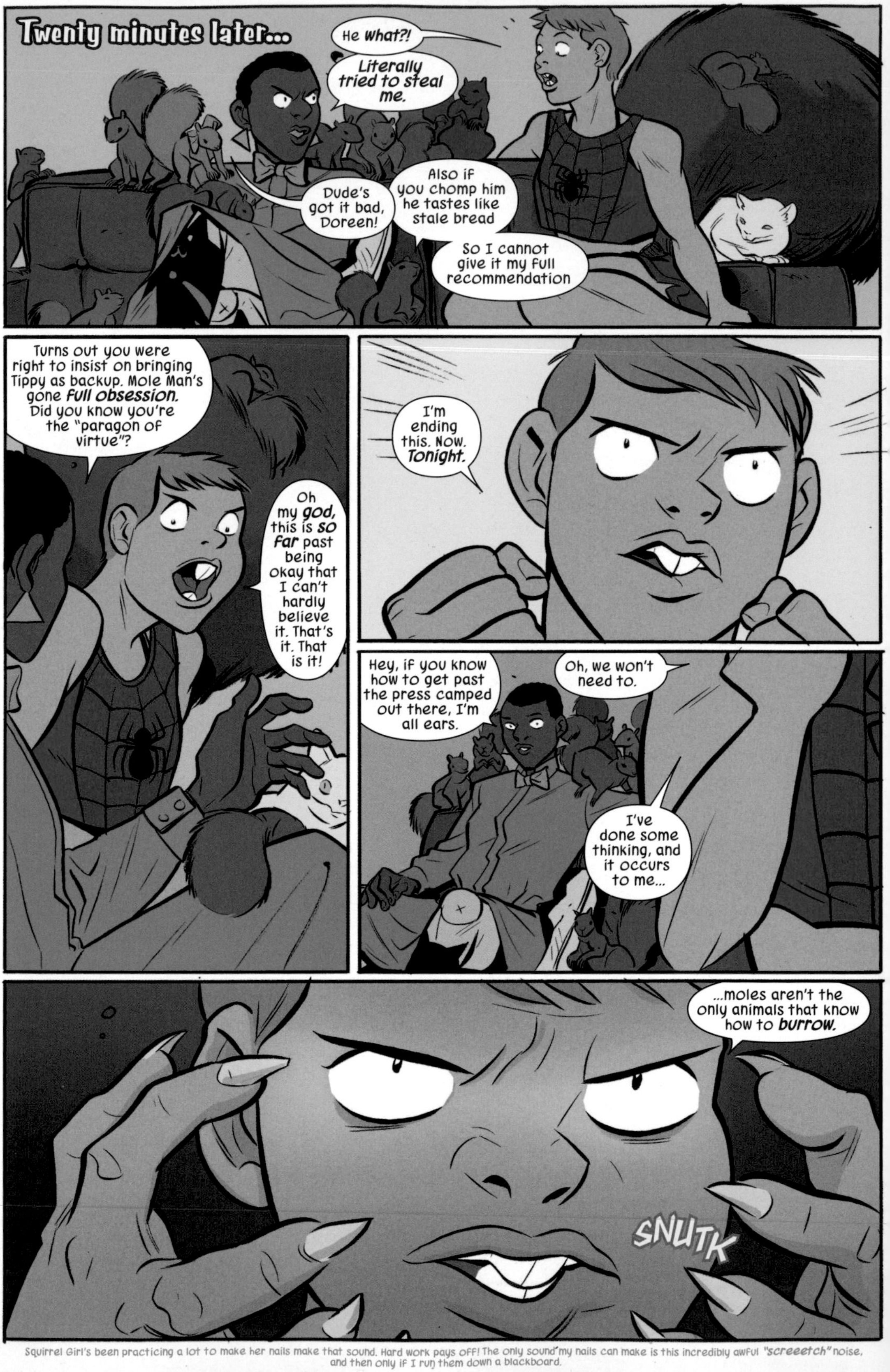
Twenty minutes later...
He *what?!*
Literally tried to steal me.
Dude's got it bad, Doreen!
Also if you chomp him he tastes like stale bread
So I cannot give it my full recommendation
Turns out you were right to insist on bringing Tippy as backup. Mole Man's gone *full obsession.* Did you know you're the "paragon of virtue"?
Oh my *god,* this is *so far* past being okay that I can't hardly believe it. That's it. That is it!
I'm ending this. Now. *Tonight.*
Hey, if you know how to get past the press camped out there, I'm all ears.
Oh, we won't need to.
I've done some thinking, and it occurs to me...
...moles aren't the only animals that know how to *burrow.*
SNUTK

Squirrel Girl's been practicing a lot to make her nails make that sound. Hard work pays off! The only sound my nails can make is this incredibly awful *"screeetch"* noise, and then only if I run them down a blackboard.

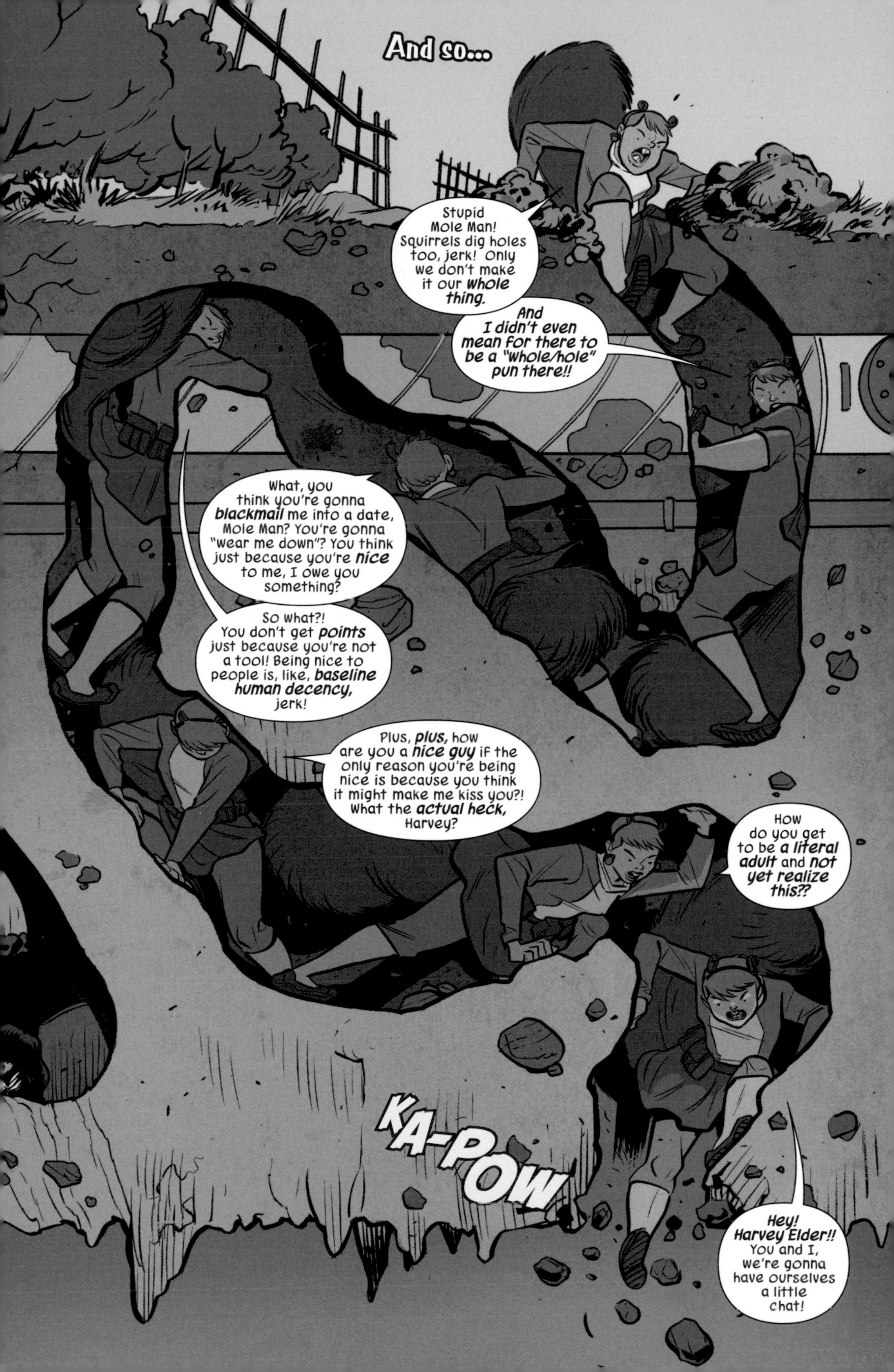
And so...
Stupid Mole Man! Squirrels dig holes too, jerk! Only we don't make it our **whole thing.**
And I didn't even mean for there to be a "whole/hole" pun there!!
What, you think you're gonna **blackmail** me into a date, Mole Man? You're gonna "wear me down"? You think just because you're **nice** to me, I owe you something?
So what?! You don't get **points** just because you're not a tool! Being nice to people is, like, **baseline human decency,** jerk!
Plus, **plus,** how are you a **nice guy** if the only reason you're being nice is because you think it might make me kiss you?! What the **actual heck,** Harvey?
How do you get to be **a literal adult** and **not yet realize this??**
KA-POW
Hey! Harvey Elder!! You and I, we're gonna have ourselves a little chat!

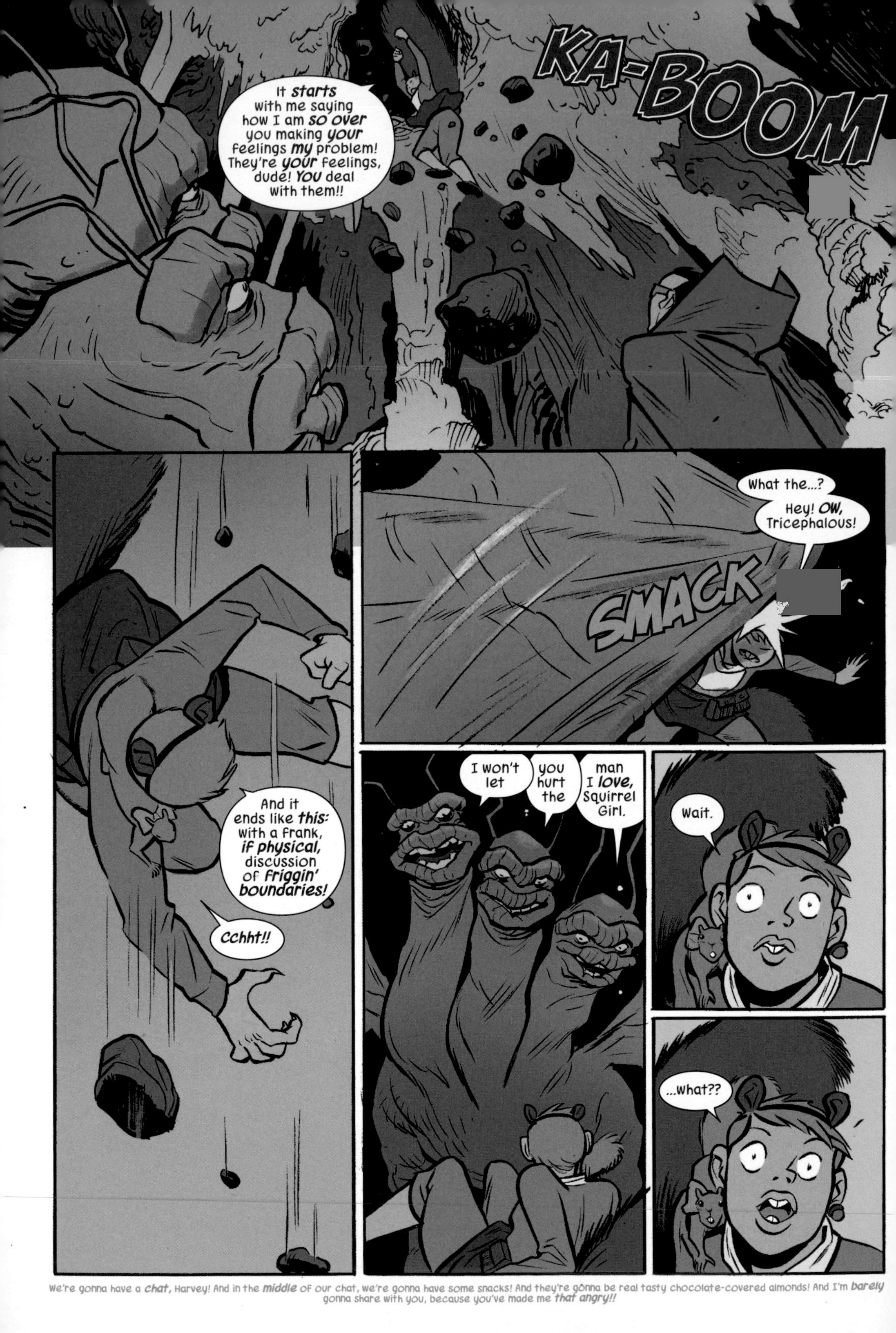
It starts with me saying how I am so over you making your feelings my problem! They're your feelings, dude! You deal with them!!
KA-BOOM
And it ends like this: with a frank, if physical, discussion of friggin' boundaries!
Cchht!!
What the...?
Hey! OW, Tricephalous!
SMACK
I won't let
you hurt the
man I love, Squirrel Girl.
Wait.
...What??

We're gonna have a *chat*, Harvey! And in the *middle* of our chat, we're gonna have some snacks! And they're gonna be real tasty chocolate-covered almonds! And I'm *barely* gonna share with you, because you've made me *that angry!!*

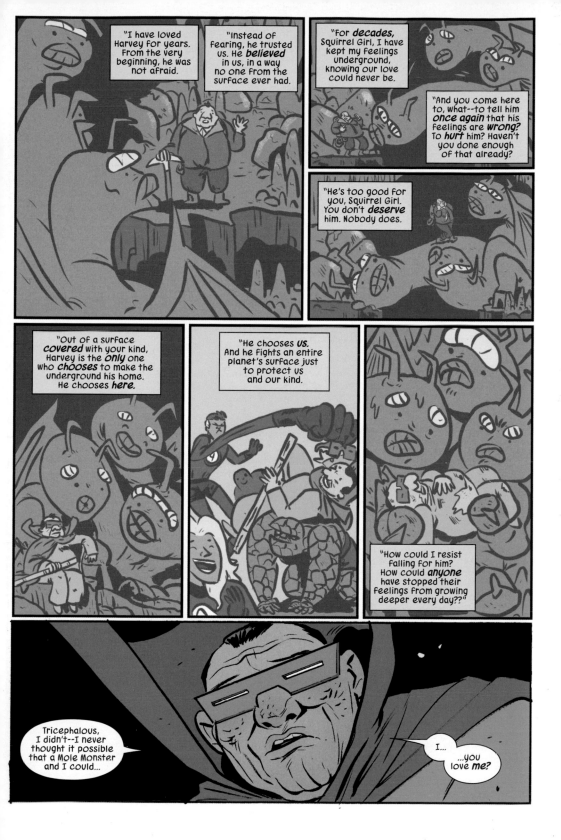

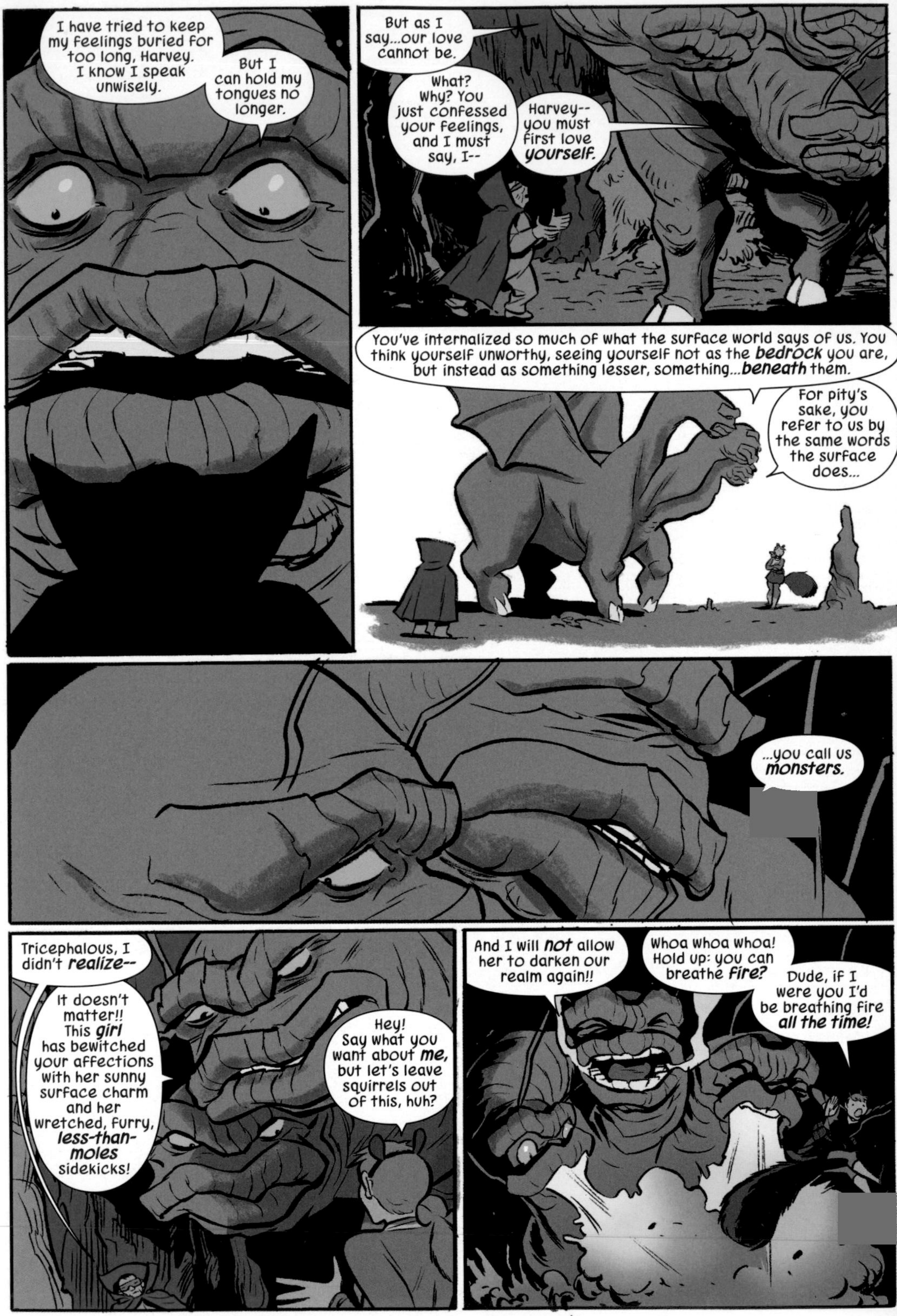
I have tried to keep my feelings buried for too long, Harvey. I know I speak unwisely.
But I can hold my tongues no longer.
But as I say...our love cannot be.
What? Why? You just confessed your feelings, and I must say, I--
Harvey-- you must first love *yourself.*
You've internalized so much of what the surface world says of us. You think yourself unworthy, seeing yourself not as the *bedrock* you are, but instead as something lesser, something...*beneath* them.
For pity's sake, you refer to us by the same words the surface does...
...you call us *monsters.*
Tricephalous, I didn't *realize--*
It doesn't matter!! This *girl* has bewitched your affections with her sunny surface charm and her wretched, furry, *less-than-moles* sidekicks!
Hey! Say what you want about *me,* but let's leave squirrels out of this, huh?
And I will *not* allow her to darken our realm again!!
Whoa whoa whoa! Hold up: you can breathe *fire?*
Dude, if I were you I'd be breathing fire *all the time!*

If I were you I'd be flying *everywhere,* breathing fire *nonstop,* and shouting "Bet you didn't know squirrels could do *this,* huh??"

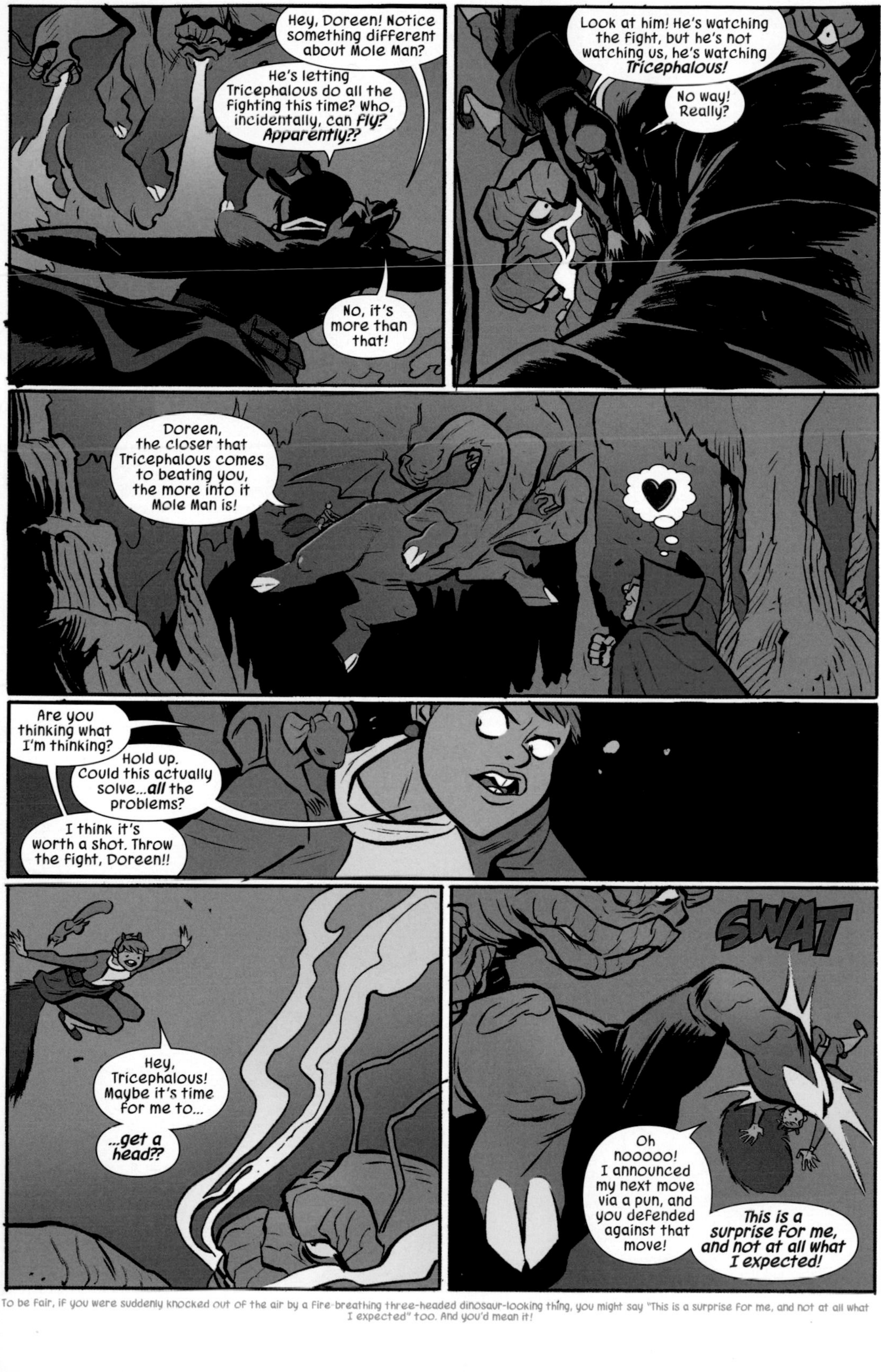
Hey, Doreen! Notice something different about Mole Man?
He's letting Tricephalous do all the fighting this time? Who, incidentally, can *fly*? *Apparently??*
No, it's more than that!
Look at him! He's watching the fight, but he's not watching us, he's watching *Tricephalous!*
No way! Really?
Doreen, the closer that Tricephalous comes to beating you, the more into it Mole Man is!
Are you thinking what I'm thinking?
Hold up. Could this actually solve...*all* the problems?
I think it's worth a shot. Throw the fight, Doreen!!
Hey, Tricephalous! Maybe it's time for me to...
...get a head??
SWAT
Oh nooooo! I announced my next move via a pun, and you defended against that move!
This is a surprise for me, and not at all what I expected!

To be fair, if you were suddenly knocked out of the air by a fire-breathing three-headed dinosaur-looking thing, you might say "This is a surprise for me, and not at all what I expected" too. And you'd mean it!

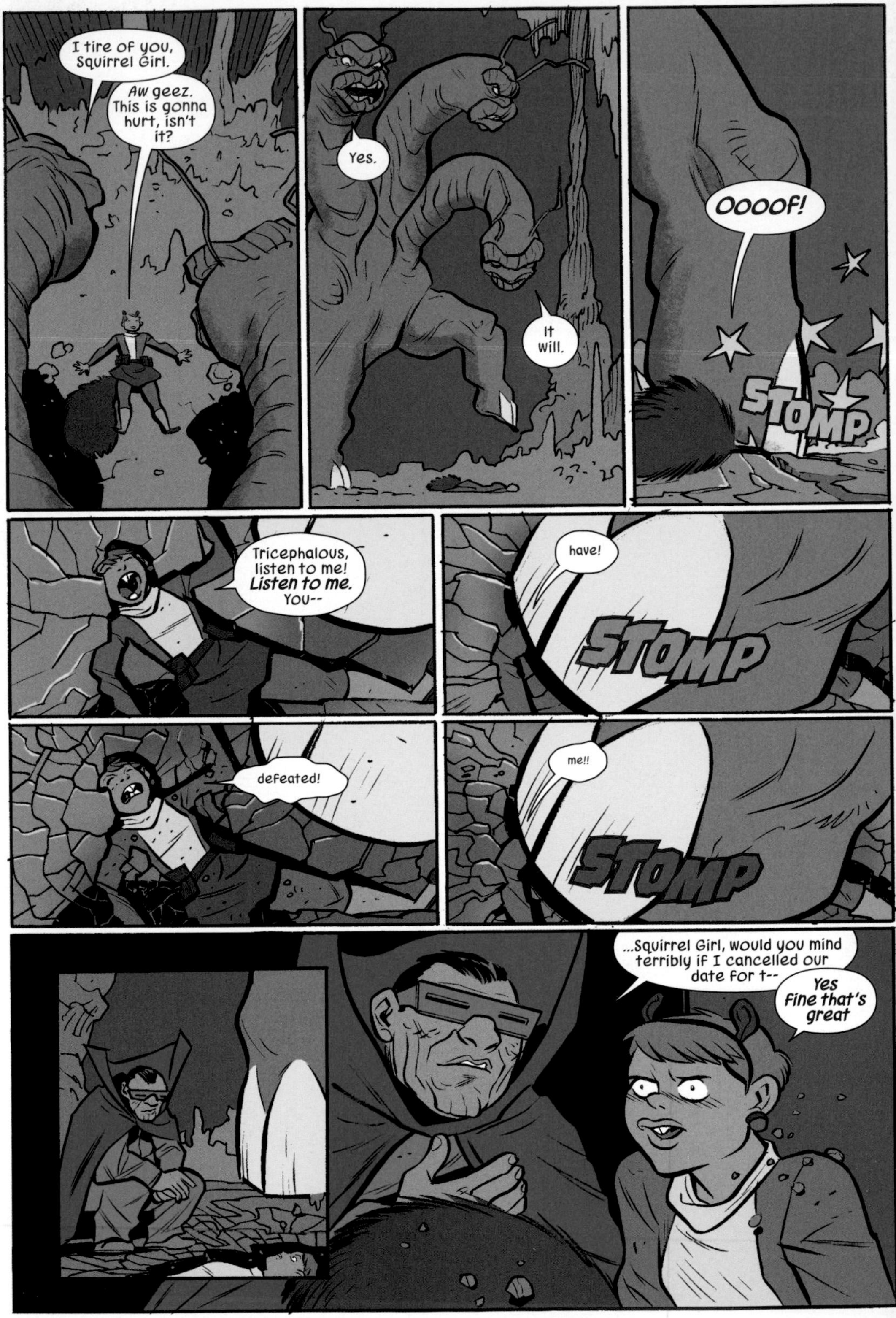
I tire of you, Squirrel Girl.
Aw geez. This is gonna hurt, isn't it?
Yes.
It will.
OOOOF!
STOMP
Tricephalous, listen to me! *Listen to me.* You--
have!
STOMP
defeated!
me!!
STOMP
...Squirrel Girl, would you mind terribly if I cancelled our date for t--
Yes fine that's great

Tricephalous, more like Trice*ailus*, am I right? Because we were ailed by it three times? Nevermind, it was--it was a stretch to begin with.

IF Tony was named Ron instead, he could be "I, Ron" Man. Missed opportunities, Tony! Get on this, Tony!

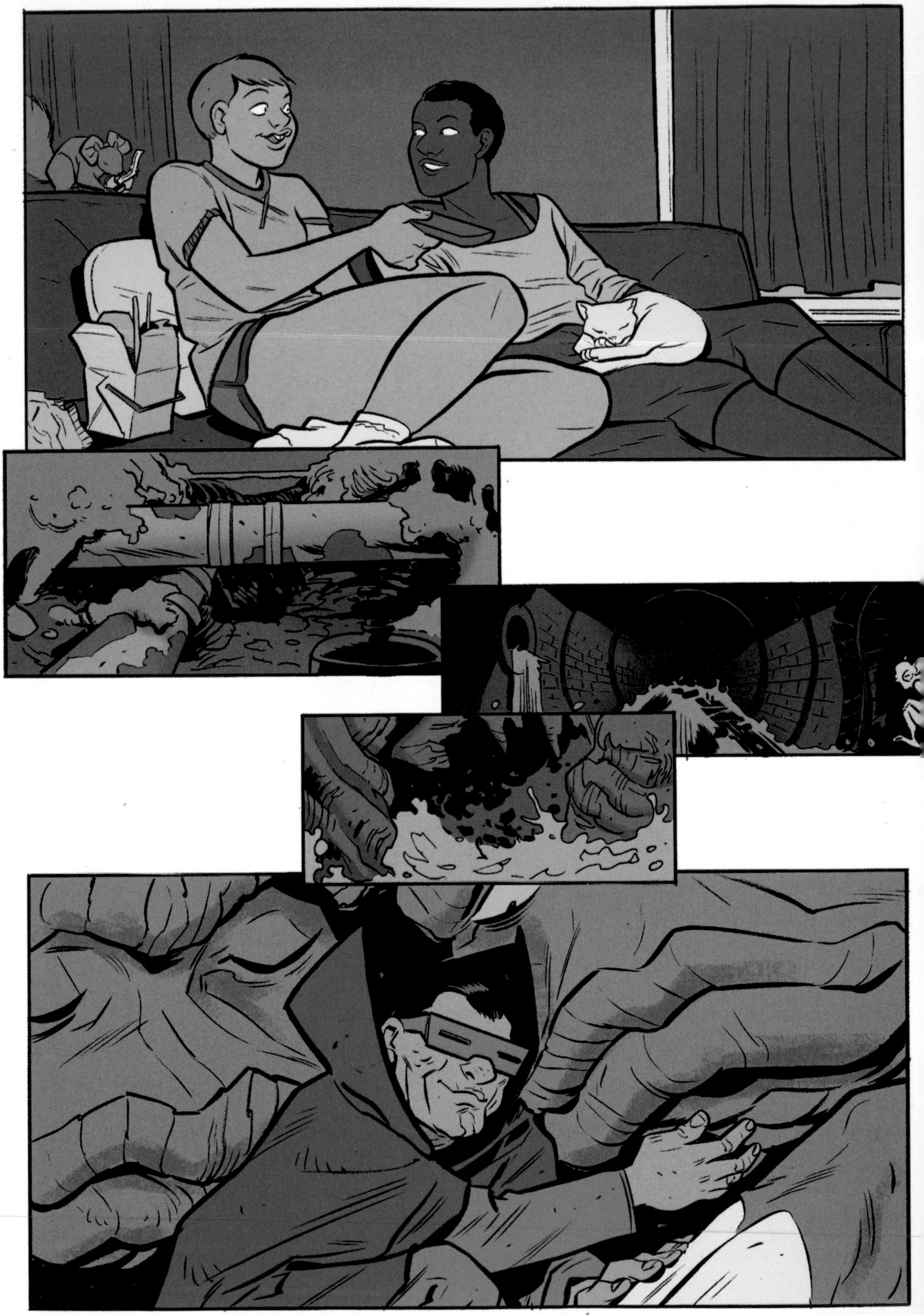

The end!

11

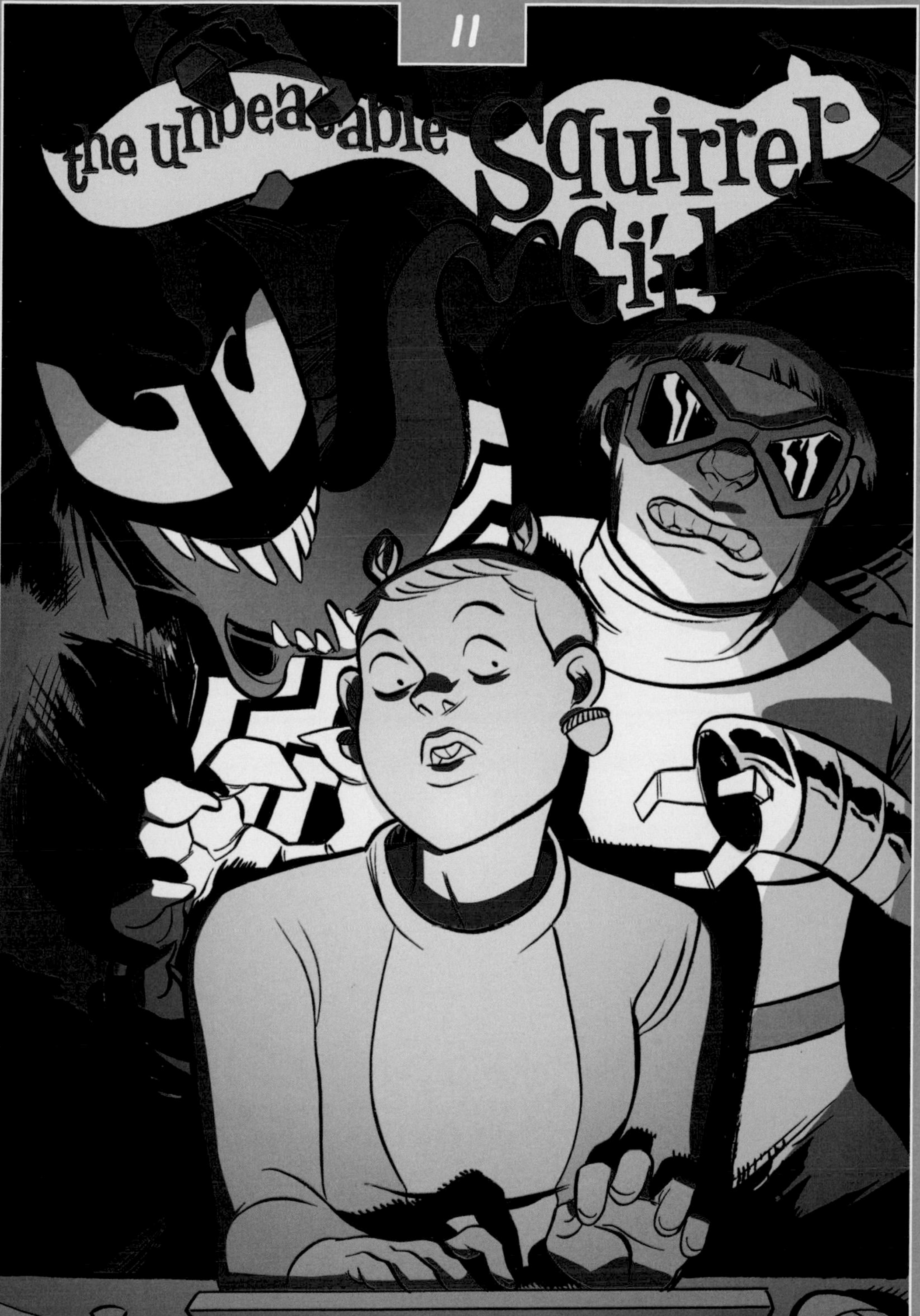
the unbeatable Squirrel Girl

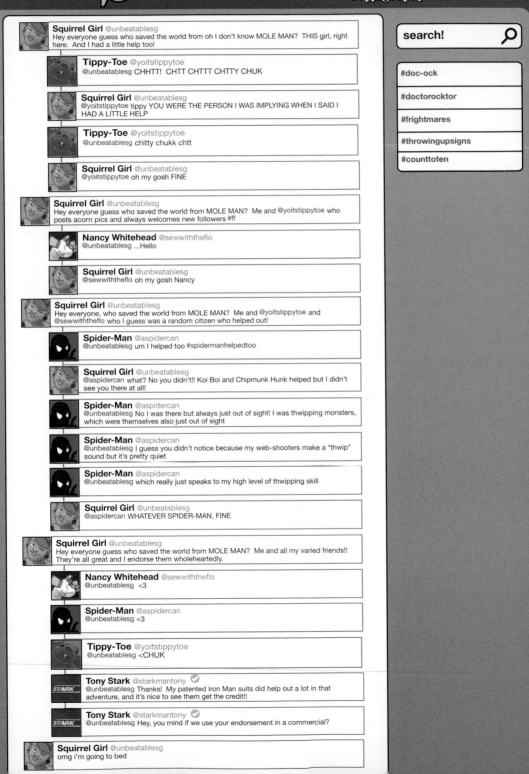

Doreen Green isn't just a second-year computer science student: she secretly also has all the powers of both squirrel and girl! She uses her amazing abilities to fight crime **and** be as awesome as possible. You know her as...**The Unbeatable Squirrel Girl**! Find out what she's been up to, with...

Squirrel Girl *in a nutshell*

search!

#doc-ock

#doctorocktor

#frightmares

#throwingupsigns

#counttoten

Squirrel Girl @unbeatablesg
Hey everyone guess who saved the world from oh I don't know MOLE MAN? THIS girl, right here. And I had a little help too!

Tippy-Toe @yoitstippytoe
@unbeatablesg CHHTT! CHTT CHTTT CHTTY CHUK

Squirrel Girl @unbeatablesg
@yoitstippytoe tippy YOU WERE THE PERSON I WAS IMPLYING WHEN I SAID I HAD A LITTLE HELP

Tippy-Toe @yoitstippytoe
@unbeatablesg chitty chukk chtt

Squirrel Girl @unbeatablesg
@yoitstippytoe oh my gosh FINE

Squirrel Girl @unbeatablesg
Hey everyone guess who saved the world from MOLE MAN? Me and @yoitstippytoe who posts acorn pics and always welcomes new followers #ff

Nancy Whitehead @sewwiththeflo
@unbeatablesg ...Hello

Squirrel Girl @unbeatablesg
@sewwiththeflo oh my gosh Nancy

Squirrel Girl @unbeatablesg
Hey everyone, who saved the world from MOLE MAN? Me and @yoitstippytoe and @sewwiththeflo who I guess was a random citizen who helped out!

Spider-Man @aspidercan
@unbeatablesg um I helped too #spidermanhelpedtoo

Squirrel Girl @unbeatablesg
@aspidercan what? No you didn't!! Koi Boi and Chipmunk Hunk helped but I didn't see you there at all!

Spider-Man @aspidercan
@unbeatablesg No I was there but always just out of sight! I was thwipping monsters, which were themselves also just out of sight

Spider-Man @aspidercan
@unbeatablesg I guess you didn't notice because my web-shooters make a "thwip" sound but it's pretty quiet

Spider-Man @aspidercan
@unbeatablesg which really just speaks to my high level of thwipping skill

Squirrel Girl @unbeatablesg
@aspidercan WHATEVER SPIDER-MAN, FINE

Squirrel Girl @unbeatablesg
Hey everyone guess who saved the world from MOLE MAN? Me and all my varied friends!! They're all great and I endorse them wholeheartedly.

Nancy Whitehead @sewwiththeflo
@unbeatablesg <3

Spider-Man @aspidercan
@unbeatablesg <3

Tippy-Toe @yoitstippytoe
@unbeatablesg <CHUK

Tony Stark @starkmantony
@unbeatablesg Thanks! My patented Iron Man suits did help out a lot in that adventure, and it's nice to see them get the credit!!

Tony Stark @starkmantony
@unbeatablesg Hey, you mind if we use your endorsement in a commercial?

Squirrel Girl @unbeatablesg
omg i'm going to bed

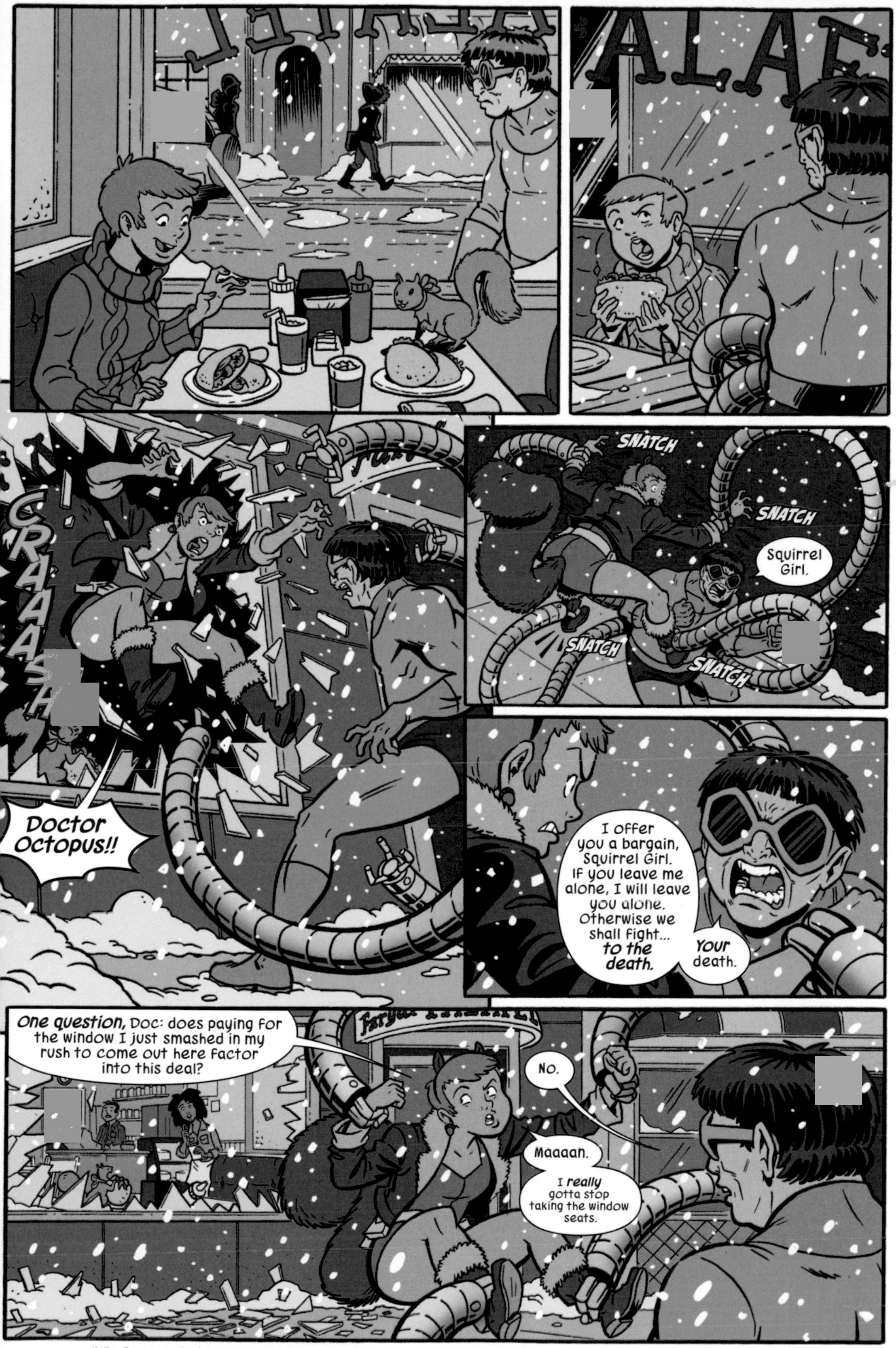
CRAAAASH
Doctor Octopus!!
SNATCH
SNATCH
Squirrel Girl.
SNATCH
SNATCH
I offer you a bargain, Squirrel Girl. If you leave me alone, I will leave you alone. Otherwise we shall fight... to the death.
Your death.
One question, Doc: does paying for the window I just smashed in my rush to come out here factor into this deal?
No.
Maaaan.
I really gotta stop taking the window seats.

Hello, I am a regular human who would like to eat falafel. Do you have a "patrons must pay for broken glass" policy? No, not "glasses": glass. Ah, I see. Well, just--just seat me at whatever table is farthest from all the windows.

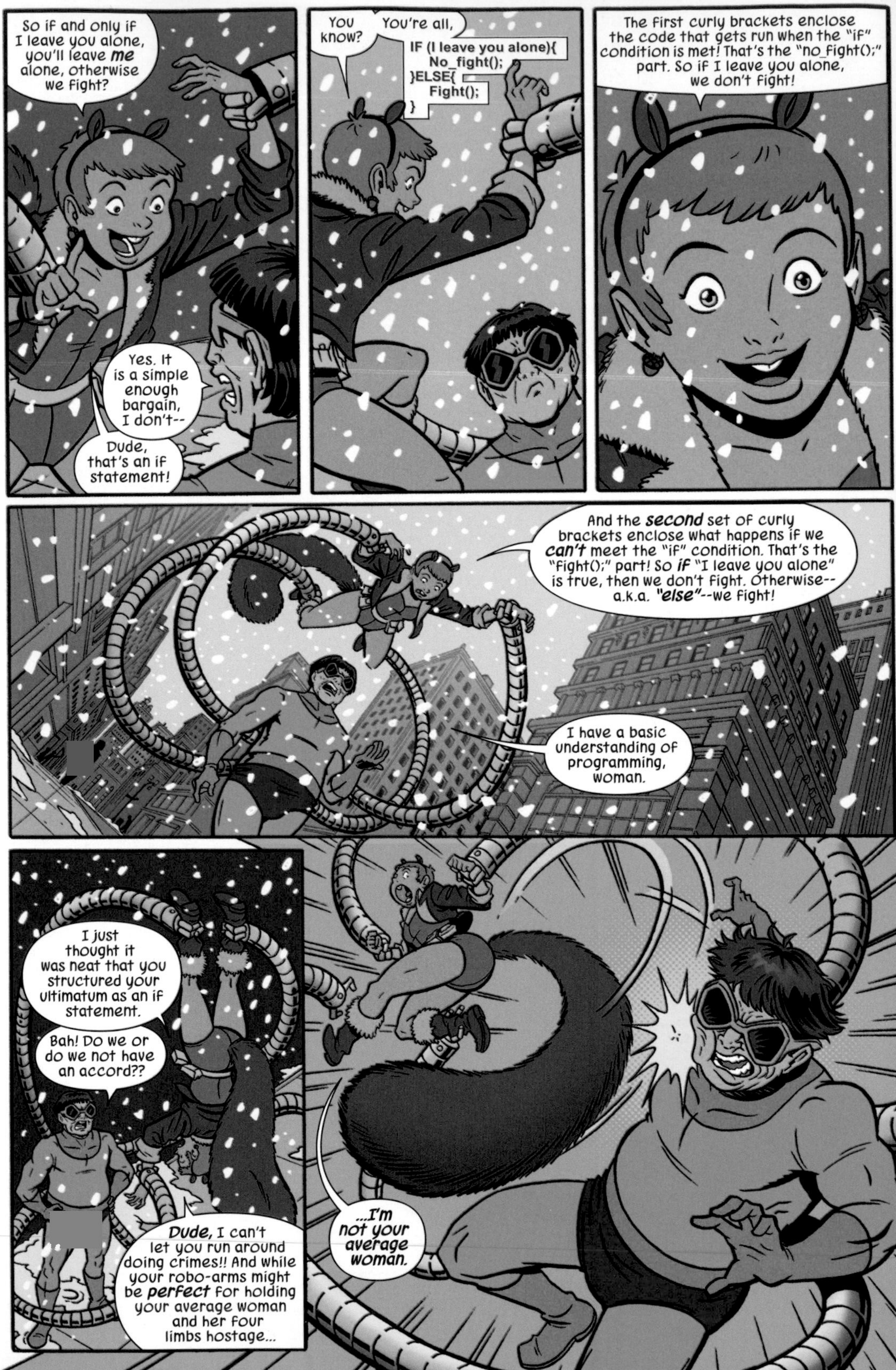
So if and only if I leave you alone, you'll leave *me* alone, otherwise we fight?
Yes. It is a simple enough bargain, I don't--
Dude, that's an if statement!
You know?
You're all,
IF (I leave you alone){
No_fight();
}ELSE{
Fight();
}
The first curly brackets enclose the code that gets run when the "if" condition is met! That's the "no_fight();" part. So if I leave you alone, we don't fight!
And the *second* set of curly brackets enclose what happens if we *can't* meet the "if" condition. That's the "fight();" part! So *if* "I leave you alone" is true, then we don't fight. Otherwise--a.k.a. *"else"*--we fight!
I have a basic understanding of programming, woman.
I just thought it was neat that you structured your ultimatum as an if statement.
Bah! Do we or do we not have an accord??
Dude, I can't let you run around doing crimes!! And while your robo-arms might be *perfect* for holding your average woman and her four limbs hostage...
...I'm not your average woman.

Spider-Man is watching this and suddenly realizing all the times having a tail would've helped him. The answer: approximately one zillion. But then they'd all be much shorter comics, so I guess the real winner is *YOU*, the reader!!!

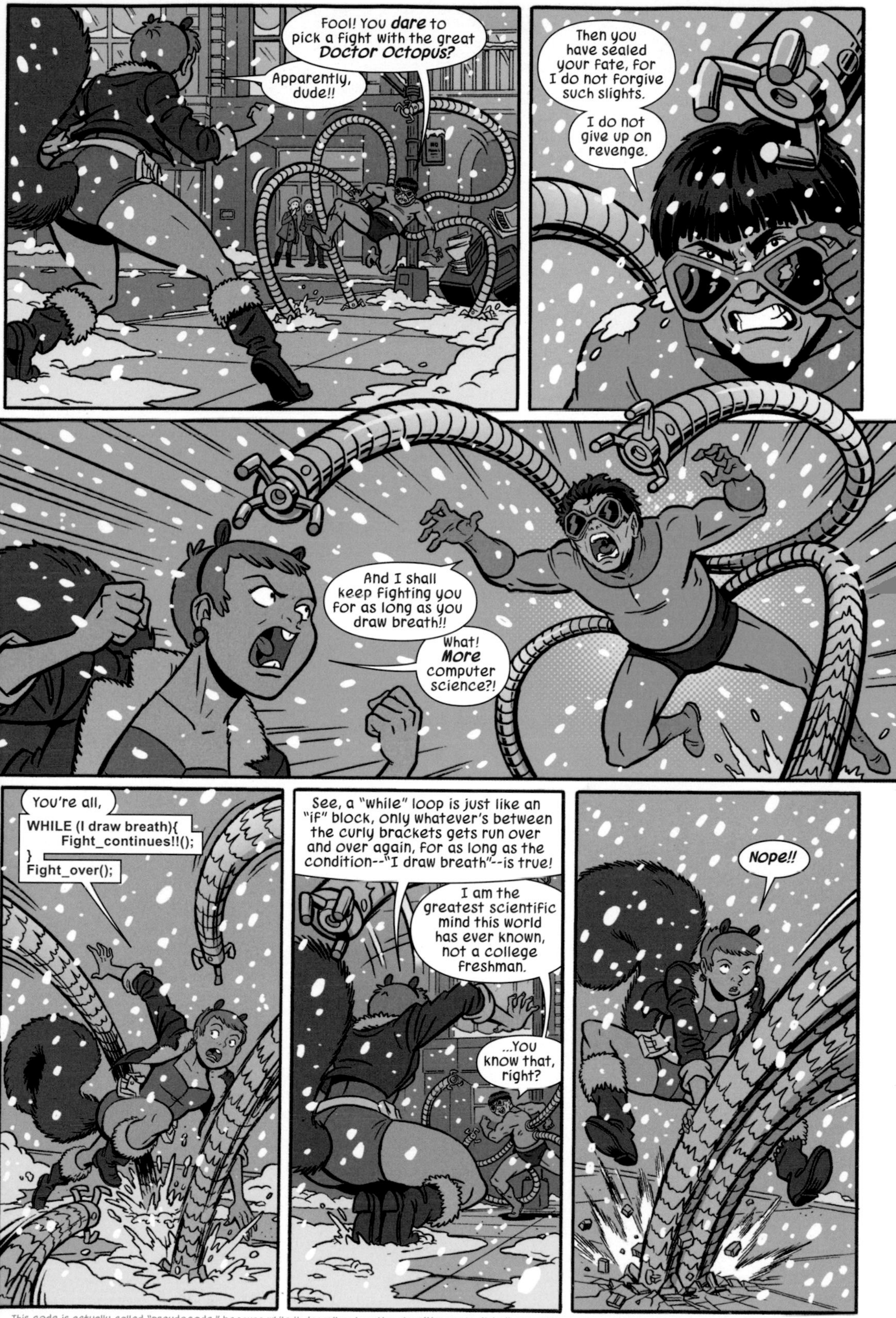
Fool! You dare to pick a fight with the great Doctor Octopus?
Apparently, dude!!
Then you have sealed your fate, for I do not forgive such slights.
I do not give up on revenge.
And I shall keep fighting you for as long as you draw breath!!
What! More computer science?!
You're all,
WHILE (I draw breath){
Fight_continues!!();
}
Fight_over();
See, a "while" loop is just like an "if" block, only whatever's between the curly brackets gets run over and over again, for as long as the condition--"I draw breath"--is true!
I am the greatest scientific mind this world has ever known, not a college freshman.
...You know that, right?
Nope!!

This code is actually called "pseudocode," because while it describes how the algorithm works, it isn't something you can just pour into a computer and then call it a day. Too bad, huh? Also, I'm being informed programming *never* works by simply pouring things inside your computer. That's *double* too bad!

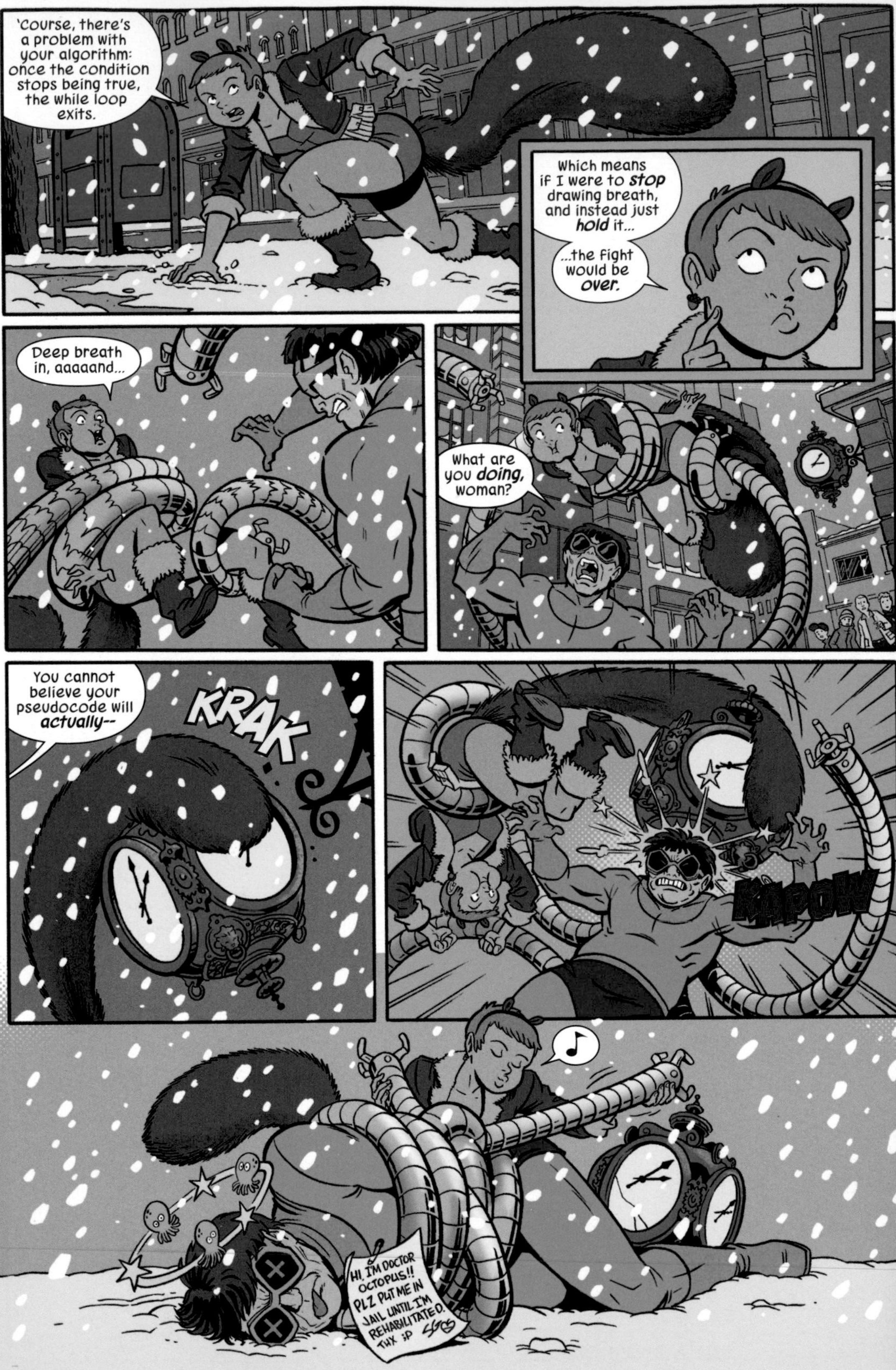
'Course, there's a problem with your algorithm: once the condition stops being true, the while loop exits.
Which means if I were to *stop* drawing breath, and instead just *hold* it...
...the fight would be *over.*
Deep breath in, aaaaand...
What are you *doing,* woman?
You cannot believe your pseudocode will *actually*--
KRAK
KAPOW
♪
HI, I'M DOCTOR OCTOPUS!! PLZ PUT ME IN JAIL UNTIL I'M REHABILITATED. THX ;P

The cops are like, hey fellow officers, look at this helpful note! It tells us exactly what we should do, including the term of his rehabilitative sentence! Done!

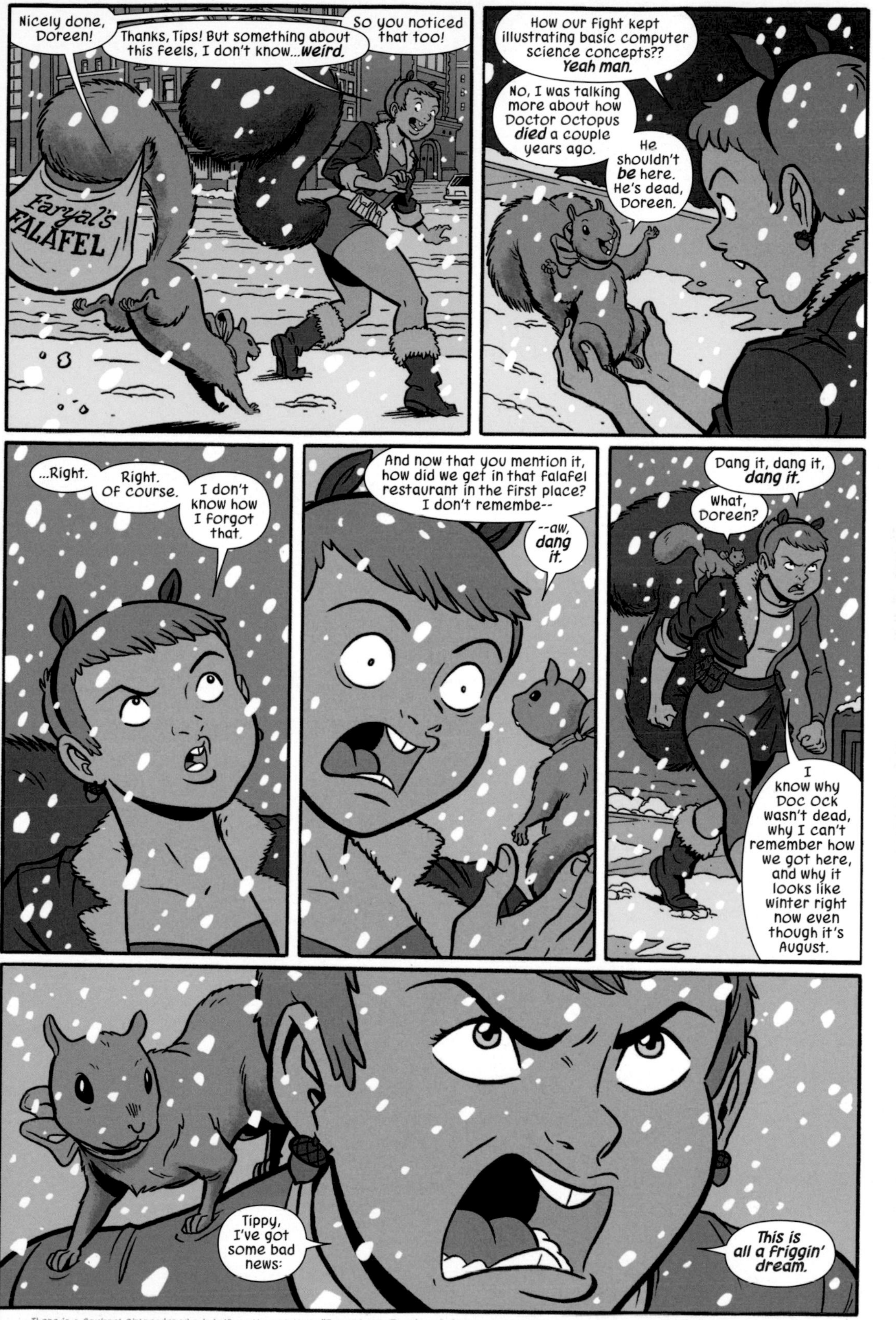

Nicely done, Doreen!
Thanks, Tips! But something about this feels, I don't know...*weird.*
So you noticed that too!
Faryal's FALAFEL
How our fight kept illustrating basic computer science concepts?? *Yeah man.*
No, I was talking more about how Doctor Octopus *died* a couple years ago.
He shouldn't *be* here. He's dead, Doreen.
...Right.
Right. Of course.
I don't know how I forgot that.
And now that you mention it, how did we get in that falafel restaurant in the first place? I don't remembe--
--aw, *dang* it.
Dang it, dang it, *dang it.*
What, Doreen?
I know why Doc Ock wasn't dead, why I can't remember how we got here, and why it looks like winter right now even though it's August.
Tippy, I've got some bad news:
This is all a friggin' dream.

There is a *Squirrel Girl* reader who is halfway through their *"Excuse me, Doctor Octopus cannot appear in* Squirrel Girl *as depicted"* letter right now who is *really* wishing they finished reading their comic before bustin' out the ol' email client. Hi there, *Squirrel Girl* reader! Thanks for reading our comic, even though you must be pretty annoyed with us right now! Just save that letter as a draft until we make some other Doc Ock mistake, okay??

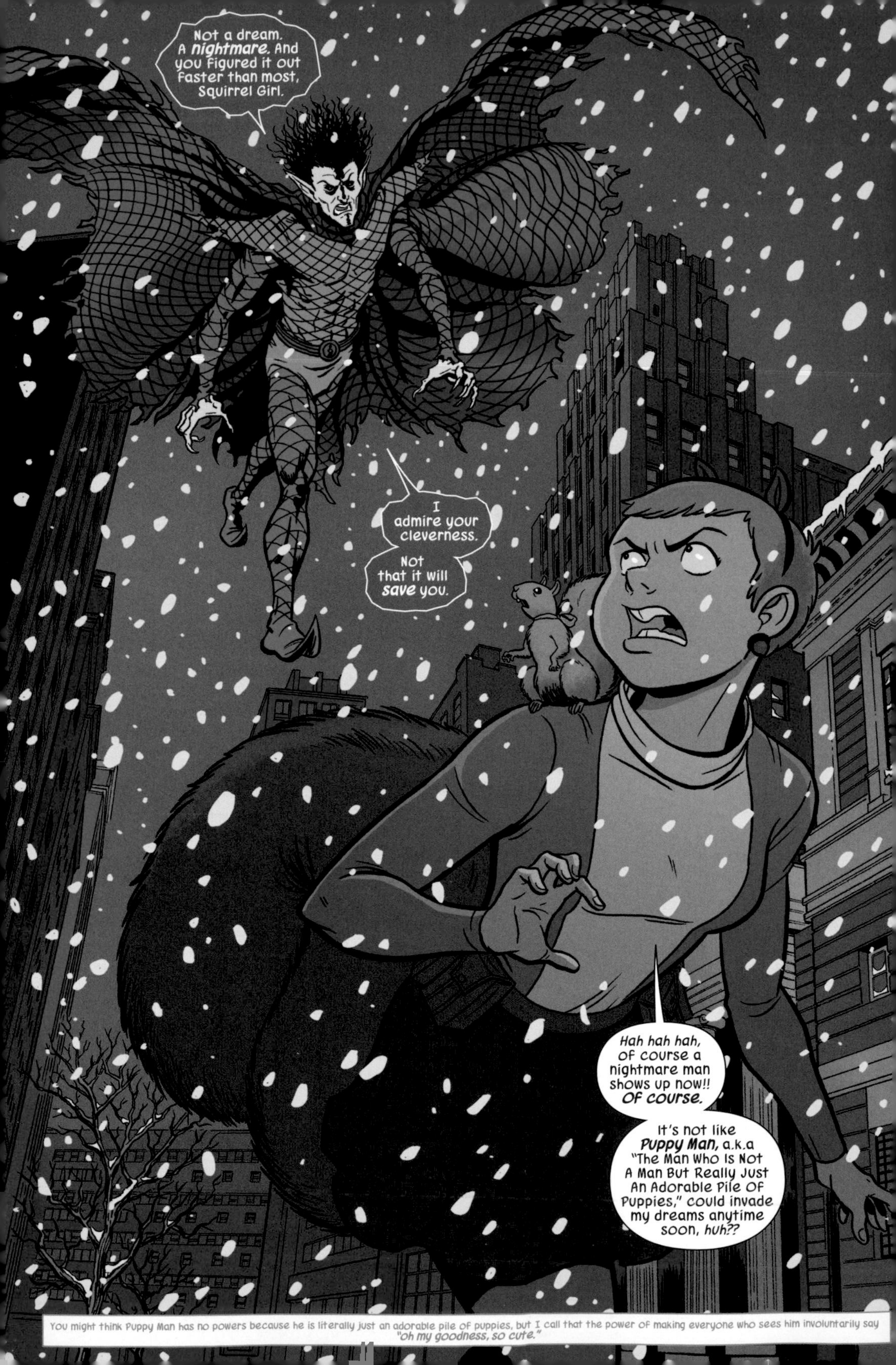

Not a dream. A *nightmare.* And you figured it out faster than most, Squirrel Girl.
I admire your cleverness.
Not that it will *save* you.
Hah hah hah, of course a nightmare man shows up now!! *Of course.*
It's not like *Puppy Man,* a.k.a "The Man Who Is Not A Man But Really Just An Adorable Pile Of Puppies," could invade my dreams anytime soon, *huh??*
You might think Puppy Man has no powers because he is literally just an adorable pile of puppies, but I call that the power of making everyone who sees him involuntarily say *"oh my goodness, so cute."*

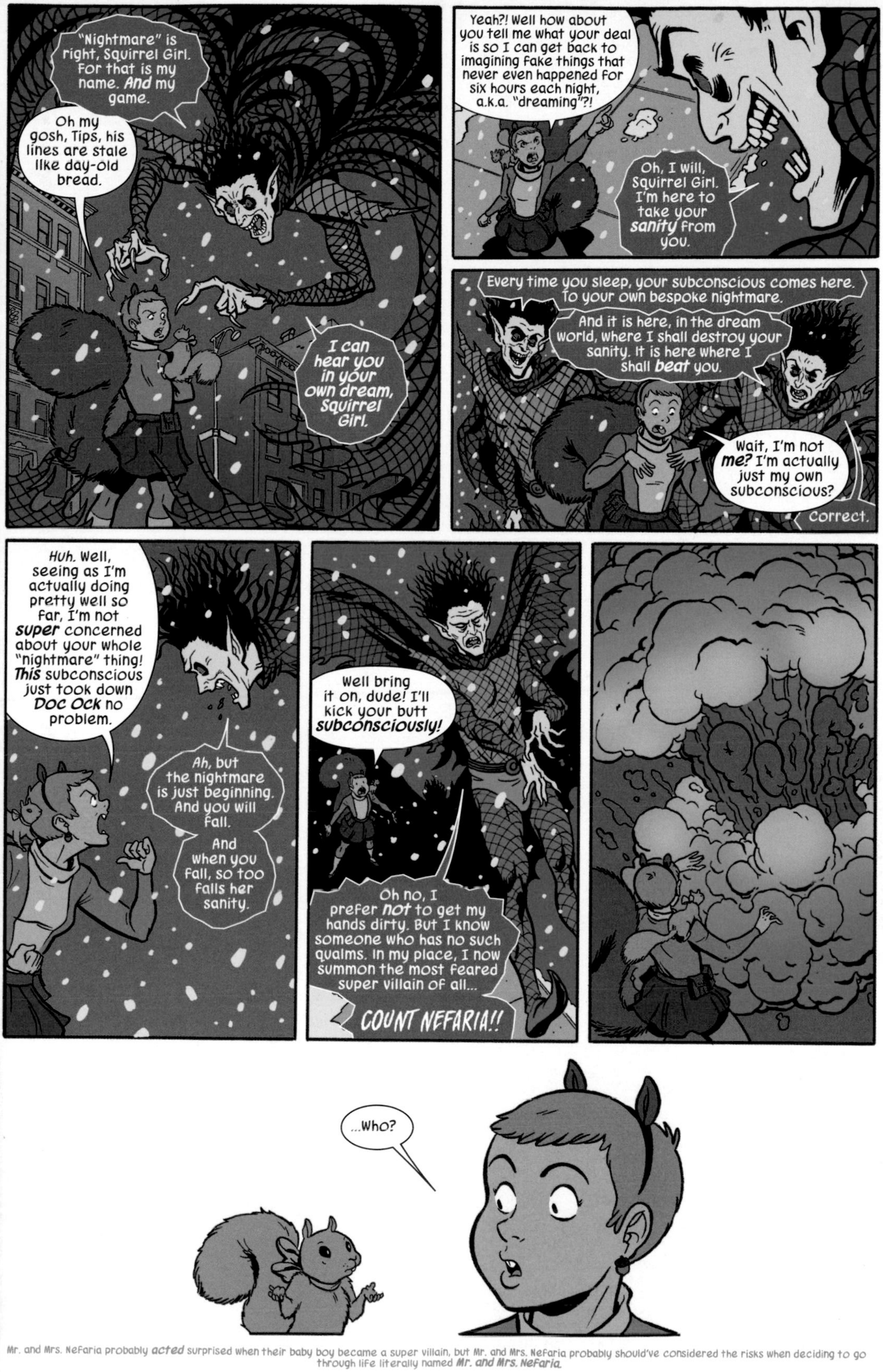
"Nightmare" is right, Squirrel Girl. For that is my name. *And* my game.
Oh my gosh, Tips, his lines are stale like day-old bread.
I can hear you in your own dream, Squirrel Girl.
Yeah?! Well how about you tell me what your deal is so I can get back to imagining fake things that never even happened for six hours each night, a.k.a. "dreaming"?!
Oh, I will, Squirrel Girl. I'm here to take your *sanity* from you.
Every time you sleep, your subconscious comes here. To your own bespoke nightmare.
And it is here, in the dream world, where I shall destroy your sanity. It is here where I shall *beat* you.
Wait, I'm not *me?* I'm actually just my own subconscious?
Correct.
Huh. Well, seeing as I'm actually doing pretty well so far, I'm not *super* concerned about your whole "nightmare" thing! *This* subconscious just took down *Doc Ock* no problem.
Ah, but the nightmare is just beginning. And you will fall.
And when you fall, so too falls her sanity.
Well bring it on, dude! I'll kick your butt *subconsciously!*
Oh no, I prefer *not* to get my hands dirty. But I know someone who has no such qualms. In my place, I now summon the most feared super villain of all...
COUNT NEFARIA!!
POOF!
...Who?

Mr. and Mrs. Nefaria probably *acted* surprised when their baby boy became a super villain, but Mr. and Mrs. Nefaria probably should've considered the risks when deciding to go through life literally named ***Mr. and Mrs. Nefaria.***

How often do you think Count Nefaria gets called Count Nefarious by his barista? Probably 100% of the time, huh. Yeah. Probably 100% of the time.

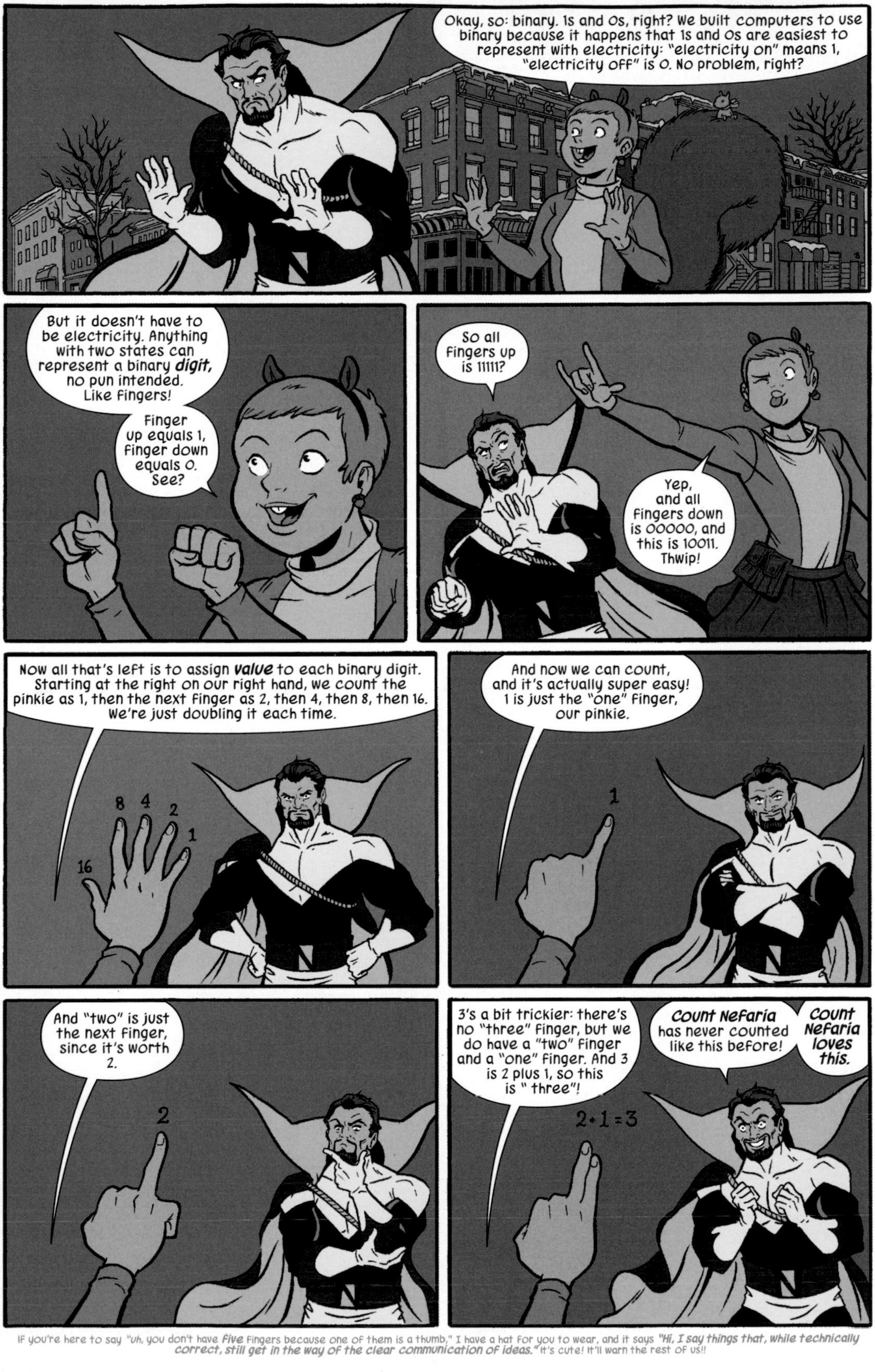
Okay, so: binary. 1s and 0s, right? We built computers to use binary because it happens that 1s and 0s are easiest to represent with electricity: "electricity on" means 1, "electricity off" is 0. No problem, right?
But it doesn't have to be electricity. Anything with two states can represent a binary digit, no pun intended. Like fingers!
Finger up equals 1, finger down equals 0. See?
So all fingers up is 11111?
Yep, and all fingers down is 00000, and this is 10011. Thwip!
Now all that's left is to assign value to each binary digit. Starting at the right on our right hand, we count the pinkie as 1, then the next finger as 2, then 4, then 8, then 16. We're just doubling it each time.
8
4
2
1
16
And now we can count, and it's actually super easy! 1 is just the "one" finger, our pinkie.
1
And "two" is just the next finger, since it's worth 2.
2
3's a bit trickier: there's no "three" finger, but we do have a "two" finger and a "one" finger. And 3 is 2 plus 1, so this is "three"!
Count Nefaria has never counted like this before!
Count Nefaria loves this.
2+1=3

If you're here to say "uh, you don't have *five* fingers because one of them is a thumb," I have a hat for you to wear, and it says ***"Hi, I say things that, while technically correct, still get in the way of the clear communication of ideas."*** It's cute! It'll warn the rest of us!!

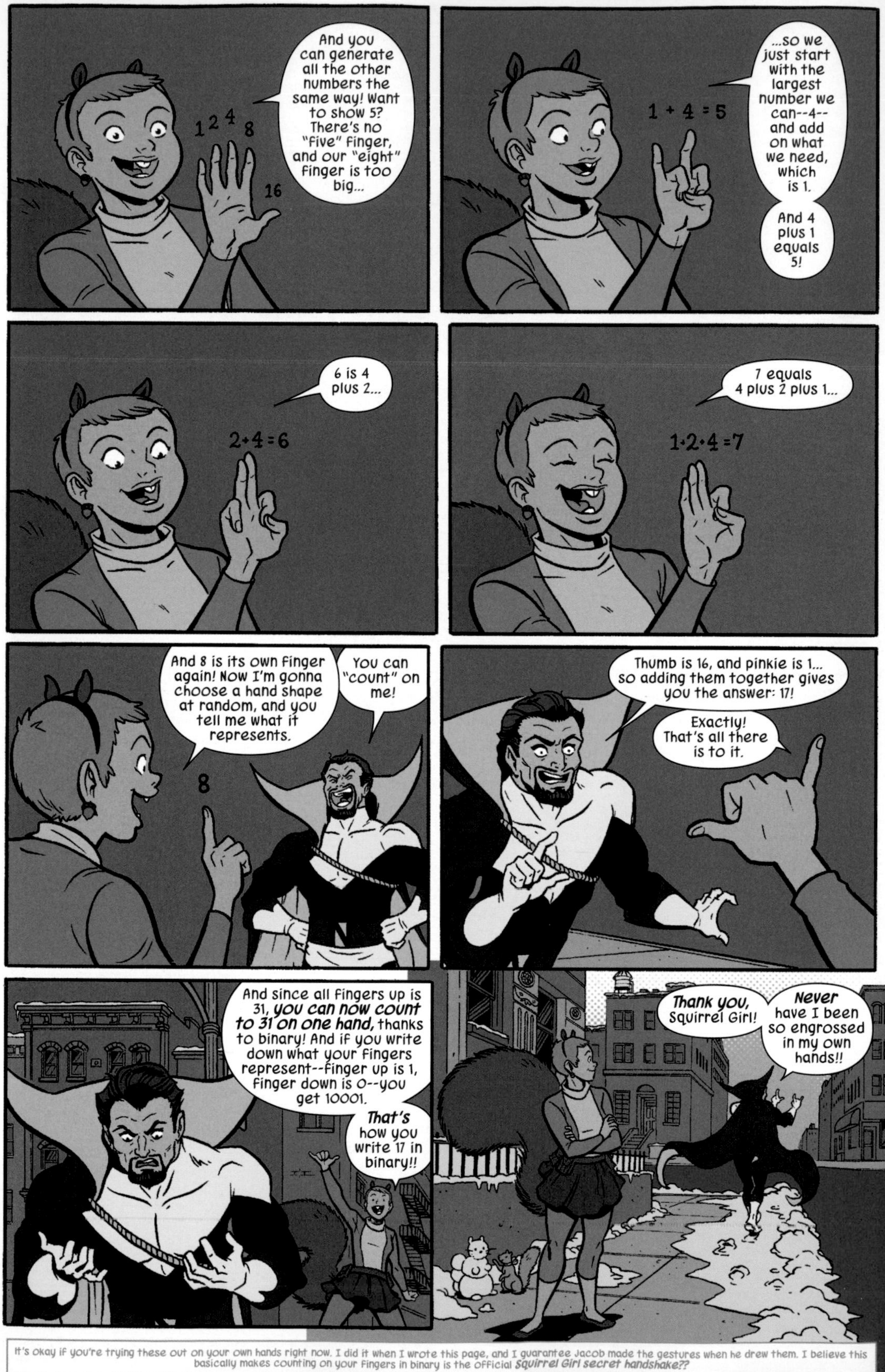

And you can generate all the other numbers the same way! Want to show 5? There's no "five" finger, and our "eight" finger is too big...
1 2 4 8
16
...so we just start with the largest number we can--4--and add on what we need, which is 1.
And 4 plus 1 equals 5!
1 + 4 = 5
6 is 4 plus 2...
2+4=6
7 equals 4 plus 2 plus 1...
1+2+4=7
And 8 is its own finger again! Now I'm gonna choose a hand shape at random, and you tell me what it represents.
You can "count" on me!
8
Thumb is 16, and pinkie is 1... so adding them together gives you the answer: 17!
Exactly! That's all there is to it.
And since all fingers up is 31, **you can now count to 31 on one hand,** thanks to binary! And if you write down what your fingers represent--finger up is 1, finger down is 0--you get 10001.
That's how you write 17 in binary!!
Thank you, Squirrel Girl!
Never have I been so engrossed in my own hands!!

It's okay if you're trying these out on your own hands right now. I did it when I wrote this page, and I guarantee Jacob made the gestures when he drew them. I believe this basically makes counting on your fingers in binary is the official ***Squirrel Girl secret handshake??***

IF you want to write crossover fan fiction about Count Nefaria and another number-obsessed Count who lives on a street that goes by the name of Sesame, let me just say that I am *way* ahead of you.

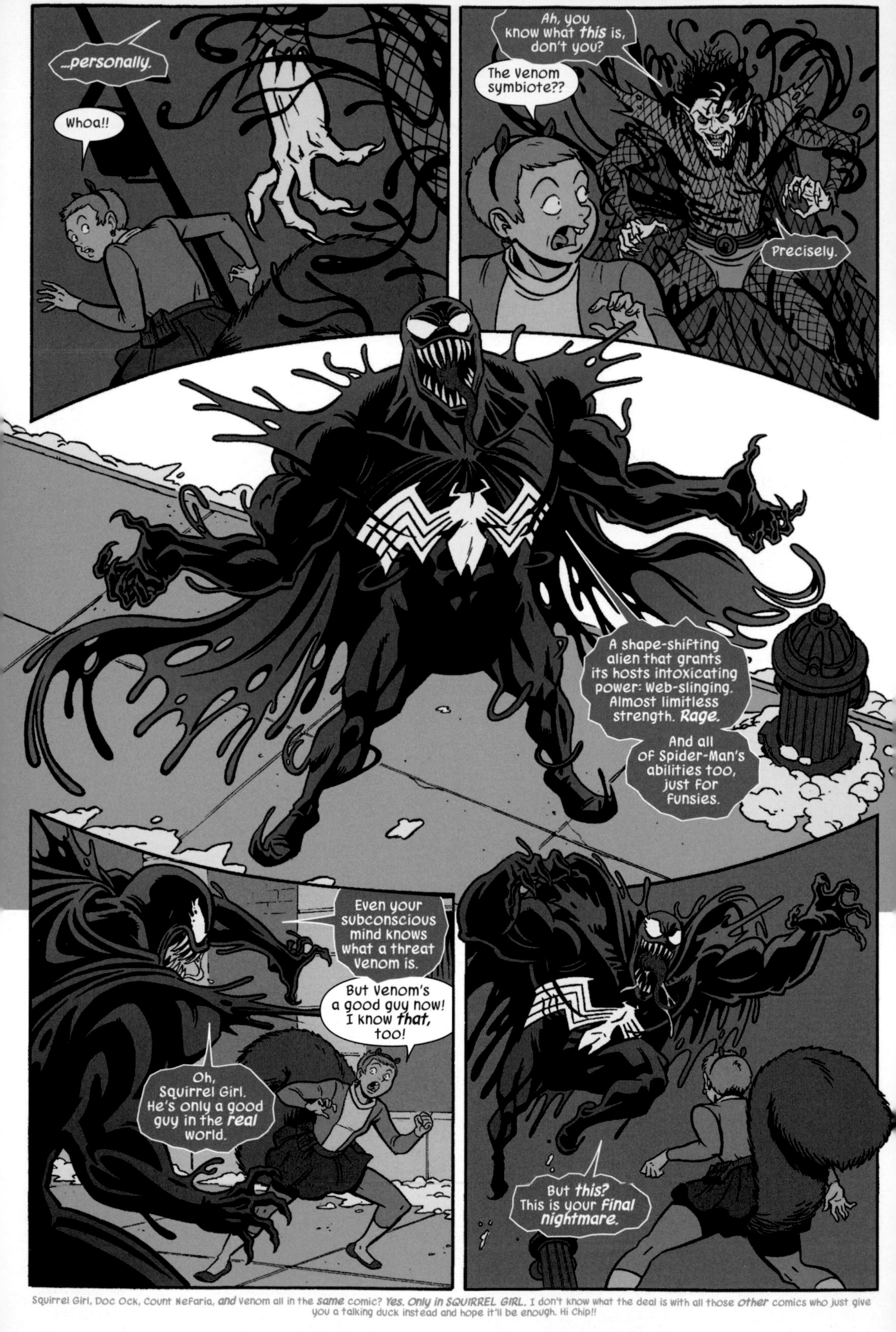
...personally.
Whoa!!
Ah, you know what *this* is, don't you?
The Venom symbiote??
Precisely.
A shape-shifting alien that grants its hosts intoxicating power: Web-slinging. Almost limitless strength. *Rage.*
And all of Spider-Man's abilities too, just for funsies.
Even your subconscious mind knows what a threat Venom is.
But Venom's a good guy now! I know *that,* too!
Oh, Squirrel Girl. He's only a good guy in the *real* world.
But *this?* This is your *final nightmare.*

Squirrel Girl, Doc Ock, Count Nefaria, *and* Venom all in the *same* comic? *Yes. Only in SQUIRREL GIRL.* I don't know what the deal is with all those *other* comics who just give you a talking duck instead and hope it'll be enough. Hi Chip!!

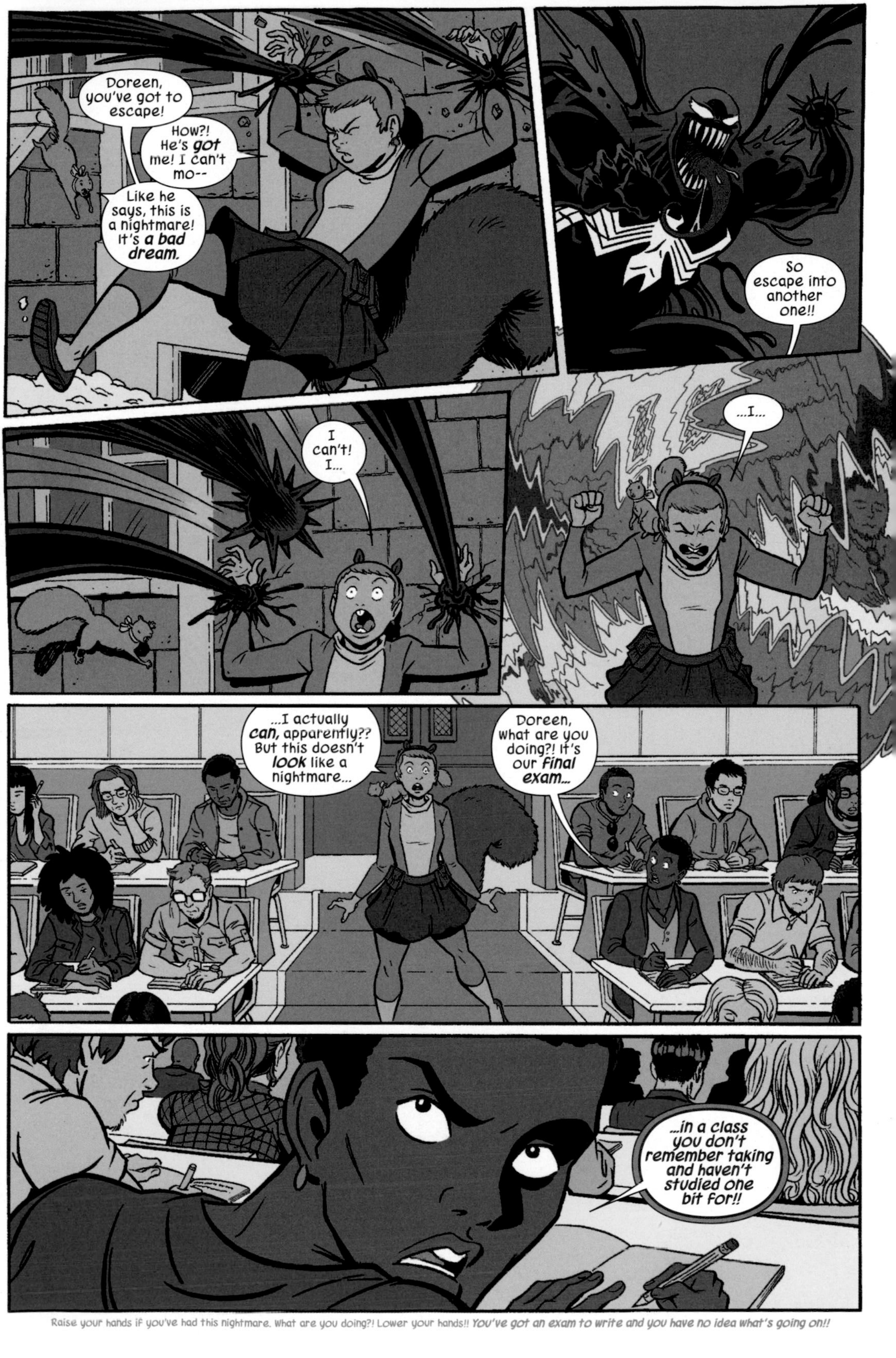

Doreen, you've got to escape!
How?! He's **got** me! I can't mo--
Like he says, this is a nightmare! It's ***a bad dream.***
So escape into another one!!
I can't! I...
...I...
...I actually ***can,*** apparently?? But this doesn't ***look*** like a nightmare...
Doreen, what are you doing?! It's our ***final exam...***
...in a class you don't remember taking and haven't studied one bit for!!

Raise your hands if you've had this nightmare. What are you doing?! Lower your hands!! *You've got an exam to write and you have no idea what's going on!!*

Kraven the College Administrator got to the top through his readiness to hunt down errors in course loads and disputes between faculty as readily as he hunts down Spider-Man, which is to say: *extremely friggin' readily.*

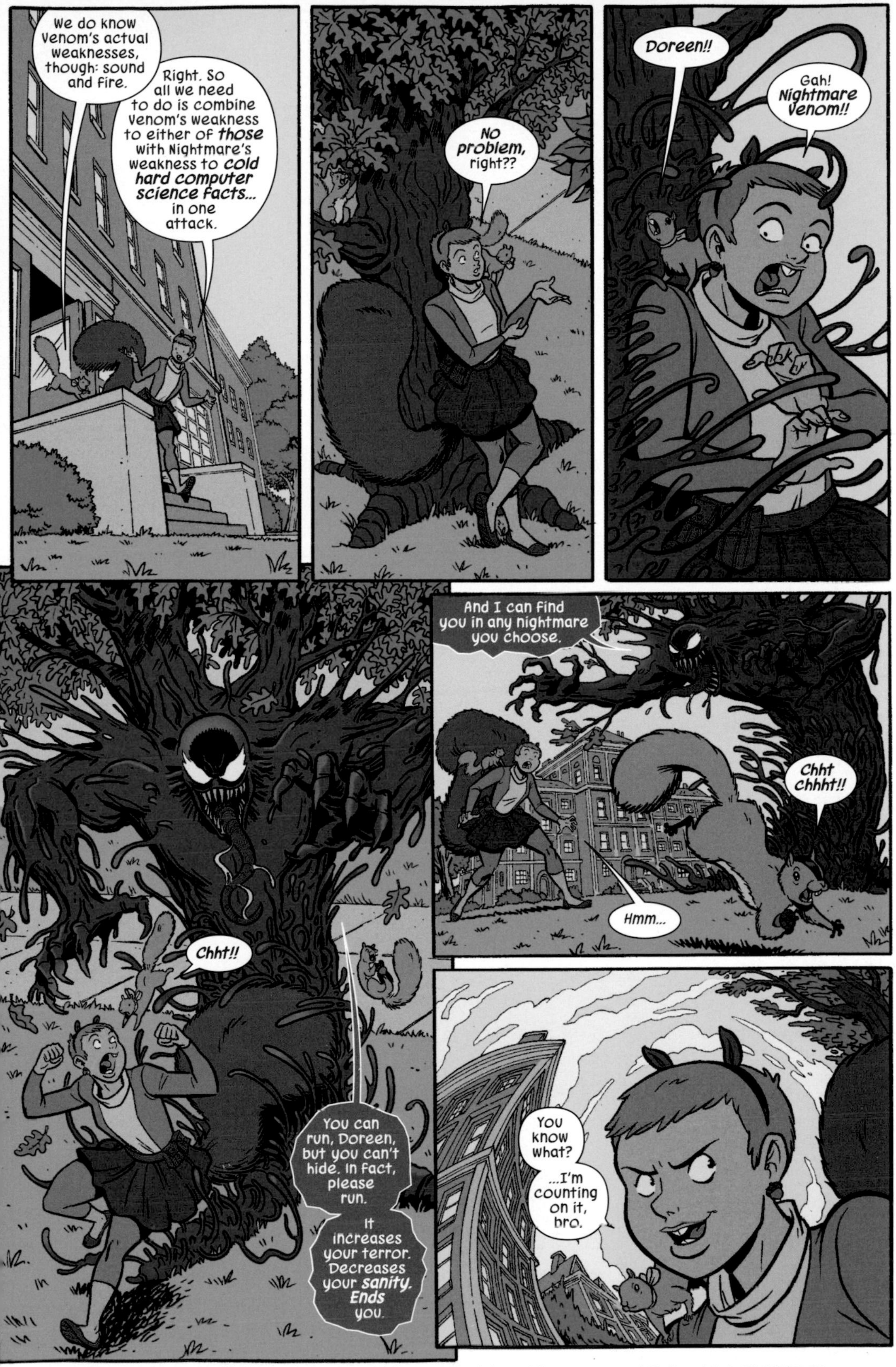
We do know Venom's actual weaknesses, though: sound and fire.
Right. So all we need to do is combine Venom's weakness to either of *those* with Nightmare's weakness to *cold hard computer science facts...* in one attack.
No problem, right??
Doreen!!
Gah! *Nightmare Venom!!*
Chht!!
You can run, Doreen, but you can't hide. In fact, please run.
It increases your terror. Decreases your *sanity. Ends* you.
And I can find you in any nightmare you choose.
Chht Chhht!!
Hmm...
You know what?
...I'm counting on it, bro.

We'll never get to see how this "didn't study for my exam" nightmare world ended up, so let's say: everyone got A's. Hooray! Grade inflation for all!!

I'm not gonna say you can recognize a computer scientist by the way they're constantly throwing up binary hand signs. I'm just saying, in a just world, you *could*.

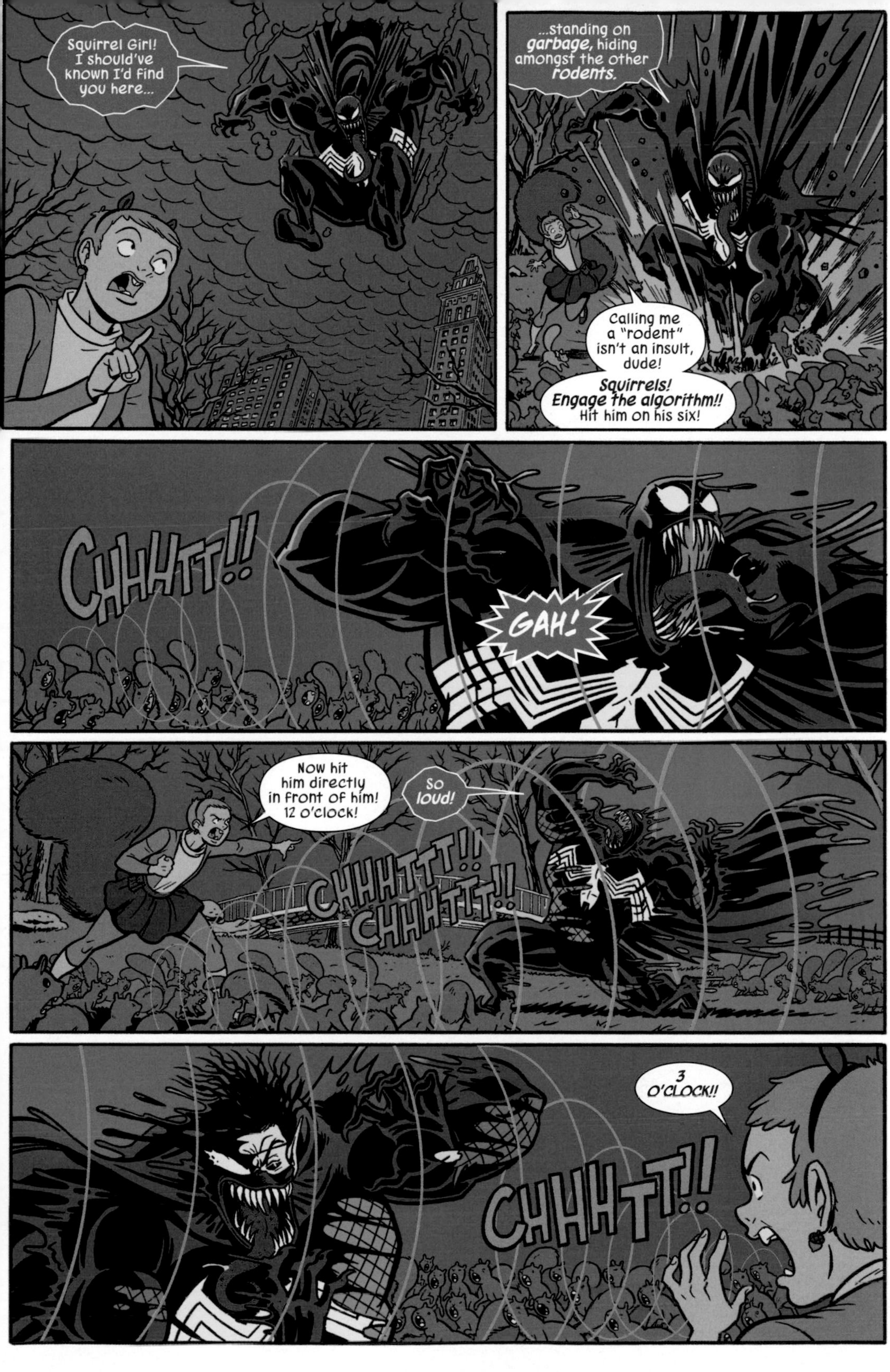
Squirrel Girl! I should've known I'd find you here...
...standing on garbage, hiding amongst the other rodents.
Calling me a "rodent" isn't an insult, dude!
Squirrels! Engage the algorithm!! Hit him on his six!
CHHHTT!!
GAH!
Now hit him directly in front of him! 12 O'clock!
So loud!
CHHHTTT!!
CHHHTTT!!
3 O'CLOCK!!
CHHHTT!!

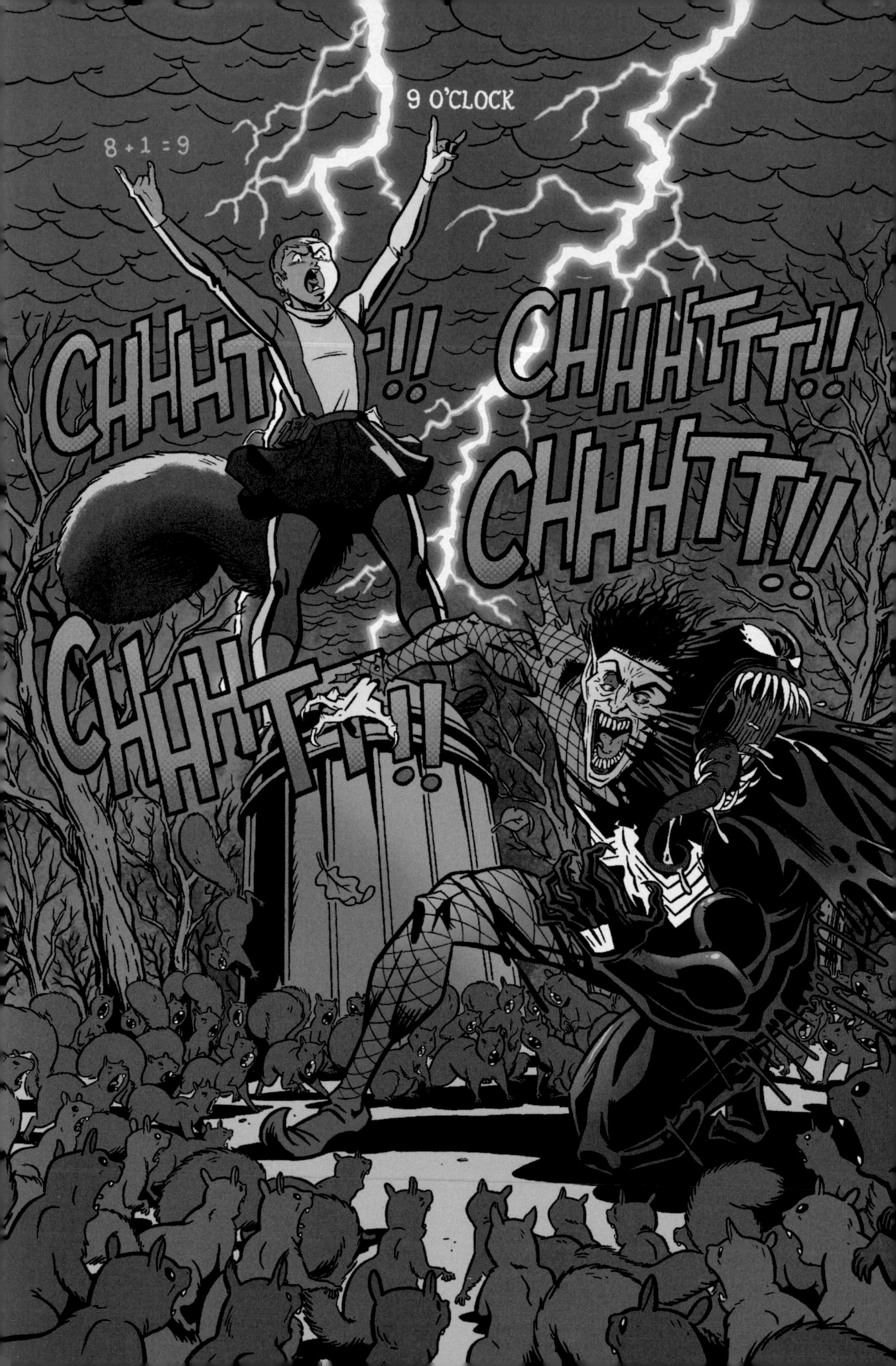
9 O'CLOCK
8 + 1 = 9
CHHHTT!!
CHHHTTT!!
CHHHTTT!!
CHHHTT!!

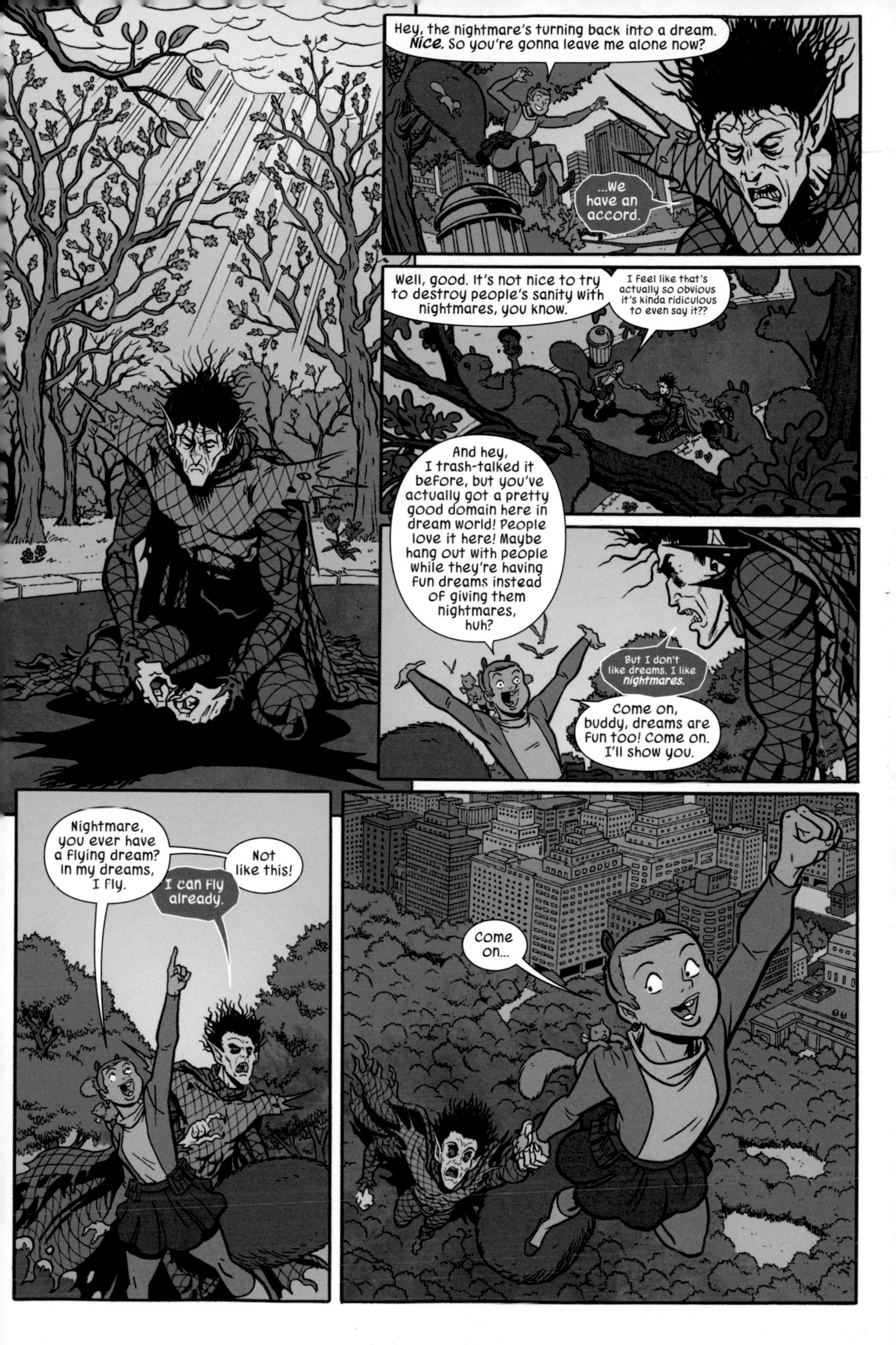
Hey, the nightmare's turning back into a dream. Nice. So you're gonna leave me alone now?
...We have an accord.
Well, good. It's not nice to try to destroy people's sanity with nightmares, you know.
I feel like that's actually so obvious it's kinda ridiculous to even say it??
And hey, I trash-talked it before, but you've actually got a pretty good domain here in dream world! People love it here! Maybe hang out with people while they're having fun dreams instead of giving them nightmares, huh?
But I don't like dreams. I like nightmares.
Come on, buddy, dreams are fun too! Come on. I'll show you.
Nightmare, you ever have a flying dream? In my dreams, I fly.
I can fly already.
Not like this!
Come on...

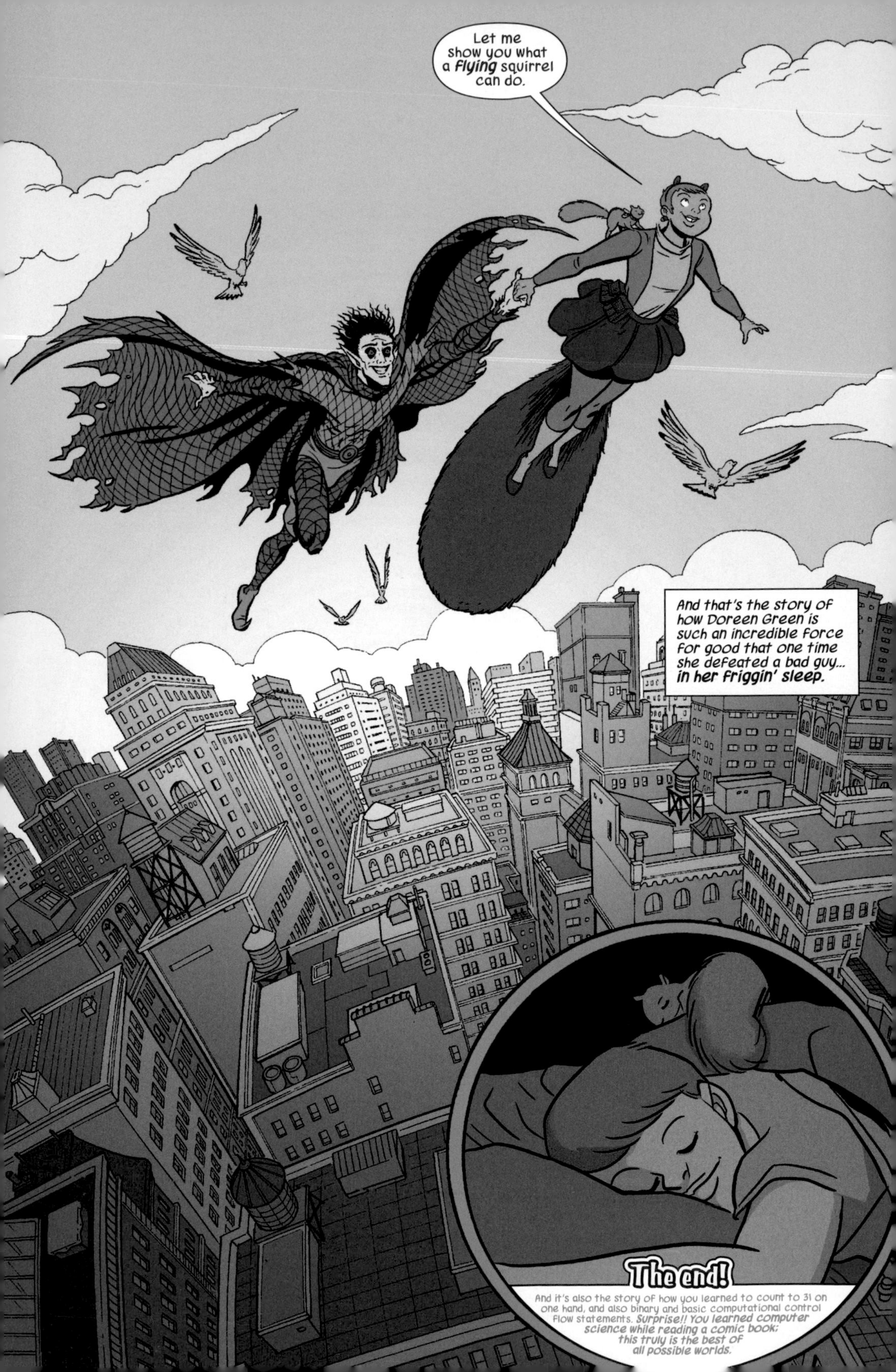
Let me show you what a *flying* squirrel can do.
And that's the story of how Doreen Green is such an incredible force for good that one time she defeated a bad guy... **in her friggin' sleep.**
The end!
And it's also the story of how you learned to count to 31 on one hand, and also binary and basic computational control flow statements. *Surprise!! You learned computer science while reading a comic book; this truly is the best of all possible worlds.*

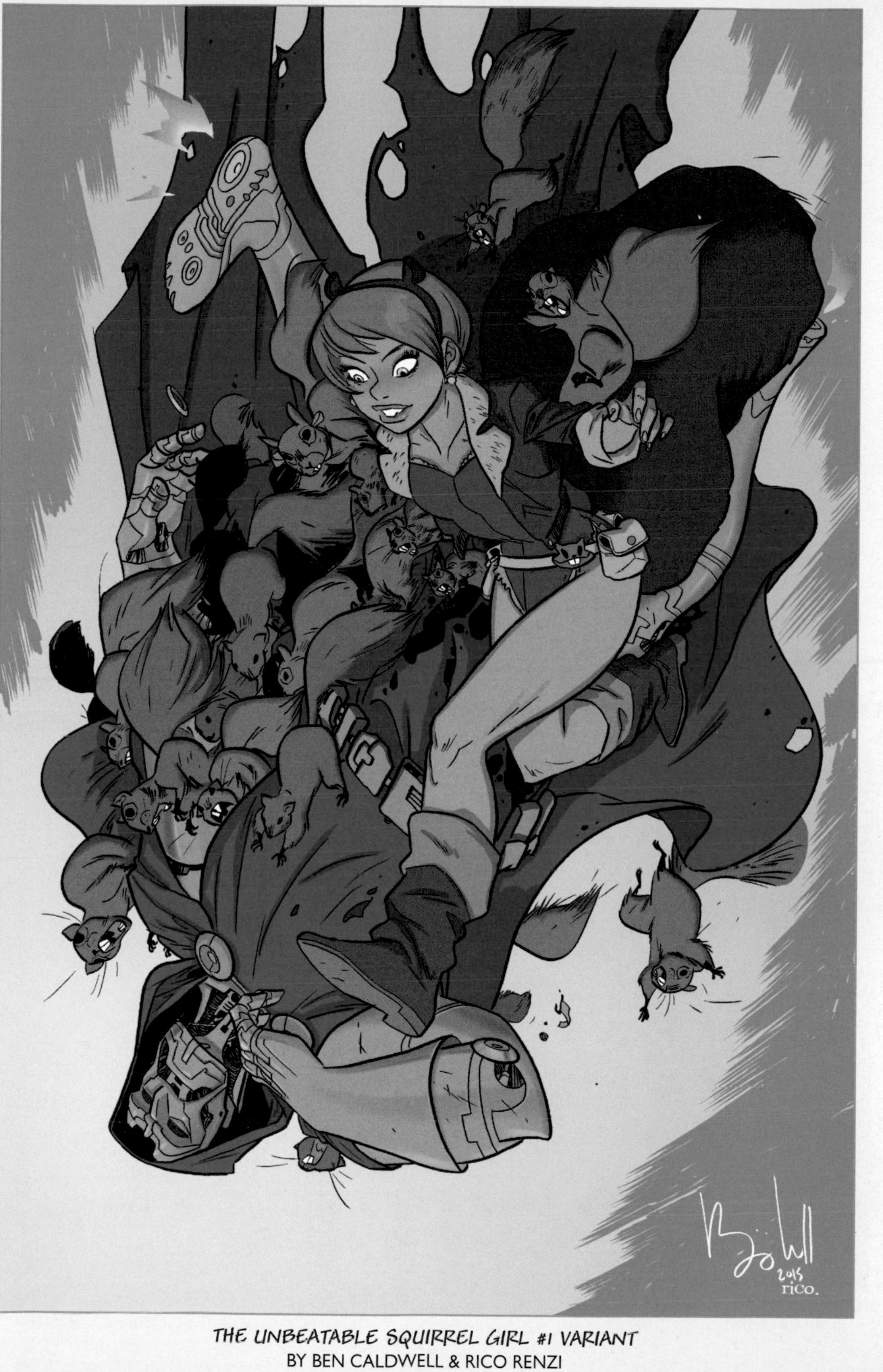

THE UNBEATABLE SQUIRREL GIRL #1 VARIANT
BY BEN CALDWELL & RICO RENZI

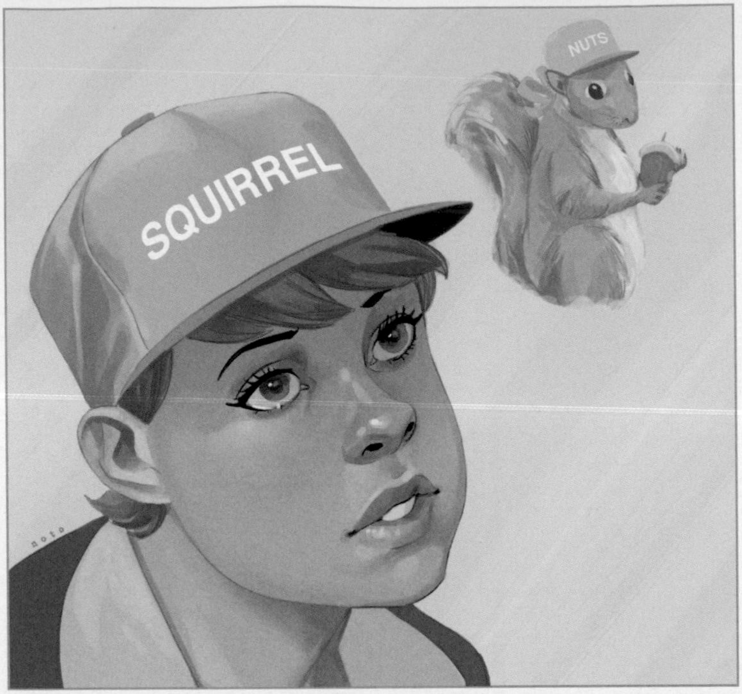
NUTS
SQUIRREL

THE UNBEATABLE SQUIRREL GIRL #1 HIP-HOP VARIANT
BY PHIL NOTO

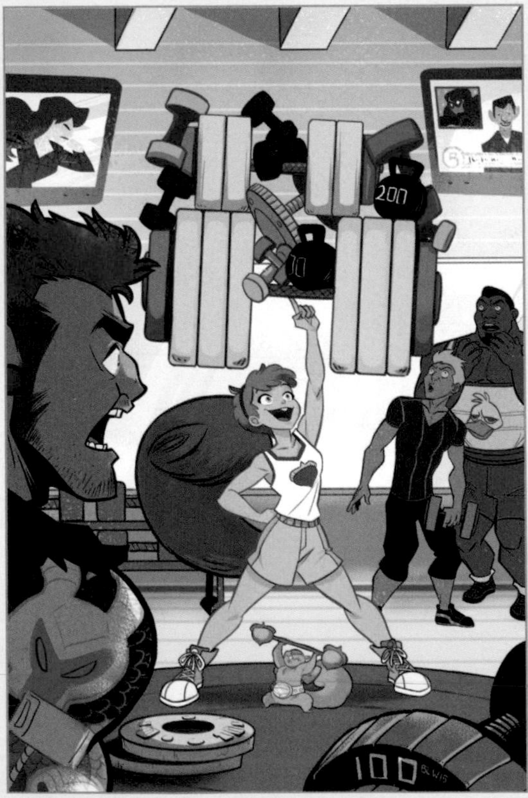
200
10
100

THE UNBEATABLE SQUIRREL GIRL #2 VARIANT
BY BRITTNEY L. WILLIAMS

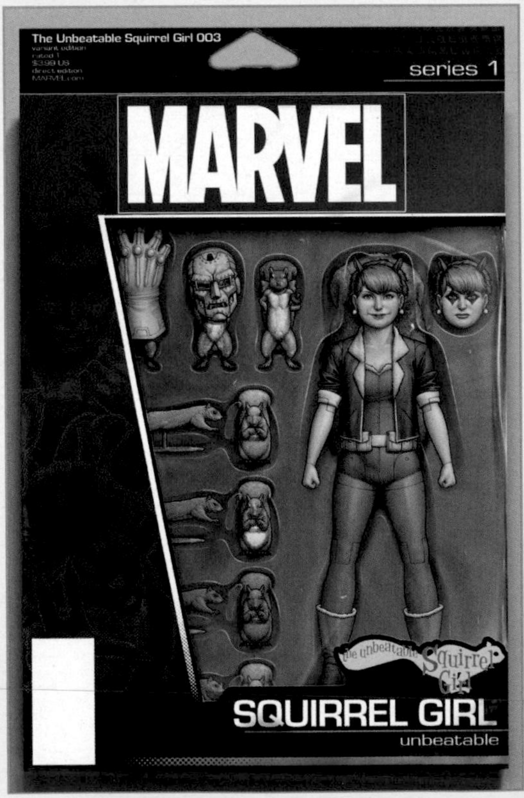
The Unbeatable Squirrel Girl 003
series 1
MARVEL
SQUIRREL GIRL
unbeatable

THE UNBEATABLE SQUIRREL GIRL #3
ACTION FIGURE VARIANT
BY JOHN TYLER CHRISTOPHER

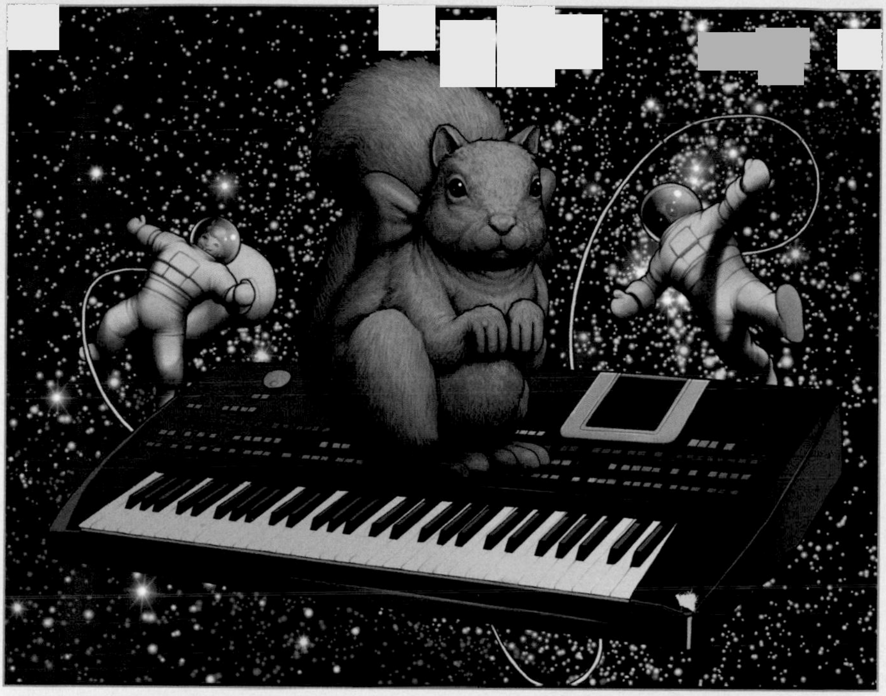

THE UNBEATABLE SQUIRREL GIRL #4 DEADPOOL VARIANT
BY JOHN TYLER CHRISTOPHER

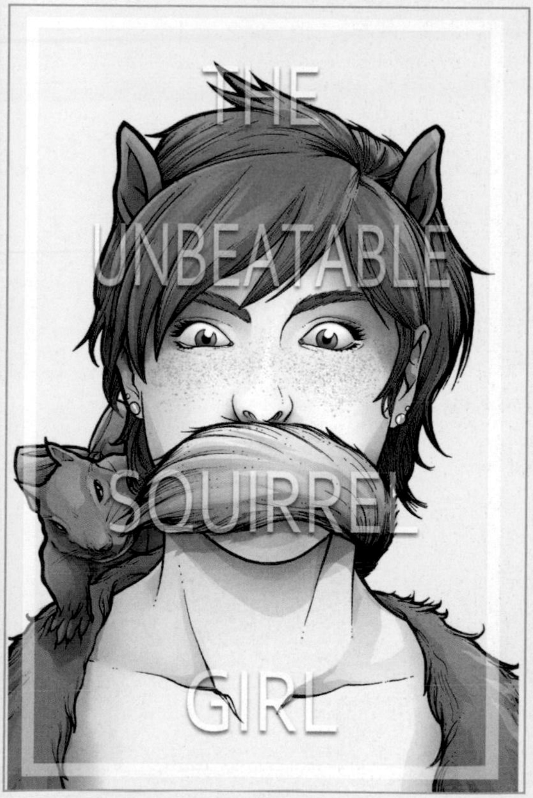
THE
UNBEATABLE
SQUIRREL
GIRL

THE UNBEATABLE SQUIRREL GIRL #3 VARIANT
BY MATT WAITE

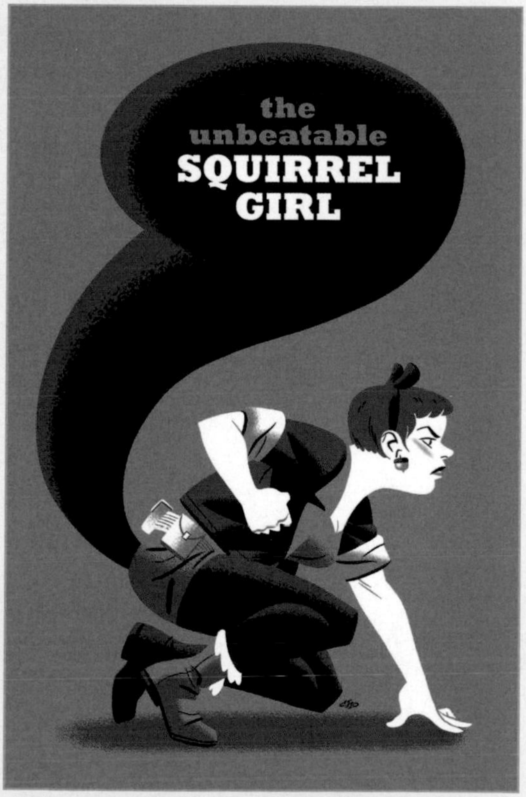
the
unbeatable
SQUIRREL
GIRL

THE UNBEATABLE SQUIRREL GIRL #5 VARIANT
BY MICHAEL CHO

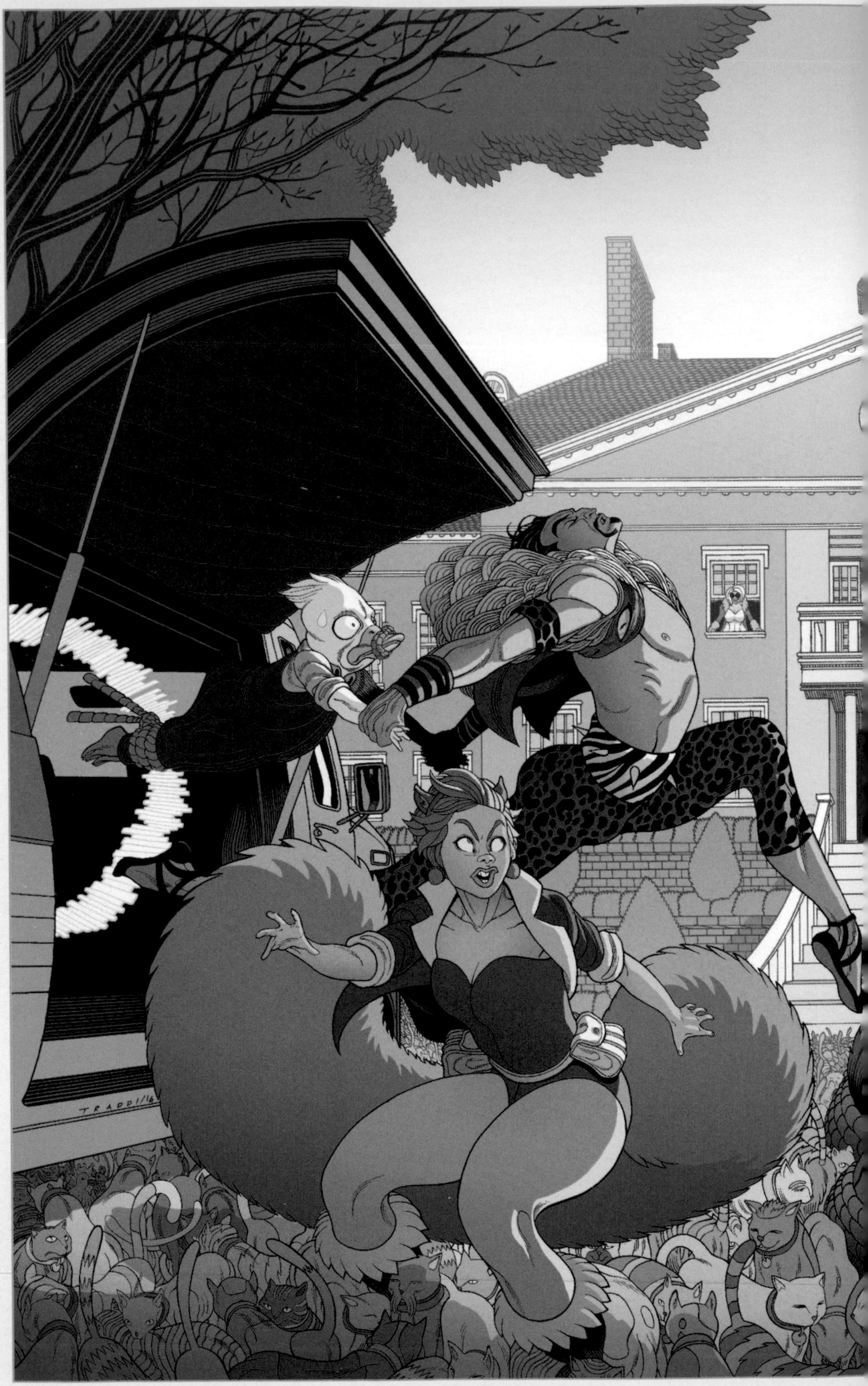

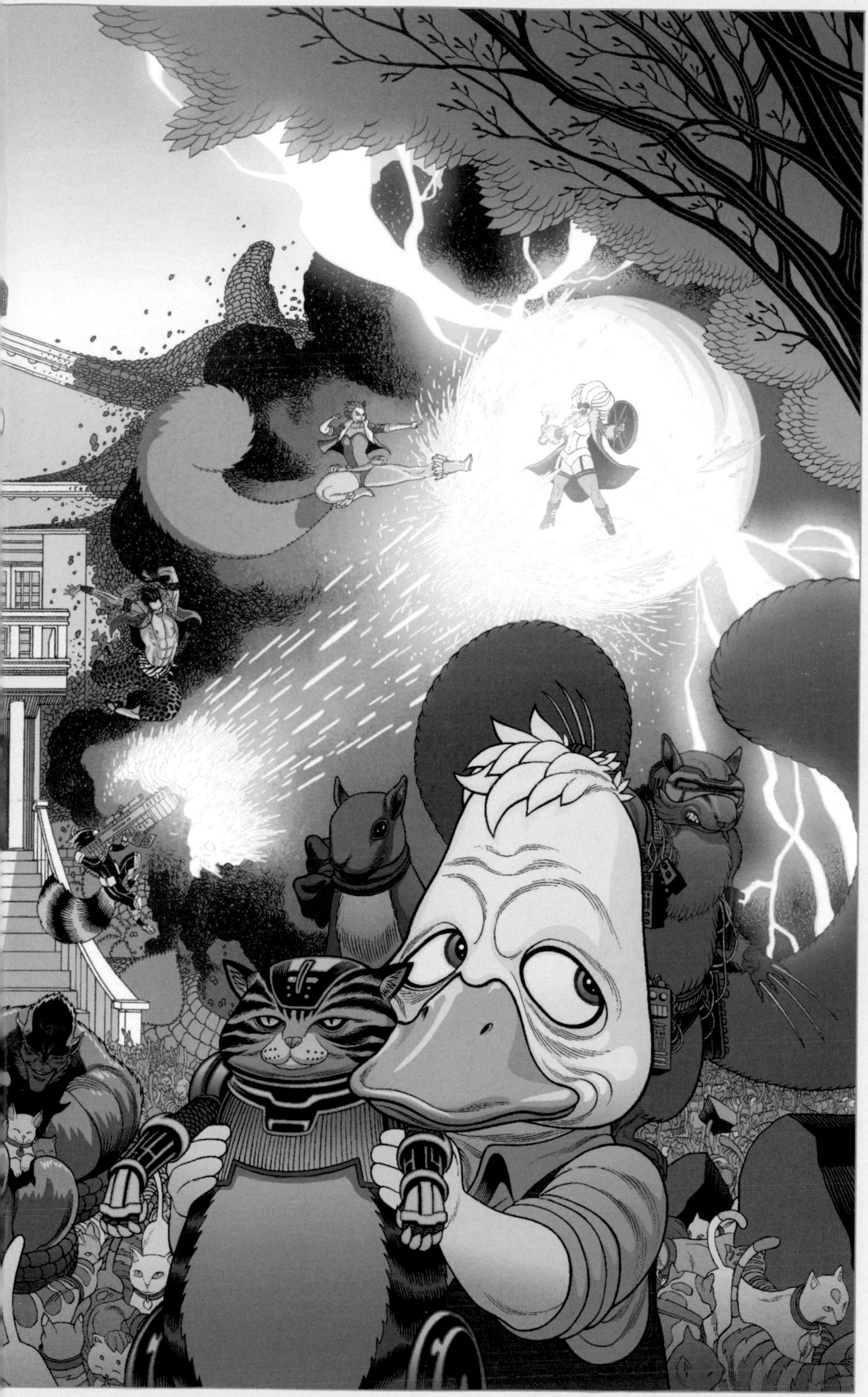

THE UNBEATABLE SQUIRREL GIRL #6 & HOWARD THE DUCK #6 COMBINED VARIANTS
BY TRADD MOORE & MATTHEW WILSON

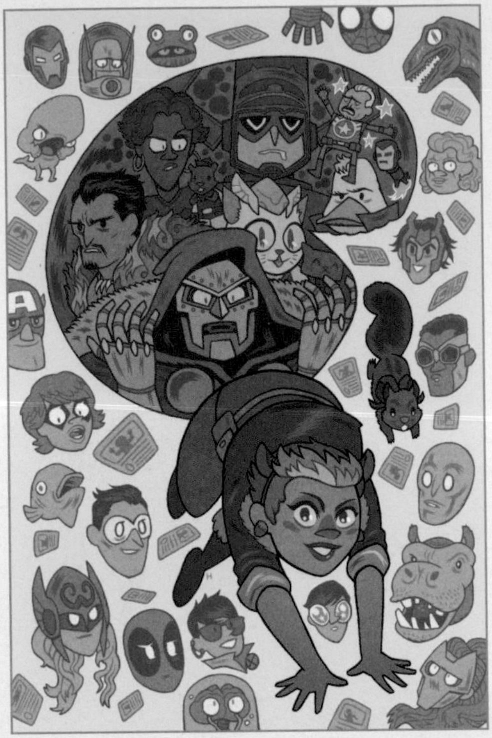

THE UNBEATABLE SQUIRREL GIRL #7
STORY THUS FAR VARIANT
BY DAN HIPP

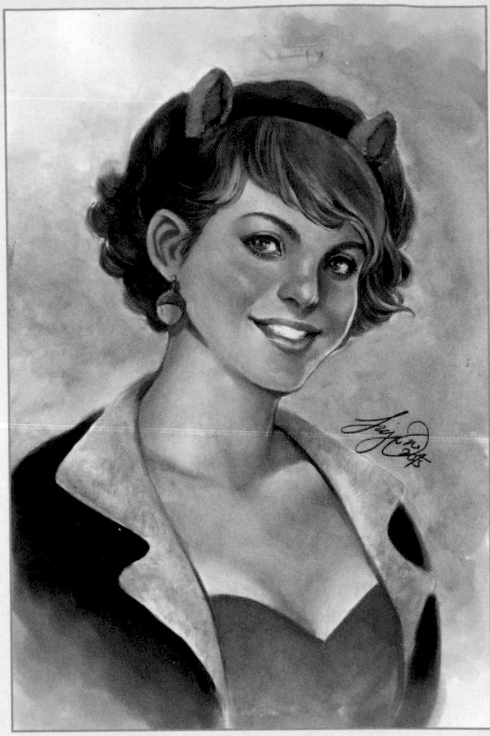

THE UNBEATABLE SQUIRREL GIRL #7
VARIANT
BY SIYA OUM

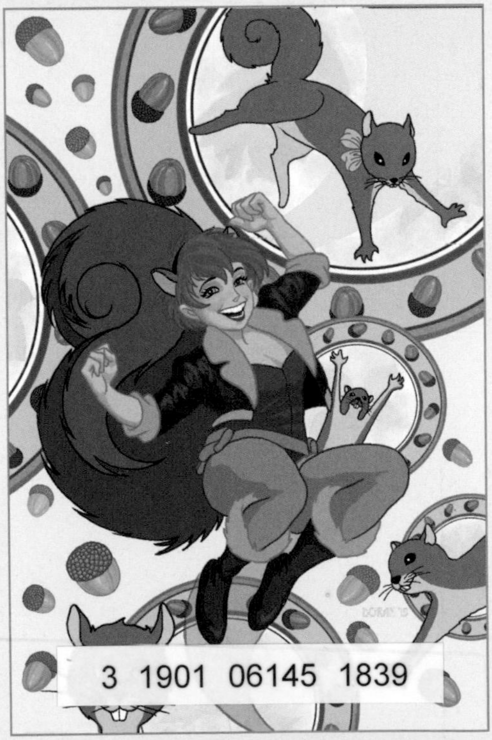

THE UNBEATABLE SQUIRREL GIRL #7
CLASSIC VARIANT
BY COLLEEN DORAN

"Delightfully inventive." — *Vulture*

"A consistently surprising, heartfelt [...] hilarious comic." — *The A.V. Club*

YOU GO, SQUIRREL GIRL!

With her unique combination of wit, empathy and squirrel powers, computer science student Doreen Green is all that stands between Earth and total destruction! Well, Doreen plus her friends Tippy-Toe (a squirrel) and Nancy (a regular human). So mainly Squirrel Girl. Then what hope does Earth have if Doreen gets hurled back in time and erased from history? Some hope, hopefully, as Howard the Duck is waiting impatiently for a crossover! And if one animal encounter isn't enough, prepare for Swarm, a buzzkill made of bees, and Mole Man, the subterranean super villain looking for love! But you're not here for flowers and kissing, you're all about computer science and super-heroics. Get both — and more — in a showdown with Count Nefaria!

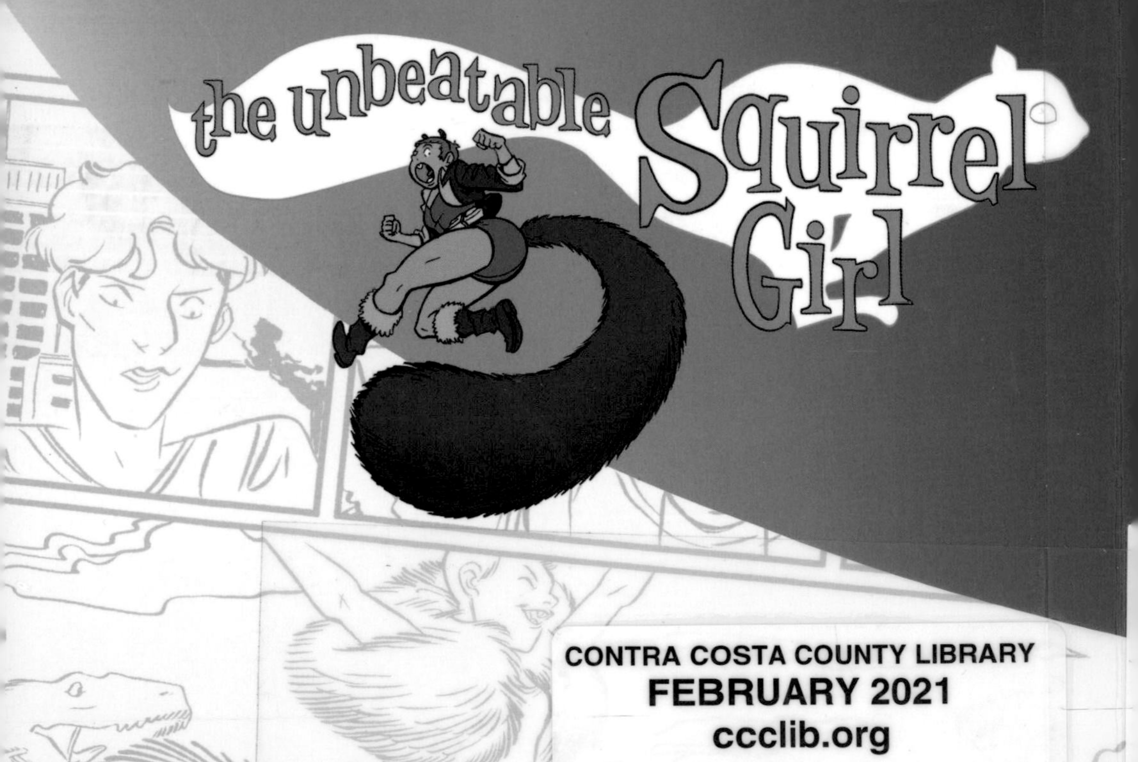
the unbeatable Squirrel Girl

ISBN 978-1-302-92116-3
51299
9 781302 921163
$12.99 US $16.99 CAN

Collecting ***Unbeatable Squirrel Girl (2015B) #1-11*** and ***Howard the Duck (2015B) #6*** — by Ryan North, Chip Zdarsky, Erica Henderson, Joe Quinones, Jacob Chabot and Rico Renzi.

MARVEL

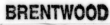